MW01591245

BEYOND THE HORIZON

A Sci-Fi Novel Collection

SCOTT MICHAEL DECKER

Copyright (C) 2023 Scott Michael Decker

Layout design and Copyright (C) 2023 by Next Chapter

Published 2023 by Next Chapter

This book is a work of fiction. Names, characters, places, and incidents are the product of the author's imagination or are used fictitiously. Any resemblance to actual events, locales, or persons, living or dead, is purely coincidental.

All rights reserved. No part of this book may be reproduced or transmitted in any form or by any means, electronic or mechanical, including photocopying, recording, or by any information storage and retrieval system, without the author's permission.

Cube Rube

Chapter 1

Jack stared at the cube, mesmerized by its iridescent color. One part of his mind calculated how long it would keep him in smoke while another part mocked him for thinking iridescence a color.

Two inches to a side, the cube stared back at him from the middle shelf of a contraption known as an oven.

He swore it stared, seeing deep into his soul, tracing his past through his three failed marriages, his four bankruptcies, his multiple encounters with the Imperial Patrol, and his constantly smoking himself into oblivion.

Ivory swirls sloshed across its surface, like laughter. The cube knew him.

Twenty minutes earlier, he'd dropped from orbit in his Salvager to sniff through the ruins of Canis Dogma Five, the old Circian home-world, for something he might hawk to the junk lords for a few hundred galacti. He'd found someplace to park the Scavenger out of sight from the constant patrols, his ship almost as derelict as the ruins he explored. Then he'd worked himself between the decrepit doors of an apartment building, one of the few still standing amidst the ruins of a city that had once housed a million people, minimum. Two floors up, he'd cracked a flat whose stale air bespoke its millennial inoccupancy. The oven was a perfect find, as valuable in its current state as it would be after being dropped out a window. I'm not carryin' it

3

down two flights of stairs, he'd thought indignantly, bending to look inside. The dusty glass pane obscured the interior, so he'd opened the door.

And stared at the cube inside.

Before he could think, he snatched it from the oven.

* * *

A scene filled his sight and a voice rang in his ears.

He was in a cavern, and a man stood before him, dressed in sequined silks of multiple colors, upon his head a slim, simple circlet, in one hand a two-inch silvery cube.

"I am Lochium Circi the Ninth, Emperor of Circi, a civilization that once reached to the outer arms of the galaxy." Behind the figure was a small table, on it a vial filled with orange fluid, and a large stone slab atop one-foot pillars. "Welcome to my final resting place, Traveler. You have now been selected for a sacred duty. You see me because you have been chosen to wield the Ghost cube." Lochium Circi the Ninth ceremoniously held up the silvery, two-inch cube. "With this modest device, the Circians spread their influence throughout the galaxy."

A remote rumble shook the chamber, and dust drifted down from the ceiling. "And now our influence is dying. Barbarians bombard Canis Dogma Five into oblivion as I speak.

"You, Traveler, have been chosen to become the next Emperor of the Circian Empire, with all the privileges, responsibilities, and obligations thereto implied, and to bring together again all the remnants of our once-great Empire under the auspices of one government, to live peacefully until the end of time under you and your successors.

"The cube has chosen you, Traveler, because you are worthy and noble and pure. May the billion suns of the galactic core light your path with brilliance."

* * *

His head spun and his face stung.

"Hold it by its edges," the girl told him.

Jack did as she bade him, the cube threatening to suck him elsewhere again.

4

He stared at her, she who had slapped him. She who knew what he held.

Because it was hers.

He wondered where she'd come from. The apartment had had the feel of having been vacant for a very long time. He also wondered why she hadn't just taken it from him. One part of him already knew, and another part ridiculed him from not considering for a moment handing it back to her. He'd be stupid to give up something that might keep him in smoke for the rest of his life.

She stared back at him, much as the cube had.

Jack saw what she was thinking. Me, Emperor?

The thought was beyond ludicrous and passing farcical.

She laughed softly, shaking her head.

He was a wretch, through and through. No amount of wealth, schooling, or breeding could remedy that. All a charm school might do is teach him how to insult people without their knowing it, something he now did without intending to.

He frowned at her. "I'm Jack, but you knew that, didn't you?"

She nodded. "Misty." She didn't extend her hand.

He might have been a leper. "Pleased."

"Likewise." Clearly she wasn't.

"This is yours, isn't it?"

"It was," she said, shrugging. "Or more accurately, I used to be its."

"And now I'm its?" He frowned at it in his hand.

"You catch on fast."

"What is it?"

"A Gaussian Holistic Oscillating Subliminal Tesseract, a ghost cube." She suddenly stood and beckoned him to follow. "Now that you're here, I need your help."

He climbed to his feet slowly, as though he'd been sitting for several hours. The quality of light through dusty panes hadn't changed appreciably.

She led him up several floors, some of the stairwells difficult to navigate, their steps mangled by time and inattention. He wondered as he followed her up what an eight- or nine-year-old girl was doing in a decrepit ruin like this by herself.

"It's been a couple weeks," she said, stopping outside a door at the end of a hall. "So he doesn't smell very good."

5

Not smelling very good was an understatement. He could barely hold his gorge. "What do you want me to do?"

Grief wrecked her face. "Help me bury him."

He knew without asking that just leaving the corpse wasn't a choice. He also knew that just leaving the girl wasn't a choice. A tantalizing lifetime of smoke-filled nights receded inexorably from his grasp. And right now, he really needed to smoke.

The blanket helped to hold together what decay was rapidly dismantling, but couldn't shield him completely from the ooze he should've expected.

She led him to a wildly overgrown park, two blocks away, where a pit had already been dug.

"I just couldn't figure out how to get him down here."

Once he'd finished, organic was the only word he could summon to describe his smell. In addition to the odors of necrosis and its associated fluids, a thick layer of freshly-turned soil now stuck to those stains. The cube was tucked in his pocket.

He'd just chunked the last shovelful to fill the pit when a distant whine alerted him. "Quick! The patrol!" He loped for the nearest building, the girl outpacing him easily and leading him toward a culvert.

They dove into it just as the craft roared overhead. Straining engines whined in complaint as it circled back.

"Stars above, they saw us. We can't stay here." He looked at her, despairing that they'd be trapped in the culvert.

Misty seemed unconcerned.

Jack tracked the incoming ship by sound as he looked her over. The backwash of the landing retros buffeted her thin, threadbare clothing, its many rents and tears each carefully stitched. Her hair fell in stringy, ungainly swatches to uneven, hacked-off lengths near her shoulders. Her cheeks were hollow with malnutrition or shock.

Maybe both, he thought. "Why won't they find us?"

Her eyes glistened with ethereal light. "You'll persuade them not to." She didn't glance toward his jacket pocket, but she might have.

Voices outside approached. "Over here. I told you I picked up a signal of an incoming ship. Probably some scavenger."

He brought out the cube.

* * *

Jack looked at the culvert. The drainpipe was three feet in diameter, barely room for anyone to have gone in. "We've picked up native signals before. Remnants of the old Circian Empire, eking out a meager life among the ruins. If it was a scavenger, where's the ship?" He turned to look at his shipmate.

The guy shrugged, his uniform immaculate.

Jack knew his own was perfect as well. "You goin' in after 'em?" He gestured at the culvert, and then picked an imaginary speck of dust off his sleeve.

The other guy shook his head. "They ain't payin' to replace uniforms, remember?"

"We'll set up monitors in a perimeter. If there's a scavenger, we'll catch 'em on the way out."

* * *

Jack snapped back into the culvert, his hand coming off the cube.

The voices outside faded.

He'd felt as if he'd been dreaming, on the one hand hearing them talk outside the pipe, on the other doing the talking. Somehow, he'd maintained an awareness of his hand on the cube.

Misty watched him, her eyes on his face.

"What *is* this thing?"

She shrugged. "Grandpa never said, but he did tell me it's old, very old. My ancestors used it to control the galaxy."

He brought his gaze up from the cube. "What ancestors?"

"The Circians."

Archeologists had long wondered at the source of Circian power. A meek, unpretentious peoples, they had somehow spread their influence from a modest-size planet with few mineral resources across the galaxy, dominating multiple constellations with far more natural resources and far larger navies. Even their home system had been insignificant, a two-planet single-star system with a young blue primary sitting astride the narrow neck of empty space between Canis Major and Canis Minor. The Dog Bone, it'd been called by the early spacers who'd colonized the area some ten thousand years ago.

But somehow, Circi had come to dominate first the adjoining

Majora and Minora constellations, then the Perseus Arm itself, and then the entire galaxy. Not by conquering anything, either.

All by persuasion.

Jack shook his head at her. "That your grandpa we buried?"

She nodded, looking sad.

"We'll go say a few words, once it's safe."

She smiled at him, looking grateful.

"Where are your relatives?"

Her gaze narrowed in bewilderment.

"You don't have any relatives?

"Grandpa never mentioned any."

"Your parents?"

"Died five years ago when the building two blocks over collapsed."

"There have to be other people around here."

She shrugged. "Grandpa always told me to stay away. There's a tribe six blocks to the west, another twelve blocks north. See them once in awhile, but they always run when I approach."

"What did he tell you to expect once he'd died?"

She brightened unexpectedly. "He told me, 'Expect the Universe. You're the Princess.' "

He was dumbfounded. What kind of upbringing was that? "Princess of what?"

"Circi," she said matter of factly.

He threw his head back in laughter and hit his head on the inside of the culvert. Laughing even as he rubbed his head, he shook it in wonder, bemused and bewildered.

She looked as bemused as he felt.

"And just how were you supposed to become the Princess of Circi?"

"Become?" She looked even more befuddled. "I already am!"

He roared with laughter all the more.

Misty looked annoyed.

Outside, the roar of engines signaled the patrol's departure.

He sleeved the tears from his eyes, his hands still grimy with fresh earth. "What the stars am I going to do with you?" He laughed some more at his own predicament, the sudden caretaker of a delightful nine-year-old.

A crusty, renegade salvage-hound too self-centered to make four

8

marriages work, not diligent enough to avoid three bankruptcies, having tangled more times than both combined with the law, and an inveterate smoker, now the guardian of this orphan.

And owner of a cube that had ludicrously chosen him to become Emperor.

"Are you all right?"

He nodded and caught his breath, sure he looked a wreck, his face red and tear-strewn. "Too ironic, is all," he said, glancing down at the cube. "Well, if this was truly the source of the Circian's power, it's clear why their Empire fell." And he laughed some more.

* * *

"I think they're gone now," Misty said, peering from the culvert.

He could barely see her outline, night having long since fallen.

They'd likely set up infrared monitors in a perimeter, but they weren't interested in the native peoples. The Imperial Patrol would be looking for him and his Salvager.

He followed her out, trusting that she knew the area and where they could flee if the patrol returned.

They made their way to the gravesite and stood beside the unmarked mound of freshly-turned soil.

Her face swung up to his, a pale shadow amidst darker shadows.

What am I supposed to say? he wondered; I didn't know the man.

The moon of her face beamed at him brightly.

He took her hand and sighed. "We gather here at the final resting place of—"

"Augustus Circi, Emperor," she supplied in the pause.

"—to honor his passing from a life of devotion. Those of us who remain behind will never forget him."

The girl beside him wept softly in the darkness.

* * *

He climbed into a clean set of formalls, fresh from a shower, wondering the whole time how they were going to get off planet without the Imperial Patrol's intercepting them.

At least I'll be clean when they arrest me, he thought.

He'd parked Misty in the galley in front of a protein mush, his synth having sized up a meal for her.

Although famished, he had more of an appetite to get out of his soiled clothing and get cleaned up.

She licked the last off the spoon and glanced at him, her eyes taking in the fresh formalls.

"Your turn," he said, hiking his thumb toward the stall.

She half-frowned in that direction. "I've never been in one before. Does it hurt?"

He chuckled, shaking his head. "It's voice-operated, so if you scream, it'll shut itself off." He glanced around. Everything looked all right. "Did you touch anything?"

"Not a thing, just like you told me." She beamed at him. "The mush was terrible."

"You get used to it. In," he said, hiking the thumb.

He took her seat, the cube where he'd set it, after admonishing her not to touch it.

"It's not mine anymore, so I can't," she'd told him.

The galley was small, with barely room for two at the table. The seamless walls hid all the kitchen gadgets, but Jack needed just two: the synth and a spoon.

"Synth on," he said, and a whirring noise trundled out a bowl of mush. "My favorite."

He devoured it mindlessly, his gaze on the cube.

Two inches to a side, its edges slightly beveled, its sides completely reflective, the cube gazed back at him.

Belching, he pushed aside the empty bowl and put his hands on the cube.

* * *

The opulence stunned him, and the feel of the silk against his body felt like a mother's womb.

The two bulges at his breast bewildered him, as did the cavity between his legs. Mammaries and a vagina! he thought, looking around.

In his hand was a hairbrush. The marble columns framed a view of manicured palace grounds, topiary-tangled gardens, sprawling out-buildings.

He knew where he was, but not how he'd got here.

Or who he'd become.

Dismayed, he looked up from his ample breasts to see a servant approach.

"My Lady looks distressed, pardon my noticing," the handmaid said.

* * *

"What am I supposed to wear?" Her voice came from the shower, bringing him back to the ship.

He hadn't noticed she was finished. Ordering up a pair of small formalls, he took them from the sizer and thrust it into the showercube, his eyes on the kitchen, averted.

"Thank you."

He stepped back to the table.

She emerged, clad in formalls, looking down at herself in evident distaste. "I'll need better clothes than this before I can be presented at the Palace."

He roared with laughter and the bewildered look on her face caused him to laugh all the harder.

"You shouldn't have laughed like that," she said a long time later.

"I'm sorry," Jack replied, kissing the top of her head. She was curled against him in the Pilot's chair, one of three places to sit aboard the Scavenger.

He'd laughed so hard he'd begun to cry, and her face had crumpled as she'd slid to the floor and gathered herself into a fetal position to weep.

He'd picked her up and sat her on his lap and wept with her until they'd both wept themselves dry.

The girl quiescent in his arms, he wondered how he'd known what to do. An orphan, reared in a brothel on Alpha Tuscana, he'd run away to work on a garbage scow at age twelve. Jack had never known a mother's embrace. The brash buxom breasts of courtesans had been a paltry substitute, the boy cast away the moment a paying customer walked in the door.

"I'll get you finer clothes than Princess Andromeda, and she'll be so envious that she'll ask who your designer is."

Misty giggled. "Liar."

He giggled too, enjoying the moment and the smell of freshly-washed child and being close to another human being.

Far too little of the latter throughout my life, he thought.

* * *

Emperor Phaeton Torgas stared at Princess Andromeda. "There's been a change in the alignments, I tell you!"

She sat on an ottoman slightly to the right of his throne, the heiress in attendance upon the troubled Emperor. "Someone dares oppose the Empire?" she asked lightly, looking as dainty as a daisy. They were alone in the throne room, or as alone as they'd ever get, servants omnipresent and perpetually underfoot. Like rats, she thought.

He scowled at her over his scepter, a gold-plated staff two-and-a-half feet long, capped with a platinum-filigreed halo, which served to house a somewhat-plain looking two-inch silver cube. "No, it's not open defiance, as if we didn't have enough of that already." His gaze was on his own satin-clad foot.

Her satin slippers, embroidered with gold and silver thread in the shapes of roses, glinted in the evening light.

"It's more an undercurrent, but a strong one, a shift in the pillars that hold the Empire aloft."

"Sounds grave, Father. No doubt a concern easily addressed." She smoothed an imaginary wrinkle from the sleeve of her silk blouse.

"If only I knew where to look! I'd place the Armada on alert, but I haven't an inkling of what to tell Admiral Camelus to look for." A shudder shook him. "When I look around the room, I see the legacy of my forebears, and I'm invigorated to build upon their achievements," Emperor Phaeton intoned. "And when I look upon you, my dear daughter, I desire to extirpate any hint of resistance, that you may rule unhindered when I'm gone."

She glanced around the room, busts of her forebears lining the walls. For twelve hundred years, the Torgas lineage had held sway over half the galaxy, occasional rebellions flaring at the edges but nearly all put asunder quickly.

"I hear you had something akin to a fit this morning?"

She drew a sharp breath. Of course he knew about that, she reminded herself. The cube tells him everything.

"The cube tells me everything."

It was an open secret that this alien cube was the source of Torgassan power.

"I don't know what happened, Father. I was brushing my hair out in my dressing room and ..." She looked at him bewildered. "Remember that time you ghosted me? That's almost what this felt like. I was in a ship galley, small and cramped, a bowl with the leavings of some mush beside me, and a girl's voice called from around the corner ..." She shook her head, unable to recall what the girl had said.

They both looked at the cube mounted on the scepter.

The alien artifact functioned by reading the minute variations in electrical fields introduced by human thought. At its wielder's behest, it also injected electrical field perturbations in resonance with the brain's neuro-electrical activity, able to do so irrespective of distance.

Which was how her father had known.

These electrical fields were known as Gaussian fields, and the device was called a Gaussian Holistic Oscillating Subliminal Tesseract, but it was usually referred to by the acronym, GHOST. Thus the origin of the term. Whenever the Emperor wanted to know something or to influence someone, he simply ghosted them.

Their gazes met over the top of the scepter.

"Is there another cube, Father?"

Chapter 2

The next morning, Jack got Misty and himself some breakfast, and then Jack looked into the cube to find out what the Imperial Patrol was doing.

Slowly, its sides lost their reflectivity and an image formed.

The cabin of the Imperial Patrol vessel.

"—no sign of activity. Maybe he's laying low until we get distracted," one said.

"With that long a criminal record, I'd say he doesn't know when to lay low. What about that girl, the one he was with on the monitors?"

"What about her?"

"Think we should report her to Captain Jenks? He did say to report any suspicious planetside activity immediately."

"What's suspicious about a girl? Especially a native brat?"

The other patrol officer was silent a moment, looking pensive. "This scavenger is a loner. She's clearly a ground-dog. Doesn't make sense, their pairing up like that."

"There you go thinking again."

"What do you suppose happened that he'd want immediate reports? He's never expressed the slightest interest in this sector, much less the planet itself."

The other man extended a hand toward a tactiface, moved a few manipules until data spilled down the screen. " 'Canis Dogma Five, former Capital of the Circian Empire, whose last remnants collapsed in three hundred BTE'—over fifteen hundred years ago—'after ruling the galaxy for nearly a millennium.' " His eyes scanned the fountain of text.

"Maybe it's Torgassan Paranoia," said the other man. Clearly from one of the subjugated worlds, he wore a Torgassan Patrol uniform, swore fealty to the Torgassan Emperor, got paid out of the Torgassan coffers, but was no more Torgassan than his shipmate.

"Listen to this: 'Despite numerous attacks by rival empires, the Circians fought very few wars. The fifty or so naval engagements they are known to have had all ended in the surrender or negotiated capitulation of their opponents. They were never the victor by means of the outright defeat of their enemies.' " He turned to his companion. "Now, that's influence!"

Influence that Emperor Torgas wished he had, Jack was thinking.

"Influence that Emperor Torgas wished he had," said the other man, his face empty of expression.

Jack jumped, and the cube turned silver again.

* * *

"They don't look very friendly."

Jack wasn't about to let that stop him. They stood on a cracked and pitted major boulevard six blocks north of Misty's tower apartment, surrounded by rag-clad natives, each bearing a weapon, every weapon aimed at them.

After they'd eavesdropped on the Imperial Patrol, they had set out to find the other natives of Canis Dogma Five. They'd followed the wide boulevard, an occasional skeleton of toppled skyscraper blocking their path. They'd have made better time if they hadn't had to climb through the detritus. The boulevard itself was a veritable forest but a pygmy one, the thin, scraggly trees barely eking out nutrients from the rock-hard surface, most of them sprouting from seams.

Jack held out his hands to show they were empty. "I come to ask a favor. My name is Jack."

A large man with a heavy spear and even heavier gut replied, "You fell from the stars two nights ago, and the Imperial Patrol looks for you. Why shouldn't we sell you to them?"

"Because I helped this girl bury her grandfather, Augustus Circi."

The man lowered the spear. "The old man finally died?"

"About two weeks ago," Misty told him.

"I'm sorry for you loss," the heavy man said. "We honor those who help with our dead. Thank you, stranger Jack who fell from the stars. Come, and ask you favor in private. Away from the Patrol's prying eyes." He looked overhead as if expecting a patrol craft any moment, then signaled to the group.

Warriors melted into the surroundings like wraiths.

"I'm Xerxes, and my home is this way." He gestured to an alley between derelict buildings that looked none too inviting.

As his eyes adjusted to the darkness, Jack realized it was free of the detritus that littered the rest of the ruins. The smells of dank and dusty decay were absent too. Misty followed obediently at his elbow. The alley turned into a tunnel, then a corridor, and beyond a heavy curtain, an abode, the scents of home and food unmistakable.

"There she is," said a woman's voice. "Didn't I tell you, Xerk, that we'd be seeing the waif? How are you, my girl? Misty, isn't it? I'm your great aunt once removed, Gertrude. You can just call me Trude." Her manner was just as robust as her girth and her voice. If her man was large then she was larger.

Trude was a good name for her, Jack was thinking.

"That's *Princess* Misty," the girl said, a hand to her hip and her shoulder thrust forward. "And I'm anything but a waif!"

"Anything but is for certain, no question there. And who's the gentleman escort, your Highness?" From anyone else, it might have been mockery, but from Trude it actually sounded respectful.

"Captain Jack," Misty said, "this is my Great Aunt Trude, once removed."

"Enchanted," Jack said, inclining his head.

"Mutual, Captain, and welcome."

"And you were right," Xerxes said to his wife. "Augustus is dead."

"Now wasn't that what I was sayin'?" she asked in an "I-told-you-so" voice. "Knew it was comin', Princess, as he hadn't been well."

"Jack helped me put him to rest," Misty said, "and then brought me here."

16

"And a right thing, too," Trude said, looking Jack over again. "A good deed sometimes gets rewarded. Anything we can do, just you name it."

"Um …" Jack looked around the lodgings, the walls clean if dingy with smoke from ill-ventilated fires, the carpets threadbare if in good repair, the furniture crude but looking comfortable even so, the walls riddled with cubbies full of useful items. "There is something I'd like to ask of you both. I brought Misty here not knowing of her relation, just knowing she needs care—care I can't give just yet. If I may ask—"

"But Jack," Misty cried, "you said you'd take me to the palace!" She looked as if about to weep.

"And I will," he protested, "if your aunt and uncle are willing, but I need a few days." He saw she wasn't believing him. "You know—to make arrangements."

"For what? We don't need arrangements! I'm the Princess!"

"But even the Princess needs the proper attire, Misty. You said so yourself. And it's much more proper and fitting if you received an invitation to the palace. Getting one will take a little time." Not bad, Jack thought to himself. I should confabulate more often, I'm pretty good at it.

Her face scrunched in disbelief. "But why should I stay here? How are you going to know if the clothes will fit if I don't go with you?"

"Well, I've got some trading to do before I'll have any money to buy the clothes. I'll be back in a few days." She still looked doubtful, so he added, "I promise."

She seemed to relent, then looked sad. "You sure you'll come back?"

"I'm sure," he said with quiet confidence.

"Oh good," she said, suddenly brightening, and then threw herself into his arms.

He couldn't help but embrace her. He didn't quite know how else to respond, but the warmth he felt deep inside made the whole trip worthwhile.

"He'll still have to get our permission, your Highness," Trude said softly.

"Of course," Misty said lightly, looking up at Jack with a smile that melted away all doubt he had about returning.

* * *

In retrospect, lodging the girl with her relative Circians had gone far more smoothly than he could have imagined.

Making his departure far more difficult than he could have imagined.

As Jack trudged doggedly back to the way he'd come, doubts gnawed at him.

I should go back for her, he thought a hundred times en route to his ship.

I'll miss her too much, he thought.

How can I do this to her? he wondered, his guilt adding to his indecision and regret.

Once you leave, you'll never return for her, he remonstrated himself. You never planned to return for her in the first place, he thought in self-recrimination.

The thought of her being left in the care of strangers was so reminiscent of how he had once felt as an abandoned orphan that Jack burst into tears and almost turned around on the spot.

He tore his gaze from over his shoulder and forced himself to continue southward, his surroundings blurry. A bystander might have thought him injured he wailed so disconsolately.

Back at his ship, hidden under a building at the base of a chute leading up the boulevard, Jack checked for signs of tampering or attempts at forced entry. Seeing none, he disarmed the gene-lock.

The ship did a quick gene analysis, then opened the hatch.

In the copilot's chair sat Misty.

"How...?" Between his befuddlement, relief, joy, and dismay, Jack didn't know what to say.

She looked abashed, as thought he might punish her.

Instead, he knelt at her feet and buried his head in her lap, weeping uncontrollably and protesting how terribly grateful he was that she'd disobeyed him and begging abjectly for her forgiveness.

"We'd better get going," she said sometime later.

He nodded mutely, wondering how he'd become enamored of her so quickly and why she had such faith in a terrible scoundrel like him. He also wondered how he could act such a fool and engage in such lugubrious buffoonery.

He looked over at her from the pilot's chair. "I'm not a very good person sometimes."

18

She looked ancient in her nine, elongated years. "You're always a good person, but your choices aren't always good."

He dropped his gaze to the controls, remembering what awaited them. He still didn't know how they were going to evade the Imperial Patrol, but he sensed he'd probably use the cube.

Setting it on the console, he gazed at it silvery sides, which promptly dissolved into iridescent rainbows. The patrol cabin materialized, the two officers scanning their instruments.

"Why do you suppose the Captain wants these ground-dog travels documented? What a waste of resources!"

"There you go thinking too much," the other one replied.

"And why electromagnetic activity? They don't have electricity. All we'll get on that is background static."

Jack looked at Misty.

"Concentrate on disappearing," she said.

He wrinkled his brow, remembering how he'd influenced them before as they stood outside the culvert, debating whether to go in after the two evaders.

"I wonder where that scavenger went. You think he's still groundside?"

"We'd know if he wasn't. A ship that size leaves a trail visible from the primary. Don't worry, we'll see it easily from geosynch."

You think I'm gone already, Jack thought.

"You know what I think? Gone already."

You think I have a cloak, Jack thought.

"If I were him, I'd have a ship-cloak. Probably has contraband aboard right now. I don't think we'll see him at all."

"I think you're right. I think he's long since gone."

Jack powered up the ship. The hum of finely-tuned engineering vibrated the seat beneath him. Hold that thought! he thought, you won't see me at all!

He steered the ship out of its subterranean parkway space and pointed it at the stars.

Aboard the Imperial Patrol, sensors alarms began to flash, blaring their warnings at the two slack-jawed, empty-eyed patrolmen.

Jack engaged the main engine and launched the ship skyward. Two incognizant patrolmen watched without a twitch as their monitors tracked the Salvager.

Just get us off planet, he told the cube. Once in space, he could evade with a series of random hops.

Misty watched placidly, if attentively, from the co-pilot's chair.

As they hit the ionosphere, a thought occurred to Jack: "How did you get past the gene-lock?" He turned to stare at Misty.

Wide-eyed, she blinked at him.

"Bogey, bearing eight-one-nine, engage!" The patrolmen came to life.

"We've been spotted!" Jack picked the Vulpecula system at random and dropped the ship into an evasion pattern.

Just before the first hop, the ship slewed.

"Tractor beam" flashed on the screen, and Jack cursed.

The stars blanked out and a new set replaced them, but the patrol clung tenaciously.

"Come on, baby, shake 'em!"

The stars blanked again, and a fiery sun appeared a parsec away. "Tractor beam" continued to flash.

"You're under arrest," blared their speakers, the patrol using an override to commandeer the Scavenger's com system.

"Kiss my black hole!" Jack said, reversing the polarity to the hull in the hopes of breaking the tractor beam's hold.

The ship hopped again, and they appeared inside a nebula briefly, the thick plasmas nearly sending the shields into overload, but also weakening the tractor beam further.

The next hop took them to the Seven Sisters, and the "tractor beam" warning died.

"We did it!" Jack said, exulting, but he let the ship complete three more random hops before he was sure.

On the fourth hop, the Tuscana constellation appeared around them, and Jack powered down the ship, leaving on only the passive sensors. Without engines or other active systems, they would look like a derelict floating aimlessly in space.

Jack looked at the cube.

The silver surface stared back at him blankly.

Just in case, he willed them to be transparent.

The cube surface turned black.

"I knew you could do it, Jack!" Misty said with a squeal.

"*We* did it, or at least I think we did. Just to make sure, we'll wait awhile. Let's get something to eat while we wait," he told Misty, "and then we gotta sell that hold full of junk before I can take you to Torgas Prime."

Chapter 3

They walked the long avenue leading into the city of Perth on the garbage planet Corolla Tertius in the constellation Coronis Australis. On either side of the avenue stood slatted fences, little obscuring what lay beyond them. Mountains of junk soared in haphazard profusion, eclipsing any sight of the horizon. The gray, sultry sky seemed inadequate to contain the voluminous discard, the detritus of a hundred thousand occupied worlds.

Corolla Tertius had been Jack's first stop after stowing away on the garbage scow from Alpha Tuscana when he was twelve years old. Undeniably, the garbage planet held a comforting familiarity for him.

The mountains of refuse on either side of the avenue appeared to be moving. Upon closer inspection, the refuse itself wasn't actually moving, but hordes of scavengers were. The gleaners, they were called, picking through recently-dumped scow-loads of garbage for materials that might be recycled or reused.

Jack had been among them when he'd first arrived on Corolla Tertius, happy to explore what had been dumped here as garbage. One person's junk ...

"How come we're walking?" Misty asked, flitters whizzing past both ways on the avenue.

"'Cause Jack can't even afford a taxi, much less all the gowns, jewels, staff, and what-not that an arriving princess will be expected to wear, not to mention the fuel needed to get to Torgas Prime." The stench of garbage on either side was nearly overpowering.

She glared at him from under her brow.

"I said I'd get you there, right?" he asked, annoyed.

"Yeah?" Her voice looped upward, the question audible.

"So you can trust me to do that, Princess Misty Circi, or you can ask someone else." He didn't expect her to understand all the variables and hurdles, but he did expect her to have some patience.

"All right, I just might."

He raised an eyebrow at her, stepping around what was clearly a gear casing for a landing strut. Must've fallen over the fence, he thought, the fence bulging precariously from the weight of junk it tried to contain. "Just might what?"

"Trust you," she said, smiling with that perfect, classic face.

A face that opened the joy in his heart. He didn't know why, but just looking at her gave him hope and instilled in him a sense of redemption and purpose.

He'd had little enough of all three in his life.

Ahead was a warefront—the front of a warehouse—whose shoddy appearance lent itself to the idea that it might have grown out of the junk behind it. The smell wasn't any better inside than out.

A weather-beaten, toothless derelict looked up from a glasma counter in better shape that he was. "That you, Jack?"

"Sure is, Busby. Look at you, workin' the counter. Moving up in the galaxy!"

The two men embraced. "What brings you back, boy?" He threw his working eye toward the girl, the glasma one remaining fixed to Jack's face.

Jack was surprised he had a prosthetic. Only then did he notice that the iris was a vertical almond-shape, probably from a stuffed, big-game cat. "This here's Misty."

"I'm a princess!" she piped up.

Busby giggled openly. "What'd you do, Jack, marry a Queen?" He threw his head back and laughed, blackened stubs where teeth should have been. His face had the puckered lemon look of the chronic edentulous.

"Not quite," Jack replied. "Hey, I got a half-a-load I need to sell. What's your rate today?"

Busby's hand shot up toward the sign, the forefinger missing its last joint.

"A quarter galacti per ton? Last I was here it was four bits, twice that."

"It's the market, Jack. You know the song and dance."

Every choreographed step of it. At that price, he wouldn't even fill his tank. He didn't have much hope of cajoling Busby to up his payout.

Misty tugged on his sleeve.

He looked down at her, saw her glance toward his pocket. Could I use the cube and have him triple his price? he wondered excitedly.

The swirling misery inside Busby's head flooded through Jack.

He stopped himself. Busby had taken Jack under his wing when the twelve-year-old orphan had been dumped from the garbage scow with the rest of its refuse, had shown him how to spot valuable glean, how to keep from being sucked into giving away what he'd collected, how to outsmart the other gleaners, who were as likely to steal his pickings as to find their own.

"Show old Busby your teeth," Jack whispered, nodding toward the trash collector and hoping he didn't get jealous.

Misty looked at Busby, smiling slowly, widening it until a full rictus had plastered her face.

Busby laughed again, joy in his eyes. "I can't tell you how good it is to see you, boy, how much I enjoyed having you at my side. How about four tenths per ton, Jack? I could do that for you."

"What a charmer," Jack told Misty as they were climbing into the taxi outside. To celebrate, they went to the fanciest restaurant on Perth.

Shredded banners hung limp in the stench-filled breeze, a stench replaced by the smell of roast beast, when the wind was right. The warped and stained wooden benches barely held their weight as they wolfed down real food, probably made from the pig-sized rodents who fought with the gleaners over loads newly dumped from the bellies of scows, the roast beast a far sight better than the flavored mush synthed aboard the ship and served in their own edible bowls.

Downtown Perth looked little different from the outskirts. The buildings were taller and the streets were cleaner, but the architecture was similar if more chic. Fancy dilapidation, the motif was called, a high-class garbage dump.

Under a statue of Captain James Stirling, who'd named Perth in the

110th century following the Diaspora, Jack and Misty fed the birds their leftovers, giggling and watching the antics as pigeons and seagulls fought over the scraps. These citified birds were far smaller version of the ones who flocked above the dumps in all directions around Perth, scattering only when a scow descended from the skies.

The inscription under the statue amused them both: "In the name of God, the Father, and his Majesty King George III, I do hereby consecrate this ground as the first free settlement in all of Coronis Australis, may its residents long enjoy clean living."

"Do you think he knew it'd be one big garbage dump?" Misty asked, and they both dissolved in laughter.

Jack stopped suddenly, sitting up, the feeling of being watched dropping dread like a lead weight into his bowels.

Half a dozen people strolled leisurely through the square. Streets bordered all four sides, their sidewalks somewhat crowded.

There, at one corner, a man looking away. At another corner, a woman browsing something in her hand a bit too intently. Jack didn't need to look toward the other two corners.

"We're being watched," Misty said.

He still found it disconcerting how well she knew his thoughts.

"Who are they?"

"Oh, variety of possibilities. Maybe the collection company hired by my first wife to get her spousal support. Half a dozen worlds think I owe them various fines—I've never been arrested on Corolla Tertius, I swear—so it can't be here. And well, I am a few months late on my Salvager payments. Come on." He stood and strode aggressively toward the man who'd looked away.

They despised confrontation, these collection agents. It was what they least expected and most feared. A hostile target was a dangerous target. Oh, yeah, they call them recipients, Jack thought. Euphemistic confabulation.

Misty a step behind him, Jack strode resolutely at the man.

He half-turned as though interested in something else.

Jack collided with him, knocking him to the ground. "Sorry," he said. He wasn't and kept on walking, crossing the street and turning west toward the spaceport.

He ventured a look back.

The man and two collection companions stood watching him from the corner, brushing the dirt off him.

Jack took the next turn, walked half a block, loped up an alley, then stepped to the curb and hailed a taxi.

"That happen often?" Misty asked, settling in the back seat beside Jack.

"Makes life interesting," he said. "They'll probably have agents at the spaceport. Only way they could have tracked me here was my landing. They're all public information."

"All landings?"

"Listen, kid, I don't make enough money to bribe every space traffic controller who happens to handle my landing requests. We'll have to think of some way to avoid them. I know you don't have much experience in this type of thing but if you've got ideas, I'd like to hear them." If this is that same collection agency, he thought, they probably know most of my tricks.

"Since they probably know most of your tricks, it'll have to be something original."

He snorted, bemused by her. "You a mind-reader, kid?"

"My name's Misty, and it's Princess Misty to you, Mister."

Jack roared with laughter, loving her cheek.

"You want any help or not?" she asked in mock pique.

"Of course, my Lady Princess Misty." He inclined his head toward her.

"That's what I thought, so check the cheek, pal."

"Yes, m'lady."

They shared a laugh as the taxi pulled to a stop across from the spaceport entrance, as instructed.

Duty free shops selling mostly memorabilia crowded the area outside the spaceport entrance. Why memorabilia might be marketable on a planet as forgettable as Corolla Tertius was a mystery to Jack. He ducked into a shop to browse.

He checked his palmcom to see if the Scavenger had been refueled yet. In a hurry to leave, he hadn't had the chance to alert the dockmaster. He keyed in the request, and an autoreply alerted him to a twenty-minute wait.

"How does this look?" Misty had draped a boa over her shoulders. It trailed to her feet in a cascade of glittery tendrils, like a furry worm.

A display of mock official uniforms stood behind her.

Jack smiled. We've got a little time, he thought.

* * *

I hoped she can do this, Jack thought, following Misty at a respectful five paces, a manservant cap pulled low over his brow, a uniform-looking suit decking him from head to toe, sans insignia.

They'd fashioned a tiara from a bracelet, found a sequined evening gown to modify to her size, and snatched the red pumps from a girl-sized doll.

She erased his every doubt in the first encounter.

"Boy," she said to the youngish valet at one concourse door, "My fool servant—" she gestured vaguely over her shoulder in Jack's direction —"has not only lost my port pass and credentials, he didn't even have the wherewithal to alert my father, King Quantus of Fornacis Secondus, of my predicament. Can you show him what competence is and get me a shuttle out to my yacht, please?"

The valet perked right up. "Certainly, Lady—"

"Princess Misty Circi," she said, and then turned on Jack. "Fool!"

He cringed obediently.

The valet jumped to do her bidding.

As they were en route to the posh side of the spaceport, Misty asked the shuttle driver to take them to the opposite end, where all the independent traders were relegated. The driver glanced askance at her.

"The fool servant of mine even forgot where we parked!" She cuffed him for emphasis, sitting behind him in the back seat.

The driver threw a pitying glance in Jack's direction and banked the flitter.

"Right here is fine, driver."

They'd seen a shadowy figure slouched against a landing strut two spaces over from the Salvager. Their paltry disguises weren't likely to work on people who had a profile on Jack. Their disguises might be thick, but that profile was pretty thick, too.

"All right, miss genius, what now?" Jack asked, peering toward the Scavenger from behind a cargo transport five spaces over. They'd spotted two additional collectors surveilling the Scavenger.

"Why don't we walk right up to the ship and say it's under contract to King Quintus?"

"They'll recognize me, even in this suit," he replied.

"Not if you exert a little influence."

"Eh? What do you mean?" He saw her glance at his pocket. He kept forgetting about the cube. And he didn't owe these hired pests an electron's worth of anything, unlike Busby, who'd helped him out when he was young. "All right, let's try it."

She led the way.

He admired how good she was. Stars above, what am I thinking? She should be practicing her social graces, not trying to finagle her way past a debt collector!

Cap down, gaze on her feet five paces ahead, he followed.

The nearest surveiller intercepted them at the Scavenger hatch.

"Jack who? You must have the wrong ship. The one's under contract to King Quintus of Fornacis Secondus. There are at least three other ships here named 'the Scavenger.' And at least two others by the name of 'Salvager.' Get out of my way!"

You don't see me, Jack thought, feeling the bewilderment. You must be mistaken. Check your records.

"Uh, pardon, your Ladyship, I must be mistaken. I'll check my records. You would mind waiting white I do so?"

"Sorry, I'm already late. If this idiot servant of mine hadn't lost my port pass and credentials, I'd have left long ago. A princess can't get decent help these days, I swear!" She kicked Jack in the shin. "Dolt!"

He cringed and cowered, holding his leg, and hopped over to the gene-lock to palm it.

The surveiller stepped aside. "Pardon, Lady Princess."

They stepped into the ship, and the hatch slid closed.

They fell into their seats, laughing to the point of tears, and Jack started the preflight checklist.

"You were wonderful, Misty!" he said, guiding the ship into orbit, still giggling.

"I was, wasn't I?" she said, grinning at him. "I'll make a damn fine princess!"

He wondered where she'd learned to curse like a sailor.

Chapter 4

The first place they stopped after leaving the garbage planet was Denebi in the Summer Triangle, near the red giant Vulpeculae. Sometimes known as Alpha Cygni, Denebi was a blue-white supergiant that bathed its fifteen planets with such bright light that humans lived under polarized domes only on the outer three planets. Denebi III, their destination, was a cold if well-lit ball of rock and ice with barely enough oxygen to sustain life. At a half-grav, it was an easy landing for even the bulkiest and most awkward of craft.

"Why are we stopping here?" Misty asked.

"I got an old associate who might be interested in some merchandise. Low gravity planets make better transshipment points, so this is a commerce center for almost all settlements in the Summer Triangle."

"Doesn't feel much like summer," she muttered.

"You stay here and mind yourself," Jack told her. "Keep yourself locked in the ship and don't open the door for strangers."

"Why can't I go with you?"

"This old associate of mine likes kids—dipped in chocolate for dessert. I won't be long."

She made a face at him and returned up the gangway at his bidding.

Jack retracted it remotely and locked the hatch with the gene lock. He was still puzzled how she'd gotten past it on Canis Dogma Five.

He closed the cargo hatch and shouldered the bundle of exotic goods he'd put together to sell, the bulging satchel easily five times his weight. Without the satchel, he'd have had a difficult time walking in the low gravity.

The spaceport tarmac was littered with variegated ships, from yachts to deep-space cruisers, the bulk of them freighters. Salvagers like his were scarce, the densely-populated Summer Triangle having been consistently occupied, even in the long interregnum between the Circi and Torgassan Empires. There wasn't much junk around to salvage.

He found a carrier at the spaceport edge and rented it with nearly his last galacti.

"Where you gonna sell that load o' junk?" the clerk asked him.

Jack frowned at the jibe. "I get a discount for letting you insult me?"

The carrier groaned and wheezed under the weight but followed him obediently, its rear blades sliding smoothly across the perma-frost ground. Cornering was difficult, the momentum wanting to carry off the carrier.

He wound his way through the markets, puffs of icy air above hucksters who offered up their wares to the crisp atmosphere, each breath freezing instantly to a glitter, lit by the bright blue primary like jewels.

Passing smoke shops and shoot shops, snort stops and shot stops, Jack felt the yearning for a lungful of comfort. Not until I make the sale, he told himself doggedly. And what about her? he asked himself yet again.

What about her? he replied to his own question, daring himself to think the unthinkable.

I can't think about her right now, he told himself. While he didn't think about her, another part of his brain plotted how he could rid himself of the pesky girl.

The unassuming storefront declared in inch-high letters the under-whelming presence who might be found beyond the door: "R. Delphin, Proprietor."

Leaving his carrier behind, Jack pushed into the shop.

The interior was immaculate. Glasma cases displaying fine antiques lined both sides of the shop. The walls displayed stills of other antiques that had once graced the premises. An old man with half a cybernetic head peered at fine stones through a high-precision oculus. He wore a sterile white coat and white satin gloves. Even his shoes were draped with sterile white cloth.

"Stop right there. You need decontamination."

Behind the door was a small decom stall. Jack stepped dutifully inside; the machine hummed and whined, and he tried not to think about the years it was taking off his life. When he stepped from the stall, the cube in his pocket felt warm. Why's it warm? he wondered.

"Jack Carson, Junkster Extraordinaire," Delphin said, looking him up and down, as if appraising his market value.

"Richard, how very good to see you," Jack said, his enthusiasm sounding forced even to him, he who lacked all nuance.

Delphin looked over Jack's shoulder. "What monstrosity are you attempting to off on me this time, Carson? I don't want any, by the looks of it from here." The proprietor turned his oculus on Jack.

"I'm not here to sell that. I got something else, requires privacy." He let his eyebrow rise a bit.

"What about that?" He stabbed a finger over Jack's shoulder. "You take your eyes off it, it'll be gone."

"Good riddance." He might have shrugged, his voice nonchalant. "It got me here."

Delphin's oculus scanned Jack from head to toe and gasped. "I've never seen one of those. This way, Carson." He spun and led the way to the rear, turned into a nearly hidden doorway. "Boy, mind the shop. In fact, put out the sign and lock the door."

A rag-haired urchin ducked past Jack, steering clear of both men nimbly.

"Caught him trying to purloin a trinket," Delphin said, leading Jack into a small laboratory. "He's working off his debt. Better that than being sentenced to three years hard labor on a garbage planet." The oculus riveted itself to a gadget that looked quite similar to the one that adorned Delphin's head. "Put the cube there, on that platter."

A mounted platter occupied the center island.

Jack put the cube on the platter, its iridescent sides swirling ominously.

Delphin swung the larger, ceiling-mounted oculus around and positioned its gargantuan lens just above the cube. The smaller oculus

31

attached to his head also peered inquisitively at the alien device. The man's hands danced across the controls.

The lights dimmed and a bright beam pierced the dark, the cube emanating no light itself. A dull, distant whine originated somewhere.

Jack wondered whether the images he'd seen on its sides had been projected from somewhere inside the cube, or whether the cube had put the images into his visual cortex. Its sides began to swirl.

"Where'd you get it?"

"Canis Dogma Five." Jack didn't have the subtlety to prevaricate.

Delphin gasped and swiveled his oculus toward him. "How'd you evade the patrols? That place is locked down tighter than a casino vault. Latitude and longitude?"

Jack told him and added, "The former Capital of the Circian Empire."

The oculus swiveled back to the cube. "How much are you asking?"

Jack's initial thought, en route, had been to get it appraised, but Delphin was already asking how much, and clearly wanted to buy it. Jack thought of a price and doubled it, then doubled it again, then for good measure quintupled that. "Fifty million galacti, ten percent now, the remainder once you've verified its authenticity."

"Done," Richard Delphin, proprietor of fine antiquities, said immediately.

"Cash," Jack added.

The hesitation was brief. "Of course."

Five million galacti cash was an inordinate sum. The trinket that the boy had tried to steal couldn't have been worth ten galacti. The baubles at the front of Delphin's shop were rarely worth more.

"I'll need a few minutes to make arrangements, of course."

"Of course," Jack replied, his feet barely touching the ground. Five million galacti was five million galacti. Even if Delphin stiffed him for the balance, Jack was independently wealthy for the rest of his life.

Delphin left him there to secure the money, turning on the lights as he stepped from the room.

The profusion of equipment lining the walls held no interest for Jack. The cube under high magnification on the platter had grown quiescent, its sides a dull pewter.

I didn't want to be Emperor anyway, Jack thought, the idea still as ludicrous as any he'd entertained. He remembered as a child—

orphaned early and begrudgingly cared for until he'd stowed away on a garbage scow at age twelve—how he'd dreamt of achieving a position of power and helping all orphaned children to find a home. Jack had shared his dream with only one person, Cherise, a fellow orphan, whose prepubescent beauty bespoke the breathtaking comeliness she would acquire as an adult. To his surprise, she hadn't laughed at his dreams and instead had told him how much she admired him. Her joining the other entertainers had ultimately led to Jack's departure.

Looking at the alien cube, which had promised him the power to change the universe, Jack felt a distant, muted sadness.

He attributed his sadness to having left Cherise in the clutches of the old harpy who'd run the Southern Birds, but something about the cube on the platter...

I'm independently wealthy, he told himself, why don't I feel ecstatic?

The sense of an opportunity lost wouldn't leave him, but it was done. He'd made the transaction. There was no turning back.

Jack looked again at the cube, at its ugly pewter color, at its flat sides, and at its slightly beveled edges. Dull and unattractive. Just like Jack.

Well, maybe I'm more than dull, he thought. It would be a disservice to all ordinary-looking people to call me unattractive. He didn't need a mirror to see the bulbous nose, the recessed chin, the beetle brow, the buck teeth, the sunken cheeks. The closest he might aspire to an Imperial position was court jester, but his wit was as dull as his looks. It would be generous to describe his intellect as a dearth of cognition.

Jack sighed. No, he thought, I could never be Emperor.

Delphin came bustling back in with a satchel. "You sure you want it in cash?"

Jack nodded. He had a knife in his boot and knew how to use it wicked fast. It wouldn't stop a blaster to his back, but he'd manage. He'd developed a sense for danger, an intuition for intrigue. "I'll be all right. Which way's that back door?" He grabbed the satchel.

"You don't want to count it?"

"No," Jack said flatly.

Delphin shrugged and led him down a cluttered corridor.

Beyond it was an alley. Jack went deeper into the alley, picked a door at random—the back door to a small, indoor shopping mall—and walked toward the front.

He stopped at a boutique for a change of clothes. Remembering to remove the tags, he donned them and left the boutique.

Lightheaded, and much lighter in spirit, Jack started back toward the spaceport, the frosty ground crunching beneath his feet.

A smoke shop called his name.

Not with all this cash in hand, he told himself.

Just one to celebrate, and then I'll take the cash to the ship, he thought.

No, not even one! he remonstrated himself.

Before he knew it, he found himself asking for a booth in the back, positioning himself so he could see the front door. "Your finest, please," Jack said.

While the waiter went to fetch it, Jack dug into the satchel. The smallest domination was a thousand-galacti chit.

It'll do, Jack thought.

The waiter returned with a bowl of smoke. The pipe was a blue glasma tulip whose petals arced out gently and gracefully from a glowing center, its stem serving both as a platform and as the inhaling tube. In the center was a dusty, dun-brown ball of c-grade smoke.

"I said, 'your finest,' " Jack repeated, glancing at the chit.

In an instant, Jack was staring at the best smoke he'd even seen. Tears of resin beaded on the cluster, and the sweet smell clotted his nostrils. Already the entire establishment knew, the aroma pervading the place. Jack felt their eyes; he was glad he'd put the satchel on the bench beside him, out of sight below the table.

Jack took a practice breath, and then put his lips to the stem. The young waiter held up the burner. Jack bade him to wait and drew a lungful.

Heavenly scents filled his lungs and euphoria settled upon him. And the stuff wasn't even lit!

Jack signaled and exhaled, and the waiter applied the burner. All it took was a half a breath. Jack capped the glowing bowl and waved to the waiter, who left the burner.

The smoke expanded, sending its soothing tendrils out to his fingers and toes. His scalp began to tingle, and the surroundings began to glitter. The ceiling peeled away to show him each successive floor

34

above him, until they too rolled aside to reveal the sky, the blue-white pinprick of Denebi like a brilliant diamond so pure that its light washed the universe clean.

The booth disappeared from around him, and he floated, the distant Imperial Capital on Torgas Prime beckoning him oddly.

Below him, the palace sprawled across a picturesque valley on the lush, semi-tropical world. Palms sprouted in small courtyards located in unlikely places, buildings of fabulous façade interconnected with colonnaded walkways and soaring fountains. Rooftops glittered with crushed crystal, walls were inlaid with intricate mosaics, and walks were paved with marble flagstone.

The sight of the palace shook Jack, as though physically. He'd never yearned for the sedentary, leisure life of a prince, only for the power of one, with which he might make the lives of others better. Why am I seeing this? he wondered, little interested in the trappings of royalty.

Again the sensation of shaking, and Jack realized that someone was physically shaking him.

The bowl of smoke, a blue glasma tulip with gently arcing petals, wobbled dangerously on the table.

"Where's it at, Carson?"

He put out his hand to steady the bowl. Somewhere, his brain was saying danger was imminent, but Jack just laughed.

"I should have known. Wake him up."

A galaxy exploded on one side of his head, and his face spun the other. A curious thing seemed to be happening; he was feeling what could only be described in conversational terms as pain, but it had no relation to any event immediately preceding it that Jack had recognized as painful.

A galaxy exploded on the other side of his face and his head spun back the other way.

This was getting annoying. A person's drug-induced euphoria was sacred. Didn't they know it was extremely bad manners to interrupt such euphoria? And what person in his or her right mind would attempt to engage in a sensible discussion with someone who was by definition insensate?

He tried to focus on the three, six, or nine faces in front of him. He couldn't tell how many there were. One was familiar in that didn't-I-just-see-you-not-long-ago type familiarity. The other two faces weren't familiar at all, but the fact that both faces sat atop bodies whose physical proportion far exceeded the human norm—and were at least double Jack's own mass—lent credence to the message his brain had been trying to deliver for at least a minute or two.

"Where's the blasted cube, Carson?"

His eyes focused on the middle figure, the familiar one. His brain supplied him a name: Delphin. "I left it with you," he said—or tried to say. He was sure it was unintelligible. He was sure his brain was unintelligible.

"What'd he say?"

Jack tried to repeat it, his lips too loosened with drugs to form proper words. A fourth blow to his head finally penetrated to his limbic cortex, and the trickle down his cheek was sure to be blood. "I left it with you, Delphin," he growled, giving the apes on either side of the smaller man a nasty look.

The oculus focused on Jack's face. "It's gone, disappeared as I was examining it. I don't know what sleight of hand you performed, and I don't care. Hand me that bag."

One of the beef balls laid himself half across the table to grab the satchel containing the five million galacti.

Jack wished it gone, and it was.

"Where'd it go?!" muscle man asked.

"The cube or the money, Carson," Delphin said. "You don't want to know the third option. Choose!"

"Shove a quasar up your black hole, Delphin. If you can't hold onto a cube, it's time they put you in a nursing home." Jack realized he was furious.

"Third option it is, then, Jack. Sorry, I can't stay to watch the show, but I don't want to lose my plausible deniability." He turned to the muscle man to the left, the one with a brain cell. "Wait till I've left the building." He spun and walked off.

Jack eyed the two lumps. And the distance between them.

"Don't even think about it," the brain-cell said.

"Think about what? Have a puff on me, boys," Jack said.

"I'm workin'," one said, "but I'll be off in about five minutes. Can I—"

The other shoved an elbow in his gut. "That's consorting. You know what the boss says."

"He does it all the time."

"He's the boss." The brainy one turned to Jack. "I'll put it bluntly, Cockroach—the cube, the bag, or your life. Which is it?"

"You can put the first two into your black hole, buzzbrain, and I'll keep the third. Now, get out of my way." Jack stood, the satchel in his hand, and took a step toward the door.

A hand landed on his shoulder. It might have been a side of pork ribs. It spun Jack around.

A fist the size of a comet careened toward his face.

He pulled to one side, and the fist sailed wide.

Another plunged for his gut.

He turned sideways, and it whistled past.

Quadruple cannons launched a fusillade of blows, which Jack nimbly avoided. Even as he pulled away from one, he saw the next coming, each blow close enough he felt its wind, none able to make contact.

He wondered what he looked like to a bystander—some puppet being jerked around by its strings, he was sure. The spasm dance left him against a wall with nowhere to go. Somewhere, his brain was telling him he'd never had reflexes that good before.

Two panting, sweating lumps of lard looked at him against the wall. If they saw the satchel in his hand, they gave no indication of it. They each threw a glance at the other and charged him.

Jack was on the other side of them as they crashed into the wall and crumpled into a heap.

That's one heap of flesh, Jack thought, striding out the door.

The crowded street held no danger for him, not a single passerby seeing him. Hovercraft hummed past, and a few ground vehicles crunched across the perpetual frost. The shuffling masses somehow parted to let him by, as Jack strode, mystified, toward the spaceport.

The commotion behind him didn't alarm him. He knew they'd probably come after him, but he was oddly convinced they'd never find him.

He couldn't say exactly what had just happened. Rolling events through his mind, each moment after he emerged from his drug-induced stupor as clear as a glasma pane, Jack found that even he could not believe that he'd moved that fast.

Satchel in hand, five million galacti richer, Jack strode resolutely toward the spaceport, convinced that whatever had happened, he'd somehow acquired a new destiny.

Perpetual loser, orphan, salvage collector, thrice divorced and quadruple bankrupt, perennially getting tangled up with the authorities, and always saturated with smoke, Jack felt that somehow his life had changed.

Maybe he'd even turned it around.

The future opened to Jack like the spaceport between skyscrapers. Ships lifted off and dropped between multistory buildings on either side. The bright glare of engines reflected off building windows, some of them evidencing the blackening of carbon burn.

He'd always wondered why they'd put such tall buildings around the spaceport.

Port security didn't look up when he strode through the checkpoint. No buzzer went off when he waltzed through the scanners. No one asked for his ID or did a biometric, genescan, iris scan, retina type, bone image, E. coli match, or mitochondria sample.

As if he didn't exist.

"I was wondering why you were taking so long," Misty said as he came through the hatch. "Ran into some trouble, eh?" She touched the now scabbed-over split to his cheek.

He winced as she dressed the wound.

"I don't know why I'm doing this," she said, "You could just use the cube."

He raised an eyebrow at her. "I sold it for five million galacti."

The bewildered look on her face turned to amusement. "You're so funny, Jack. You know, the way you tell jokes without any change in expression, you ought to consider comedy."

He stared at her. "Actually, I sold it for fifty million galacti, but all I could get was ten percent in cash. It's in the satchel." He gestured at it. "Go on, look."

Doubt working its way across her face, Misty knelt. "Where did you get this, Jack?" She held up a bundle of thousand galacti chits.

"I told you, I sold the cube."

She giggled at him, her green eyes mischievous above her girlish grin. "Stop, Jack. You're incorrigible. You did no such thing."

"Yeah, I did. Why would I lie to you about something so important?" He wondered where she'd learned a word like that. Probably the ship's teacher machine, something he'd never had the discipline to use on long flights.

She giggled again. "No, you didn't. It's in your pocket."

He felt the lump before his hand got there. The cube felt inert—body temperature—and swirled placidly in his hand as he brought it out.

He stared at it, stunned.

* * *

"You're sure?" Emperor Phaeton Torgas stared at his prime Minister, stunned.

"I alerted you as soon as I could, your August Highness," Custos Messium said, dropping his forehead to the floor.

It was the fastest Torgas has seen him bow.

The Emperor held up his scepter.

Cradled in a circlet of platinum was a plain silver cube. If he stared at it, its sides became translucent and iridescent, as though secrets within bubbled to get out. It was a literal source of Torgassan power. With the Cube, his family had ruled half the galaxy for fifteen hundred years.

Half ruled the galaxy, or ruled half the galaxy.

"You're sure?" the Emperor asked, realizing he'd repeated himself.

"I am, your August Highness."

Whenever they'd attempted to extend their dominion to the far side of the galactic bar, an insurrection had erupted on this side. On one occasion, during the reign of Letus XI, the Empire had given a rebellion little attention while pursuing its expansion across the bar, and very nearly had lost Torgas Prime to the rebels.

The literal source of the Emperor's power, the cube facilitated their exercise of near-absolute dominion—to an extent.

How the Circians had ruled the entire galaxy with the cube was a mystery, unless there was another cube or a series of cubes, as several historians had speculated.

Rumors flared from time to time of another such cube, but none of the rumors had been substantiated.

Phaeton stared at the cube, its mysteries predominantly hidden, like a dormant plague awaiting the right conditions before spreading its contagion through a vulnerable populace. It allowed him to delve into others' minds, no matter what their distance. To see what they saw, hear what they heard, feel what they felt, taste what they tasted, and smell what they smelt. More importantly, it allowed him to become them, to take over their minds and direct their actions, a phenomenon called ghosting.

With ghosting, rebellions might be averted and sometimes subverted.

"Where?"

"Denebi III, your August Highness. An antiquities dealer of high repute, a Richard Delphin, was approached by a salvager of ill repute, a Jack Carson, who said he'd recovered it on Canis Dogma Five."

Emperor Phaeton went white.

The former Capital of the Circian Empire, Canis Dogma Five was a derelict world, its surface laced with the crumbling infrastructure of a once-thriving civilization. Nearly two millennium had passed since the Circian Empire's fall, and still the successor Empire, the Torgassan, kept the Circian homeworld under close surveillance.

For precisely this reason.

"And the Dogma Five patrols?" the Emperor asked.

"A curious thing, your August Highness. Not a single report of anomalous movements, unless one reviews the sensor recordings oneself. The sensors clearly indicate the descent, landing, two-day stay, and departure of this very same scavenger, but all the reports indicate only his arrival. They are glaringly mute regarding his departure. The sector commander is investigating the discrepancies. When asked, patrols and monitoring-station crews exhibit remarkable similar responses."

"That must be hundreds of personnel."

"Precisely, your August Highness."

"What are the responses?"

"They mumble, 'I didn't see anything, Sir —even from those crew members with female commanders. Their eyes lose focus, their voices become flat and emotionless, and their faces lose all expression."

"As though they're hypnotized."

"Precisely, your August Highness."

Ten years before, just after Phaeton assumed the throne from his just-deceased father, Tilbury II, the subsector adjacent to Canes Venatici

40

had erupted in rebellion, and in the first major test of his power, the new Emperor had ruthlessly subjugated its peoples.

With the cube.

He had ghosted the planet with the compulsion to bow to the least sign of Imperial rule, including the Imperial banner, a stylized depiction of the scepter in his hand.

In the first few months after the ghosting, the populace of Venatici the Outer had spent so much time genuflecting to ubiquitous symbols of Torgassan power that their economy had ground to a halt, crops went to seed for lack of anyone to harvest them, assembly lines stood idle, transport ground to a halt, and the rebellion fizzled. Everyone spent so much time on their knees that nothing got done. The people had nearly starved.

Served them right, too, the Emperor thought. We should have let them starve. Young and inexperienced, he'd let his ministers overrule his decision to extend them no help. Reports from the planet surface had consistently reflected the same perception: "They all look hypnotized."

Emperor Phaeton frowned, the Prime Minister forgotten. "Eh? What'd you say?"

Custos Messium, a tall man who'd served Phaeton's father before him, bowed in slight apology. "Pardon, your August Highness, I meant not to disturb your thoughts," he said, a slight smile upon his slight face above a slight form, "but this scavenger, Carson, appears to have retained the cube after purportedly selling it to the antiquities dealer. It disappeared as the dealer was examining it, and his efforts to recover it were met with an unusual level of evasion. It seems Carson made off with both the cube and the five million galacti that the dealer paid for it."

"You said this Carson appears to be held in low esteem. Why would a reputable antiquities dealer even entertain such a scoundrel?"

"Why indeed, your August Highness?"

Unless the scavenger had ghosted the dealer.

"Where did he go?"

"No one knows, your August Highness. Spaceport personnel are being remarkably mute on…"

"Yes, Prime Minister?"

"Pardon, your August Highness. Clearly the sensor data needs to be examined, as it appears the salvager hypnotized his way off planet."

"Clearly." The dolt!

"Pardon, your August Highness, if I may be excused...?"

"Certainly." Phaeton watched with increasing impatience as his usually sharp-witted Prime Minister removed his dull-witted self from the Imperial presence, bowing three times as he backed from the throne room.

The scepter beckoning, Emperor Phaeton quickly forgot the man. He looked deeply at the cube's swirling sides, as though a storm brewed beneath the smooth surface. Held immobile by a platinum ring, the cube was rarely touched by human hands.

Carefully, Phaeton released the catch and pulled aside the hinged, platinum circlet. Four of eight mounts came away.

"Grasp it by the edges if you must handle it at all," he remembered his father saying.

Nearly three inches from corner to corner, the cube would easily fit between the thumb and forefinger of a normal adult human hand. What purpose or intent there'd been in its alien manufacture had long since been lost when the aliens themselves had departed from this universe.

He placed his thumb and forefinger at those opposite corners. "The cube root of the sum of the cube of its sides is the length between the corners," he'd been told. The slight beveling of its edges made the corners comfortable in his grip.

He lifted it out of its mounts.

The universe inverted, and the fabric of time warped and skewed. The weft stretched and yawed but did not break or rend. And then all of it snapped back into place.

Where is this scavenger Carson? he asked the cube.

Unresponsive silence was his only answer.

Chapter 5

The Southern Birds sat at the end of a wooded lane outside a small metropolis on the southern hemisphere of a swampish world orbiting Alpha Tuscana. Jack could never remember the names of the lane, the city, or the planet, but the name of the establishment was forever etched into his memory.

The brothel was where he'd grown up.

Abandoned as an infant, he'd been given succor if not much guidance throughout his childhood by a bevy of women (and a few men) whose constant chatter frequently veered toward the bawdy banter common to such environs, the boy often forgotten as simply a constant presence underfoot. As such, Jack's education was weighted toward the idiosyncrasies of sexual behavior, the fleeting nature of relationships, the inevitable anxieties of aging, and the occasional invasion of Imperial law enforcement.

Not comely enough to attract customers' interests—in fact, rather the opposite—Jack had been spared indoctrination into the lifestyle and had remained an observer, getting rare glimpses into a complex and often tragic world. Not alone in this unconventional upbringing, Jack was one of half a dozen such orphans, all the others female, and all of them acquired as potential apprentices.

Misty looked quizzically toward the building as they approached. "What do they do here?"

"They're in the entertainment business." He'd come back on occasion since leaving at age twelve, but the last time had been nearly eight years before.

The house was quiet as they entered, almost deathly so. Midmorning was the deepest part of their night, nearly everyone asleep. Jack wondered if his childhood friend, Cherise, were still here. He rather doubted it. She'd been exceptionally beautiful and accomplished, and that even before she arrived at the Southern Birds at four years old.

The foyer was all etched glass and brass, shiny wood-grain floors, and gilt-framed portraits of nudes sprawled in somnolent leisure. The chandelier hung heavy and dark from three floors up.

"May I help you?" a girl not much older than Misty asked, appearing at their elbow.

"Uh, yes, please. I'm Jack, Jack Carson," he said. "I'm here to see Madam Mariposa."

"Certainly. Please have a seat. She's not prepared for visitors, so she'll be a few minutes."

"Of course, and please extend my apologies for not comming ahead."

"Certainly. And may I know the name of our other guest?"

Before he could stop her, Misty said, "I'm Princess Misty Circi, of Canis Dogma Five."

"Thank you." The girl nodded, evincing no surprise, and retreated soundlessly the way she had come.

Carson was the name they'd come up for him, confabulated for no other reason than he'd needed another name. Jack stepped into the reception room, where the guests chose their liaisons. A corridor blocked off by a curtain led to the "nesting rooms," as they were known at the Southern Birds. Around the walls were couches and loveseats and chaise longues, all so overstuffed as to invite comparisons to corpulence. In the center, cordoned by velvet ropes, was the viewing area, now empty. In this area, the courtesans would parade themselves, displaying their charms and looking amongst the customers for their next assignation.

Jack remembered with a twinge seeing Cherise parade herself for the very first time at age thirteen. A year younger than she, Jack had nearly ruined her first night in the rotation as he'd watched from the second-floor balcony. Madame Mariposa had stopped him from rushing downstairs, grabbing Cherise, and carrying her off to safety. He'd left soon after.

"You probably shouldn't introduce yourself that way," Jack said.

Misty turned her big blue eyes on him. "Why not?"

As he pondered that, imagining the thousands of political prisoners whose only crime was to oppose Emperor Torgas, and the millions who'd been slaughtered when they'd rebelled against his rule, whose worlds had been reduced to smoking cinders when their occupants had refused to capitulate to his demands. "Well, it's not safe," he said, looking at her directly to impress upon her the gravity of what he was saying.

He was just getting comfortable in the corpulent chair when the woman walked in.

He knew instantly who it was and he felt flabbergasted just the same.

"Jack."

That one word captured the entirety of his latency. The six most formative years of his life and their terrible culmination in having to watch his best friend and most loved companion prance and preen before a voracious audience all came rushing back to him in that one word.

In the six months before he had left, he and Cherise had become lovers, their liaisons quick and hurried and away from the watchful eyes of Madame Mariposa.

Cherise hadn't been around the other three times he'd visited, and he hadn't asked about her, afraid to open that door, afraid of what lay beyond.

Jack stood to greet her, and she stepped into his arms as though twenty years hadn't passed. If only, he thought. He pulled back to look at her, blinking away tears, seeing the same youthful innocence and purity that had always taken his breath away, seeing the simple joy of life in her soul, that capacity to be here now, fully, without a thought for the past or the future, without a care but for the one she beheld.

He knew she loved him still, as they stared into each other's eyes.

He also knew she wasn't free to pursue that love, just as she hadn't been free twenty years ago, when they'd stolen precious moments from their owners to be with each other. "You look wonderful," he said, his voice inaudible.

She beamed with his admiration, blush creeping up her neckline. She wore a chemise robe over a silk camisole, both of them a deep burgundy. "It's so good to see you, Jack. I've missed you terribly."

He nodded. For twenty years, he'd regretted leaving. He also knew he couldn't have stayed. "You're so strong and brave. I'm sorry to have been such a coward. If I'd—"

She shushed him with a smile and a finger across his lips. "Regrets keep us from living our lives today. Your courage has kept me going for many years, that and the joy of your companionship. You taught me just to be myself and honored me when I was completely truthful with you. Thank you." She took his hand and cradled it to her breast.

The empty years of his life spilled down his face. Companionship had been difficult to find, two of his three wives vulpine harpies who'd sucked his bank accounts dry. Trust had been difficult to build, even in simple transactions with other traders, a deep abiding mistrust of everyone around him undermining every exchange of goods.

"Who's your friend?"

"Misty, her name is Misty," Jack said hurriedly, before the girl could respond. "We're waiting to see Madame Mariposa."

Cherise threw him a slight smile and turned to the girl. "Misty, I'm Cherise. Jack and I grew up together."

"You were really important to him, you know," she said matter-of-factly. "And you still are."

Cherise threw him another look, as if to ask, "What have you been telling her?"

Unless I've started talking in my sleep, Jack thought, wondering how she'd known.

"Well, Madame Mariposa died a few years ago, and now, I'm Madame Mariposa. But you can call me Cherise. Come this way."

She led them to a door simply marked "private," one very near the entrance. Inside, one half the room looked like the perfect sitting room, overstuffed chairs around a low table. The other half was the compound security center, multiple monitors giving glimpses of every corridor and every exit. The girl who had greeted them moved through the monitors by turn, as though physically doing rounds.

46

"Morning rounds," Cherise said.

He saw the front stoop. "You saw us coming."

"But I didn't recognize you. You've changed, Jack."

"You're as beautiful as ever."

She laughed lightly and bade them to sit.

Facing her, Jack found himself suddenly at a loss for words. He needed her help, but now all he wanted was to remain here with her. Sell the Salvager and settle down as her business and domestic partner, running the brothel and starting a family.

"Jack's going to take me to the palace," Misty said.

Cherise's light laughter was little different. "It's a place everyone should visit at least once, I'm told."

"I'm not going there to visit. I'm going there to live."

"Oh, that's fabulous! It's what I'd do if I had the opportunity. But that requires an invitation from the Emperor himself. I'm too far beneath his notice to get an invitation."

"Jack's going to get me one."

Cherise turned to look at him.

"And I will, as soon as I can."

"And how, might I ask, will you be doing that?" Cherise had that what-have-you-been-telling-her look again.

"Jack's very persuasive," Misty told her.

"Yes, he is, isn't he?" Cherise laughed that soft, disbelieving laugh again. "And how might I help?"

"I don't know where I'll get the wardrobe necessary to live in the palace. Whatever will I do?" Misty didn't put the back of her hand to her forehead, but she might have.

Jack and Cherise both laughed aloud. His heart warmed to hear genuine laugher from his childhood friend.

"Stand up," Cherise told the girl, who did so. Then she twirled her finger, and the girl spun in a circle. "Show me a waltz."

Misty looked bewildered. "What's a waltz?"

Without a blink, Cherise stood and demonstrated a few steps. "Ta, da, da, ta, da, da."

And Misty aped her perfectly.

"Well, I think I have a few outfits to start with. A young woman not much more substantial than you left us abruptly a few weeks ago. Unlikely to be returning. And you'll be needing a bit more than a wardrobe, if you don't know what a waltz is. The Cherise School of Charm has its first official student. Jack, will you be joining us?"

About all he could do was charm a cat out of a bath.

"He's got half-a-hold of junk to offload."

Jack was getting annoyed, the way Misty was answering questions directed at him. He shrugged at Cherise.

"At least stay a day, and get a little rest."

He saw the promise in her eyes.

* * *

Jack had two stops to make in town before going back to the Southern Birds. Both were within easy walking distance of the tarmac.

The alley he approached looked the same as it had when Jack was twelve.

His heart aching, Jack had come to this alley and had approached the proprietor of the hock shop, Ignatius Argonavis. The two of them had struck up a conversation on one of the man's visits to the Birds, and Jack had taken a liking to him.

His life-long friend, Cherise, had just taken her first turn parading herself around the Southern Birds parlor.

"Get me a berth on the next garbage scow out of here, Ig!"

"What do you be wanting to do a fool thing like that for?"

Young Jack had stared across the chipped glasma counter into the wrecked face of the former spacer. Both of them were a sight to sore any eye, and they'd become fast friends. Ig, as he'd insisted Jack call him, had lost part of his face and most of his left shoulder and arm to the blast of an attacking Imperial Patrol. The injury hadn't stopped the Empire from convicting him of piracy and sending him to prison for ten years, but it had ended his spacefaring days.

"Cherise, you say?" Ig asked, his one eye searching Jack's face. "Many the tale's been told of the folly of falling in love with a whore, but—"

"She's not a whore!" Jack insisted.

"Of course not! Forced into it because she's an orphan like yourself. Something you'd have done if you weren't so downright repulsive."

"I'm not repulsive!" Jack insisted.

"And I'm a beauty queen, too!" Ig threw his head back and roared with laughter. "But you've gone and done it in a way that's quite original," Ig continued, as if Jack hadn't interrupted. "A fine fix, it is!"

And Ig had gotten Jack aboard a garbage scow, but not before Jack had extracted a promise from Ig that he'd stop frequenting the Southern Birds.

Now, twenty years later, Jack approached the same alley shop, headed for the same ill-repaired door, the sign above it in grimy letters declaring, "Argonavis Hock and Lucre."

Jack reflected what a fool he'd been. The rough years had followed, Jack working ship to ship, keeping to himself, avoiding trouble, staying away from smokeshops, snortshops, shootshops, drinkshops, and bodyshops, and somehow working his way to pilot, getting his license (forged), and taking out a loan to buy his own Scavenger.

I made it work, he told himself, pushing the door open.

The lumpy wreck behind the chipped glasma counter just grunted and mumbled, "Whatcha got?"

"Get me a berth on the next garbage scow out of here, Ig!"

The remaining eye swiveled toward him. "Jack!" And the old man barreled out from behind the counter and wrapped Jack with one arm.

Quite a powerful arm. Jack gasped for breath, laughing and hugging the man back.

"What brings you to town, boy?" Ig asked, holding Jack at arm's length to look him over, a woman peering at them from the back room.

He could see Ig blinking back tears, and he blinked away his own. "Just comin' to see that you kept your promise about the Southern Birds. Looks to me like someone made an honest man out of you, impossible as that may seem."

Ig nodded vigorously, his head only coming to Jack's shoulder. "Meet the missus, Jack. Sweetie, come and meet the boy I was always tellin' you about. Jack, this is Gretchen."

The two greeted each other.

"I told Ig he'd have to stop going to the Southern Birds," Jack said, "so I guess he got married instead."

"That ain't stopped him," she said, laughing as loud as Ig, her face as much a wreck as his.

"I go to see Cherise, make sure she's all right," Ig said. "You been out there? Runs the place now."

"I arrived yesterday, and Cherise looks wonderful."

"Aye, doesn't she?" And Ig winked at him. He turned to his wife. "I'm takin' Jack to the smoke shop. Mind the store while I'm gone, would you?"

"Startin' early today, are you?"

"Quit your gritching, Gretchen. This is a special occasion."

"Get on with ya, and be back before nightfall or I'm comin' to find you again."

"All right, all right!" He winked again at Jack and escorted him to the door.

He and Ig went to Jack's second stop on the way to the spaceport.

The place was nearly empty, and the walls reeked of old smoke and old sweat, but they greeted Ig like a conquering hero and got them a booth in the far corner where they could watch the door and the spaceport across the street.

The smoke was harsh, dry, slightly musty, and poor quality, but Jack breathed deeply, and his stress fled him as he knew it would and a slight euphoria settled in.

Jack calmly put his cube on the table between them, his arm beside it, blocking any view of it. "What is this thing, Ig?"

Ig's eye went wide, and his mouth full of rotted stubs dropped open. He rubbed his perpetual three-day stubble and whistled softly. "Pre-Circian technology," he said. With one finger he gestured Jack to put it away, an eye throwing a glance toward the smoketender.

Jack put it in his pocket.

"I've heard tales of like objects, traders comin' through, bedazzled looks in their eyes. A tesseract, isn't it? I seen people brought low in their search for such, dreams of untold wealth in their gaze, not a thought for their safety, their reason obliterated in their lust for power. I'm told you can read people's mind with one of those."

Jack met the one-eyed gaze and didn't nod. Didn't need to.

"And change it, too." Ig just nodded. "Quite the find. Couldn't happen to a better man." His eye misted over, and he grasped Jack's hand cross the table. "But there's more, isn't there?"

Jack nodded. "A girl, an orphan."

Ig threw his head back and laughed. "Got a thing for orphans."

"Moth to a candle, I guess. Anyway, the little girl thinks she's a princess, wants me to take her to the palace on Torgas."

50

The eye dropped to the table, as though to see through it to the cube in Jack's pocket. "With that in hand? Might as well be filling the coffers of the mightiest thief we know."

"I tried leaving her, but I felt so guilty, orphan and all." He didn't tell Ig about her unexplained reappearance aboard his ship. "Anyway, Cherise is going to help with a wardrobe, but I got half-a-hold full of jack I need to unload."

"I'm a hock, not a fence," Ig said.

"It's not stolen, it's just junk. Salvage."

The eye peered at him without a waver.

"I swear." Jack held up a hand as if in a court of law. "Well, half-salvage."

Finally, the eye relented. "For you, Jack, for you, but only the salvage, all right?"

"Thanks, Ig."

Somehow, Jack had extracted himself from the smokeshop before he'd become completely obliterated, but the poor quality of the smoke had helped. He suspected the shop kept its finer stash for the tourists and served its regulars its second-hand smoke.

Silently, Jack blessed Ig for buying half his load sight unseen as he supervised its transfer from his cargo hold to the lorry, beside it a fueler pumping the Salvager's fuel tank full.

On leaving the spaceport, Jack decided to take a detour through town. "Take me past the best place in town to get women's clothes," he told the driver.

"Take you past it?" the beefy hovertaxi hack asked, his jowls jiggling as he spoke. "Where you goin' from there?"

"Southern Birds," Jack said. He buckled himself in as the flitter pulled away from the terminal.

"Yeah? Pickin' up a mink stole or a fine pair of earrings for one of the girls out there?"

Disinclined to discuss his business, Jack shrugged. "No, actually, something for my daughter. You take a lot of people out there?"

"Yeah, busy place. That new Madam really knows how to entertain. Don't let them see what you're gettin' your daughter. Many a customer has left without all his belongings."

"Well, I don't know enough about clothes to get her anything. You ever try to buy clothes for a nine-year-old girl? I'll probably take her to the boutique and turn her loose."

"Sounds like a great plan," the hack said, "if you got a bottomless wallet. She sounds like a real princess, your girl."

Jack snorted. "She's a real princess, all right."

Chapter 6

Jack looked longingly out the glass storefront.

No matter where he went, there they were. And if it weren't a smokeshop, it was a shoot shop, or a snort shop, or a slug shop. They were all over the place.

I'd swear they're stalking me, Jack thought.

Cherise and Misty were in the back of the boutique, trying on something or other. They'd been at it for hours, prancing out on occasion to preen themselves in front of him, demanding his opinion, generally miffed that he wasn't effusively delighted, and then sailing back to the dressing room for the next outfit.

He didn't know how long they could keep it up. All he knew was that he'd long since had his fill, and absolute utter boredom had set in.

Then he'd spotted the smokeshop.

Quit lying to yourself, he thought.

He'd seen it when the taxi had brought him past the boutique yesterday. Every single smokeshop in the city had been calling his name for days, since he and Misty had returned to Alpha Tuscana. Five million galacti worth of smoke danced through his dreams like sugar plum fairies (whatever those were).

His interrupted smoke session on Denebi III and the few brief puffs he'd had after seeing his old mentor, Ig, had done nothing more than whet his appetite. All he wanted now was to plunge himself into a smoke-induced oblivion.

Which he'd been plotting since leaving Canis Dogma Five.

Jack looked over his shoulder toward the dressing rooms.

Neither had come out to preen in front of him for the last few minutes. Probably trying on some undergarments, he thought, or other such unmentionables. He could hear them twittering to each other, a clerk nearby twittering happily back.

They'd forgotten completely about him.

His plan had been—yes, he'd planned his obliteration by smoke to the last detail—to leave the Southern Birds in the morning, telling the other two he was going shopping, and spend the day in a cloud of smoke, and return to the evening, no one the wiser. What was he going shopping for ... something, it didn't matter, anything would suffice. Why did he reek of smoke ... well, er, uh, you know ...

Almost to the last detail.

The difficulty, when he was thinking things through, was the girl, Misty. How could he tell her he just needed a little release? A little break from the constant pressure? After all, it was quite a shock to find himself suddenly burdened with the responsibility of keeping the girl safe and fed and clothed and housed. It wasn't as if she were his actual child, whose care had been his responsibility since she was born. He wasn't accustomed to this, and he needed time to adjust. A day of smoke-induced oblivion was the perfect way to make such adjustments.

Jack was convinced she wouldn't understand.

In his experience, few people did. None of his wives had understood.

He tried to recount how many divorces he'd had. Got them confused with his bankruptcies. Was it three divorces and four bank-ruptcies, or four divorces and three bankruptcies? Maybe three bank-ruptcies and four divorces. No, it was definitely four bankruptcies and three divorces.

He shook his head, all of it a blur.

Any wonder why it was a blur? he asked himself, gazing out the boutique window at the smokeshop across the street. Throughout it all, he'd either been intoxicated, coming down, or crawling with craving. No one understood the craving.

The door to the boutique was opening before he knew it, and Jack nimbly dodged a flitter as he crossed the street, flipping an obscene gesture that general direction when the horn bleated.

The interior was dark. "A table in back, please," he said.

A fancy, "please wait to be seated" sign declared how formal the establishment was.

Maybe they'll have some quality smoke to match, he thought, the aromas wafting through the air already hinting at the palette of fine varietals available.

Himself, Jack wouldn't have come to such a place. For Misty to find the couture she needed for her arrival at the palace, they'd had to find the finest boutique on Alpha Tuscana.

When they'd arrived at the shop, Misty had planted a hand on her hip, shoved her nose in the air, and stomped her foot. "I can't believe this is the best available."

Colonnaded faux-marble framed glasma so thick that the models behind it looked smaller from distortion. The one man and three women donning and shedding the finest clothing on the planet seemed oblivious to their near nudity. Their finely-sculpted bodies, eidolons of the human physique, seemed inadequate frames for the finely-crafted clothing they displayed.

At her comment, Jack had almost turned into the smokeshop. Strategically placed right across the street, of course. While the spouse was in one establishment being immersed in a forest of fine fabric and chic design, the distinguished patron might indulge himself in an analogous immersion into seas of exotic exhaust and voluptuous vapors.

Jack browsed the smokeshop menu, the booth's low lamp outshone by the handheld pad showing the shop's array of fine smoke. He swiped through the long list of choices, from Aldebaran delight to Zosma Zoom, then reorganized it by price, most expensive on top.

He whistled in disbelief at the top one, Torcularis Titillation, supposedly the best available.

Putting a thousand-galacti chit on the table, Jack signaled the waiter. "That one," he said, pointing.

"If you'll note, Sir, the menu clearly specifies that the Torcularis requires a deposit."

"What's that on the table, emu excrement?"

The waiter sniffed indignantly and found a spot on his sleeve that merited more attention.

Jack put another chit on the table.

The waiter brightened. "Right away, Sir."

The bowl arrived, an elaborate fleur-de-lis wrought in Vulpecula Salacia ceramic, a material that was both unbreakable and impervious to heat. At the base of the fleur-de-lis was a reservoir. "And what liqueur would the monsieur prefer?"

Jack found it amusing that the pronunciation of "liqueur," "monsieur," and "prefer," all ended the same as the word "sewer." In the finer establishments, one's choice of liqueur for the reservoir was what separated the wheat from the chaff. "Anise is de rigueur," Jack said, pronouncing it the same, "but I prefer water with a slice of lemon."

"The titillation is best experienced with the least of accents, Monsieur. Good choice." The waiter soon returned with the condiment, filled the reservoir, then poised himself, a dainty tongue just reaching the corner of the mouth, his hand holding the striker above the bowl.

Jack wondered what perverse individual had instituted the custom whereby the waiter was required to apply the first flame to a bowl of smoke. But only in the finer establishments.

Jack gave the waiter a nod, and a flame kindled to life at the end of the striker. Jack drew and half-filled his lungs. The waiter capped the bowl and set down the striker, then bowed to Jack.

Euphoria filled him, and his corporeal existence fell away.

* * *

Disembodied voices intruded upon his euphoric obliteration.

"What should we do with him?" A girl's voice.

Jack knew he'd had too much, and he couldn't understand how he heard anything.

"What *we* do," said the waiter's voice, "is put people like this out in the alley, with the rest of the trash."

"Certainly is tempting, isn't it?" A woman's voice. Cherise?

His brain was so saturated with drug that he wasn't able to walk.

"I can't believe he just left us there."

Or talk.

"What was he thinking?"

Or think.

"Only of himself, clearly."

It was heaven.

"Why would he put himself through such hell?"

It's not hell, he wanted to say.

"Why would he put us through such hell?"

Put who through what? he wondered.

"You're nine, you can't say that."

"You did."

"I'm an adult. Stars above, I felt like such a fool, standing there with thousands in purchases, looking around for Jack. If the clerk hadn't mentioned it, I wouldn't have thought to look here."

"Did you see her face? If we hadn't been right in front of her, she'd have been laughing herself silly."

"Happens all the time," she said, "but not to us! The scoundrel! What a complete waste of time! What a complete waste of space!"

"I wonder if he can hear us."

"He's so thoroughly intoxicated, he probably thinks we're aliens come to do biological experiments on him."

"Can that stuff hurt someone?"

"You mean if they smoke too much? Eventually, but I've never heard of someone overdosing on it, not by smoking it, anyway. Oh, Jack, what are we going to do with you?"

"We're closing, ma'am. He'll need to leave." The waiter again.

"Could you get us a taxi, please? Is that the back door? Have it pull up into the alley."

"Yes, ma'am." Steps receding.

"Here, help me. I want to make sure they didn't filch everything from his pockets."

"Would they do that here? A place like this?"

Silence. He didn't even feel them tugging on his clothes, although by the sounds of their efforts, his pockets were difficult to get to.

"You know, what we're not finding is the cube." Cherise voice was low and secretive.

"If it doesn't want to be found, we wouldn't find it anyway."

"Huh?"

"Here comes the waiter."

"The taxi will be here momentarily, ma'am."

Sounds faded and Jack sensed little else but the cosmic rays of drug-exaggerated neural activity. He felt some sensations of motion but assumed it was the momentum of his blissful flight across the galaxy.

"Southern Birds?" A man's voice. "First time I've taken someone there in *his* state. Picked up quite a few. Quite the reversal. You're Madam Mariposa, aren't you? The trip is on the dash. Huh? I mean it's free. No, no, least I could do. Thank you for all your business. No, don't worry about him. I get regular calls from that place, happens…"

"All the time," the two women chimed in.

* * *

The sensation of rolling, and then the floor struck his face hard enough to hurt. He tried to squint, but the light was too bright so he kept his eyes closed. He tried to talk but the dirty rags in his mouth stopped him from talking.

Was I kidnapped? he wondered, his thoughts sluggish.

No, not rags in his mouth, just a dry, swollen tongue. Might as well be a rag for all it obeyed him. His brain wouldn't either, and he wondered what he'd been doing.

And where he was.

More than once, he'd awakened in an alley, his pockets emptied, along with his bowel and bladder, plunged so deep into an abyss of withdrawal that he'd lost track of where he was or how he'd got there.

He recognized enough of the feeling now to know he'd been severely intoxicated to the point of being insensate.

Cold water doused him, cold enough to elicit a gasp. He spasmed in shock. The light still too bright, he turned again to speak, a hand out and up as though to ward off more dousing, which did nothing to stop the next bucket.

It filled his open mouth, set off a fit of coughing, washed the gum from his eyes, dissolved some of the resin coating his brain cells, and got his tongue working.

"Stop!" he said, and his face filled with water again.

Coughing and spluttering, he sat up, trying to distinguish his attacker from the bright blaze of light.

A darker blotch against a blazing patch of daytime sky set down a bucket. "All right, I think that'll do."

"Awe, come on, one more," Misty said. "He deserves a lot more."

"He certainly does," Cherise said, kneeling.

He saw they were out in the shed, the two women in the doorway, two more buckets at the ready. The morning sun blazed in through the open doors behind them, blotting out all else. He recognized enough of the shed at the Southern Birds brothel, having played in and around it as a kid.

Morning.

That meant he'd spent the night out here.

He saw a blanket beside one door, bits of debris still clinging to it. He guessed they'd at least covered him with it. "How'd I get here?" He couldn't tell if his speech were intelligible.

"Scraped you out of a booth at the smoke shop," Cherise said.

"After you abandoned us at the boutique!" Misty chimed in. "We didn't have any way to pay so we had to leave all those beautiful clothes!" And she began to weep with rage, fists clenched at her sides, face twisted up like a dust devil.

Oh, he thought, realizing only now that he'd been carrying all the money. A hand of his flopped toward the pockets of his formals.

"I checked; they got it all, including the cube."

He felt it in his pocket, and he tried to show her, but his hand wasn't coordinated enough to extract it.

"We'll, at least you didn't lose that."

He blinked helplessly at them both.

"Maybe he should have," Misty snarled. "Maybe someone else would have found it, someone more responsible. How could you do that to me, Jack? How could you? At this rate, I'll be an old woman before I get to Torgas! Just lose the cube, Jack, 'cause anybody would be a better Emperor than you!" Weeping, she ran off, her wails interrupted by sobs, until her crying faded, and was cut off with the slamming of a door.

He flinched at the sound. Shame and contrition washed over him in hot waves, and he resolved never to smoke again, then instantly rebuked himself for telling such lies.

He was doomed. He'd always screwed up his life, and he didn't know how to fix it. Worse yet, his every attempt to make things better just screwed them up worse.

He glanced at Cherise for any sign of compassion.

"Nice work, Jack," she said, then stood and left him to his misery.

* * *

He sat in his squalor for days, numb.

Oh, he functioned, after a fashion. He ate, slept, showered, and changed, but he didn't talk to anyone or look at anyone.

Mostly, they just left him alone. He found a cot in an outbuilding and slept there, shaved at the crude, industrial sink nearby, slunk into the dining hall after everyone else had gone—finding a plate left for him—and cleaned up after everyone else, in spite of the staff whose job it was. They seemed to know and just moved aside when they saw him coming. It was a job he'd done as a kid, anyway, and it seemed a suitable punishment.

On the third day, he went to town and found the boutique.

The young female clerk who'd helped Cherise and Misty kept giggling while Jack paid for everything. He was sure she overcharged him, but he didn't care.

He set everything outside Misty's room, not daring to disturb her. There, the packages remained, untouched.

On the sixth day, he wrote Misty a note saying he was taking the Scavenger to Tertius Diamond look into getting some suitable jewelry, and that he'd return as soon as he could.

Just as he was climbing into the taxi, Misty tore out of the house, hurled his note at him, and yelled, "Don't bother coming back!"

En route to the spaceport, Jack couldn't keep the blur out of his eyes.

The taxi driver kept looking in his review mirror, paying far less attention to where he was flying than Jack thought he should. "Having a tough time with the smoke?" the driver asked, his voice oddly familiar.

"How'd you know?" Jack mumbled, looking out the window, and seeing none of it.

"Seen a lot of good people wreck their lives with that stuff," the driver said.

60

"Don't tell me: Happens all the time."

"How'd you know what I was gonna say? Talent like that, you ought to play the lottery."

Jack snorted, thinking he'd really hit the jackpot this time—all the misery he'd ever want or need in one foul roll of the dice.

* * *

Jack peered through the glasma pane, the lettering etched into it distorting his view somewhat, but it was easy to see that the proprietor was in.

He tightened his grip on the satchel and took a deep breath. With his other hand, he reached into his pocket and grabbed the cube.

Better get it over with, he thought, his vision replaced with that of the proprietor.

The binocularity of Delphin's sight was disconcerting. Through one eye was the normal view of the workspace, tools strewn across the workbench, his hands on a mount which held the precious stone he examined. Through the oculus, mountains of blue crystals marched into a blurry distance, the short focal length giving him a crisp view of the subject area.

Crisp and close. Jack knew this was the surface of the smooth, blue stone mounted in front of Delphin. Smooth to the naked eye, mountainous jags to the powerful oculus.

You will not see or hear me, Jack thought, slipping into the antiquities shop.

Delphin instantly looked up. "Who's there?"

Ghosting him, Jack knew he couldn't see anything. There are entire universes around us, Jack recalled someone saying once, if we only have the eyes to see or the instruments to measure.

Jack moved into the shop, careful to remain silent.

"I know you're there, and I know you know I can't see you. If that's you, Carson, I want you to know you'll never do business in the Southern Triangle again. You're finished. I've reported your theft to the Imperial Patrol, and they're not averse to taking a few bribes. You're ruined and hunted, Carson. I've been this business too long to let a hoodlum like you defraud me. Your little prestidigitation may have cost me some money, but your loss and my gain in the way of reputation will show who came out ahead on that deal." The oculus moved around the room while he spoke but turned up nothing, despite the enhanced visual acuity.

Jack almost turned around and left. This man had come after him with two gargantuan trolls and had ordered them to kill him. This man had bribed Imperial Patrol officers, most likely to shoot Jack on sight. This man had ruined Jack's reputation, preventing him from returning to his previous if meager employment.

It wasn't Jack's fault that the cube had refused to be sold. Why can't I sell it? he wondered, knowing he had as little use for it as it had for him.

Me, Emperor? Jack thought, scoffing mentally at such a ludicrous thought.

But in his efforts to turn an unfortunate event into a slight advantage, Jack had found the obstinate cube in his pocket, instead of its remaining in the possession of the person he'd sold it to. Was that my fault? he wondered, bitter at the trouble it had caused him.

No, it's not my fault, Jack thought decisively.

But it wasn't Delphin's fault, either, the antiquities dealer just responding the best he knew how to circumstances that had placed his livelihood—if not his life itself—at risk.

Which was why, at the heart of it, Jack had come back.

Quietly, Jack set the satchel on the floor. A satchel incrementally lighter and a few thousand galacti slimmer than when he'd left the shop with it a week ago.

Delphin in the meantime had turned back to his work, his thoughts far away, Jack already dismissed from his mind.

Jack stopped himself with his mouth half-open. The damage was done, and an apology wouldn't undo it. I can't make him forgive me, he thought. I guess I probably knew that the cube wouldn't let me sell it. I don't know why I tried.

Quietly, Jack backed out of the shop.

Delphin paused at one point, but didn't swing his oculus in Jack's direction.

Once he was outside, Jack continued to concentrate on keeping the satchel concealed until he'd nearly reached the spaceport.

There, the Scavenger sat, seeming to watching him as he made his way through customs.

He climbed into the pilot's seat and requested liftoff clearance from the tower.

"You took the money back, didn't you?" Misty asked, coming out of the galley.

"How'd you get aboard? I left you on Alpha Tuscana!"

She grinned at him and eased herself into the copilot's seat. "I'm glad you took the money back."

A little while later, the ship clearing the atmosphere, Jack gave her a small smile, mystified but still glad she was here.

"That must have been difficult," Misty said.

He shook his head at her. "That was the easy part." He didn't know how long he'd be able to hold his craving at bay.

Chapter 7

"Where are we going now?"

He glanced over at Misty in the copilot's chaise, her feet in fuzzy shipboard slippers, her hair pulled straight back at the temples.

Cherise had told them to go on ahead, their preparations for Misty's arrival on Torgas Prime likely to take some weeks. "In the meantime, the Southern Birds still needs my guidance, at least until I train my understudy."

And so, reluctantly, Jack had left his childhood friend behind. He knew he'd be returning for her. He'd always known.

"You and Cherise make really good companions, you know," Misty said. The classic Athenian lines of her face held an ancient wisdom, and her clear blue eyes evoked the limitless sky.

Well, the Terran Sky, he thought. Jack had never seen the sky on humankind's homeworld. Supposedly, it was breathtaking. The skies Jack had grown up under had been variously dull green, pale gray, amber, and lemon yellow. The other thing her eyes suggested was innocence. "You're too young to know the half of it," Jack said. Well, she'll soon be disabused of that, he thought, especially if she really wants to be Princess.

"I really want to be Princess, so I hope wherever you're taking me has something to do with that."

"A Princess has to have a set of crown jewels, right?"

"Damn straight she does!"

Who taught her to cuss like that? he wondered. "So we're going to the Jewel Box, otherwise known as Kappa Crucis. Inside the constellation are forty occupied worlds, each specializing in one type of precious stone or metal. We're headed for Tertius Diamond, the third planet orbiting the Diamond star, a blue-white variety super giant. I, uh—" he peered at her to gauge her reaction—"have an ex-wife who's a broker."

Misty shot him a look. "Do you owe her money, too?"

"Now, why would you even think that? I don't owe everyone I know, you know."

She giggled. "So she didn't loan you any money and didn't sue for spousal support during the divorce?"

Jack frowned. "Ever consider interrogation for a career?"

"I'm pretty good at it, aren't I?"

"You'd have to develop that wicked gleam in your eye. Since you'll never have the bulk to be physically intimidating, you'll have to rely on something else."

"I'd rather be princess, which is intimidating enough."

He conceded the point and brought the Scavenger out of uberspace.

The Jewel Box filled the screen, and Misty gasped.

A hope chest filled to overflowing with precious and semi-precious stones with multiple kliegs lights shining upon it might look thus.

Jack upped the filters, the stars so bright that it hurt to look at them, the heat coming off the screen causing him to sweat. He browsed the profusion, one of the most magnificent that the Milky Way had to offer. No matter how many times he came here, he never tired of the sight.

"Where are we headed?"

"Tertius Diamond is that one." He pointed to a blue-white super-giant, a star that one Earth writer from Russia had compared to the Orlov Diamond, the preeminent jewel in the Royal Scepter of the Romanov Crown Jewels.

"What's that one?" She pointed to a star. "Why's it changing colors rapidly, like some casino marque?"

"It *is* a casino marque. That's the Vega Strip," Jack told her, shaking his head. "We won't be going there." He'd already been there, and it'd nearly ruined him.

"What happened to you there?"

How did she know? he wondered. "The inquiry queen, they'll call you. Vega is one big gambling joint, whole worlds with nothing but casinos. Nothing there for us."

The third planet orbiting the Diamond Sun was a cold, blue ball capped on either end with ice two-thirds of the way toward the equator. The planet itself sat nearly in the Oort cloud of the massive blue-white primary, a supergiant so bright and hot that it had seared away the atmospheres of its two other planets, both of them now reduced to big, smoking cinders.

Jack brought the Salvager into orbit and commed for permission to land.

They took the shuttle from the spaceport into the Capital, Pretoria, Jack too cheap to spring for a taxi. A few blocks from the Capitol rotunda were the markets.

Shops like jewels lined the perimeter of a vast square. Crowds meandered past scintillating displays of diamonds, each display more breathtaking than the last.

Jack stopped at a kiosk decked entirely in red velvet and shaped like a crown, each inch displaying a blue-white diamond of "flawless" or "internally flawless" variety.

Jack could tell Misty was impressed.

"May I help you?"

The woman at the kiosk was looking intently at Misty, as though not seeing Jack at all.

He smiled at the sight of her, realizing he still loved her.

Daria Osborn stood six-two, was blond and fair-skinned as a Norwegian, with similarly honed features as Misty but heart-shaped. "You look like a Princess in search of a tiara," Daria said to Misty.

"How did you know?"

"I'm Daria, Jack's ex-wife. And if you're here with him, it means you've asked for his help. And there's only one thing a girl your age would ever want to be: Princess."

Misty shot him a glance. "You didn't say she was smart, too."

"Did I forget to mention that?" Jack grinned and turned to his ex. "How's business?"

"It's good. Those disturbances on a border are causing a spike in diamond sales. A little insecurity usually spurs investment. You look well, Jack. Let me guess. Orphan, found on one at those utterly derelict worlds you're always finding junk on, and you're needing some help with her, yes?"

Jack nodded sheepishly. He wouldn't just turn up for a social visit.

"Come with me." She called to a coworker to staff the kiosk, then led Jack and Misty around the red velvet crown to a door set in its back.

A small jeweler's workbench occupied one wall, a lever-mounted oculus suspended from the ceiling. Daria pulled up a stool. "Here you go, my dear, only chair in the house. Jack and I will stand." She then raised an eyebrow at him.

"Well, it's like this—" Jack began.

"If I'm going to be princess, I'll need a set of crown jewels," Misty interrupted, climbing onto the stool. "By the way, since Jack lacks the social sophistication to introduce us, I'm Princess Misty Circi, and Jack's taking me to Torgas Prime so he can claim the crown and be the Emperor."

Daria, he could see, was trying not to laugh.

"I don't want to be Emperor."

"The cube says you'll be Emperor, so you'll be Emperor," Misty said matter-of-factly. "And I'll be your princess."

"And how, if I may ask, your highness," Daria asked, "will you pay for all the clothes, jewelry, servants, and other necessities of being a princess?"

"Jack will figure it out. He's good at that."

Daria looked at Jack as if he'd lost his mind. "Did you tell her about your three bankruptcies?"

"Four," he corrected, and shook his head.

"And about your little problem on Vega?"

Jack cleared his throat and swallowed. He'd nearly ruined Daria's business by gambling away all their money. It wasn't a mystery to him why she'd divorced him. "Sorry about that."

"Foolish of me to trust you with the company's books."

"Even so, you didn't deserve that. I was wrong." Jack shuffled his feet, sure he looked like a child being admonished by a parent.

"We saw Vega on our way here," Misty said, glancing between them. "Get into trouble there, Jack?" She grinned.

"The inquisition queen, they'll call you," Jack told her. He was already flagellating himself. He didn't need her to salt his wounds. "Anyway, I was wondering if you could help us out."

Daria glanced between them. "Well, since you're unable to purchase a set of crown jewels, you'll have to lease them."

"Lease?" Jack hadn't thought of that. "Great idea!"

"Which is still a substantial amount, with a surety deposit, of course."

"Of course."

"For which some type of collateral might be accepted—"

"Like my ship?"

"Which the bank already owns, so Osborn Diamond would be a secondary lienholder, not adequate for a lease of this magnitude. No, Jack, I'm afraid I have to insist on cash. And I'm guessing your credit's not very good. How far behind are you on your ship payments?"

"Just two or three months." Jack shrugged.

Daria smiled. It might have been a wince.

"But I could catch up with my next load. Just sold half-a-load to Busby—"

"That toothless old man on Corolla Tertius? Jack, he's a blood-sucker. I can't believe you're still doing business with him!"

"He, uh, paid a premium," Jack said, glancing at Misty.

On cue, the girl looked at Daria and began to smile a slow creeping smile that spread like molasses across her sweet face.

Daria seemed to soften and relax.

"So, how much for a two-hundred piece set of crown jewels?"

Daria didn't look away from Misty. "Fifty thousand galacti per month with a five hundred thousand galacti deposit."

"Usurious!" Jack said instantly. "Don't I get a discount?"

"That *is* the discount rate, Jack. A set of crown jewels is easily worth half a billion galacti, pieced out. Together, as a collection, one billion."

"Done," Jack said, wondering where he'd get the money.

"I should be able to assemble the set in six weeks, maybe a month. I'll com you the contract." Finally, Daria looked away from Misty. "Jack?"

Jack perked up and met her gaze, hearing a note of concern in his ex-wife's voice.

"Be careful."

"What did she mean?" Misty asked as they boarded the shuttle back to the spaceport.

Jack shook his head as the glittering city of Pretoria slipped away, the tundra surrounding it like an ice cube. Jack felt a hollow place inside him grow larger, as though something precious slipped away, the ice cube surrounding his heart like tundra.

He realized Daria loved him just as much as he loved her, even now, five years after their divorce.

For the first year, before they'd married, they'd had a wonderful romance. All her friends of course had questioned her choice—a pinch-faced troglodyte with nothing to his name, a nasty divorce and a harrowing bankruptcy already behind him, four previous arrests for trafficking in illicit trade, and no family to speak of except a brothel Madame who'd relegated him to the kitchen because of his repulsive countenance, forbidding him show his face in the parlor if customers were present. Jack wasn't exactly marriageable.

But he'd adored Daria from the moment he'd met her, and he'd successfully given up smoke the entire time he was with her. For two years, they'd had a wonderful marriage, a fairly prosperous one, his salvaging business taking a brief hiatus. He'd taken over managing the back office of Osborn Diamond, while Daria—beautiful to the point of breathtaking and statuesque besides—managed the front office.

But the back office had been a small affair and he'd sold the Scavenger a year into the marriage and boredom had set in, travel rare, new sights and new worlds now replaced with new invoices and new transactions.

The wagers had started small, always from his own pocket, his company salary generous, and Jack found he was fairly good at sports betting. Reviewing a field of contenders in an Ostrick race—the forty-foot arcans from the Rara Avis constellation not terribly different from the large flightless birds from Earth known as ostriches—or assessing two opposing teams in murderball, Jack seemed to have a knack for picking the winner.

Only later, as he found himself in court, first for the divorce and then for bankruptcy, did Jack realized he'd been targeted.

He still kicked himself that he hadn't seen it then. The regular stream of shysters casually bumping into him at trade shows and shopping malls, grocery stores and immersi-theaters, all striking up conversations about some sporting event being held in the Vega Sector, hinting at the bets they were laying money on, and Jack finding himself lucky at the beginning, making huge wins on outlier competitors.

Initially.

* * *

His first visit to Vega should have alerted him to the scam.

They met him at the spaceport and greeted him like a conquering hero. He'd thought to himself at the time, I don't know these people; what are they doing here?

His escort, Whitey, had met him on occasion before, but now, on Vega, Whitey seemed stuck to his side like a Siamese twin, taking him to the most lavish casinos, whose overwhelming glitz left their employees with permanent suntans, where earplugs were de rigueur and sunglasses required at night. Whitey guided him to the high-stakes tables, the sluttiest slots with the putah putouts, the keynote keno games.

And everywhere that Jack went, he was sure to win.

Two days later he went home to a furious Daria. Until she saw all the money he'd won.

"It's too good to be true, Jack. Promise me you won't go back."

He'd promised, but the off-Vega bets on races, sports games, and powerballs continued, Jack having an infallible sense to his picks.

Then Whitey showed up on his doorstep.

The lurch in the pit of Jack's stomach should have alerted him as he stood just inside the threshold, looking at bedraggled figure before him, Daria right behind him.

Known as Whitey for his pure-white ice-cream suits, which glowed even in the darkest, most sultry of casinos, he looked rumpled and unshaven, his hair unkempt, a hollow I-can't-believe-this-is-happening look in his eyes.

"Jack, you gotta help. Here's the deal." He claimed to have been swindled into placing all his assets in a surefire, too-big-to-fail, one-time-only wager being staged by the biggest and most prestigious gaming house on the Vega Strip, Ballsy Palace.

70

"And you lost."

Whitey broke down and wept, hurling epithets in the general direction of the Vega Strip, swearing revenge. "But I got it all figured out, Jack. Here's how I can get it all back, doubled."

"Sounds illegal," Jack said, when he heard the plan over a cup of stim at the local breakfast bar. Daria had refused to let Whitey in the house.

"It's not, Jack. It's not only legal, it's exactly what they deserve."

"But you need my help."

Whitey spread his hands in silent plea, looking pathetic.

Jack forked over all his winnings in the past few months.

"Is this all you have?"

"Every cent," Jack told him.

Whitey disintegrated in front of him, melting to the floor in a blubbering puddle of warm ice cream. "It won't work, Jack, we need at least twice that." Whitey ranted and railed about the injustice of it all and how the universe was deliberately persecuting him and how Jack was part of the conspiracy to reduce Whitey to a pathetic, impoverished street derelict. "What about your business?" Whitey asked, suddenly perking up, completely composed.

"Huh? Osborn Diamond? Can't do it, Whitey, not mine to bet."

For the next six hours, Whitey harangued and pleaded and pontificated and moralized. "These bastard casinos have been bilking the likes of ordinary folks like you and me for ages, and if someone doesn't show 'em which side the butter is breaded on, they'll continue to lay it on thick!"

By the end, the metaphors were so mixed that they sounded to Jack like homogenized milk. Finally he relented, wondering if in this circumstance Daria might be acquitted of justifiable homicide.

"So here's what you gotta do, Jack."

" 'Me?' What do you mean, 'me'?"

"You think they're going to let me on the property, knowing they've already milked me dry? Look at me! Not a drop to be squeezed from my sponge. They'll have me arrested for trespassing. No, Jack, I'm too well known on the Vega Strip. They'll bounce me out on my skinny behind." Whitney was nothing if not skinny. "It's gotta be you, Jack. They gotta think you're a new mark. You've got to blind them with your innocence. You're the one, Jack. Make 'em suffer!"

And of course, Jack had lost it all.

Afterwards, Whitey was nowhere to be found.

All through the divorce proceedings and bankruptcy, Jack had berated himself. Why didn't I see it coming? How could I be such a fool?

Slowly, he'd realized that he'd been targeted from the very beginning, from that very first bet, all of it orchestrated toward convincing him he couldn't lose, building the drama until they could persuade him to place it all on a single wager, Whitey having engineered every last detail.

Now, five years later, riding the shuttle from Pretoria to the space-port, Jack still couldn't believe he'd let himself be swindled on such a grand scale.

He didn't blame Daria for driving such a hard bargain. Considering the worth of the Circian Crown Jewels, Jack really hadn't expected Daria to agree to anything. I don't exactly have a sterling track record, he thought, grateful to his ex-wife for her forbearance.

Jack looked at Misty, sitting across from him, sighing and wondering where he'd get five hundred thousand galacti.

Chapter 8

"Uh, looks like a bit of a problem, Jack."

A bright orange boot was bolted to the Salvager's landing strut.

Misty looked it over, as though inspecting how it worked. "What is it?"

"Repossession boot. I'm afraid I've been a little delinquent on my payments. First thing the bank does is have a boot put on so the ship can't be taken anywhere."

She looked over at Jack in disbelief. "But it's not attached to anything. Not even the ground! How will it stop us from lifting off?"

He really didn't expect her to understand the mechanics of such a device. Nor did he have the patience to explain it to her, not right then. "We can't take off with that thing attached, all right? Take my word for it."

"All right." She put her hands on her hips. "How are we getting to Vega?"

He'd told her about his idea on the shuttle. Frowning, Jack looked at the boot. Frustration and helplessness built inside of him, feelings that reminded him of when he was twelve.

At the brothel, he and Cherise had become constant companions. She was a year older than Jack as beautiful as the wind and just as dainty. While Jack worked in the kitchen and yard, Cherise had worked the parlor, serving the guests their drinks, and shadowing the working women when they took their gentlemen customers into the nesting rooms. Cherise typically would wait behind a screen in the room, ready to get help if the encounter should go awry.

Thrown together frequently because of their similarity in age, Jack and Cherise became close across their five years together at the Southern Birds Brothel, and he'd been her first, and she his, the both of them so young and inexperienced it was by turns amusing, anxiety-ridden, and awkward.

But then Madame Mariposa had insisted that Cherise join the other working women. And Jack, feeling overwhelmed with frustration and powerlessness, had stowed away on the garbage scow, vowing he'd make a million and return for Cherise someday.

The same frustration and powerlessness beset him at the bright orange boot bolted to the landing strut.

He couldn't even think.

Misty went over and kicked the boot. "I'm so mad!"

Down the sewer, all of it.

Without a ship, Jack couldn't do anything. They weren't going to the Vega Strip to reclaim Jack's losses from the Ballsy Palace Casino, they weren't getting Daria's surety deposit for the Circian Crown Jewels, and they certainly weren't getting to Torgas Prime.

The entire scheme collapsed around their ears.

Like the house of cards it was, Jack thought.

He remembered back to the moment he'd found the cube in the derelict building on Canis Dogma Five, when the ancient holojector had pitched onto the wall the image of the deceased Emperor Lochium Circi IX, telling him, pathetic Jack with the pinched Paleolithic face, ineluctable charm, and cursed life, that the Circian Empire was destined to rise from its ashes and be restored to its former glory, Jack as its next Emperor.

Jack looked at the bright orange boot and knew none of it could happen now.

The sight began to blur, and he began to weep.

Hope had been so bright recently. For most of his life, Jack had struggled to find a flicker of hope in the perennial dark, some hint that life might hold something better for him than persistent poverty and unremediated suffering. The few periods of joy in his life—six months of awkward bliss with Cherise, somehow finding Cherise again and rekindling their romance, and two years of wonder with Daria—had been welcome respites in a life of penance, poverty, and privation. And to have spent these last two weeks with a girl who knew boundless hope in spite of her own nearly insurmountable circumstances, Jack felt privileged.

And now it was over.

"Uh, Jack?"

He wiped away his tears and focused on Misty. He was sitting cross-legged on the tarmac at the Pretoria spaceport on the planet Tertius Diamond, his ship booted by some repo thug, and no hope of ever getting back aboard and getting off this rock and getting on with his life.

I wish I'd never found this cube, he thought. "What?" he asked her listlessly, sniffling and pulling his jacket tight against the cold.

"If someone put the boot on, someone can surely take it off."

"Where am I gonna get the money to bring the payments current?"

"You can do that later, when we get back from the Vega Strip."

He gestured helplessly at the bright orange boot. "But—?"

"Whoever put it on can take it off, right?"

"I wish it worked that way." He shook his head at her, admiring her persistence, especially in the face of futility.

She frowned at him. "Maybe they're still close by." She stood and peered toward the tower, a phallus against the cold, white sky. "What's that?"

He peered the direction she pointed. Beside the main terminal stood a service building, its many bays half empty of vehicles, flitter craft flittering in and out, and a large, black vehicle sitting squat and menacing nearby, its portals deeply tinted. It was a Crown Dictoria, known among law enforcement agencies as simply the "Crown Dick," their predominate choice for transportation, even among clandestine units, one instantly recognizable as an undercover vehicle, and a pretty common pick among repo agents, too.

"That's the bank repo rep if I ever saw one," Misty said.

He refrained from asking where a nine-year-old orphan from the derelict planet Canis Dogma Five had ever seen a bank repo rep.

"Come on," she said, pulling him to his feet.

Indolently, listlessly, he followed her.

Besides the vehicle was a burly man with a butch haircut. If he'd been any more militarized, he'd have had epaulets on his shoulders. He was talking to security, oblivious to the two people walking up behind him "…booted this guy's ship two other times, always late on his payments. Never met the man, but his dossier headshot is ugly as sin. Looks like a caveman."

The security guard spotted Jack and Misty. "Uh…"

The repo man turned. "Sweet suffering stardust!"

The sights of Jack's face had been known to blow video circuits.

"Are you the gentleman who put the boot on my friend's ship?" Misty asked.

"Uh, yeah, I guess that's me."

"Would you be so kind as to remove it, please? We'd like to get going." Misty nudged him.

Jack turned to look at her, puzzled.

"Uh, sorry, can't do that." The big man spread his hands apologetically, one of them holding a doc-cube. "This here says the payments are in default, and the bank's gotta reclaim its property."

"And you've got triple-sided copies, I assume?"

The repo rep looked at her funny. "Uh …"

"I'm sure you can make an exception, Sir." Misty elbowed Jack in the ribs.

"Ouch!" Jack said.

"Afraid I can't do that, miss," the man said.

She put a hand on her hip. "That's your Highness, Sir. Don't you know how to address a princess properly?" From the side of her mouth, she muttered to Jack, "The cube, blast it, use the cube!"

"Sorry, your Highness, but even if Mr. Carson were the Emperor, I'd still have to boot his ship."

"But he is the Emperor—or he soon will be—and I'm Princess Misty Circi, and you'll take the boot off his ship immediately!"

Jack put his hand into his pocket.

The beefy repo man grew a dazed look, his jaw going slack and his eyes becoming unfocused.

The man's thoughts flooded into Jack's mind, the catalogue of repos on his itinerary long enough to fill a small encyclopedia. Despite the number times he'd been on the receiving end of a bank's repo order, Jack was dismayed by the number of ships headed for repossession. Furthermore, their methods—logging payments late and adding excess "surcharges" for superfluous administrative tasks like taking a com from a customer—infuriated Jack. He didn't know how many times they'd weaseled in a balloon payment clause, and then invoked it if a payment was a single galacti short or a single minute late.

"Yes, your Highness, I'll attend to it immediately," the man said, and he staggered like a zombie toward the Scavenger.

While he was unbolting the boot from the landing strut, a robotow arrived and hovered expectantly, its caution lights flashing.

"Hey, Jack," Misty whispered. She pointed toward the repo man's Crown Dick.

He grinned, shooting a glance at the short-haired big man.

The repo guy carried the bright orange boot over his own ship and started to attach it.

"Hey, what are you doing?" the security guard asked.

Jack threw him a look, and his face went slack.

When the repo man finished, the robotow attached itself to the Crown Dick and lifted off, leaving its owner on the tarmac.

Jack grinned at Misty. "Let's go to Vega."

* * *

Misty was the perfect foil, particularly at the gaming tables.

Jack knew he couldn't win big. That'd be defeatist, since the casinos would likely deploy their recovery experts. And like their Whiteys— their lead draws, the ones who preyed upon likely victims—their recovery experts had entire repertoires at their disposal. Jack knew he wouldn't leave unscathed with more than a hundred thousand galacti.

The casinos couldn't afford the kinds of wins that Jack needed.

They fell into a routine, Misty chatting up a dealer while Jack played fifty to a hundred hands. He set himself a pattern, enough in wins to make it worth his while, then on to a new table or new casino before the pit boss became too suspicious.

He was careful, but he knew he couldn't escape detection. His best strategy was to fly low enough that he didn't raise a lot of concerns. He felt them watching, and at the edge of their minds was a suspicion that he was gaming them, but Jack always made sure he lost some games, that he never had a streak of too many wins.

He also found he needed to have a human dealer. The robotic

dealers didn't lend themselves well to ghosting, their circuitry sometimes indecipherable through the Gaussian interface. Like the human
brain, cyborg bio neurology emitted electrical fields, but the Ghost
cube wasn't well adapted to interpreting those fields. So when the
management substituted a robotic dealer for the human one, Jack
would often take that as a signal that he'd better move on to the next
table.

Win, win, win, lose, win, win, lose. Again and again. Jack's
winnings began to accumulate.

But as he worked the tables, he kept his eye on the prize, the one
bet in which he could simultaneously recoup his losses from five years
ago and exact his revenge on the iconic industry gorilla: The Ballsy
Palace Casino.

Word of him spread, enough to have earned him a constant
shadow, but no one could figure out how he was doing it. He never
brought out the cube, of course, but he always had it with him. They
tried separating him and Misty, by enticing her away to a kid's play-
ground, but soon found that didn't alter his pattern of winning. When
the surveillance grew too thick, he simply moved on.

Jack also learned from them, as well. He discovered that they even
surveilled the slot machines, and that any overly generous machine
could be tightened up at a few taps by the slot monitor, one operator
typically supervising hundreds of machines. Further, they would
sometimes loosen a machine to entice a customer into staying and then
recoup those losses afterward. They also had shills, gamblers on the
floor who were plants, put there by the casino to win and win big, and
thereby sucker other nearby gamblers into putting more money into
the slots.

Then there were the hawks.

These were interlocutors whose seeming-random, spontaneous
exchanges with customers might entice one or two to up the ante—to
play the games with better payouts but steeper odds. They were meant
to look like ordinary customers, but they always gave themselves
away. They'd sit down for a hand or two, tell Jack he was pretty good,
say they'd just come over from the torqueball table where someone just
won three quarter mil.

Even those games of seeming random chance—like torqueball or
roulette—had nothing random about them. Magnetized cushions and

micrograv nodes might subtly redirect a ball into a hole or deflect a die from landing a particular number. Those mechanized machinations weren't used overtly, since a casino might be fined if caught, but enforcement was difficult and complaints were lodged at far higher rates than they could be investigated. The casinos gamed their regulators too.

Jack bided his time, his wins slowly growing.

Misty didn't seem to tire of the routine, and since Jack never went back to the same casino, she never seemed to get bored. Her role was simply to ask questions about everything and provide that low-level irritant distraction that allowed Jack to do his work relatively freely.

The independent sharks inevitably got word of him. The house sharks were a clique to themselves, frequently sharing information from house to house, many of them moonlighting elsewhere. They knew who the current marks were and how much they could be milked; further, they'd often tag-team to wear customers down. There was some predatory, casino-to-casino sharking, where a shark from one casino would lure a mark from beneath the noses of another casino, but most of them tried to discourage this practice, abiding by the general dictum that if the mark was inside your doors, he or she was yours.

But the independent sharks weren't beholden to such rules. They worked only for themselves. That was Whitey, who'd sent numerous fishing boats into Jack's waters when he was married to Daria. He'd finally figured out that it wasn't him Whitey had been after; it'd been Osborn Diamond. Whitey harvested the big fish, luring them to swim in Ballsy's corner of the pond. He had a heart of larceny pumping avarice to his every thieving extremity.

Only this time, it was Jack who was fishing for Whitey.

About two weeks later and a hundred thousand galacti richer, Jack was working the floor at the Carnival, Carnival Casino, drifting from blackjack to poker, about five grand to the better for the day, when a ghost in a white suit sat next to him.

Whitey looked so gaunt that Jack's heart almost went out to him.

"You look terrible," Jack said, noting the disheveled suit, the thin cheeks, the deep-set eyes ringed in black, the straight, sheared-off teeth. And the pouch mounted on the shoulder.

A vein sack.

Whitey was an addict, a port now permanently in a vein, a sack of fluid mounted on his shoulder. "I've had it rough, Jack. Look, I, uh, I'm surprised frankly that you'd even speak to me after what happened. I'm truly sorry. We both got the sharp end of that stick. I couldn't get out of bed for two years after that—and well, I started on the injectable, too. Trying to wean myself off now, but it's so hard, Jack, so hard. How about you? You seem to have recovered somewhat. Who's the girl?"

"I'm his daughter, Misty, and I'm a princess!"

Whitney didn't even blink. "You certainly are! What a darling girl, Jack, she's a sweetie. Perfect for a place like this, help you milk a few thou out of em! More unscrupulous than I am! What a scoundrel."

Jack grinned, not sure whether to be proud or insulted.

"Sir, can I ask you not to bother the customers?" the dealer said.

"He's not a bother," Jack told her, shrugging.

Even so, she pointed her double cannons toward the pit boss and waved.

The pit boss sauntered her double barrels over.

Jack mused that he'd never seen a flat-chested female casino staffer. Probably made them wear twin prosthetics as a condition of employment. "I said he's with me," Jack told the twin-peaked pit boss.

"You don't understand, Mr. Carson," she said.

He hadn't introduced himself, his name known already along the strip.

"This man is forbidden by the management from associating with any of our guests. His unseemly activities are well known. Aren't they, Whitey?"

"They certainly are, Zelda. It's all right, Jack, I'll be going."

Jack held up a hand. "Zelda, I'm asking Whitey to stay. I know what he does, and it doesn't bother me. Thanks for the warning but it's unnecessary. Even if he wanted, he couldn't bilk me for a single slick galacti. And if you insist he leave, then I go too."

Zelda relented and faded into the background, but her eyes remained on them, Jack knew.

Whitey watched her retreat. "Awful nice of you, Jack. I don't deserve a free moment of your time, much less a defense like that."

Jack shrugged. "We were both fools once. I'd offer to buy you a bag —" he glanced at the one on Whitney's shoulder—"but I'm guessing you'd prefer not. How about joining me for a few hands, eh?"

"Oh, Jack, I couldn't."

"Sure you could," Misty piped up. "Daddy'll pay your bets, won't you?" She grinned at Jack.

"Little pipsqueak knows what I'm thinking," Jack told Whitey.

"No, I can't, Jack, not even a single hand. It gets to me, even worse than this." He threw a thumb at the shoulder pouch.

"Not even one? Come on, Whitey, for old time's sake." Jack patted the stool next to him. "I insist."

After a little more cajoling, Whitey sat.

Jack pushed a stack of chips in his direction. "Use only what you need."

Whitey's eyes glistened. "You're a kind man, Jack, more kind that I deserve."

"We all deserve a little kindness, no matter what."

They both bet against the house, and they both won, turning black-jacks. Jack grinned. "You keep the proceeds for spending money. No, no, I insist. Stay and watch if you want—it'd please me if you did—but don't bet anymore. Wouldn't be good for you."

To his surprise, Whitey stayed but only to observe.

Jack lost the next hand, but kept his bet small, then won the next three, each time ending his bets in a little higher. Three wins, one loss, two wins, one loss, four wins, one loss.

"Nice little routine, there, Jack," Whitey said. "You know they're onto you."

He nodded and glanced at Misty.

"Not enough to accuse him of counting cards," she said, "and not enough to persuade him to leave."

"Teaching her all my old tricks, eh, Jack?"

He grinned. "Two more hands here, and they'll replace the dealer with a borg, which is my cue I've outstayed my welcome."

Two more hands, and the dealer cleared her throat. "Excuse me, gentlemen, it's my break time. Bennie the borg will assist you while I'm gone. Not much of a conversationalist, but he can make a mean martini."

Jack gathered his chips to go. "Nice to meet you, Bennie, gotta go." He turned to look at Whitey. "Pleasure. See you tomorrow maybe?"

"Probably not, Jack. Not good for my moral redemption, these places. Been good seeing you. And quite nice meeting you, Misty." He shook hands with them both and faded into the darkened casino.

"He'll be back," Misty said.

* * *

The next day he was back.

Jack had moved on the Palms Palisades, a desert-themed, light-festooned palace whose floors were covered with sand, but somehow Whitey found him anyway.

"Thought I'd come to watch you work," he said to Jack, "and frankly, it was quite a pleasure yesterday to see you walk out of that place with fifty grand. Bilked the snot out of 'em before they knew what was happening."

At the Palms Palisades, Jack settled himself at a poker table, deuces wild, playing two house opponents and two human competitors. His strategy here was different, five-player hands subject to far more variation. The house in this case had rigged the game, the dealer having remembered the cards, a fact known to Jack by his ghosting the dealer. The house had been expecting him.

Patiently, Jack worked the game, letting the house win most the initial hands. Then Jack changed tactics, drawing one more or one less card than the dealer expected, and confounding the resulting hands, to make the dealer lose. His two competitors began to win to their delight, Jack exhibiting a slightly puzzled looked at his apparent lucklessness. His bets small, he didn't lose much, but the house was losing significantly.

The pit boss pulled the dealer and put in another gentleman, who by his drab looks was probably sharper than a rocket scientist.

"This could get ugly, Jack," Whitey whispered to him.

"Daddy's already ugly," Misty whispered back.

The first thing Jack noticed about the new dealer was how furtive his thoughts were, as though in his efforts to keep his thoughts off his face, he actually kept them out of his mind. There was an economy to his movements which betrayed his intimate knowledge of the game. As though he'd seen every gambit ever played and had remembered its nuances. Further, the new dealer didn't appear to be counting cards.

Formidable, Jack thought. The house had upped the ante.

One of his competitors didn't like the change. "I'm out."

Jack shot Whitey a look, and the thin man took a seat beside Jack.

Two against the house, always better odds.

The pit boss appeared instantly, a man so thick through that he stretched the seams of his jacket. "Oh, no you don't, Whitey."

"He stays," Jack said, "or I go."

The pit boss glanced between them. "The cameras are rolling, gentlemen. Any hint of collusion, you both get the boot." He said something unintelligible into his wrist. "Capisce?"

The old languages die hard, Jack thought. "Capisce." He could see Whitey hesitating. "Just for today, old friend, just so these mother buggers don't win."

"You got it, Jack." Whitey grinned.

The other competitor bowed out, glancing appreciably at Jack and Whitey.

Now it was two to two. The dealer and the house player against Jack and Whitey.

As tempted as he was, Jack didn't let the upped ante get his goat. With the evened odds, two against two, Jack was able to work the house, he and Whitey winning two, three, and four in sequence, then losing one. He controlled their losses.

When next he looked up, two hours had passed. He was drenched in sweat. But he and Whitey each had impressive stacks of chips beside them.

They'd drawn an audience, he saw. Odd how he hadn't noticed before. Usually a sign he was winning too much.

Jack saw several pairs of knowing eyes in the spectators. He and Whitey together were far ahead of the progress Jack usually made on his own, and he didn't like the attention it was generating.

Se he began to lose.

Gradually, subtly, but still losing, working his stack down until it was barely larger than when he started.

"I gotta step out, gentleman," he told his opponents. "Salvage my dignity, at least." He was guessing he'd cleared only a thousand.

Whitey easily had seventy thou in front of him. "It's all icing to me, Jack, if you want to continue." He gestured at his stack to indicate that Jack could have whatever portion he wanted.

"You earned it fairly, Whitey, I couldn't." He grinned at Misty. "Daddy didn't do so well today, did he?"

"Quitting ahead, at least," she said brightly. "But you're right, it's time to stop."

Together, they walked to the cage to cashier out.

Hand in hand, Jack and Misty headed to the entrance, where they ran into Whitey, tucking a stash of chits into his pocket.

"Dinner on me?" Whitey asked. "It's the least I could do." The drip bag at his shoulder was nearly empty. "Gotta stop for a refill, but how about it? What's a little chow between chums?"

Morose, Jack agreed reluctantly, letting himself be talked into it.

"I'm hungry, Daddy."

That convinced him.

* * *

Over dinner, which Whitey dove into with gusto, they talked of old times, Jack barely touching his food.

"All right, Jack, you can lay it out for me now. No cams or mikes here." The nearest table was at a casino one block over. "What brings you back to the strip, really?"

Jack was taken back. "Brings me back? What do you mean?"

"What are you playing for? What's your stake, what's the goal, what's the wager you're wanting in on?"

He waved dismissively. "I'm just playin' it day by day, putting a little aside for a rainy day. I'm not trolling for any big fish, Whitey. I know better than that. We both know these big casinos have entire arsenals they can aim at us. There isn't a fish big enough to risk my life on, or my daughter's life."

Whitey shook his head. "Great job thus far, making them think so, especially by bringing her along. But I don't buy it, Jack. You're too good not to be working some angle. Don't tell me if you're not comfortable. It's all right. I understand. There's a streak of luck or skill or something that's kept you in the black for the last few weeks, and it just doesn't make any sense if you didn't have a plan."

Jack shrugged in bemusement. "But I don't, Whitey."

"At the poker table today, you lost deliberately. Why?"

"We were winning too much too fast, drawing too much attention."

"See? If you didn't have some long game in mind, you wouldn't have done that. But it's all right. I can see you're not comfortable telling me what it is. I don't begrudge you that for a moment. Whatever you've got in mind must surely have Ballsy Palace as its goal. Don't tell me you haven't plotted your revenge…"

Jack laughed aloud. "But I haven't, Whitey. Look, sure, I've thought about it. Of course, I was angry. But I'm not here for that and any grudges I might have harbored initially just don't interest me anymore. It's past, and I'm done with that." Jack smiled at the thin, older man. "I've got my daughter and I'm enjoying life. What more can a person ask?" He looked at Misty and winked.

"But if someone hatched a scheme to filch a few million from their vault," Misty said, an evil gleam in her eye, "you know you'd go along with it."

"No, I wouldn't, not if it would put you in danger."

"But you'd certainly consider it," she chided, grinning at him.

Jack smiled at her. "Of course I would, wouldn't you?"

* * *

"Listen, Jack, I've got a lead on something, but I gotta know what I'm working with."

Jack was mid-morning through a day at the Triple Trump, a card house sitting glumly amidst the glitz like a dour older sister, her décor all in clubs, hearts, spades, and diamonds. He'd been raking the tables in pinochle, the opportunities to win fewer and farther between, but far higher in payoff. He and Misty hadn't seen Whitey in a couple of days, so he was surprised when the ice-cream suited old man sauntered in and sat beside him.

Intrigued, and guessing he wouldn't want to talk at a table, Jack glanced at the clock. "Join me for lunch in an hour or so?"

Whitey hesitated then agreed somewhat reluctantly.

The casino restaurant like the casino itself was decorated all in playing cards, some of them large than life. A talking suicide king took their order, while a pair of deuces cleared off a nearby table.

"What do you mean, 'you gotta know what you're working with'?" Misty asked Whitey point blank. "You think Jack is just gonna tell you how he's skimming thousands off these bastards?"

"Don't get cheeky with me, midget. All the casinos know you aren't his daughter. And you certainly aren't a Princess, so you can put your pretensions up your exhaust port."

"Listen, you fatuous fathead—"

"Hush," Jack said, his hand on her arm. To Whitey, he said, "She's right and didn't deserve to be addressed that way. She deserves an apology."

Whitey made a face.

"An apology doesn't cost you a dime, but the lack of one might lose you millions."

Whitey sighed, his gaze on Jack. "Sorry, Misty, I shouldn't have called you a midget."

"Apology accepted. And the question still stands." She smiled cutely. "But you're right. I was getting cheeky. Sorry about that. Jack keeps telling me I don't have a filter."

"Thank you, and no, I don't expect Jack to tell me anything. That'd be a breach of my professional ethics."

Jack kept his face expressionless, somehow.

"But whatever you've got, Jack, it might be useful." Whitey looked at Misty. "Maybe it's the same as what you got, girl. You mentioned filching a few mil from the Ballsy Vault the other day. Guess what came my way this morning? Word that someone has its blueprint."

Misty glanced between them, her blank look in high contrast to the eager expressions of both men.

"It means knowing how to get in and out, what the security devices are and where they're at, how the place is laid out." Jack looked at Whitey. "How do we know it isn't a set up?"

"I'll know." Whitey leaned close and whispered, "I've been there."

Jack sat back, the possibilities sending his heart into the heavens. "What if word gets back to Ballsy? They'll be expecting something, and they may lay some traps."

"It's an inside source, Jack. Someone with a knife to sharpen. You can't make billions without upsetting somebody. The other piece, Jack, is what you got. We've got to exploit every edge available to us, 'cause their security is the finest. They've got more layers of security than the royal palace on Torgas Prime. The vault is six stories underground, with more checkpoints than the Imperial Bureau of Investigation compound on Alpha Tuscana. We're talking geno-typing, iris-scanning, retina-typing, facia-metricking, bone-imaging, E. coli-matching, mitochondrial gene-sampling, strip-searching, and even anus-imaging."

"No two assholes alike," Misty quipped.

"Where'd you learn language like that? Jack, what have you been teaching her? Anyway, that's why I'm asking, Jack," Whitey said, shaking his head. "I wouldn't ask otherwise."

"A caper like this is a one-time thing," Jack said, hesitating. "We'll have contracts on our lives for the rest of eternity."

"We'll be so filthy rich, we'll be able to buy our own rogue planets." Whitey was grinning from ear to ear.

He hated to be the naysayer, but there just wasn't any help for it. "Sorry, Whitey. I can't." He grasped Misty's hand. "I don't want my little princess to be on the run for the rest of her life. It's just not worth it."

"Aw, come on, Jack, with your talent, we could score big. Just tell me you'll consider it, Jack. Don't let me down!"

Jack could see the pitched fit coming. He remembered the tearful breakdown he'd witnessed at his front door on Tertius Diamond, pitched with just enough finesse to beguile Jack into playing along with Whitey's scheme. "Save it for the mongrels, Whitey," Jack said bluntly. "You flamblasted me once with that routine, and it ain't gonna happen again. Unless you have a way to bring down Ballsy Gaming and put it out of business, I don't want any part of your scheme."

* * *

Whitey caught up to them the next day at the Galloping Galaxy Casino, themed upon a period in ancient Earth history called the Wild West. Staff wore boots and outrageously large hats called ten-gallon hats, sported a pair of projectile-emitting barrels of metal known as guns, and spoke with drawls so elaborate that your food grew cold while you waited for the end of the word.

Texas hold 'em seemed to be the house specialty game, with mock "gun" fights going on after accusations of marked cards or other cheats. Long mustaches and longer games, bowlegged and bow-armed posturing, made it all look so ridiculous that Jack and Misty spent their first hour just watching.

It was afternoon when Whitey spotted them at a table.

After the usual pit boss threats and Jack's insistence that Whitey stay, the white-decked man settled on a stool beside Jack.

"You look different, somehow," Misty said.

Jack had noticed it, too.

"What's it to you, midget?"

"No, I'm serious, Whitey," Misty said, stopping Jack by lifting her finger.

Jack waited, Misty sometimes full of surprises.

"You don't have a bag on your shoulder." Misty raised an eyebrow. "Have you stopped using the juice for good?"

Whitey looked half-bewildered, half-suspicious. "So?"

"So, congratulations," Misty said. "Quite an accomplishment."

Jack seconded that. "You're looking better all around."

Whitey glanced between them. "Why, thank you. That's quite kind of you. Guess I didn't really notice, so preoccupied with other things."

Jack gestured Whitey to join in a hand.

Whitey picked up his cards. "I found a way," he said, placing his bet.

Jack placed his, hold 'em even worse than pinochle, more difficult yet to win and more lucrative. He had a stack of almost a hundred thousand galacti beside him. "Found a way what?" Jack said. I'll probably have to lose some, he thought, the crowd in spurred boots and ten-gallon hats getting thick behind him.

"You know, what we talked about."

Having ghosted him, Jack did know. "What's the way?"

The dealer laid out the first of three community cards, the "flop," calling out each in turn.

"My insurance policy. Every shark has one." Whitey grinned.

"Didn't know you could find a policy for that sort of thing," Misty said.

Jack signaled her to zip it. "Tell me about it."

"Tell me about yours."

Jack didn't need to look around. Too many eyes and ears. "Over dinner, eh, old friend? I don't like talking business while doing business."

"Over dinner, then."

And for the next hour, Jack lost steadily, getting more and more upset as he did so. By the time he withdrew, he had only twenty thou beside him, and he was red-faced with rage. Most of his previous winnings seemed to have migrated to Whitey.

"Don't say I never did you a favor," Jack told him as they cashed in their chips.

The management approached Whitey at the door, a small dapper man with two bulky bulls behind him. "Don't come back, Whitey. It won't be pretty if you do."

"Put your Galloping Galaxy into your back black hole," Whitey said amiably.

Outside, on the busy, blazing-bright boulevard, Whitey threw his head back and laughed. "Gotta say, I'm sure been enjoying your company, Jack. Good times, friend!" He patted him on the back and laughed the whole way to the bank. From there, they went to a restaurant.

"So, when I started doin' this some thirty years ago, I made sure I had something on each employer. I've worked for just about every corporate gamer on the Vega Strip. Every conversation, all the nasty little schemes, and yes, even that entire episode with you and Osborn Diamond. All the marks I've brought in for Ballsy—recorded every single one of them. Must be a million hours of video and audio, half a billion coms, fifty million stills, all of it booby-trapped."

"You mean, set for release to the public if Ballsy should try to eliminate you?" Misty asked.

Whitey grinned, nodding. "Way too smart to be anything but a midget."

Misty stuck her tongue out at him.

"Dropped into the hands of a reporter or filed with the Vega Strip Gaming Commission—and Ballsy's out of business."

Jack smiled. "You'd risk implicating yourself?"

"I could turn state's evidence or disappear like a wraith. It's about time I retire anyway. Before Ballsy decides to retire me."

It all sounded too good to be true. But if it were true, then Ballsy could be crippled right after he and Whitey had cracked their vault.

"Where's the booby-trap?" Jack asked.

Whitey gave him a look of pure indignation. "What, and show you the goose that'll lay my golden egg? Not happenin'." Then Whitey brightened. "But I'd sure like to know how you're doing this, Jack."

The hook is baited, Jack thought. But who's handling the fishing pole? Me or Whitey?

"Tit for tat, Jack," Whitey sniggered.

"Sounds too good to be true, Jack," Misty said to Jack, sneering at Whitey. "For all we know, Whitey's workin' for the Gaming Association to try to put you out of business. We haven't seen any blueprints or this booby-trapped stash of dirty Vega Strip laundry. He's full of flambé."

"Suit yourself," Whitey said, and he stood to leave. "Very nice seeing both of you again." He bowed and turned to walk off.

"Uh, Whitey—?"

The thin, white-suited man turned, one eyebrow raised.

"Have a seat," Jack said, gesturing across from him.

"Jack, don't!" Misty protested. "You're giving away your edge, throwing away all your advantage."

He looked at her. "Ballsy came after me. I happened to be married to the owner of a lucrative diamond business, and they targeted me as an easy source of money. They systematically lured me into their web with the full intent of bilking me and my wife for very galacti they could. I've dreamt ever since of nothing more than finding some way of putting them down, permanently. So they can't do the same to anyone else. Now, finally, I have a change of doing that, and recovering the money they stole from me and Daria. I'll do everything I can to protect us both, Misty, but this is something I have to do.

"I have to." He looked her straight in the eye. "Are you with me?"

Misty smiled. "I'm with you."

They shook.

Jack told Whitey about being able to ghost someone's thought, but didn't tell him about the cube. "So I can read what's going on in their minds, and sometimes I'm even able to see what they're seeing."

"That's the stuff of science fiction, Jack. How are you doing that?"

He smiled and shook his head. "Leave me an ace or two in the hole, would you, Whitey?"

The older man shook his head. "I knew it was something. I knew you had some gimmick." Whitey sat back. "That's phenomenal, Jack. You could'a really cleaned house with that kind of skill. So why the low level wins? Why the gradual approach?"

"Ballsy," was all Jack said.

Chapter 9

Ballsy Palace stood solitaire in the desert, surrounded by dunes hundreds of feet high. Turrets ringed the resort compound like sentinels. The main casino tower soared above all else for hundreds of miles around, a gigantic inverted pyramid held aloft by antigrav units, its underside ablaze with multi-colored lights.

The thick column where the pyramid peak met the ground housed multiple elevators shafts.

On the grounds between the column and the ring of turrets were the outdoor sports: an ostrich track, a golf course, a murderball diamond, a crippleball gridiron. Underground, beneath these playing fields, were the administrative offices of Ballsy Gaming, themselves in the shape of an inverted pyramid. And at the peak of this pyramid, six stories underground, was the vault.

One elevator went there, an armored elevator. Six keys operated this elevator, one person at each level receiving the elevator from the floor above, inspecting its contents, and then sending it to the floor below. Each day's take was sent to the vault below for counting and storage, and then once per week, the week's take was loaded back onto the elevator in a sealed, secured container. The weekly deposit was sent up from the vault level by itself to the fifth level, where six suited thugs boarded. At each level, the sealed, secured container was reinspected for tampering and the six thugs reidentified for veracity before being sent up the next level. Atop the building, the container was loaded onto a freighter and sent under heavy guard and multi-ship armada to Metropli Bank on Dorado Quintus, where banking laws were so stringent that no one knew who banked there.

Once this container was safely delivered to Dorado Quintus, a journey that took only a day, the six thugs returned under continued blackout to the Vega Strip and the Ballsy resort, having done their job. Two days work out of seven, five days off, living expenses paid and leisure on the house. What more could a muscle-bound pea-brain ask for?

Entrance to the vault was restricted to four people, including Leticia Ballsy, the Chief Financial Officer and scion to founder Leonard Ballsy. The other three were virtual prisoners, going into the vault only to count the money and living Spartan lives on level five underground, right above the vault itself. Not even Leonard Ballsy was allowed into his own vault.

Leticia Ballsy lived in one corner of the above-ground pyramid, on the top level, her suite taking up the entire corner, rumored to be palatial, that corner of the roof given over to her personal golf course. She wagered on her own golf games, and nearly always won.

At one point in the not too distant past, Leticia Ballsy had developed an interest in one of those six thugs, a not-so-pea-brained fellow named Carmody Carruthers. For a time, when Leticia wasn't counting profits in the Ballsy vault, she could be found straddling Carmody's considerable bulk. Much as they tried to keep their impassioned liaisons under the covers, word soon spread throughout the resort staff. All might have remained copasetic, since the pair was discreet and didn't engage in public displays of passion, nor betray by look, word, or gesture that their nocturnal activities might have provided footage for the most salacious of adult films, but for the cupidity of Carmody Carruthers.

Which actually became the title of one such adult film.

An individual with an impressive physique, Carmody had worked all his life to defuse the myth that he was dumb. So in his carousing with the CFO of Ballsy Gaming, he mentioned after a particularly invigorating coupling one sweat-soaked night that his one ambition in life was to assume command of the six-thug unit that guarded the weekly deposit.

And Leticia's response was what ultimately put the chink into the armor that had thus far proved impenetrable to all schemers seeking to subvert the security surrounding the weekly Ballsy deposit. She laughed and said, "We already have the smartest possible man for the job."

She didn't intend to insult him. And few people would have taken either the laugh or the comment as insult. In fact, either by itself might have only pricked Carmody's delicate ego. But both together pierced the thin veneer of competence and burst the blister of his infectious insecurity. Carmody grew discontent and his long-festering inadequacy regarding his intellect became the suppurating boil upon the buttocks of Ballsy Gaming. After a time, Leticia tired of his titillation and acquired other boy toys but had not an inkling that beneath Carmody's stoic surface stirred the venom that ultimately proved deadly to her organization.

Whitey was well known among the Ballsy Gaming staff, the number and range of marks he'd managed to get in the door having enhanced Ballsy's bottom line significantly. He'd even been granted an honorary tour of the Ballsy vault.

And it was Whitey who'd been given first pick when Carmody sought to sell the vault blueprints.

When Jack, Misty, and Whitey arrived by shuttle on Vega 14, the "Biggest little Star System in the Galaxy," they caught the casino flitter at the spaceport and were whisked along with the hundreds of other gamers to the Ballsy Palace complex.

The flitter crested a towering dune and dropped toward the turrets, the inverted pyramid already dominating their view, the flitter top a single sheet of glasma.

Jack realized when they were still a quarter mile away just how large the Ballsy pyramid was.

It hovered directly over them.

The top floor, their brochure declared, was a full half-mile square, the roof large enough for a full nine-hole golf course, Leticia Ballsy's private course, and a swimming pool the size of a small lake.

It looked as if it would fall over and crush them at any moment.

The three of them were the Jones family, Mr. Jack Jones, Mr. Whitey Jones, and their daughter Misty Jones. Whitey for this operation had set aside his ice cream suit and now wore the de rigueur flower-print touristy formalls that everyone else wore.

He looked positively ghostly, his skin a nasty, nearly-translucent hue of colorless white. Jack guessed that only the ice cream suits gave him any relief from the near-death look.

"Cute outfit, Whitey," Misty had said at the outset.

"Cork it, midget."

They'd also brought all the requisite equipment that any tourist of middle class means would have: camera, sunblock, polarizers, audio-players, vidtexts, and of course the inevitable ignorance.

The moment they got off the flitter, they all three looked up at the edifice dangling precariously by a thread above them and exclaimed, "How does it stay up?" The central pillar which housed all the elevator shafts looked (and was) far too insubstantial to hold up its bulk.

Crowds of people just like them streamed in and out of cramped elevators, and Jack knew that the largest of them, the central elevator, the armored one which took the day's take to the vault and the week's take to the launch pad, was used exclusively for moving money and was never utilized to relieve the crush of patron.

One elevator had been set aside with velvet ropes and red satin carpet. A single, impeccably-dressed young man strolled leisurely toward the gold-plated elevator door, blithely ignoring the crowds of sheep-like people being funneled systematically into already cramped elevators.

"That's how we should have arrived," Misty said, looking up between Jack and Whitey, that princess pout plastered to her face.

"Exactly the kind of attention we don't want," Whitey said.

"Maybe you don't want it, but a princess demands it."

"Pipe down, pipsqueak."

The check-in process at the most popular gaming complex on the Vega Strip took hours, but the staff were most accommodating, making sure the guests' needs were attended to. The aromas of smoke, drink, snort, and shoot were all around them, waiters and waitresses floating among the guest with trays of all the best mind-altering drugs. Jack could smell the fine blends in the smoke they were serving, but as tempted as he was to obliterate himself with huge lungfuls of the stuff, he refrained.

Oddly enough, he identified with Whitey's sentiment that he

simply had too much else to think about and had mostly forgotten or at least set aside his cravings.

Room key in hand, they toted their bags from an elevator to their room on the sixteenth floor, the numbers on the buttons going all the way to one hundred twenty, the most expensive suites at the top. Yes, they might have afforded one such suite, but would have garnered that unwanted attention.

Their modest suite was already labeled "Mr. and Mr. Jones," and a bouquet of flowers adorned the low, living room table, a welcome card stuck prominently among the stems.

Misty went immediately to the door with her name on it, looked into it, and promptly "oohed" and "ahhed."

Fir for a princess, apparently, Jack thought. The master bedroom across from Misty's room was certainly plush by any measure if somewhat shy of palatial. Then he looked at the bed.

A single king size bed.

He swore, knowing he'd rather sleep on the floor of Misty's room than leave himself vulnerable to Whitey's knife between his ribs. They'd asked for separate queens, a request they were sure had generated a good deal of sniggering on the part of the hotel staff. Jack was almost relieved that the request had either been ignored or had gone astray. Now, he wouldn't have to find an excuse to sleep on Misty's floor.

Whitey shrugged when he told him. "Better that way," he said.

They laid out the blueprints on the living room floor after scouring the suite for surveillance devices, then rehearsed their plan once again. Verbally, Carmody had alerted Whitey to a few security measures that had been added since the facility had been built, primarily cameras to monitor blind spots, motion detectors, and the like.

One feature of the security system—and its primary flaw, in Jack's opinion—was its reliance on human video monitoring. Each camera's signal was routed to four different monitoring stations, the quadruple surveillance intended to obviate any vulnerability. What they'd overlooked was that all four monitoring stations relied on the same ventilation system.

Their intent was to introduce a gaseous, odorless soporific and then shut down all the communications and security apparatuses including the laser-trip beams, the retinal- and iris-scanning, the geno-typing, and all the other identification checks.

"And especially that anal-imaging," Misty said. "I know no two assholes are alike, but stars above!"

"Midget," Whitey muttered.

"So we place canisters here, here, here, and here," Jack said. "Did Carmody get those maintenance orders in?" They'd badged and uniformed themselves as HVAC maintenance techs.

Whitney in his gray-striped suit looked like a prisoner. "Maintenance orders placed. Complaints of dust in the vents. Probably haven't been cleaned since the place was built."

"They go off at twenty-two hundred, two hours before shift change. We then have ninety minutes to disable communications and security apparatuses, gather the take, and get out the door. If all goes well, we'll have a thirty-minute lead to get to the escape yacht. Everything ready with that, Whitey?"

Whitey had secured a modified Mercury Orbit—touted as the family's family car—but all its emblems and registrations removed and its engine hypercharged. It awaited them at the Vega 14 spaceport. "The Orbit's ready," Whitey said, winking.

"Let's go," Jack said.

* * *

They changed in a utility closet, even putting a "company" skirt on their tool cart. Misty wore an outsize wig and head piece, taking Whitey's "midget" insult to that next level. They'd parked the "company" flitter near the service entrance.

Whitey led the way, the service elevator stopping at the first floor underground. "Work order to clean the ducts," he told the security guard. When the guard balked, Whitey pushed him. "We got four floors to do today, pal, and I ain't ready for a coffee break yet."

"Why the midget?"

"You ever try to crawl into a vent? Ain't easy. What's the hold up? That's your own blazin' work order."

The guard waved them through, and they wheeled the cart to their first stop. Jack helped Misty up into the vent, where she installed the canister, then they spent the next hour acting as though they were cleaning the duct.

"They've even got motion detectors farther along in the duct," Misty whispered, one of the modifications that Carmody had told them about.

Methodically, they worked their way down to the fourth level below ground, the security getting thicker at each level. By the fourth level, word had spread among the staff, and the sight of this crew in gray-striped formalls with a cart and a midget was by then somewhat familiar.

On the fourth level, as Misty was installing the canister in the vent, Leticia Ballsy herself stepped off the elevator. "What are they doing here? I didn't approve any maintenance!"

Floor security babbled something inane.

Jack began to sweat, Leticia's gaze on his face. They'd done what they could to obscure Jack's features behind a scruffy beard, his visage a frequent feature of intergaming communiqués for the last few weeks. Any winner working the strip was profiled for the major gaming houses.

"Let me see that work order!" She didn't take her eyes off Jack.

He swallowed nervously, and he felt her scrutiny in the prickling up and down his spine.

She was as beautiful as she was deadly. She shoved the work order back at the security guard. "Get me Marcuse," she said.

Marcuse Narvone was the smart man whose position Carmody had coveted, a meticulous man with a face of stone. Carmody had warned them he was a prick, as likely to shoot someone as he was to smile.

Jack knew their flimsy work hadn't truly been approved but only filed in the right places by Carmody. It would never pass Narvone's inspection. Jack concentrated on the cube in his pocket, and the swirling thoughts of Leticia Ballsy surged into his mind. You've got better things to do, Jack thought, imagining the golf course atop the casino itself.

"Never mind, I've got better things to do," she told the guard. "Keep your eyes on them at all times until they're done!" And she was gone.

He and Whitey exchanged a glance, and Misty poked her head from the vent. "Bitch needs a good schtupping," she muttered.

Whitey's mouth formed the word, "midget."

"Let's wrap it up, guys," Jack said. "You done with that sweep up there?" he asked Misty.

They packed up and prepared to go.

"Hey, these dates don't match," the guard said, her brows drawing together.

Exactly the kind of thing that might give them away. "Let me see," Jack said. He hadn't really looked closely at the flims. He didn't look closely now. "Well, one's the day someone called for a quote, and the other when they placed the order."

The guard's thoughts were filled with images of Leticia's voluptuous figure.

Jack pushed her thoughts that direction. You can't wait until your shift ends, Jack told her, feeding her an image of Leticia unclothed.

The guard's nipples grew turgid even under the thick uniform. "Oh, yeah, I see." She ran her finger around the inside of her collar. "I can't wait to get off, today. You about ready to wrap up?"

"Yeah, we're done. Come on, you two, step it up." He gestured supervisorly in their direction, then looked at the guard, "Ain't she something?" He gestured at the ceiling.

The woman nodded, "She got it all!" They shared a laugh, and Jack gestured his crew toward the service elevator. Beside it, the armored elevator door opened, and he stepped that direction.

"No, no, no," the guard said, "don't want to take that one." She herded them into the service elevator and pushed "ground." "See you next time." The doors closed across her face.

All three of them heaved huge sighs.

* * *

The waiting was the worst.

Between four and ten—sixteen hundred and twenty two hundred, in the shipboard parlance of spacers—all they had to do was wait. No one felt much like talking, and none of them was hungry. All Jack could manage was a cup of stim, which just frayed his already-frazzled nerves.

The below-ground offices began to empty, the swing shift coming on only enough to staff the four monitoring stations, one on each floor.

The clock ticked off time with mindless precision, and defiantly refused to go any faster, despite their pleas.

"Five years," Jack muttered, looking out their solitary window at the brightly-lit sports fields below them, the dining-area floor a clear sheet of glasma.

"Eh? What?" Whitey said, blinking haughtily his direction.

"Five years since this place destroyed my marriage and my life," Jack said, the lights below making his face look ghostly.

Whitey in his pallor didn't need any such lights to look ghostly. "Ballsy will burn in hell," he said. "I'll be glad when they've finally gone down. It'll be a relief to be outa this business. You know, Jack, I do believe that this corrosive lifestyle might have eventually corrupted me."

"Might have," Jack said.

* * *

When ten o'clock arrived, it seemed they were completely unprepared.

They weren't, but it just seemed that way.

They returned to the service elevator, and instead of exiting on the ground floor, they climbed through the ceiling and boarded the armored elevator through the top.

By now, everyone at all four monitoring stations was unconscious. Donning gas masks, they overrode the elevator controls, retrieved their cart, and stopped at each station in turn to shut down all the security system on level six, in and around the vault.

They had to shove aside a few bodies laying across the control consoles, but otherwise it was quick work. Each monitoring station controlled separate and duplicative security systems on level six, so each had to be visited in turn.

After shutting down the last of those systems on level four, Jack punched up a system scan, which alarmingly alerted them that all systems had been disabled. Jack then ghosted all four levels to insure not a single staff person was still conscious.

Jack, Whitey, and Misty stepped off the armored elevator on level six and wheeled their cart into the vault without a hitch.

Satchels of cash in a pile reaching Jack's shoulder sat in the middle of the floor, receipts stapled to each satchel, awaiting tomorrow's accounting of today's take. Tucked into wall cubbies were previous day's takes, awaiting the weekly shipment to Dorado Quintus. Each satchel had a prominent Ballsy emblem on it.

Thirty million galacti, easy. They didn't gloat too much, not yet.

Swiftly, they loaded the cart, first with the satchels in the middle, then with those in the cubbies.

The cart loaded, they pushed it toward the elevator, so heavy they all three had to push. The elevator had no complaints about the weight, Jack guessing it was antigrav augmented. The inside was dead silent, insulated by two-inch thick steel plate. None of them spoke, nor even looked at each other.

They took the cart out the service entrance, their "company" flitter nearby. They'd rigged a winch inside the van and pulled the cart directly in, the winch whining under the strain.

About to close the van doors, Jack got a sudden thought. "Hey, Whitey," he said, "pose with this for me, would you?" He put a satchel with the Ballsy emblem into Whitey's arms and backed away to snap a still.

Whitey grinned at the camera, the open flitter hold behind him, several dozen Ballsy satchels visible.

Snapping the still, Jack reached into Whitey's mind with the cube and suspended Whitey's volition.

Whitey froze in place with catatonic rigor, the satchel still in his hands.

Misty hopped into the driver's seat and Jack climbed in beside her. The flitter complained but lifted reluctantly, carrying them past the silent turrets at the Ballsy Palace perimeter.

Behind them, a frozen Whitey stood vigil with a satchel of cash.

Twenty-five minutes out into the desert, and just five minutes from the spaceport, Jack watched through Whitey's eyes as lights blazed and alarms went off, the entire grounds flooded with a brilliance brighter than day, "Intruder alert, intruder alert," repeated inanely by robotic voices loud enough to deafen. Armed crews spread out to the perimeter, one squad quickly finding Whitey near the service ramp. A cadre surrounded him, their weapons raised.

"Drop the satchel," the commander said.

Jack released Whitey.

The thin, paste-white huckster in gray, pinstripe formalls dropped the satchel, shoved his hand into the air and defecated all over himself. "It was them," he screeched, "I had nothing to do with it!"

Jack withdrew and smiled at Misty. "How about the drop?" Whitey's damning information would release any moment.

Misty checked her palm com. "Data dump set for five, four, three, two, one—data transferring." She looked over at him. "Did Whitey really crap all over himself?"

Jack grinned and nodded, the lights of the spaceport ahead. "I almost pity the guy," he said. "But not for long."

"Data transfer complete," Misty said, pulling the flitter up to the checkpoint at the tarmac gate.

Jack briefly ghosted the security guard. All good, he thought.

"All good," the guard said, a dazed look on her face as she waved them through.

Jack remotely opened the Salvager's cargo hold, and Misty drove the flitter directly into it. He commed for permission to lift off even before he got to the pilot's seat, while Misty secured the cargo. That much mass loose in the hold might easily cause the Scavenger to wreck.

Misty climbed into the copilot's seat, and Jack engaged the engines. The Salvager leaped for the skies, he and Misty giggling inanely.

But the time they reached escape velocity, Jack and Misty were laughing so hard they couldn't see anymore.

Thank the stars for autopilot! he thought.

Chapter 10

"Where did you...?"

Jack shook his head at Daria. He'd just put down five hundred thousand galacti for the Circi Crown Jewels. "You don't want to know."

"That man I saw on the news yesterday!" The realization spread visibly across her face, her grin at Jack broadening. "Arrested for grand larceny—sixty-five million gone from the Ballsy Palace vault, and only one satchel of fifty thousand recovered. You didn't have anything to do with that, did you, Jack?"

"Not a thing."

"I thought I recognized him," Daria said, as though Jack had answered otherwise. "He came to our door, didn't he?"

He was glad the three of them were alone, Misty in front of a mirror trying on a tiara. "And here's something else for you." He handed her a flim.

"Certificate of Deposit," she read. "Metropli Bank, Dorado Quintus, the contents of one cubic yard, belonging to Daria Osborn of..." She looked up at Jack. "What's in the container?"

"Everything that you lost five years ago." Jack watched the blood drain out of her face.

Then tears welled up in her eyes. She shook her head and wiped them away. "I can't, Jack, you know that."

"Not right now," Misty said, rejoining them at Daria's desk. "And you shouldn't, not for five years, at least. But it's money that Ballsy stole from you by exploiting Jack. It belongs to you. It's yours."

How can you tell a princess no? Jack wondered.

"How can I say no to a princess?" Daria said, sniffling. She looked at Jack and smiled. "Thank you. You're as wonderful as I always thought you were." Daria embraced him.

"You're welcome," Jack said, an awful rent in his heart finally healing.

* * *

The first punch came out of nowhere and put out his lights almost instantly. He felt the Ballsy goons dragging him somewhere as the last shreds of consciousness left him. I hope Misty's safe, he thought as he plunged into darkness.

He and Misty had left Tertius Diamond in the Kappa Crucis constellation and had stopped at a diner in the middle of nowhere, one of those places that had sprung up from the ether simply because two heavily-traveled space lanes happened to intersect nearby.

The Erehwon Diner hung suspended from nothing like a holiday ornament that had lost its tree. Spines of glittering light shot out like flaming lances from the diner core, an asteroid that had been towed to the spot. Along these spines were docking bays, most of them occupied with ships in a myriad of sizes and varieties. The long-haul shippers, those tractor-trailer units too large to dock anywhere, stood in ranks a few points away, a diner shuttle ferrying their crew in for a meal and then out when they were done.

Jack had berthed the Scavenger near the end of one such spine, and he and Misty had walked the long glasma tube to the diner itself, occasionally dodging retro-clad waiters and waitresses taking dock-side meals directly to ships.

"Why didn't we order dock-side?" Misty asked.

"You ever been to a place like this? It's half the entertainment."

"When are we going to start using our new identities?" she'd asked.

Jack had purchased two pseudodents, one for her and one for him, but he hadn't quite figured out what to do about the Salvager. He'd had the ship for three years and really liked it. It was home, and he was reluctant to part with it. If he could somehow figure out how to transfer its ownership to his new pseudodent, he wouldn't have hesitated.

The diner itself was gravitationless, effectively, the asteroid's mass so small it exerted no pull at all. The dining tables were suspended in three dimensions along geodesic girders, the wait staff navigating the maze with a combination of guide rail, grav nodes, and retro blasts.

They cycled through an airlock to the maître d's desk, the restaurant chaos inundating them with noise. Jack signaled for a table for two, not even trying to outshout the cacophony.

The kitchen glowed with flickering flame, rivaling a steel foundry, and seated at the counter facing the kitchen were the usual suspects: bloated long-haul freighter pilots in grease-stained formalls, bleary-eyed and poorly-groomed, their portly forms perched precariously on stools so small they threatened to slip between the abundant buns they were intended to support. Had the gravity been any greater, they would have.

One bulky pilot, more brawn than fat, threw an eye toward the door.

Jack dismissed it as random. He considered ghosting the place, but decided that he'd probably find the cacophony of thought to be comparable to the auditory one.

The host seated them, helping them navigate the weightlessness. Nearby was a sign indicating the restrooms.

The vids placed ubiquitously throughout the restaurant caught his attention. "Breaking news from the Vega Strip in the multimillion-galacti heist of the Ballsy Palace vault," The bobbing head of a reporter said, "The Gaming Commission has received a virtual jackpot of information spanning twenty-five years of Ballsy Gaming operations, information so shocking that the commission has issued a preemptive order to halt all gaming at all Ballsy resorts throughout the Strip until its investigation is complete."

The mic was shoved into the face of a smartly-dressed woman, the caption identifying her as President of the Vega Strip Gaming Commission. "The tactics depicted in this documentation are so egregious as to warrant immediate action. That's all I can say right now."

The reporter returned. "Oddly, the information was gathered by the same individual who is charged in this break-in at the Ballsy Palace vault, Peter Whitey Van Schluss. When asked about criminal charges against Ballsy, the commission stated that the entire cache had been turned over to law enforcement."

Jack grinned at Misty as the vid broke for a commercial. Jack motioned that he was headed to the restroom, and Misty indicated the same for herself to the ladies' room.

He had just finished emptying his bladder into the suction urinal when he turned into the fist that turned off his lights.

* * *

Somewhere, pain pricked his consciousness, and Jack swam upward from the depths of oblivion.

Into hell.

Although not a stranger to pain, Jack hadn't known anything close to *this* level of pain. The left side of his face throbbed with the unending bass-drum beating of his heart. The wet stuff on his upper lip was sure to be blood.

He turned his head toward a light, and his nose flopped that way like a beached fish, a spike driving itself into his brain through his nostrils. He was convinced the facial reconstructions wouldn't do much to improve his appearance.

An attempt to speak caused a fresh gout of blood to burst from his nostrils.

"Where is it, Carson?" A low, menacing voice said from beyond the circle of light. A fist the size of a freight train leaped to his face and sent his head rocking back. "Where's the money?"

Focus! Jack told himself. I have to focus.

Focusing sharpened the pain and the pain consumed his thoughts and his brain wouldn't work. A tiny part of his mind pitched in some sarcastic remark about never having your brain when you needed it most.

But he knew they didn't want him to think. They just wanted their money. The Gaming Commission's shutting down Ballsy's gambling activities hadn't, apparently, extended to their enforcement or intimidation operations. Jack suspected that Whitey's info dump would slow down Ballsy, but not cause it to implode completely.

"What'd you do with it?"

The blow came from the other side and sent his head the opposite direction. Focus! he told himself, despite his overwhelming desire for the oblivion of unconsciousness.

His assailant was male and right-handed. Jack recalled the long-haul freighter pilot who'd glanced over from the restaurant counter as he and Misty had entered through the airlock, the one who was more brawn than fat. Jack tried to match that with the vague glimpse he'd gotten just as he was turning from the urinal and the fist collided with his face.

There must be others, Jack thought, unsure if the person pummeling him now was the same as the one who'd assaulted him in the restroom or the more brawn-than-fat long-haul freighter pilot at the counter.

It didn't matter.

What mattered was they'd captured him and now tortured him in an effort to recoup some of their losses.

How many are there? he wondered, another question and another blow distracting him momentarily. The sharp spikes in pain made it difficult to think, but he was becoming accustomed to the dull throbbing that he suspected he'd have as constant companion for at least the near future.

Where am I? he wondered. Another question and another blow spun his head the other direction.

The room came back into focus, and Jack guessed he'd lost consciousness momentarily. What was I doing? he wondered.

"No more blows to the head," said a distant, disembodied voice. "We want to know what's in it. Here, use these on his hands."

His hands, limp at the ends of arms tied in three places to a chair that felt bolted to a deck that vibrated with the deep thrumming of a starship engine.

"Where's the money?" A hand grasped one of his fingers, a pinky, and placed it in the jaws of some tool—pliers?—and squeezed.

A shock went up his arm, and his brain reported dispassionately that the knuckle on his left pinky had been reduced to a mangle of flesh and bone. The pain reached him a moment later, and he screamed.

"He has a voice," the disembodied voice said. "Let's see if he can talk." The face shoved itself into the light. "Jack, my name is Bill. I am your Dante—your guide through purgatory. Are you familiar with the

106

ancient work? If not, I'll acquaint you, one torture after another. You know what we want—our money. What you get is your freedom. And what good is freedom, Jack, if you have to spend the rest of your life recovering from your injuries? Don't make us hurt you further, Jack! Just tell us where it's at. Where's the money, Jack?"

He stared at Bill through two eyes that refused to line up, one of them nearly swollen shut. The two images, one of them somewhat fuzzy, went different directions, and Jack dived into the gulf that opened between them.

Water full in the face brought him back to consciousness. The evaporation cooled him and relieved some suffering, although it stung his lacerations too.

"Where's the money, Jack?"

A hand grasped his right pinky carefully, as though performing some delicate operation that Jack was too disoriented to follow. He managed to focus his good eye on his pinky just as the fingernail disappeared, leaving behind bright pink flesh that turned quickly red. Like a thunderclap that followed a lightning strike, the pain ripped into Jack's brain a moment later, the pinky on fire.

"How many fingers would you like to lose, Jack? How many toes?" The face poked into the light again. "How about your manhood, Jack?" The laughter was wicked and cut into Jack's soul like a shiv into his bowels. "It's so simple, Jack. Tell us where the money is, and we let you go. No harm, no foul."

It was tempting, simply because the pain was excruciating, but Jack knew they'd never let him go. He was dead meat, and the only thing that kept them from killing him was his knowledge. He wondered how he could have ever been so stupid. He should have begun using the alternate identity immediately after the robbery. Of course, Ballsy Gaming would send its agents after him, if not its entire private armada. What was he thinking?

Jack prayed that Misty was safe. He suspected she was, since his captors hadn't mentioned her. If they had captured her, they would have tortured her in front of him to extract the information they wanted.

"How could you have been so stupid, Jack? You should have used that alternate identity immediately."

So they'd captured the Scavenger as well, had searched it thoroughly, and had found the documentation.

What about the cube? Jack wondered. Why didn't I think of it a long time ago?

The bucket of water to his face must have cleared his thoughts.

He tried to channel his interlocutor's thoughts but all he was aware of was his own. And pain, of course. He didn't have the cube, apparently. He couldn't feel it in any of his pockets, and he could assume they'd searched him thoroughly.

A chill coursed through him, and all hope abandoned him.

If these unscrupulous criminals knew what the cube could do, he thought, they wouldn't hesitate to use it to take over the Empire.

Then he remembered what Misty had told him immediately after he'd found it: "I used to be its." The cube had chosen Jack.

To be the Emperor, besides.

A thought so ludicrous at the time that he'd dismissed it outright. A thought that grew more improbable yet as the interrogation proceeded. A thought so beyond the realm of possibility that Jack, in excruciating pain, deep in debt, pursued by the bank's repo agent, being chased for the alimony he owned his first wife, and now in the clutches of a criminal organization intent on extracting information before killing him, a thought so far beyond reason that Jack began to laugh.

Because it also meant they couldn't use the cube either.

The vibration from his laughter exacerbated his pain.

And incensed his captors.

"You dare laugh! I'll give you something to laugh about!" And Bill whipped out a blasma pistol and blew off Jack's foot.

And the chair leg and a foot-size piece of floor.

"Fool!" And someone knocked the blasma pistol from Bill's hand.

Jack stared at the place his foot had been, in his head an inane thought that he should be falling forward. The Criperor, they'll call me, he thought giddily. The Limperor! Then every nerve that had occupied the now-missing foot sent its pain into his brain. Fire now engulfing his stump, he wondered why it didn't emit a fireball.

He remembered with some long-forgotten part of his mind that the chair was bolted to the floor. The stench of fried flesh filled his nostrils. As the smoke cleared, he realized that a woman stood before him. He'd seen her face and knew he should recognize her, but the pain had pushed him past knowing and past caring.

He prayed to all the gods ever created to kill him now and relieved his torment.

"We're doing this all wrong," the woman said, her posture one of command, her focused gaze one of privilege. She shoved a palmcom into his face. "Tell us where the money is, or we kill your ex-wife." On the screen was Daria Osborn.

"Jack!" Daria writhed as though in pain.

He knew what she'd say if he were to ask: "Don't let the bastards win! Don't give in to them for my sake, Jack!" And he could see it in her eyes as well, but he also knew they'd do to her exactly what they were doing to him.

"Tell us!" Leticia Ballsy said, grabbing pliers from the table. She ripped off his little toe, the small one from his remaining foot, a fleabite to an elephant stomp.

"Tell us!" And she twisted the ring finger of his right hand into a neat little knot. He didn't know a finger could bend like that.

With each digit, Daria on the palmcom screamed as well, and he saw they were doing the same to her as to him. All he could think was, "I have to stop them."

It was also occurred to him with clinical precision that they wouldn't stop not matter what he told them, that his and Daria's mutilated bodies with their tortured faces would end up gracing the headlines of all the broadcast tabloids, their lurid deaths fodder for the masses and a memorable lesson to every shyster contemplating a caper similar to the one Jack had pulled on Ballsy Gaming.

Ballsy had no choice, and neither did the industry. They had to lay down in full graphic color what the consequences were for trying to bilk a casino—any casino.

So even if Leticia Ballsy were to release him now, the other gaming houses would finish the task out of principle, from the very moral fiber of their convictions.

"All right," he gasped, "I'll tell you." He could barely get a breath, his lungs seeming compressed by sheer pain.

"Jack, no!" Daria said, and a cry of pain was cut off when Leticia ended the com.

"Tell them to stop!" Jack spat. "I said I'd tell you!"

"So get on with it, Carson." Leticia hung a finger over her palmcom. "Only you can stop her torture."

"I have to use the bathroom." He'd noticed awhile ago that he'd already lost control of his bladder. Now his gut was cramping and a bowel movement was trying to force its way forth.

"You can sit in your own feces, Carson. You aren't going anywhere, so if you have to go, then you can go right where you're at." Then Leticia smiled. "And your ex-wife's torture continues until you tell me where the money's at."

Jack couldn't hold it any longer, and he began to weep as he voided all over himself. Warm chunky liquids spread around his behind and down his legs. The aroma of feces joined that of burning flesh. Shame and helplessness flooded through him as he sobbed at the indignity. "Not telling you now," he choked out between sobs, rage pouring down his face, his breath coming in huge gulping gasps.

Then put his head down and let his weeping take control.

Amidst his weeping, he felt a hand on his arm. And then someone put the cube in his hand.

"Here you go, Jack," said a voice, as ethereal as rain.

It sounded like Misty, and he wanted to yell at her to flee, but then he noticed that the only sound was his weeping. Through his tear-streaked vision, he saw Leticia, her expression fierce, ferocious, and frozen. Even the thrumming of engines through the floor had been silenced.

His hands and arms, he saw, had been freed. How did that happen? he wondered.

His legs, too. Both of them.

And they were intact.

So were his fingers. The chair leg was still a molten strip where it hung over a foot-wide hole in the floor, but his leg that had been vaporized by the blasma blast was intact again.

Glowing softly in his hand, the cube stared at him.

He was still covered in feces and urine, but his body was intact—completely intact.

Rising unsteadily, he pushed away the bright lamp they'd shoved into his face. The shadows emerged. Three others besides Bill and Leticia had been watching from the perimeter, and along one wall was a workbench with an arsenal of implements ready for use.

No one stopped him as he took a tentative step forward.

They all stood still as stone, unmoving.

He glanced over at the table of implements they'd been ready to use on him. He glanced among his erstwhile captors. The ghost of pain was still unimaginable, but the shame and humiliation sat on his chest like an alien parasite eating into him.

Jack very badly wanted to subject them to the same indignities.

And to what end? he asked himself.

Jack stepped around the statue Leticia and found his way into the corridor. In a daze, barely recognized what he was doing, he found a cleansall and a clean pair of formalls. The person who looked back at him in the mirror was a ghost of Jack Carson, haunted by the harrowing experience.

He made his way to the bridge, where a crew stood frozen at their posts. In one vid, his ship trailed the Ballsy vessel, the Scavenger attached with a tractor beam.

Jack deactivated the tractor beam, left the bridge, and maneuvered toward an escape pod. He flew it toward the Salvager. With his palm-com, he opened the Scavenger's hold and maneuvered the escape pod inside. He didn't wonder how he'd found his palmcom. He was so far beyond wonder that he couldn't question anymore what came his way.

Setting the cube on the console, Jack brought the Salvager to life and set a course for Tertius Diamond, thinking he needed to make sure Daria was safe.

During the day-long journey there, he stared sightlessly at the ship around him and the cube beside him, all of it so surreal that he couldn't take it in.

As though his sensory processing circuits had been blown.

All that remained was shame, humiliation, and pain.

He knew he needed to attend to these but he held them at bay somehow.

At one point en route, he slept the dreamless sleep of the dead, a deep restful sleep, refreshing and invigorating. He knew he'd have nightmares, but somehow they too were held at bay.

On Tertius Diamond, Jack took a flitter taxi from the spaceport, which stopped down the lane from Daria's home, the home he'd once shared with her. The place was surrounded by Crown Dicks, and the street was blockaded. A hover buzzed overhead, bristling with weapons.

"Who are you?" the officer at the checkpoint asked him.

"Her ex-husband," he said. "Jack Carson."

She looked at her palmcom. "You're not authorized, sorry."

He looked toward the house, about to ask the officer to check with Daria on that, when Misty emerged.

Jack brightened immediately. He'd somehow known she was safe but to see her brought him profound relief. He remembered the voice, ethereal as rain, telling him, "Here you go," and her putting the cube in his palm.

Misty stepped through the checkpoint into his arms.

"I'm so glad you're safe," he whispered, wonder and awe, bewilderment and bemusement, pain and relief all floating through him in chaotic catharsis. "How's Daria?"

"She's safe." Misty pulled away and looked up at him, a wisdom beyond her years in her eyes. "How are you?"

He nodded and looked along his arms to his fingers, down his legs to his toes. "I'm intact, thanks to you." He grinned at her.

She grinned back. "Sorry I couldn't get there sooner."

"I'm glad you got there. That's what's important. But how'd you do it? How did you find me, and then get here from there?"

She shrugged, the classic lines of her face heavy with gravity. "I'm still not sure, Jack. But I had to it, because you wanted me to."

He stared at her, not understanding, and knowing at some level that he probably wouldn't ever understand. There had been a lot of things he'd wanted as his captors had inflicted more painful and degrading tortures. He'd wanted, under duress, to do far worse to them in retaliation, to subject them to inhumane indignities beyond imagining. But we all want our deepest darkest desires fulfilled when we're under duress, he thought.

"Because you needed me to," Misty said.

Jack nodded, accepting that. "Thank you." He held her in his gaze, letting gratitude shine through his face. Her face became blurry with his tears. He wiped them away and looked across the barriers toward Daria's home. "I should go see her, but I'm not authorized."

"You made sure she was safe," Misty said, "and now she's in protective custody. Did you see the news this morning?"

Jack shook his head. "I can barely function, can't believe I'm alive, and intact, and free." He glanced again at his foot, then at his fingers.

The right ring finger had been tied into a knot, he remembered. And now, there it sat at the end of his right hand, functioning perfectly, as straight as it'd always been.

He wiggled it, giggling.

"They captured Leticia Ballsy, arrested her for a slew of offenses. Somehow, vids of her torturing someone were leaked to the police. They're still trying to find that person."

He blinked at her, and then looked at the officer not ten feet away at the checkpoint. "Shouldn't I turn myself in?"

Misty shrugged. "They also have a vid of Daria being tortured, and she'll testify at the trial. There's no shortage of evidence. Leticia and her crew have all been denied bail."

"What about Ballsy Gaming?"

"Confiscated as evidence. They'll never do business again."

Jack sighed and looked again toward Daria's home, on whose very doorstep Whitey had given the performance of his life, convincing Jack to risk all his and Daria's assets on a bet he was sure to lose. "I guess I really don't need to see her. But won't they find me eventually?" He looked again at the officer not ten feet away.

"They can't find any information on Jack Carson. It's as if he never existed."

Jack looked at Misty.

She looked at him innocently, once again a nine-year-old orphan sans awareness of galactic matters.

He didn't know how she'd done it, and he didn't care.

Because it meant he was free.

Chapter 11

Monique "The Bruiser" Brewster watched from Sedition Control Forty as the hapless junker loaded a set of pristine-looking crates aboard the Salvager. Much too pristine for a junker of his caliber. She was guessing it wasn't junk.

A Sedition Control Investigator with more than five thousand subjects under surveillance, the Bruiser had been alerted to the junker's activities when he'd slipped past a Galactic Patrol on Canis Dogma Five. The entire episode on the Vega Strip, and especially his bizarre escape from his Ballsy Palace captors, had convinced her he was the slimiest trickster she'd ever encountered.

The vids of his departure from Canis Dogma Five would have been hilarious had she had any disposition toward mirth. Two slack-jawed, drool-slathered patrol officers had watched insensate as the Scavenger belonging to Jack Carson had roared right past them, their alarms and buzzers going off unheeded. The officers had been suspended and were undergoing neuralizing, neither one remembering the incident, both swearing they hadn't taken their eyes off their monitors for a moment.

Maybe they should be tested for intelligence, Monique thought, or have some sense beaten into them. "What's going on at the Birds?!" she roared.

A tech jumped visibly in his chair. "The Southern Birds team has apprehended the proprietor, Cherise Mariposa, but they're still searching for the girl."

"Find her! We've got to tack this slippery junker to the tarmac, before he turns his persuasive energies on us."

Monique had had the Carson Junker under direct surveillance since his first visit to Alpha Tuscana. Who was the girl? Monique wondered for the thousandth time. She'd rechecked Jack's profile, but he'd never had a child by any of his three wives, nor had he shown the slightest skill in nor inclination toward rearing a child. The man can barely care for himself, she thought, let alone a child. Never had a home, she knew, the brothel the closest he'd ever come to actually living someplace permanent. Four bankruptcies, a ship about to be repossessed due to default, an empty bank account, petty charges pending on half-a-dozen worlds, and a cargo hold filled with girls' clothes sitting between him and starvation.

And why did the Torgassan Empire even consider this worthless Junker worth surveillance? It might have been a question for social critics, and it might someday be a question for historians, but it wasn't a question for Monique "The Bruiser" Brewster.

It was what she did.

After any act of sedition toward the Torgassan Empire—be it rolled eyes during an Imperial event or an obscene gesture toward the Imperial banner—her job was to pursue and detain the seditionist. And if the suspect somehow got hurt in her custody, well, that was just too bad. The same was true for any of her staff who flubbed the job.

"Birds team, report!" Monique was getting nervous.

On the tarmac, the fuel truck was pulling away. Unwilling to risk the bird flying away, she'd ordered the fuel replaced with water. Even if Jack Carson tried to lift off, the Salvager would take him nowhere.

"We can't find the girl anywhere," said Montgomery, the site lead.

"What do you mean, you can't find her? We had the house cordoned tighter than a black hole! Who's second in command? Is that Wallace? Put him on!"

A pink, scrubbed face popped up on the monitor. "Wallace here."

"You're in command. Get a camera on Mariposa and put a lazgun to her head. Make sure the lazgun's visible."

"Yes, Ma'am. Uh, what about Montgomery?"

"Fire that bitch!"

The former commander of the Birds team got on the horn. "You can't do that!"

"You're fired, Bitch!" And Brewster silenced Montgomery's com.

Monique couldn't actually fire anyone under her command, but everyone knew Montgomery would soon be out on medical leave. The Bruiser ground her fist into her palm in anticipation.

"All right, people! In we go!"

* * *

Jack palmed the gene-lock on the Salvager door, finished loading the last of Misty's wardrobe, which she'd enhanced significantly now that they were filthy rich. He'd left Misty and Cherise at the Southern Birds, hoping to be back quickly. Just a quick trip to see about a retinue for Misty, he thought, whistling tunelessly.

He'd given himself a week to recover from his escapade with Ballsy gaming, and he still felt a shock to his system whenever he thought of gambling, cards, dice, and ice-cream suits.

He'd had a week of the paradise in Cherise's company, Misty learning at her elbow as Cherise continued to train her understudy. Not exactly the kind of education he'd been hoping Misty would get. He wanted to turn the brothel into an orphanage, but he wasn't sure how to tell Cherise. With the money he'd filched from the Ballsy vault —the bulk of it going to Daria—Jack felt that he and Misty might have enough to finance an entourage fit for a princess.

"I can't arrive by myself!" she'd pouted two nights ago. "I have to have a full entourage of personnel, Jack. For stars' sake, what will Emperor Torgas think?!"

He'd looked at her, feeling so flustered he wasn't able to speak. "What are we talking, here?" he finally forced past his perplexed lips.

"Just the usual personnel any princess would have, Jack. You know, land steward, house steward, housekeeper, butler, chef, lady's maid, valet, first footman, second footman, head nurse, chamber maid, parlor maid, house maid, between maid, nurse, under cook, kitchen maid, laundry maid, page, tea boy, head groom, stable master, groom, stable boy, head gardener, game keeper, grounds keepers, governess, and gate keeper."

Misty took a deep breath. "But to truly impress his highness

Emperor Torgas, I'll probably also need chauffeurs, kneemen, legwomen, coiffeuses, coutures, stockinglasses, chaperones, equestrians, scullery maids, enderlasses, chimney sweeps, fishmongers, nannies, tinkers, tailors, soldiers, spies, nincompoops, dunces, jesters, and jokers. And of course there's you, Jack. You'll go with me, won't you?"

His mind shuddering at the litany, he just nodded dumbly. "But what'll you call me?"

She scowled in consternation. "Hell, I don't know! You ask such hard questions! I'll try to think of something."

And he'd arranged a trip to an old Britannia estate on Cor Caroli in the northern constellation Canes Venatici. If anyone could assemble a menagerie of servants with such intricate gradations, it was the Britannians.

The Scavenger all fueled and ready to go, Jack pulled the hatch closed behind him. He stepped into the cockpit and stared.

Misty sat in the copilot's chair.

He blinked at her, as though she might disappear between blinks.

She blinked back at him, a hint of a smile on her face.

"You could have just said you wanted to come with me."

"I wanted to come with you."

"Better late than never." He glanced toward the Salvager hatch— the gene-lock secured hatch. "How'd you get past the gene-lock?" It was only the fifth time it'd happened.

"You know," Misty said, "you should really make a decision, Jack."

"Huh? About what?"

"Whether to call your ship Salvager or Scavenger. The way you're calling it both, sometimes in the same sentence makes you seem … schizophrenic!"

Shrugging, he snorted at her, not having realized until she pointed it out. "Why should I? It's fine with me, whatever I call it. Are you going tell me how you get in and out through that gene-lock?"

Shrugging, she snorted at him. "Why should I?"

"Mutual, darling."

"Glad we agree on something."

The vidscreen filled with a bulldog's face, and a voice boomed from the ship's intercom. "Jack Carson, you're under arrest for sedition!"

Pounding commenced on the Scavenger hatch, a distant voice shouting, "Open up in the name of the Emperor!"

Sedition? Jack wondered. Trafficking in contraband, trespassing on secured archeological sites, absconding on spousal support orders, defaulting to his creditors, breaking and entering, grand theft, larceny, fraud. His list of offenses was lengthy, but sedition wasn't among them.

The bulldog on the screen growled at him. "We've got your woman, Carson! Don't even think about squirrelling out of this one!"

The bulldog face was replaced with Cherise, a handful of hair sprouting from between her captor's fingers, a lazgun to her head. "They swarmed the house after you left, Jack! And they can't find Misty!"

Dogface replaced Cherise. "Give up, or we shoot the woman, Carson!"

"You can't do that!"

"Look at me, Carson!"

He couldn't help but do so, her face filling the screen.

"I'm Sedition Control Investigator Monique 'The Bruiser' Brewster —" her badge flashed briefly on the screen—"and I do whatever it takes to capture my suspect. You give up or she gets hurt. Which is it?"

"I give up," Jack said quickly.

* * *

Sighing, Jack let himself fall back on the bunk, exhausted.

"What are you doing?" Misty asked him. "Now's your chance to escape!"

He looked at her in disbelief. Things had gone from ludicrous to bizarre in the last eight hours. He'd been hand-cuffed, strip-searched, geno-typed, iris-scanned, retina-typed, facia-metricked, bone-imaged, E. coli-matched, and even mitochondrial gene-sampled.

And for good measure, a still shot of his anus, for all the toilet cams they'd deployed throughout the Empire. "No two assholes alike," Misty'd quipped.

Jack looked around the cell where they'd just deposited him. Blank, featureless walls broken only by the door, the cot, and the all-in-one sanistation. His journey here had been through a labyrinth of gene-coded doors, iris-coded gates, badge-checked apertures, and even a foot-thick airlock. He couldn't imagine trying to get back out the way he'd come, the route alone enough to disorient a bloodhound. And through all the myriad checks, scans, imaging, and typography, Misty had followed, everyone around them blithely ignoring her.

Jack had been made to change clothes no less than three times, the two jumpsuits each a different color, but somehow he'd held onto the cube. No one asked him for it, nor had they tried to take it.

He frowned at Misty again. She'd seen him in his full, naked, slouchy glory thrice over, at no time evincing any change in expression. On the second full disrobing, he'd said, "Can't you look someplace else and spare a guy his dignity?"

One of the three officers doing the strip search looked at the other two and then back at Jack. "Who you talkin' to?"

Jack had glanced between Misty and the officer, but hadn't replied.

"Talkin' to unseen persons, they call that," one officer said to another. "We got a certifiable cuckoo." After that, they gave him a bit more room.

Looking at Misty, Jack shook his head. "Where am I going to escape to? And why didn't they see you?"

"Cause you willed them not to—with the cube."

He brought it out of his pocket, surprised the jumpsuit had a pocket. The opaque, silvery sides of the cube stared blankly back at him. "I'm doin' a good job of getting you invited to the palace, aren't I?"

"You're making progress," she said sans irony.

"So, if I can persuade them not to see you, why couldn't I persuade them not to capture me?"

"You gave yourself up," Misty replied.

He pondered that, knowing they had Cherise someplace. "And why would I try to escape, when they'll harm Cherise if I do?"

"We'll have to escape together, all three of us."

He thought about the multiple layers of security, the compound obviously meant to contain high-value detainees. It was impossible for a single person to escape, much less three.

"You can do it," she said. "Here, put your hands on the cube like this." She wrapped thumb and forefinger along opposite edges, then placed her other thumb and forefinger similarly but offset by ninety degrees.

He took it from her and did the same, and the world slammed into his brain. Cacophonies of sound and kaleidoscopes of light inundated him.

"Concentrate," she said, her voice impossibly far away.

He focused on her, and saw a scruffy drudge staring at him from a low slouch. Oh, that's me, he realized.

"All right, well done. You're ghosting me, now."

"Ghosting?" The lips of the drudge moved in time with the word.

"Yeah, it's a ghost cube, remember? Now, concentrate on the surrounding rooms."

Somehow, he knew what to do. In the adjoining rooms beyond two-foot thick walls were guards. Also above and below, more guards, all of them stationed in empty cells identical to the one he occupied. One featureless corridor served each set of cells, and the cell block itself was set six stories below ground. Odd, I don't remember descending that far, Jack thought. It occurred to him that they'd deliberately distracted him while delivering him to his destination.

He searched the compound, looking for Cherise and for the control monitoring station. If they were smart, they'd have two monitoring stations, each monitoring the prisoner and each other.

"If they're smart, they'll have two monitoring stations, each monitoring each other as well as you."

He could have told her that.

"And you have to find Cherise."

He stopped himself from telling her the obvious.

There! Four floors up and to the west end of the compound. Cherise lay on a bunk in a cell identical to his, weeping softly.

He sent her his comfort, and she sat up suddenly, looking around. Her gaze fixed on the door, where he observed her from, and her lips formed a silent word: "Jack?"

Quickly, he withdrew and scoured the compound for monitoring stations. He found three of them, one for the perimeter and two for the prisoners. Both were filled with stern-looking Imperial guards, eyes glued to vidscreens.

He'd have to keep his attention on all three of them, remembering his near-capture when leaving Canis Dogma Five. He focused on the main monitoring station, however, chiefly because of one occupant, a woman. A large woman with the face of a bulldog and a disposition to match.

"I got here as fast as I could," Bulldog said. "What are you grousing about? You brought him in, didn't you?" Brewster was saying to a silver-haired gentleman with a few more epaulets than everyone else. "First, I'll meet with Montgomery, and then I'll interrogate the prisoner."

"Montgomery," Jack discovered, was four cells over and one level up from his.

Brewster looked at the compound commander. "Absolutely no one in or out of the cell except me, under any circumstances. Got it?" She poked a finger into his chest.

The man tried his best not to recoil as she stomped from the room. "I think I have a broken rib," he said after she'd gone, rubbing where she'd poked him.

Jack ghosted Brewster through her escort, reluctant to infiltrate the woman directly, following her progress as she descended the stairs and passed through multiple checkpoints. Her escort changed several times, and Jack changed his ghosting to match.

At one point, Brewster stopped and cornered the escort he was ghosting. "What are you starin at, Newfuss?" She clocked him, and he slithered down the wall to the floor.

Jack was kicked back to his cell, but he soon reacquired the woman as she emerged onto level five.

"Why the hell am I being kept here?" Montgomery demanded as Brewster entered the cell.

The big woman glanced at her escorts. "We'll need a moment alone, thank you."

The two escorts fled.

Brewster looked up at the ceiling. "This is a private conversation, Captain."

In the monitoring stations, screens went blank at the Captain's nod.

Jack ghosted through Montgomery's eyes.

"And now *you're* looking at me funny," Brewster said with unconcealed disgust. "What's wrong with you people here? Does everybody on Tuscana have an IQ of two?"

"What's this about, Brewster? Arrest me for interfering with your investigation if you think you have to, but don't just hold me in a cell without explanation!"

"Explanation? You want explanation? You let that girl escape, is your explanation. You failed me."

The punch landed and Montgomery's lights went out before Jack knew what had hit him.

Back in his cell, Jack heard Misty saying something to him, but he was too disoriented after being knocked unconscious twice to understand what she was telling him.

He repositioned his hands on the cube and located the escorts outside Montgomery's cell. The sounds coming through the foot-thick door weren't pleasant.

"Now's the time, while she's distracted," Misty said.

Jack zeroed in on the two internal monitoring stations and wondered how he could do this. I have to get them to open the cell door, he thought. What better way than to have the prisoner disappear? He took himself off their visual cortexes.

"Captain, the prisoner!" Twenty people gawked at an empty cell.

"Escape in progress!" the Captain shouted. "Get in there and found out where he went! Lockdown on floors one through five! Quintuple the security at each checkpoint."

"Uh, Sir?" said a two-chevroned woman.

"Yes, Lieutenant?"

"Detective Brewster ordered no one in or out of the cell except her."

"Fuck that bitch! I run the place. Get in there!"

"Yes, Sir. Oh, uh, and lockdown means Brewster can't move either."

"About time someone put her in restraints!"

The two guards outside Jack's cell opened the door and rushed in. Jack nimbly stepped into the corridor, Misty at his elbow. They slithered down the corridor toward the two guards at the checkpoint. Both guards in fighting stances had their weapons in hand. Behind them was a clear glascreet door reinforced with poly-alloy bars.

A voice came from Jack's cell. "Not a trace, and not a mark on the walls. What about the vents?"

"Too small," said a voice from the monitoring station. "And vent shows clear."

He figured they probably had visual there. Probably in the crapper too.

"What about the toilet?"

"Crapper's clear!"

How are we going to get to the next level? Jack wondered.

Somewhere, a radio squawked.

"Open this blasted cell, Captain!" It was Brewster, who'd found some communicator. "What the hell is going on, anyway?"

The Captain signaled the door to be opened. "Escaped prisoner, Brewster. You're on level five. Get down to level six, maybe you'll see something no one else has. He just disappeared off the monitors."

"And you sent the guards in to inspect visually, didn't you?" Brewster sneered, her voice dripping with venom.

Jack saw her exit the cell, glimpsing the bloody pulp she'd left behind. He ghosted her escort to the checkpoint on level five, where they did a gene-scan, retinal scan, facial metric, iris check, and badge scan.

"What are you lookin' at?" Brewster snarled at the guard Jack was ghosting.

He withdrew before she punished the guard. "Here she comes," Jack whispered to Misty.

Brewster descended the stairs. Both guards at the checkpoint looked her direction.

One of them opened the door for her, and Misty skipped between Brewster and the door.

"What was that?" Brewster looked around, her nose knotting up, sniffing audibly.

You will not see us, Jack willed.

Brewster stepped forward, pulling the door closed quickly behind her. She took one step toward Jack's erstwhile cell and froze. "What's that?" Again her head swiveled on her neck, her gaze coming to rest right on Jack's face. "I'd swear if my eyes didn't tell me otherwise that he's right in front of me. Can't you smell the fear?"

"Right where?" a guard said, staring at the blank wall behind Jack.

"Right there." And Brewster unfurled a blunt bludgeon known on anyone else's physiognomy as a finger, and jabbed it at Jack's chest.

Somehow he sidestepped, and the finger dented the wall.

It's got to be solid block! Jack thought.

Brewster looked at her bent finger. "Ow, that hurts."

Jack could have told her it was broken.

"Let's look at the cell." And Brewster was gone.

The Captain came down the stairs and demanded entry.

Jack slipped into the stairwell before the door closed.

Misty looked at him with eyes bigger than moons. "That was close," she lipped at him.

They worked their way upward, slowly, having to wait at each checkpoint until someone came through, strobes flashing and alarms pinging the whole time. On the first level below ground, where Cherise was being held, a bevy of guards stood between the checkpoint and her cell.

Misty tapped his arm, and with a variety of pantomimes, indicated she would create a distraction. She descended a level and moved to the far end, away from the stairwell.

Watching her through the cube—and keeping her off everyone's visual cortices—and doing the same for himself—took a level of concentration quite at the limit of his power. Drips of sweat ran down his back. His arms and legs felt leaden.

He had to time this just right.

"Now, Jack!" Misty shouted.

Jack revealed her to the station personnel.

"It's the girl! Where'd she come from?" Brewster shouted, her voice echoing from the multiple pickups. "Get her!"

A series of instructions went out, including the order for the first floor contingent—the closest guard besides those at the second floor checkpoint—to investigate.

Misty raised her fist to the camera. "Come and get me, Bluster Brewster!"

And Jack slipped past checkpoint one as guards tumbled out and down the stairs.

Then he took Cherise out of the picture.

"Captain, now the woman's gone!"

One of the guards rushed into her cell, and Jack followed.

Cherise looked frightened, watching the guard, who dashed back into the corridor and yelled to his companions, "Vanished! And no sign of an exit!"

"Come with me," Jack said to her, his voice low.

Cherise jumped, her fright turning to terror. "Jack?"

He took her arm. "It's all right. Come on," he whispered, and pulled her into the corridor.

"The girl's a decoy!" Brewster shouted. "He's after the woman!"

Another series of instructions were issued, and guards bunched up at checkpoint one on both sides, Brewster ordering them to cut off Jack's escape.

On level two, a guard cornered Misty, and Jack made her vanish. Now holding himself, Cherise, and Misty invisible to the visual cortices of everyone in the compound, he began to feel faint, and sparkle began to cloud his peripheral vision.

"I can't hold it," he whispered to Cherise, knowing they were doomed.

"If you can make yourself disappear, you can make yourself appear elsewhere," she whispered back, her gaze not quite focused on him.

Jack saw Brewster pounding up the stairs, her bulk like a charging bull. He knew they'd never escape if she cornered them on the first floor. There was only one thing he could do.

He projected an image of himself in his sixth floor cell, and confusion erupted.

"It's a decoy!" Brewster shouted.

"No, it's not!" the Captain replied. "All the rest of it is an illusion!"

"All personnel to checkpoint one!" Brewster ordered, rounding the stairwell to checkpoint two.

"Belay that order!" the Captain roared. "I'm in command of this compound! Shut down checkpoints two and three, and shut off that bitch's mike!"

"That's my prisoner and if you let—"

Brewster went silent.

"All right, everyone," the Captain said, "Let's slow it down. First things first. We make the assumption that our prisoner has somehow compromised our video surveillance system. Second, we inspect every cell on every floor systematically by feel, and we access everything below level one through the maintenance tunnels."

Had Jack known about them, he might have escaped through the maintenance tunnels. I can see only what other people are seeing, he reminded himself. Backing to the end of the corridor, taking Cherise with him, Jack looked up.

A maintenance hatch.

How to get up there? he wondered, seeing no ladder, just blank, featureless walls. Must be mechanical, he thought, some switch somewhere that lowers a ladder from inside the hatch.

On level two and three hatches opened and ladders lowered, the guards already scrambling down them.

Jack searched the control room, found a bank of lighted switches, the ones numbered "two" and "three" blinking. He ghosted the technician, who punched the other four switches.

The hatch above his head opened, and a ladder descended.

"Who ordered those hatches opened?" the Captain roared.

But Cherise was already climbing, Jack right behind her. The piping-ribbed tube took them to a cramped landing, beside it a larger tube extending all the way down.

And up.

Freedom, Jack thought.

A quartet of soldiers dropped into the tube, and stopped just below the ground floor threshold. "All right, we hold here unless we're ordered elsewhere."

Below, on level two, Misty had crawled out into the larger tube, Jack saw.

And the girl began to climb downward. "Jack, if you can hear me, show me now," she whispered.

But if he did, and these four guards went after her, she would never escape.

He and Cherise would, but then Misty would be their prisoner. How could he let that happen?

"You have to, Jack," Misty whispered. "Let them capture me so you and Cherise can escape!"

He remembered leaving her with Xerk and Trude on Canis Dogma Five, and then with Cherise at the Southern Birds, how guilty he'd felt, especially that first time, how all he'd wanted was to turn around and fetch her with him and never part company with her again.

How can I leave her? he wondered.

"Because I'm asking you," Misty whispered.

She hadn't asked him to leave her those first two times, had only begrudgingly accepted it as necessary. This time she was asking him to leave her. Sighing, Jack made her appear.

"Sergeant, look! Isn't that the girl?"

Below them was a squeal, and she dropped rapidly down the ladder.

"Let's go," the sergeant said, and they all dropped past him and Cherise.

Jack poked his head out. The way was clear. They climbed up and quickly slipped behind some throbbing machinery as another guard headed into the maintenance chute.

From the maintenance room, Jack and Cherise made quick time out through the service entrance. The compound itself was surrounded by wire-topped cyclone fencing which hummed and crackled.

At the gate, a mesmerized guard opened it without a hint he was doing so, and Jack and Cherise ran across the road.

"Let's get out of here," Jack said, sweat pouring off him, his breathing rapid. "They've got her cornered on the sixth floor. She's giving herself up now."

"Can't you stop them?" She led Jack into an alley.

"I can barely stand," he said, his vision clouding. "She told me to leave her behind."

"So we could escape?" Cherise looked perplexed. "That's no help."

"Listen, we'll have to come back for her. There's no help for it. I'm not strong enough to get her out of there now. Just get us to the spaceport." Jack was barely aware of what she was doing, struggling to stay conscious. He knew she left for a few minutes, but that was all.

"Ok, come on," she said, helping him to his feet.

Jack didn't know whether he'd lost consciousness. He staggered from the alley and practically fell into the back of a flitter taxi. He heard the words she spoke to the driver, but he didn't understand what she was saying.

"Oh, I'm glad it's you, Mack. Listen, we need a bucket to get off this rock, and we'd better make it look like a hijacking, or the Imperials will start arresting people for conspiracy. And we'll need to change taxis a couple of times to make sure we're not being tailed. Me 'n' my friend just escaped from the compound back there—"

The driver mumbled something as they heaved around a corner.

"Yes, that compound, and there's a frightful agent named Brewster—"

Again the driver mumbled something.

"Well, I guess that's Brewster. Sounds like it anyway, and she's got a friend of ours, a girl!"

The unintelligible driver spoke.

"I don't know if she'll do anything to Misty."

More mumbling.

"All right, good plan, Mack. Thanks for your help. What? First stop already? Come on, Jack, changing taxis."

He had the sense that he'd put only one foot to the ground in between flitters. All he really knew was that the light was too bright and the colors were all wrong.

Then it all went away.

* * *

He had the sensation of being carried, twice, and then Cherise was shaking him.

"Jack, you've got to wake up!"

He struggled out of the darkness and noticed immediately how beautiful Cherise was.

He smiled beatifically. He was aboard a ship of some sort, he saw, like a freighter, perhaps. A small shape occupied the co-pilot's seat.

"You'll never guess who's already aboard."

"Misty?" he mumbled through his own thick mist.

"I'm here, Jack," the girl said, and her arms were around him and he felt her shaking and knew she was crying and he'd have cried too if he weren't so exhausted and he let consciousness slip away because he was with the two people he cared most deeply about and he was safe and he was free.

* * *

Emperor Phaeton Torgas stared at the two people kneeling before him, trying to control his features.

Another ghosting cube has been unleashed!

The strong undercurrent, that shift in the pillars upholding the Empire, the change in alignments he'd first felt about three months ago, now beset his rule.

The gold-filigree, platinum-haloed scepter holding his own

ghosting cube lay hidden beside his thigh on the throne, his hand on the armrest just above it.

He hated not having his hand on the scepter. Many were the nights the Emperor awoke in panic, the cube fading from his sight, disappearing right out of the scepter, the dream dissipating as he awoke, scepter in hand, the cube securely ensconced in its setting, having gone nowhere.

His fingers twitched with the desire to grab it and blast these two supplicants into oblivion. They're only the messengers, he told himself.

But they'd bungled the capture of Jack Carson and his two companions, and for that they deserved oblivion. Perhaps they're useful yet, he thought, but he doubted it.

Emperor Phaeton had restrained himself during the interview from delving into their minds to sort through the true sequence of events, although the surveillance vids had given him a fairly complete picture. He thought it odd that the girl, Misty, hadn't appeared in a single vid.

"How do you think he did it, Captain Lang?"

"Your August Highness," Captain Caeneus Lang said, bowing deeply, "At first, I thought he had some device that disrupted our video surveillance system. After I reviewed the vids however, I'm convinced he used some sort of neural disruptor."

"Detective Brewster?"

Monique "the Bruiser" Brewster put her forehead completely to the floor. "Your August Highness, forgive me for declining to speculate. I don't know, but I do know the threat that such abilities pose to the Empire. And that Carson must be exterminated quickly, whatever the cost."

Yes, she would know that, the Emperor thought. She's a snake poised to strike. Emperor Phaeton glanced at Captain Lang, he who'd ordered Detective Brewster confined in a stairwell and had cut off her communications.

Perfectly within his rights to do that, the Emperor knew, but also the decision that had ultimately allowed the miscreants to escape.

Now or later? he wondered.

Phaeton glanced at Brewster. No, he thought, let her hear later how horribly the Captain dies. Not only that, but let her see it. "See Captain Lang to his quarters," he said to no one.

A servant appeared and waited until the two supplicants had

exchanged pleasantries and the doomed-but-didn't-know-it Captain made his obeisance, then escorted him from the throne room.

Prime Minister Custos Messium, whose name translated from the ancient tongue as "keeper of Harvests," chose that inopportune moment to appear. "Your August Highness," Messium said, bowing with such grace and elegance that it might have been mocking for its obsequiousness.

I should have rid myself of him long ago, Phaeton thought yet again.

A holdover from his father's administration, Prime Minister Messium knew the Empire from its edge at the outer Scutum-Centaurus Arm to the Galactic Bar. He'd made himself useful with that knowledge and so had spared himself a one-way ticket to oblivion.

The perfectly-proportioned Emperor scowled.

Messium stood six-foot-four and was thin as a pole. Silks draped the lanky frame, protrusions hinting at the gaunt, ethereal body beneath. The hair was a short, unruly halo of gray, the face pinched in constant pique. "Forgive my intrusion, your August Highness, but I thought it prudent to insert myself into the weighty matter that now confronts my liege, His August Highness, whom I'm sworn to protect."

"Really?" Phaeton asked bluntly, "They why didn't you capture Carson yourself?"

"His August Highness amuses himself by taunting a humble man. Like him, the humble man has only recently become aware of certain forces at work. And may I introduce myself to the supplicant, your August Highness?"

Viper meet Cobra, Phaeton thought idly, a single finger waving assent.

While the two greeted each other, he mused that neither species was an appropriate comparison for the Bruiser. No, a far more appropriate reptilian analogy would be Python. Yes, much better. Python.

"Eh? What?" He realized he'd missed something.

"Pardon, your August Highness, but I asked whether Detective Brewster was being considered for the task of capturing this rogue trash monger?"

Stupid to let your attention lapse, the Emperor admonished himself, especially in front of these two. "You have an opinion about that?" His tone was clear he'd asked for none.

"Pardon, your Highness, I meant no offense, only to acknowledge the reasonableness of such a course. The Detective's background is recommendation enough, and her knowledge of the suspect a bonus."

But you have something else you wish to point out, don't you? Phaeton thought.

"But I wish to point out, if I may, your Highness, that Detective Brewster has not been cleared."

Emperor Phaeton suspected she wouldn't pass clearance. "Superfluous, Lord Minister. Her background is enough recommendation, as you pointed out."

"There are procedures in the clearance process that are disregarded only at great risk to yourself, your August Highness."

"Risk that I'm perfectly capable of evaluating myself, Minister."

Messium dropped to a knee instantly, and even Brewster put her face to the floor.

Phaeton's jaw rippled, and he opened his hands from the fists he'd made. He pulled himself back from the brink of blasting the upstart into the next universe. "Now that you've inserted yourself where you weren't welcome, you may remain there. Detective Brewster, Prime Minister Custos Messium will be your Liaison. All requests for resources will go through him, and all will be granted, won't they, Prime Minister?"

"Indeed, your August Highness."

"Be gone, before I beridst myself of you."

"Indeed, your August Highness." Messium bowed and backed from the throne room, his gaze upon the floor.

"Disgraceful behavior," he muttered to himself. "I'd apologize to you, Detective, except that I don't apologize." He'd have called her "Lady," too, if her visage had contained the least vestige of feminism. "You'll report daily or more often as events require. Please see Admiral Camelus for a vehicle. He has a prototype fighter he's eager to field test."

"Yes, your August Highness," Brewster said, looking around as if sensing she'd been dismissed.

Then he looked at her directly.

"Yes, your August Highness?" Brewster asked, looking suddenly nervous.

I'd imagine if I'd just witnessed an Emperor admonishing his Prime

131

Minister, I'd be nervous, he thought. He dropped his hand to the scepter.

Something fuscous, something furtive, something insidious, something feral. Her mind surrounded him like a carnival attraction—a funhouse filled with distortion mirrors. The world was warped and twisted. Innuendo and intrigue lurked behind every façade. Every person recited encyclopedic detail of his or her life. People poured out their hearts to her, their secret and most base desires, those yearnings found utterly abhorrent by society, the predilections to torture and dismember, the pure joy in seeing others suffer. These were the untold and unexpressed—and often unacknowledged—desires writ eternal upon people's souls, open for her vicarious viewing.

Phaeton snapped back into his body. "The faster you capture this miscreant, Detective, the greater your reward."

"Yes, your August Highness, and thank you." Detective Brewster bowed and backed from the room, her gaze on the floor.

The Emperor stared at the spot where she'd been sitting.

Depraved, was all he could think.

I'll have to rid myself of her the moment she captures this scavenger.

* * *

"But how did you escape?" Jack realized he'd asked the same questions now for the third time.

Misty shrugged. "They acted like they didn't see me."

"What I don't understand," Cherise said, "is how you found the ship. How could you have known I'd secured this freight tractor? I did it after we left the compound, while you were still trapped inside."

Misty shrugged at them both.

"And then you somehow got inside without anyone knowing," Cherise added.

The girl was beginning to look distressed.

Jack watched her from behind the controls of the freight tractor, their load of Tania Steele en route to Chamaeleon, to the planet orbiting Alpha Chamaeleontis, a planet encrusted with manufacturing, roboticized nearly to the point of no longer needing its human creators, and a virtual dead zone of human activity.

As such, it was the perfect place to lay low for a while, no one the wiser. The freight tractor would be put on auto-pilot for its next load—ten thousand widgets for the fashion-conscious widget-wearer, all the rage on the central worlds of the Torgassan Empire—and by happenstance absent its pilot and two passengers when it left Chamaeleon.

"Tell me about this," Jack said, putting the cube on the console between them.

The girl didn't even glance at it.

Cherise's eyes went wide. "Is that what I think it is?"

"A ghost cube," Misty said.

"You said the name stands for something?"

"Its full name is Gaussian Holistic Oscillating Subliminal Tesseract."

Jack glanced at Cherise.

"What's that mean?"

"Just that it reads, emulates, amplifies, and sublimates the electrical fields given off by a human brain."

"So it can tell what we're thinking and cause us to change our minds? Or persuade us to do things we wouldn't normally do?" Cherise looked at Jack suspiciously. "You didn't..."

"I swear, not for a moment," Jack said quickly. He saw she still harbored doubts. "And I wouldn't, not to you, my friend."

Her face softened, and she stepped to his chair to put her arm over his shoulder.

"Hell, I couldn't even ghost Busby, the old bugger." Jack looked under her breast at Misty. "When I met you on Canis Dogma Five, you told me it wasn't yours anymore."

"I wasn't its," she corrected.

"So why did it select me? Why did it select you?"

"After Grandfather died, there wasn't anyone but me." Misty looked pensive, her gaze on her hands in her lap. In their two days aboard the freighter, Cherise had given her a makeover, and then had declared she'd done all she could. Misty's hair was cut to a pageboy with a fashionable curl at the end and a single lock swirled back on her forehead. She wore a pretty pink jumpsuit with matching shoes, sequined lapels, and a pair of diamond-stud earrings.

"I don't know why it selected you," she told him finally, with a sigh.

"Maybe it knows that Jack's in the best position to care for you."

Jack and Misty looked at Cherise and said simultaneously, "I am?" and "He is?" respectively.

"Well, what's your one goal?" she asked, looking at Misty in a motherly way.

"To live in the palace on Torgas Prime as the Princess."

Jack smiled. They'd had an exhaustive conversation yesterday with Misty, trying to dissuade her from this course, but she hadn't been dissuaded.

"And your name is—?"

"Misty Circi, Princess Misty Circi."

"You said you're princess of the Circian Empire, didn't you?"

She nodded vigorously.

"Only the Torgassan Princess can live on Torgas Prime."

"I'll rename the empire when I become the Empress."

Misty wouldn't be deterred.

"And we know that the old Circian Empire dominated the Milky Way not by force but by persuasion."

Jack looked up at Cherise, wondering where she was going with this new line of reasoning.

"Inordinate persuasion, even of inveterate enemies bitterly opposed to their rule, even of entire constellations committed to secession. They never persuaded anyone to love them—stars forbid anyone try that with a human being—" Cherise gave Jack a poke— "but they did defuse animosity toward their rule and convinced nearly all of humanity to live placidly under them for a very long time."

Jack frowned at her.

"And maybe," she added, "maybe the cube selected Jack because he's your best hope, Princess Misty Circi, of reestablishing the Circian Empire."

Misty looked skeptically at Cherise. Jack looked skeptically at himself. "I don't think so," they both said.

"Well, maybe of getting you to Torgas Prime," she amended, looking deep in thought.

"Yeah, but what then?" Jack asked, having wanted not to breach the subject before. "You'll upset a lot of people when you show up on Torgas Prime and say you're the Circian Princess."

"Not if you're with me," Misty said.

"If I'm with you, even more people will be upset, especially that detective."

"But you'll persuade them to like me, won't you?"

"I'd have to go to charm school to do that." Jack snorted.

Cherise hid her smile behind her hand.

He raised an eyebrow at her. "Wouldn't help, would it?"

* * *

Later, after Misty and Cherise had gone to bed, Jack set the cube on the console.

Fuscous gray swirls roiled beneath its smooth surface, turgid with possibility.

"What can you do?"

Jack wasn't sure it was a question he'd asked aloud, but the cube didn't need it articulated.

He snapped into the body of a tall man, whom he knew was tall by the impossible distance to the ground. He wore fine silks and strolled through a garden whose topiary was just as immaculate as it was intricate. Even the sidewalk was etched with arabesques.

Jack pulled himself back, knowing there were subtleties to the cube he'd have to master. Getting them out of the Imperial compound on Alpha Tuscana had exhausted him, and without Cherise's resourcefulness, they'd have never gotten off-planet.

"How do I ghost someone without taking them over completely?"

The cube sides manifested a view of elaborate topiary and etched walkways. The tall one was having a conversation with a man bedecked with insignia.

"He's quite lost his reason, Admiral, putting that animal in charge of capturing this rebel."

"Hush! How do we know he isn't listening?"

"What if he is? Let him throw me into a singularity! Better that than having to watch the Empire unravel because the Emperor has lost his hold on his faculties. I'm not advocating rebellion, Lord Admiral, just a period of observation—to see what other areas his August Highness might be not so 'high' in." The tall man chuckled at his own pun.

"The Emperor's infallible," the Admiral insisted.

"Stardust! And you know it! You're saying it because you think he's listening. I'm sure someone's listening, but I'm not convinced it's the Emperor." The tall man peered into the cube. "You are listening, aren't you?"

Jacked looked away and the cube went dark. He was almost sure the tall man had seen him. But how could that be?

Remembering the detective at the Imperial compound, Jack wondered how Brewster had sensed Jack had been ghosting the person near her. And she'd done so not once, but thrice.

Then he realized what the tall man had said. "Putting that animal in charge of capturing this rebel."

Brewster? Capturing me?

Jack went cold, intuiting that indeed Detective Monique "The Bruiser" Brewster was out to capture him.

I'm not a rebel, Jack thought immediately.

Another part of his mind sneered, You're taking an upstart princess to the Imperial Capital, one who claims she'll be Empress, so that makes you a rebel.

He frowned. From what he'd seen of Brewster's methods, he was sure she'd never rest until he was a puddle of pulp in some hospital bed, or worse, some coroner's freezer.

Where's Brewster now? he wondered, and he looked at the cube.

Its sides grew dark and turbid, as though some storm gurgled beneath the smooth surface.

Jack waited, urging the cube to show him Brewster.

Striations appeared, as though a cyclone roared inside the cube, but no images formed.

Composing himself, Jack relaxed in the pilot's chair and reached for the cube, picking it up by its corners. He took a deep breath and placed his hands flat on its sides.

The galaxy spread below him like a whirlpool, the galactic bar like the filament of a halogen lamp, too bright to look at but irresistibly beautiful. Spiral arms pinwheeled outward, leaving tails of flame and dust, fading away the farther they got from the core, until mere wisps remained.

Show me Brewster, he thought, but nothing happened. As though Brewster doesn't exist, he thought idly.

Show me the Southern Birds, he thought. The brothel was in full swing, a lively tune playing, women strutting and men leering, drink and smoke abundant.

Jack pulled back, reminded that he hadn't had anything to smoke in nearly two months.

Show me Torgas Prime, he thought. The palace ballroom glittered brightly, almost as lively as the Southern Birds' parlor. Gentleman in spats or uniforms escorted ladies bedecked in sequins and diamonds. Jack looked toward the throne, catching a glimpse of the Emperor. Like the galactic bar, the figure at the rear of the ballroom was too bright to look at.

Jack pulled himself back into the freighter, puzzled. Why couldn't he see the Emperor? Why couldn't he ghost the Emperor?

He looked down at the cube. Show me the Emperor. Its side grew dark and turbid but showed him nothing.

Jack thought of Xerxes on Canis Dogma Five. Instantly, he was inside the dun, dingy abode, Trude across the table from him, remonstrating him for some imagined fault, declaring how faultless she was.

He thought of Cherise, and instantly he was looking at the inside of their cabin doorway, seeing the light from the cockpit seep underneath, wondering why Jack was taking so long to come to bed, and wanting him deeply, thoughts of him …

Jack looked over at the door separating them.

One more, he thought reluctantly. Misty.

The cube stared back at him, unresponsive. The dark and turbid surface swirled aimlessly.

Odd, he thought.

Brewster, Emperor Torgas, Princess Misty.

Why wouldn't the cube allow him to ghost those three? he wondered.

I'll have to look into it tomorrow, Jack thought. Cherise was awaiting him now.

* * *

Before he went to bed, Jack checked the lifeboats from long habit. Whole crews had been lost on ships with poorly-maintained lifeboats.

This freight tractor had two lifeboats, one on either side of the bridge.

The lifeboat to starboard, Jack saw, had a transponder offline. I'll have to fix that in the morning, he thought. The transponder was a beacon whose signal was automatically activated upon launch, so even if the occupants were injured or unconscious, rescuers could still find the survivors.

Yawning, he readied himself for bed.

"What were you doing?" Cherise murmured in his arms.

"Trying to figure out what the cube does," he replied, the feel of her against him like the touch of sunrise. "I can't ghost Misty. It's very odd. I wonder—"

She smothered his words with a kiss.

And he forgot what he'd been saying.

Chapter 12

The first blast was a glancing blow to port, but it still hurled Jack and Cherise from bed.

"Lifeboat," he screamed at her over the screech of wounded steel and injured ship. He shoved her that way and pulled himself toward the cubby where they'd made Misty a makeshift bunk.

"What is it?" she squealed over the noise.

"I don't know," he said, but he did know, and he expected a second blast any moment.

The gravgen failed, and Misty went tumbling.

"Just ball yourself up," he told her, demonstrating by pulling his knees to his chest.

Practiced at moving around in the absence of gravity, Jack maneuvered her quickly toward the lifeboat.

Cherise was already strapped in. She grabbed Misty and strapped her in the other seat. There were only two.

Jack braced himself as the second blast landed. He hit the launch, and they were flung away from the wreckage, tumbling.

Jack only got a glimpse, glimpse, glimpse of the disintegrating freighter as the lifeboat spun away uncontrollably.

But they were clear of the wreckage. And alive.

Jack relaxed against the lifeboat floor, confident their transponder would signal their position to any rescuer.

But would it also alert any attacker?

"What was that?" Cherise asked, glancing him up and down.

Jack realized he was completely naked. In his hand was the cube. He didn't remember picking it up, and he tried to recall if he'd had it when he went to get Misty from her cubby.

Cherise was naked, too. "There must be some formalls in this tub."

Misty giggled at them both, a knowing look on her face.

"I think we were attacked," Jack said, reaching for a kit beneath the seat. As expected, the kit contained two sets of formalls. Inside were emergency rations for two people for a week, first-aid supplies, and a back-up transponder.

Jack knew they were aboard the starboard lifeboat, the one with the inoperable transponder. He realized he'd known even before they boarded, the first blast to port having forced them to starboard.

He struggled into the formalls and switched places with Cherise so she could dress too. Their changing positions slowed the spinning somewhat, but the motion was still upsetting.

From the direction of the disintegrating freighter, a bright ball of light flared.

Cherise shot him a look. "That didn't happen on its own, did it?"

Jack shook his head. "Someone destroyed the freighter. Looks like a pocket nuke. We probably shouldn't stop our spinning until we're sure the area is clear. Let's hope this tub looks like another piece of debris." He traded a glance with Cherise, wondering what their fate would be if they were captured.

Their attacker had taken care not to leave any survivors.

"I don't feel very good," Misty said, looking wan and green.

Jack handed her a bag from the kit, in case she had to vomit. "Let me see what I can do." He positioned himself in the middle of the pod and did his best to gauge the direction of their spin. Bracing himself in a ball, he used his arms to spin himself the same direction.

After a few iterations, the lifeboat seemed to have slowed.

Jack eased himself to the floor.

Misty still looked miserable.

Without much else to do but wait, Jack encouraged them both to sleep.

He contemplated the cube in his hand.

Why couldn't he ghost Misty? Brewster? The Emperor?

140

He recalled their escape from the compound on Alpha Tuscana, and how he'd projected an image of his empty cell into the visual cortices of all the observers, including Brewster. How had he been able to do that, but still not have the ability to ghost her?

Perhaps it was a matter of degree.

What we need is someone to explain how this works, Jack thought.

An alien technology, a relic from before the dawn of Humanity, the cube operated on principles barely within the grasp of those who'd wielded it. The Circians had openly used the cubes to rule the galaxy, and the Torgassans were using the same cubes, even if there wasn't much evidence of it. They used their vast navies to put down rebellions and maintain control of their far-flung domains.

And what did it mean, Jack wondered, as he watched her sleeping face, that a young girl would come forward, declare herself a Circian Princess with the full intent of becoming Empress, wielding one of the very same cubes that her forebears had used to rule the galaxy?

And why had it chosen him?

A quadruple-divorced, thrice-bankrupt, and nearly always askirt-the-law junk collector, constantly on the run from creditors and courts, without a courageous bone in his body, nor a charitable thought in his head.

Why him?

Jack sighed, unable to say.

The slightly nauseating but somewhat soothing motion soon lulled him to sleep.

* * *

He dreamt he was hurtling through time, backward to the last vestiges of the Circian Empire. Barbarian navies prepared to bombard Canis Dogma Five into oblivion, the planet ravaged after nearly a century of war, the galaxy no longer a unified human civilization but a pastiche of a hundred thousand occupied constellations, each struggling to stay connected with each other as technology regressed and hostile ecologies rid themselves of this pestilential invasive species known as human.

Jack watched the last Circian Emperor descend deep unground into a bunker that would soon be his tomb, carrying the last known cube with him. Also with him was a microfusion projector containing a recording of his last will and testament and his proclamation that the finder of the cube was hereby conferred all the titles—and attendant duties, responsibilities and obligations—of the Circian Emperor, and exhorted that person to build anew the Circian Empire of old.

Suddenly, Jack was in the Emperor's mind.

Emperor Lochium Circi IX looked around the chamber, knowing what exactly he would need to do to escape detection and preserve this ark, this last Circian time capsule.

He would not fail.

Sensor field disruptors already encapsulated the ark, their microfusion batteries able to last five hundred years. But these disruptors would fail if he continued to occupy the bunker.

Lochium the Ninth would soon be Lochium the Last, as he laid out the implements he would need. The gasses he planned to use would dissipate over time, absorbed into the surrounding rock, and he wasn't concerned at the decades this would take. If by some chance, the barbarian hordes discovered this chamber in spite of the sensor field disruptors, they were in for a nasty and fatal surprise.

He laid out the copper band whose change in color would signal the release of hydrogen sulfide, and he prepared the divan where he would take his final repose.

Then he lay down and broke the ampule.

The smell of rotten eggs pervaded the chamber immediately, and the copper band turned green. His eyes watered, and he began to cough, his lungs quickly filling with fluid. The smell went away as his olfactory nerves were paralyzed, and he lost consciousness soon afterward.

Jack slipped from Emperor Circi's mind.

Within minutes, the necrosis to the basal ganglia was irreversible, and he died.

Emperor Lochium Circi the Last. The cube rolled from his hand and fell to the floor, where it awaited its next host for almost a millennium.

The sensor field disruptors failed at four hundred and fifty years post-collapse, but civilization had regressed locally to Paleolithic levels, and no means of remote sensing existed to find the underground chamber. Writing on stone with blunt instruments had once again become the primary means for recording events. For those who achieved some semblance of literacy.

At nine hundred ninety years post-collapse, an enterprising young woman dug up the hatch to the buried chamber. After she opened the hatch, the faint odor of rotten eggs dissipated, and she dropped into the tomb.

Her presence activated the microfusion projector. The holographic figure of Emperor Lochium Circi the Last appeared before her and conferred upon her the title of Emperor with all its attendant duties, responsibilities, and obligations.

She understood most of the speech in spite of its odd inflections and stilted pronunciation, although some of the words were quite beyond her comprehension. She carried the projector and the cube to the surface and declared herself the Empress of the Circian Empire.

She and her descendants were regarded for the next five hundred years as local lunatics cursed by their forebears to haul around a bulky projector and an odd-looking cube. Throughout that time, not a single craft dropped from the skies, and no contact was made with their near-Canis neighbors, either Majora or Minora. An occasional local convert or adherent might swear fealty to the self-declared Emperor, and an occasional miscreant might attempt to purloin either sacred object, but these erstwhile rulers of a long-bygone Empire most often lived out lives of lonely eccentricity and rarely ruled much more than the amount of land they themselves were able to cultivate.

In due course, the projector wore out, grew distorted and fuzzy, and finally stopped working altogether.

Then the strangers from the sky began to visit, saying they were from Torgas, a place impossibly far away. Initially, they were friendly, but soon began asking questions that indicated they were somehow afraid of the local lunatic.

Protective of their own, the people of Canis Dogma Five did their best to hide the crazy Emperor, and since the cube itself did not want to be found either, the Torgassans were never able to locate its bearer.

* * *

Jack woke with a start, the constant wobble having invaded his dream.

Cherise looked over at him from her seat, secured in it by her straps, she and Misty looking over the excretory hoses with horrified fascination. "Oh good, you're awake. We were hoping you could explain how we're supposed to use these."

He blinked several times and thumbed the sleep from his eyes. He glanced out a porthole, where stars wheeled past with undaunted regularity. Somehow, their escape pod hadn't been found by the attacking ship. Jack was certain if they'd been found, they'd have been destroyed.

He opened his mouth to explain how to use the tubes but realized he had no experience with one of them. And that he'd probably find it embarrassing to try and show them. He closed his mouth, not knowing what to say.

"Maybe if you could stop the spinning, we could sort this out," Cherise said.

Misty held up a curved trough like a banana with its inner half sliced off. "How's this supposed to work?"

Jack took it from her and started to position it, but then flushed with embarrassment and handed it back to her. "I'll try to stop the spinning."

"Quickly, please," Cherise said, squirming.

He realized he had to go too, and they'd been awake longer. Bracing himself, he rose slowly and found the covered control panel. There was barely room for him to lie down. Standing, he took up even more space.

The cover swung back and almost took out his eye. He recoiled from it and hit his head on the hull. Fixing the cover open, he activated the external retros, seeing he had thirty minutes of blast time.

Thirty minutes of thrust to get them to some destination.

Used efficiently, he'd probably need only a few minutes to stabilize the craft with the retrorockets.

But the crude controls and complete lack of sensors made his task difficult. He guessed the direction of their spin by the angle of the stars wheeling past, found the retro closest to the equator of their spin and repositioned it, only to have their slight wobble take that retro off their equator.

He muttered an imprecation.

As he tried to gauge the equator's position, he realized that their axis itself was variable. They were like a spinning top with a moving center of gravity.

"Uh, everyone has to hold as still as possible."

The wobble seemed to diminish when everyone was bracing themselves.

And now! He hit the blast briefly.

Stars still wheeled past, but more slowly.

"Once more," he said, waiting until the equator aligned once again with the retro.

Now! The retro flared, and the stars subsided to a slow cascade.

"That better?" he asked.

Both his companions nodded.

"I think that one fits like this," Cherise said, unbuckling herself to demonstrate.

"Oh, I see," Misty said. "Here let me try." Then she pointed a finger at Jack. "Eyes closed until I say so!"

He dutifully closed his eyes, his own bladder burning.

Once they were done and he'd taken his own turn—their eyes dutifully closed and Misty having a giggle fit—Jack wondered how they were going to be rescued. The lifeboat clearly didn't have enough fuel to get them anywhere near civilization, nor even the navigation equipment necessary to tell them where the nearest civilization might be.

"We'll having to assume whoever attacked us didn't stay to rescue any survivors," he told them. "An explosion like that is sure to be investigated, and the freighter's transponders surely activated at the first hull breach."

"Then there'll be rescuers in the area, searching for survivors."

"Imperial rescuers," he told Cherise. "And we were lucky." He told them about the inoperable transponder he'd found aboard the starboard lifeboat before he'd gone to bed, the lifeboat they were now on.

"So if it had been working, we'd probably be dead now," Cherise said, her gaze hollow. Then she frowned, "So what do we do? We can't just drift forever through space. There's only so much food, water, and air aboard this tub."

He nodded. "About five days of food and water." He looked up at the control panel, its hatch still fixed open, and made a quick calculation based on the amount of oxygen remaining versus the time they'd been aboard. "And about three days of air." Three occupants were consuming more oxygen than the lifeboat's usual capacity.

"So what do we do?" Misty asked.

Jack stared back at them blankly. "I say we risk capture by an Imperial patrol, take over their ship, and try to escape to the other side of the galactic core."

"And what are we going to do there?"

Jack shrugged at Misty. "Find a habitable world, or an inhabited one. Must be thousands of viable planets still populated after the Circian collapse."

Misty pouted. "Then how am I going to become Empress?"

Jack tried not to laugh or even smile.

Cherise was also suppressing a grin.

"You said you'd take me to Torgas." She looked miffed.

"Emperor Torgas just tried to kill us. You know going there means your death, don't you?"

"Some things are more important than life, Captain Salvager."

He winced, his life not exactly a paragon of ambition and achievement. He glanced at Cherise, hoping for reinforcements.

"You said you would," Misty insisted.

Cherise was silent.

Jack sighed, his choices limited. So much had changed since he'd first met her on Canis Dogma Five. Doing so aboard his Salvager—a ship with modest cloaking and maneuverability—had been a possibility. Taking her there aboard the freight tractor would have been extremely risky, but still doable. To try and land on Torgas Prime abound a hijacked Imperial Patrol vessel would get them instantly blown to bits in orbit, if they got that far. More likely, we'd be intercepted as we entered the system, Jack thought, and perhaps even as they entered the constellation, the Empire so paranoid of attack that the Capital was ringed with defense bases for a thousand parsecs around.

Don't fool yourself, pal, that other part of his brain told him. You know you had no intention whatsoever of taking her anywhere near Torgas Prime. Not for a moment.

"Well, we can't do it aboard a hijacked Imperial Patrol," he told her. "You tell me how we're going to get there."

"Why don't we ask them?" She pointed out the porthole.

Jack nearly broke his neck whipping his head around. The lifeboat's rotation took the object out of view. "Who?" he asked, waiting for it to appear again.

A black blot occluded the stars, and then was gone.

Jack reached for the controls and stopped the lifeboat's spinning. Then he adjusted their position to put the blot in the viewport.

"What is it?" Cherise asked.

The blot on the field of stars was a solid black featureless disc. It appeared completely inert, emitting no light nor reflecting any light. Its presence was notable only for the absence of everything behind it.

Jack watched carefully, his breath threatening to fog the inside of the glasma.

The blot was slowly getting larger.

"Why's it getting bigger?" Misty asked.

"It's not," Jack said. "We're headed directly toward it."

"But what is it?" Cherise asked again.

Jack shook his head. "A derelict space station, a rogue planet, I don't know. From this distance it looks perfectly spherical. We may be able to avoid it using our retro, but if it's too large, like a rogue planet, then we may not be able to avoid its gravity well."

"What's a rogue planet?" Misty asked.

"A planet that isn't orbiting a star. Sometimes planets are torn from their orbits, and they just drift through space until they're captured by another system, or destroyed."

"I've never heard of them," Cherise said.

Jack shrugged. "They're not very interesting. No atmosphere, or if there is one, it's locked up in ice. Without a primary, no heat or light or energy, unless you burrow hundreds of miles into the crust to reach the molten core."

He looked out the porthole and realized their approach was far faster then he'd initially thought. He reached for the retro controls. "Hang on, everybody!"

"Look!" Misty said.

Something flared from the disc rim, a flare or—

"A ship!" he and Misty said at the same time.

Cherise glanced between them, smiling.

The flare bent toward them, growing gradually larger. Twenty minutes later, it filled the porthole, and a tinted viewport slid past them. Jack and Misty waved excitedly, each trying to crowd out the other.

A cargo bay door opened on the ship's side, and it backed over them, the lifeboat sliding smoothly into the larger ship's cargo bay.

While Jack and Misty sang and danced, overjoyed to be rescued, Cherise watched them, looking somber.

"What's the matter?" Jack asked.

"How do you know they're friendly?"

Chapter 13

At first, the cargo hold of the larger ship was black, pitch black.

Then light flooded the hold.

Jack blinked rapidly until his eyes adjusted. What little he could see out the porthole looked like empty cargo bay walls. A hissing soon commenced—the cargo bay filling with air. Jack watched the external pressure reading increase gradually to one atmosphere.

"What if they're not even human?" Misty asked.

When humans had left their Earthly cradle some ten thousand years ago, they'd embarked on an exploration of the Milky Way, full of dread and excitement in equal measure—dread for the evil predatory races that would feed on humans until their stomachs were full and humankind was extinct, and excitement at the new and fascinating civilizations they were sure to find.

Neither had been the case.

Not that humanity hadn't found other creatures, but none of those species had been at an evolutionary par with these new interlopers. The closest they'd found was a semi-literate biped invertebrate on Yahoo Sextuplus who'd either hid from the visitors or had thrown their feces at them.

There was also evidence—Jack's cube part of that evidence—of a species who'd once occupied a three-dimensional, sub-light, body-based consciousness, but whose current whereabouts was unknown. It was speculated, and heavily debated in intellectual circles, that this species had transcended the bounds of corporeal existence and now floated in some ethereal ether ominously known as the Purity of Thought Itself.

"Well," Jack told Misty, "if they aren't human, I'd prefer feces-throwing invertebrate bipeds over the inventors of *this* cube."

He saw the puzzled exchange of glances between the other two, but ignored it.

A figure shuffled forward from a hatchway, Jack barely able to glimpse the person before he or she left his field of vision. "Anybody in there?" they heard.

Jack exchanged a glance and a shrug with the other two. "Three of us," Jack said. "Opening now." He cycled the lock, the pressure nearly equalized.

The hatch opened.

"Oh, hell," the young man said. "Three of you. In a space not fit for one. I'll bet there's a tale behind that dog." He laughed at his own pun. "Come on aboard. I'm Sammy, Sam Kinkaid. Mother will be glad to see the three of you!"

Jack climbed out and thanked the young man, Misty and Cherise right behind him.

"Looks like you've been in there a day or two at least," the boy said. He didn't wrinkle his nose.

Jack had overestimated the age, and now, based on development, he was thinking the other couldn't be more than fifteen years. "At least three days," Jack replied.

"Seems like longer," Cherise said, looking around the inside of the cargo bay.

"This way," Sammy said, "Let's get you to your quarters while Mom pilots us back to Chiron. You've time to freshen up if you'd like before we get there."

"What's Chiron?" Jack asked, not familiar with any local planet or outpost with that name.

"A dark planet, our home," Sammy said over his shoulder. "Other-wise known as a rogue planet—one that doesn't orbit a star. Here we are." He stopped an intersection. "Modest accommodations, to be sure, but then the last visitor we had was my father—but that was a few years ago."

About fifteen years, Jack guessed. Four doors at an intersection faced each other, three of them open.

Jack took the one across from the other two, throwing a glance at Cherise.

"Misty, you take that one," she said, "and I'll take this. Just tap on the wall if you need anything."

Jack felt a slight lurch under his feet. "Feels like we're underway. Thank you, Sammy." He couldn't wait to get into the cleansall, convinced he reeked of old sex, rank fear, and cramped quarters. He could barely stand his own smell.

He attended to his toilet, evacuating with immense relief, something he hadn't dared do aboard the lifeboat. It was one thing traveling alone to let one's hygiene go for several days. Aboard his Salvager, he might not shower for a week or shave for a month. But to do so aboard a cramped lifeboat with two others—repulsive!

The cabin was spare, just room for a sleeping net. Modest was an overstatement. He found formalls where he thought he might and donned them, and had just slipped the cube in his pocket when he heard a tap on the door.

The woman stepped in without waiting for an invitation.

I'm glad I'm dressed, Jack thought.

"I'm glad you're dressed," she said. "Claudia, Claudia Kinkaid." She extended her hand.

He'd have had difficulty not shaking it, the cabin crowded with one occupant. "Jack Carson. Pleased."

"Thought I'd butt in since I didn't want to say this in front of Sammy. You're the passengers aboard that freighter, eh? Blew up three days ago? Thought as much. No survivors, according to the local authorities, but I'm guessing you had the transponder off for a reason." She held up a hand to stop Jack. "The less I know the better. That wasn't an accident, that freighter blowing up. Someone wanted you dead, and still would if they knew you were alive. The rest I don't want to know. Having you on Chiron puts me in a bind, so I'm getting you off as fast as possible. The main question, of course, is which way do you want to go? You're welcome to stay for a day, but not a moment longer. I can't put my home at risk any more than that."

Jack nodded appreciably. "Surprised you're able to risk that long." He estimated her age about ten, fifteen years his senior, and smart.

Scientist smart. He noted the efficient clothes, precise haircut, clipped speech. Further, she was accustomed to doing everything herself. He saw she knew he was appraising her. All women knew, he knew. "It's very kind of you to offer any hospitality. And Sammy too. Sweet boy, by the way."

"Thank you."

"We'll discuss where we're going amongst ourselves and let you know well before tomorrow morning. Needless to say, but I'll say it anyway, thank you for rescuing us and especially for not turning us over to the Imperials. If there's anything we can do—beyond getting off Chiron as fast as possible—please let us know."

"Thank you. Landing in three minutes. For safety, please use the nets." And swiftly, she was gone.

Odd, he thought, how a person of the opposite sex can give off no signals of any kind, as though completely sexless. He strung up the net and climbed in, just as the ship began to descend toward Chiron.

* * *

"There are worlds around us on multiple levels if only we have the eyes to see or the instruments to measure," Professor Claudia Kincaid told her guests over dinner. Wines from Lorraine—a plain on ancient Earth in a region to the southeast of what was once known as France— and silver from Lepus Secundus, translucent ceramics from Vulpecula Salacia, and crystal forged deep in the Virgan gas giants, Claudia knew how to lay out a table.

The finely-sculpted sythemush couldn't be helped, however.

No matter how she dressed it up, it still tasted like mush.

She was annoyed she couldn't obtain anything better. She owned her own exoplanet. She ran her own business. She conducted her life with the utmost efficiency.

But she couldn't get real food.

"Do you know what I mean, Captain Carson?" She looked across the table at her guests.

The ugly troll who'd alighted from the lifeboat with the fabulously beautiful woman and the mysterious girl looked up from his plate in bewilderment.

The luxurious layout was surely wasted on troglodytes like him, Claudia was thinking.

"I agree, never thought I'd eat from a Salacian plate." He tapped it to elicit a dainty ping. "Fabulous dinnerware. But you're referring to aliens, aren't you? Like the microscopic life on Chiron—living in the liminal zone between the hot molten core and the near absolute zero of cold, open space."

Perhaps he just *looks* like a cave dweller, she thought. "As one example, yes. And then we have the ancient race that left behind that little bauble you brought with you."

The silence was profound.

Claudia might have smiled. She was bemused that they hadn't expected her to know about it. She knew everything that happened on Chiron. "Believe me, Captain Jack, my interest is only academic. But for edification purpose, I would like to see it, as I imagine Sammy might also."

Her son looked up suddenly at hearing his name, his head swiveling around. He and the mysterious girl had been having a private giggle over some adult inanity.

He's been isolated from his peers far too long, Claudia thought, knowing he'd soon need to look into universities. Just she and her son on Chiron, it was a special occasional when they had guests such as these.

The ugly man put the cube on the table.

Some trick of light caused it to fade from her vision when she wasn't looking at it directly. If she hadn't told him to put it there, she wouldn't have seen it. As if it occupied an entirely different dimension.

"This is a ghost cube, isn't it?" she asked.

The exchange of looks between the trio confirmed that it was.

"A Gaussian Holistic Oscillating Subliminal Tesseract," Claudia said. "Worth more than Chiron in its entire. And a star if it were orbiting one. The species who manufactured it gone without a trace—or at least no trace but this. As if they occupied an entirely different dimension." She turned her gaze to the woman, briefly groping for her name. "Cherise, you've seen it at work, when you three were escaping the Imperial compound on Alpha Tuscana—" she smiled at their gasps, again bemused that they didn't expect her to know such things—"What's your impression?"

"Just that it represents a level to technology we'll never likely achieve, Professor."

Not an intellectual giant, Claudia thought. She looked over at the girl, Misty.

Unfathomable, that one, the Professor knew. There was some quality about her that—like the cube itself—was just outside the range of human receptivity or comprehension.

But then we're all a bit beyond comprehension, aren't we? Professor Kinkaid thought idly.

"You have an Empire that wishes you dead and thinks it may have annihilated you," she said, addressing all three of them, "And a device whose capabilities make it among the most valuable of alien artifacts. Where will you go, my ineluctable guests?"

She watched them glance amongst themselves, as though deciding which of them would speak. As if she hadn't listened in on their conversation and knew the substance of their decision already.

Earlier, she'd escorted Captain Jack to the cavern where she kept all her vessels.

Ice crystalized on every surface like lichen. The air was thin due to absorption and leakage. Their breath fogged in front of them like the finest of powdery snow, but the floor was warm beneath their feet, huge pumps circulating magma-heated water throughout the rooms in her underground compound. Here at five miles beneath Chiron's ice-entombed surface, it was still cold enough to freeze everything instantly. The liminal zone—that place in the planet crust where basic proteins might form, warmed naturally by the magma but not too hot to boil water—was easily five miles below them. Few creatures lived outside the liminal zone.

"Here's the ship I can loan you," she'd told him, showing him the two-person sport yacht she'd bought right before she'd become pregnant with Sammy. She'd used it half a dozen times since, and had been meaning to sell it for years, but somehow hadn't gotten around to it.

His eyes went wide as he'd gazed upon it. "But that's a Quasar."

One of the most expensive brands, built for speed and able to outrun any Imperial patrol no matter what its load.

She'd held up her hand to stop any protest. If he weren't so ugly, she'd have demanded sex from him in payment, and considered it anyway in spite of his repulsive physiognomy. Mating practices on outlying colonies where men predominated had given women substantial bargaining power. It's been too long since I've had a man, Claudia thought. "Just remember that I helped you. If you're able at some point to pay me for it, or return it, that would be even better." She'd smiled at his continued objections.

Now, over dinner, she watched her three guests closely. She knew they'd considered the far side of the Galactic Bar, and she knew they weren't going there. She also knew they were unlikely to tell her. Perhaps it was better she didn't know.

"Perhaps, it's better you don't know," Misty said nonchalantly.

Claudia gazed placidly at the girl, who grazed placidly on her dressed-up mush. "And why would that be?"

"You know why," the girl said slyly, a gleam in her eye. "You don't own your own rogue planet by being ignorant."

Claudia chucked, surprised at the girl's depth. There was a fine sophistication to Misty's face, a translucence to her checks, a patrician authority to her nose, and a knowing mischief in her eyes. "Perhaps I do know why. You might consider searching for the origins of your little toy." She noticed it was already gone from the table. Prudent, she thought.

"You said there isn't a trace of them left," Cherise said.

"A trace that we have eyes to see or instruments to measure," Claudia added, smiling. "But you have in your possession an instrument that half-exist in other dimensions."

"You're suggesting that we try to enter those dimensions?" the woman asked.

Claudia raised her initial estimate of the woman, too. All three of them more intelligent than she'd expected. "The Empire would certainly find it difficult to pursue you, wouldn't it?"

* * *

The Emperor Phaeton Torgas looked down into the chamber and smiled at the guest adjacent to him. "It does appear you were successful in annihilating this scavenger, Detective Brewster," he murmured, pitching his voice so that only she could hear.

As if his every word weren't instantly seized upon, analyzed ad infinitum, and sieved for the slightest nuance.

But at least his other guests weren't privy to his remarks.

The arena was small, an intimate affair constructed for the Emperor's entertainment. The field itself was a cube—not ironically—which looked impervious from the inside, its inner surfaces mirrored. Around its four sides were seats, cascading theater-style from a round, raised circumference. The field might be viewed from any angle, above or below in addition to all four sides. From the outside, the field looked to be completely open, as the polarized glasma permitted light to pass through from only one direction—from inside to out.

No light passed from outside to in.

In each corner of the cube was a glowb, lighting the interior and its contents. Live plays, musical concerts, duels to the death, and orgies of every stripe had been preformed for the Emperor's edification and entertainment on multiple occasions, but the subject of this evening's show hadn't been arranged for the Emperor.

It had been arranged for his guest.

And inside the cube was Captain Caeneus Lang, erstwhile commander of the Imperial compound on Alpha Tuscana. He still wore his uniform, but all the elements of insignia—epaulets, chevrons, decorations, and medals—had been ripped from the fabric, raveled edges outlining slightly darker fabric spared exposure by the appliques sewed directly on the uniform.

"It has come to attention that certain spectacles are a predilection of yours, Detective. I bring you one such spectacle, in honor of your accomplishment."

"Your August Highness, you do me too much honor." The big woman with the bulldog face inclined her head his direction. "I did what any humble Imperial servant would do."

Someone's been coaching her, Phaeton thought, his Prime Minister the likely culprit. The Emperor did not look in Custos Messium's direction, the other man in attendance and sitting smugly back in the shadows almost directly across from the Emperor.

Present also were the Admiral, Sophocles Camelus, a childhood friend of the Emperor, if friends could be had by such, and a bevy of the Emperor's consorts, who in his opinion needed regular reminders of what he was capable of.

Phaeton smiled.

Of all the human expressions, the smile was the least honest. A frown was rarely mistaken for much else, universally represented displeasure or discomfort, and never masked a person's true feelings. A smile often indicated amusement or pleasure, but just as often indicated something far different. A smile might represent a decision, particularly one with unpleasant consequences, a task undertaken in the face of obstacles or repercussions. A smile might simply be an ambiguous expression, sowing confusion and uncertainty. Or a smile might be dissimulation, utter obfuscation, a feint meant to mislead the observer. A smile could dissemble fear, hatred, malice, avarice, or any among the litany of human excesses. In particular, a smile was the mask worn in the theater of human drama, a character whose true face remained hidden in the play of life, an anonymous actor whose true motives remained murky, and whom audiences continued to wonder about after the curtain fell and the theater emptied, a character whom audiences still imagined upon the stage long after the last bow had been taken.

Audiences will wonder about me long after I've taken my last bow, Emperor Phaeton thought, smiling.

He held up his cloaked fist, a gold-embroidered silk kerchief covering over his hand and the object in it, his scepter.

Both the symbol and the source of his power, his scepter held in the center of a circlet a two-inch silvery cube, slightly beveled along its edges, a plain and unassuming cube, but one whose looks—quite analogous to a smile—were often deceiving.

If a person noticed it at all.

Scepter in fist, a cloak over it, the Emperor ordered the event to begin.

A woman rose from the audience, long robes cascading to the floor. She descended the tiers like a wraith, smoothly, without the suggestion of legs. She stopped at the arena wall, and a portal formed in the side of the cube.

She stepped into the transparent cube, and the portal collapsed behind her. "I am Justice Minister Janis Astraea.

"Captain Caeneus Lang, you have been condemned to death for dereliction of duty. As arbiter of innocence and purity, I do hereby proclaim that your death will cleanse us of the smirch that your deeds have left on our souls. Only your death will balance the scales. So it shall be, so it is done."

The portal opened behind her, and she backed from the arena.

"So this is it? Nothing else?" Lang asked the reflective walls, his own image mirrored back to him on all sides, ad infinitum, his own words echoing back to him from all sides, until distance itself distorted the sight and sound beyond recognition, a transmogrified representation of a life lived well, a life ended badly.

"No hearing, no court martial, not even an opportunity for me to face my accusers? What monumental cowardice! Hide behind your mirrors! Hide behind your sterile glasma walls! My death cleanses you of nothing, I tell you! Your failures are writ large by my death. You will suffer the torments…"

The Emperor yawned, not deigning to give succor by responding to the increasing vitriol. "It has always been a subject of some interest, Detective Brewster, how people choose to die. Don't you think?"

"I've not had the pleasure to study such, your August Highness," she replied. "I'm honored to have that opportunity."

"Do you prefer spams, Detective?" The Emperor flicked a gaze at the prisoner.

Waves of muscle contractions washed over the Captain, stopping the obloquy. He flopped across the floor like a fish.

"Perhaps contusion," the Emperor murmured.

Visible skin sprouted violet-red abrasions, and the Captain tore at his clothes, a half-strangled scream gargling from his throat.

"Ataxia?"

Captain Lang stood with an ungainly wobble and ambulated puppet-like around the cube, his movements jerky and disjointed, his speech garbled and slurred beyond intelligibility.

"Or no muscle tone at all?"

The man in the cube collapsed in a heap, like a rag doll. Moisture spread at his crotch as his bladder emptied. His face was lump of clay, his eyes looking different directions.

"Or simply pain?"

The Captain went rigid and screamed, leaped to his feet, and ran in tight circles, as though to escape the inescapable, his face a rictus of agony.

"Well, Detective Brewster?"

Captain Caeneus Lang dropped to the floor, his face beaded in sweat, his lungs gulping huge volumes of air.

"Pardon, your August Highness, I must have missed the question."

Just as you missed your target, the Emperor thought. Even the finest of tools needed refinement. "How would you prefer to see Captain Lang die?"

"Pardon, your August Highness, but my wishes in this circumstance are immaterial. I would defer to you, Lord."

He considered annihilating her for the breach in address. How dare she refer to me with lowly "Lord," he thought. But he needed her and that galled him all the more. He reminded himself he was sharpening this instrument, not breaking it. "It appears your interest lies in inflicting the indignity yourself. Very well, Detective Brewster, perhaps on another occasion you might do me the service of showing me how you work." The Emperor flicked an eyelash toward the prisoner, never taking his eyes off Brewster.

In the arena, the Captain in the torn and soiled uniform began melting from the feet up, puddles of ooze forming around the stumps he stood on, their length lessening even as he watched, the molecular cohesion of his flesh releasing and turning into the ninety-percent fluid that it always had been.

"Know, Detective Brewster," Emperor Phaeton said, watching as horror crept onto her face, her eyes riveted to the spectacle of someone melting away right in front of her, "know that this miscreant, the scavenger Jack Carson, escaped your bungled attack on the freight tractor. Know, Detective Brewster, that I require you to eliminate him. Know, Detective Brewster, the fate that awaits you if you fail."

A bubbling puddle of plasma was all that remained on the area floor.

Chapter 14

Jack felt the barely-tamed power of the Quasar under his hands as he guided the yacht delicately up through the narrow shaft toward the planet surface.

"Good luck, Jack," Professor Claudia Kinkaid had told them just before they'd boarded, a hint of mischief in her eyes.

Cherise had suggested how Jack might compensate their host for her untoward generosity.

Misty nudged Cherise. "Jack didn't sleep much last night."

"When you get older," the woman told the girl, "you'll find that there are things more restful than sleep." And she winked.

Misty laughed and threw a grin at Jack.

Who tried to ignore them both. Having spent nearly all his formative years in a brothel, he wasn't embarrassed by nocturnal machinations. He simply didn't want to discuss it. "It was very thoughtful of you," he told Cherise, knowing he had thought of it, too.

But he was male, so of course he hadn't mentioned it.

The Quasar interior was mahogany inlay and satin fabric. The seats were form-fitting and articulated to each person's frame, the buttock and upper thigh areas riddled with vibrating nodules for comfort and massage. The controls were tactile-response glasma, mounted at the ends of his armrests, his hands fitting inside them like gloves, a backup set of manual controls in front of the copilot's chaise. The visual display was semicircular seamless glasma whose edges included a shrunken view of the ship's stern. The engines were turbo interpellant vectoring fusion thrusters, whose hydrogen conversion to lithium produced temperatures nearly equal to those of a solar surface.

They ascended a narrow shaft toward the planet surface, its frequent turns preventing rubble from pouring into the compound located ten miles below, an occasional maintenance bot slipping into a side crevice to let them pass. The shaft walls glittered with frozen particles, all gasses instantly crystallizing, and only methane able to maintain any liquidity in the near absolute-Kelvin temperatures around them.

A sensor blared when they got too close to the shaft wall, and Jack guided the craft back toward the center. The journey was mostly just tedious, as long as their pace was slow. If they'd tried to hurry, it might be hazardous, but the shaft itself had to be wide enough at all points for the largest of Professor Kinkaid's supply ferries, a craft easily thrice the Quasar's bore.

The shaft expanded into a canyon, a deep rift in the planet surface whose jagged sides were coated with diamonds of ice.

The cube sat on the Quasar dash, just within Jack's reach, to one side of the controls.

Cherise could easily reach it as well, equidistant. "Where are we going?

"He's going to throw the cube away."

Jack glanced over his shoulder at Misty. It didn't surprise him that she knew. He wasn't subtle and he'd never learned to hide his feelings. He was guileless and lacked the finesse to obfuscate his intentions.

"You can't do that, Jack," Misty said. Her voice carried that resigned ennui of a person who argued in spite of the futility.

"I am anyway," he said, determined.

"Oh, Jack," Cherise said, biting her lip and looking away.

"It wants you to Emperor," Misty said, her voice higher, her tone imperative.

"Well, it forgot to ask me what I want!" he snarled. His voice boomed around the cabin as though amplified by a megaphone. He instantly regretted raising his voice when he saw Misty blink away tears. He saw Cherise wince, too.

She took his hand. "I'm glad you don't want to be Emperor. You wouldn't be the sweet gentle man I love."

He melted inside a little, knowing how disappointed she must be at his relinquishing all that wealth and power. He'd never wanted it anyway, at least not for himself. Until Cherise had mentioned it, he'd forgotten the late night longings he'd once articulated to an orphan girl who like him yearned only for the comfort of a home and a family to call her own. And perhaps to help others in similar circumstances find the same.

It hadn't been a lot to ask of the universe, but the pitch black emptiness of space had turned its cold shoulder to him and left him to fend for himself.

Oh, he'd tried to make a home and a family three different times, but each time, those homes and wives had had demands which he'd found impossible to fulfill, priorities at odds with his own, conflicts he lacked the skills to resolve. Most the marriages had ended in acrimonious divorce, two of three wives begrudging him the time away from home to earn a living the only way he knew how. Often, he'd found the homes empty of the warmth and welcome he so badly needed, welcoming he'd only found twice in his life, once when he was very young, in the arms of Cherise, and once when he was somewhat older, with Daria.

Warmth he had somehow found again when he'd returned to Cherise on Alpha Tuscana.

He looked over his shoulder toward Misty, grateful she'd brought him on this journey, grateful she'd insisted he bring her to Torgas Prime. "Thank you," he said, quietly.

"Thank you, Jack," Misty said.

Jack nodded, blinking away the blurriness in his eyes. He hoped she wouldn't miss him when she was princess.

"I'll miss you when I'm princess."

Do I have a megaphone in my head that shouts out all my thought? he wondered.

"You have a megaphone on your face that shouts out all your thoughts," Misty said, giggling.

Another reason he could never be Emperor. No dissimulation, not a shred of disingenuousness. A person as open-faced as he was could be manipulated easily, forged to the will of those more crafty and less scrupled.

"Can I come to visit?"

Misty nodded, smiling. "I still think you're being unwise. There's a reason the cube chose you to be Emperor, and you're not as easily swayed as you think."

"With all due respect, Princess Misty, I'd say it's rather difficult for a nine-year-old to imagine the degree of duplicity or the depth of depravity among those who crave power."

"Maybe," she said. "With all due respect, Emperor Jack, I'd say it's rather difficult for a man accustomed to abandonment and rejection to embrace the purity and innocence inside his own soul, particularly one who's had so few chances to express that."

He didn't believe her for a moment, looking at her for the least sign of mockery.

The classic lines of her face held the sincerity of ancient philosophers.

"Somehow," Cherise said, "you've managed to become a decent person in spite of insurmountable obstacles and a complete absence of allies."

I'm such a scoundrel, he told himself, not believing either of them, incredulity of his face.

"What's the matter with him?" Misty asked.

"An incurable case of self-deception, perhaps." Cherise reached across the console and brought his hand to her lips. "If only you could see yourself through another's eyes."

He snorted dismissively and turned his attention to the controls.

The cube on the console showed his ugly mug on its sides.

"Vulpecula Salacia," Jack said.

"Setting course for Vulpecula Salacia," the ship responded. "Course plotted. Engage?"

"Engage."

* * *

"What's down there?" Cherise asked.

"You'll see." Jack requested permission to land from the Spaceport Authority.

Below them, hot rings of fire encircled lush, green continents and rimmed blue-gray seas as shiny as mirrors. The vegetation on Vulpecula Salacia III had adapted to the volcanic climate in a way rarely seen elsewhere. Chemolithotrophs had developed the ability to siphon sulfur and its poisonous variants—the sulfetes, sulfites, and sulfodes—and had proliferated on the highly volcanic planet, turning an otherwise unlivable hellhole into a tropical paradise.

The stench of rotten eggs pervaded the place.

Across the eons, the fine particulate filtering ability of the chemolithotrophs had left behind large deposits of silicates, and where those deposits had escaped metamorphic pressures, beds of clay had accreted, clay so fine and pure that it could be fired in layers thin enough to be transparent. Impervious to heat, these ceramics were utilized throughout the Empire for a variety of industrial purposes. Tableware from Vulpecula Salacia was in such high demand that it could hardly be obtained, but once it was obtained, it lasted forever, never chipping, breaking, nor succumbing to temperature stresses, the repeated heating and cooling that eventually led to the weakening of most materials.

Navigational beacons guided the Quasar to a greenbelt forty degrees north of the equator, a region Jack knew to be almost unbearably humid and tropical. Along the coastlines of this continent, volcanos belched ceaselessly, but their ash plumes fell almost immediately to the ground, intact. Airborne chemolithotrophs—themselves as heat-resistant as the ceramics manufactured in such abundance here—bound with the volcanic ejecta almost immediately upon its departure from the vents.

The Quasar dropped like a stone between turgid fountains of glowing ash and rock, plasmas of fire dancing around them like demons. Jack couldn't imagine trying to navigate between the multiple volcano plumes, the ship's course plotted and controlled from the ground, a course that changed as necessary, as the plumes themselves changed with prevailing winds.

"You should see this place at night," Jack told the other two.

Both of them wide-eyed and sweating, they looked as if they had no interest at all in seeing it during the day.

Their landing pad, one amongst thousands, was a small square of tarmac barely larger than the ship's footprint. Jack was somewhat surprised that the authorities let anyone land, some planets requiring everyone to dock their vehicles at orbital stations and use shuttles to get groundside. Vulpecula Salacia had less habitable land than most planets with livable climes.

Jack looked among the yachts around the Quasar. Bentleys, Jaguars, Porsches—a veritable concours d'Elegance of vehicles. The glitterati in Maseratis flocked here for both the fine ceramics and the tropical delights, volcanic tourism in vogue.

Exactly what Jack was looking for.

* * *

Their hotel suite was a significant distance to the north at the peak of the continent where three tectonic planets collided, where a chemolithotroph-enhanced jungle thrust its greedy leaves high to grasp the last bit of sun and sulfur-laden air, where stasis fields stabilized soaring hotel towers, built above a mantle so unstable that earthquakes scaling ten plus on the Pictor scale were a daily occurrence, and where volcanic plumes hurled their hellish vomit skywards on three sides. The skies were so full of soot they could not be navigated with any known craft.

One cone stood silent, not even smoke issuing from its caldera.

Their tram rocketed into the city on a stasis-field suspended tube, the ground too unstable for a road, the air too thick with particulates for a hover craft.

The moment Jack disembarked from the tram, the tectonic activity was unmistakable. The ground shook under his feet constantly, a dull, teeth-rattling rumble.

"You'll get accustomed to it," their taxi driver said, loading their bags onto an odd-looking ground vehicle. Sporting four large, round, rubber tori, two on each pair of axles, a noisy, smelly engine rumbled fitfully and spewed noxious, oily, gray smoke. The vehicle looked too fragile to get them anywhere. Further, the roads leading away from the tram station looked like puzzles that had once been assembled but then had been thrown haphazardly back in the box, many of the pieces canted out of place at various angles.

The vehicle took the puzzle-piece roads with surprising equanimity, the large balloon-like tori climbing right over chunks of displaced roadway.

It pulled to a stop under their hotel, a massive column of steel and glass whose base was linked to the ground only by conduits of coolant necessary to keep its occupants in comfort. The structure did not actually touch the ground, suspended by stasis fields a few hundred feet above the jungle canopy. Even here, this far north, the humidity was oppressive, and the pervasive smell of rotten eggs permeated everything.

"Who farted?" Misty asked.

"The planet itself," Jack replied, smiling, the smell worse here than at the spaceport. Soon they and their luggage were climbing up the hotel side in a glasma-enclosed platform, belching volcanoes occupying all one hundred eight degrees of their view. One cone stood silent.

"We came here to see those?" Misty looked bewildered.

"Sort of," Jack said. "You'll see."

Cherise glanced askance at him, also looking bewildered.

* * *

Cerasma tubes formed a perimeter just inside the ring of volcanoes. Made of the same heat-impervious ceramic for which Vulpecula Salacia was famous, the cerasma tubes carried ferries full tourists to and around the volcanoes, the four-hundred mile tour itself taking an entire day, at minimum. Side tours at the largest volcanos might themselves take an entire day, spider webs of smaller, walking tubes catacombing the three largest volcanoes among the twenty-five that ringed this northern cape.

Jack followed one plume, tracing it from its caldera, where the ejecta column launched into the sky, where it plateaued and began to spread, then narrowed again as it turned white, as though cooling somewhat, then formed a tail which dropped from the plateau to the jungle below, the tail like a chute or a hose, propelled side to side by the force of what it ejected, leaving everything in its wake coated with a fine grit of ash, nutrient rich and ready for absorption, a constant cloud of it billowing around the point of impact, miles away from the caldera that had spewed it into the sky.

"The cerasma wall is just a quarter-inch thick," their guide was telling them as their ferry trundled along, taking them toward the first of the six volcanoes on their itinerary today.

Nervous tourists clad with cameras and already sporting Vulpecula memorabilia glanced apprehensively amongst themselves, wondering if such an insubstantial barrier were adequate to protect them.

"When we get closer to the columns of ejecta, additional outer cerasma tubes will be added, and special cooling systems designed for these extreme environs will help to keep us comfortable in spite of the thousand-degree-plus temperatures just inches away."

A brisk wind funneled through the open-top ferry, as much to oxygenate as to ventilate, Jack able to see several similar ferries as intervals both ahead and behind them.

Ahead, through the cerasma distortion, Jack saw the dormant cone he'd seen on arrival.

"We have a special treat today for everyone," their guide said. "One of our cinder cones has gone silent, and has just today been deemed safe by park management for tours. Already, cerasma tubes are being lowered into place, and we'll have the opportunity to walk down into a caldera."

"You mean nothing between us and that?!" Misty asked, pointing to the ejecta column adjacent to their trolley.

Jack squinted toward the pulsating pillar of molten mush belching into the sky. At least a quarter mile away, the width alone was over-whelming to apprehend, and Jack hadn't even looked up to see the plume traveling miles into the sky.

Near the column was a mist that seemed to form right at the base, where the ejecta left its funnel, a mist that was sucked immediately into the vortex created by the high-speed ejecta rocketing skyward.

"To the ferry's right is the spout whose geologic age makes it a comparative youngster. Pliny the Younger we call it, for its similarity to the eldest cone in this chain. The light fog that you see gathering at the vortex where the ejecta leaves the spout isn't a fog at all, folks, but a colony of chemolithotrophs, those microscopic creatures who metabo-lize the sulphs and make Vulpecula Salacia livable for us. In that colony alone are an estimated one quadrillion chemolithotrophs, whose life cycle still is not completely understood, but whose breeding depends on the chemicals first released there, at the vortex of cinder cone and ejecta, a class of molecules called sulfodes."

"Are you on vacation?" a woman of advanced years asked Cherise from across the aisle. Beside her was a man of similar years, one of his eyes having that permanent droopy wetness indicative of declining health.

Cherise nodded and introduced herself.

"So nice to see a family on vacation," she said. "We have two children about your age, both with families." She turned her adorning eyes on Misty. "And I have a granddaughter about your age. You're what? Nine or ten years old?"

Misty nodded bashfully.

"You've got a face of a princess."

"I am a princess," she said.

Jack nearly panicked, looking around for anyone who might have overhead. Imperial spies could be anywhere. He was hoping that as public a place as the volcanoes of Vulpecula Salacia was the absolute last place they would think of looking for him.

Cherise had put a hand on Misty's arm.

"So cute, your daughter," the old woman said, "reminds me of my own at that age." Then she said in a loud stage whisper, "They all should think they're princesses, shouldn't they?"

Misty glanced between them, looking either amused of offended or trying to decide which, while Jack sighed in relief.

He knew what she wanted to say, which was, "And I would be princess if Jack would just agree to be Emperor, humph!"

"And I would be princess if –"

Jack shushed her. "Not here, not now."

She looked crushed. "All right." She bit her lower lip and dropped her gaze to her lap.

He really disliked rebuffing her, and could see her feelings were hurt. Pulling her to him, he put his arm around her. Her head buried in his shoulder, they watched the passing cinder cone giants, their tour guide droning on about chemolithotrophs.

"Such a cute family," the old woman murmured from across the aisle.

* * *

Just after lunch, they arrived at the quiescent cinder cone, the one that had ceased erupting five days before. Seismic readings indicated no imminent eruptions, according to their tour guide, "and therefore it's completely safe."

As safe as an Emperor who sees treachery in every nuance, Jack thought.

Lunch had been cacophonous affair at a pavilion suspended between two belching calderas. Volcano-fried steak and volcano-grilled potatoes had been served, unique only in that they'd been cooked in the heat belching forth from the planetary core and seasoned with sulfur. "Fine source of minerals," the menu had proclaimed.

Misty had been delighted.

Watching her now, as their ferry docked at an unloading platform across from another tour just departing, Jack wondered how she'd respond. He'd found himself intrigued and delighted with her responses thus far, her awe and excitement infectious.

At one cone, the cerasma tube approached an ejecta column within fifty yards, the column a solid wall of volcanic blow—lava, steam, smoke, ash, and magma—rushing upward at unbelievable speed. Three layers of cerasma protected them from the heat, as high as 2900 degrees Fahrenheit (higher than that would vaporize the rock, their guide told them). Between them and the pyroclastic column hovered a cloud of chemolithotrophs.

Misty had seemed fascinated with the concept that a creature could not only survive in such an environment, but thrive. In addition, their ability to wrestle such incomprehensible power as contained in a volcanic plume, and tame the wild magma to their own purpose amazed her. All by a creature who at the individual level could not be seen by the unaided human eye. It defied comprehension.

Jack admired the girl. She had seemed to rebound almost instantly from his earlier rebuke. He wished he had that kind of resilience. Even at her age, Jack had found himself deep in despair for days on end after some slight, even ones he'd later discovered he'd imagined. Predisposed already to dwelling on a topic, Jack had been frequently called morose by the adults around him. It was only much later, after he'd run away from the brothel and got himself a berth on a garbage scow that he'd learned it might have saved him from a lifetime of employment as an escort. His irredeemably ugly face wasn't necessarily a deterrent to his entering the trade, as sometimes a sunny disposition might overcome a lack of physical attractiveness. But the combination of a sour disposition and an ugly face had practically guaranteed he wouldn't be considered for the pleasure trades. Madame Mariposa had attempted on a few occasions to cajole a smile from him, but had been so remarkably unsuccessful that she'd quickly relegated him to kitchen and grounds-keeping duties.

Misty was quite the opposite.

"What?" she'd said, looking abashed, a fry perched at the tips of her fingers, about to be plunged into her mouth. "What did I do now?"

He'd smiled and shaken his head. "Nothing except be yourself. I want you to know how much I admire the joy you find in almost everything around you."

She'd giggled and smiled. "I can't wait to get down into a caldera. Our guide did say we'd be going into one, didn't she?"

Jack'd nodded. "I'm excited too." He hadn't let himself think why.

Hand in hand with Misty, Cherise a few steps behind them, Jack walked down the long, sloping cerasma tube toward the sere landscape of the recently-quiescent volcano.

"As you'll see, even in this harsh environment," their guide said, "sprouts are already growing from an area that just days ago was a pyroclastic flow."

A thin green coat of fuzz covered the blasted ground, which Jack had thought a byproduct of the sulfodes.

The tube brought them to a platform which arced out over the vent, a waist-high railing separating the tourists from a plunge into the abyss. Around them, cameras whirred and clicked, Jack feeling somewhat naked without this standard tourist accessory.

The three of them walked out to the end, a point directly above the bubbling cauldron of newly-quiescent lava. The roiling surface looking anything but quiescent.

Cherise and Misty to his left, Jack leaned over the railing.

"Hey, not too far," Cherise said.

Jack grinned at her, the hot, viscous mud burbling discontentedly below them. "How hot do you think that is?"

"Hot enough to melt anything we know about," Misty said, eyes fixed to the turbulent liquid rock some eighty feet below.

"Anything?" he asked.

"Anything," she replied, nodding emphatically.

He reached into his pocket, pulled out the cube, and hurled it into the lava, where it disappeared with a small splash.

Vertigo seized Jack, reality warping around his head. He grasped the railing and thrust himself back, nausea roiling his lunch.

Cherise gasped.

He glanced at her, was surprised to find her gaze on the lava below, where the cube had disappeared, a look of shock and dismay on her face.

Where'd Misty go? he wondered.

"I'm right here," she said, stepping from behind him, her hand on the small of his back. "Are you all right?" Her face was turned up toward his, full of concern.

"You do look a little green," Cherise said, her face full of wonder. "I'm flabbergasted you did that, Jack, and I'm proud of you." She stepped to his side and kissed his cheek, Misty pressed between them.

Jack held onto them, looking at the increasingly active surface below them, shocked at what he'd just done, but knowing he'd planned it. He supposed the duality of mind necessary to plan such an act and to keep it secret even from himself was a skill he'd honed after years of being addicted to the smoke. One part of his brain had constantly planned his next episode of smoke-drenched delirium, while the rest of his brain had gone about his usual daily activities.

"What's the matter? Why are you crying?"

Soft sobs shook him, and he didn't know why. He felt as if he'd thrown away his dreams. He hadn't really hoped to become Emperor, had he? How ludicrous. Loser Jack Carson, orphaned who knows when, reared in a brothel, runaway on a garbage scow, triple divorced and quadruple bankrupt, and more petty offenses on his record than excrement had maggots, Jack couldn't imagine what he'd been thinking. He'd done the Empire a favor to spare it his stewardship!

So why was he crying?

"Evacuate! Evacuate!" their guide yelled. The mountain rumbled ominously below them. "Seismic readings are spiking! She's about to blow! Evacuate! Evacuate!"

Jack pushed Cherise and Misty ahead of him, and the three of them ran for the tube. They hadn't felt the rumbling, the platform suspended about the caldera by a stasis field. It sure didn't look stable, Jack thought. The smell of the sulfur became an overpowering stench, one that clotted the nostrils.

Halfway to the tube, running as fast as he could, he realized he couldn't breathe.

Misty and Cherise both had their hands to their throats.

Weariness washed over Jack. It wasn't just sulfur fumes, it was also carbon monoxide!

All three of them stumbled fifty feet from safety.

We'll never make it, Jack thought, his vision clouding. Inanely, he wished he'd never thrown the cube away. He pushed the thought aside and held onto Cherise and Misty, darkness closing in on him. The only two people who'd ever loved him … it seemed right and good that he should die with them.

A cloud enveloped them, the mist so thick that it soaked their clothes, and Jack snapped his eyes open, suddenly alert again. He could breathe, although it felt humid.

"Come on," he said, peering through the mist. He pulled the other two to their feet and urged them on. He couldn't see the tube entrance but he knew it was there.

They stumbled along the platform, the side railings keeping them from plummeting into the percolating brew below.

"There they are," Jack heard, and hands grabbed them. And pulled them forward. Jack stumbled and fell onto a smooth-as-glass surface.

They'd made it! The cerasma cold on his cheek, Jack watched licks of lava lurch from the pool below. The tube itself began to move, retracting from the caldera.

A surge of lava leaped upward and engulfed the platform that the tourists had just vacated. Slugs of slag crumbled into the hungry maw.

The last of the mist dissipated from around him. The three of them were surrounded by other members of their tour, including the nice elderly couple.

"You made it!" the old woman beamed. "I can't believe you made it! We thought for sure you were gone, and then those chemo things swarmed around you. It's a miracle!"

172

The Mist! Must have been the chemolithotrophs, Jack thought, the flying bacteria able to breakdown the lava and release the oxygen.

He checked Cherise and Misty, saw that they were all right.

Winded and scared, but all right.

"Let's get you to a hospital, just in case," their guide insisted.

At first, Jack objected, but then he relented. "But we go together, all three of us."

He held onto Misty and Cherise all the way to the infirmary.

Chapter 15

"She saw it with her own eyes, your August Highness!" Prime Minister Custos Messium bowed his head to hide his disquietude. "And surveillance cameras also verified he threw something into the caldera, an object very nearly what you described." What other proof does he want that it was destroyed, its very cinders? he wondered.

The Emperor had grown increasingly paranoid of late.

"Your August Highness," Custos said, "perhaps I may better assist if I knew your concern in more detail." He gave a small bow, as the Emperor had been more fickle of late, more arbitrary.

"No, you may not ask. Spies and cameras are sometimes unreliable. I want proof! Bring be its very cinders if you can!"

Custos glanced at the scepter. He'd long known that it was the source of the Emperor's power—the power to see anything anywhere in the universe, and the power to influence people to his causes, even against their will.

What he hadn't known was that another just like it existed, had been found on the planet Canis Dogma Five, the former Capital of the Circian Empire, whose fall had preceded the rise of the Torgassan Empire by some fifteen hundred years.

Had been found by a luckless scavenger who couldn't maintain a marriage, keep himself out of hock, or even keep ahead of the law. A feckless fool who'd duped an antiquities dealer for five million galacti with the sale of a plain, reflective cube of alien manufacture. The same feckless fool who'd bilked all the major casinos on the Vega Strip and had finally stolen nearly seventy million galacti from the Ballsy Palace Casino. The same fool who'd somehow eluded capture on Alpha Tuscana, actually escaping a high-security Imperial compound.

The same feckless fool who'd just been seen hurling that cube into the caldera of an active volcano.

And if one other exists, Prime Minister Custos Messium thought, then perhaps there's a third or even a fourth. It had long been a mystery how the Circians had held the entire galaxy under their sway for almost two millennia while the Torgassans had been unable to extend their influence beyond the galactic bar. Only a quarter the size of its predecessor, the Torgassan Empire constantly chafed that they seemed doomed to the shadows of the once-great Empire that had gone before.

Salt on the wound. A decubitus of the soul.

And now to find out there'd been another cube all along.

Dismayed, Custos was careful to keep the emotion off his face. "One slight difficulty with the latter request, your August Highness. The volcano which had been dormant for five days began erupting again, and in fact, almost killed this scavenger and his family. Not possible to recover the ashes of this artifact, sorry to say."

"Well then, we don't know it's destroyed, do we?"

It was not the royal "we." He specifically means me, Custos knew. "No, your August Highness," he replied dryly, "we don't."

He didn't begrudge the Emperor his stubborn refusal to believe that the scavenger had destroyed the cube, after all—

"There was that antiquities dealer, who was convinced this scavenger somehow spirited it away from him from under his very nose," the Emperor said.

Custos had long since grown accustomed to the Emperor's filching his every thought. The Prime Minister was mystified he hadn't been eliminated long ago, some of those thoughts bordering on perfidy. But he hadn't navigated the Imperial whim across forty years and two successive Emperors because he was blindly loyal.

He'd done it because he was effective.

"If I may suggest, your August Highness?"

The Emperor looked up suddenly, as thought he'd been deep in thought. "What is it, Lord Messium?"

"Whatever the events on Vulpecula Salacia, whether he destroyed the cube or not, it would behoove us to insure he did not employ some fantastical prestidigitation, as it appears he did on Alpha Tuscana. And the Vega Strip. And Denebi III. In fact, we would be prudent to insure that this scavenger never finds another cube again, your August Highness."

"We would be prudent, yes," the Emperor said. "Make it so."

Custos smiled, knowing that this kind of efficacy was precisely what the Emperor desired of him.

About to bow and take his leave, Prime Minister Custos Messium paused, feeling his palmcom vibrate in his pocket.

It wouldn't vibrate during an audience with the Emperor unless it were really important. He read the message and smiled. "Good news, your August Highness. Our recently acquired source confirms events on Vulpecula Salacia."

"The source you told me about just yesterday?"

"Indeed, your August Highness, the one whose veracity is unassailable."

Tension visibly left the Emperor, and a slight smile emerged. "Well, then, perhaps that final step won't be necessary."

"Perhaps, your August Highness." Custos said. But rather than taking his leave, he waited.

Knowing he was clear about what needed to happen.

"You still think it prudent, however."

"I do, your August Highness," Custos said, bowing and backing from the chamber.

* * *

Brewster stared at Prime Minister Custos Messium and knew what she was being ordered to do.

She also knew what it meant for her.

Detective Monique Brewster wasn't under any illusion that this hadn't been coming. The moment she'd been summoned to the Imperial Capital, Torgas Prime, she'd known that this was her fate. To some extent, she welcomed it. The worst part was not knowing when the

Imperial ax would fall, not having the wherewithal to gauge how much longer she would be of use to the Imperium.

It was all she'd ever asked for—to be of use.

But this—being under the direct orders of the Prime Minister—was far more use than she could ever have hoped for. A life well-lived was a useful one, she'd always believed, and the Imperial Bureaucracy, like every government before it, sought at all costs to preserve itself primarily, and secondarily to provide for the needs of its citizens.

Which was why Brewster knew that she'd be eliminated the moment she'd eliminated the scavenger. Her killing him made her a liability to the government, a liability that had to be eliminated.

"What about the recently acquired source?" she asked. If it were disclosed how Brewster had leveraged the source, the headlines might not reflect well on the Imperium.

"Yes, well, it would be the most efficient disposal," the Prime Minister said dryly, coughing once.

Brewster wished he'd just say it. She knew she was out of her league, that the subtleties of communication at these rarified levels of the bureaucracy left her gasping for meaning, the air that they breathed composed exclusively of plausible deniability.

Brewster breathed concrete, pure and simple. Tell me what to do and get out of my way while I do it, she thought, disinclined to use nuance and even less receptive to it.

He wants the inside source eliminated, she divined.

And if he didn't, he could always deny he'd told her that.

"What about the other one?" Blunt, like a bludgeon, Brewster knew she made the Prime Minister squirm. She wasn't some bureaucrat he could consign to the bowels of a distant archive housed several thousand feet beneath an inhospitable planet surface, as much a symbolic as a literal burial. No, she was dangerous, and he knew it. She knew he knew it and knew he'd see to her elimination once she'd completed the job.

"Other one?" Messium asked, looking mystified for a moment. "Oh, yes, the innocent one. Well, as they say, innocence exculpates."

"Huh?" Blunt described Monique in many ways, her vocabulary among them.

"The answer was no," the Prime Minister said, looking around as though for the door.

She could take a hint. "Very well, Lord Minister. I'll have your results soon." She wanted to summarize what was instructed, but sensed he'd have none of it. Precisely the specificity he wanted to avoid. They were, after all, at the Hall of Justice on Torgas Prime. The Capital.

She nodded and bowed to him, and watched him leave.

The interview room was pleasant if spare, vague pastels to the furniture which might match any other furniture vaguely pastel in color. A serving cart to one side, two pitchers on it, cups, implements, condiments. Four chairs around a low table.

She pulled the stiff blue suit away from her neck, hating having to wear it. An escort would arrive momentarily to guide her from the building.

An escort had greeted her when she arrived. The escort had brought her here and asked her to wait for her host, no indication given that the escort knew who she was meeting with.

The blue suit, the escorts, the waiting, all part of the machinery. Not that she couldn't have left the building the same way she'd come in, but that a visitor wandering a secure building was both compromising and in bad taste.

It wasn't that she didn't understand, which others might suspect from her stoic demeanor and blunt persona. She just didn't have any use for it. She'd have gone berserk long ago if she'd had to work in such an environment, needing her feet on the ground and her hands on a suspect. A suspect's neck, if possible.

There was a certain thrill and satisfaction in both.

The escort was the same person who'd brought her into the building, a young man whose eyes saw everything and whose face gave away nothing.

"This way, please." He wasn't incordial, impolite, or insouciant, but simply uncommunicative. As he guided her from the building, down seventeen floors, past ten checkpoints, across three foyers, and through a gigantic waiting room—government buildings all had to have waiting rooms—he didn't inquire as to her business nor even how it had gone, he didn't ask after her wellbeing or as to the weather, and he made no mention of the uprisings in progress at two places on the periphery.

"Wait here, please," "Through here, please," "Step up to the scanner, please," "Speak your name slowly and clearly, please." Instructions precise but pleasant. Having hints of an oft-repeated tone but tinged with a consideration that his escortee had likely never heard them before. Not a hint that what he was doing was boring, superfluous, or unnecessary in any way.

Until they reached the main lobby, a four-story, glass-walled, marble-floored mausoleum intended concurrently to crush any vestige of human spirit and declare the absolute hegemony of the Torgassan Imperiosity. Diamond slabs of marble tessellated the floor in all directions, interrupted by but a single pillar. Diamond sheets of mirror tessellated the ceiling similarly. A central pillar of elevators was all that interrupted these parallel planes of impersonality.

"Have arrangements for all your comforts been made for your evening on Torgas Prime?" the escort asked quietly over his shoulder.

It was the longest sequence of words she'd heard from him, ascending or descending. She was caught off guard by their profusion. Then she assembled their meaning, and she was shocked. "Only the early evening. Later comforts are still lacking."

He extended a comcube. "Completely discreet, of course."

She took it, grateful. "Of course. Obliged."

"My pleasure." No hint of it in his voice, just simple information.

She looked around the dolorous lobby, at the numerous bureaucrats going multiple directions. It was unlikely that anyone had overheard, and would have been quite difficult to monitor, the cavern an echo chamber. Intentionally so.

They were the last words he spoke to her before she left the building.

She didn't ask if he'd been prompted to offer, and she wondered who'd originated the idea.

Probably the Prime Minister Custos Messium himself.

The more she thought about it, the more convinced she was that he had.

* * *

"More them likely, it was the chemolithotrophs that saved you," the doctor said.

Jack, Misty, and Cherise exchanged glances, none of them having realized how close to death they'd come.

"The volcanic gasses are noxious, certainly, but it's specifically the carbon monoxide that's lethal. It's colorless and odorless. It binds with the available oxygen in the air until there's nothing to breathe. For a person in an enclosed environment, such as a room, an increasing lassitude sets in, followed by somnolence, and then sleep, quickly followed by unconsciousness and death. Fortunately, calderas emit other gasses along with carbon monoxide, alerting you to their presence. What drew the chemolithotrophs was the presence of sulfodes."

The doctor shook her head. "We get one or two cases similar to yours nearly every time a volcano goes dormant. I've been trying to get the tour companies to put in gas detection sensors for years. You'll find you're a bit logy for a few days while the residues dissipate, but there'll be no lasting effects. If you have continued fatigue for longer than a week, please see your physicians. Enjoy the rest of your stay." The doctor shook hands with each of them and left the room, consulting her palmcom before she'd reached the door.

Jack looked over at Misty, then at Cherise. The room was crowded with three hospital beds, but they'd insisted. "I guess I could have done that while you weren't there," Jack told them.

"Why are you saying that?" Misty asked. "You think the cube caused the volcano to erupt?"

Jack nodded, frowning. "I put you both in danger, and that was wrong of me." He pulled at his hospital gown and smirked, wondering where his clothes were.

"Doesn't seem like it could do that," Cherise said.

"Besides," Misty said, "you didn't even know the other part of your brain was going to do that until right then."

He smiled, finding comfort in the fact that she knew him so well. He located his clothes. "I'm getting dressed. I'd like to get out of here." He pulled his wraparound curtain closed.

From beyond came the sounds of their getting dressed. "Where are we going, Jack?"

He was still thinking when they'd finished dressing and had signed all the hospital discharge papers, collected all their belongings, and were out the door.

He was silent all the way to the hotel, the night sky pale with the light of both erupting volcanos and the plant's lunary, an orb half the size of Vulpecula Salacia itself, which contributed to the instability of the planet's crust.

"You just want to go, don't you?" Cherise asked, looking around their hotel suite.

Jack nodded.

The tube-shuttle ride across the moon-lit planet was roller-coaster past hundreds of volcano spouts, liquid fire pouring from each like hoses.

"Where are we going?" Misty asked.

Jack frowned and shook his head. "Someplace we can hide, while we get you ready for your Imperial presentation."

"And what then, Jack?" Misty asked. "What will you do?"

He looked over at her, having heard the catch in her voice. It was a long ride to the spaceport near the equator.

She was blinking tears from her eyes.

Jack blinked them from his own. "I don't know, Misty. All I do know is that you and Cherise are the only family I've ever known, and I'll feel terribly sad when I leave you on Torgas."

She came over and sat beside him and put her head against his shoulder. "I'll miss you terribly, too."

Jack saw Cherise wiping a tear from her eye.

"You wouldn't consider a position in my administration, would you?"

He chuckled and shook his head. "Chief Sanitation Engineer? I don't think so."

"Not even Chief Garbage Collector?" Cherise asked.

They all three shared a laugh, and Jack bent to kiss the girl's hair.

"What if I wanted you to be my regent?" Misty asked.

Jack liked how close she was, the warmth and glow of her fine-boned face near his, the twinkle in her eye like magic fairy dust on his soul. "Regent? You mean rule the Empire for you until you're old enough?"

Misty nodded.

"I remember a boy I knew when I was young," Cherise said, "who talked for long hours deep into the night how he dreamed one day of all the things he would do when he became Emperor, of the great navies he would muster and the huge battles he'd fight as he spread his influence to the far corners of the galaxy, of the distant places he'd explore and the great engines of manufacturing he'd build, and how he'd provide every family with enough to eat and every child with all the clothes he or she wanted and a safe place to live and a family to live with.

"I remember a boy who wept with the determination to give to everyone all those important things that had been missing from his life, and from mine.

"I remember that boy," Cherise said, "and how much I loved him, for his generosity, for his compassion, and for his determination. I loved him then and I love him now for the wonderful person he is. I'm glad you threw away that cube, Jack, so that we can be together, just us, ourselves. It wouldn't have been the same if you'd been Emperor. Thank you, Jack."

The multiple, erupting volcanoes were blurred by the memories of deprivation that spilled down Jack's cheeks. He held Cherise to him for the rest of the ride, Misty snuggled between them.

He'd remembered to com ahead, so the Quasar was fueled and ready for departure. Jack paid the dock fees and loaded their luggage, and then they boarded.

On the dash sat the cube.

All he could do was stare at it. Over and over in his mind, he played the scene back to himself, suddenly reaching into his pocket, grabbing the cube, and hurling it into the caldera, where it splashed into the lava, a lick of molten goop arcing up at the impact. Jack could feel Misty's and Cherise's gazes upon him.

He couldn't comprehend its being here.

The human mind was flexible if nothing else, in both active and reactive ways. Even when confronted with enormities that appeared beyond apprehension, such as an erupting volcano, its ejecta column but inches away, or the universe in its sixteen-billion-year entirety, more galaxies in the universe than the stars in the Milky Way, the mind somehow found a way to accept and to cope.

But not with this. How am I supposed to understand this? Jack wondered.

You're not, said that other part of his mind, the one that had plotted his getting rid of it, the one that arranged for his smokeouts without his knowing it, the one that operated just below the level of consciousness, occasionally poking its little self up above the blue event horizon of awareness to alert him to the nasty things it had been up to. His savior and his nemesis.

Don't even try, that other part of his mind told him. Don't let it bother you. It's not worth it.

He reached for the com and requested permission to lift off.

Cherise and Misty scrambled for their seats as Jack stepped through the preflight checklist.

The cube stared at them, quiescent.

Just like the volcano, Jack thought.

Permission was granted and Jack launched the Quasar.

"Uh, Jack?" Misty asked.

He looked over his shoulder at her, her seat behind and in between his and Cherise's. "Yes?"

"Where are we going?"

He smiled. "You know where. You know me far too well, Misty. You tell me where we're going."

"The Imperial Capital, Torgas Prime."

"And why is that, Princess Misty?"

"Not because you promised to take me there!" She stuck out her lower lip. "What you're thinking is, 'If I can't throw it away, maybe I can give it away—to the Emperor himself.'"

* * *

Brewster felt the gush inside her and a spasm seized her too. She threw her head back in ecstasy and slammed slammed slammed her hips into his, pulled back a ham-sized hand, and with her next spasm, brought it across like the bludgeon it was, and smashed his face.

He went limp at the dull pop from his neck.

Which excited her more and she continued to buck above him until her spasms subsided, and she fell across the corpse, her breathing rough from exertion.

Beside the bed, her palmcom went off.

A message alerting her that her quarry had left Vulpecula Salacia.

She was off the bed and into her clothes with nary a thought. She took the stairs five at a time and had hailed a taxi for the spaceport, excitement of different kind now pumping through her veins.

Chapter 16

The scene filled his sight and the voice rang in his ears.

He was in a cavern, and a man stood before him, dressed in sequined silks of multiple colors, upon his head a slim, simple circlet and in one hand a silvery, two-inch cube.

"I am Lochium Circi the Ninth, Emperor of Circi, a civilization that once reached to the outer arms of the galaxy." Behind the figure was a small table, on it a vial filled with orange fluid, and a large stone slab set a foot off the ground. "Welcome to my final resting place, Traveler. You have now been selected for a sacred duty. You see me now because you have been chosen.

"With this cube," Lochium Circi the Ninth said gravely, holding up the silvery, two-inch cube, "the Circians spread their influence throughout the galaxy."

A remote rumble shook the chamber, and dust drifted down from the ceiling. "And now our influence is dying. Barbarians bombard Canis Dogma Five into oblivion as I speak.

"You, Traveler, have now been chosen to become the next Emperor of the Circian Empire, with all the privileges, responsibilities, and obligations thereto implied, and to bring together again all the remnants of our once-great Empire under the auspices of one government, to live peacefully until the end of time under you and your successors.

"The cube has chosen you, Traveler, because you are worthy and noble and pure. May the stars light your path with brilliance."

* * *

Jack stared out the viewport of the Quantum as though he might discern their destination from the void around it. In the copilot's chair sat Misty, sleeping fitfully, and behind them both, snoring softly, was Cherise.

He shook his head, still disbelieving. Every fiber of his being screamed at him that this was a mistake, that he should turn the ship around and head the other direction and put as much distance between them and their destination as he could.

The cube had told him he would be the Emperor, an idea still as incomprehensible as it was ludicrous. An idea that fit him with the comfort of an iron fist—shoved into his back passage.

An idea that hadn't changed from the moment he'd first touched the cube some three months ago. The one reason he'd not gone about living his desultory life was Misty's insisting he take her to Torgas Prime so she could be princess.

And not just any princess, but Princess Misty Circi.

The Circians hadn't ruled in two millennia. By what logic or right or heavenly mandate did she think she could just go to Torgas and depose Emperor Phaeton from a throne that his family had occupied for five hundred years?

Because the cube had told Jack he'd be Emperor? And that he would naturally adopt her and make her his princess?

Jack glanced over at Misty.

The relaxed pose softened the classic lines of her face. The imperious manner was nowhere in evidence as she slept.

He looked at the cube on the console, where he habitually placed it when piloting a vessel.

The dull silvery cube stared back at him, quiescent.

It had exhorted him to become Emperor through the recording of the last Circian Emperor, Lochium the Ninth. Then it had stymied his every effort to rid himself of it.

As had the girl.

185

He looked at her again, unable to fathom the faith she had placed in him.

He looked at the cube again, unable to fathom the faith it had placed in him.

The feeling of déjà vu seized him, and Jack didn't know why. A shiver shook him from tailbone to neck, and his skin crawled.

He sighed and put his head down.

All of it had seemed so farcical—or would have if his life hadn't been in danger. The Imperial patrols he'd evaded, the gaming gangsters he'd escaped from, the Imperial compound he'd slipped out of, the freighter that'd been blown from under his feet, the volcano that had nearly annihilated him.

All of it farcical. And yet entirely consistent.

Jack's life had been anything but consistent. Orphaned at an early age, taken in at a brothel, running away on a garbage scow at age twelve, working his way into the ownership of his own Scavenger vessel, marrying three times disastrously, bankrupted four times, and arrested more than both combined.

If there were some theme or meaning to the chaos he called his life, it might be noted as defiance. Defiance of his origins in coming so far, defiance of convention in living at the edge of the law, defiance of the perpetual beating that life seemed to inflict on him.

No matter how many times life had knocked him down, he'd always rolled to his feet and danced away to live another day, his spirit undaunted.

He glanced over at Misty, who in that way at least reminded him of himself. Whatever had come their way, she'd remained undaunted in her quest to reach Torgas Prime. Her grandiose delusion of becoming Princess aside, she was a lot like him.

Behind Jack, Cherise stirred.

He was glad he'd returned to the Southern Birds on Alpha Tuscana and found her. The dreams they'd shared as youths had helped him to see now that his life did have a pattern and a purpose, that he could be a part of something greater than himself, that his latent dream of making the universe a better place for those less fortunate had not been just a dream.

Misty and Cherise were with him for a reason.

Jack wiped away a tear of gratitude, something deep inside healing just a little at the thought of their devotion. Incredibly, they believed in him.

He didn't know how it'd happened, and he couldn't say why—but they did. And he could accept it. He might not believe in himself, but he could accept the fact that they did.

And somehow, so did the cube.

Which was why he was flying a course toward Torgas Prime, and not running as fast as he could the other direction.

Afraid?

Of course.

But facing his fear, as he'd always done, confronting his challenges.

Jack thought it bizarre that not long ago he'd considered his life an abysmal failure, and the path he'd taken through it to be strewn with the detritus of its hurricane, a swath of destruction that was as irreparable as it was inevitable.

Somehow, he'd learned otherwise.

Playing his trump against the casino and repaying his ex-wife the money he'd lost, and then giving back to the antiquities dealer, Delphin, the five million he'd inadvertently swindled from him. Not irreparable at all.

And certainly not inevitable.

"When I'm Emperor," he'd once said to Cherise when he was but nine years old.

Little had he known he'd been given the opportunity.

He stared at the cube. "But you knew, didn't you?"

The cube stared back at him, silent.

* * *

Returning to the spaceport on Tertius Diamond, Jack got out of the flitter taxi and stepped toward the terminal entrance.

And froze.

Brewster stood just inside, saw him, and came his way.

Jack didn't need to turn and look. He was already surrounded.

"No use in running, Jack," Brewster said, her bulldog face watchful. She stood two inches taller than he and outweighed him by at least fifty pounds. "Where's the cube?"

"Hole it, Brewster."

She signaled, and officers converged, pinning Jack's arms. Swiftly, they cuffed and searched him and found nothing. A Crown Dick flitter replaced the taxi, stripped of markings but sprouting so many antennas that it was unmistakably an undercover law enforcement vehicle.

They bundled him into the back seat, Brewster getting into the front. She half-turned as the vehicle took off. "Where's the cube, Jack?" Her voice was muffled through the glasma partition.

He laughed at her. "Really? As if anyone in his right mind doesn't know how I've tried to get rid of it?"

"Then you won't hesitate to hand it over, will you?"

"I'd be delighted to give it to Emperor Torgas, his August Highness, himself."

Brewster laughed at him. "Really? As if any ruler in his right mind would allow you on the same planet?"

"Seems we're at an impasse," Jack told her. "But we still want the same thing. Certainly gives a person something to think about, doesn't it? On, and I assume you have Cherise in custody?"

Brewster's sharp look indicated that very fact.

"You won't ever capture Princess Misty Circi, Brewster, so stop trying," he said, knowing that the source of the Detective's concern.

"So even if we do capture her, it'll be because she wants to be captured?"

"The answers to how many engineers it takes to change a light bulb," Jack quipped. "How many times do we have to play this game, Brewster? You know you can't win."

She stared at him through the plasma partition.

He pulled his hand from behind his back and held up the restraints between two fingers. He'd ghosted them into thinking they'd closed the restraints. "You can't win, Brewster." He ghosted the driver and sent the flitter off the road and into a culvert. The vehicle landed on its passenger side, trapping Brewster. His door—never fully closed—flew open, and Jack leaped out.

The multiple vehicles from their escort pulled to a stop on the road above.

Jack ghosted himself off their visual cortices and climbed back up to the road. One of the escorts vehicles—identical to the one that Jack had just wrecked—stood idling, its driver door wide open, its driver attempting to free Brewster from the wrecked vehicle.

Very kind of them, he thought, climbing in and taking off.

No one saw him leave.

He ghosted the Quasar on the tarmac. A bevy of Imperial Secret Service beefs stood around it, a bright orange boot fixed to one of its landing struts. They all stood in defensive postures, crouched and weapons drawn, looking as if they expected attack from any quarter. An unmarked Crown Dick buzzed overhead.

He ghosted the mind of the squad commander, and learned they'd taken Cherise under heavy guard to the local detention center, these Imperial compounds ubiquitous throughout the Torgassan Empire. When I'm Emperor, I'll get rid of them entirely, Jack thought, forgetting momentarily he didn't want to be Emperor.

At the compound just outside the city boundary, Jack parked his blatant undercover Crown Dick and got out.

It looked like an Imperial compound. The usual triple-layer cyclone fencing with barbed wire curls coifing its crown, the watchtowers every two hundred feet, the pole-mounted cameras as thick as a forest, and the elaborate checkpoints both inside and outside the gate, the low-brow building whose bulk was underground.

Knowing the compound similar if not identical to that on Alpha Tuscana, Jack walked in past the slack-jawed guards staring dumbly at their frantically beeping alarms. He located Cherise on level six, below ground. Ghosting a guard on that level, Jack puppeted her to open Cherise's cell and escort her up.

Jack met them in the foyer, the multiple glasma barriers between the elevator and the entrance now flung wide open in spite of the strobes and klaxons declaring their protest.

"Oh, Jack," Cherise said, throwing her arms around him.

"Are you all right? Did they hurt you?" He knew Brewster capable of torture. A single glimpse into her mind had shown him that.

"No. I'm fine. What about Misty? They kept badgering me about her. I thought she was right beside me when they converged on the Quasar, but then she was gone."

"Well, I suspect she'll be joining us soon. Come on."

They walked out of the compound together through the lights and the noise. Cherise giggled at the guards staring insensate at their berserking devices. "I'm surprised they aren't drooling," she said.

"I could throw that in just for fun," Jack said, grinning.

En route, a multivehicle motorcade of Crown Dicks roared past them the other direction, toward the compound, all their lights blazing and sirens blaring, Bulldog Brewster clutching the controls of the lead vehicle, her face fierce and determined.

Jack watched in his rearview as chaos erupted behind them, Brewster belatedly recognizing Jack in his Crown Dick. A pile up ensued as Brewster braked and all the vehicles following her swerved to avoid her.

Flying the flitter back to the spaceport, Jack ghosted the squad surrounding the Quasar. He had them remove the bright orange boot from the landing strut and attach it to one of their own vehicles.

Jack pulled onto the tarmac, activating the Quasar remotely with his palmcom, and parked the Dick as close as he could, the Quasar surrounded by other similarly unmarked Crown Dicks.

He and Cherise threaded their way through them and the several-dozen Imperial officers staring dumbly at them. The Quasar hummed in anticipation of takeoff.

Misty was already buckled into the copilot's chair. "I was wondering where you'd got off to," she said.

Jack put in a request to lift off and went through his checklist.

The ghosted space traffic controller gave Jack the go-ahead in a voice that was almost robotic.

A single Crown Dick pulled up just as the Quasar lifted off. Brewster fired a blasma cannon in their direction but her shots went wide, the Quasar already in the stratosphere.

"I think we'll be seeing more of her," Misty said, grimacing.

"Much to our dismay," Jack replied, nodding.

Chapter 17

The acquisition of the Circian Crown Jewels seemed to trigger a cascade of support. Coms poured in from across the Alpha Sector, each one with an offer of resource or materials.

"We need a cruise ship," Misty insisted. "No self-respecting princess would arrive on Torgas Prime in anything less pretentious."

Sorting through the offers, Jack found one from the Vice President of Heiress Cruise Lines, Johanna Phoenicia.

"I've got the perfect suggestion," she stated over the com. "If you're willing to work with a few negative connotations." She explained that their cruise liners were named after members of the English Royal Family from old Earth, but as they'd begun to exhaust this theme, they'd had to expand this to any ruler of England. "By virtue of its being our least popular cruise liner, it also happens to be available, and at a fraction of the usual cost."

"The Oliver Cromwell?" Misty replied indignantly. "Wasn't he some usurper?"

Jack tried to explain that there really wasn't another cruise liner of such proportions available anywhere on such short notice.

"I want the Queen Victoria!" she demanded.

Not available for another ten years.

"How about the Queen Elizabeth I?"

Extremely popular, not for another fifteen.

"And the King Henry the Eighth?"

Fully booked by philandering fraternities for the next five years.

"All right, then, but at least paint over the name."

Jack sighed, one logistical nightmare resolved. And in leasing the Oliver Cromwell from Heiress Cruise Lines, Jack was spared the onerous task of finding a crew for it.

But it was one chore on an exhaustive list of logistical tasks that Jack had no patience for and no experience in. There was the honor guard—which needed uniforms, weapons, a commander, a Royal Crest. There was the coterie of servants: chauffeurs, kneemen, legwomen, coiffeuses, coutures, stockinglasses, chaperones, equestrians, scullery maids, enderlasses, chimney sweeps, fishmongers, nannies, tinkers, tailors, soldiers, spies, nincompoops, dunces, jesters, and jokers.

"Of course, I need all that staff. A princess needs to be prepared for anything!" Misty said when Jack complained.

"But they won't all fit on the cruise liner!" he told her sarcastically. When filled, the cruise liner with its full contingent of passengers and staff would hold nearly a million people. Of course they'd all fit, but he just wanted to see her reaction.

"Then they'll just have to follow in the lifeboats," Misty declared.

The other worry constantly on Jack's mind was Brewster. When was the next attack coming? When would she try next? What would she try next? How could she not be aware of the flurry of activity taking place in orbit of Alpha Tuscana as the Imperial Menagerie of Princess Misty Circi painstakingly assembled itself?

Fortunately, the Oliver Cromwell was an optimal place to assemble such a menagerie, its numerous decks and multiple bulkheads creating easily compartmentalized societies within the hull. The expenses mounted horrifically, one of but a billion worries that Jack had to contend with, one that seemed magically to take care of itself. Nearly a week passed before Jack realized that Cherise had invited Daria aboard to handle the financial logistics of the enterprise.

The cruise liner fully stocked and all the personnel aboard, Jack commanded that the ship prepare for launch.

"Hey, wait a minute," Misty said. "You didn't ask my permission."

Jack thought ruefully how he'd run afoul of the law more times than he'd been divorced or gone bankrupt combined, but he hadn't ever really violated the law intentionally, nor ever contemplated doing so—one of the hazards of living in a law-obsessed society. Upon hearing that from Misty, however, he found himself plotting her murder.

I'll think about that later, he told himself, and promptly asked her permission.

"Granted." She grinned at him, fetching in her diamond tiara and sequined royal dress. "Now, what about you?"

"Me?" Jack asked. He'd had not a spare moment to think across the last month, and in the circumstances, he couldn't fathom what she was talking about.

"You'll accompany me when I land on Torgas Prime and escort me to the palace for the formal Imperial introduction, right, Jack?"

"I, uh, guess. I thought I was just taking you there."

"And you'd abandon me on the palace doorstep, like some orphan?" Tears welled up in her eyes.

"Well, I hadn't quite thought it through." In fact, he'd been plotting his thorough obliteration in some unseemly smoke shop somewhere far away from Torgas Prime. And what about the cube's exhortation that you become Emperor? Jack asked himself. Don't be ridiculous, he told himself. It's undignified to consider such an irrelevant idea. "If you insist, your August Highness," Jack said.

She fled, wailing disconsolately.

"What did I say?" Jack asked Cherise.

"It's what you didn't say," she told him. "Now, go find her, apologize, and tell her you'd be deeply honored to escort her to the palace and present her to the Emperor, that you can think of no higher honor than being asked by her August Highness to perform this sacred task."

This, Jack knew, was his blind spot, that place in his character that seemed to be absent, a hole in his soul that no charm school could fill, a gap that could not be remedied.

He found her and apologized and swore his fealty and begged her forgiveness for his thoughtless remarks from both knees.

In the end, she begrudgingly accepted his apology and acceded that without him, she was a waif without standing or status, and she was grateful for all he'd done, and she'd soon release him from her service once the Imperial introduction had been made.

"You're sure you don't want to be Emperor?"

Jack nodded and frowned. "I'm sure." As much as he might have pined away in his youth about his beggarly circumstances, Jack was so thoroughly unfit for such authority as to provoke more laughter than Misty's declaring she was a princess.

"Well, we have to make you something if you're going to escort me to the palace and introduce me to the Emperor."

"Captain Jack will do," he said.

"No, it won't, not grandiose enough." The she grinned at him. "How about Paladin?"

"Never heard of it."

"It means Champion, particularly in battle."

"Princess Misty Circi, arriving aboard the Usurper Oliver Cromwell, introduced to the Imperial Court by her Paladin Jack." He shook his head at her. "Guaranteed to get me killed."

"They wouldn't dare."

"What's the Emperor going to do, step off the throne and invite you to take it?"

"Of course not, Jack. You're so silly. But we have to give you a title, and Paladin it is."

* * *

"Your August Highness," Admiral Sophocles Camelus said, his tone grave, "the upstart Princess Misty Circi informs us that she is now en route with her Paladin, Captain Jack Carson. Her curseliner, the Oliver Cromwell, landed moments ago."

Emperor Phaeton Torgas looked around the room. "Curseliner?"

"Er, uh, sorry, your August Highness. My apologies for the typo."

"Does anyone here doubt she comes to claim my throne?" the Emperor asked.

No one spoke. They had been debating the issue for weeks while the cruise liner with the ironic name was being prepared openly in orbit above Alpha Tuscana. While there was general disbelief amongst them that an unarmed and unescorted cruise liner could do a smidgen of damage to Torgas Prime in a direct frontal assault, not a one of them doubted what the arrival of a rival princess meant for Torgassan rule.

Phaeton looked among his advisors, the Ministers of his various cabinets, among them the Prime Minister Custos Messium, the Chief

Justice Minister, Janis Astrea, Admiral Camelus, and the Emperor's daughter, Princess Andromeda Torgas, the heir to all his domains.

"There is only one way to deal with upstarts like her! Slaughter the bitch!"

Everyone turned toward Andromeda.

Phaeton held up his hand at the multiple objections, nearly everyone aghast at the brutality of annihilating an unarmed cruise liner. Even Admiral Camelus had been shaking his head. Phaeton had noticed however that Prime Minister Custos Messium had been notably silent. "Lord Messium," Phaeton said, "your silence speaks volumes. Do share your thoughts with us."

The tall aesthete looked among his peers, then bowed to the Emperor. "It should be as her August Highness says," Messium said. "If it can be done."

"What do you mean, 'if it can be done'?" Andromeda said immediately, venom-like rebuke in her voice.

The thin face turned slowly her direction, "I mean, your August Highness, that all previous attempts to kill or capture this purported Princess and her Paladin Jack Carson have failed miserably. Yes, I agree that an immediate assault upon the cruise liner Oliver Cromwell needs to be mounted, *and* we need to be prepared for its failure."

"Our Armada will not fail!" Admiral Camelus declaimed. "Not like your sniveling clandestine agents!"

The Prime Minister sneered at the Admiral. "When the Armada fails, you'll find out how effective my clandestine agents are!"

"Stop it, both of you," Phaeton said, wanting to egg them both on to mutual blows, neither one much to his liking. They'd both been inherited from his father and both reminded him of rotten, hard-boiled eggs. "So, Prime Minister, what will we do in the unlikely event of a failure?"

"Your August Highness," Admiral Camelus interjected, "we won't fail."

Phaeton tried to contain his annoyance. "I'm sure you won't, Admiral." He turned to Messium. "But if that should happen, what then?"

"Why then, your August Highness, then we invite her August Highness Princess Misty Circi—"

"Don't call her that!" Andromeda shouted, launching herself from her chair at the Prime Minister.

"Hold!" Phaeton said.

Andromeda's dagger was inches from Messium's heart.

The Prime Minister hadn't flinched. "We invite her to Torgas Prime," he finished, as though he hadn't been interrupted.

"Next time, Messium," Phaeton said, "I'll consider it treason and I'll kill you first. Daughter, put away the knife."

Slowly, she retracted it, murder never leaving her face.

Phaeton wondered what he'd have done if she had disobeyed him. Probably thanked her for ridding him of the snake. "Invite her here to do what?"

"Forgive me, your August Highness, for not being clear. We invite her to the Palace." Messium picked a speck of invisible dust from his sleeve. "We then have multiple means at our disposal with which to attend to hers."

Phaeton made a distasteful face, as though he disliked having to take out the trash. "And an upstart who has eluded both capture and frontal naval assault will be so easy to dispose of?"

"By no means, no, your August Highness," Messium said. "She and her Paladin Jack will prove as slippery as rotting fish. But at least we'll have them in our net."

* * *

The bridge aboard the Oliver Cromwell was brazen.

Polished brass flooring reflected sepia-toned images. Polished brass ceilings reflected those reflections. Polished-brass cloth upholstered chaise lounges sitting at polished-brass control consoles. Viewports lined with polished brass showed a view out the bow. A polished-brass serving cart held polished-brass pitchers and polished-brass goblets.

Two navigators sat forward of the Captain's chaise, while behind it sat the operations engineer and the environmental engineer, respectively. The Captain's chaise swiveled on its maglev in all directions, a palmcom mounted at the end of one brass-cloth armrest.

"Bring the helm round to point two-seven-five degrees at warp point-five," Jack said.

Both navigators repeated the course instructions.

"Engage," Jack ordered.

"Course engaged," both navigators said simultaneously. Ships the size of the Oliver Cromwell were required to have two human navigators in addition to their multiple redundant computer navigational systems, each rechecking the calculations and measurements for safety.

They had just steered clear of local traffic in the Southern Birds constellation and had entered the interstellar traffic lanes on the Imperial Highway, that conduit of space traffic for all travelers coming to and from the Imperial Capital, Torgas Prime.

A vessel so large as the Oliver Cromwell could not exceed warp two, even if it were able to achieve such a speed. Even completely empty, Jack doubted it could get to warp one-point-five. With Princess Misty Circi's entire retinue, and its full complement of crew, the Oliver Cromwell was only at a quarter capacity, only five of its twenty pods occupied.

Jack looked almost regal in his white spats and brass tacks. Why these were traditional Captain's wear was beyond him. He felt ridiculous wearing such archaic clothing. Just gimme a pair a plain formalls, he thought. Furthermore, his hair had been coiffed to the style most recently to rage through the Capital Ignorati, a halo of curls not too terribly dissimilar to the halo of platinum encircling the top of the Imperial scepter.

He might have found it ironic had he known that in that platinum circlet was mounted a cube identical to the one in his pocket.

The short, sharp whistle of the Boson's Mate signaled the entry of the Captain onto the bridge.

Captain Jack Carson stood and saluted, Captain Seamus Starswinger having relinquished his duties temporarily to Jack for the launch. He gave the oncoming Captain a status report and then stepped aside as the other man took command of the bridge.

The Boson's Mate blew another short trill as Jack stepped off the bridge.

Cherise was waiting for him in the Captain's lounge. "You look wonderful," she said, giving him a hug. Behind her, the monitors showed the bridge real-time, Captain Seamus Starswinger doing a status check of all systems.

"Thank you. A brilliant idea to broadcast our journey, by the way." He smiled at her.

An unarmed cruise liner approaching Torgas Prime carrying her August Highness Princess Misty Circi was a momentous event, but one broadcast to a watching Empire was pivotal.

Like him, Cherise was dressed in the latest fashion, her couture assembled in consultation with five designers frequently seen among the Capital Ignorati, her hair coifed more elaborately if similarly to his, a veritable penumbra of a lion's mane.

"You look fabulous," he said.

"The companion to the Lord High Paladin Jack Carson must be properly attired and groomed, no?"

"As the Lady High Duenna to the August Highness Princess Misty Circi, you'll have to be more than properly attired and groomed. You'll have to be properly behaved as well."

"Then you'll be lonely and sad," Cherise objected, pouting.

Jack giggled. "There'll be time." He looked into her eyes and saw eternity.

"We're sitting ducks," Misty said, bursting into the lounge. She stopped short as seeing them in an embrace. "Bad timing, looks like."

Jack let go of Cherise. "You have a talent for that."

"I do, don't I?" She grinned. "We should have an armed escort, at least. Not that the Emperor would try to do anything, but what about pirates?"

"Don't worry, Misty," Jack said, "Nothing will happen to us."

Chapter 18

"Attack!" Admiral Camelus ordered.

Armed with a blasma pistol, Prime Minister Custos Messium watched from the rear of the bridge, intent on the viewscreens and the single undefended cruise liner, the Oliver Cromwell, that cruised obliviously toward Torgas Prime.

They were aboard the Torgas Armada Flagship, Lepanto, named after a naval battle between ocean-going vessels back on Earth in the Christian Era year 1571. The Lepanto was a small city unto itself, its capacity equal to that of its prey, the Oliver Cromwell. Unlike its prey, the Lepanto bristled with guns of all sizes. And if she fired all weapons on one side, she could have launched herself into a spin.

The armada that Admiral Camelus had just ordered to attack was comprised of twenty fighter carriers with each three hundred fighters, fifty destroyers, thirty battleships, forty-five battle cruisers, two hundred scouts, and five hundred patrol cruisers, as well as over a thousand logistical supply ships. Such an armada was only deployed in the event of a direct threat upon the Imperial Capital, Torgas Prime.

Before the attack, Admiral Camelus had addressed the entire fleet over secured comchannels. "My fellow Torgassans, sailors, gunners, pilots, and crew, we are about to embark upon an assault on an enemy far more powerful than any we've ever faced. The cruise liner Oliver Cromwell may look like a helpless beached whale, but it is precisely that supposed vulnerability that makes this ship and its occupants so dangerous. You may have heard rumors that aboard the Oliver Cromwell is a nine-year-old princess. She claims to be Princess Misty Circi. Yes, Circi, a name once heralded as great, a family who once ruled the galaxy two thousand years ago. These upstarts who have commandeered this name for its gravitas would have you believe that she approaches Torgas Prime on a mission of peace. Usurpation is her only goal, the usurpation of Imperial power from his August Highness Emperor Phaeton Torgas. Therefore, we will withhold no weapon, will leave no gun unmanned, and will bombarded this cursed vessel the Oliver Cromwell with the utmost fusillade of blows until our magazines are emptied. Once you begin firing, you are not to stop until nothing is left of this cruise liner but its detritus. Nothing! Keep firing until it's gone!

"My fellow Torgassans, sailors, gunners, pilots, and crew, go forth and destroy!"

Prime Minister Custos Messium had listened with cynicism. He'd heard a thousand rousing speeches in his lifetime, and the Admiral's wasn't terribly different. He'd come aboard the flagship Lepanto with his bulldog assassin, Detective Monique "The Bruiser" Brewster to insure with his own eyes that the upstart Princess Misty Circi and her Paladin, the scavenger Jack Carson, were obliterated once and for all. Like Admiral Camelus, Prime Minister Messium did not underestimate the threat posed by this pair.

And even though the nine-year-old girl proclaimed herself princess and seemed the more prominent threat, it was Jack Carson, the scavenger of ill repute, with three divorces, four bankruptcies, and more arrests than both combined, who posed the most danger.

How had he acquired a cube? Custos had asked himself a thousand times. How do we get it from him or obliterate him or both?

"You know this assault will fail," Brewster had told him yesterday as the Armada had converged on the cruise liner.

"Eh? You speak treason." He stared at her, alarmed.

"Is it treason to prepare for all possibilities?" She stared back at him, calm.

He was glad they were alone. He'd have had to kill her if anyone had overheard. "No, no, of course not, but you can't be so sure that it will fail."

"The Junkman has eluded me three times. Me, Detective Monique Brewster. No one's ever eluded me once. What makes you think some bludgeon-minded dolt like Admiral Camelus will be any more successful against the Junkman? Sheer force of arms?" Brewster snorted.

She even sounded like a bulldog, Custos thought, careful not to let the thoughts reach his face. Although he was taller than her by an inch or so, she outweighed him nearly two-to-one. Prime Minister Custos Messium was very thin.

"So you must be prepared," Custos had told her.

"I am," she'd told him. "While you're on the bridge, watching the charade, I'll be in my Viper in launch bay two thirty-seven, waiting until it's clearly a debacle."

Watching from the rear of the bridge while Admiral Camelus launched the attack, Prime Minister Custos Messium feared Brewster was right.

On screen, phalanxes of ships launched volleys of laser, phaser, and blasma bolts, sunlight cannons, uberlight torpedoes, pseudolight mortars, and epithets in all the vernaculars. The side of the Oliver Cromwell erupted with constellations of light, each pinprick of light a huge gout of flame.

The deck shook under Custos in time with the blows. How odd, he thought, the flagship Lepanto not among the attacking ships.

The armada surrounding the cruise liner continued to pummel the helpless ship. The deck under the Prime Minister's feet continued to shake.

"Lord Admiral, we're under attack!"

Custos realized what was happening, remembered the Admiral's exhortation to keep firing, and left the bridge at a dead run.

Behind him, he heard, "Our own armada is bombarding us!"

Chaos erupted, the deck under him lurched as the gravgens failed momentarily, the lights died, and emergency lighting kicked in, klaxons blared, sailors scrambled up and down corridors, and Custos headed for the nearest escape pod.

Brewster was right, he thought, hoping she'd been able to launch successfully. How Princess Circi and Paladin Jack had done it, Custos didn't know. Somehow they'd deceived the entire armada into thinking that the flagship Lepanto was the cruise liner Oliver Cromwell.

The Prime Minister struggled along the corridor, battling the flickering gravity and a steady stream of sailor going the other direction. The deck under his feet bucked and slewed in the continuing bombardment, and he crawled the last fifty feet to the escape pod hatch.

"This one's mine, mate!" the terrified sailor inside said.

Custos pulled the blasma pistol from his belt and blew the sailor's head off.

Getting the body out became much easier when the gravgens failed completely. Now covered with blood, Custos sealed the pod and strapped himself in before hitting the launch sequence. He prayed his escape pod was somehow missed in the all-out assault. The pod launched, shooting him into space and safely beyond the offensive line of attacking Imperial vessels.

* * *

Brewster checked her anchors once again and looked past the Viper toward the stern of the Oliver Cromwell.

Just visible astern was the flaming wreckage of the Imperial Flagship Lepanto. Tiny streaks continued to spear the already battered and blistered flagship, the Imperial armada as yet unaware they were bombarding their own ship, and not the cruise liner.

She had launched at the first sign of trouble and had escaped the offensive perimeter, had guessed—and found—the cruise liner a parsec away, placidly continuing on its leisurely course toward Torgas Prime as though nothing usual had just occurred not far astern.

Brewster had then matched pace with the Oliver Cromwell in her Viper and had brought it in for a smooth and undetected landing on the larger vessel's underbelly.

Her airshell crackling at having to repel the vacuum around her, Brewster searched the hull for a maintenance hatch. Before leaving Torgas Prime, she'd obtained the Cromwell's blueprints and access codes through Imperial intelligence, an oxymoron and conundrum simultaneously.

Armed with the ability to access any part of the huge cruise liner, Brewster found a hatch and opened it with an access code, carrying on her back all the tools she needed to sabotage the vessel, her palmcom easily storing the Cromwell's schematics.

Inside the hatch, she paused to reconnoiter.

The trilithium core was only two bulkheads over. She couldn't have asked for a more propitious landing. I'll be in and out of here in less than an hour, Brewster thought. She dropped from the access tube into a corridor.

Empty.

As she'd thought, the crew whittled down to its skeleton, their passenger manifest limited to the "Princess" and her entourage, which though vast was barely a quarter of the cruise liner's capacity.

Brewster strode brazenly down the corridor toward engineering, wearing a nondescript uniform similar to those worn by Heiress Cruise Lines crew members.

The hatch to the engine room was locked and coded.

Brewster held her palmcom to the reader, and both beeped. The hatch swung aside.

A Boson looked up from a control panel that took half the room.

Brewster blasma'd him, and the figure crumpled. She dragged the body out of sight and made her way into the engine core, ignoring the warning signs, overriding the "No access permitted" locks.

She hoisted the pack from her back and set it on the floor. Above her pulsed the trilithium drive, a fusion reactor that forced three molecules of hydrogen into one molecule of lithium and harnessed the energy thereby released.

She got the timer and pushed the pack up against the cerasma barrier, that clear layer of heat- and impact-resistant material between her and obliteration. She could barely look at the turbid nuclear soup just beyond the cerasma containment vessel.

Brewster smiled and backed out of the fusion chamber, then made a hasty retreat to the access tube where she'd entered.

Detaching the anchors and boarding the Viper, Detective Monique Brewster navigated away and put as much distance between her ship and the Oliver Cromwell.

Her palmcom beeped to inform her of the impending detonation, and she dimmed her vids in anticipation.

"Three," it told her, "two, one, now."

At first, nothing happened. The Oliver Cromwell looked unchanged. Then a ripple moved across it from amidships toward bow and stern, bright cracks spreading across the hull like hot flowing lava underneath the brittle shell of cooler, hardened rock. Then an explosion engulfed the Oliver Cromwell, and the blast sent debris in all directions, flaming shards spreading out in a small nova with the shockwave. They're dead! she thought.

The shockwave jolted Brewster as though waking her from a dream, and she watched helplessly as her obliterated Viper disintegrated before her eyes, illuminating the hull of the Oliver Cromwell under her with its explosion.

Panicking, Brewster looked around. Then she started pounding on the hull. "No! No! NO!" she screamed each time she struck the cruise liner's intact hull.

A figure appeared nearby, a blasma gun aimed at her. The one-armed man whose left shoulder and face had been half-blasted away at some point in the past grinned at her. "Jack said I'd find you here, Detective Brewster. I'm Ignatius Argonavis, Ig for short. You can come with me peacefully, or you can die. Which is it?"

* * *

Emperor Phaeton Torgas stared morosely at his minister of interior affairs. "Destroyed? The flagship itself? By our own armada?"

"How could that happen?!" Andromeda demanded, leaping to her feet. "We just saw the cruise liner being destroyed!"

The Emperor and his daughter had just watched the vid feeds of the battle and had seen the Oliver Cromwell disintegrate under a barrage so intense that Phaeton had for the tiniest period of measurable time felt pity for its occupants.

But it had passed quickly.

Relieved, he had been grateful to be spared the guilt.

And now, and few minutes later, he was being told otherwise. "Minister," he said, "explain yourself!"

The interior minister, newly appointed to her position after being abruptly vacated by its previous incumbent, abruptly vacated her bowels and began to weep. "Please don't kill me like you did my predecessor, please, your August Highness!"

"Tell me what happened! Stars above, just say it!"

"That's just it! We don't know. One minute, they launched the attack, and the next, the cruise liner was a parsec away, intact! And the armada flagship Lepanto had been obliterated! By our own armada!" She broke down in tears and threw herself on the floor at his feet.

Andromeda held her nose in disgust. "Get her out of here!"

The Emperor waved at the servants to do this daughter's bidding, the overpowering stench of voided bowel nearly causing his eyes to water.

"Incoming com from Prime Minister Custos Messium, your August Highness."

Servants cleared away the interior minister and her mess, and a vidscreen descended from the ceiling.

"Your August Highness," Custos said, his thin, ghostly face gigantic. "Forgive me. I should have anticipated the subterfuge. Brewster warned me something would happen. You were right from the very beginning, your August Highness. This scavenger is more of a threat to your rule than all your enemies combined."

"So it's true then, Lord Minister."

"Yes, your August Highness."

"But we just saw the cruise liner go up in flames!" Andromeda protested. "How can this be?"

"Forgive me, your August Highness," Messium said, his face drawn and sure, "but he has in his possession something that until a few months ago we thought was unique. He has a cube."

Andromeda's gaze went to the scepter in the father's hand.

Emperor Phaeton nodded to her to try to dispel the disbelief in her gaze. "Yes, daughter, one of these. A Gaussian Holistic Oscillating Subliminal Tesseract—a ghost cube."

She recoiled in shock and horror. "What are you going to do, Father? You have to stop them!"

He frowned. "Since we can't stop them from coming here, we go the next step better." Then he brightened and smiled. "Prime Minister Custos Messium, would you do the honors of inviting Princess Misty Circi and her Paladin, Captain Jack Carson, to attend upon the Imperial Court here on Torgas Prime?"

Chapter 19

"Jack, it's a trap!"

He glanced over at Misty, Cherise looking drawn and pale. They had just receiving a com from the Prime Minister Custos Messium, in which he had invited them to Torgas Prime to meet with his August Highness Emperor Phaeton Torgas at the palace itself.

Jack smiled. "Of course it's a trap."

"And knowing it's a trap," Misty said, also smiling. "You'll know exactly what to do about it."

Two days ago, he'd have panicked and whined and hemmed and hawed and found some excuse to turn tail the other direction and find the nearest smokeshop.

But after diverting an armada into attacking its own flagship and deceiving Brewster into blowing up her own Viper, Jack felt confident he could do anything.

At the approach of the armada, he'd noticed the similarity in size between the Oliver Cromwell and Lepanto. The rest had been easy, it seemed, his ability to maintain the illusion with one part of his mind undistracted by events swirling around him aboard the Cromwell.

And during the bombardment of the flagship, Brewster's viper had come shooting out a launch bay and had veered toward the Cromwell with unerring accuracy. How she'd found them, Jack didn't know, but with a little concentration, he'd altered her reality just enough for her to think she was destroying the cruise liner. Brewster now occupied a makeshift brig down in the bilges.

The thought of walking into the palace on Torgas Prime—and into a trap—didn't bother him much. He felt he could handle whatever the Emperor might have lying in wait for them.

* * *

An Empire watched, nervously quiescent at this self-proclaimed princess who'd evaded two attempts to stop her cruise liner and who now approached the Imperial Capital, presumed usurper but virtually unarmed and defenseless.

The paparazzi printed stories about the princess and her cortege faster than the Treasury presses printed money. Wild and lurid—and wildly inaccurate—descriptions of Misty's life on Canis Dogma Five, of Jack's and Cherise's lives on Alpha Tuscana, of Jack's adventures roaming the galaxy in search of salvage, of Jack's nasty divorces and despicable bankruptcies and innumerable arrests by the Imperial patrol, rippled across the airwaves by the hour, providing the cruise liner with a little comic relief if not much in the way of accurate information.

In the five days from the armada attack gone awry and their arrival at Torgas Prime, fictionalized dramas about the three of them had become the main fare of evening vidcom entertainment, but by far the most popular and successful shows were the sitcoms about Jack. Which he might have found funny if they hadn't been so accurate.

"It's almost as if they were looking over your shoulder," Misty told him after seeing an episode of "Gambler Jack, Card Shark."

The cruise liner settled into orbit above Torgas Prime, a bright green-and-blue tropical world without ice caps, circling a young blue primary. A smaller secondary star, a red dwarf, orbited the primary far beyond the habitable zone, tracing its lurid arc across Torgas Prime's night sky for fifteen years at a time, and adding a purplish tint to the daytime sky the other fifteen years.

The attacking armada had turned into both an escort for the Oliver Cromwell and a funeral procession for all the lives lost aboard the flagship Lepanto.

On the day after the attack, Misty had dressed in her royal couture, a dainty tiara upon her fashionably-coiffed hair, a few choice selections from the Circi Crown Jewels adorning her person, and had addressed the Empire. "Citizens of Torgas, I am Princess Misty Circi, and I bring to you my condolences over the loss of your fellow citizens in the wreckage of the flagship Lepanto. I feel greatly aggrieved at your loss, and while nothing can compensate for the deaths of your sons, daughters, sisters, brothers, fathers, and mothers, please know that I share in your loss and pray for their salvation in the next realm." She'd then bowed her head and had shed a single tear.

The Emperor had followed moments later to address the Empire from the palace, his manner grave. He too had expressed his condolences but in comparison to the broadcast but moments before, he had come off as insincere and shallow, frustrated and awkward. Princess Andromeda sitting just to his left had looked homicidal.

It had been that vision, the face of a princess contemplating murder, that had most disturbed Jack right up to the time of their arrival in orbit above the Torgassan Capital.

Their ground transportation was a limoshuttle from the Emperor's fleet—not the Imperial limo, reserved for the Emperor himself, but the next best thing: Princess Andromeda's limo. The sequined limo with its diamond-encrusted exhaust flukes, platinum wings, and gold-thread upholstery seemed appropriately lavish for an arriving princess. Jack found it ironic that an arriving, usurping princess would descend from orbit in the incumbent princess's limoshuttle.

They landed on the tarmac just beyond the terminal, the Prime Minister Custos Messium prominently visible above the other cabinet minister assembled to welcome the arriving guests, his white hair and conspicuous height emphasizing his gaunt, familiar features.

Epaulets of gold, cufflink diamonds, and rainbows of insignia accenting his uniform, Jack marched off the boarding ramp and stopped at its base, saluted the gathered government officials, and then stood at attention beside the ramp while a band struck up the Torgassan Imperial Anthem.

We should have composed our own, Jack thought, as Misty emerged from the limoshuttle.

"Her August Highness, Princess Misty Circi of Canis Dogma Five," Jack intoned in his most sonorous voice.

The assembled diplomats bowed, Custos at their head going to one knee.

Misty descended the ramp, resplendent in her evening gown, her dogstone bracelets and necklace glittering in the afternoon light of the young blue primary, her Duenna Cherise carrying her silken, sequined train.

Prime Minister Messium stood to greet her, kissing her outstretched hand as she curtseyed. He looked twice as tall as she, a contrast exacerbated by his rail-thin form.

Her smile was perfect as she accepted his obeisance and greeting.

"On behalf of his August Highness the Emperor Phaeton Torgas, and his daughter her August Highness the Princess Andromeda Torgas," Custos said, pausing dramatically, "a thousand welcomes." His smile was perfectly mischievous. "Enjoy your stay, your Highness."

A small gasp among the audience was quickly stifled, his addressing her as simply, "Highness" and not "August Highness" clearly denying her status equal to that of Emperor Torgas and Princess Andromeda.

"Thank you, Lord Minister Messium," she replied, a mere flicker in her gaze indicating she'd noticed anything.

It was exactly such subtleties that would have been lost on Jack three months ago, when he'd first laid his hands on the cube. It was exactly such subtleties that reverberated in his consciousness since.

Now wait a minute, he told himself. Covert hostilities had been a daily feature of his for as long as he could remember, and such slights had frequently burned in his thoughts deep into the night, inflicting their shame and humiliation long after the person had administered the slight and left Jack's presence.

"Your flitter awaits this way, your Highness." Messium gestured at the bunting- and banner-bedecked walkway, a plush red carpet so thick it was almost a berm leading through the terminal to the waiting flitter beyond. Messium bowed again, and stepped aside.

Misty nodded. "Thank you, Lord Minister Messium, you're more than kind." She stepped along the plush walkway.

Messium fell into step behind her, right next to Jack.

"Lord Paladin, I presume?"

"Lord Minister Messium, a pleasure," Jack replied.

The two men nodded to each other without breaking stride. "A pleasant trip, Lord Paladin?"

"Quite, Lord Minister, barring a mishap or two." He glanced over his shoulder. "I've brought you a present."

Ignatius Argonavis and his charge, the hulking bulk known as Detective Monique "The Bruiser" Brewster, were just exiting the limoshuttle behind them.

"Very kind of you, Lord Paladin," Minister Messium said, his smile perfect but his gaze giving away his fury. "May my personnel take custody?"

"She's not a bother, Lord Prime Minister," Jack said, loud enough for the Imperial flunkies around them to hear.

"Oh, but I wouldn't presume to bother you with her keeping any further, Lord Paladin."

"She's collateral against your good behavior, Lord Prime Minister." Jack smiled.

The pale skin turned beet-red, then subsided. "As you wish, Lord Paladin."

Misty in the meantime was smiling and waving to the crowd as bouquets flew overhead and landed on the carpet, marigolds and roses, chrysanthemums and camellias, daisies and lilies. Servants gathered the bouquets, their scent quickly overpowering the stench of betrayal coming off the Prime Minister.

"What do you and the little usurper want?" Messium asked.

Jack admired the man's steel, remembering that the Prime Minister was on his second Emperor, having served Phaeton's father and having survived the transition. Both considerable accomplishments. "Time will clarify all, Lord Minister," he said cryptically. Not that he hoped to compete in cryptics with one so experienced, but simply that the die had been cast and all the galaxy awaited their fall.

The open-top limoflitter was equipped with a place for the honoree to stand. Jack sat on one side, Misty standing a few feet forward of him, while Custos Messium sat on the other side, level with him. Several other vehicles would load with the remaining personnel of Misty's retinue and follow at their leisure.

Sitting behind Misty, Jack realized just how slight she was, how vulnerable and ethereal, small even for a nine-year-old girl. Sharp, savvy, and smart, but an insubstantial nine nevertheless.

The wide boulevard between spaceport and palace was crammed on each side with spectators all the way to the palace. A vertical city, antigravs suspending its insubstantial arches, colonnades, skywalks, and crosspaths, the Capital was a chaotic vertigo of intricate architecture. At night, it was purported to look like a swarm of fireflies. On every available surface, faces looked down upon the flittercade, the tiny form of Princess Misty looking up and smiling and waving. Building sides were plastered with close-ups of her face, with occasional momentary cutaways to Messium or Jack.

For all the waving the crowd did back, it was remarkably silent.

"Are they always so lacking exuberance?" Jack asked.

"My question is their question. The uncertainty ties their tongues."

As it certainly should, Jack thought. He held his smile fixed to his face and continued to wave, but inside was an insidious anxiety. What did he and the little usurper want?

At that moment, Jack couldn't have answered.

She was adamant she was the Princess, and the Emperor might confer that status upon her and legitimate it as only an Emperor could. But what about Jack?

Jack Carson, orphan adopted into the bosom of a brothel, runaway it age twelve, pilot of his own Salvager by twenty two, thrice divorced and quadruple bankrupt, more arrests than both combined, the finder of an alien artifact that exhorted him to be Emperor.

What did he want?

At the moment, Jack couldn't have answered.

He sighed under his smile and looked at the crush of humanity around him, their anxieties infectious. By what right or mandate did he have to insinuate himself between them and their security?

By the word of a feisty, nine-year-old girl?

Nearly as ludicrous as Jack's becoming Emperor.

The journey finally ended at the palace entrance.

The vertiginous city restrained its impulse to soar the closer it got to the palace, and the infrastructure abutting the Emperor's home assumed an obsequious note one would expect from anyone approaching his August Highness.

The palace itself was fortress and home, administration center and cultural beacon, the sprawling complex four small cities within a city. At its center was a throne room for his August Highness Emperor Phaeton Torgas, a towering rotunda of glasma and steel, atop the rotunda a replica of the platinum circlet at the head of the Imperial scepter.

Inside it a cube.

The limoflitter pulled up to the gate, which swung wide onto a circular drive, a fountain dancing in the middle.

A band struck up the Imperial Anthem as Misty stepped down from the flitterlimo and was greeted by a woman who introduced herself as the interior minister. A small knot of civilians stood nearby, their presence a puzzle to Jack.

After he was introduced to her, a pleasant smile possessed her face. "Oh, *you're* Jack. I was wondering who these people were asking for. Seems you have visitors already."

The small knot of civilians rushed at him.

"You, Jack Carson, are hereby served a summons to appear—"

"You owe your ex-wife Felicity Carson—"

"Payments of your salvage vessel are five months—"

"The department of revenue recovery on Denebi III—"

"You're under arrest for failure to appear—"

"Hey!" Misty shouted, louder than them all. "You'll just have to wait!" she said, hand on her hip. "How can a princess be presented to the Emperor without her Paladin?"

The solicitors looked amongst themselves, befuddled.

"Upon my word, you may serve your summonses once the ceremony is over." Misty looked among them. "You have my oath. I, Princess Misty Circi, do hereby swear to make Jack Carson available to you to serve your various legal citations at the conclusion of today's ceremony." She looked at them one by one until she had them cowed. "Thank you." She turned to him and bellowed, "Stars above, Jack, couldn't you have taken care of all that before we got here?"

He followed her abashedly, falling into step beside the Prime Minister again.

"Sounds like a heap of trouble," Messium murmured, his tone not unsympathetic.

"Seems to follow me," Jack muttered.

Their procession threaded between two lines of an honor guard, saluting soldiers in dress spats and white gloves, and then they were in the palace.

The first thing Jack noticed was the silence. It seemed to enfold them like a tomb. Much of it to increase discretion, nearly every surface was designed to absorb sound. Their progress was deathly silent.

The second thing Jack noticed was the subtle opulence. Silk wallpapers whose fabric itself was embossed with its own pattern, gold filigree threading through carpet and drape, elaborate trim embedded with silver thread, portraiture framed with intricate trim, lighting that appeared source-less, as though seeping from the walls and ceilings through osmosis. An opulence intended not to overwhelm but to assert itself subliminally.

The subliminal opulence obscured the third observation from Jack for the first few minutes: That their course was a windy one, meant to confuse and befuddle, intended to be irretraceable.

Oddly, he had no impression at all that they were being watched. Footservants stood sentinel at every corridor intersection, their faces impassive, their gazes unwavering and obsequious, dropping to a knee at the Princess's passing. Wait staff were everywhere, yet unobtrusive as furniture, their genuflections as silent as ghosts. Jack knew that there had to be cameras everywhere and multiple monitoring stations actively tracking their progress through the labyrinthine palace, but Jack found no evidence of either, neither visual nor intuitive.

Then their procession entered a long corridor; at its end a terrible long distance away were a pair of double doors. The corridor itself grew gradually taller and wider, but all in such perfect proportion that the doors to the throne room at its expansive other end were impossibly small—much too small for a human being and probably too small for a mouse.

The Lilliputian guards besides these doors lent the corridor its only perspective. Above these doors was that platinum circlet again, in relief, the cube at its center. This emblem dwarfed all else. This, too, all intended to impress.

Jack felt as he strode the long, expansive corridor that he was gradually shrinking, being diminutized to the size of the Lilliputian guards.

Whatever spirit or pride or stature that a person possessed before entering this corridor was slowly worn away until the spark of one's spirit was compressed to a pinprick. Not until you are completely humble may you attend upon his August Highness the Emperor Phaeton Torgas.

Their party stopped at the double doors, and Jack stepped forward. "Her August Highness Princess Misty Circi of Canis Dogma Five."

The guards all bowed and the doors opened wide.

Onto a corridor whose foreshortened dimensions mirrored the corridor behind them, as short as the other corridor was long, at the far end a throne that looked gigantic, and upon that throne a man, alone.

Robust and ramrod straight, he held a scepter capped with a platinum circlet, a plain silver cube suspended inside it.

Jack stepped forward five paces and knelt to touch his head to the floor, then he stepped one pace to the side. "Her August Highness Princess Misty Circi of Canis Dogma Five."

Misty entered the chamber, her robes resplendent, the full complement of Crown Jewels making her look oddly lighter despite their nearly fifty pounds of heft. She stepped forward effortlessly, elegantly, and bowed, knee to carpet.

"Pathetic," the Emperor said. "You and your newt-faced Paladin," he added, the sneer in his voice matching the contempt on his face.

Jack would have hurt his neck had he looked, per protocol keeping his gaze on the ground at Misty's feet.

Misty laughed lightly, then ceased abruptly. "Then why not kill us outright?" She smiled slyly. "Because you can't. Really, Emp, you must know you're defeated. You must! And yet you've brought your entire cabinet to witness your last attempt to hold onto power, and put your daughter behind you to kill us in case you fail somehow." Misty spread her hands.

The wall retracted to expose on either side several rows of chairs, bureaucrats of all shapes and sizes—but predominantly round and fat —occupying them all.

"And failing that," she added, "you then put your own personal assassin in charge of our escort, the redoubtable Prime Minister Lord Custos Messium.

"All in vain, of course, your August Highness. So your calling us pathetic is like a red dwarf calling a blue-white supergiant a dim bulb. Really, Emp, you're supposed to be the brightest bulb in the chandelier, or at least in the galaxy. What happened?"

The Emperor's hand on the scepter clenched and unclenched, the knuckles white. A muscle rippled in his jaw and a vein wriggled at his temple. His eyebrows seamed to grow together of form a single line of hair.

"We're not a threat to you, Emp," Misty said, an impish smile on her face. "So why the attack on our ship? Pity Admiral Camelus didn't survive. The real tragedy was the five thousand sailors who died alongside him. His own armada killing him did you the favor of ridding you of his incompetence."

"You insufferable little witch!" Torgas exploded, leaping to his feet. He looked ready to hurl the scepter at her.

"Pipe down!" she said, and pushed an open hand at him.

He was hurled back into his throne, the front two legs coming off the dais momentarily.

"You'll probably want your bulldog back at some point." Misty gestured over her shoulder.

Ignatius Argonavis guided his prisoner forward.

Detective Monique "The Bruiser" Brewster looked two sizes smaller right then, as she was turned over to the palace guards.

"Detective Brewster's many attempts to capture or kill us failed miserably, of course. Including her last attempt, in which she tried to breach the cerasma containment vessel of the trilithium reactor aboard the Oliver Cromwell." Misty grinned. "And blew up her own Viper instead."

Then Misty backed to the side by a pace. "And finally we arrive at the most insidious betrayal of all." She looked at Cherise, kneeling just two paces behind her.

Jack stared aghast at his friend.

Cherise began to weep, her face crumpling. "Oh, Jack, I'm so sorry! They threatened to kill everyone at the Southern Birds if I didn't spy on you."

He watched as though through a sterile glasma pane as she crumbled, begging his forgiveness and weeping disconsolately.

"Worse yet, Emperor," Misty continued, "you have two more attempts up your sleeve to avoid your fate, but both will prove futile."

"Salacious succubus!" he screamed. "Want do you want?!"

"One would think at nine years old that I'm much too young to know what you mean. But duck, weave, squirm, and dance, Emp, because none of it will avert the fate that is already written on the stars for you and your Empire."

"What do you want!?" he screamed again, his face red and bulging, his neck tendons straining as though he struggled against some invisible restraint.

"Ah yes, the central question. Well, since you put it bluntly, I'll answer it bluntly. We want you gone.

"Abdicated, overthrown, assassinated, suicided. Whatever means you'd prefer, Emperor. Pretty simple, isn't it? Your Empire is finished."

Princess Andromeda stepped from a hidden doorway behind the throne and blasted Misty with a blasma pistol.

The girl crumpled to the floor, and chaos erupted.

"No!" Jack leaped to her side and held her. "No!" and began to weep.

"Jack," she rasped, a trickle of blood seeping from one corner of her mouth. "Jack, listen."

He suppressed his sobs, seeing she was fading fast. The blast had struck her in the abdomen, eviscerating her.

"Jack, it's up to you now. You can do it. You must take the Emperor's cube from him."

"Misty!? No, don't ..." He could see her eyes were glazing.

"It's all been for you, Jack." She coughed up a gout of blood. "All for you. Everything I've done. To help you gain the confidence you needed. Jack, look at me."

He blinked away his tears.

Her gaze seemed to clear for a moment. "You have all the resources you'll ever need inside you. You always have. You just needed to be shown. I'll be with you from beyond, Jack. Rule justly and well, Emperor Jack."

And she died.

The bolt seemed to take a long time to reach him.

Jack knew what it was before it struck, but he seemed helpless to prepare. Misty had just died in his arms. What could possibly be more important than that? Couldn't they see he was devastated and disconsolate?

As the bolt struck him, Jack apprehended its nature and its source and its essence in ways that had eluded him since he'd placed his hands on the alien ghost cube three months before.

Yes, the power behind the Emperor's blow might have killed him.

And as much as Jack might have liked to prepare for the blow in the eternity between Phaeton Torgas's launching the attack and the blast actually striking him, there really wasn't any way to prepare.

Not for this.

The Milky Way reeled below him, the local galaxy group not far behind.

The alien race that had manufactured the cubes weren't extinct, per se. Neither did they exist any longer, either. Not in the dimensions accessible to the Human Race, anyway. And as might be expected, the ethnocentric blindness of humanity had masked its ability to grasp the incorporeal planes of existence all around them, those places of being impossible to measure, observe, or even know.

When this blow of ethereal energy from the Emperor's ghost cube struck Jack, it did kill him, in one manner of speaking. It displaced his soul long enough from his body to launch it on a journey through time.

I always thought that time was static, Jack thought, as the universe shrank before him.

The idea came to him in words because language was how Jack integrated the reality. But he realized that the alien presence who'd imparted the idea hadn't communicated in words.

The universe shrank to a single point in time.

Jack was the point in time.

Jack was god.

Again, the words, but transmitted along some medium that defied the limitations of language. He was omnipotent, omniscient, omnitemporal.

And still unalterably, ineluctably, insufferably human.

He slammed back into his body and channeled the blow into an alternate universe. He might have encapsulated himself and let the energy wash past him, but everyone behind him would have been obliterated.

Phaeton struck again and Jack opened a door to elsewhere between them.

Andromeda fired her blasma pistol at him, but its energy was a glow globe to her father's supernova.

Jack was no longer in its path when the blast struck. He lifted the blasma pistol from her hand. "You won't need that."

Her open hand whistled through air through the space where his face had been.

The momentary distraction allowed the Emperor's next bolt to land.

Jack had a choice, and he thought long over the dilemma.

Let the real-time energy destroy the molecules of the body that his spirit had occupied for thirty-two years, or save his body by deflecting it, killing Andromeda with the eddy?

He ached at Misty's death, she who had been all but a daughter to him, and he hesitated to inflict similar suffering on Phaeton Torgas, who for all his Imperial pretensions was also another human being. Me or Princess Andromeda? Jack wondered for a short eternity.

And even though Jack now knew he would survive the destruction of that collection of molecules which had housed his spirit so faithfully, he elected to preserve it, even though that meant Andromeda would die in the backwash of the blast.

The universe had its own immutable laws of action and consequence. Time started again, and her body liquefied and splashed the floor behind him.

"No!" the Emperor wailed, reaching a hand her way.

Jack lifted the scepter from his other hand as Torgas lunged toward her remains.

The robust man who'd ruled an Empire shrank as he crumpled where his daughter had fallen, where nothing remained but a liquid muck, vaporized by the blast.

Jack sighed and stepped to Misty's body, tears filling his eyes. "Here, help me out," he told Cherise.

The woman he'd loved when young and had lost and regained and lost again stared at him through fearful eyes, tears streaking her cheeks, and knelt beside him.

He brushed away her tears. "They'll never be able to hurt you again, Cherise."

Together, they lifted Misty's body and placed it at the foot of the throne. Together, they knelt and bowed.

"Princess Misty Circi of Canis Dogma Five, I hereby posthumously name you inheritor of all my domains, and honorary Empress Misty the First, may you rule wisely and well."

Jack held the ghost cube he'd found on Canis Dogma Five in one hand and the ghost cube he'd taken from Emporia Phaeton Torgas in

218

the other , and he launched himself into time and space to search for Misty's soul.

But it was nowhere, and nowhen, to be found.

She was irrevocably, irretrievably gone.

Emperor Jack wept inconsolably.

Epilogue

"Jack, you won't believe this."

He glanced over at Cherise from his favorite spot on the balcony of their suite high in the palace. Below, the vertigo Capital city sparkled, never sleeping.

The glow of her palmcom lit her face from beyond the rounded bulge of her abdomen. They'd married soon after his coronation, and now she was six months pregnant.

Jack's first year as Emperor was drawing to a close. He couldn't remember feeling so tired. The moment he'd taken the throne, every long-simmering dispute, every suppressed grudge, all the local conflicts, and every politician or military leader who'd pined for that next rung of the power ladder, had erupted in rebellion. Many had harbored long-standing resentments at having been subdued under the Torgassans, but some simply sought to expand their spheres of influence.

"Every single vid—and the Torgassans had a lot of surveillance vid —is lacking the one person it should have."

He frowned in her direction. "Huh?"

Nearly every rebel had backed down after a personal visit from Jack. With the two ghost cubes, Jack was able to suspend the constraints of time and distance and place himself where and when he needed to be. Sensing he might alter the universe in terrible ways if he were to reverse time at all, he chose only to suspend it for short periods. But when confronted with an Emperor they couldn't kill, or one who might catch them in compromising circumstances, most rebels hesitated in the headlong rush to war.

"I've been reviewing all the surveillance vids from the time you found the cube on Canis Dogma Five," Cherise said.

Jack nodded. "What prompted that?"

The few rebels who'd continued to defy Imperial rule after such a visit frequently found their adherents scattering inexplicably. Jack would simply ghost those adherents with an aversion to their intransigent leader. Without fellow insurgents to carry out orders, most rebels found their rebellions fizzling quickly.

"Do you remember," Cherise said, "how Misty would mysteriously appear different places? Didn't you tell me you'd tried to leave her behind on at least three occasions? And when we escaped from Brewster at the compound on Alpha Tuscana, somehow she not only spirited herself out of the facility, but also located us at the freighter in spite of having no way to know where we'd gone."

Jack nodded, remembering all that, missing her still. They'd held a quiet funeral service for Misty, ensconcing her ashes in a lonely crypt behind the Southern Birds, the erstwhile brothel now an orphanage. And every time Jack visited some obstreperous rebel whose intransigence seemed insurmountable, Jack would bring to mind what Misty had told him.

"You have all the resources you'll ever need inside you."

He smiled at the memory.

"So I started looking at all the vid to see if I could figure out how she was doing it."

Jack looked over at Cherise when she didn't continue. The ghost cube was in his pocket, slightly warm. The other cube, nestled in a platinum circlet atop the Imperial scepter, remained in the throne room and was used primarily for ceremonial occasions.

There were only three rebel leaders who were so fanatical in their opposition to Imperial Rule that Jack had to do more than visit or ghost their adherents. When he ghosted each of those three rebels, he discovered that each was in one way or another so severely imbalanced that they shouldn't have been granted any influence whatsoever. And no amount of cube-induced influence was going to deflect them from their goals. He'd killed them, much to his dismay. Looking back on his first year as Emperor, their executions were what he regretted most.

"Also, I've been thinking how she always knew what was on your mind, how she'd say things that you'd just thought of."

Misty would have handled those three rebels differently, Jack was sure. "So what did you find?"

Cherise shook her head at him. "So you *were* paying attention. I got the distract impression you hadn't heard a word I said."

"Oh I heard it all." Then he grinned at her sheepishly. "I just didn't listen."

"I thought as much." Cherise sighed. "Whatever will I do with you, Jack?"

He shrugged. "Love me forever and hate me occasionally."

They shared a laugh and Cherise shook her head. "I certainly will." She ran her hands across her abdomen. "Do you think she'll be like her namesake?"

"Misty?" Jack shook his head. "I don't know. I hope she's her own person, more than anything."

Cherise nodded. "Me too. So, what I found isn't nearly as important as what I didn't find."

"Didn't find?"

"Jack, in every single vid of you, there isn't a trace of Misty."

He'd known that that's what she was going to say. By tacit agreement, Jack never ghosted Cherise and never had. Still, he'd known.

And he didn't believe it, not wanting to believe it.

"What about the Imperial compound on Alpha Tuscana?"

Cherise shook her head. "That place has more cameras than a porcupine has quills, and she doesn't show up once in their vids."

"But dozens of people saw her on the vid monitors."

"And even now they swear she was there, Jack. The investigation of our escape is rife with descriptions of what she did, what she wore, what she said. But not a bit of it is on video or audio."

Jack stared at Cherise, his mind stumbling toward meaning, his disbelief refusing to yield.

"One final question, Jack."

"Uh huh?"

"In the moments before you put your hand on the cube for the very first time on Canis Dogma Five, did you have any hint that anyone was nearby—any hint at all?"

In his memory, Jack retraced his route from the Scavenger into the relatively intact apartment building and up two floors. Although the memory was hazy, he did remember distinctly having an awareness of feeling totally alone. "No one," he told Cherise. "In fact, I remember wondering where she'd come from."

"That's what I thought." Cherise sighed and shook her head. "Jack, do you remember how old you were the first time you told me you wanted to be Emperor, just so you could give every child a home?"

"I was nine. I'd just turned nine, in fact."

Cherise took his hand in hers. "Jack, I don't think Misty was real. I think she was a projection, a manifestation of that horribly traumatized nine-year-old boy who was determined to see that no one else had to endure what he'd endured."

"What do you mean, 'a projection'?"

"The cube, Jack, a Gaussian Holistic Oscillating Subliminal Tesseract. It integrated your sublimated desires and tesseracted them into the persona we came to know as Misty."

Jack stared at her. "How do you know that?"

"I *don't* know, Jack. It's just a guess. But it's the only one that makes any sense. It's why she doesn't appear on any of the surveillance vids. It's why you couldn't leave her behind. It's why she always knew what you were thinking."

Jack pulled the cube from his pocket. The cube he'd found on Canis Dogma Five, the one that had belonged to Emperor Lochium Circi, the Ninth and Last, rested in his hand, quiescent. Its silvery, reflective sides were quiet and contemplative.

"That's not possible," Jack said. He blinked away his tears, missing her still. He knew with dead certainty that Princess Misty Circi from Canis Dogma Five had not only been real, but had changed the course of history. "Misty was as real as you or me," he told Cherise.

Emperor Jack looked at the cube in his hand. "Isn't that right?" he asked it. "Misty *was* real, wasn't she?"

The cube stared back at him, silent.

Doorport

All points in space exist at one point in space.
All points in time exist at one point in time.

Chapter 1

Janet Thompson stepped through the doorport and gasped. This isn't San Diego! What went wrong? she wondered, jostled by a passerby, overwhelmed by the noise, offended by the stench, chilled by the cold, and half-blinded by the light.

Blinking, she turned to read the sign above the doorport that she'd just come through.

"Downtown Sacramento Transit Plaza," it said on the lintel.

But I just came from Denver! Janet thought. She pulled her collar tight against the cold and looked around, wondering where she was. The cold was a wet, soggy rag, so unlike the crisp, dry cold of Denver. The classical cathedral dominating the square looked oddly familiar, but the steep pyramid piercing the sky behind it was the landmark she needed. The Transamerica Pyramid, San Francisco.

I step into a doorport in Denver headed for San Diego, and I end up in San Francisco, stepping out of a doorport that says I came from Sacramento.

The system's gone haywire, Janet thought, pulling her comcard from her purse. With a few thumbpresses, she dialed central California dispatch, the back line to the supervisor, her old friend Charlie Goodrich.

She looked around as her call went through. Doorports lined the square, people popping in and out of them every few seconds, the ports shimmering as they bent the fabric of space-time to bring two points together. The mid-morning doorport traffic heavy, all the people looked as if they belonged, none of them disoriented, as she was sure she looked. The usual knot of protesters stood down the street, waving signs predicting the apocalypse. Supercilious sacrilege! she thought, disliking their inflexible intolerance.

"Charlie here," the voice said. "Janet, wonderful to hear from you."

Janet held up her comcard so he could see her. "Hey, Charlie, how are you, old friend?"

Charlie was in his fifties, a bit overweight, balding and red-faced, a competent troubleshooter and Janet's typical go-to when anomalies like this cropped up. "What can I do for you, young lady?"

"I got a bad one, Charlie," Janet said, the wind whipping her hair into her face. At least it blows away the urine smell, she thought. "I was in Denver, stepped into a port for San Diego, found myself here, stepping out of a port from Sacramento."

"Uh-oh," Charlie said. "Let me get a trace on that one. That the doorport behind you?"

"Yeah, sure is." She'd made sure he could see it over her shoulder.

"Quite a snafu, that one. I hope Old Man Douglas doesn't get word about this. He'll give birth to extraterrestrials." Charlie looked at something off screen, his hands moving across his tactile interface, the tacti-face beeping at his every touch. "Say, you weren't playing with that prototype you and the boys are developing at Corporate, were you?"

"The recalibrator? I wouldn't dare; Old Man Jackson would excoriate me for using untested equipment. You know how careful he gets about R&D."

"You mean, 'anal.' " Charlie smirked.

Janet smiled. "Exactly what I meant." Charlie always knew what she meant. They'd worked together for ten years on system maintenance and troubleshooting on the west coast before her promotion last year to VP of R&D.

"Nothin's comin' up, Janet," Charlie said. "All systems read normal; those two doorports both pass a self-check. I'll do a reset for both and then recheck. It'll inconvenience our customers for about thirty seconds, so if you hear complaints, that'll be me. But you know what I'm not finding …"

"The record of my going through, right?"

"Right," Charlie replied, frowning.

All ports were tracked and billed accordingly. A port from LA to SF was $35 one way. Wave your comcard at the sensor, wait for the green, step on through, pay your bill each month.

Great. No record. "Look, Charlie, I'm freezing, where's the nearest doorport to San Diego? The rest can wait."

"Yeah, let's get you going." He waved at his tactiface. "Forty feet west of you."

"Left, right, up, down. I don't know west or east," she protested.

"Sorry, to your right."

Janet spotted it, headed that way. "Thanks, Charlie. I owe you one."

"Pleasure to be of service. Say 'hi' to the family."

"Likewise on your end. Bye." She thumbed off the call, and his face was replaced with an alert. One new voicemail, three new emails, four new vidmails. Probably all of them wondering where I am, Janet thought, sighing and stepping to the right doorport.

She waved her comcard across the sensor, the light turned green, the doorport shimmered, and she stepped on through to San Diego— four doorports down from where she should have emerged fifteen minutes ago.

With a sigh, she headed through the Transit Center toward the local doorports, dodging a protestor and wondering what had gone wrong.

Alterlude #1

Officer Anthony Stewart checked that he had everything ready, scooped up his three-year-old, shouldered the day bag, and kissed his wife goodbye. "I'm so lucky to have you," he told her. "C'mon, Suzy," he said to his four-year-old and headed for the garage.

"I'll pick up the kids at three," Sharon said as he stepped into the garage. "As usual."

"Thanks, Honey," Anthony said, the door closing between them. His hands full of child, bag, lunch, and briefcase, he managed to extract his comcard from his pocket and swipe it across the doorport sensor.

Space-Time Harmonic Aperture, it said across the lintel.

Fancy name for a doorport, Anthony thought. The light turned green, the surface shimmered, and he stepped from his garage into the nippy Denver morning. Making a beeline across the neighborhood square for the childcare doorport, Anthony saw that a line had already formed.

"Daddy, slow down," Suzy complained, hanging onto his hand.

In his arm, his son Dustin giggled.

"Sorry, Honey," Anthony said, his breath fogging up in front of him. "You both warm enough?" he asked, heading for the back of the line, looking around the square. Several doorports had lines in front of them. Rush hour. The bank of five doorports labeled "downtown

230

Denver" was fifteen people deep. Anthony sighed, knowing he'd be there after dropping off the kids at daycare.

A woman with a child in her arms slid into the line just before he did. The child grinned over his mother's shoulder and stuck his tongue out at him.

Anthony flipped back his lapel to expose his badge. "All right, you're under arrest."

The boy burst into tears, and his mother spun as though to rebuke him. Suzy giggled, and Anthony told the woman, "You're up," pointing to the open doorport in front of her.

The mother scowled at him, waved her comcard across the sensor and disappeared through the doorport.

He swiped his comcard, the light turned green, the doorport shimmered, and he followed.

The mother with the bawling child entered the daycare center ahead of him, throwing dismayed glances over her shoulder.

Sheepishly, he entered behind her and set down his wriggling three-year-old son. "Sorry about that," he said, his kids dashing off to play with their friends. "He stuck his tongue out at me." Anthony stuck the day bag into his daughter's cubby.

"Oh," the mother said, trying not to smile. She handed him the sign-in wand. "Jackie," she said, offering her hand.

"Anthony," he said, shaking it and turning. "Bye, Kids." He waved.

"Bye, Daddy," five kids replied, maybe one of them his.

He held the door for Jackie, and they headed up the walk for the doorports.

"County Sheriff?"

"Yeah," he said, knowing the badge visible under his lapel.

"D.A.," she said.

"Oh? Deputy or big cheese?"

Jackie smiled bashfully. "Assistant."

"So I bag 'em and tag 'em, and you—"

"Lock 'em up and throw away the key," she finished.

They both laughed and took their turns at the doorport.

Back at the neighborhood transit point, Anthony saw that the line to downtown was much shorter. After a couple minutes of talking shop, they'd stepped through the doorport into Civic Center Park. Across the street, behind yellow-striped sawhorses, a cadre of protestors chanted in unison and waved signs. "Doorports will be the death of us all," one sign said. A cloud of steam rose above them, the protestors were so numerous. While Jackie headed to the courthouse, Anthony turned toward the County Jail, the Sheriff substation attached to the backside.

At his desk, Anthony sorted through the missing-persons reports filed overnight in the county. He scratched his head at the number, which had increased recently for no apparent reason. As the open squadroom came to life for the day, Anthony browsed through files on his tactiface.

"Hey, Stewart, did you find that 84-year-old who lost herself in her own closet?"

Anthony didn't even look. He just held up a single finger. A cackle of laughter followed. He didn't care; he liked what he did. No one else wanted missing persons, considered a promotional backwater at the department. Of course, having a hysterical wife call about a husband who'd been missing only four hours and was just checking out of a motel with someone who wasn't his wife, or an old man looking for "Bessie" who later turned out to be a forgetful basset hound so old she didn't know how to get home anymore, wasn't exactly detective work.

Some of it included matching a John Doe at the morgue with a missing persons report. A new body had come in, and some of the circumstances triggered his memory. Sorting through reports, he matched one to the John Doe. Per protocol, he personally had to port to the morgue and match it to the specs given him by the worried family member. Anthony pulled the profile onto his Sheriff's comcard.

Near the john was the doorport to the morgue.

Anthony swiped his card and stepped through the shimmering port.

"Stewart, got a match already?" Ruth the receptionist asked.

"I think so," Anthony said, following her back to the meat locker.

"Column five, door three," she said, gesturing him into the refrigerated area. Shiny aluminum panels mirrored their progress down the banks of drawers toward the one he wanted.

He slipped his comcard into the tactiface nearby, then pulled open the third drawer down.

An elderly male stared up at him with a bewildered expression, a mole on his left cheek.

On the tactiface, a drawn, bewildered face with a mole on the left check looked at Anthony.

"Biometric," he said.

"Analyzing," the tactiface replied, then the screen began to flash. "Match."

"Let's get you back to your family, old guy," Anthony said to the body, then covered him back up and slid the drawer back in. He shook off shivers outside the meat locker. "Thanks, Ruth."

"Glad you found him, Stewart."

Back at his desk, his tactiface began to flash, indicating he had an incoming call. He tapped the screen to answer. "Missing persons, Stewart here," he said.

The face on the screen was that of a young man. "Hi, I'm calling from St. Louis, and I can't get a hold of my father in Denver today. We talk every day."

Anthony nodded, smiling. A person wasn't considered missing until forty-eight hours had passed. "All right, Sir, I'll need to get some basic information." He shrank the face to a corner of the screen and began putting in the information the young man was giving him.

Within seconds he had a match. Anthony verified all the major demographic details, then said, "Sir, my apologies but my records indicate your father died—"

"Last week, that's right. I did it again," the young man said. "I'm sorry, I keep forgetting, it was so sudden, I must have dreamt about talking with him yesterday. Look, I didn't mean to waste your time."

"Sorry about your loss, Sir, and it wasn't a bother at all."

"I can't believe I did that, forgetting my own father died. My therapist says sometimes people do. You ever get calls like this before?"

"It's happened," Anthony said, thinking they'd been all too frequent recently. His tactiface flashed, indicating another call. "I've got to go, Sir." The caller hung up after another apology and Anthony picked up the next call.

The daycare.

Oh, great, he thought.

"Hi, Mr. Stewart, just wanted to remind you that the kids need to be picked up at three. I'm calling because of what happened yesterday."

Oh, yeah, Anthony thought, I was supposed to pick them up but thought for some reason that my wife was going to. Been forgetting a lot lately. "Thanks for reminding me," Anthony said. His therapist had told him to expect some of that around the anniversary. "I appreciate the reminder. So much to juggle, doing this all on my own."

Anthony hung up, saw it was already noon. Seems like hours had passed without his having noticed. Looking up, he saw Captain Jameson approaching, the precinct Chaplain in tow. Father McClanahan had been to the house a number of times in the past year, but not recently.

"Captain Jameson, Father McClanahan," Anthony said.

"Stewart," the Captain said, his hand on Anthony's shoulder. "Why don't you join the Father and me in my office in about five minutes?"

"Certainly, Sir." Anthony nodded to them and returned his attention to his reports. He could feel the looks of his coworkers, and he knew they could see he was suffering. It used to be they'd rib him about finding someone who'd lost themselves in their own closet. They hadn't done that for the last year. He thought it ironic he'd miss something he used to find so annoying.

He knew his work wasn't as thorough, and the Captain was probably going to suggest he take some time off. The tactiface told him how many reports he still needed to sort through. How can I take any time off? he wondered.

With a sigh, he headed for the Captain's office.

"Anthony," the Captain said.

First names, Anthony thought, wants to keep it informal. "Captain, Father." He nodded to them both.

"How are the kids, Anthony?" Father McClanahan asked. As precinct Chaplain, he knew all the officers, all their spouses' names, all their kids' names. "Dustin's four now, and Suzy three, eh?" And their ages.

Anthony hesitated, thinking at first that McClanahan had it backward. Why did I think that? Of course Justin's four and Suzy's three. "Uh, yeah, yeah, they're, uh, fine, Father. Thanks for asking. They still sometimes ask for their mother, but that's to be expected."

"Tomorrow's the anniversary, Anthony," Father McClanahan said. "Got anything planned?"

Anthony blinked back a tear. "I hadn't realized. No plans, since I guess I forgot. Funny how you forget things like that."

"Anthony," Captain Jameson said, "it's the forgetting that's got everyone concerned." He sighed and looked away. "And how you sit there for hours not moving, man! It's unnerving!"

The Father put his hand on the Captain's arm.

"Maybe I could take the kids to the crypt," Anthony said, not really seeing them anymore. "Yeah, I'll do that. Thanks, Father, for the suggestion, and thanks for the day off, Chief."

Anthony found himself back at his desk without a memory of returning. It's just the grief, he knew.

His tactiface alerted him to the time. The squadroom was subdued as he rose and tidied his desk. He felt their eyes again and wished his suffering weren't so apparent.

His walk to Civic Center Park seemed to take no time at all.

"Hey, Anthony, put on your coat, it's freezing," Jackie said, standing in line at the doorport.

He smiled, liking her, remembering their date two weeks ago, remembering he'd enjoyed himself for the first time since his wife … I can't think about that right now, he told himself.

At the daycare, he held the door for Jackie and they walked in together.

Justin glanced from Jackie to him. "Are we getting a new mommy?" he asked, Suzy watching wide-eyed beside him.

All Anthony could do was kneel, gather his kids to him, and weep. As though he hadn't wept at all since his wife had died.

Chapter 2

"Space-Time Harmonics," Janet said, squinting into the lights, her voice echoing from the back of the auditorium, "allows us to bend the space-time fabric between two points and open a doorway between them. When first deployed forty years ago, doorports altered the fabric of our society. Planes, trains, and automobiles suddenly became obsolete. In less than ten years, the United States changed its primary mode of travel from hydrocarbon-powered vehicles to electricity-powered doorports, and the industrialized world is now but a few steps behind us. Doorports line our streets. Instead of cars in our garages, we now have three to five doorports each. Our houses used to be valued in part on how many cars fit in the garage. Now, it's doorports.

"But even that may become superfluous.

"Our current infrastructure requires two fixed doorports, one on either end, both finely calibrated to insure the safe arrival through that space-time aperture of its valuable human transit."

Janet smiled, barely able to see past the glaring stage lights. "But what if, ladies and gentlemen, what if each doorport might be recalibrated for a different destination each time?"

A buzz began in the room. These are sector chiefs and division managers, she reminded herself. They know precisely what that means. "Less maintenance, less infrastructure, less real estate, less energy, greater flexibility, fewer transfers."

"What about system instability?" shouted someone from the back.

Janet recognized the voice instantly.

Old Man Douglas, co-founder turned apostate.

Janet didn't hesitate. "Instabilities are an anachronism. Our network hasn't had a single anomaly in the last forty years." Before today, she thought. "We have within our grasp the next generation of doorport, one that will leave our competition gasping and our customers smiling. Thank you, everyone!" Janet waved and walked off stage, trying not to run, hoping she didn't trip.

Backstage, she wiped her face, breathing roughly.

Old Man Douglas, twin brother to CEO Jackson Weintraub, was ninety years old, had been one of the two senior engineers responsible for developing the first generation of doorports and, on the eve of their rollout, had abruptly resigned from the project, had declared the technology dangerous, and had denounced the company engineers as charlatans, his twin brother among them.

He can think what he wants, Janet thought, having grown up with doorports. A forty-year-old engineer at R&D, she knew the reliability of the technology. He's a fool, she thought, making her way to the reception area, wondering how she was going to handle all the questions she was sure to get. Her secretary greeted her in the back corridor. "You look like you've seen a ghost." The young man frowned and led her to a chair.

"No, just Old Man Douglas." Janet sat, feeling somewhat disoriented.

"Who let him in? I had him escorted to the sidewalk just an hour ago!"

Janet shook her head. "He's irrepressible. Listen, Stan, any questions about my being late?" She had run onto the stage, hopelessly unprepared.

Stan shrugged. "Old Man Jackson was a bit miffed, watching on com from Denver, but he's always that way. Let's get you freshened up for the reception. You're still pale."

"I'm not going—indisposed, all right?" Janet had to figure out what went wrong this morning. "I got that noon at Corporate anyway."

"Old Man Jackson will be a bit miffed."

"But he's always that way," they said together, sharing a chuckle.

"Look, Stan, I called Charlie about ... a glitch. I'm going to forward the call to you. You have to keep this under wraps. Got it?" She thumbed her comcard.

Stan's eyes went wide. "Haven't had a 'Charlie' in a year. That bad?"

Janet nodded. "Really bad, this time. I need a tight lid on this one, all right?"

Stan nodded, his eyes wide. He pulled out his comcard, which beeped. "Got it. Be careful. I'll cover for you here. Exit's that way." Stan pointed.

Her coat over her arm, Janet stepped from the service entrance into an alley fifty feet from the street. Once outside, Janet breathed a bit easier, and headed for the nearest doorport. She checked her watch, the time ten-thirty PST. She was due back in Denver at noon MST, a half-hour hence.

Her husband Frank often chided her about the anachronism around her wrist, a self-winding mechanical watch, a relic from the pre-doorport age of internal combustion engines, smog-choked air, and climate change.

At the sidewalk, standing against the building as though stalking her, was Old Man Douglas. "Come with me," he snarled, taking her elbow roughly and towing her down the street.

Janet planted her feet and tore her elbow from his grasp. "Lunatic! You don't know what you're talking about and haven't in forty years. None of your catastrophizing has any basis in reality, and none of your predictions has or will come true."

"Latent effects of space-time perturbations might not be seen for another hundred years—or another day. Just because you can't see it coming doesn't mean it isn't there. Have you worked through the progressions? No! Because they won't let you!" He handed her a memchip and was gone before she could give it back.

Perturbed, Janet watched him as he scurried away, hunched over, his pink bald spot above a grey crown all she could see above the collar of his trench coat, his feet taking steps too rapidly for a frail, ninety-year-old man.

She headed toward the doorports lining the middle of the street, putting the chip in her pocket.

"Repent!" a bearded young man said, nearly striking her with his sign. "You're bringing about the end of time!"

She stepped nimbly around him, resisting the temptation to grind her heel into his instep. He sounds so certain, she thought, shaking her head. Medieval nut-job!

Reading the signs above the doorports, she continued walking, not finding the doorport labeled "Denver." Albuquerque, Phoenix, Houston, Kansas City, Salt Lake City, De Moines, but no Denver.

She sighed and pulled out her comcard. In the corner was the icon for the prototype—she smiled, then shook her head. Thumbing for a map, she saw that the nearest Denver doorport was a twenty-minute walk. I'll never get there in time, she thought. Janet could have ported to a neighboring city and found a doorport for Denver there, but she didn't know what the distance between doorports was in that city.

Well, she thought, pulling up the prototype, wish I didn't have to use this. It hadn't been field-tested but had proved flawless thus far in lab tests. We'll have to start field tests soon, anyway.

Janet stepped to the nearest doorport, one labeled "New Orleans," and used her corporate override to pull the doorport offline, a tool she carried from her maintenance and troubleshooting days with Charlie. She waved her comcard across the sensor pad. Thumbing the activate on the prototype, she watched the comcard screen as the prototype recalibrated the doorport in front of her to Denver, and recalibrated the destination doorport in Denver to align the space-time harmonic aperture.

The sensor beeped and flashed green, and the doorport shimmered.

Janet smiled and stepped from San Diego to Denver.

Civic Center Park greeted her with its cheerful bird calls, vendor bells, and bare, rustling trees. And of course, the cold, crisp winter day. The State Capitol dome gleaming under the noon-time sun, she stopped to don her jacket, then looked for the doorport that would take her to Corporate.

I could have ported directly to Corporate, she thought ruefully, checking her watch. Fifteen to eleven Pacific, she saw, rolling the watch ahead an hour to Mountain Time, striding toward the bank of local doorports, no protestors in sight.

A bell tolling from a few blocks away caught her ear. The Cathedral Basilica of the Immaculate Conception sounding the hour, she thought, enjoying the bells, having lived as a child within earshot of the Basilica, having heard its bells all through childhood.

She froze, startled, and looked at her watch.

11:45.

She searched between the trees for the Basilica tower.

12:00 noon.

Her throat tightened, her heart raced.

She held up her watch just under the tower clock face, the latter's hands vertical. Pulling out her comcard, it too stated the time was noon. The bells stopped tolling and her comcard started beeping, telling her she needed to be at Corporate.

My watch is never wrong! she thought, wondering what happened.

She found the doorport for Corporate and stepped out onto the sidewalk in front of the building. Across the street stood a cadre of protestors, behind yellow-striped sawhorses, chanting in unison, waving signs, a cloud of steam rising above them. Fanatics! she thought, flummoxed.

In the building foyer, the concierge nodded.

"Can you tell them that I'm on my way up, please?" Janet asked him, and stepped into the elevator.

"Running late?" the woman beside her said. Maxine, from finance. A royal bitch, Janet remembered, but hammered out contracts that were airtight. "Not like you at all," Maxine said, eyes on the floor counter. "Stan says you're the queen of on-time. Admires that in you."

Janet shrugged out of her jacket and snorted. "Late twice today for whatever reason. See you."

Maxine nodded and got off.

The elevator dropped Janet off at the fifteenth floor.

The Vice President of Operations, Evan Jonas, Charlie's boss, swore under his breath as he whisked past her into the board room. The wood-panel, plush-shag silence of the executive suite was unnerving to her, in spite her having occupied an office here for the last two years.

The chaos and bustle of an operations nerve center for ten years had hard-wired her for excitement.

She slid into her chair in the boardroom, wondering why Evan had been late also. But then, Evan was always late, and making up excuses about missed deadlines, shoddy work, and poor compliance. If I were boss, Janet thought, first thing I'd do is fire him.

Old Man Jackson cleared his throat, eyes darting between Evan and her in silent rebuke for their tardiness. Jackson's gray crown below the pink scalp reminded her she'd seen his twin brother Douglas on a San Diego street not fifteen minutes ago.

Jackson and Douglas Weintraub had pioneered the technology, moving it from laboratory to world-wide implementation in a matter of years, Douglas having decamped on the eve of the doorport's simultaneous deployment in a hundred cities across the U.S.

"How was San Diego, Janet?" Jackson asked, voice gravelly with age.

"Splendid, sir." She smiled.

"Saw my brother, I hear."

While Old Man Jackson had built the doorport network, Old Man Douglas had promulgated research that purported to show the system would eventually collapse, that space-time perturbations would cause a rift that would swallow the Earth whole. No one had been able to replicate Old Man Douglas's research.

"Heard him at the back of the room, yes. Despite our efforts to keep him out."

But the combined Weintraub research had been replicated across the globe, and thirty years ago, they'd been awarded the Nobel Peace Prize in physics. Jackson had used his half of the award to expand the network, and Douglas to decry his brother's ambition and to proclaim an impending apocalypse.

Jackson grunted. "We should have Legal look into a restraining order. Soon he'll be assaulting our staff. Evan, what's going on? You're late!"

"Doorports at San Diego and Downtown Denver went off-line for no apparent reason, sir. We're looking into it."

"That'll be my doing, Evan." Janet held up her comcard. "I had to use the prototype recalibrator to get here on time, and I was still late. I'd have warned you but didn't have—" Janet smiled "—time."

Those in the room chuckled.

"How'd it do?" Jackson asked.

"Perfect, sir," Janet said, thinking, I must have misread my watch, or set it wrong.

Jackson lifted an orange folder from the table. "Excellent work, Thompson." Her report on the lab testing, submitted just yesterday. "How soon to complete field-testing?"

"Three months max, sir," Janet said, having suspected he might ask.

"Make it two. Coordinate with operations. Evan, get R&D whatever they need. Since this will require a large scale redeployment of resources, get me an estimate of how many doorports will go idle within the year. Include projections of where these idle ports might be redeployed—and think vertical, for godsakes! I hate those blasted elevators!" Jackson pounded the table. "Report on my desk in the morning, Evan!"

"Yes, sir!" Evan looked as if he'd been struck by lightning.

Two hundred million doorports in the United States alone.

He'll be up all night, Janet thought, knowing her task would be equally difficult.

"Yes, Mr. Weintraub?" Janet asked, entering his office.

Those dreaded words during the meeting had come just afterward —"Please see me immediately after the meeting, Ms. Thompson"—and she'd waited as everyone else had left, then had followed Old Man Jackson to his office.

"Call me Jackson, goddammit," he said, as usual.

"Yes, Jackson goddammit," she said, smiling sweetly.

He threw back his head and roared. "Glad our corporate stuffiness hasn't diluted your piss 'n' vinegar. Hate those suits. You know how many Vice Presidents we got? Twelve! I could fire 'em all and not a thing would change. How are you, Janet?"

"Wonderful, Jackson." She didn't remind him she was Vice President of R&D. "How are your boys?"

"Eh? Can't get the Senator from Massachusetts to return my calls, and the Attorney General of Florida keeps our lawyers hoppin'."

Bragging by complaint, she thought, liking him greatly. Earlier, confronted by his twin brother, she'd had to summon her courage to defy him, forgetting momentarily that she worked for Jackson, not Jackson's twin brother.

"How's Frank? Job's still open when he's done with that fathering."

Janet shook her head at him. "You knew one of us would have to be at home with the kids. Why him and not me? He's as smart as I am." Although an engineer, Frank had gone into finance and was CFO.

"You're the visionary," Jackson said. "And he and I get in too many tiffs, both of us too strong-headed." Then he glanced out the window.

Downtown Denver, the Capitol dome gleaming not far off, beyond it the Basilica clock tower. The office was floor-to-ceiling window on three sides, along the fourth wall, two doors. One led out, the other to Jackson's personal lair, where no one but Jackson went.

Janet had never seen the inside of the lair. It was rumored a pigsty, filing cabinets bursting with paper, diagrams crowding each other for wall space, not a single window, and one glaring, uncovered incandescent lamp.

"How's my brother?" Jackson asked.

"Didn't have the opportunity to ask; he was waiting for me when I came out, started spouting his usual drivel. Said, 'They won't let you see the projections. They won't let you see the equations.' Then he handed me this." She tossed the memchip onto his desk.

He raised his eyebrow at her. "That's the reason I snatched you from your post-doctorate at MIT, you know?"

"What?" Janet was surprised. She'd never fully understood why a conglomerate like American Doorport would offer a twenty-eight year old brainiac without a moment of private-sector experience a whopping salary at a management-track technician's position.

"Take a week. Turn your duties over to your team. Look at those equations." Jackson pushed the chip back toward her with the eraser of a pencil, as though it might be infected. "Decide for yourself if there's any merit to what he's propounding. I can't see it, but your Space-Time Harmonics are sharper than mine. That's what I saw in your work at MIT."

She looked at the chip. She looked up at him. "You have some doubts."

"Keeps me up at night, Janet."

He looks old right now, she thought, seeing his sloped shoulders and slouched posture as though for the first time. "You're not gonna like this, Jackson."

He met her gaze, the weight of the ninety years clear in his eyes. "Out with it, whatever it is."

And she told him about the two incidents earlier.

"That was the other reason I snatched you from MIT—your bluntness. Who else knows?"

"Charlie Goodrich, but only about the first."

Jackson nodded. "You trust his work? Everyone else thinks it's sloppy."

Janet shrugged. "I do. In a pinch, he comes through like no one else."

"Good enough. On that second one, you used the prototype?"

She nodded. "Don't know if that's what introduced the anomaly."

"I want you and Charlie on this—just you two, all right? Think he'll transfer temporarily to Denver without problem?"

Janet shook her head. "He hates the cold. I'll go there. Fewer distractions."

"One week," Jackson said.

"One week," Janet said, standing and retrieving the chip.

"Oh, by the way," Jackson said, standing also and stepping around the desk. "Here's some additional information you'll need." He handed her another chip. "Give my regards to Frank."

"Certainly, Jackson." She pocketed both and stopped at the door to look back.

He stood looking out the window, his back to her, slouched forward, only the pink scalp and grey crown visible above his collar.

He's already forgotten me, Janet knew.

Chapter 3

Janet couldn't believe they were talking about her like that.

"As an only child grows up, competition occurs only in extra-familial settings," Frank said, speaking to her father. "In families where there aren't other prominent issues such as alcoholism, chronic illness, or workaholism, an only child doesn't have to compete for the parents' attentions." Frank had studied psychology before getting into physics. He and her parents were conversing after dinner. "Without such competition, an only child can more easily think that he or she is more deserving or entitled, may become more demanding and self-centered, less empathetic toward others and less insightful into the effect they have on other people."

"That doesn't happen with all one-child families, does it?" her mother asked, her grandchildren curled up beside her and sleeping peacefully.

"No, no," Frank said, "of course not. The parent's skills have a far greater impact than the lack of competition for parental attention. When there's a distinct absence of those skills and a lack of other protective factors—grandparents aren't present, daycare or school or other systemic agents don't respond—then it's more likely to happen, but it's not a certainty by any means."

A frown on her face, Janet wasn't completely sure they weren't referring to her.

"Doesn't a lot of that depend on the child?" her father asked. A former Denver County Sheriff, he was a big, busty man. "After all, Janet knew what she wanted from the moment she was born."

"Daddy!" she said, giving him a mock scowl. She didn't know whether to be miffed that they were talking about her, or that they weren't.

"It very much does," Frank said. "High energy versus low energy, extrovert versus introvert, externally guided versus internally guided —all factors in whether the child responds well or badly to being the only child."

Janet yawned, envying her children, remembering how she'd always liked curling up on the couch next to one parent or the other.

"Well, I suppose we should be going," her father said, "I know you're out of town for the next week or so, Janet, so we'll let you turn in early."

"Thank you, Dad, appreciate it," Janet said, standing to see them to the doorport, while Frank took each of the sleepy children to bed.

"I heard an interview with Douglas Weintraub yesterday," her father said on their way to the garage.

"That lunatic," Janet said, snorting dismissively.

"Sounded reasonable to me," he replied.

"Scientifically unsound," Janet replied, knowing she hadn't yet reviewed the information he'd given her that morning. "Are you and Mom going to be all right? It's pretty late. You sure you don't want someone going with you?"

Not all of the doorport transit points were safely guarded or secure. Some, such as the sprawling complex near New York City, housed in the terminal that used to be JFK airport, were self-contained communities, operating 24/7, cameras everywhere, and staffed by TSA security guards. Others, such as neighborhood hubs, were open plazas.

"We'll be fine, dear," her mother said. "We'll take a few more door-ports to avoid the risky ones."

"All right, since it's not that late," Janet told her. "If it were much later, I'd be concerned."

"Well, thank you," her mother said, looking at the doorports in their garage. "Oh my, you've added one since we were here last. How can you afford it, with Frank on leave?"

"Company doorport," Janet explained. "Takes me right to Corporate. They insisted on installing it."

"Must think you're important, or something," her mother said.

Janet shrugged, suppressing a smile. "I deserve it."

Her mother and father laughed and stepped to the correct doorport, arm in arm.

"Here, let me," Janet said. She waved her comcard across the sensor. "No charge. Bye!"

They waved and stepped through the shimmering doorport together.

Frank was just coming out of the kid's room when Janet got upstairs.

He greeted her with a kiss. "I'm glad they only had one of you," he said.

"I'd have *never* gotten along with a sibling," Janet said.

"I've *never* gotten along with my sister," Janet said, looking at Charlie over her cup of coffee. They were sitting in Charlie's office in the Systems Maintenance Headquarters West, the nerve center for operations, overseeing nearly seventy-five million doorports from Denver to Honolulu. Out the window to the east was the Sierra Nevada Mountain range.

They'd hauled in a desk for Janet to sit at for the week while she and Charlie sorted through the anomalies she'd encountered and looked closely at the two chips given to her, one from each of the Old Men Weintraub.

"She sure seems to have taken a dislike to your work," Charlie said, viewing a newsfeed on his tactiface. "Listen to this: Cynthia McLoughlin, leader of the Divine Church of the Temporal Apocalypse, is ironically the younger sister of Janet Thompson, Vice President of Research and Development at American Doorport. The two sisters, each highly regarded in her own field, appear to have embarked on careers at polar opposites to each other, and ones about to collide—"

"Charlie, cut the drivel. Sounds like you're reading from the pages of the National Inquisitor, not the business section of the New York Times. What'd she do to make the news?"

Charlie chuckled. "Protest rally in Times Square. Drew a hundred thousand people. Her'n Old Man Douglas pairin' up a few years ago seems to have sparked a movement."

"Her crackpot theology and his crackpot science," Janet said, holding the two chips in her hand. "She left her post-doctorate studies at Harvard Divinity School just a month after I graduated MIT. We haven't talked in years, her and I."

"Doesn't sound cordial, your relationship."

Janet frowned. "Not at all. My parents were over last night, begging me to give her another chance. At the same time she's holding a rally to denounce the very work I do!" She sighed and sipped her coffee. "I feel sad for them. Seeing their daughters clash the way we do must tear them apart! I had a dream last night that my husband and parents were talking about my being an only child. A form of wish fulfillment, I suppose."

Charlie regarded her from beside his tactiface.

"I know that look," Janet said.

Charlie smiled and looked down at his hands.

"C'mon. You want to say something and don't want me to take it wrong."

"That's the look." Charlie said, nodding. "Janet, you've changed. In the year since you headed to Corporate, I don't know what's happened. There's an edge to you that wasn't there before. Now I know R&D has a rigid side to it, and frankly, you're better suited to rolling up your shirtsleeves than you are to wading through paper, but that doesn't account for it, either."

Janet mulled it over for a moment. "I was thinking yesterday about the wood-panel, plush-carpet silence of Corporate, and how much I miss the chaos here." She could feel his scrutiny, and she reminded herself that she had worked alongside Charlie for nearly ten years, up until her transfer to Corporate two years ago. "Sounds like you miss the old Janet."

"Yeah, I guess I do," Charlie said, sighing.

"Thanks," Janet said, smiling wistfully.

"Hey, uh, Janet?"

She heard the change of topic in his voice. "Yeah?"

"Why'd Old Man Jackson send you out here?"

"You mean, 'Why couldn't I have commuted?'" She stood and stepped to his desk, showing him the two memchips in her hand. "Old Man Douglas gave me this one, said it had equations they won't let me see, and when I told Old Man Jackson about it, he handed me the other, saying, 'Here's some additional information you'll need.' "

"And you haven't looked at either, have you?"

"I swear, Charlie, sometimes I think you know me better than my husband. Besides, Old Man Jackson wanted me to take a week off before we start field testing the prototype."

Charlie held out his hand to take one. "Old Man Douglas gave you this one?" He whistled tonelessly. "And Old Man Jackson didn't blow you into the next century for talking to him?"

"Oddly enough, no. In fact, he sounded concerned." Janet looked at Charlie and they stared at each other for a full ten seconds.

"What do you suppose is on this one?" Charlie held up the other memchip.

Janet shrugged. "Let's take a look."

Charlie popped the chip into his tactiface. Multiple pictures appeared, and he tapped one.

The photograph was unremarkable, a head shot, underneath it a name, beside it basic demographics, at the bottom a narrative.

Charlie read it off. "Thirty-seven year old Caucasian male from Minneapolis Minnesota, disappeared January twentieth, twenty-one thirty-five, stepped into a doorport in downtown, never reappeared at the doorport in the suburb of Water Park, cause attributed to a lightning strike at the moment of transport, which knocked out the receiving terminal."

Charlie swept his hand left to right across the screen, bringing up the next profile. "Fourteen year old African-American female from Raleigh, North Carolina, disappeared August tenth, twenty-one thirty-three, stepped into her home doorport to the Oakwood Park transit plaza during a category-three tornado, receiving terminal knocked out by the storm at the moment of transport."

"How many are on there, Charlie?"

"Let's see." He minimized that screen, then minimized again, and again, each time showing more profiles. Finally he tapped "List All" and read the number to her.

"And that's all that's on there?" Janet asked.

Charlie nodded. "Pretty obvious why Jackson would give that to you."

"He mustn't think these are accidents." Janet went back to her tactiface, Douglas's chip in her hand, ruminating. "Charlie, can you get me a doorport activity trace on a couple of those?"

"Like a list of ports by date and time? Yeah, I can do that. It's all on the mainframe."

Janet smiled. Odd that we still call it that. An old term from the twentieth century when computers emerged, mainframe referred to the old warehouse-sized array of tubes and wires. Now of course, quart- to gallon-size biological protein soups stored a quintillion times more information. Furthermore, the company biocomputer was itself housed inside a harmonic aperture to keep it safe from natural disasters, with multiple redundant databases backed up real-time in five other harmonic aperture locations.

Janet was about to plug in the Douglas chip.

"Hey, hold up," Charlie said. "I pulled a profile at random. Listen to this:"Twenty-eight year old Caucasian female, resident of Albany, New York, died of cancer of the throat after a long, protracted illness. Multiple daily portations between Princeton, New Jersey, where she was a research assistant, Times Square, where she was an entertainer, and home. Died October twenty-nine, twenty-one thirty-nine."

"Guess a girl's gotta work her way through college," Janet said.

Charlie nearly choked on his coffee.

"How could she be going to school and work—and *not* to doctor's appointments, radiology, chemotherapy—when she's dying of cancer? Why don't you run a doorport activity trace on that one? Pick out a few more while I look at Old Man Douglas's chip."

"All right," Charlie said, his hands flying across the tactiface.

Janet plugged it in, and her tactiface displayed a single file. On the screen was a schematic showing the mathematical progressions for space-time harmonic physics. Twelve years ago, she had danced through these progressions in her post-doctoral studies at MIT, but as she worked the progressions in her head now, she felt slow, as though wading through mud.

Her comcard in her pocket buzzed. "This is Janet," she said, pulling it out and cradling it in her lap.

"Hey, Janet, Stan, listen, we got an odd request. A Denver County Sheriff's Deputy is asking for records related to a missing persons."

Janet looked at the face on her comcard. Her personal secretary knew when to bother her and not. This is important, he was saying.

"Sorry, it's important."

"All right, and why not route his request through legal?"

"Says he knows your father. I said I'd try but I didn't promise anything."

Janet frowned. "All right, then. Send me his contact, and I'll call."

"Sure, and thanks, Janet." Stan smiled and his face shrank as the call disconnected.

Janet returned her attention to the progressions. A mainframe the size of the company's processed one calibration—once through the entire sequence in front of her—in less time than it took her to blink. Quintaflops per second, she'd been told. Two hundred million doors in the United States, most of them used multiple times per day. Ten to the power of fifty calculations, minimum.

"Hey, Janet, you gonna break for lunch?"

The sun outside glared off the snow-capped mountains to the east. She nodded, unaware three hours had passed, the equations coming back to her slowly. "You going out for something?"

"Yeah, sure. Come with, or you'll drive yourself crazy."

She smiled. "I promise I'll stop at dinner. Bring me something, would you?"

Charlie rolled his eyes but nodded. "Back soon."

Alterlude #2

Suzanne Jacqueline Roberts, Esq., Attorney at Law, Inc., frowned at life, disgusted.

She looked out the window of her old brick office building and sneezed. Oh, no, she thought, not another cold. But she knew from the rush of heat that followed it was too late—she'd already caught it. That's the third one this year. That's what I get for sitting in a cold, drafty building, day after day, in the middle of winter.

She blew her nose and shook her head at herself, then returned her attention to the legal brief in front of her. The Friend-of-the-Court brief had been filed on behalf of a plaintiff suing Mountain Power for destruction of habitat on her twenty-acre farm downhill from a power-line clearcut, the runoff from a cloudburst a year ago having washed away the topsoil and the plaintiff's barn and back acre preserve with it. She'd won a similar case last year, which had garnered enough in the way of fees that she'd been able to afford an office, rather than work from home. She still had to do all the work herself, unable to afford law clerks or secretaries.

A beat-up tactiface perched precariously on the right side of the desk. The left side was piled high with docupads, cases she'd agreed to take on the behalf of mostly poor clients against primarily rich corporations with legions of lawyers at their disposal. Out the window, the frames peeling paint, the State Capitol was barely visible above other surrounding buildings. The office had seen better days, the carpet worn and shedding nap in a couple places, the furniture mismatched and stained, the ceiling missing a few tiles.

All that, and I awoke this morning in a cold bed, alone.

Looking around her office, Suzanne sighed at how screwed up her life was, rubbing her bare ring finger.

Suzanne's last date had been with a County Alderman ten years her senior whose philandering ex-wife had made him look like a pimp, and that date had been eight months ago to a Nuggets basketball game where the box seats had given her butt cramps and the smell of beer wafting from below had made her nauseous and the noise had given her a migraine. The date five months before that had been with a physician so full of himself he hadn't the slightest interest in anything except the wart on her cheek which she'd always thought cute and he'd said might be cancerous. Eighteen months ago was the last time someone had asked her out and that had only been to try to seduce her into a compromising photo shoot at a seedy motel to derail her prosecution of a defamation suit against a newspaper. And the last time she'd had rousing sex was that college quarterback who'd happily gored her at her request but had been dumb as an ox and just as clumsy.

At least he'd been nice about it, Suzanne thought. But then he'd never returned her calls.

She straightened the collar of her limp tweed jacket, smoothed her impossibly wrinkled skirt, and decided to get some lunch. She pulled on her coat and went out the door, barely able to pull it shut behind her because of the wood-swell. Two blocks from her office was the nearest set of doorports. She tucked her face into her lapels and pushed against the biting wind, her walk as brisk as the noonday weather.

Not many pedestrians in this area, the buildings mostly old and neglected.

No lines at the doorports, she saw. Not like other areas. She waved her comcard across the doorport sensor, and as the light blinked green, she stepped into the shimmer and out into Civic Center Park.

The first pushcart vendor she came across was hawking hot dogs slathered with chili.

Hot comfort food for a cold winter day.

Suzanne strode among the trees, enjoying the chili dog, knowing

253

she'd have heartburn later. With a belch, she finished it off, wiped her face the best she could, and turned toward the bank of doorports. Towering above them was the State Capitol. Suzanne looked at some of the surrounding buildings.

I'd just die to have a view of the Capitol, she thought.

Sighing, she turned to the doorports, found hers, swiped her comcard, and stepped through.

Her office building was a few steps from the bank of doorports. She entered the lobby, noting some of the looks she drew, her suit the finest Armani, her shoes Italian leather, her jewelry subdued silver-and-diamond Giorgio originals. Sometimes, she even drove her Jaguar XJ-9.

Yes, in these days of doorports, the price of gas at forty dollars a gallon, Suzanne still drove a car. Once per week, home to office, a distance of a mile, and then office to home, each mile taxed at a hundred dollars, a GPS locator measuring the distance she drove.

She rode the elevator to the top and stepped into the marble-floored foyer.

"Suzanne Jacqueline Roberts-Carter, Esq., Attorney at Law, Inc." emblazoned in six-inch gold letters across the lintel.

Her staff awaited her just inside the doors. Law clerk, Junior Partner, Secretary.

She smiled and snarled at the law clerk. "I want the brief on Delaware vs MacDougal, twenty thirty, now!"

The clerk fled.

Suzanne scowled at the inch-thick folder that her Junior Partner had handed to her. "Is this EPA vs BP, Exxon, et. al., twenty seventy-five? All right, now how about the summary? Think I can read a hundred-page decision in five minutes?"

The Junior Partner was clenching his fists, a vein pulsing at his temple, his color not quite yet the shade Suzanne was looking for.

"What are you waiting for?!" she roared, and flung it at him. "Summary back to me in ten minutes, dammit!"

He caught it awkwardly, his glasses half off his face. He stomped back to his office, his face precisely the bright crimson Suzanne had wanted.

She snorted in pleased disgust. "I'll take my messages in my office."

"Yes, Ms. Roberts," her secretary said.

Suzanne was already striding away.

The carpet was thick, without a flaw, and silent under her heels.

She entered her office, strode around her desk and contemplated the clearly-visible Capitol Dome a few blocks to the west. *Top corporate defense attorney, and I can't get decent help. What kind of morons are law schools churning out these days! I've got a deposition to decimate in Federal Circuit Court of Appeals in two hours, a civil suit entering closing arguments tomorrow against Mountain Power that won't stand a chance after I'm done with the rebuttal, twelve requests from regional and national firms wanting me to save their asses from regulatory mires that they walked into face-first like blindfolded fools, and four subpoenas from the Colorado State Legislature wanting my testimony on water diversions by companies I represented in the last Colorado River watershed negotiations.*

Suzanne heard a soft knock behind her. "Yes, Pamela?"

Her secretary stepped into her office. "There are two voicemails, three vidmails, and twelve emails."

"I can't believe people are still using voicemail!" Suzanne hissed. "Let me hear those first." She continued to stare out the window.

"Certainly, Ms. Roberts," her secretary said.

"Ms. Roberts," the frail voice of an old woman said, "I need your help. My husband disappeared into a doorport a year ago and hasn't been seen since. The police haven't been able to find him—they laugh at me when they look up his name. They call me senile and say he died three years ago, but I know he didn't. I want your help in suing American Doorport. They caused him to disappear. I've got proof. Please help me. I'm seventy-five years old and I don't have much money. It's not about the money. It's about their taking from me the only source of happiness I've ever had in my life. No, it won't bring my husband back, but maybe it'll stop them from making other people disappear. Please, Ms. Roberts, please help me."

Somewhere deep in memory, as though in a dream, Suzanne saw herself arguing a case against American Doorport. Of course, she was already on retainer with them. Suzanne wasn't averse to suing big corporations, but her specialty was in defending them.

From little old ladies like this one.

"Have that new clerk look into it, Pamela. What's his name?"

"John, Ms. Roberts."

"Might as well see if American Doorport needs a little defending. Next message, please," Suzanne said.

"Hi, Suzanne, this is your sweetie saying I love you and that wonderful little thing you did last night with that string of pearls, oh my—"

Her secretary shut it off, turning red. "My apologies, Ms. Roberts, it wasn't marked confidential, and—"

"Not to worry, not your fault," Suzanne said, warmed by the message and trying not to blush. "Just transfer it to my personal box, but do send dear Tommy a dozen roses for me, would you?"

"Yes, Ms. Roberts," her secretary said, giggling.

Suzanne smiled, remembering his warmth and fullness last night. She caressed the pistachio-size diamond on her left ring finger, their wedding last year having been the social event of the decade, their reception held at the Hyatt across from the State Capitol and all the socialites from the region attending.

Suzanne Jacqueline Roberts-Carter, Esq., Attorney at Law, Inc., sighed at how perfect life was for her.

Chapter 4

Charlie frowned at Janet when he came through the door. Bright rays slanted across her desk, the sun barely clearing the Sierra Nevadas.

"How do you do it?" he asked.

Janet smiled. "Look so refreshed and clean after working "til midnight, sleeping on a cot, getting up at dawn, and having none of my usual beautification appliances around me?"

"Yeah! I can barely function with all that. Take it away and I'm a helpless doddering old fart!"

She shook her head. "Leave a girl a few secrets, would you? I made you some coffee, oh, and I brought the crew some donuts—in the break room." She'd enjoyed seeing all her old acquaintances, people she'd worked alongside for five years, and then had supervised for another five.

"Thank you." He shook his head. "You always were the first one in. Set a hell of an example for everyone else." Charlie parked himself at his desk.

Janet browsed the equations given her by Old Man Douglas. Yesterday, she had borrowed a biocomputer from corporate to have it run simulations all night with these equations, using yesterday's real-time requests for harmonic aperture calibrations.

Among the equations on the memchip were long-term projections of harmonic integrity, based on predisposing assumptions that bore little relation to actual conditions. The summaries all indicated disasters beyond reckoning, some of them so wildly fantastic that Janet had laughed aloud. Among the projections however was a common theme: Since space-time perturbations had never been experienced nor documented, people would not necessarily know they were happening. People's subjective experience of both space and time being fixed and concrete, any distortions in either would be rationalized to fit into that subjective experience, and unlikely to be recognized as anomalous to those frameworks.

"You want to hear what I came up with yesterday?" Charlie asked.

Janet looked over from her desk, enjoying the sunshine. "On those glitches I encountered the other day?"

Charlie nodded. "There's indication of a power variation at the moment you stepped into the doorport. Denver Con Edison reports a transformer blew a half a second before the port, perhaps introducing enough of a voltage variation to send you astray. Pretty similar to some of those vignettes collected by Old Man Jackson."

"But we've had back up on every set of doors for twenty years for precisely that reason."

"I know, I know," Charlie replied, "and that's the part I still haven't figured out. Voltage regulators on the Denver port were replaced last year during regular maintenance. And it wouldn't have been the electromagnetic field disruption either—the transformer was just a couple feet from the doorport—since all doorports are shielded."

Janet frowned. "What about the protein components?"

Charlie raised an eyebrow at her. "Do you think the amylase-transferase magnetic alignment might have been disrupted?"

She shrugged. "Have your guys down in the biochem run a few tests. Just in case. And let's get a rep from Con Edison to give us GPS coordinates of all their transformers. We've got enough headaches without this becoming one."

"I'll get on it," Charlie said. "Now about the other one."

She looked at him when he didn't continue. "I'm not gonna like this."

"You're not gonna like this."

She sighed. "So why'd I arrive in Denver fifteen minutes after I stepped into the doorport in San Diego?"

Charlie smiled. "Based on doorport records—recorded on two

different bioprotein servers mind you—you spent fifteen minutes in some sort of harmonic limbo."

The silence ticked away between them, Janet trying to reconcile the "limbo" within the framework of the space-time harmonic progressions. Then she tried to match one of the predisposing assumption scenarios on the memchip to the "limbo" in which she had spent fifteen minutes of her life.

She turned to look at Charlie. "All right, I give up. This doesn't fit either our known harmonic framework, or these wild assumptions that Old Man Douglas describes on this chip."

Charlie looked at her tactiface behind her. "Any substance to those 'crackpot' predictions?"

Janet shook her head. "The predisposing assumptions that serve as base points are so extreme that they bear little resemblance to real-world conditions. But there is one global assumption that Douglas makes that isn't borne out: That people won't recognize space-time perturbations because our views of both phenomena are so fixed."

"Sounds like the 'It doesn't make sense to me so I'll make something up so it does make sense' rule."

Janet nodded. "People do it all the time. It's when they do it in the face of changing reality—like time or space—that worries me. Clearly it doesn't always hold true, but if I hadn't had my grandmother's old mechanical watch, I might have rationalized away the missing fifteen minutes. But the fact is, I was noplace, notime for fifteen minutes. And we can be sure of two things—it isn't the first time it's happened and it won't be the last."

Charlie and Janet stared at each other, thinking the same thing: Just how safe is the doorport network?

Janet and Charlie walked up the steps of the old Victorian on the south side of Albany.

"Parker" announced the lighted sign under the mailbox.

The fiftyish man who answered the door asked, "Who wants to know?"

"My name is Janet Thompson, and I'm Vice President of Research and Development at American Doorport." She held out a business card.

"And I'm Charlie Good—"

The door slammed in their faces.

Janet and Charlie looked at each other, their breath fogging the space between them, the walk from the local transit plaza slippery with ice, a fine powder beginning to fall.

Janet pulled out her comcard. "Hi, Mr. Parker? We're here because we think we've made a terrible error. May we come in?"

A few minutes later, Mr. Parker returned to the door. "You hounded us for months after our daughter died." Mrs. Parker stepped up behind him. "And then you sent the bill to collections and sued us in court."

"And on behalf of American Doorport, I'm here to apologize," Janet said. "We compounded your loss terribly, and it was wrong for us to do that."

Mr. and Mrs. Parker stared at them for a few minutes, standing on the stoop in the cold gray afternoon light.

Janet blinked back tears when she realized Mrs. Parker was crying softly.

Mr. Parker guided his wife back into the house, leaving the door open for them.

Janet and Charlie followed them in and stood in the entryway. Mrs. Parker had found a chair and held her face in her hands, inconsolable. Mr. Parker turned toward them. "Come on in," he said, gesturing to the couch. A tear dripped off his chin as he reached for a tissue. "I'm Charlie, too," he said, extending a hand.

"Like the bassist," Charlie said.

Charlie Parker nodded. "My great grandfather. Didn't know anyone remembered him."

Janet looked around. The oval rug extended under the sofa on one side and the two armchairs on the other. A third wall was a window to a quaint backyard. A stairway beside the door led upstairs, the railing a polished pine. Opposite the stairway was what looked like a kitchen door, a dinette just visible from where Janet sat.

"Your home is beautiful," she said. "Your daughter must've been happy here."

"She was so active, she was hardly here," Mrs. Parker said, sniffling. "I'm Eileen."

"Nice to meet you both," Janet said. "When did your daughter have to give up her studies because of the throat cancer?"

Charlie scratched his temple. "Couldn't have been more than a year before she died." He looked at his wife. "She stopped going to

Princeton in December, just one semester shy of her Master's. Isn't that about right?"

Eileen nodded. "We were so proud of her. Didn't borrow a dime, not from the government, not from us. Well, not until she got sick, that is."

Janet nodded. "Probably couldn't work anymore."

The Parkers shook their heads, exchanging an uncomfortable glance.

"And she didn't have any health insurance, did she?"

Again the Parkers shook their heads.

Charlie cleared his throat. "Janet and I, we need some information."

Eileen frowned. "We've sent you everything already. Doctor's appointments, radiology, chemotherapy, dates, times, com numbers, addresses. What more could you want?"

Janet smiled. "The bills themselves."

The Parkers looked at each other and then looked at her. "I don't understand," Charlie Parker said. "Why would you need those?"

"We can't reverse what's happened. There isn't anything to be done, because nothing's going to bring your daughter back. If nothing else, in apology for doorport charges that she clearly could not have accrued and that we should never have billed in the first place, we'd like to offer to pay those bills."

Janet held up a picture.

Professor Turnbull waved it away. "One of my best research assistants and well on her way to becoming my protégé—one who would have far exceeded her teacher. What do you want to know about Angelica Parker?"

"When did she have to quit because of the throat cancer?"

"December, twenty-one thirty-eight. Only lived ten more months. By November, she was dragging herself here. She had gaunt, deep, dark circles under her eyes, her throat bandaged all different ways, wore turtlenecks to spare the rest of us from how bad it really looked. Fainted three or four times at her desk, and nobody knew. Nary a word of complaint." Professor Turnbull shook his head and thumbed a tear from his eye.

"Thank you, Professor," Charlie said.

Janet approached the young woman as she headed for the back

door, up a Times Square alley that stank of urine and rotting vegetables. Charlie waited at the alley entrance.

"What do you want? I'll be late!" The young woman stepped past her, eyes running up and down Janet's body.

Unaccustomed to being undressed by a woman, Janet shivered. "I'll come with you," she said, pulling her coat tight. "Tell me about Angelica." Janet followed her into the rear entrance.

"Who?"

Janet held up a photo.

The young woman giggled. "I've never seen her without make up. Look, I can't help you, all right?" She tried to escape down a hallway, doors lining one side of it.

Old sweat, loud thumping and sour beer wafted to Janet from the other end. Determined, she tried to follow.

"Hey, Danielle, can you get this bitch off my ass?"

A six-six blonde with a garish top and no bottom came around the corner at the other end. Blonde on top only, she saw instantly. "Awwright, what ya want?!" In two strides she towered over Janet.

At six-even, Janet was more accustomed to the opposite. "Can you tell me about her?" she asked, holding up a picture, about to pee her pantsuit.

"Awww, it's Missy. She could really shake it." Danielle said, taking it from her. "Whatever you want to know, it'll cost you." Danielle held out her hand.

"When did she last work?" Janet asked.

Danielle scowled. "You don't get it, do you?" The leggy blonde with carrot bottom lifted one of her tree trunks straight over her head and put her foot on the ceiling. "You see this," she said, pointing to the pink gaping clearly between the orange. "That's my bank account. I don't do anything without a deposit in my bank account. Now for you, since you are such a nice lady, I'll let you put your deposit in my hand." Danielle dropped her leg and opened her palm.

Janet swallowed, trying not to retch. "When did she last work?" she asked, groping in her purse.

Danielle just grinned at her, obviously enjoying her discomfiture.

Janet put a hundred-dollar bill in her hand, reluctant to make even that contact.

"Whassa matter? I ain't got cooties. Missy there worked up until

September. By then she was so thin her ribs were showing, emphasized her nicely, but the customers started razzing me about makin' the sick girl work. Customers asked about her for months after she stopped dancing. Nice girl, smart as a whip, gave it her all. You look like you're a sharp one, too. Ever show yourself off?"

Janet felt undressed again. "Thanks," and she bolted as fast as she could.

Janet looked at Charlie as soon as they returned to the office.

"Either our billing system has gone on a rampage," Charlie said, "or all those people are crazy."

Janet frowned, thinking back to her days at MIT. "I had a professor who insisted on starting every seminar with one admonition. He said, 'All points in space exist at one point in space. All points in time exist at one point in time.' And he would say that there's a third possibility." She smiled at Charlie.

"That both are true?"

"Uh-huh. The billing system is accurate and all those people did experience what they say they did."

"What about the discrepancies? This girl had to have used door-ports to get to her doctors' appointments. Where are those records? And why does the mainframe have records of ports that the young woman never took?"

"I guess that's what Old Man Jackson wants us to figure out." Janet frowned at Charlie.

Alterlude #3

Zachary Hempstead arrived at home, cold, hopeless, and depressed.

I should just kill myself and get it over with.

His day at the newspaper had been horrific, his boss at the suburban weekly wanting him to write a puff piece on a strip-mall owner, while his exposé on kickbacks to the local alderman gathered dust.

"It was trash like that that got you fired at the Denver Post!" she'd told him. "When you walk in front of a train, all you'll become is a hood ornament on a locomotive!" The crotchety old lady always spoke in outdated analogies, which was part of the reason she managed a suburban weekly, and not an inner city daily.

His apartment above the pawnshop was a wreck. Clothes strewn across the couch, some washed and others long since needing it; dishes stacked in the sink, perhaps the source of the faintly odorous miasma; garbage not quite contained by the cabinet under the sink, also the possible source of the distasteful aroma; flecks of dust, paper, hair and other daily detritus leaving the area with telltale signs of disorganization; stacks of unopened correspondence, among the pile a likely summons for unpaid loitering and disorderly conduct fines, a hazard of the work he did; and silence.

Blessed, cursed silence.

The silence of singularity. Not loneliness, which he had long since set aside as irremedial, but of certainty that he would always be alone. The silence of isolation. Not quite self-sufficient, which he had long since abandoned as being impossible to achieve, but of that resentful resignation that he had to depend on others, much to his profound disgust and dislike, and which he did only reluctantly and only when he had to.

Always the silence.

But never where he needed it: in his head.

In his head there was no peace, a fact evident on his face. But to ask him would earn the rebuke: "Nothing." Consistent amidst the noise was the self-recrimination: "I could have had a Pulitzer."

At the Post, five years ago, he had caught wind of the source of the terrible toll heroin abuse was taking in Philadelphia, New York, Boston, Washington DC, Atlanta, Miami, and every other U.S. city above five million. Heroin was flooding the streets, leaving junkies and occasional users dead from overdose in droves, the powder so pure that the slightest mismeasure was easy to make even for the most experienced mainliner.

The war in Pakanistan had done nothing to stem production for the worldwide heroin market. The tribal warlords ensconced as they'd always been in the Hindu Kush were hungry for cash to fuel their warring. And they'd found an ally in the Central Intelligence Bureau.

Zachary, a veteran reporter for the Denver Post, had stumbled across a young, newly-emigrated Pakani who'd told a wild tale. Old fashioned aeroplanes taking off from airstrips in Iran and Bangladesh to Hong Kong and Turkey, laden like wallowing sows with bales of black, sticky poppy blossoms so heavy the planes barely flew, the tar leaving black trails on the tarmacs. Crews of bare-chested Pakanis loading these bales into cargoports. Refineries in the Mexican Sierra Madre Mountains and the jungles of the Yucatan Peninsula rendering the sticky blossoms down to the finest white powders. Bricks of compressed powder, ported into inner-city destinations. Small, white packets of the finest, purest heroin seen on an American city street costing a fraction of its nearest competitor.

And each link supported and protected under subcontracts with shadow corporations set up by but run independently of the Central Intelligence Bureau.

Zachary Hempstead would not have believed it, if the young

Pakani had not shown him the records regarding one such shipment. The Pakani had died the next day, and Zachary had gone underground for a year, working his way backward through the supply chain, carefully documenting the doorport numbers, the transit dates and times, the employee and subcontractor names, the tailfin numbers of the old fashioned aeroplanes. In addition to drugs, there was the flow of money, which had to be laundered, likewise through CIB shadow companies and contractors.

And then there were the weapons purchases. The handheld rockets gone astray en route to other hotspots, the weapons mimickers in Indonesian and Indian sweatshops, whose poor manufacturing standards often resulted in the trigger puller being as likely to die as the target.

For a year Zachary had documented it all, and in one lightning month he had compiled a book complete with names, dates, and amounts, ready to publish. He had made the mistake of offering first publishing rights to the Denver Post and its parent company the Blackstone Publishing Empire. The series set to be published four Sundays in a row, the first installment of the expose was considered so inflammatory that the second part never saw the light of day, killed by the publisher, Editor and CEO of Blackstone Publishing, JK Blackstone.

The Denver Post was immediately excoriated in print, video, audio, web, blog, tweet, com, and blurb. The Blackstone Publishing Empire was threatened with Federal confiscation and defamation lawsuits, if it did not print a thorough retraction and an uncompromising repudiation of its author.

And thus Zachary's career had plummeted in flames, like one of those old aeroplane analogies used anachronistically by the Old Dame.

Zachary looked around his nearly empty apartment, wondering why he continued to live this nearly empty life. He shuffled to the kitchen, shedding his scarred leather jacket over the back of a chair whose stuffing was bursting from multiple rips in its fabric. He looked into his nearly empty refrigerator. One frozen dinner left. He looked into his nearly empty flatware drawer. One olive fork left.

With a sigh, he threw the frozen dinner back in the freezer, threw the olive fork back in the drawer, and walked to the closet beside the door.

He stood in front of the open closet, looking at the upper shelf. He knew what was up there. He didn't know if he had the courage.

I won't know if I don't try, he thought.

After clearing a place, he sat on the couch, then cleared a spot on the coffee table to set the box he'd got off the shelf.

He stared at the lid for a period of time that escaped measure. His arms felt like lead as he lifted. Underneath the pistol gleamed. The gun felt light in his hands—as light as his arms felt heavy. He looked in the magazine. One single bullet left.

He wondered if he should eat first. The irony of a last dinner, with a last fork, before shooting himself with a last bullet, was lost on him.

The gun metal was cold comfort.

With a sigh, he threw the gun back in the box, threw the lid back on the box, threw the box back in the closet.

Not tonight.

He ate doggedly, tasting nothing, and then he belched and set the empty foil tray on top of the stack at the end of the table.

His eyelids grew heavy and he wondered if he should go to bed.

Maybe I'll sleep forever.

Maybe I'll wake up a different person.

His alarm went off at its usual time, and he rolled over and put his feet to the floor, his despair flooding through him again.

He slogged through his morning routine, then slinked out his door and down the stairs, the smell of urine more pungent this morning, fresh stains at the base of the stairwell.

The line at the doorport was mercifully short. He waved his card, and the light changed to green. The doorport shimmered, and he stepped through into Civic Center Plaza, two blocks from the Denver Post, giddy at his having been promoted to Senior Investigative Editor yesterday after winning the Pulitzer Prize for his investigative series on CIB-backed heroin sales in America's inner cities, his book based on his newspaper exposé having hit number one last week on the New York Times bestseller list.

And Zachary Hemptstead strode briskly along the sidewalk, glancing at headlines on his comcard, vaguely remembering an awful dream about having contemplated suicide.

Why would I have a dream like that? he wondered, his life better than he could ever have dreamed.

Zachary jumped and nearly dropped his comcard when it vibrated, indicating he had a new message.

The message was from a cub reporter interning under him at the Post. "I got a voicemail from an old woman who says her husband disappeared into a doorport a year ago. Says the police call her senile and tell her her husband died three years ago. Says she has proof that they caused him to disappear, and that she's hiring an attorney to sue American Doorport."

Normally Zachary might have dismissed such a phone call as quackery, delusion or worse, but for some reason he couldn't name, he felt intrigued.

This might be worth looking into, Zachary thought.

Chapter 5

On her first morning back at Corporate, Janet looked up from her desk. "How did you get in here?"

A Denver County Sheriff's Deputy stood before her desk, an envelope in his hand.

Janet had instantly recognized the uniform, her father having worn one for years.

"Deputy Anthony Stewart," he said, stepping forward and handing her the envelope. "A subpoena for the doorport records for one Barnaby Thornton, date of birth twenty sixty-nine, January second."

Janet didn't even blink. "My apologies for not returning your call last week. I was indisposed on special assignment in California. Please, Deputy, have a seat, and tell me how I can help." She gestured to the sitting area on one side of her office.

Deputy Stewart did blink. Twice. "Uh, well, of course." He sat and blinked at her again.

Janet tried not to smile. Into her com, she said, "Coffee, Stan." She smiled warmly at the Deputy. "How long did you serve with my father before he retired?" She stepped around the desk.

Stewart cleared his throat. "Uh, maybe four years, sir, uh, Ma'am."

"Please, Deputy, call me Janet. Father continues to tell fond stories of his years with the Sheriff's Department. What's your detail? Missing persons, you mentioned in your message."

The coffee arrived, Stan carrying it in with his usual aplomb.

"Thank you, Stan," she said, pressing the envelope into his hand. "I'll serve us," she said, nudging him out of the office. "Cream? Sugar?" she said to Stewart. She poured for them both, adding cream to his and taking hers black. Settling into a chair near his, she handed him his coffee, picked up her own and turned her gaze on him. "Please, what can I do for you?"

The cup clattered against the saucer. He lifted it gingerly, as though the nearly translucent cup might leap from his hand at any moment. He sipped just as gingerly and lowered the cup, then used both hands to guide the cup and saucer to the low table at his side. Finally he looked at her and gave her a wan smile. He reached under his lapel. "As the subpoena asks…" His gaze went blank, and he lifted the lapel to look inside his breast pocket. "I, uh, seem to have, uh, misplaced—"

"The envelope? You gave it to me already, but please, there's no need for a subpoena. I'd be happy to provide whatever information you're seeking."

"Oh? Well." Deputy Stewart looked relieved. "Well, then, I'll just—"

"What are you seeking?" Janet asked, interrupting him.

"The Doorport records for Barnaby Thornton, D.O.B January two, twenty sixty-nine."

When he did not continue, Janet said, "There must be some probable cause or complaint under investigation, yes?"

"Oh, uh, yes, uh, his widow, Yelena Thornton, states that her husband disappeared into a doorport one year ago on December third, one month shy of his seventieth birthday." Deputy Stewart ran his finger under his collar. "Problem is, our records indicate he died three years ago, and while it would seem she might be suffering from a memory impairment of one sort or other, she insists she doesn't have dementia."

Janet gestured with an open palm. "And does she?"

"I'm not qualified to make—"

"Of course you aren't. But surely you have some sense of that, having spoken with her, yes?"

"My sense of her is that she's as lucid as you or me."

Janet put a look of concern on her face. "Sounds like you need records of his ports between the date of his recorded death, presuming it's false, and his supposed disappearance a year ago, a period of not more than two years?"

Deputy Stewart frowned, scratched his head, looked at her and shrugged. "I guess so."

If what he requested verbally differed substantially from the subpoena, the legal department could always argue for a continuance. "And of course Mrs. Thornton must be experiencing substantial distress as a result of her husband's disappearance, presuming it happened?"

"Substantial," Deputy Stewart said doubtfully.

"Perhaps enough to warrant some kind of care?" Janet asked. "From a professional?"

Stewart raised his eyebrows. "I hadn't thought of that."

"Doesn't the County have some sort of service for victims and witnesses? Both groups must have significant trauma, wouldn't you say?"

"Oh, significant," he said, looking puzzled.

"And as you investigate such offenses, don't you or your fellow officers sometimes feel some empathy for them, even to the point of secondary trauma?" Janet didn't mention the evenings tiptoeing around the house when her father would sit silent in the living room for hours, not moving. Once a month, once every six months, not frequent, but often enough to cause consternation among family members. "And don't you sometimes feel, Deputy Stewart, that if you could just help a little more, that if you could alleviate a bit more suffering, that somehow your own suffering wouldn't be so severe?"

"Um, well, yes, certainly, but—"

"And when did you last seek counsel yourself?"

"Two months ago, but that's—"

"What for, Deputy Stewart?"

"Well, my wife." He looked at the floor and bit his lip.

"My apologies. I'm sorry for your loss. I meant not to pry. Thank you again for helping me to understand what you're requesting. We'll have it to you as soon as possible. Come with me. Stan can see you to the door. This way, please."

She caught Stan's eye as she led the Deputy to her outer office, and with a flick of her gaze, she indicated the restrooms rather than the elevators. "Again, thank you, Deputy."

Back in her office, Janet responded to her flickering tactiface, knowing what awaited her.

The list of doorport transmissions from Barnaby Thornton ended, as she had feared, on December third, twenty-one forty. Beside the list of transmissions on her tactiface was the death certificate, dated almost two years before.

Janet went white.

She hurried into Old Man Jackson's office. "We have to talk."

He smiled, as though expecting her. "Yes, Janet, we do."

Not the rebuff or resistance she'd expected. She looked around to make sure they were alone. "The system's unstable."

"Yes, Janet, it is." His face was serene, his eyes untroubled.

"Well, what are you goddamn going to do about it?"

"What would you do about it?" He was remarkably unperturbed.

Janet stopped short, not expecting this response. She looked at him. "Somewhat cavalier about this, wouldn't you say?"

"I've had a bit more time to consider the situation."

She regarded him, sitting in front of the floor-to-ceiling glass, the city of Denver stretching out behind him, the Capitol dome easily visible, the Cathedral Basilica among the other towers. She sighed. "Sorry to burst in here like this."

"You're concerned." Jackson shrugged.

"There's a subpoena." Janet nodded to the tactiface beside his chair.

"How would you respond to it?" His placid gaze was unnerving.

Janet considered. Why was Jackson directing all her questions back to her? "Get legal on it, see how we can delay. Find out more about Yelena and Barnaby Thornton, see if there's ever been a neurological evaluation on Yelena, track down whether their bank records reflect payments for these ports he supposedly took after he died, find out from legal if there might be some precedent under which we might withhold records, such as trade secrets, dig up some dirt on this Deputy, who's a bit unstable himself."

Janet caught her breath, not quite believing the verbal obfuscation coming from her own mouth. "Well, we can't just admit publicly that the system is unstable, can we?"

Jackson turned his head a fraction. "Can't we?"

"The panic, the lawsuits, the regulators." Janet shook her head. "There's little way to control the damage from such an announcement.

We'd end up like Enron or Adelphia from the early 2000s, or Citibank from the 2020s, or EXMOBP from the 2050s. Textbook implosions. And we can't return to hydrocarbon transport. We almost choked ourselves just from burning them, not to mention the manufacture and disposal of all vehicles powered by HC's."

"Isn't it unethical not to?" Jackson asked.

"Is it ethical to unleash a worldwide economic collapse? Cargo transport is ninety-nine percent doorport. Stop that, and world production grinds to a halt. Returning to hydrocarbon transport would take another twenty years to reach economies of scale—and with far greater hazard to public health, regardless of cost. Is it ethical to replace an existing mode of travel with a miniscule degree of hazard with one known to cause far greater damage? Private and public pressure would mount almost immediately to restore doorport service if regulators decide to shut it down. Ethical considerations would be set aside in the face of practical considerations. People would simply decide—eventually, mind you—that the benefits outweigh the risks."

"How do you know that the degree of hazard is as miniscule as you say?"

Janet frowned. "I don't, and that bothers me. Those vignettes you gave me—but a fraction of the anomalies. The perturbations are nowhere near as severe as your brother and my sister predict, but for every anomaly we know about, we can be certain there are ten to a hundred more that we don't know about."

She looked at Jackson. "Twenty-eight. Research assistant, working on her Master's, dancing on the side. Throat cancer, supposedly. Why her, and not someone else?" Janet put the back of her hand to her mouth, blinking back tears for reasons she couldn't name.

"You were twenty-eight, once," Jackson said.

"Why her at all?"

Jackson regarded her.

I feel as though I'm in his fishbowl, she thought. "And we don't know if doorports caused her cancer, triggered some metabolic dormancy that might have lain unactivated throughout her life, or if she was just unlucky."

She sighed. "But even if the number of anomalies is a hundred-fold of what we know, the degree of hazard is still far less than that of hydrocarbon transport." Shaking her head, she looked out the window.

Her eyes happened to alight on Invesco Field at Mile High, home of the Denver Broncos.

"Your sister will be here soon," Jackson said, following her gaze.

"Your brother will be here soon," she replied.

"What does Charlie know?"

She wrinkled her brow at him. "What's your concern?"

"What could I possibly be concerned about?"

"Leaks. Inadvertent, but leaks none the less. Our siblings would denounce us from major media outlets instead of from pulpits, soap-boxes, and stadiums.

"What about the anomalies? You brought me on board from MIT for a reason. I haven't found any abnormalities in the sequences that Douglas gave me, but then I haven't applied any of his more extreme assumptions. And where I was for fifteen minutes—whatever limbo or purgatory or liminus it was—we don't know. Jackson, what if I can't correct these anomalies?"

"What if you can't?"

Janet looked at Jackson. "You've turned my every concern or question back on me. Why? What are you thinking?"

Old Man Jackson didn't smile, but he might have. "What do you think?"

Janet let the question hang between them. "I'm not ready for those answers. One day, perhaps, but not today."

"No," Jackson said, a hint of a smile reaching his eyes, "Not today."

Alterlude #4

Doctor David Winters looked in the mirror, thinking it would be the last time he might call himself that. His face drooped, his eyes were puffy, his cheeks were bristly, his brow was lined. He slogged through a shower and a shave, then dressed himself. He went through the motions of getting ready for the day, feeling as though he were preparing for his own execution.

Today, the Medical Board of Colorado would decide whether to rescind his license to practice. A death sentence for a doctor.

He hadn't slept well in months, not since his mother died. His depression had been deepening for about two years, since his father died. Losing both of them in eighteen months had devastated him. Losing his license for his role in their deaths would probably finish him off.

His father Doctor Samuel Winters had been Professor of Clinical Psychiatry at the University of Colorado, Denver, and Medical Director at the Vail State Hospital for the Clinically Insane. A gentle man who would eagerly intercede with a patient who had been wrongly committed or poorly diagnosed, Samuel Winters was widely regarded as one of the most brilliant medical minds west of the Mississippi. And then he began to forget things.

At first it was small items. "Well, it seems I set my keys some-where," he'd say, and they'd be in his hand. Since his two elder sons,

David included, were both doctors, the signs were apparent to them far sooner than for most people. When shown just how frequently he was forgetting, Doctor Sam acknowledged what was happening. Unfortunately, the variant of dementia that Doctor Sam had contracted was swift and relentless.

And incurable.

Geriatric medicine being David Winter's specialty, he knew how the disease would progress, and his father had understood what to expect in the coming months when David described the etiology.

As in life, so in death.

Doctor Sam and his wife, Doctor Lila Winters, had come up with a plan to minimize his suffering and preserve his dignity to the greatest possible extent in his last six months.

Doctor Lila Winters, Professor of Microbiology at the University of Colorado, Denver, and Medical Director of Infectious Diseases at the State Department of Public Health, was then diagnosed with lymphoma, which by the time of diagnosis, had already metastasized to the meninges, the lining of the spine and brain. While she began an aggressive course of chemotherapy and radiation treatment, Doctor Samuel Winters entered his final months of decline.

Doctor David Winters could not have done otherwise but to step in where his mother now could not. Their plan for his father had been so logical, obvious, and compassionate, that David felt obligated to help them carry it through. Doctor Lily, as she had become known, was too ill from chemo and radiation to help, so David took a lead role in his father's care.

David didn't know what was worse, seeing his father become hostile and combative, or having to apply the restraints himself. The only redeeming moments were the times when both his parents were feeling well enough that they could, if briefly, enjoy each other's company.

"It's time, David," his mother said to him one day. They'd not seen Doctor Sam lucid in two weeks.

David knew what to do, never mind that the instructions were written out, and had been for over a year, and had been reviewed by Doctor Sam's treating neurologist, and a second prominent neurologist, and notarized and filed with the courts as his last living will and testament.

David mixed the cocktail, assembled the IV, inserted the line, and placed the button in his father's hand. Then he gave his father a hug, and left them both, going home for the first time in three months.

His mother commed him later that day, and Doctor David returned to find the coroner already there.

A month later, his mother handed him her own last living will and testament.

And even though she fought with all her resources, and had access to the best medical interventions possible, Doctor Lily withered across the next eighteen months.

"It's time, David," his mother said to him one day. He had not seen Doctor Lily eat or walk in two weeks.

David knew what to do. He mixed the cocktail, assembled the IV, inserted the line, and placed the button in his mother's hand. He gave his mother a hug and left her alone, going home for the first time in three months.

This time, it was he who called the coroner.

Doctor David Winters looked himself over one last time before leaving, wondering how he could look so good when he felt so bad. He sighed.

They might take my license to practice, but they can't take my dignity!

He knew he could not have acted any differently, that faced with a similar circumstance in the future he would do the same, and gladly. And damn the consequences!

The Medical Board of Colorado had already communicated its intention, had asked him to present himself this day with his medical license to practice before their august body to relinquish unto their possession this hallowed document, thereby rescinding his capacity to practice medicine in the State of Colorado.

Doctor David Winters checked in his briefcase one last time to insure indeed that he carried his license.

A drop of water splotched the Governor's signature.

Am I crying? he wondered, turning his face into his sleeve.

He dabbed his eyes dry and blew his nose into his kerchief, methodically refolded it and inserted it back into his pocket, looked at the splotched signature on the medical license and smiled.

It didn't matter anymore.

He closed his briefcase, straightened, and walked into his garage. He swiped the sensor with his comcard and stepped through the door-port. The chill struck him but he felt it not at all, walking toward the "Downtown Denver" doorport. Stepping into Civic Center Park, Doctor David Winters blinked at the Klieg lights and flashes, the press crews obviously expecting him as he turned toward the State Capitol. The usual protestors waving their signs were nowhere to be found.

They lobbed questions his direction, and to most of them, he just smiled, his heart soaring, his life goal achieved before he was sixty.

Doctor David Winters walked into the Capitol Rotunda, and applause erupted at his entrance, his colleagues standing and cheering. Doctor David had to stop and dab at his eyes again. Then he shook hands with Governor and sat beside him.

The Governor stood and silence fell. "Fellow citizens of the State of Colorado, I am humbled and honored today to stand before you with Doctor David Winters, Professor of Geriatric Psychiatry at the University of Colorado at Denver, and Medical Director of the Institute of Geriatric Studies, to enshrine into Law the principle that we, each one of us, has the right and sometimes the obligation to hasten our own demise.

"Doctor David Winters, won't you please stand beside me?"

David rose and stopped beside the Governor's podium.

"Because of your hard work and personal sacrifice, the State of Colorado may now consider itself amongst the most compassionate and progressive in its treatment of those suffering from terminal illnesses. On behalf of the residents of the great state of Colorado, I offer our gratitude. With this signature, we move into a new era— indeed, what may even be described as the next evolutionary step—in the ethical handling of death and dying."

It wasn't until later that afternoon, when he'd returned to his office at the Institute of Geriatric Studies, that he realized his degree of elation.

This must be akin to a religious epiphany, he thought with a smile.

As he walked in the door, he noticed a Denver County Sheriff's Deputy and a tiny elderly woman in his lobby.

Doctor David looked quizzically at his secretary.

"Wants an eval," the young man wrote on a note pad. "Insisted."

Bewildered but intrigued, he took a few minutes to settle himself in his office. He opened his briefcase. What's my medical license doing there? he wondered. And how did the Governor's signature get smudged? I can't think about that right now, he thought, closing his briefcase. Then he asked his secretary to send them in.

The oddly-matched pair settled themselves. "Deputy Anthony Stewart," the officer said. "And this is Yelena Thornton."

Doctor David Winters smiled at her.

"Doctor," she said. "My husband disappeared into a doorport a year ago..."

Chapter 6

Janet greeted her parents warmly as she stepped from the doorport into their garage, her husband right behind her.

"Frank, how are you?" her father said heartily, throwing his arms around the smaller man enthusiastically. A former Sheriff's Deputy, Bill McLoughlin was a big Irish man. "It's good to see you, and there's never enough of that."

It amused Janet that Frank had never really become comfortable with her father's arms-wide-open blustery manner. Florid described everything about her father, his complexion, manner, outlook and speech. Frank's reservedness was nary the match.

They entered the house and Janet saw her on the couch and froze.

"Now don't you two be getting your hackles up like wet cats under my roof," her father said.

"Billy McLoughlin!" her mother said.

He turned to her, "Well, 'tain't right these sisters don't act sisterly, and I won't have it, not here. You two don't want to invite each other into your lives elsewhere, that's your business, but I'll not it have here even if I do have to spring it on ya, now go on and hug your sister or I'll give you a lickin like you ain't had since elementary."

Janet tried to suppress a smile but couldn't and walked over.

Cynthia McLoughlin stood, also trying not to smile. "He's irrepressible, ain't 'e," she said, the classic Athenian lines of her face softening.

"Incorrigible, ain't 'e," Janet replied, hugging her sister. "For him," she said in her sister's ear.

"For him," Cynthia said.

"I don't give a toot what the blarney it's for," Bill said, wrapping his arms around both of them.

Janet found herself laughing for no reason, and for the next while it seemed that her feud with her sister was somehow remote. She also saw as the evening progressed that Frank seemed uncommonly attentive to her, as though he were seeing her for the first time. And in truth, Janet felt relaxed as she hadn't felt in months—not since she'd taken the Vice Presidency of R&D at Corporate.

Charlie was right, Janet thought, I've changed.

As they sat down for dinner, Janet chose the seat across from her sister, enjoying her company for the first time in memory, the two of them three years apart, just long enough to have emphasized their different developmental stages, but not long enough to have kept the younger from borrowing everything of the elder or wanting to know her business or wanting to tag along.

What a pest she was, Janet was thinking.

Look how beautiful she is now, she thought, admiring the golden cascade of her long blond hair and translucent skin, and Janet felt again as she had throughout a childhood of having a much prettier younger sister who always got her way with either a dimpled smile or a quick tantrum, felt as though somehow all her accomplishments simply could not measure up to the princess that her younger sister was.

And Janet reflected for a moment that Cynthia might have had an analogous experience—and might still be having it. Janet saw Cynthia was looking at her and thinking deeply.

"It hasn't been easy, has it?" Janet asked her.

Cynthia raised an eyebrow at her.

"Being my sister."

Cynthia shrugged. "I never could be as smart as you or as accomplished or as nice. They'd say, 'Why can't you be like your sister?' And I'd have to do something to show that I wasn't."

Janet smiled. "I couldn't stand how you'd get what you wanted without blinking an eye, and I had to work so hard to get the slightest bit of recognition while you just smiled and got all the attention a girl could want."

Cynthia shook her head. "It was all the wrong kind of attention. I admired how smart you were and I wished I was that smart but everyone wanted me to be pretty and it was such a curse."

Janet looked at her sister. "I didn't realize. I'd have traded anything to be as pretty as you."

"I'd have traded anything to be as smart as you."

The two of them began to giggle.

"Bunch 'o fuss fer nuthin'," their father grumbled in a low voice, trying not to smile.

Dark glasses with large lenses shading her eyes, and a tight wool cap pulled as far over her head as she could get it, hair tucked underneath, Janet stepped out of the doorport at Invesco Field at Mile High, wearing a denim skirt, calf-length leather boots, and a plain turtleneck sweater with a plaid vest thrown over her shoulder. Janet felt uncomfortable without her usual formal business attire.

She'd been to Invesco Field at Mile High year after year for fireworks at Independence Day and New Years since she was a young girl.

The marquee above the stadium entrance declared, "The Divine Church of the Temporal Apocalypse, Saturday, December 11."

She had come to see her sister speak but didn't want her to know she was there. She prayed she wouldn't be recognized. I'd die of shame, Janet thought. And if it were reported in the press ...

Janet shuddered, thinking the stock price would plummet.

She noted sardonically the number of people also stepping out of doorports. The irony that these followers of a movement to eliminate the use of doorports would themselves use doorports to arrive at a rally where their use would be denounced brought a smile to Janet's face. The usual protestors weren't present, as though they knew they'd be preaching to the choir. Or calling the choir's attention to their out-of-tune singing.

Janet found her way in and chose a seat in the lower rows of what might have been the fifty-yard line, a crowd on the field, the stage directly opposite her, and the stands behind her not a quarter full, perhaps five thousand people total.

The program noted a number of speakers, her sister the keynote. I should have come toward the end, Janet thought, not caring to hear anyone else.

She wasn't sure if she could handle the drivel and hypocrisy.

As the event commenced, clearly intended to be as much a religious revival as a protest rally, the speakers by turns inveigled against evil and exhorted an embrace of the Church. While clearly components were Christian in origin, none of the established orders would have claimed this apocryphal, apocalyptic sect, their views so extreme as to challenge a reasonable person's suspension of disbelief.

But whatever the fiction they pedaled, Janet could not discount the hundredth monkey, that lone soul whose commitment to his or her own vision eventually drew enough followers that it tipped the balance of conventional wisdom to become the accepted ideology.

Protestors at most major doorport transit hubs was evidence of a tipping balance, of a deep dissatisfaction with existing social, economic and political structures. Something was beginning to manifest.

Janet was drifting off when they announced her sister. She sat up, startled.

"... Of the Divine Church of the Temporal Apocalypse, Cynthia McLoughlin."

All those around her stood, applause filling the air. Belatedly, Janet stood as well.

Glowing in robes of gossamer white, her hair cascading down her back to her waist, Cynthia McLoughlin floated onto the stage, gathering the bouquets left for her or thrown to her. An assistant help her to arrange them behind her.

"Thank you, everyone," she said, her voice full and rich with adoration. "Surely the next world is upon us, and our freedom now approaching." Cynthia spread her arms, looked around the stadium and brought her gaze back to rest directly on Janet.

"It is our fate," Cynthia said, her voice echoing back from the empty stadium seats, "to have the beast rampage among us—alas as yet unseen but that beast rampages none the less. It is a beast we cannot see, hear, or feel, for that beast lurks in the veils of time, between the liminal thresholds of space, and its sound is obscured by the blathering of supposed scientists who belabor ceaselessly about this abomination called Space-Time Harmonics."

The crowd hissed, and Janet jumped, startled.

Cynthia, although easily fifty yards and a thousand people away, appeared to have her gaze fixed on Janet.

"This beast cannot be sensed because it changes our past, and because the change is in the past, our memories change with it, and what we really experience fades as though we dreamt it, and what we are left with is the illusion of having lived, a fake memory of a changed past, and an uncertain future, an abyss of approaching chaos, in which nothing is predictable, in which the very fabric of space and time begins to fray.

"Stop!" Cynthia threw up her hands. "Every step across geographic distances causes the space-time fabric to fold in unnatural ways. Every doorport you use tears the fabric that much further. Every time we take a linear property like space or time and bend it to our will in violation of God's law, we invite the apocalypse closer. Even now, lives are being thrown into chaos, and the only reason we don't know it yet is that human memory is an imperfect thing."

She lowered her hands and lowered her voice. "A police officer with a wife leaves home and arrives at work without one. A lawyer leaves a successful practice for lunch and returns to a floundering career as a public defender. A Pulitzer Prize-winning journalist leaves for his post at a nationally-known daily and arrives disgraced at a neighborhood weekly. A prominent physician about to be lauded for exemplary practices finds that he is about to lose his license for those very same acts. A low-level bureaucrat goes to lunch and returns as a high-powered regulatory investigator. A floridly psychotic young woman ports to her doctor's office and arrives at her corporate position of R&D VP. All of them—hear me carefully—all of them unaware that space-time disruptions caused by their use of doorports have changed their destinies!

"Unaware!" she repeated, letting the word echo around the stadium. "And how many of us here at Invesco Field at Mile High today have had our lives changed without our knowledge? Unaware!"

Cynthia looked around. "We are not here to bewail our fate. We are here to change our fate! To act!

"I hear you say, 'what can I do?' Well, I'll tell you what you can do! ..."

Janet slid out of her seat and headed to the exit, having heard enough. Hyperbole, she thought, all hyperbole. None of that could possibly be happening! Janet wondered what involvement Old Man Jackson had with the Church of the Divine Temporal Apocalypse.

Janet didn't worry that the anomalies were as severe as Cynthia had described. Janet *did* worry that they might be perceived as such. If such a perception became widespread, American Doorport would collapse. As Janet walked out of the stadium and toward the bank of doorports, she looked for the one labeled with her destination: Downtown. The office wasn't open, of course, but Janet always had things she could be doing.

Multiple doorports were labeled "Civic Center Plaza." Janet chose one but stopped.

She thought through the process, moving through the equations in her head with the alacrity she'd had when she was a post-doctoral researcher at MIT. In her head, she saw once again the very holo-boards she'd used, equations layered in different colors one atop the other, floating in the middle of her laboratory.

Alongside that, she brought to mind the sequence given her by Old Man Douglas as she'd last looked at it on her tactiface, moving through the pairs of equations with the same facile fluidity.

"Hey, lady, you all right?"

Janet looked at the gentleman. "Uh, yeah, thanks for asking." She waved her comcard across the sensor and stepped through the door-port into Civic Center Plaza.

No protestors here, either. Probably all at the rally, she thought, the wind brisk and the afternoon chill. The Corporate doorport was a short walk, the pairs of equations flipping through her mind.

"Hey, lady, you all right?"

Janet looked at the gentleman. "Uh, yeah, thanks for asking." She waved her comcard across the sensor and stepped through the door-port onto the sidewalk in front of Corporate.

Shaking off an odd sense of déjà vu, Janet unlocked the front door and shut off the alarm, then did a double take. She had just turned on the alarm. Shutting it off again, she wondered who was in the building already.

Walking to the elevator, she pulled out her comcard and contacted the security company.

Evan Jonas, Vice President of Operations, they told her.

Odd, she thought, riding up in the elevator. He never comes in on Saturday.

Evan swore under his breath as he whisked past her and into the boardroom. He stopped in the doorway and looked at her over his shoulder. "Bad news, Janet. Old Man Jackson is dead."

Chapter 7

Janet waited beyond the boardroom door, with the Vice President of Operations and the other ten Vice Presidents. All of them just standing around. Outside, dusk was falling.

She had been on autopilot, numb at the news. She and Evan had gathered those they could of the Board for American Doorport at the Corporate offices, and had set up comcard links for those unable to port themselves there.

All thirty were in attendance, either personally or by comcard.

Beyond that door.

And beyond that door, they were selecting, per Old Man Jackson's instructions, the next interim CEO of American Doorport. The Board of Directors would decide who had the best balance of skills to guide the organization until a permanent CEO could be found.

Likely from among the twelve Vice Presidents outside the boardroom.

None of them looked at each other. Janet looked at none of them. If they hadn't been present, Janet would have wept. Certainly at the death of Jackson, who in the last year had personally mentored her, but more at the change and loss of support that his death represented.

She looked among the other eleven Vice Presidents, gauging to what degree that person was likely to be chosen, and what degree of support that each might provide her.

Tired of sitting, Janet stood and stepped to the window. Lights were coming on across the Mile High City, and the air was deceptively clear. Which means terribly cold, Janet thought. In the distance glowed Invesco Field at Mile High, the bright stadium lights due east of the west-facing windows.

The noise of activity vibrated through the floor under her.

They've decided.

She turned toward the boardroom door. Glances her way, conversations ending, silence growing.

The boardroom door opened, and out stepped the media mogul, RK Blackstone, President of the Board of Directors. "Ladies and gentlemen, as you can imagine, the board has had to make its most difficult decision to date since the founding of American Doorport forty years ago, a decision that in a few months will be superseded in difficulty yet again, one which few boards make willingly or happily. The first decision of course will be choosing the person to lead the company in between the death of its founder and the appointment of its new permanent Chief Executive Officer. In some ways, the interim CEO is the tougher decision, as it requires someone who can maintain the confidence of the shareholders and the public, and who can push forward all the initiatives instigated by the founder.

"In its deliberations, the board has been fortunate to have at its disposal a candidate whose persistence of vision has brought American Doorport to the threshold of its next evolutionary age, a candidate perfectly suited to carrying the Corporation through its own space-time harmonic aperture toward its future.

"Ladies and gentlemen, it is with pride and hope that I introduce our next interim Chief Executive Officer, Doctor Janet Thompson."

Who? Janet wondered.

I don't believe it, Janet thought.

Why are they staring at me? she wondered.

And her last thought: I'd better say something.

"Mr. Blackstone, Directors of American Doorport, Vice Presidents and colleagues, I must say I don't deserve half of Mr. Blackstone's praise, but if I'm able to bring us part way into our next stage of evolution, I'll have earned some of it." She smiled, still trying to gather her thoughts. Some kept their gazes on her, others wouldn't look at her, and a third group looked at her, then away, at her, then away.

288

"Jackson Weintraub held us all to high expectations, and we all felt his keen edge of his wit when we disappointed him. Let us all carry through with his vision for American Doorport lest we tempt him to return from the dead."

A few chuckles, a few nods.

"Let's start now." Janet held up her comcard. "A prototype recalibrator. You've seen the lab tests. Jackson wanted two months worth of field tests. I want the field tests finished in one month. Evan, procure a team by Monday morning who can manufacture and distribute one recalibrator to each employee of American Doorport by the time the morning commute begins this next Friday, December fifteenth, each coded to its bearer's thumb and retina prints.

"Evan," she said again.

"Huh?" he said, as though he hadn't been paying attention.

"Friday morning, and I'll have none of your foot-dragging."

"What foot-dragging?" he protested.

"You can drag your feet all the way to the unemployment line, or you can get a recalibrator into every employee's hand by Friday morning. Make it happen, Man!"

"But... but..."

"Well?" She scowled. "Yeah or nay, will you or won't you? Decide now, or I'll decide for you."

"But... but..."

"You're fired."

The sky behind her exploded, dull thumps in the distance following soon after.

Janet turned from the window back to the room. "One month to test the prototype."

On Monday morning, bright and early, Janet pulled her tactiface over from the side of the desk and punched up Charlie.

"Charlie Goodrich here," and the face appeared.

"Glad to see you, Charlie, listen, there's a vacant position here at Corporate that I need to fill interim ASAP. What do you say?"

A smile split Charlie's face. "I been waitin' since yesterday for this call. What took you so long?"

"Always a step ahead of me, aren't you?"

"I know what you're thinking before you do! Of course, I accept, and of course we'll get those recalibrators out by Thursday midnight. And don't worry, when I heard Old Man Jackson died on Saturday, I told my wife you'd be appointed interim, that you'd fire foot-dragging Jonas, and that you'd ask me over to Corporate. I can be there in fifteen minutes."

"See you then, Charlie," Janet said, laughing and killing the call. Relieved to have someone she could count on at Corporate, Janet remembered Old Man Jackson's comment not two weeks ago: "We got twelve Vice Presidents. I could fire 'em all and nothing would change."

Janet smiled, wondering who else she could fire.

Research and Development could do without a Vice President for now.

Then a yawn struck her. She looked out over downtown Denver, the bright morning sun glaring off snow-capped buildings. She hadn't slept, working through the night, poring over balance sheets, employee rosters, purchase orders, and contracts. Yesterday—a Sunday—she'd spent meeting with her ten remaining Vice Presidents, gauging the depth of their commitment to the company, instilling in each her vision for the company and asking whether they were with her or whether they would be seeking positions elsewhere.

None had the potential for Operations, the largest and most demanding Vice Presidency, and thus her drive to have recalibrators in the hands of every employee by Thursday midnight was already twenty-four hours behind schedule.

But Charlie can pull it off, Janet thought.

She looked around the office, needing some distraction. Already 10:30, Janet had waited until Charlie's usual arrival time of 8:30 pacific before contacting him. For a Monday morning following the CEO's expiration, it was preternaturally quiet.

Her eyes alighted on the forbidden office, the separate space that Old Man Jackson had kept from his pre-deployment days, whom few people even knew about, and even fewer had seen. Janet had not.

Where's the key? she wondered.

Where would Jackson have kept it?

In the right hand drawer, in back, to the left, Janet was thinking.

She opened the right hand drawer as far as it would go, and looked in the left rear corner.

A key.

She smiled.

Tarnished, unremarkable, unmarked, nary even a key ring.

She knew without trying that it was the right key.

Her intercom rang. "Charlie Goodrich to see you, Doctor Thompson."

"Send him in, please."

Charlie came in, grinning, his suit rumpled as ever, his bald head gleaming.

Janet came around the desk, the key in her hand. "Welcome aboard, Charlie. We'll have you go down to personnel to load the clearances onto your comcard, sign your contract, get your job description updated, but all that can wait."

Charlie shrugged, as though to say, "What for?"

"Let me show you." She held up the key and strode to a door that no one to Janet's knowledge had seen open in five years.

"The Old Man's inner sanctum, eh? I'd heard rumors, but never heard that anybody'd seen it. You don't want to talk about the recalibrator deployment?"

Janet shook her head, inserting the key in the lock. "More than anything, I want to know what Old Man Jackson's vision for the company was." She turned the knob and opened the door.

Musty, dark.

She groped for the light switch.

A single, uncovered incandescent light bulb flared to life in the center of the room a foot above their heads.

To one side, three filing cabinets barely contained the papers stuffed into them, none of the drawers able to close all the way.

To the other side, a desk stacked high with documents, some bound, others not, in the center a few rough sketches.

On the far wall, diagrams competed for space on a wall that would have been crowded with half their number, push pins tacking papers in constellations so random they might have been stars.

On the floor, more stacks of documents, research briefs, technical documents and trade journals.

"That's a pretty chaotic vision," Charlie said.

Janet nodded, stepping into the room, gesturing Charlie to follow. There was barely a path to the desk, and little enough room for two people to stand. On one desk was an envelope, "Janet" written hastily across it. Janet picked it up, thinking to look at its contents later, and put it in her pocket.

She closed the door behind them.

On the back of the door were three diagrams.

One was a crude drawing of a one-way doorport—a doorframe on one side, no doorframe on the other, the sequence clearly indicating a space-time harmonic aperture without a fixed destination.

The second was an illustration of a frameless port—a doorport without a door on either end.

The third illustration was a diagram of the solar system, exploded out of another diagram of the Milky Way Galaxy.

"Space travel," Charlie said.

"He didn't dream small, did he?"

"He didn't dream there'd be anomalies, either."

Janet frowned at Charlie. "Maybe that's why he didn't push this." She gestured at the back of the door. "Wanted me to fix the anomalies first."

Charlie looked at her. "Did you hear what you just said?"

"Yeah, I guess," she said, bewildered.

"Old Man Jackson wanted you to fix the anomalies, eh? And I suppose the next thing you'll tell me is you know how?"

Janet laughed and shook her head, gestured Charlie from the room and turned off the light. "Of course not, but then there's Yelena Thornton, who's likely got dementia, saying her husband died a year ago, disappeared into a doorport, even though his death certificate says three years ago."

"And doorport records substantiate what she says?"

Janet spread her hands in befuddlement. "And I have to check on the subpoena; she's pursuing a missing person's case, got this gung-ho deputy involved."

"Yeah, but dementia?"

"Doesn't add up, does it?"

Charlie shook his head.

Janet could tell by the look on his face he was percolating.

"As though the space-time fabric is intentionally bringing this to our attention," Charlie said.

"Intention isn't something I'd attribute to Space-Time Harmonics. Unless it's viewed on systems level," Janet said, musing. "All systems seek homeostasis—which is about as intentional as a system could get. So all these anomalies are simply events within a system out of balance, events whose result is to bring the system either closer to or back into balance."

Charlie nodded. "Makes sense on a systems level."

"How about those predictions by Old Man Douglas and my sister dearest?"

Charlie waved them away. "We don't have the ability to put the system so out of balance that the fabric of space-time would swallow the Earth whole."

Janet nodded. "Even so, I don't like even one anomaly. And we need to get someone else involved before this gets too big."

"Someone else?"

"Who do you know over at NTSB?" Janet asked, the National Traffic Safety Board often sending regulators to monitor the safety of the doorport network.

Charlie smiled. "Met someone at a conference six months ago, who grumbled about our never having problems."

"Axe to grind?"

"I don't think so, just seemed bored."

"Why don't you contact that person, ask for a site visit." Janet smiled. "Maybe we can tell her about Yelena Thornton and at least let her know we're investigating."

The bells rang their mournful tones above her as she followed the casket into the Cathedral Basilica of the Immaculate Conception, mourners lining either side of the grand stairway leading into the church, and the surviving Weintraub brother walking beside her, looking much, much older than when she'd seen him in San Diego.

Twelve tones rang their declaration of the hour on this Tuesday, and Janet knew this to be the blackest Tuesday she'd ever faced, one that had begun with a call at dawn.

"Janet," her secretary Stan had said, his face on her comcard looking worried, "Deputy Anthony Stewart insists on seeing you immediately."

What now? she wondered.

First the phone call, two weeks ago, saying he wanted to speak with her, then the search warrant last week, demanding records.

What was he going to do now, arrest her?

"Stan, tell him I can see him at three pm today after the funeral."

"But he's insisting on seeing you now."

"Tell him I'll have all the records he requested last week at three pm, and not a moment before. And please ask if he'd like to join us for the service at noon."

Stan had frozen his face to speak directly with the Deputy.

A minute later, Stan came back on. "He agrees, but only out of respect for your grief."

Janet had choked back tears.

As she strode up the aisle of the four-hundred-year old Cathedral, Janet let loose a few of those un-cried tears, knowing a thousand more threatened to flood down her face.

Old Man Douglas walked beside her, daubing his cheeks.

Behind them was the upper crust of Colorado and everyone of note for ten states around. Jackson Weintraub had been unbelievably wealthy, often called the Bill Gates of the twenty-fourth century. His near monopoly of the market had funneled the entire earnings of the hydrocarbon, vehicle, and road-building markets into his pocket. Regulators had hounded the company since its founding, but a token licensing of the technology to competitors had been just enough to stave off nationalization. With wealth had come power, and Jackson Weintraub had used that power with finesse to achieve his objectives.

Even before his body had grown cold, lawyers had lodged enough claims against the estate to cause the Colorado State Court Bioservers to have multiple protein aneurisms.

But nothing could stop American Doorport, not if Janet had her way. As she turned along the first pew, the coffin now settling upon the altar, Janet calculated her next area of expansion.

Emerging markets, particularly those still on fossil fuels, were ripe for the recalibrating doorport. The major barrier to doorport deployment in poor countries with unreliable infrastructures was the drain on resources that would be caused by the installation, operation and maintenance of the banks of doorports frequently seen in nearly all major metropolitan cities. Most impoverished regions could only support a door or two, and with fixed destinations, these doorports were too inefficient to build an economy of scale. But a doorport that could be recalibrated to any other doorport tipped the balance to make their installation viable in nearly every corner of the world.

And a doorport with a solar collector mounted on top ...

Janet smiled, taking her seat in the Cathedral Basilica.

Paeans to those who have passed, euphonic eulogies, triumphant tributes, all serve to connect us with our sadness, Janet was thinking, but what about our guilt, anger, and remorse? Obscuring the unpleasantries about the dead does nothing to address our ambivalence about their passing.

Janet felt guilty about getting Jackson's position.

In the days since the board's decision, she'd had no time to think about it. This moment was her first waking moment without ten thousand concerns weighing her down. She hadn't slept until last night, having worked forty-eight hours straight.

"Honey, you've got to sleep," Frank had said to her last night.

His speaking had startled her out of a nap in which she'd dreamt of arriving at work that morning with Jackson greeting her as she walked in the door at Corporate.

The pew hard beneath her, Janet felt the tears as they burned their way down her cheeks.

Douglas patted her hand, seeming oblivious to his own tears.

Toward the end of the service, Douglas asked if she would come with him to the cemetery to see his brother laid to rest, the memorial service public, but the burial private.

Janet tried to think of a polite way to decline and couldn't. "Certainly," she said. "I would be honored to come with you. I feel privileged that you asked."

The casket was loaded into the hearse, and as Janet turned to follow Old Man Douglas to his limousine, a voice stopped her.

"Doctor Janet Thompson?"

She turned.

"Deputy Anthony Stewart." In his hand was a piece of paper.

She remembered his visit, had liked his gentle concern. "I've got the information—" she started to reach into her purse.

"Freeze." His hand flew to his pistol. "You're under arrest for obstruction of justice, contempt of a court order, and interfering with a police investigation. Please come with me quietly."

The blood left her face. "Of course."

He gestured toward a doorport cage, the dimensions just short of those needed to get through a standard doorport.

"Please, Officer, I'll go willingly." Janet looked around. A circle had already formed around them.

"Protocol, Doctor, my apologies."

Douglas re-appeared and strode right up to the Deputy Stewart. He was easily six inches shorter and fifty pounds lighter. "The lady said she'll go willingly." He pushed his face into the Deputy's. "You've got enough gall disturbing a funeral. The least you could do is leave her her dignity. If you insist on the cage, I'll insist you take me too, youngster."

Deputy Stewart shrank from the tiny old man. "Can I have your word, Doctor Thompson?" he said, not taking his eyes off Old Man Douglas.

"Of course, Deputy," Janet said. "I'm sure this is a misunderstanding. I've got the information you want."

"It's more serious than that, Doctor Thompson. This way, please," and the Deputy led her toward the nearest set of doorports, the crowd parting reluctantly.

"What do you mean?"

"Please come with me. Anything you say can and will be held against you in a court of law. You have ..."

Booking was humiliating. Strip search, jail jumpsuit, photo, fingerprint, retinal print, endless demographic questions, repeated five times at each hand-off, separated from her belongings, bars, uniforms, cameras, guns, chains all around her. Each segment of the process was held in a different physical location, two deputies on either side escorting her through each doorport to the next step in the process, each form of indignity designed to deflate an ego.

As was the Perp Walk, a custom resurrected from the twentieth century, of being paraded publicly in chains through a glass cage, forty feet long, open only at the top to let noise in, covered with a grill, two deputies patrolling the walkway above.

For Janet, it was insult to injury, and all the while, she wondered, What have I done?

And all the while, seeing again and again as though standing outside looking in from the circle of onlookers, watching herself get arrested at a funeral, in full view of the illuminati of Colorado and beyond.

Great way to start a career as a CEO, she kept thinking.

And under those feelings, the warring grief, disbelief and guilt.

The bars clanged shut behind her one last time, a stinging reminder that they had taken her freedom.

The cell was forty feet square, empty save five women who looked and smelled like they belonged here.

The one with the bushy orange hair stood.

And kept standing, the big hair blocking out the lights.

Janet thought her head was going to bump the ceiling.

"Hey, it's Missy's friend!"

The voice sounds familiar, Janet thought, staring up into the big woman's face.

"You know, at the CUNY Lingua!" The leggy woman lifted one of her tree trunks straight over her head.

"The dancer!" Janet said, so relieved to see someone she knew and not caring it was someone she'd never be seen with if she could help it.

"Yeah," then Danielle said in a whisper, "that's what I'm in for."

"In Denver? I saw you last two blocks off Times Square."

"Got here yesterday to show off my mile-high canyon, but you folks around here ain't got much humor. That officer didn't like it when I told him he might be tall enough to wear my hat on his head—" She pointed and dropped her leg "—went and arrested me just for saying it! Key Rist! Wasn't like I tried to show him or anything. What about you? What are you in for?"

Janet found herself giggling at the big woman's banter.

"That sounds serious," Danielle said. "Say, did you find out what you wanted when you was askin' after Missy?"

She shook her head.

"C'mon over and sit yourself down."

Sitting beside her, Janet saw that they were equivalent in height. Sitting.

Truly tree-trunk legs.

"Company lawyer will be here shortly to bail me out. How about you?"

"No family, no friends, not here, and no money either," Danielle said. "I'll have to stay until my hearing. Your company gonna bail you out?" She whistled tonelessly. "Must think you're valuable. What did you want to find out about Missy, anyway?"

297

"Whether she continued dancing until the day she died or whether she stopped before then."

"Funny, had a couple of dreams about that very thing. What is it? You seen a ghost or something? What's the matter?"

Janet shook her head. "Nothing." But in her heart she knew it wasn't nothing. She knew Danielle hadn't dreamt.

"Her, too?" Suzanne Jaqueline Roberts-Carter, Esq., said, looking as if she'd drawn a lungful of some foul miasma.

"Her, too," Janet replied.

"What division she work in?"

"I'm sorry?"

"Of American Doorport?"

"Oh, my apologies, I didn't know what you meant. She doesn't work for the company."

"Then I can't bail her out. I'm the company lawyer right now. Conflict of interest to do something for you personally. Sorry."

"All right," Janet said. "I'll just get dressed. Thanks for your time. You know where to send the bill?"

Suzanne nodded. "You don't want me to wait?"

"No need, but thanks for offering," Janet said. "I'm going to be here awhile."

Suzanne pointed to the leggy redhead just visible through multiple panes. "Really?"

Janet nodded, smiling.

"Uh, hi," Frank said, smiling at Danielle but looking quizzically at Janet.

"Danielle's going to stay with us for a few days," Janet said.

They shook hands, Danielle grinning from ear to ear. "Miss Janey bailed me out, too! Wasn't that nice? I can see you're wantin' to talk with your wife in private, 'cause you probably think she's got a screw loose, but there ain't a need for that, 'cause you don't need to worry about me. I got that bank account I told you about, Miss Janey, and I'll be just fine, but get out your comcard so we can stay in touch, which is what you're wanting anyway now, isn't it? Listen, Mister, that's quite the jewel you got there, an' I'd do anything to keep a hold of her, if that's the way I went, so you just take care of her, or you'll have to answer to me, all right? All right, I'll see you both soon, I'm sure. Taa, taa!" And she was gone.

Janet watched her go, checking her comcard to insure she got Danielle's number.

Frank threw his head back and laughed.

Grinning, Janet looped her arm in his and pulled him along from the County Jail toward the nearest bank of doorports.

"What was that all about?" Frank asked, wiping a tear from his eye.

"I'll tell you later, all right? And what are you doing here?"

"I came to get you because our house is surrounded by reporters. I took the kids over to your folks, and I'd suggest we go there too, if they haven't found the place, that is."

"Reporters?" Janet snorted, exasperated.

"Not everyday a CEO gets arrested." Frank shook his head.

"Not a great start to my tenure at American Doorport," Janet said, shaking hers.

"You didn't look well when that Deputy arrested you."

"Healthiest moment of my life. No idea what you're talking about."

Frank pulled her close, his eyes on the doorport lintels. "I'd have fainted too, in that situation. Wish I had been close enough to do hear what Douglas did. Scandalized everyone, that Deputy arresting you right then. You should sue."

"I forgot about the search warrant. We should have replied days ago, if that's all it's about." They located the right doorport.

"I wonder if the press corps found your parent's house."

"Doesn't matter," Janet said, pulling out her comcard. She activated the recalibrator, set the doorport to align with the one in her parents' garage, and waved it across the doorport sensor. The light blinked red, red, red, green, the doorport surface shimmered, and they stepped through into her parents' garage.

"Mommy, Mommy, you were on the vid!" her oldest leaped into her arms. "Why did you look so unhappy? Did that man do something bad to you?"

While Janet reassured her daughter, Janet's family reassured her, her parents greeting her with hugs.

Janet sighed and thought, with their help, I can endure anything.

Later that night, the kids asleep in the upstairs bedroom, Janet and Frank laying on the sofa bed downstairs, lit by just a night light, she told him what was happening.

"So you had these incidents—very minor, comparatively—and a

few other people have had loved ones die of natural causes, but their deaths don't correspond to our record of their activities. How many were on that memchip Jackson gave you?"

Janet told him.

"And so," Frank said, "even if those represent a tenth of the anomalies that are actually occurring, it's still one anomaly per million transactions, if even that."

"But we don't know if the doorports themselves are at fault, or whether these anomalies signify a much larger, more horrific perturbation in the future. What if Old Man Douglas is right? What if Cynthia gets a hold of this information? What if the apertures are responsible for these people's deaths?"

"How could they be?"

"I don't know. But I do know that if a dancer like Danielle has dreams about her co-worker Missy, then thousands of other people have some subliminal level of awareness about similar circumstances. And if Yelena Thornton remembers because she has dementia, it suggests that these are physiological phenomena which we have no way to measure, access, or anticipate. If the harmonic apertures have subsequealae because we're transferring matter across space beyond the natural linearity, do those ripples resonate with larger space-time fabric and cause harmonic perturbations of the degree that might bring the fabric to the point of collapse?"

Frank frowned. "Like the temporal equivalent of the Tacoma Narrows Bridge?"

Janet nodded. The classic engineering example of elementary-forced resonance between the natural structural frequency and the wind's external periodic frequency, the collapse of the Tacoma Narrows Bridge in 1940 was precisely the kind of harmonic perturbation she feared. "Exactly."

"The actual cause of failure was aeroelastic flutter," Frank replied. "But I see your concern. You mentioned some equations that Douglas gave you? Difficult to believe that he refined the equations after he and Jackson parted ways."

"What if he didn't?"

The brows narrowed.

"What if Douglas felt, at the outset, that the technology was inherently unstable, couldn't convince his brother of that, couldn't get anyone to listen or look at the permutations he'd developed. The predisposing assumptions bear little relation to actual conditions, of course, but I'm sure he had no means of developing long-term sequelae for a little-tested technology, so he had to introduce predisposing assumptions at wild variance to reality."

"And you feel that the cumulative sequelae are beginning to alter the space-time fabric?"

Janet shrugged. "Something certainly is."

"Let's find out."

"How?"

Frank grinned. "You said that the Parkers kept getting bills for doorport trips that their daughter never took, and then they never got billed for doorport trips that she did take to and from doctors, hospitals, and specialists, right?"

"And the reason they got the bills for trips to Princeton, Times Square, and home up to the day she died is that she actually took those trips. And the reason she didn't get billed for medical trips was she never took them in the first place."

Frank shook his head and drew a line on the blanket in front of him. "Here's her life without cancer." He drew a second line parallel to the first. "Here's her life with cancer." Then he made an indentation to the right of both lines. "And here's our bioprotein computer. All three exist in parallel but distinct space-time sequences."

"Parallel time lines," Janet said. "Shmirnov's theory."

"Which postulates that multiple timelines run parallel to each other, each timeline a slight variation on the next timeline. Our bioprotein server sits in its own space-time harmonic aperture for a reason—so that it can't be tampered with by cyberpranksters. So, if Miss Parker lives this non-cancerous timeline, her ports captured by our server, and then later a perturbation in the space-time fabric gives her throat cancer a year before, causing her life to jump to this timeline with cancer, what happens to the data already recorded by our server in this completely-separate aperture?"

"It only records the one sequence!"

"But only if—and this is a big if—that perturbation doesn't have some ripple effect that then changes the aperture where the server is stored."

"Given the billions of transactions that it monitors, seems like it would be affected in some way or another."

"Seems like it would. But, if we assume that it hasn't been affected …"

"Then we have a way to discover when these larger perturbations started and how widespread they are." Janet sighed. "I knew there wasn't a conflict. I knew it." She kissed her husband. "Gosh, I love you."

Alterlude #5

Ashley McArthur looked out her office window onto K Street Mall in Washington DC, glum at the snow-covered buildings, disliking all the Christmas lights, wondering if the sun would come out before noon, or whether it would stay gray all day.

Assistant inspector general at Housing and Urban Development, Ashley brought her gaze back to the materials strewn across her desk. Three tactiface screens cluttered with information added their chaos to her desktop. Balance sheets, requisitions, invoices, correspondence, all added up to the massive fraud investigation into Colorado State Department of Housing and Community Development. She had personally spearheaded an audit into what was proving to be the biggest case of fraud at HUD in a hundred years, all because Colorado had contracted its federal housing appropriations to an innocuous non-profit, joint-powers agency called Cottage Home, Inc.

At HUD, auditing was rare. Its twenty-billion dollar yearly budget appropriated these monies to the states based on complex income-by-population formulas. When audits occurred, they did so because of glaring inequities. Four years ago, Cottage Home had begun reporting astounding results in its yearly data versus the services that they had been projected to provide. In the first year, their services were lauded as exemplary, but as federal regulators had begun to analyze the service delivery methods, the reality was quickly revealed to fall short of the reported results. Far short.

So they asked for HUD's Inspector General to look into the issue.

For two years, Ashley had been looking into the issue. By January first, she expected to have a final report to Congress, the last pieces on her desk ready to assemble into its final form. She smiled out the window, wondering if she might step outside for lunch, get a hot chocolate, and return to the office for her final push to assemble the remaining pieces, and package it for the Inspector General.

She glanced at the clock. 11:30.

Good enough, she thought, standing. At the door, she grabbed her hooded parka, stepped out into the larger office to the sign-out board, and headed for the stairs. On the ground floor, she waved at the security guard, slipped into her parka, and stepped out into the brisk Washington cold.

The K Street sidewalk crunched underfoot as it did for the other thousands of bureaucrats, lobbyists, and businesspersons headed somewhere for lunch, lines forming at many of the doorports in the center of the street already, despite a time somewhat shy of noon.

Ashley joined a line for the Dining District, an enclave of the finest restaurants, negotiation booths, and shakedown spots in Washington, where a snack from a vender cart was ten times the price elsewhere but a sighting of a Cabinet Secretary, Senator, and on rare occasion even the President might be had, making that snack worth ten times what a person had paid. I deserve the best hot chocolate I can find, she thought, proud of her work on the Cottage Home investigation.

She swiped her card, the light turned green, the doorport shimmered, and she stepped through to the Dining District. The aromas enveloped her like a warm blanket, of cinnamon and barbeque and garlic and rosemary.

Ashley thought, Why in the blazes did I come here? I always find it disorienting, and if I'm anywhere close to a foul mood, this place is sure to send me plummeting into one!

And I've got plenty to be foul about!

She circled around the line of doorports toward the one that would take her back to her office on P Street, the backwater of federal offices, where the nearest window was five cubes over and covered with soot from the foundry next door pumping out its noxious smoke as they built parts for the submarines at Norfolk just across Chesapeake Bay. She remembered the odious report her boss wanted from her by two pm and how she hadn't started on it, and besides, what was there to report to the NTSB chief except that doorports continued to operate flawlessly across the nation in transporting both people and freight, and how she wished she had something to report on, but her agency, once one of the largest and most powerful in Washington, governing the safety of all modes of transport and having power to police all the major manufacturers of those now-outmoded hydrocarbon vehicles collectively known as planes, trains, and automobiles, was now one of the smallest in Washington without a hint of its former influence.

Now a political backwater, the National Transportation Safety Board was death to a bureaucrat. Its chairperson appointed by each new administration was either long past his or her zenith or on a rapid descent to a nadir in the dungeons of the bureaucracy.

Ashley found the doorport, waved her comcard and stepped back onto P Street, the avenue nearly empty of pedestrian, her stomach empty of lunch, her life empty of excitement, her career empty of purpose.

Depressed, Ashley made her way back to her desk, her threadbare parka now thrown over her arm.

The unit secretary Doris looked up as she went past. "Ms. McArthur, you have a message from Charlie Goodrich, Division Manager at American Doorport. He says he'd like to speak with you at your earliest convenience."

"Thank you, Doris, I'll return his com as soon as possible."

Remembering Charlie from a conference six months ago, Ashley was thinking, I wonder what this is about?

Chapter 8

Janet knew by Doctor David Winter's eyes that he'd seen great suffering. She also knew that in spite of the suffering he'd seen, it hadn't reduced his capacity for compassion. Instead, it had deepened it.

"Doctor Winters," Janet said.

"Doctor Thompson," David said.

"Wonderful legislation the Governor signed last week. Congratulations. Work that leaves me in awe."

David's gaze dropped to his desk, his eyes misting. "You're very kind. Your own work is highly admired in your field, I'm given to understand."

"Kind of you to say, if my arrest hasn't dimmed that admiration, that is. A procedural oversight, but entirely my fault, as I didn't follow through to make sure the company responded in a timely fashion to the subpoena."

Doctor Winters shrugged. "It happens that a patient of mine has an interest in your work—a delusion, actually, that her life has been stolen from her. Persecutory ideations and religious preoccupations. She speaks very highly of your work, if not your morals."

Janet felt ambivalent, disconcerting and reminiscent of her sister. "Doctor Winters, I need your help."

"Regarding the subpoena?"

Janet shrugged. "That and others. I know a young woman who complains of dreams that a friend of hers worked alongside her until the day she died, despite her parents having substantial unpaid medical bills indicating a degree of illness that would certainly have prevented her from working. I have doorport records consistent with the dreams and inconsistent with the illness."

The Doctor's eyebrows climbed his forehead.

"And I believe," Janet said, frowning, "that you already know Ms. Yelena Thornton." Janet saw him start. "Doctor Winters, I have doorport records that support her claims, in spite of her, uh, cognitive difficulties. But as I said, I need your help."

David Winters studied her from across his desk. Slowly, he stood. "Why don't you have a seat?" To one side of his desk were three chairs, one of them sprouting a number of gadgets. "No, not that one," he said, amusement emerging on his face.

Janet took one of the regular chairs.

David took the other. "Please keep in mind, Doctor Thompson, that I have two issues that constrain how and to what degree I can assist you with this matter."

"Confidentiality, I'm sure is one of them."

"Just so. And the other is legal as well. I've examined Ms. Thornton, as you're aware already, but that was done within the context of the forensics investigation, which was ordered by the same Grand Jury that executed the subpoena."

"So you can't tell me the results of your examination."

"I cannot."

"I would like you to examine this young woman I know."

"Barring requests for comparison between the two, I would be delighted, as I must say I'm intrigued. But may I ask, what is your intent in requesting this examination?"

"Our doorport network is beginning to have problems. I wish to solve them, but to do so, I need to pinpoint the problems. I won't ask further into the results of Ms. Thornton's examination except to request that your analysis of Danielle take into account or at least consider that their issues may originate from similar places."

"What are you expecting to find?"

Janet examined his face. The face of a scientist, one of high integrity and deep moral resolve. His integrity and resolve are just what I need, Janet thought.

She sighed. "On Monday morning, some thirty-six hours after assuming the reins at American Doorport, I asked my Vice President of Operations to report to the NTSB that anomalies are beginning to emerge, small variations in the accuracy and reliability of doorport transmissions. By your analysis of Danielle, I hope to have something that will help me explain—and to correct—these anomalous events, and perhaps, why we have been unable to detect them before this."

Doctor Winters stared at her for a full five minutes, blinking occasionally, and even once starting to speak. Finally, he did speak. "I wonder whether I'll understand enough of your physics to explain these anomalies."

"By turns, I wonder that I'll understand enough of your neurology."

Doctor Winters nodded, a slight amusement reaching his face. "As long as you ask nothing more than that, I should like to meet this Danielle."

"Doctor Winters," Janet said, "if all that you provide is a slight clue as to how a doorport record validates a young woman's dreams or an old woman's assertions, I won't have come to you for naught." And Janet was thinking, Already I've gained by being here, by seeing his integrity and resolve.

"Already you have not," Doctor Winters said, "come here for naught."

Janet smiled, liking him.

"I'll give you a general description. Will that work for you?" Doctor Winters asked, and at her nod, he continued. "Dementia is a term used to describe general cognitive decline, usually of older people. The three basic types—vascular, myelinar, and those due to infectious agents— each have different causes and different etiologies but result in similar symptoms: difficulties with retention, language impairments, cognitive processing problems, inability to generalize, disorientation, confusion, poor impulse control, motor disorganization, and the like.

"Vascular dementia usually is a result of transient ischemic attacks across time, small virtually-undetectable strokes, where blood vessels burst and deprive neurons of oxygen in multiple locations, resulting in vascular lesions. Each lesion is so small that it goes unnoticed, but the cumulative effect results in the symptoms noted above. Myelinar dementia, sometimes called glial dementia, results when the brain's 'glue,' the glial cells, begins to malfunction. Glial cells surround neurons and hold them in place, supply nutrients and oxygen to neurons, insulate neurons from each other, destroy pathogens, remove dead neurons, and modulate neurotransmission. When they malfunction, it is analogous to an autoimmune disorder, such as rheumatoid arthritis or lupus. Those due to infectious agents include Creutzfeldt-Jakob Disease or CJD, which can be contracted by eating the tainted cerebral matter of other animals.

"The most prominent form of Glial-cell dementia develops from the breakdown of the waste-product removal system in the brain, a process called demyelination, in which glial cells physically separate dead molecules from live ones. When demyelination breaks down—when glial cells either cease to function or themselves begin attacking live neurons—plaque begins to build up, dead cells begin to accumulate on the surface of live ones. The plaque build-up then prevents neurons from growing new dendrites, and prevents dendrites from emitting and receiving neurotransmitters, and reduces the conductivity of the dendrite itself. On a macroscopic scale, this accretion of plaque results in slower and fewer completed neural signals.

"Human memory is notoriously fickle. Learning and memory are distinct processes, keep in mind. One is simply the recall of information taken through the senses, while the other is the processing of information stored in complex arrays called schemas, whose interrelated links reinforce each other for long-term retention. Typically, learned information is static and concrete at first, but as that information is used, reused, re-associated with other information and other memories, it makes a transition to what is known as fluid. When plaque builds through the failure of demyelination, learned information does not as easily get reused or re-associated, particularly if the schema is little used, as we often see in patients who spend their days watching vids or other non-upper cortical activities. For someone suffering from dementia, their learning rarely reaches that transition to fluidity, and their thinking is rarely able to transcend that concretion. That doesn't mean they aren't able to learn—simply that their learning takes place more slowly and often requires external strategies such as extensive notes, prompts, or reminders.

"Now, please keep in mind that this brief description of dementia discloses nothing about Mrs. Thornton, nor a shred of content from her examination. But hopefully, it helps you to puzzle through your conundrum."

Janet frowned. "Doctor Winters, is the onset of dementia gradual and mild, or rapid and severe?"

"That depends on the dementia." Doctor Winters smiled. "My father had virulent CJD, and his decline from fully-functioning psychiatrist to blithering idiot took less than a year. Alzheimer's can take ten years from the first signs of onset to complete incoherence. Alas, I cannot disclose what Mrs. Thornton has—or if."

"Of course, Doctor Winters. Given that the disease is progressive, I'd question how far her dementia had progressed at three years ago and at one year ago. Without knowing the degree of decline, I'm still left in somewhat of a fog. Help me to understand something: What might be the operative issue where Yelena would remember something and Danielle would not?"

"Cognitive dissonance," Doctor Winters said immediately. "A concept from the early days of psychoanalytic development. Essentially, an idea incongruent with one's self perception cannot be held for long without distress. When we feel distress about something, our coping skills engage to reduce that distress. Rationalization—in this case the process of rectifying two sets of conflicting memories—almost requires a person to dismiss memories incongruent with experience, not to belabor the subjectivity of our experiences. Now, we can compare the two situations, Danielle's and Yelena's, but to do so we have to suspend judgment regarding what's true. We don't know what's true and we may never find out. We have to set aside what's true as immaterial, at least for the time being.

"So Danielle's friend died of throat cancer, and Danielle remembers her friend's dancing up until the day she died, two mutually incongruent experiences. One is irrefutable: Her friend is dead. The other, to be congruent, has to be rationalized in one way or another."

"So she dismisses the memories as dreams."

"So it sounds," Doctor Winters said, nodding.

Janet nodded. "So, Mrs. Thornton's husband disappears into a doorport a year ago, but all the records indicate he died three years ago in completely different circumstances. Unlike Danielle's situation, neither of Mrs. Thornton's memories is irrefutable. Either set of memories can be discounted, but they are still incongruent, so Mrs. Thornton has to decide which one is true."

Doctor Winters smiled. "It is and would naturally be ego-syntonic for her to choose the former, as those memories are more recent and more emotionally charged."

"More distant memories being more easily dismissed," Janet added.

Doctor Winters nodded. "And our officialdom, when presented with the incongruity between Yelena's assertions and the official records ..."

"Tells her she has dementia," Janet supplied.

"Your words, not mine," said Doctor Winters. "Please be reminded, that I still have not revealed the results of my examination."

"You haven't," Janet acknowledged. "Well done. How soon could you see Danielle?"

"I'd imagine I have appointments beginning next week. See my secretary, would you? I try to reserve at least two days of the week for the direct examination of patients." He smiled. "Keeps my mind fresh."

"Thank you so much, Doctor Winters, for all your time." Janet stood and shook his hand, then stopped at the secretary's desk on her way out of his offices, sorting through the space-time harmonic sequence in her head to try to rectify what Yelena Thornton remembered versus what official documentation declared.

How could she remember her husband's disappearance into a doorport but not his death two years before that?

Janet pulled her jacket tight as she left the Institute for Geriatric Studies, and her comcard buzzed in her pocket to alert her. Next meeting in five minutes with the President of the Board, RK Blackstone.

She looked at her grandmother's gold, mechanical watch. 10:55. Her comcard out, she strode toward a bank of doorports a half-block away.

Protestors. Paleolithic imbeciles, she thought.

Thumbing through her schedule as she walked toward them, Janet saw they were blocking one doorport rather than all of them. Usually, they just carry signs and yell at people, she was thinking. The one doorport they were blocking read across the lintel, "American Doorport."

Janet stopped beside a planter, pretending to be absorbed in her comcard, wondering how she was going to get back to corporate. For a minute or two, she thumbed through messages on her comcard, then pulled her calendar back up, wondering if she should call RK Blackstone to let him know she was delayed. Moving her thumb up to the previous appointment with Doctor Winters at 10:00 to mark it done, Janet suddenly remembered the recalibrator.

She thumbed it up on her comcard, strode to the nearest unblocked doorport and swiped it. The light blinked red, red, red, green, the doorport shimmered, and she stepped through to the sidewalk in front of Corporate just as the bells of the Cathedral Basilica began to toll in the distance.

The sound a comfort, having grown up within earshot of it, Janet took a moment to listen to the melodious chimes, and then the tolling of the hour began. One, two, three …

She stepped toward the building, and as she put her hand on the door, expecting the toll for the eleventh hour, all she heard was silence.

All I counted was ten.

Thinking she must have been mistaken, she checked her Grandmother's watch. 11:00 exactly. Shrugging to herself, she entered, made her way to the elevator, smiling at her coworkers.

On the twelfth floor, she stepped off and greeted the unit secretary, who seemed surprised to see her.

"Is Mr. Blackstone here yet?" Janet asked.

"No, Doctor Thompson," the secretary said, looking bewildered.

Janet strode toward her office.

Stan looked up from his new desk outside the CEO's office. "Janet, er, uh, Doctor Thompson."

She waved it away and rolled her eyes. "Just Janet, please."

Stan chuckled. "Sure. Back early from your ten o'clock?"

Janet stopped, her hand on her doorknob. "No…" Frowning, she asked, "Any sign of Blackstone?"

Stan frowned, his brow wrinkled. "Wasn't that at eleven?"

Janet looked at her watch. "And it's two past by my Grandmother's old watch. Unlike Blackstone to be late. Did he call to say he was held up?"

Stan just blinked at her, then swallowed. "Uh, Janet, it's two past ten."

Janet stared at her secretary, not comprehending. "I just spent an hour with Doctor David Winters at the Institute of Geriatric Studies. That can't be right."

Stan showed her his comcard, then pointed at the clock on the wall. They both said 10:03.

Janet whipped out her own comcard. 10:03.

She blinked at it, uncomprehending. "I was just talking with Doctor Winters. He met with me right at ten. I'd told him I had back-to-back meetings this morning and he promised me he'd be punctual. I spoke with him for at least an hour." Janet realized she was beginning to sound frantic.

Stan frowned. "I know you've been under some stress lately, but …"

"No, no," Janet said, speaking too quickly. "I must be mistaken." But her Grandmother's watch insisted it was 11:03. It's never wrong, Janet thought. What if it isn't wrong? "Or maybe I've just invented time travel," Janet quipped.

At Stan's laughter, she entered her office and got settled, then tapped her tactiface to get Charlie.

As his face swam into focus, Janet pulled off her watch.

"I don't like that look on your face," Charlie said.

"Come in here, now, please."

A minute later he was there, his tie askew, his shirt wrinkled. "What's the ruckus?" Charlie jerked his thumb over his shoulder. "Stan's telling me you've lost it."

She handed him her watch.

His eyes bounced between her face and the watch face. "I'm not making any sense of this. And this is the watch that's never wrong, right? Your grandmother's watch."

Janet nodded and told him about her morning.

Charlie whistled tonelessly. "An hour or so with Doctor Winters starting at ten am, and then you got back here at ten am?"

Janet shrugged. "I don't know what happened."

"And you ported back here?"

Janet and Charlie looked at each other.

The silence stretched, and finally Charlie rubbed his face with his hands. "I have an idea. It's ten fifteen now, right?"

Frowning, Janet nodded.

"Let me send somebody to the doorport that you used at eleven.

Which one was it? All right, and I'll ask them to watch for you, not to try to speak with you, but just to watch. And then have them report to me, all right?"

Janet nodded. "I want you here when I meet with Blackstone, Charlie. You know as much about this as I do."

"I'll be here," he said, and left her office.

Janet turned to look out the window at downtown Denver, anxiety chewing at the edge of her sanity.

"I've asked you here, Mr. Blackstone, to alert you to a few emergent issues," Janet said.

Charlie had taken a seat near the door. The time was 10:55, Blackstone having arrived early.

"Call me RK, Janet," RK Blackstone said. "What issues? Couldn't have anything to do with being arrested at your boss's funeral, could it?"

Janet threw her head back and laughed.

"Jackson told me he had some concerns and had you looking into them. What do you have?"

Janet described the Missy Parker situation.

"And you offered to pay her medical bills? Glad to hear it, would've done the same, myself. What else do you have?"

Janet told him about Yelena Thornton, the subpoena, and the neurological testing done by Doctor Winters.

"Won't tell you the results, eh? Well, other ways to get that information. What do you make of the dementia?"

"I can't put it together just yet, but one related piece regarding Missy Parker—her coworker Danielle says she dreamt that Missy danced all the way up to her death."

"Even through chemo, radiation, and all that? Not likely she did, wouldn't you say?"

"Doorport records support that she did. Same with Yelena."

RK Blackstone looked at her, looked away, looked back at her.

"And just this morning—"

"Hello? Charlie here." Charlie was looking at his comcard. "You see Janet stepping into the doorport now?"

In the distance, the bells of Cathedral Basilica began to toll.

"All right, thank you so much." Charlie looked at Janet and RK.

"What the bloody hell?" RK said, looking quickly between them.

"Just this morning," Janet continued, feeling faint, knowing her face was white, "I met with Doctor David Winters—"

"Which you told me."

"—and on my way back to meet with you, I stepped into a doorport outside his office just seconds before eleven am, and stepped out of the doorport right here in front of Corporate to the sound of those same bells, except for one small incongruity. Those bells tolled only ten times as I stood in front of Corporate."

Blackstone frowned at her.

"That comcall I just got," Charlie said, "was from a technician I sent to watch for Janet, to make sure she indeed was stepping into the doorport in front of Doctor Winters' office at precisely eleven am."

"But you were right here the whole time!" Blackstone said, an edge of panic in his voice.

Janet and Charlie just stared at him.

RK Blackstone sat down, looking pale. "You used the prototype?"

Janet nodded. "This is a new development, one which I've only had a few minutes—sixty, to be exact—to grasp. If it means what I think it does ..."

"Time travel," Blackstone whispered.

"Exactly." Janet shook her head. "If it's at the expense of lives, we can't have it. For every Missy Parker or Yelena Thornton, there are thousands we don't know about."

"I agree. What's our exposure?" Blackstone asked.

To legal liability, Janet's mind automatically supplied. "Slim, but growing," she said. "I asked Charlie to contact the NTSB, and we'll file an incident report. Wasn't until we got served the subpoena that we even knew about Yelena Thornton. They don't know about Missy Parker or the others." Janet saw Blackstone start. "Jackson didn't tell you about this?" She held up a memchip.

Blackstone shook his head.

"Handed it to me two weeks before he died, the same day his brother handed me this one in San Diego." She held up the other memchip.

"Old Man Douglas." Blackstone shuddered.

"Exactly. There's our vulnerability. If he or Cynthia McLaughlin get ahold of this information, our stock price tanks, and we'll have regulators crawling all over the place. And that's where we need your help."

The media mogul grinned. "All right, let me find a reporter who can slant this our way. Who've you retained for counsel?"

"Suzanne Roberts-Carter," Janet replied.

"Good, good, knows the region well, knows the aristocracy, knows the judges and legislators. Let me know if you need someone national, though. Sounds like you've got it contained. How about the field testing on the prototype?"

"Ready for a Thursday evening rollout," Charlie said. "We can have it on every employee's comcard today if Janet wants it."

"My concern is today's anomaly," Janet added, "especially if it's part of the larger pattern. Any way we can isolate the prototype?"

Charlie and Blackstone both looked at her. "Instead of uploading it to everyone's comcard?" Charlie asked.

Janet nodded, knowing this end of things to be Charlie's expertise. She held up her comcard. "I was looking at my schedule at the time I activated the prototype and stepped through the doorport. I'd prefer that we issue new comcards to everyone, instead of uploading the prototype."

Charlie's face scrunched up. "A one terabyte comcard costs a hundred dollars. Fifty-six thousand employees. Order, copy, distribute, register." Charlie stopped muttering to himself, looked at them. "All told, a full week at five-point-six mil just for parts. Labor another mil."

Janet considered. The prototype recalibrator was her baby, the culmination of a year of work. "I can wait another week," she said, sighing. "Further, I want an opt out and a hold harmless on file for each employee. Oh, and a confidentiality. If things go haywire, we'll want to keep it under wraps."

RK Blackstone smiled at Janet. "Jackson was right about you, Janet. Said you'd be the one to take over in his place. Well done."

Alterlude #6

Janice Thomas walked into Doctor David Winter's office for her monthly scheduled appointment. "Hi, Shireen," she said to the receptionist. "Sorry I'm late. You know how it is getting here without using doorports—takes awhile."

"Please have a seat, Janice. Doctor Winters is with another patient."

Janice moved away from the window. No one else was in the office, just the secretary behind the window, which snicked shut as Janice found a seat.

"She closed the window because she wants to talk about you," a voice said from across the room.

When Janice looked, no one was there. "Oh, just shut your trap," she replied, feeling annoyed.

"You don't need to be here; there's nothing wrong with you," said a voice beside her.

Janice didn't bother to look, knowing she wouldn't see anyone. "I know there's nothing wrong with me, but I still need to see Doctor Winters."

"Of course you do," said yet a different voice on the other side of her. "You need to tell him about the apocalypse."

"The doorports are ripping apart the space-time fabric," Janice said, "Doctor Winters doesn't believe me. I tell him every time but he never stops using them."

"But you won't stop telling him," said another voice across the room.

"Of course, I won't," Janice said, seeing no one there. "Why don't you show yourself? What are you afraid of? You never show yourself. Like that bitch who took over my life. She never shows herself, she wouldn't dare."

"She's paranoid, isn't she?" said a voice beside her.

"Yeah, paranoid. They call me paranoid, but she's the one who's paranoid. I ought to go see her sister. She'll believe me. She already knows what the doorports are doing to us. The space-time harmonic sequence is flawed. I tried to tell them at MIT, but they told me I was ill. I came to Denver to tell Jackson Weintraub, but they locked me up and put me in restraints, then they jabbed me in the butt and put those medications in me."

"The medications are poison," said a voice across the room.

"No, they're not," Janice replied. "You keep telling me that, but the last time I listened to you they took me back to the hospital because I was so crazy."

"You're not crazy. There's nothing wrong with you."

"Of course, there isn't," Janice replied. "But I'm gonna see Doctor Winters anyway because he understands."

Somewhere a door opened. "Hi, Janice. I'm glad you could make it today."

Janice saw Doctor Winters across the room. "Oh, hi!" Abruptly she stood. "Sorry, I didn't see you. The voices are really loud today."

"Yes," Doctor Winters said. "I could hear you in the next room. Come on in." He gestured.

She bounced into his office, liking the sun that streamed through the windows. "Sorry I'm late. I rode my bike. I didn't want to take the doorports."

"Still feeling afraid of them?"

Janice nodded. "I know you tell me it's paranoia, that there's nothing to be afraid of, but I've got a Doctorate in Space-Time Harmonics from MIT and—"

Doctor Winters held up his hand.

"Sorry," Janice said. "I know you think that's part of my delusion, but how come I can write out the sequence forward and backward if I'm not a Doctor? Where did I learn that?"

"You went to MIT, Janice. That's where you learned the equations." Doctor Winters smiled. "And that was when you had your first break. Twenty-eight is a late age for anyone to have a first psychotic break, but you were also under tremendous pressure, just starting a post-doctorate, putting out your vitae to different research institutions, looking for a tenured position, considering a private sector position—the strain you told me was overwhelming."

Janice nodded glumly. "I didn't handle it so well, did I?"

"You did the best you could," Doctor Winters said.

"I probably should have studied my bible more. God doesn't want us to mess around with time and space like that. You should stop using the doorports, you know."

"So you've said on other occasions."

"I've told you that every time I've been here."

Doctor Winters smiled. "Yes, Janice. Looks to me like the voices and ideas are stronger today."

"How did you know? And so are the liminal forces. The fabric is beginning to come apart. Did you read about Yelena and Barnaby Thornton? How tragic. Disappears into a doorport a year ago, and then they have a murder-suicide on the day he returns, no one sure who killed who. That's the doorport system at work, Doctor. You know she was involved somehow, don't you?"

"I didn't read about a murder-suicide, Janice. Tell me a little more about your symptoms. When did they start getting worse?"

"Last week sometime, when that woman was arrested. They won't be able to make anything stick, you know. And I'll bet you've forgotten it was murder they arrested her for."

"No, Janice, they didn't arrest her for murder. It was just contempt of court. Now, we both know what your diagnosis is, right?"

"Paranoid Schizophrenia," Janice said immediately.

"And you recognize the types of delusions you have, right?"

"Persecutory delusions," Janice said.

"And what is the one fixed delusion you have?"

"But it's not a delusion. She really *did* steal my life at MIT. She did! And she made my roommate Stacey move out because she couldn't stand her cat! I know you don't believe me, and I know you're going to give me another shot today to try to make that belief go away, but it doesn't matter what you give me, your medications can never make reality go away, and oh, why do I keep coming back because I know the result is the same, oh why won't you believe me, Doctor Winters, why won't you believe me?" And Janice bit her lip to stop herself and wiped away the one tear that leaked from her eye. With a sigh, she looked up at Doctor Winters. "Can I ask you something?"

"Certainly," he said.

His gaze was as gentle as she'd always found it, and she felt warm and comfortable in his presence in spite of the fact that he never believed her or heeded her warnings or let her hold onto especially that one belief which she knew deep in her soul to be true. "What would you do if she told you that it could be true, that anomalies are beginning to emerge, small variations in the accuracy and reliability of doorport transmissions? Would you believe her?"

"I would certainly feel compelled to do so," Doctor Winters said, his face looking troubled. "Janice, given the strength and persistence of your ideations at present, would you consider being in the hospital right now?"

"I don't want to go back there, Doctor Winters. I really don't."

"If you were to leave here now, how would you go about finding something to eat?"

"Nearest fast food, grocery store, food in my fridge—I've got it all."

"And if the clothes you're wearing got dirty, how would you go about finding clean clothes to wear?"

"Clothing store, clothes closet—lots of good free stuff there—or I'd just go home and look in my own closet."

"And if you didn't have a place to sleep tonight, how would you go about finding a place to sleep?"

"I'd ask you if I could sleep on your couch. And rightfully you'd refuse of course but it wouldn't stop me from asking."

"What's today's date?"

Janice told him. "And I'm at your office in Denver, it's the middle of winter, and my name is Janice Thomas, and I'm forty years old. I don't want to kill myself, and I haven't had a thought about harming myself for at least five years, and I don't want to hurt anyone else, and I have no history ever of assaulting anyone." She paused and smiled. "See, there's no basis for holding me involuntarily for treatment. I'm happy to accept whatever voluntary outpatient treatment that you recommend—within reason, of course—so I don't need to be in the hospital."

Doctor Winters sighed. "Very well. Please see my nurse for that shot, and I'd like to increase your PRN supplement of that same medication. In fact, let's make it daily. Would that work for you? And rather than four weeks until your next appointment, how about two weeks?"

"Okay! I'd be happy to come back in two weeks. You've such a nice man and a wonderful doctor. No wonder you're the Medical Director of the Colorado State Hospital and Professor of Neuropsychiatry at the University of Colorado at Denver. Thank you, Doctor Winters!" And Janice took the prescription he'd written to the front desk, where she found the nurse waiting.

"Jeanie!" she said, happy to see the nurse again. Together they went into the exam room, where Janice dutifully raised her shirt a little, unbuckled her pants and leaned over the exam table. "Ouch!" she said, the needle not really hurting.

"I'll send the prescription to the pharmacy," Jeanie said. "And they'll deliver tomorrow. Oh, and I'll ask them not to use doorports."

"Oh, thank you, Jeanie," Janice said, straightening her clothes. "See you in two weeks."

As she walked out the door, a faint voice to the right of the doorway said, "They never believe you."

"No," Janice Thomas replied, "but one day they might."

Chapter 9

That night, drifting off to the soft sounds of Frank's breathing, Janet Thompson sighed, that lethargic bliss after deep, satisfying sex with the man she loved spreading through her body.

Everything in place, all her cares addressed, her family safe, her man happy, Janet said a blessing under her breath, thanking the spirit for all that was well and wonderful, and for all that wasn't, for she knew that facing challenges would take her to her next point of growth.

For even though all systems sought homeostasis, they also experienced continual growth and continual decay, and because of that, homeostasis might be achieved but it was always transitory, always brief, and in that imbalance, the pressures themselves were homeostatic with the degree of imbalance.

And whatever the anomalies or perturbations in the space-time fabric, the forces in play to correct them were equal and opposite to those perturbations. And if one calibration to align one space-time point with another space-time point shifted that fabric ever so slightly, so too did the natural resilience exert its force to restore the original positions of those space-time points.

And in those equations as they floated through Janet's head as she drifted just above the threshold of sleep, she saw that it was the work exerted by the space-time fabric to restore itself to its original position after a harmonic aperture was created that caused the perturbations themselves, and her immediate thought was, Why not have the sequence of equations themselves restore the space-time fabric rather than making the fabric restore itself?

Janet snapped awake a moment before the alarm went off and knew what she had to do.

The solution glowed vividly in the forefront of her thoughts.

She rose and stood next to their bed in the dark, and looked down upon her husband, his warmth lingering inside her still, tempted to climb back onto him because even after fifteen years of marriage, he still left her gasping, and she loved his every touch, and his gaze made her melt inside, as it had the first time their gazes had met. And in the dark, she sighed.

And she heard him sigh too.

"I love you," she whispered.

"I love you," he whispered back.

And she moistened but right then her comcard buzzed, reminding her she had an early meeting that morning and couldn't climb back into bed. She shut off her alarm and reached for a bathrobe to start her morning routine.

Once the coffee was brewing and the shower warming up, Janet consulted the weather report on her home computer, synched her comcards—the one she used everyday with the one she kept in her shoe for safekeeping, and stepped to her closet to lay out her clothes.

Under the water, she felt as though she were in Frank's arms again and she wanted him right then as she always wanted him after just having had him and knew he felt that way too and would be as ready for her as she was now for him, and she was grateful for the need to wash because it distracted her from her desire.

She hurried into her clothes from the brace of cold hitting her as she climbed from the shower, and partly dressed, retrieved some coffee before returning to the bathroom mirror to do her teeth and face.

Lucky that her face needed nothing more than mild repair, Janet smiled at herself when she was done.

Satisfied, she finished dressing and accessorizing, making sure to slip that extra back-up comcard into her shoe, then kissed her husband goodbye. Stopping at the kid's rooms, she kissed them each, barely disturbing their sleep, then slipped downstairs for a bite, her coat and briefcase, one more shot of coffee, then to the doorport in the garage.

All I have to do is revamp the entire harmonic equation progression, and all these anomalies will disappear, Janet was thinking as she activated her recalibrator and swiped her card.

The sensor turned green, and the doorport shimmered.

Janet stepped onto the sidewalk in front of Corporate and into a crowd of protestors.

"Thieves and murderers!" They screamed as one.

Janet side-stepped a blond woman but she wouldn't let Janet pass. Then she saw it was Cynthia, and Janet remembered the expose in yesterday's Denver Post by the Pulitzer-prize winning reporter Zachary Hempstead.

"You've taken your last life!" her sister yelled in her face. "You cold-blooded killer!"

Once free of the protestors, Janet stepped to the quadruple doors leading into the building.

A twisted face thrust into hers. "You've screwed your last man. He was my husband! Mine!"

Belatedly, Janet recognized Charlie's wife, and her face grew deep crimson as she remembered the encounter she'd had with Charlie last night on the floor beside her desk.

"You cold-blooded slut!"

Once inside the door, Janet walked through the foyer, dismayed at all the yellow "caution" tape.

A young woman with a badge at her lapel strode up to Janet. "We knew we'd get you on something. You've ported your last person into the void."

Janet recognized her as Ashley McArthur, Assistant Inspector General at NTSB, and then Janet remembered the judge's ruling yesterday that had placed American Doorport into Federal receivership.

"You cold-blooded CEO!"

Once at the elevators, Janet was stopped at their open doors by a hand on her arm.

"You're under arrest, Doctor Thompson," Deputy Anthony Stewart said.

"What for?"

"Suspicion of murder. You have the right…"

And then Janet remembered the newspaper story, how the Denver Post reporter, Hempstead, had got ahold of doorport records, and that just before Barnaby Thornton had disappeared into a doorport, Janet herself had gone through that same doorport, the maintenance record indicating repairs right after the disappearance.

Repairs that Janet herself had ordered.

"You cold-blooded killer!"

Booking was humiliating, far worse the second time.

The Perp Walk, that public indignity resurrected from the twentieth century of being paraded in chains past a voracious press crew and a scornful group of citizens, had been the worst part for Janet the first time around.

"Can we do the perp walk before the strip search?" she asked her captors. "Those jumpsuits make me look fat."

They looked amongst themselves, then to Deputy Stewart.

"They'll recognize me much better if I'm in my suit and heels," Janet added.

Deputy Stewart nodded to the booking clerk. "Alert the jail. We can do the strip search and printing there." He took her by her elbow, her wrists in chains behind her back. "Don't try anything. I'll be watching your every move."

"Don't be an idiot. My arrest is the highlight of your career. You'll never nab such a high-class criminal as me again, and we both know it."

"Uppity bitch," he muttered under his breath, signaling his partner to grab her other arm.

They hauled her over to the doorport.

"Take it easy," she said. "I don't move as fast in my heels."

The deputy waved his comcard across the doorport sensor, and the first deputy stepped through. Then Stewart waved again, and pushed Janet through.

The first deputy grabbed her arm on the other side, and Janet blinked away the after images as camera flashes flickered randomly, fractions of a second apart. The barrage of flashes was disconcerting.

Stewart stepped into the perp-walk tube behind her, the forty-foot glass cage, open only at the top to let noise in, covered with a grill, two deputies patrolling the walkway above. The yelling and hissing reminded Janet of a vaudeville performance. Here, though, people were yelling for her blood in earnest.

The deputies on either side were smiling for the cameras as they escorted her slowly through the tube.

Halfway along, she tripped, fell, and tumbled, her high-heeled shoes flying off. Unable to reach her feet herself, Janet snarled at the Deputies, "Help me up, you media hounds."

They hauled her to her feet, and Deputy Stewart retrieved her shoes.

"I'll carry those," Janet said.

He put them in her hands behind her back, then put his hand back on her elbow. "Don't be trying to sue us for brutality, lady. This was your idea."

Her shoes in her left hand, Janet reached into one of them with her right.

Her back-up comcard.

She activated the recalibrator by touch, pulling up a random destination.

They escorted her the remaining fifteen feet, and Deputy Stewart waved his card. The doorport shimmered and he stepped through.

The second Deputy waved his card, and the doorport shimmered. Janet feigned a stumble against the jamb of the doorport, her back to the sensor, her shoes close enough for her comcard to be read.

"Clumsy, aren't you?" The deputy said in disgust, shoving her through the shimmering doorport.

And into the open public square, jostled by a passerby, over-whelmed by the noise, offended by the stench, chilled by the cold, and half-blinded by the light.

Ecstatic, Janet giggled, and her first thought was, I did it!

Ecstasy quickly turned to anxiety.

Her second thought was, I'm a fugitive!

Her third: In handcuffs.

She looked around. A classical cathedral dominated the square, and poking into the sky beyond it was a steep pyramid.

The Transamerica Pyramid, San Francisco.

She stepped to a bench and sat. Who can I get to help me? Janet wondered, struggling to get her arms under her feet and out in front of her.

A few minutes of contortions left her panting, and Janet decided she simply wasn't limber enough to get her hands in front of her.

Who do I know who might help me with these handcuffs? she wondered.

Danielle!

Quickly, not knowing how long before national and international alerts were issued for her capture, Janet fished her back-up comcard out of her shoe, twisted her neck to see it over her shoulder, and pulled up Danielle's contact info.

Danielle's face swam into focus. "Miss Janey! Boy, you sure got people mighty upset. You go, girl!"

"Listen Danielle, I need your help. I've got to get these handcuffs off."

"That ain't the least of your worries, Miss Janey. I'll be there straight away."

The face faded from the comcard, and Janet sat up straight on the bench, trying to look as comfortable as a person in dual, silver bracelets possibly could.

The mid-morning pedestrian traffic was light, thankfully, and she didn't look terribly out of place in her pantsuit. The drunk with the rotted teeth sitting near the fountain twenty feet across from her was glancing her way all too frequently and smiling his wrecked grimace at her in a way-too-friendly way. As he stood, a slight reel to his stance, Danielle strode up behind him, spun him around, pulled his face into her cleavage and said. "Don't even think about it, or you'll have to deal with these!" She shoved him back to the bench he'd stood up from and strode over to Janet with her mighty tree-trunk legs. "We gotta stop meetin' on the wrong side of town, or law, or what have you! I swear, Miss Janey, I don't know what's gonna happen to my reputation if we keep meetin' like this!" Danielle threw her head back and laughed.

Janet threw her head back and laughed with her.

Pulling a pin out of her hair, Danielle had her out of handcuffs, on her feet, back in her shoes and headed for the bank of doorports in seconds. "No, no, don't use yours, 'cause they're probably on your tail already." Danielle pulled a handful of cards out of her purse and grinned. "I always have a back-up plan to my back-up plan."

She waved one across the "Bangkok" doorport and dragged Janet through.

The chaos of lights, bicycles, rickshaws, and stir-fry at Bangkok Central assaulted them. Ignoring it, Danielle hauled Janet to another bank of doorports, glanced among her cards, waved a different one across the "Lima" doorport sensor and stepped through with Janet clutched to her side.

They waded through a herd of sheep to the bank of doorports opposite, Danielle picking out "Sydney" and waving yet a different card.

London, Moscow, Anchorage, Boston, Madrid, Tel Aviv, Tokyo, Honolulu, Houston, Cairo, Bhopal, Phnom Penh, Buenos Aires, and finally, New York City.

Times Square.

Danielle led her into an alley. "No way they'll untangle that trail. Come with me, Miss Janey. Let's get you some normal clothes."

Janet followed her. "Look, you don't have to risk your own freedom. I should be all right from here."

Danielle stopped and turned. "If that's what you need, Miss Janey, all right, I guess. But you're gonna need counterfeit comcards if you want to keep your freedom."

"I have a few ideas, places I can go that they can't follow."

Danielle looked doubtful. "I don't know about that, Miss Janey. They're probably howling for your blood right now. Wouldn't surprise me to see your face on that vid right there." She pointed to the massive Times Square screen above them.

Dutifully, Janet's face appeared, under it a warning message.

Janet swore. "All right. But just tell me something. Why would you *want* to help me?"

"I heard from Mr. Parker, told me what you did. Whatever they're saying about you, it ain't right. A murderer doesn't pay a family's medical bills for them. You helped to set things right for Missy Parker, and you'll set all the rest of it right, of that I'm sure. I don't know how but that don't matter. You'll do it 'cause you've set your mind to it. That's what matters, that's why I'm helpin'. Now dry those tears and come on with me before someone recognizes you."

Chapter 10

Janet stared out the window on the afternoon of her second day at the Homestead Studio Suites, a slightly seedy motel in New Jersey that Danielle had picked out "'cause I never been there before."

She was getting a quick case of cabin fever, having gone nowhere in two days, having done nothing in two days, having spoken to no one save Danielle in two days.

Her sole source of information had been the vid, which at a place like this still had non-interactive channels, but whose content was so salacious Janet shuddered at the thought of watching. And the content that wasn't pornographic was inevitably tabloid.

Which for the last two days had been all Janet, all the time.

A nation searched for Doctor Janet Thompson, her image on every vid screen, newsie, and billboard. The CEO of the fifth richest corporation in the world on the lam for murder, last port to San Francisco, whereabouts unknown.

Murder! she thought with disgust.

Her company, American Doorport, now under federal receivership, its assets frozen, its foreign subsidiaries now under scrutiny for similar allegations, worldwide travel now in chaos, the company's dominance of doorport transmissions widely derided.

As though a world-size microscope had focused on her and would not let up.

Which was the reason she hadn't used any of the interactive channels, nor the tactiface, nor her comcard.

The worst part for Janet was having to think.

Not about her predicament, or how the company's stock price had tanked, or how her position at the company was now jeopardized.

But how mortified and betrayed her husband must feel, and how abandoned her kids must feel, and how ashamed her parents must feel.

She'd cried so many times already, she didn't think she could cry anymore. As much as she tried to rationalize it, she couldn't get away from the feeling that she'd betrayed the most sacred trust a woman could have—that with her husband.

And Charlie.

A tear trickled from her eye.

And she'd betrayed her husband with Charlie. Her friend, Charlie.

In her head, she struggled to keep in mind that it was a harmonic anomaly, that she hadn't screwed Charlie's brains out on the floor beside her office desk. But her memory insisted she had. And she'd enjoyed it.

Her face flushed with shame at the memory.

Odd, Janet was thinking, as tears poured anew from her eyes, how that memory was divorced from the company's being ordered into receivership earlier that day by the Federal District Court of Colorado, a ruling temporarily upheld by the Tenth Circuit Court of Appeals later that same day, the NTSB moving in the very next day to take over operations. Suzanne Roberts-Carter had not been able to obtain a preliminary injunction to stop the takeover.

At no point during her seduction of Charlie later that evening had she even considered the impending takeover by the NTSB. In spite of this miniscule validation of the possibility that both events were the result of harmonic anomalies, Janet was still a wreck.

Danielle had come back to the room late last night after her "show" at the "off Broadway theater," exhausted. But she had taken one look at Janet and had perked right up. "I been thinking, Miss Janey," Danielle had said. "You're gonna be needin' a few things. Without your comcard, you can't get money or nothin'. We're just gonna have to do something about that."

Janet just about hadn't paid attention, she was so caught up in her own misery.

But when she'd awakened, Danielle had been gone already.

Janet had panicked until she remembered what Danielle had said late the night before.

Now, Janet could feel her panic rising. Danielle had been gone for several hours, and there wasn't a thing to do except watch trashy vids about what a terrible mother she was, based on interviews with "friends" of hers whom she'd never met. Or interviews with "coworkers" whose names were unfamiliar, listening to them disclose the terrible things she'd done to them and other employees.

What if she doesn't come back? Janet wondered, pacing the floor, her anxiety heightened by her inability to do anything about it.

What if they traced my call to her in San Francisco? What if someone saw me stepping into a doorport with a six-six, orange-haired female? What if they indentified her and tracked her using her comcards? What if they were watching Danielle now and about to follow her back to the seedy motel in New Jersey?

The questions wouldn't stop, and soon Janet's heart was racing, and her chest hurt, and she couldn't breathe, and first she was hot and then she was cold, and she felt she was just going to scream at the top of her
…

Danielle burst through the door. "Hi, Miss Janey!"

A distant voice called her name but "Janey" wasn't her name and no matter how many times she insisted, the person kept calling her that and it was so annoying.

Janet's eyes snapped open.

"Oh dear Jesus Lord thank you she's awake!" Danielle said in one swift breath.

The room skewed and warped but snapped back into place when Janet sat up.

"Gave me a mighty scare when you dropped like that!"

Janet tried to speak but her mouth wouldn't work, so she gestured vaguely toward the door.

Danielle stood and bent down to help Janet up, her bust nearly bursting from her blouse.

Janet was instantly reminded of childhood, unable to recall having been lifted bodily from the floor by anyone since then.

Danielle pulled her into her ample bosom. "You just relax now,

331

you're in good hands, everything's all right, Mama Danny'll take care of you."

If you don't smother me first, Janet thought, trying to breathe around the cleavage mashed into her face.

"Listen, Miss Janey," Danielle said, holding her at arm's length. "I stick out like a sore thumb, and I'm as likely to draw attention to you as you are, but I know you ain't equipped for this kind of life like I am, so I went an' got you a few things to help out." Danielle nodded toward the door. There sat a bag, which Janet hadn't noticed until now.

"What things?" she asked, finally catching her breath, her heart rate slowing somewhat.

Danielle emptied the bag on the bed; wigs cascaded atop each other, some sliding onto the floor.

Bemused, Janet began to giggle.

"Now the trick, Miss Janey, is to change your wig as often as you use the bathroom. An' you gotta do it in the stall, otherwise their cameras will catch you changing your hair in front of their eyes."

Janet picked up a blond wig, so unlike her dark brown hair, and threw it on her head.

"The other thing you gotta do," Danielle said, "is change your face, and that's where this comes in." And she fished a bag of cotton balls out of the pile of wigs. She ripped open the bag and stuffed one into her cheek, up by the cheekbone. "Now this ain't very comfortable, but they darn sure aren't gonna recognize you, either with their eyeballs or with that bio metric scan they got."

Janet tried one, and the gritty taste almost made her gag.

"Your face is everywhere, you know, and you gotta do something to change it. Unless you got the time and money for some plastic surgery. Speakin' of money, that's one thing I can't help you with. My bank account—" she jabbed her thumb toward her vagina "—ain't *that* big."

Janet tried not to giggle and shook her head. Like nearly everyone else, all her credit information, contacts, email addresses, phone numbers, bank accounts, bills, and personal documents were on her comcard. In addition, Janet had had a prototype doorport recalibrator imprinted on her comcard. She held it up to Danielle. "This is all I got. That and my purse." She gestured to the dresser, where it lay.

And froze.

"Uh-oh. What's goin' on, Miss Janey. You got your wheels turning, I can tell."

Janet grabbed her purse and upended it as Danielle had her bag. Out tumbled the contents, among them the envelope she had found on the desk inside Old Man Jackson's inner sanctum. Ripping open the envelope, she dumped it out on the bed. Comcards, a dozen of them at least, different names imprinted on each. She scooped them up, threw everything else back in the purse, and turned to the tactiface. Pulling it toward her, she looked at the back, sorted between the wires, and unplugged the network.

"Where'd you git those? Looks like the stack I always keep with me."

Janet inserted the first comcard into the tactiface reader. The name and face that appeared were unknown to Janet. She swiped through the records on the card, saw encyclopedic personal information, including a rather impressive bank balance. She wondered what Old Man Jackson had wanted with a bunch of comcards that weren't his. Telling Danielle where she'd got them, Janet inserted the next card.

Danielle picked up the card from where Janet had set it.

Janet swiped her hand across the tactiface, seeing similar information, but for a different person. The next card, the same; similar info, different person. The next, the same. What struck Janet as odd was that each had bank balances in the hundreds of thousands of dollars. And they were all female.

"These comcards don't have thumbprint protection, Miss Janey." Danielle had picked up each one as Janet had removed it from the reader. "They're just like the one's I got."

"Why do you have cards like these?"

Danielle shrugged. "Protection. So I don't get found too easily. Remember that globe-trotting we did the other day? I used four different comcards on the doorports, and I didn't use mine, not that my name's really Danielle, either, but that's not the point. Why do you suppose your old boss had those in his office, anyway?"

Janet smiled, putting the last comcard into the reader.

The tactiface flashed in objection. Invalid format, it protested, prompting: Reformat Comcard?

Frowning, Janet pulled it out of the reader and thumbed the "On" button. The comcard lit up—no name or identity printed on it. Instead

333

of the usual demographic information, there appeared to be a number of applications imprinted upon the card. Janet tapped into one of them. "A recalibrator!" she yelped.

"A recombobulator?" Danielle replied.

Janet giggled. "Yeah, something like that."

But it was unlike the one she had on her comcard. She was about to tap a few buttons.

BAM! BAM! BAM!

Janet nearly peed on herself.

"This is the manager," said the voice beyond the door. "Why did you unplug the tactiface?"

Janet snatched up the cards, grabbed the wigs and her purse and dashed into the bathroom.

Through the door, she heard Danielle. "It wasn't working so I jiggled the wires. I think I broke it."

Janet heard a muffled, angry voice.

"But I can't. I'm not decent."

If dancing in front of a crowd doesn't bother her, Janet thought, an ornery motel manager shouldn't either.

Then there was a crash and Danielle screamed.

Janet dug into her purse, pulled up the card with only applications, thumbed up the recalibrator, punched out a destination, said a brief prayer and activated it.

The shimmer of an activated doorport appeared in the wall.

A frameless doorport!

Something crashed against the bathroom door.

Janet stepped into the shimmer and onto a Florida beach. Relieved, Janet looked around.

"Hey, where'd you come from?" The young man in sweats behind her looked as if he'd been standing there the whole time.

Janet frowned. I can't leave Danielle there, she thought, and thumbed up the seedy motel in New Jersey. She knew in her frumpy blond wig and disfigured face, the cotton ball still wedged between her upper molars and the inside of her cheek, that she probably looked pretty weird. "Sorry," she told the young man, "another time." And she activated the doorless port.

On the walkway outside the motel room, Janet summoned another doorless port behind her and then peered into the room. Two burly suits in dark glasses stood over a cowering Danielle. "Where is she, bitch!?" One said, drawing back his fist.

"No!" Janet shouted instinctively.

They both turned.

Janet dashed into the port and onto a crowded, Los Angeles city street. Reprogramming the motel as passers-by irritably stepped around her, Janet changed the coordinates slightly and activated it. The shimmer appeared on the building wall next to her.

She stepped onto the second-floor walkway five doors down from their room.

The two government goons were just running from the room.

Janet programmed another port, this one into the room where Danielle was, then she positioned the port to appear thirty feet further away on the second-floor walkway.

Leaning out so the goons could see her clearly, Janet called to them. "Over here!" And she waved prettily at them.

They both turned, saw her, and ran her direction, reaching for their hips.

Janet ducked and ran for the port.

It was the longest run of her life.

One ricochet, bang! And then two, bang!

She felt the squirts and didn't care and hit the port at full speed which gave her no time or room to stop her collision with Danielle and they both tumbled to the floor and Janet reached for Danielle's mouth to cover it with one hand while she thumbed up a new doorless port on the comcard.

The shimmering appeared a few feet away.

Janet pushed herself to her feet, watching the empty doorway, grasped Danielle by the hand, and together they leaped through the port and onto the Florida beach.

The young man in the sweats behind them looked as if he'd been standing there the whole time. "Hey, where'd you come back from?"

Janet just smiled at him, turned to Danielle and stood on her tiptoes to kiss her.

"Why didn't you say so in the first place?" The young man said, snorting and walking off in disgust.

Janet and Danielle dropped to the sand, giggling uncontrollably, both of them out of breath.

Chapter 11

Pushing aside the tactiface, Janet pulled the comcard from the reader and slipped it into her pocket. The casual pants and thick sweater felt uncomfortable, and she checked her appearance one last time. Too bad Danielle can't see me now, Janet thought, the taller woman having returned to her dancing.

Wavy golden hair, almost strawberry, spilled past her shoulders. High, rouged cheekbones graced a face dominated by two green, glowing eyes. Her executive clothes had been replaced with more casual ones.

Janet smiled at herself in the mirror and turned to gather her things, the layout of the apartment in Pompano Beach already familiar, despite her having leased it just three days ago. And she loved the view.

Furnished apartments easy to find, Janet had had no problem finding those basics needed for a household. The difficulty had been finding a tactiface that she could jimmy to her specs, disconnect from any wired or wireless external interfaces, and use without fear of being identified.

She'd had to transfer her personal comcard to the tactiface, strip any personal information, and load it onto the recalibrator card that she'd found in Old Man Jackson's office.

Hopefully this works, she thought, donning her thick coat in preparation for the Denver winter. She pulled out the recalibrator, thumbed up the date she wanted, zeroed in on the desired doorport and activated it.

A shimmer appeared in the apartment living room, and she stepped into it.

Civic Center Plaza was no less cold than she'd remembered it from five days before. Protestors were absent, she saw with relief.

Setting her recalibrator to make as quick a getaway as possible, Janet walked toward the doorport she wanted, reading the lintels. Finding the one she wanted, she stopped beside it.

A picture-perfect woman strode toward her, and Janet caught her breath at how beautiful the young woman was. On her left wrist was a slim gold watch, which she checked as Janet watched.

Belatedly, Janet realized that the watch was identical to her Grandmother's, which she had on her wrist right now. She grasped her left wrist with her right hand and turned to look past the other woman.

"Pardon me," the woman said, "you look vaguely familiar. Do I know you? I'm Janet Thompson."

"You must be mistaken," Janet replied, "I don't recognize you at all."

"My apologies," the other Janet said. "Good day."

Janet nodded and looked across the square, seeing an older man coming toward them.

The other Janet stepped to the doorport. With an odd glance over her shoulder, she stepped through the shimmer.

Janet strode toward the older man. "My apologies, Mr. Thornton, may I have a moment of your time?"

He stopped, raised his gaze, said, "No!" and strode toward the doorport.

Janet intercepted him, standing between him and his destination. "Please, sir, it's not safe."

"You one of those lunatics!? You look like one! Get outta my way!" And he shouldered her aside.

She leaped to the doorport, slapping aside his card and swiping her own. He yelped, and she pushed him through and followed into her Pompano Beach apartment.

"What the hell? Let me out of here! Where am I?"

"Shut up and listen!" she said, suddenly furious. "You were about to walk into your death. I know because I've been accused you of murdering you." She waited for his response, saw he was listening. "I couldn't let you walk into your death, Mr. Thornton. Your wife, Yelena, will miss you terribly."

He watched her warily. "Where have you brought me? Who are you?"

Janet couldn't have lied to him if she'd wanted. "Pompano Beach, except it's a year after you died, and my name is Janet Thompson. I'm the CEO of American Doorport, or I was, anyway, until I was arrested five days ago for your murder."

"And they just let you go?" Barnaby Thornton snorted. "You probably got that hot shot corporate lawyer Roberts-something to bail you out, didn't you?"

Janet frowned and shook her head. "I had to escape, actually."

"And if it's a year after I died, then somebody forgot to tell me!"

Janet smiled. "Look, I just want to correct whatever went wrong. The doorports themselves are creating problems—one of them was your disappearance. Now I think I've got a solution ..."

"Can't think of anything better than accosting old men and taking them from their wives?"

The obnoxious old fart, Janet thought, can't imagine why she wants him back. "So you want to go home?"

"Yeah, that's what I want. What's so difficult about that?"

"All right, let's go." Janet thumbed up the coordinates of his house, current time. "Just remember to tell everyone it was me who saved you." She activated the doorless port, and a shimmer appeared.

"What's that? A doorport? Where's the frame? And where'd it come from?"

"Go on. Quit your yapping." She gestured at the shimmering.

With a growl at her, Barnaby Thornton stepped out of her living room.

With a sigh, Janet wilted to the couch.

That was harder than I'd thought.

Glad it was over, she wondered how long she should wait before she might expect some result. The reappearance of Barnaby Thornton would force them to drop the murder charge, but she was still being hunted for evading arrest.

Janet stood and looked at the huge bay window. She'd never lived by the sea and could see why people chose to.

She walked to the tactiface and wondered what her next step should be.

Her wig blond and her cheeks stuffed, Janet stepped from the doorport onto the transit plaza nearest to her house and saw Frank returning from dropping the kids off at daycare. She intercepted him halfway toward the downtown doorport, where a long line had already formed.

"I need a moment of your time, Frank," she said, walking beside him and staring straight ahead. She heard him gasp and saw him start.

"What ... you ..."

"It's an anomaly, it's not me. You know it's not me. You know it." She turned to look at him, knowing he was struggling. Then she took his arm. "Walk with me—you know we're being watched."

The line downtown was growing mercifully short, mercifully fast.

She saw him nod and dab at his eyes. He looks gaunt, she was thinking. "We'll get through this, you know." She blinked back tears to see him in such pain. "Let the kids know I'm ok. God, how I miss all of you."

Frank stifled a sob, leaning close to her. One more person ahead of them.

"I'll go first, but I just wanted you to know that I love you terribly." Janet swiped her recalibrator, and stepped back into her living room in Pompano Beach, praying that Frank would understand.

If anyone could understand, Janet thought, Frank will.

She turned her attention to her next step—finding Old Man Douglas.

At the Pompano Beach library, logged on under one of the pseudonyms left for her by Old Man Jackson, Janet pulled up a list of possible contacts, both for Douglas himself as well as for the Church of the Divine Apocalypse—the one led by her sister, Cynthia.

The Denver office for the Church appeared to be beside, or perhaps in the same building, as the Cathedral Basilica of the Immaculate Conception.

Why don't they just call it the Immaculate Apocalypse, Janet wondered, dismayed at the irony. The church bells she'd heard all her life proclaiming the apocalyptic vision of a few misguided zealots with a distaste for doorports. It galled her that they might be right. And that her pesky little sister led them.

For all these reasons, Janet left the library with trepidation for the nearest set of doorports, programming her next location on the recalibrator.

Next stop—The Cathedral Basilica.

The windblown streets of Denver struck her backhanded with their chill. Janet remembered a time when it had exhilarated her, but now she felt only foreboding.

The classical lines of the ancient cathedral soared into a clear, crisp sky, the nearby deciduous trees all long since bare of leaves, the naked branches stark against the blue above.

Janet strolled past once, looking for addresses.

None other than the church itself.

On her way back, she saw the plaque at waist height, the tarnished brass almost invisible amongst the ivy growing over the low flagstone wall. Beyond the squeaky metal gate stood a doorway, the roof above it standing out in relief against what appeared to be the side wall of the main church itself.

The small "open" sign hanging from a string inside the diamond-framed panes was barely visible.

Janet pushed open the door, setting some bells ringing in a distant room.

No one in the vestibule, a small, six-by-six chamber with a chair, a display rack of literature, and a coat rack. Crowded with a single person in it, the room was uninviting.

She shrugged out of her jacket.

"Ah, you've decided to join us."

Janet turned to look at Old Man Douglas. "Hardly."

"In a physical sense, at least," he replied, gesturing her into the office.

It looked and smelled like an ancient scriptorium, the one regular chair outnumbered by scrivening stools in front of rostrums, on each a thick book or sheets of half-filled manuscript. Shelves lined three walls, floor-to-ceiling, full of books, their variety remarkable in antiquity, heft, and quality, and the fourth wall was a waist-high window, bisected with a door.

"Meant for study," Old Man Douglas said.

Janet was still startled by his similarity to Old Man Jackson. Why she found it disconcerting when they had been, after all, identical twins, mystified her.

"Coffee, hot chocolate, schnapps?" Douglas asked.

"Listen, Mr. Weintraub—"

"Do me the honor, dear Janet, of calling me Douglas."

"Your brother would've said, 'Call me Jackson, Goddammit.'"

Douglas smiled. "If it helps you to feel more comfortable. 'Call me Douglas, Goddammit.'" He imitated the intonation perfectly.

Janet smiled, "I miss him."

Douglas nodded. "So do I. Please, be seated." He took one of the high stools.

As did Janet, feeling a comfort in his presence similar to what she'd felt around Jackson. "Thank you."

"So sorry to hear about your recent arrest."

"I'm getting used to it." Janet shrugged. "But I needed my freedom and I need your help."

Douglas frowned and put a hand to his chest. "My help? Why would I give you that? Isn't it enough that I haven't called the police? I'm fairly certain I'd be richly rewarded for turning you over to them."

"The fact that you haven't indicates you're at least interested in hearing me out."

"It does. But beyond that, what could possibly interest me in helping you?"

"You and your brother parted ways because you found flaws in the equations—ones which will result in mayhem on a large scale, if not the complete destruction of Earth." Janet looked at Douglas for dissent. Seeing none, she continued. "I have a solution to those flaws. I can make the door-port network safe, eliminate those flaws and prevent that mayhem."

"How?" he asked immediately.

"Sir, a gentleman allows a lady a few secrets. But to make the door-ports safe, I need access to the biomainframe—to adjust the programming. Access that I can't obtain because I'm a fugitive."

"And how am I supposed to help with that?"

"We both know—as did Jackson—that you absconded with more than just the equations when you and your brother parted."

"Such as passcodes? Ridiculous, and even if I did, I'm sure he changed them long ago."

"I'm sure that he didn't."

"What? Preposterous! Outright stupidity!"

"Not at all. He wanted you to have access." Janet watched him closely, his face changing as he assimilated the information.

"So he left the system vulnerable to my changing it so that if I ever did find a solution, I could implement it without needing to go through him." Douglas frowned. "You attribute to my brother a far greater degree of faith and trust than he was capable of, you know."

"You underestimate him. Try it." She gestured at the one tactiface in the office. "Log onto the biomainframe. You'll get right in, I assure you."

Staring at her, he sat down at the tactiface. With a few touches, he had the company interface on screen. A few more and he was in. With a sigh, he looked at her. "How'd you know?"

"Jackson was as concerned as you are about system instability, and beyond his gruff façade, he was gentle and nurturing. He simply wasn't willing to allow a few glitches to stop the rollout."

"A few glitches!"

Janet shrugged. "Motor vehicle accidents didn't stop Henry Ford from producing cars. Accidental electrocutions didn't stop Thomas Edison from setting up an electrical grid. Jackson did everything he could to stop anomalies, including putting into place all the safeguards he could. And twelve years ago, he hired me to find and correct these system imbalances."

"And you've got a solution?"

"I do."

"And why should I help you?"

"You'd allow more deaths to take place? Are you so immoral that you'd deny me the opportunity to remedy those very flaws that you've decried for forty years? Perhaps I attribute to you a far greater degree of faith and trust than you're capable of."

They stared at each other.

Janet waited, so sure of her moral bedrock that she felt she could wait forever. She looked into his wise blue eyes.

A spark of interest lit them. "What's your solution?"

"So you'll help me?"

"You don't give an inch, do you?"

"Not for a heartbeat."

Old Man Douglas chuckled and shook his head. "All right, I'll help."

Solemn, Janet said, "Thank you. On behalf of all the Barnaby Thorntons, thank you."

His eyes went wide. "You did that?"

Janet smiled.

Douglas whistled tonelessly. "I hope your 'solution' doesn't involve more like him." He moved things around on the tactiface screen and turned it toward her, starting the vid.

The face of Barnaby Thornton was streaked with tears, several microphones stuck in his face. "First she kidnaps me, says she saved me from certain death, then returns me to Denver only moments after my wife has blown her head off with a shotgun. I'd rather that she left me dead!"

Janet sighed and closed her eyes.

She stood in front of the quaint house that the Thorntons occupied. It was a few minutes before Barnaby Thornton was expected to step out of the doorless port from her Pompano Beach apartment.

She thumbed up an aperture on her comcard, positioning it right in front of the first doorless port, her new one designated to take Barnaby back one hour.

The shimmer appeared.

Behind her she heard a "whump" from inside the house, and she felt sick, knowing what it was—Yelena taking her own life.

A shimmer appeared beside the first one, the two so close Janet could not see between them, and then both ports collapsed.

I hope it worked, Janet thought, turning toward the house. As she walked up the sidewalk, faint but strident voices reached her, one male and one female, and then she heard a "whump" from inside the house. Feeling sick, Janet ran to the door, her own voice in her head chanting, NO! NO! NO! Her hand on the knob, a second "whump" rattled her, the vibrations reaching her heart through her hand.

Janet wished she hadn't opened the door.

The shotgun lay on the floor between the two bodies.

She retched into the flowerbed.

Chapter 12

Back in Pompano Beach, strolling at the waterline, Janet saw none of the beauty in front of her, her hands tucked into her jacket pockets.

Try as she might, the image would not leave her mind. The salt in her tears was similar to that in the ocean, but burned so much hotter. Had they inflicted actual burns they might have rendered the sort of physical disfigurement that she felt she deserved.

Though the charges of murder had been lifted in Denver, she stood convicted in her own mind of murder-suicide. Nothing would lift from her soul the plain fact that her acts had led to deaths of two people.

The doorport to Hell is an aperture of good intentions.

If the backlash to her stopping Yelena's suicide was the murder-suicide of the Thorntons, what would the backlash be to her trying to stop the murder-suicide? She had debated trying to correct the devastation she'd wrought. To what extent will system equilibrium revolt against any attempt I make to undo what I've done? To what extent does my wish to correct things obscure the pain?

The waves lapped at the sand a few feet away from her, their answer as ambivalent as the ocean of emotion in her mind.

System equilibrium, she had forgotten, wasn't a fixed point. The two forces of liminality and abeyance exerted their influences as well. Liminality was the process by which an element of the system was pushed to the threshold of ejection, a place where that element stood poised for elimination. Abeyance was the force that sought to ameliorate the conditions that forced the element toward ejection or that sought to strengthen the barriers to ejection. Liminality and abeyance worked in an action-reaction dialectic, very often emphasizing what appeared to be a false dichotomy in their work to reach a new equilibrium.

Janet was under no illusion that she operated outside the system, that she was somehow immune to liminality. The system could, at any time, decide that she herself was exerting too much influence, introducing too much instability, that no amount of abeyance could stop the system from forcing her beyond liminality, ejecting her completely from the system.

She also knew that she herself was a force of abeyance, that her role was to keep the system from tearing itself apart. Her concern was that the system had become so ensconced at its new point of homeostasis that her efforts to restore stability would be met with defiance.

Yelena's killing herself was a reaction to Janet's rescuing her husband, and the deaths of the Thorntons was a reaction to Janet's trying to prevent Yelena's killing herself.

Walking and weeping, Janet could not say whether the system instability had reached the tipping point, where the descent into chaos could no longer be avoided, where the immaculate apocalypse was inevitable and unavoidable.

All she knew was she had to try to stop it.

The lone woman walking along the water's edge toward her looked oddly familiar. The blond hair was windblown, obscuring her features somewhat, but even so Janet could see the classic Athenian lines.

Cynthia!

Janet stopped.

The line of eyeless windows on the faces of apartments, condos and beach houses gazed upon the pair sightlessly.

There was no place to run.

Her sister, her nemesis.

A month ago, after seeing her at her parents, Janet might have thought otherwise.

"There's nowhere to go," Cynthia said, stopping a few feet away.

Janet shrugged, knowing any response would sound defensive. "How did you find me?"

"Immaterial." Cynthia's face was Athenian marble, cold as stone. "I'll destroy you eventually."

"Even if working with me will achieve the same goal?"

"You assume you know my goal."

"You've never been able to mask your true intent," Janet said. "You've always sought to undermine my every success by any means at your disposal." In her jacket pocket, Janet thumbed her comcard.

Cynthia smiled.

"You have such perfect canines, dear sister, always have. So tell me, why come here to tell me what I already know. To gloat, perhaps? To make sure I know that you'll have your vengeance? Is the taste of revenge sweeter when your target knows you've exacted your vengeance?"

"All of those," Cynthia said, grinning broadly.

"I think you'll find instead that revenge is at best bittersweet and I pray you'll see that the way to your own salvation doesn't include anyone else's destruction." Janet considered tapping the comcard in her pocket. What am I afraid of? she wondered. I've dealt with my vengeful sister all my life. "I'm not your enemy, Cynthia." Janet could see bewilderment in her sister's eyes. "Your enemy is and always will be your resentment of me."

"You salacious bitch!" Cynthia screamed, her face an inch from Janet's.

Janet made her face sad, stilling her initial response. "I feel so terribly sad you're not able to see that. I can't help you resolve your resentments."

"God damn you, you whore, who in your absolute righteous certainty do you think you are!?"

Spittle sprayed Janet's face. Janet said, her voice dead calm, her words even and measured, "You'll find your salvation on the other side of those resentments, and you'll trap yourself inside them if you exact your revenge. I'll pray for you."

Janet turned and walked the other way, her head down, tears pouring down her cheeks anew, while the person she called sister screamed invective after her.

It isn't my place to help her, Janet told herself, but at least I can choose how I respond. She knew that responding in kind would only escalate the enmity. At peace with herself in that, Janet was bothered by something much more alarming.

How had she found me?

At the Pompano Beach neighborhood library, Janet browsed through doorport records on the biomainframe using the passcodes Old Man Douglas had given her. He too had been as concerned about the murder-suicide and what it had implied.

The doorport network would not respond happily or willingly to Janet's attempts to resolve the anomalies.

Just as Cynthia would not respond happily or willingly to Janet's attempts to resolve the conflict between them.

She's the force of liminality, Janet thought, and I'm that of abeyance.

Looking through Cynthia's recent doorport transactions, Janet saw she'd made a trip to the Thornton's—or at least to the transit plaza in their neighborhood. Janet looked at the date and time.

A half hour after Barnaby Thornton had arrived home after a year-long absence!

Shaken, Janet looked for the next transaction, the one that would have taken Cynthia out of the neighborhood.

A half an hour after the murder-suicide.

White, her fingers shaking, Janet traced Cynthia's ports backward in time. They all looked as though they were routine transports between destinations of logical explanation for a religious zealot.

I've got to find out how she knew where I was!

Then it occurred to her.

Barnaby Thornton.

Janet had told Barnaby Thornton after he'd asked where he was. Cynthia must have spoken with him just after his return to Denver. Sitting back and looking across the library over the top of the tactiface, Janet wondered what she'd said to them.

And whether that had triggered the murder-suicide.

I wonder if an anonymous tip on Deputy Stewart's voicemail might interest him in investigating a little further?

But then, someone may have seen me at the Thornton's front door.

Disguised, yes, but thus far, media reports indicated no foul play, the theory being simply that Barnaby Thornton had disappeared for a year, and upon his return either he or she had shot the other and then had turned the gun on self. No record existed of his death three years ago.

On a whim, she swiped the database aside and searched gun ownership records for the Thorntons.

None found.

Surely, that'll trigger suspicion, Janet thought.

Pulling the doorport records back on screen, she downloaded a file extraction of Cynthia's transports and dropped them into the comcard she was currently using. Something about the file struck her as odd.

Too small.

Wouldn't a thirty-eight year old adult like my sister have taken far more doorports than that?

Janet opened the file.

A month ago.

Janet blinked.

Cynthia McLoughlin, first doorport transmission, one month ago, about the time that Janet was telling Charlie how she'd never gotten along with her younger sister.

Janet turned back to the records on the biomainframe.

Nothing further back than that.

Why? she wondered, bewildered.

The biomainframe occupied its own space-time harmonic aperture, placed there as a protection from real-time disasters, power surges, info-pandemics, and human infiltration.

Her memories of her childhood, constant catfights with her sister over clothes, make up, privacy, territory—and even men, Cynthia having once stolen a boyfriend of Janet's. They had deserved each other, Janet remembered with a smirk. Why do I have all of these memories but the American Doorport biomainframe has no record of her before a month ago?

Homeostasis. Abeyance. Liminality.

Systems theory predicates that a system cannot remain unbalanced for a sustained period without some extraordinary, extrasystemic force holding it imbalanced. Unless... Could a system create its own antagonist to force external change? Had Space-Time Harmonics created Cynthia McLoughlin?

The implications staggering, Janet closed out of the tactiface, retrieved her comcard, and fled for the exit.

Chapter 13

"Law offices of Roberts-Carter."

"This is Doctor Janet Thompson. I'd like to speak with Suzanne immediately, please." The tactiface at the downtown Phoenix Public Library was toward the back of the second floor, isolated enough that Janet felt she had a reasonable chance of privacy.

"One moment, please." The secretary looked closely at her face. "I'll get her immediately."

Janet had entered the library disguised, scouted out the tactiface, found the nearest restroom to remove her disguise, and then returned to the tactiface to make her call.

Late last night, while watching the news in her motel room just outside of Phoenix, Janet had seen a news report that the District Attorney in Denver was dropping the murder charge against her, due to "convincing exculpatory evidence."

Janet had snorted. Like a body with a gunshot wound at the scene of a murder-suicide, she'd thought. And then she'd wept in relief. Compounded by guilt that in her efforts to save one person, two people had died.

The news report had said nothing about her escape from jail, and Janet was sure she still topped the FBI's most wanted list.

"Janet, where are you?" Suzanne said, behind her the Denver Capitol.

"Phoenix. Listen, Suzanne, I want to turn myself in."

Suzanne looked at another part of her tactiface. "Who's Doris?"

"A pseudonym I've been using."

"You look terrible. You all right?"

"I'm… better. It's been rough."

"I'll bet. So you saw the news? Doesn't mean you're in the clear, but as you've guessed, your turning yourself in will help tremendously. I'll call the DA and see what I can do. Can I com you back on this same number?"

"Yes, please. And thanks, Suzanne."

"Certainly. Lay low until I negotiate something. Call you soon."

The com died, the face collapsing.

Janet removed the card, the tactiface logging her off immediately. She picked up her purse and headed to the ladies room. In a stall, she donned a wig and stuffed cotton balls into her cheeks.

Phoenix was a natural bowl, the surrounding mountains mostly devoid of trees, the high desert drab, the wide roadways in their precise grid deflating any charm that the Spanish/Mexican architecture might have promised.

Janet chose a direction at random and walked, her coat over her arm, the mid-winter clime at sharp contrast with that of Denver, not seven hundred miles to the northeast.

She yawned, having slept fitfully, her dreams haunted by blood spattered walls and the smell of a fresh gun discharge. In between the dreams had been periods of wakefulness, in which she'd either wept or stared unseeing out the window.

She looked a wreck, dark circles under her eyes, her cheeks gaunt from wads of cotton and not eating, her hair mussed and her clothes disheveled. She hadn't had the energy to do more than throw on the clothes she'd worn the day before and throw her hair under a scarf.

In her pocket her comcard buzzed.

Pulling it out, she measured the declension of the sun. She'd been walking awhile, she saw. Tapping the comcard, she watched the face materialize.

"Hi, Janet. Listen, I was able to negotiate a three o'clock time today, but the DA wouldn't budge on either a later time or a nice, quiet booking. He insisted on making it as public as possible. A spectacle might actually work to your benefit. I could have gotten you in sooner, but with no less of a circus, but I figured you'd want to clean up a little, right?"

"Yes, I would. Thanks. That's a bit of a relief. Where do I meet you?"

"I've had reporters camped at my door since you escaped. How about your house? We can go to the courthouse directly from there."

Janet wanted to say she could be anywhere, but elected not to. "All right. I'll send the passcode to our doorport by email. Suzanne?"

"Yeah?"

"Thanks."

Suzanne nodded. "Glad to be of help. I'll be at your house at two-thirty, all right?"

"See you, then." Janet killed the call, feeling immensely relieved.

Switching cards to her own comcard, she thumbed up her husband.

"Frank here," he said. Behind him was a skyline very similar to that visible behind Suzanne. The skyline that Janet had grown accustomed to seeing behind Old Man Jackson.

"I love you."

He tugged on his tie, blinked rapidly, cleared his throat. "I love you, too," he said finally, with a heavy sigh. "I'm glad you're ok. You look terrible."

"I'm turning myself in," she said giving him a hint of a smile.

"Why'd you escape in the first place?"

"I thought I could fix things on my own." Her voice choked, and she almost wept. "But now, I know I can't."

Frank nodded. "I can see you're suffering. Do you want me to be there when you turn yourself in?"

She shook her head. "No, you should be with the kids, tell them what's going on. Suzanne negotiated a three o'clock time for me, so I have time to look presentable. How are things there?"

"A mess, but don't worry about it. Charlie'll be dropping the lawsuit, realizes it's the anomalies. His wife isn't convinced, but she'll come around."

"Lawsuit?"

"Sexual harassment."

"Oh." Janet shook her head. "To all appearances, I really screwed up my first try at CEO, didn't I?"

Frank tried not to smile. "Not everyone gets fired in such a blaze of

351

glory. You're safe and that's what's important. I love you terribly, you know."

It was awhile before Janet could speak. She couldn't see him through her tears, but it was a comfort just knowing he was on the other end. "Thank you," she was finally able to say. "Hopefully, I'll be home tonight."

"I'll see you then," he said, dabbing at his eyes.

His face faded from her comcard, and she thumbed up her recalibrator and stepped to the nearest doorport.

The third time through booking was less onerous, almost pleasant.

"Sorry about the last time," Janet said to Deputy Stewart.

He shrugged, looking resplendent in uniform, the same uniform Janet had been accustomed to seeing her father in for years. "Thanks for the apology. And thanks for coming back."

They allowed her to do the Perp Walk in her heels, after a thorough search, of course. Her hygiene was immaculate, and the circles under her eyes obscured by make-up, but there was no hiding her gaunt looks.

On the far side of the perp walk, she was changed into an orange jumpsuit and ushered into a holding tank.

"Good Lord Almighty!"

Janet didn't even have to look. She soon found her face mushed into a bosom three times the size of her own and one full foot higher. Giggling, she pushed Danielle far enough away to catch a breath. "I'm so glad to see you."

"So am I. Just sorry it's here." And Danielle threw her head back and laughed. "Well this time, I did try to put my bank account over the top of the officer's head. More interested in an arrest than my nookie. I'm so disgusted! His loss, I say. How are you, girl!" Danielle turned to other women in the cell. "This's the one that saved my life in New Jersey that time I was telling you about. What the hell you doin' back here?"

"Turned myself in."

"Them finding the body a year after you supposedly kilt him put a hole in their case you could throw a fit through, now didn't it? So they just want to trump up their resistin' arrest is likely, but don't you put up with none of their guff. 'Course, with that fancy-panty, high-priced lawyer you got, they won't have enough to hang a coat on you. Uh-oh." Danielle looked over Janet's shoulder. "Looks like you're already bein' bailed out."

Janet gave Danielle another hug. "Call me the moment you get a chance, all right? All right, I'll talk to you soon."

The two beefy female deputies escorted her out, gave her time to change, walked her over to property, where Suzanne was waiting. "There's a wolf pack out front. You ready for them?"

Janet shook her head, repacking her purse. The comcards with the fake identities she had left at home, knowing they'd be confiscated by jail staff. "Any way to avoid them?"

"None that I know of. Doorports are on the other side of them."

In the jail lobby, Janet asked to use the restroom, and she gestured Suzanne to come with her.

Thumbing her doorless port app to life, Janet said, "Give me your hand." A shimmering, person-sized oval shimmered on the wall. "Come on." And she stepped through it into Suzanne's office.

"Can I get one of those?" Suzanne asked, watching the doorless port collapse. She stepped around her desk, shaking her head. "More resourceful than I gave you credit for."

"Are we alone?" Janet looked around.

Suzanne looked at the door to her office. "Give me a minute." She stuck her head out the door. "Pamela, I'm with a client. We're not to be disturbed." Pause. "Oh I came in the back way." She closed and locked the door, then turned. "What is it?"

And Janet told Suzanne what she'd been doing since her escape from jail.

Suzanne's eyes got wider and wider.

And then told Suzanne about her confrontation with Cynthia.

"No transactions beyond a month ago?" Suzanne said.

Janet shook her head.

"In my world, that means someone impersonating someone else. I suspect it means something else to you."

"If my hunch is correct, I didn't have a sister a year ago."

Suzanne whistled. "I'm getting a headache. How's that possible?"

"It means my sister's right. It means Old Man Douglas is right. It means that the system is unstable. And it's probably getting worse. How would we know, unless some discrepancy alerts us—like the doorport records, or Yelena Thornton's dementia? But for everyone else, their memories have changed. I remember fighting with my sister all throughout my childhood. We have never agreed on anything. And I remember fucking Charlie's brains out and enjoying it—even though I'd never do that to my husband, to Charlie, to myself, to my kids, to my coworkers."

"That little gizmo you have in your pocket that got us here, is that the same as all these doorports?"

"Just without the frame."

"You mean we could get right over to your boss's office without stepping into that rat's nest of reporters in front of American Doorport?"

Janet smiled. "We certainly could." She thumbed up the destination and activated the doorless aperture. A shimmering oval appeared in the middle of Suzanne's office. Janet and Suzanne stepped through it.

Frank spun, the State Capitol visible through the windows behind him. "Where'd you come from?"

Janet stepped into his arms. "I'm so sorry you've had to go through all this." She held him tight, oblivious to Suzanne behind her. "I've missed you so much."

"I've missed you too." His voice was a strained whisper.

She pulled back and looked into his face, and saw the gentle man she'd married. He did understand, she saw, but she also saw that it was costing him. "I came directly because it's much worse than I thought."

"What is? The anomalies?"

Janet nodded.

Frank sighed.

"But I dreamt up a solution." Then she smiled. "No, I really dreamt it, I swear, but I need Charlie's help." She realized Frank was looking at her funny.

"I keep having to tell myself it wasn't you," Frank said, his voice breaking. "But I'm not believing it much anymore."

Janet nodded, biting her lip. "You won't have to do that for much longer, I promise."

Frank hung his head, took a deep breath, and looked at her. "What if Charlie says, 'No'?"

"I don't think he will."

"Charlie," Frank said to his tactiface.

"Yeah, boss?" came Charlie's tinny voice.

"Come in here."

"Be right there."

Janet felt extremely awkward when he entered. "Hi, Charlie."

His face beet red, Charlie nodded and wouldn't look at her.

"If you can't do this, Charlie, I can leave the room, but you've got the skills to do what we need. Tell me how I can help you to be more comfortable."

He shook his head, his chin pressed into his neck, the top of his balding head reflecting the ceiling lights.

"Charlie," Frank said.

He looked up at his boss.

"We're all suffering, and Janet has a way to end that suffering, but we need your help."

Charlie looked at Janet hopefully. "You do?"

Janet nodded.

"I knew you could, and Jackson knew it too! He, er, uh, visited when you spent that week in California, told me you'd find the flaw."

"Well, it's not a flaw," Janet replied. "The harmonic aperture sequence equations are incomplete. They bring together the two space-time points, but then they let the natural elasticity of the space-time fabric restore the two points to their original locations. The loss of elasticity is causing parallel time-lines to cross."

Suzanne snorted. "You mean, we could be living different lives than we were when we left the jail, and we wouldn't know it?"

Janet nodded. "This morning you could have been an impoverished environmental defense attorney working out of a drafty office."

Suzanne was silent.

"Are you all right?"

"Must have been a dream," Suzanne said to herself.

Janet shivered, knowing already. "Can I use your tactiface?" she asked Frank.

"Certainly, but why?" He frowned at her.

"You'll see. Charlie, if all we do is add an additional sequence to force the points back into place, then we minimize the loss of elasticity to the whole fabric." Janet moved things around on the tactiface, pulled up the doorport server, did a search on Suzanne. "When did you move into your current offices, Suzanne?"

"Five, six years ago, why?" the lawyer asked.

"Up until very recently, doorport records indicate an office in the Glen Elder area."

"But Glen Elder's over by the warehouse district, near all those goody two-shoe nonprofits." Suzanne caught her breath, her hand to her mouth. "You mean …?"

Janet nodded. "Your life has been changed by a doorport anomaly." She looked over at Frank and Charlie. "For every Yelena Thornton, there's a thousand Suzannes whose lives have been irrevocably changed."

Frank looked over at Suzanne. "She looks like she's seen a ghost."

Janet nodded. "And Cynthia."

Frank's eyes went wide. "Her, too?"

"She didn't even exist a month ago!" Janet said through gritted teeth. And she told him what had really happened with the Thorntons.

"You traveled back a year?" Charlie asked.

"With disastrous consequences. So I need the additional coding added to the sequence."

Frank looked around the office.

Janet could see he was evaluating the idea. Well, he's not going to like this next piece, she thought, but before I tell him… "Charlie can do the coding."

"So just add a sequence to restore the points to their original locations?" Charlie asked. "Easy!" And he hustled over to Frank's tactiface.

Frank looked at her sharply. "What about the regulators? If we attempt to change the coding, they'll be crawling all over us."

"I can distract them," Suzanne said. "You can defend their being excluded on the basis of trade secrets, tell them the upgrade is simply scheduled system maintenance. Or just give me five minutes in front of that judge next week, and I'll have drilled so many legal holes in the NTSB's case that it'll sink faster than a lead-filled Russian sub."

"They may not even need to know," Frank said. "A week ago, they didn't know anything. Why not install the additional coding then?"

Janet frowned. "The consequences."

Frank nodded but Suzanne looked puzzled.

"It may already be too late," Janet said. "The system's highly unstable—more than we know already. It was quite by chance that I discovered Cynthia and Suzanne. That memchip that Jackson gave me was based on searches he'd conducted with the information he had

356

then. Get finance up here, get a run on the number of delinquent accounts—probably a far better indication, but only for people who've disappeared."

Frank nodded. "And that won't include people whose lives have changed in subtle ways, or people who didn't exist at all."

The four of them exchanged glances.

"People who didn't exist at all," Janet repeated. "Just one measure of just how unbalanced the system is." Watching Charlie, hunched over like a gnome at what had once been Jackson's desk, Janet was reminded how much she missed Jackson.

"Got a memchip?" Charlie asked.

Janet pulled out the one that Old Man Douglas had given her, the one with the space-time harmonic equation sequence on it.

Charlie plugged it in, moved things around with a few swipes, pulled it out and handed it back. "There's your new sequence."

She hadn't expected it so soon. "That easy?"

"That easy," Charlie replied, grinning.

"What won't be easy," Janet said, looking at the other three, "is replacing the coding on the biomainframe."

"Seems like that'd be the easiest part," Suzanne said.

"Backlash," Janet said. "The suicide of Yelena Thornton was the backlash of my having returned Barnaby Thornton to present time. Their murder-suicide was the backlash of my trying to prevent her suicide." Janet saw that Frank and Charlie understood, but that Suzanne did not. "Whatever I do to correct the anomalies will be met with an equivalent effort to keep them the same. The system has reached a new balance in its imbalance. The baseline has changed, and the backlash to my trying to restore the baseline to its original position will be severe indeed." Janet looked at Frank. "That's why I need to return to the rollout."

"Eh? What? The rollout?" He looked frightened.

Janet strode to the window, picking out the Cathedral Basilica from the Denver skyline, the clock tower and her grandmother's watch having been unsynchronized for days. If you could call it that, Janet thought, her excursions to try to correct the past having thrown time itself into a conniption fit.

"Parallel time lines." She looked at Frank. "You yourself said it. Shmirnov's theory predicts that multiple timelines—even an infinite

357

number of timelines—run parallel to each other, each a slight variation on the next but distinct, never touching, never intersecting. Rubicon's theory of space-time postulates the fabric model, where the distance between two points is simply a function of time, and that if time can be stopped, distance can be reduced to nothing, and thus all points in time exist at the same point in time, and all points in space exist at the same point in space."

"All I know is you've left me in the Stone Age," Suzanne said.

Frank, Charlie, and Janet exchanged a chuckle. "Let's just say that both theories could operate simultaneously, and we'd never know it. If both do operate independently of each other, neither mutually exclusive of the other, then the variations in people's lives are infinite and interchangeable."

"You mean I could become a poor, goody-two-shoe, windmill-tilting, non-profit lawyer at anytime? Yikes!"

Janet nodded. "And I could be cursed with a sister who bedevils my every endeavor. But keep in mind: These changes aren't random. They're purposive. Our every doorport transmission has consequences. Currently, our system relies on an inherent elasticity in the space-time fabric to restore two points to their original positions."

"And that's causing a strain, right?" Suzanne said.

"Exactly. Any strain to the system has consequences. One of them, if we follow Shmirnov's theory of parallelity, is that parallel timelines might trade—the first twenty years of one person's life in one universe becomes the first twenty in that same person's life in a parallel universe. Human memory being what it is, our brains supply us with the information we need to make sense and logic of our existence, in spite of its being patently false."

"So my brain is telling me that my memories about being a bleeding-heart lawyer are so inconsistent with my current position that I think I must have been dreaming."

"Something like that." Charlie said. "In a parallel universe, you were that lawyer. In this one, you're a blood-sucking vampire."

"Thank you," Suzanne said to Charlie, not a hint of sarcasm in her voice.

"So my suddenly getting a sister is a direct result of a response to and an effort to correct those very same strains."

"And you want to eliminate those strains, right?"

Janet nodded.

"That segment that I added to the biomainframe sequence," Charlie said, "should supply the work to return to the points to their original positions, and eliminate the reliance on the elasticity—and hopefully eliminate the strain."

"The trick," Janet added, "will be inserting the sequence at the initial rollout forty years ago."

"And you can't just install it now," Suzanne said.

Janet glanced at Charlie, as though to say, "She gets it."

"The backlash," Charlie said.

"There'll be backlash whichever way it's done," Janet added. "What we have to do is to minimize that backlash, which won't be easy. Forty years ago, doorports were rolled out nationwide using incomplete software. The complete software must be installed then, before anomalies occur." Janet looked at Frank.

"And that's why you need to return to the rollout?" Frank asked.

Janet Thompson nodded, seeing in his eyes that he knew exactly what that meant.

Chapter 14

"Are you all right?" Frank asked.

Janet stared at him blankly, not knowing how to articulate what she had just discovered.

"Listen, we can delay this. One day, even twelve hours won't make a difference."

He's right, Janet thought, her mind reeling.

Frank and Charlie exchanged a glance.

"I know what you're thinking," Janet said. If they insist, I won't have the energy to fight, she thought, but if I don't do this now, I know because of what I know that I won't ever be able to do this.

The three of them were in the maintenance office in the basement of Corporate, the only place they felt that they might be safe from discovery. Charlie had brought into the room a two-sided doorport. For safety, he had wired it directly to its own biomainframe, not the corporate one which processed all the calibrations and did all the billing. Built into this biomainframe was a new harmonic sequence.

Janet had dressed for the usual Denver winter, so she was sweating, the building heat plant taking up most of the basement. She carried a bag with a couple of changes of clothing. She also carried three comcards: Her own, a comcard with only applications, and a third with multiple fake identities all matched to her appearance and thumbprint.

Each of the fake identities had associated bank balances of over a half a million dollars.

"We just need to do this," Janet said, the silence as difficult as their remonstrative looks.

Frank stepped close to her and cradled her face in his hands. "I hear that you need to do this. I couldn't convince you otherwise, even if I wanted to. I can see that you're afraid. Anyone would be. I certainly am. But we're both more afraid of what will happen if you don't do this."

Janet nodded. "There isn't any way I can tell you what it really means."

He shook his head. "No, there isn't. I don't have a way of comprehending how deeply you need to do this. I just know that you do." He held up a finger to shush her. "Yes, I know it means you might not come back, but we're taking every precaution we can to insure that you do. What's the back-up plan?"

Janet sighed and looked away. *I just can't tell him, because if I do, he'll forbid it outright.* "From here, you and Charlie will open a doorless port at the door of the Cathedral Basilica, every year at midnight for the five years following my arrival then." She had the doorless port program on one of the three comcards she carried, but because her task was to change the programming on the biomainframe forty years in the past, there was no predicting how that would change the future.

"Right," Frank said, sighing.

Janet sighed too, leaning into his embrace. Last night, holding him as though she'd never held him before, she had fallen asleep, their bodies one, their souls nearly touching, and she'd awakened that morning, fully confident that she would have set everything right by evening, the doorport programming fixed, the anomalies corrected, the space-time fabric stabilized, and the space-time apertures harmonizing flawlessly.

Neither Janet nor Frank had felt that they should risk destabilizing the system any further by using their recalibrators. En route to work, however, had been the inevitable protestors, which seemed to have grown in numbers since the consent decree for the temporary takeover by the NTSB had taken effect.

One protestor, a manic-looking woman about Janet's age, intercepted her just as she stepped out of the doorport from dropping the kids off at childcare.

The woman carried a hand-painted sign. "MIT Life-Stealer," it read.

Janet tried to step around her, but she moved to block Janet's path. "You stole my life at MIT," the woman screamed.

Janet stepped the other way.

The woman blocked her. "You swiped the research I did for Doctor Armstrong!"

Janet looked one way and moved the other way.

"You made my roommate Stacey move out because you couldn't stand her cat!"

Fear seized Janet.

And the woman swung her sign at her.

Janet dropped to the ground, the sign whistled harmlessly overhead, and a police officer tackled the protestor before she could strike Janet again.

Another officer helped her up. "They told us this would be a nonviolent rally," he said. "Here, let's get you going." And the officer escorted Janet to her doorport. "Gave you a fright, it looks like."

Janet could barely speak. "Th... Thanks, off... Officer." She stepped through the doorport and onto the sidewalk in front of Corporate.

Into more protestors.

Maybe it was the look on her face. None of them bothered her.

She walked into the building unobstructed, stepped past the concierge's desk. "May I use your tactiface?" she asked.

As though he might refuse. He let her into his office behind his desk.

Oblivious, her face bloodless, her mind racing, Janet activated the com, her hands shaking. She had never told anyone about the cat, or about her roommate, Stacey.

How had the protestor known? Stole her life?

She commed Doctor David Winters. "My apologies," Janet told the receptionist. "I need to speak with him, immediately. Please, oh please!" I'm probably starting to sound like a frantic mental patient, Janet thought.

"Doctor Winters here. Oh, hi, Doctor Thompson, how can I help you this morning?"

"You told me you had a patient with an obsession—that her life had been stolen from her. Do you have a picture of her?" She realized the concierge was looking at her funny. Mercifully, he closed the door between them, leaving her alone in his office.

"Janet, I do," Doctor Winters said, "but unless there's a compelling need, such as a safety concern, I can't disclose that information."

"But you know who I'm talking about, right?"

"I certainly do, but—"

"Someone tried to assault me just ten minutes ago, swung her sign at me during a protest."

Doctor Winters pursed his lips and wrinkled his brow.

"She said I'd stolen her life at MIT." Janet realized her voice was becoming shrill.

Doctor Winters shook his head. "My apologies, Doctor Thompson, but—"

"You don't understand! She mentioned a cat that I've never told anyone about!"

"Who's cat?" Doctor Winters asked.

"Stacey's cat!" Janet nearly screamed.

Doctor Winters had gone as white as she had. He was shaking his head tentatively. "Can't be," he whispered. "You must be mistaken, Doctor Thompson."

"I'm not. It's her, isn't it?!"

Swallowing heavily, Doctor Winters moved things around on his tactiface and pulled a picture onto his screen so Janet could see it.

"That's …" Janet knew now, and wished she didn't know. "Yes, Doctor Winters that's her. Tell me about her."

In a stumbling voice, blinking rapidly, Doctor Winters began. "Janice Thomas, forty-year-old female, native of Denver, Doctorate from MIT in Space-Time Harmonics, first psychotic break at age twenty-eight, just after earning her doctorate, found screaming one evening in a lecture hall about flaws in the doorport technology that would cause world-wide disaster. Hospitalized for six weeks, never really did recover, returned to Denver, where I began treating her, multiple hospitalizations since, auditory hallucinations, persecutory delusions, plus one prominent fixed delusion that no amount or combination of antipsychotics can touch: That her life at MIT had been stolen." Doctor Winters looked away, swallowed, pulled at his collar, and coughed.

363

"What would you think, Doctor Winters, if I told you that it could be true," Janet said, "that anomalies are beginning to emerge, that small variations in the accuracy and reliability of doorport—"

"No!" Doctor Winters held his hands over his ears.

His face became blurred by her tears. "Tell me, Doctor Winters," Janet demanded. "Tell me why didn't the antipsychotics work on that one delusion?"

"I don't know, Doctor Thompson."

"Yes, you do, Doctor Winters!" Now she was screaming. "You know exactly why, don't you, Doctor Winters?!"

"No, I don't!" he yelled back.

"Why didn't they work, Doctor Winters? What's the one condition in which modern antipsychotics don't work, Doctor Winters?! Say it, goddammit!" Janet was now weeping openly.

Doctor Winters wiped his cheeks free of his own tears. "I'm sorry, Doctor Thompson. If you insist, I'll say it."

Janet's voice was strained but low. "Please, Doctor Winters, I need you to tell me, no matter what the cost. Please, Doctor Winters, please."

Doctor David Winters nodded, his face gentle. "It means, Janet, that it's not a delusion."

"It's not a delusion," Janet said back to him, nodding, and knowing she really hadn't needed Doctor Winters to tell her, knowing already what she would find in the database, having known on some level since hearing those words from that crazed protestor who wasn't crazed at all but who had had taken from her one of the most precious things that could be taken from a person: her future.

"It's not a delusion," Janet said again, no longer able to see Doctor Winters' face. "Thank you, Doctor Winters, and my apologies. I'm sorry I yelled at you, I'm sorry—"

"No, Janet, no apology necessary," Doctor Winters said. "Yours is a burden no one should bear. When people ask me how I can work with people who are so tormented by their delusions, I know that there is one redeeming fact: the fact that they are having delusions. For you, Doctor Thompson, there isn't that redemption."

"Because it's not a delusion," Janet said.

Chapter 15

"Are you sure you're all right?" Frank asked.

"Of course not," Janet said, wiping fresh tears from her face. "But that won't stop me."

After the phone call to Doctor Winters had ended, Janet had searched the biomainframe and had traced her own history of doorport transmissions back to age twenty-eight.

But no further.

Janet Thompson hadn't existed before age twenty-eight.

"I love you so much, Frank Thompson," Janet whispered.

"I love you more than you know, Janet Thompson," he replied.

She wept into his shoulder as she'd never wept before.

When she pulled away, he wouldn't look at her.

"I know you don't want me to go."

Frank bit his lip. "What I want isn't important. It's what you need to do. It's what you were meant to do."

Spoken truer than you know, Janet thought, nodding at him. She turned to Charlie. "I'll see you on the other side, my friend."

Charlie smiled at her. "Yes, you will. Whether we have to go back after you or not. We'll be here."

Janet sighed and gave him a hug, then turned to Frank. "Give the kids my love."

"And your parents."

"And my parents." Janet shook her head. "And my sister."

"Her, too," Frank said.

Janet smiled, looking into his eyes. "See you then. I love you."

Frank just nodded, lip between his teeth. "Good luck."

"Thanks." Janet stepped to the center of the room, stood just a few inches from the doorport.

Charlie tapped a few times on the tactiface screen.

The doorport began to shimmer.

She threw Frank a kiss and stepped …

… into chaos.

The world warped and skewed, three horizons twisting around Janet, and the wind blew snow at her from three different directions, and Janet pulled her lapels tight around three different throats with three different pairs of hands, the overnight bag hanging from three different elbows in three different directions.

Turning her heads sent her worlds reeling, so she held still for a moment.

"Hey lady, you all right?" three men's voices said to her, all slightly mistimed.

"Fine," she said too fast, her voice sharp, but reverberating. "Fine, but …" The echo was disconcerting. "But can you direct me to American Doorport?"

"Certainly," "Be happy to do so," "You betcha," three different voices said all at once. "It's that way," they said, pointing in three different directions.

She chose one direction, trusting that she would go the right direction. "Thank you," she said, nodding to the one young man, the nod setting all three worlds a jiggle.

The first step was a nightmare; she felt she was stepping into an abyss of sky, and when her heal found cement she sighed. The second did not fill her with quite so much trepidation, the third better, the fourth better yet.

I'll never get accustomed to this, Janet was thinking, but she was still moving, trying to read the signs along the storefronts through the snow.

As best she could understand, she occupied three different worlds all at the same time, received the sensory input from all three, maintained a physical presence in all three, and processed all the sensory input in one brain.

Words on fluorescent signs floated past her vision in three different directions, fonts, luminances, colors, sizes, all different, and it wasn't until one eye had picked out "Door" from one of three signs from among six eyes that she realized she had found the building.

The three hands that reached for three doors confused her, and she had to stop. All three buildings were different, she realized.

Which was the right one?

She retreated a step to try to determine which building was the correct one. Oddly, they were all two-story buildings, none of them the multi-story edifice that occupied an entire city block in downtown Denver.

Had she been able to see a single skyline clearly, she might have known where these three offices were, but the visual signals were so jumbled, any object of any distance away was obliterated by the snow falling in every direction.

Just choose, she told herself. I have to trust I'll find the right one. And she focused on the one door with the silver lettering on the glass. She watched the hand collide awkwardly with the handle, the glass deceptively close.

The door opened, quite without her exertion.

"May I help you?"

The head was shiny, the rim of hair brown, the eyes behind the spectacles full of mischief.

All three faces were mercifully the same.

"May I speak with you, Mr. Weintraub?" And then Janet grinned. "Or shall I call you Jackson, Goddammit?"

After an initial moment of surprise, he threw his heads back and laughed. "This way, please," he said, gesturing her into three differently decorated offices. Closing the doors behind her, he got her coats, set her bags beside the coat racks, insisted on getting her cups of tea, and said over his shoulders, "Find yourself a seat in the next room. I'll be back in a spiff."

Janet shook her head slowly and stepped toward brighter doorways, stopping to put her hands on the pine/oak/mahogany doorjambs. Tenuously she found her way to three chairs, three blazing fireplaces facing the rooms from different angles. An arc of fire warmed her quickly, the barrage of light nearly overwhelming.

Jackson bustled in with tea, setting three different cups on the low tables in front of her.

"I'm sorry, Jackson, would it be possible for me to face the other direction?" and she pointed her fingers over her shoulders.

"Ah! Don't want the fire on your face, but of course." And he maneuvered three chairs into equivalent positions. "How about this?"

Janet smiled and nodded, rose slowly and stepped to the other chairs.

Jackson pushed the cups across to where she sat and settled himself into the chairs she had abandoned. "You look somewhat piqued, Miss. Please, have some tea and take a moment."

She smiled at him, seeing in the younger, fifty-ish Jackson the same warmth and comfort she'd come to like in Old Man Jackson. "Bless, yes, a bit piqued, to put it mildly." She had to grasp the cups of tea with all six hands to get them off the table. The taste of three different herbal teas went down her throats and she sighed. "Thank you, Jackson, you're such a dear."

"You're too kind, Miss—?"

She smiled. "I'm Doctor Janet Thompson, and I'm interim CEO of American Doorport in the year twenty-one forty-one, and I'm here in your time to ask something of you."

His six eyes lit up. "Time travel!" They all three said. "We did it! I knew we would!"

"Ah, but there's a catch." Janet held up three index fingers. "I'm under a bit of duress at the moment," she said, "because anomalies have started to appear after forty years of space-time harmonic use."

Two Jacksons frowned. "My brother is right?"

Janet also frowned and asked the third Jackson. "You don't have a brother?"

Two Jacksons looked bewildered and the third said, "Should I?"

"What year is this?" Janet asked, instantly intuiting that Old Man Douglas was himself an anomaly.

"Twenty-one"—"oh-one" "oh-two" "oh-three."

"To give you a sense of the confusion that's occurring," Janet said. "I now exist simultaneously at three different points in your life, Jackson, each of them one year apart. Or perhaps three different parallel time-lines."

"How could that be, if I've never met you before?" all three replied, "unless I'm the first one."

"The first one is in twenty-one oh one," Janet told all three.

The Jackson who didn't have a brother said, "This brother I'm supposed to have—is he there in twenty-one-oh-two?"

Janet repeated the question and then answered it. "Yes, he is. And twenty-one-oh-three."

All three of them looked solemn. "These anomalies—how widespread are they in twenty-one forty-one?"

"No one's really sure. It was only through illness that we discovered them at all—an eighty-four-year old with dementia and a forty-year old with schizophrenia. But billing records indicate a far higher saturation of anomalies than all of our projections, and far worse than any religious zealot could have imagined."

They all three looked remorseful. "We have to fix it. We can't keep using the technology until it's fixed."

Janet smiled.

"You know where the flaw is?"

"It's actually not a flaw, per se," Janet said. "The technology bends space-time to bring together two points that don't naturally touch, then releases the two points to return to their original positions. The natural elasticity is what snaps those points back into position. It's that elasticity that's becoming brittle in twenty-one forty-one."

The three Jacksons nodded. "So simple," they all three said, and then two of them added, "that my brother didn't see it either."

Janet pulled a memchip from her pocket.

"What's that?" they all three asked.

"The harmonic sequence with additional coding to move the two points manually back to their original places."

All three Jacksons grinned then frowned. "That won't fit my tactiface."

Janet pulled out three comcards, the ones with the apps. "Got a reader?"

They breathed an audible sigh. They took the comcards from her. "You say you exist at three points simultaneously in my life? If all three

369

of me drop this coding into the biomainframe at the same time, more chaos is likely, not less."

"I agree," Janet said nodding. "Twenty-one-oh-one should install the coding. Would you do the honors, Jackson?"

"Certainly," one Jackson said, and he stood. Then all three of them spoke. "What will happen to you?" they asked.

Janet bit off a sob. "I'm … not important. I'll be all right."

The three Jacksons just stared at her.

A tear slid down her cheek.

He leaned across the table. "In one tear," he said, dabbing her cheek, "a thousand sorrows." He too blinked rapidly. "Such courage, fragile lady. Thank you."

"Thank you, Jackson," Janet replied, sniffling. "Now, twenty-one-oh-one, it's time. Please, do it now."

And Jackson stepped across the room, slid the card into the slot, and began to move objects on the tactiface.

"Thank you, Janet. Implementing in five, four, three, two, one."

The faces in front of her began to spin, and the vertigo nearly made her retch and the air left her lungs before she could scream and blackness enveloped her.

Janet awoke, and the room refused to focus.

The tiny creature beside her bed emerged from a blur and smiled at her. "Welcome back," she said, sighing, her gray hair a nimbus around her head. "You're going to be all right."

Hospital room, Janet thought, then the room faded again.

The squeak of wheel woke her. The gray-haired woman pushed the meal-cart to a spot beside the bed. "We'll have to start with soft foods."

Janet's throat was sore. Tube feeding? she wondered. And who is this old woman?

"I'm Yelena," she said, as though answering Janet's thought.

Did I say that out loud? And why does that name sound familiar?

"So nice to meet you, too." Yelena took the cover off a bowl of what looked like porridge.

The swallows were painful, and Janet felt so helpless at having to be fed. She also knew she was too weak to do it herself. "What happened?" she asked, her voice a croak.

"Doctor Winters will be able to speak with you shortly."

How long have I been here? Janet wondered, but her weariness washed over her and the room faded from view.

Somewhere a throat cleared, and Janet looked around.

A gentleman with a nice smile and bushy eyebrows sat beside the bed.

Doctor David Winters, Janet thought.

"Welcome back, Janet," Doctor Winters said. "You gave us all quite the scare."

"What happened?"

"You had an episode of catatonia after Jackson Weintraub died. You became so depressed and psychotic that you wouldn't eat. You kept raving about Yelena and Barnaby Thornton and a murder-suicide— quite the disturbing delusion you were having. You've been ill for about a month, but you're getting better now. I can see it in your eyes."

She smiled at him, although her smile was wan and weak.

"That's the first smile in a long time. Any auditory hallucinations?"

She shook her head. "No, no voices, not right now." Weariness, just weariness.

"You look tired. Go ahead and sleep. I'll come back after you've awakened."

And she slipped into a dream.

The squeak of wheel startled her out of sleep.

Yelena pushed the meal-cart up to the bed.

"I dreamt about you, Yelena," Janet said, sitting up and taking the bowl from the old woman. "I dreamt that your husband died. Is he all right?" She began to eat.

Yelena, eighty-four and tiny, looked up at Janet and grinned. "Barnaby might be a sour old grape, but he's my sour old grape, and I'm grateful, so grateful, that you brought him back to me. Thank you."

Janet smiled, remembering something vaguely about the space-time harmonic sequence. "I'm not sure what I did, Yelena, but I'm glad he's safe."

"I'm not sure what you did, either, except that it brought him back." Yelena patted her hand. "And don't worry a bit about what they say."

"What who say?"

"Oh, you know," Yelena replied, looking Janet in the eye. "They say I have dementia, they say you have schizophrenia, but we both know the truth, don't we?"

371

"I'm sorry?"

"Don't mind me. The basic fact is, you saved us all, even though no one else knows it."

"Huh? What do you mean?"

"Just never you mind, Janet dear. Right now, you need to focus on recovering your strength. Lie down, now, and don't listen to a bit of my babbling, all right?" Yelena took the half-empty bowl from her.

"All right," Janet said, weary again, not understanding. She lay back, not strong enough to continue sitting upright. What she did understand as she slipped off to sleep was that the episode was behind her, that she had been re-stabilized, and that she was looking forward to returning to her position as Vice President of R&D at American Doorport.

Inoculated

Acknowledgments

Thanks to the following beta-readers:
Anne Potter
Elise Abram

Chapter 1

Lydia brought the amoeba-class ship out of sub-ether above a cloud-shrouded planet in the Mnemosyne Constellation and threw a glance at her companion. "I swear, Xsirh, I don't know what those Homo sapiens are thinking. Look at her! Ugly as pondscum! Why does she get to become Empress?"

On the holo, a dainty tiara glittered in the human female's dishwater hair. Her skin was white and rough as plaster. Her lips were the color of rutabagas and poised in a perpetual pout. The nose was squished into the face, a wart the size of a snail perched on a cheekbone, the close-set eyes peering from beneath a unibrow. The holonet was alive with the upcoming coronation of the Homo sapiens Empress, and it didn't matter where Lydia surfed or what program she watched, the hype inundated all the media.

The blob of protoplasm in the copilot's chair, Xsirhglksvi Xlmhgzmgrmrwvh, nodded in agreement. "With your radiant beauty, you're far more deserving to be Empress," Xsirh said. A series of slurps, burps, and chirps comprised the language of her companion, inviting inevitable comparisons to human flatulence. Xsirh's green exoderm mottled with laughter, cilia writhing around his face.

Detecting sarcasm, Lydia glanced at the upper portion of his physiognomy, where his optical organelles were located. "And you became an expert on human beauty when?" Reared by the Kziznvxrfn, she knew their language better than any other human, and sometimes better than they themselves did.

"When I met you, Lydia." His coloration took on a blue shade, a sign he was blushing. "I knew you were special from the moment I saw you."

Mollified, she smiled. "Thank you, Xsirh." He was the father she'd never had, the mother she'd always wanted, and the brother she was always competing with, all in one. He gets maudlin at the oddest of times, she thought. Of all the Kziznvxrfn, he knew her the best. He'd reared her since she was four. The Paramecium way of life had been difficult for her to adapt to. Without his protection, she would have perished. He'd risked censure and ostracism to help her, relations between human and Kziznvxrfn tenuous at best.

She replaced the holo with a view of the planet below. Their destination outlined, the capital Helios occupied an archipelago on the water-bound planet. Lydia and Xsirh had come to negotiate a contract for its didinium exports, which the Kziznvxrfn considered a delicacy.

One of the few humans who understood the Kziznvxrfn's near-addictive craving for the unicellular protists, Lydia had started buying didinium harvested on human worlds for the Kziznvxrfn market and now was the number-one supplier, with a seventy-five percent market share and a fleet of cargo transports. Always on the lookout for new sources, she'd come to Mnemosyne with her adoptive father to scout out the quality of its product.

"Atmospheric entry in one minute," the ship computer blurted. "Zgnlhksvirx vmgib rm gdl nrmfgvh," it repeated in Kziznvxrz.

She checked her five-point and glanced at Xsirh.

A transparent shell dropped from the ceiling to cover him, his periplast far more permeable than her epidermis and his body lacking bones. In a multi-g descent, he'd ooze right through five-point restraints, even with anti-grav absorbing the brunt of the torsion forces.

The ship began to shudder and shake. Lydia concentrated on breathing deeply, atmospheric entry the worst part. Twenty-four years ago, during just such a descent, she'd been orphaned on Kziznvxrfn, her parents dying in the crash. She gripped the armrests with both hands, sweat breaking out on her brow, her stomach doing pirouettes up to her craw, her heart hammering in her ears.

Then the shudder ceased.

"Imperial Infection Control to inbound Paramecia vessel, please assume a holding pattern at fifty-thousand feet while your ship is being imaged."

"Acknowledged," Lydia said, barely finding her voice in time.

"Imaged?" Xsirh said, the shell retracting into the ceiling. "Why do they need to image our ship?"

"Contraband, probably." She shrugged, frowning. She'd commed with a complete flight plan and had been cleared by the authorities. She couldn't imagine what the holdup was.

"Oh, I'll bet it's the coronation."

Intuitively, she knew he was right, the hoopla reaching even Theogony on the galactic rim, a hoopla they couldn't avoid no matter how hard they tried.

"Infection Control requesting visual contact," the ship computer said. "Rmuvxgrlm Xlmgilo ivjfvhgrmt erhfzo xlmgzxg."

"On screen," Lydia ordered.

"Commander Sarantos here, Imperial Infection Control. Lydia Procopio, I presume?" A smile lit up his face. "My, aren't you pretty!"

Prettier than that pondscum Empress of yours, she thought. "What's the hold-up, Commander? All the clearances are in the flight plan filed a week ago with Space Traffic Control."

"We've had some changes in protocol due to the recent outbreaks, Ms. Procopio, clearances or not. We're detecting alien life aboard the ship. We'll need to sterilize the vessel."

"Of course there's alien life aboard—my Kziznvxrfn companion, Xsirh."

"Kzizn? You have a Kzizn aboard? We'll need to do a visual and the alien will have to be dealt with."

"He's been inoculated per protocol, Commander. We've both been inoculated. It's all on file." Humans everywhere were paranoid about infectious agents and invasive species. Recent infectious outbreaks had ratcheted up their paranoia to a persecutory fervor.

"Prepare to be boarded," Commander Sarantos said. The screen winked out.

"I don't like the sound of this, Lydia," Xsirh said.

Her stomach ground and heaved, and not from the rough atmospheric entry. "It's never been a problem before. We've been to how many worlds belonging to these supposed Sapiens?" She frowned at him, dreading the inspection. And what had the Commander meant by "the alien will have to be dealt with"? Lydia and Xsirh had learned how difficult relations could be, their first few attempts to establish trade contacts having failed spectacularly.

"Not very sapient, are they?" Xsirh said. "I'd better get into my envirosuit before they board." His exoderm extended as his periplast retracted, protecting the attached cilia. He looked as if he were folding himself inside out. Xsirh slithered to the floor and squirmed toward his cabin on his exoderm, the mucousy periplast better suited to semi-aquatic environments.

The ship lurched violently to one side. "Tractor beam," the amoeba said, its voice eerily calm. "Gizxgli yvzn."

Thrown against her restraints, she wondered if Xsirh was all right. "Xsirh?" She tried to look over her shoulder. "Xsirh?" Unable to see him, she unbuckled herself. Bracing herself to keep from sliding down the slanted floor, she made her way into the corridor.

"Just a bruise," he said, holding twenty tentacles to a mottled patch of his periplast.

"Nothing broken?" she asked.

He shook his head and laughed, his optical organelles meeting her gaze. He had no bones to break. "Right in the micronuclei, though," he added, his organelles squinting in pain. His micronuclei were the equivalent of human gonads, one of four ways that Kziznvxrz reproduced.

I wish we'd been using the sub-ether drives, Lydia thought. They'd have put us beyond reach of any tractor beam.

"Unauthorized entry being attempted," the ship said. "Fmzfgsliravw vmgib yvrmt zggvnkgvw."

Infection Control, she thought. "Entry authorized. Let them in." She turned to Xsirh. "Better that than they blow our hatches."

"This won't be pretty."

She knew that as well as he did. The amoeba-class vessel righted, and she stepped toward the hatch, which opened.

The face of Field Commander Sarantos was a mix of a leer and a wretch. "What's that stench?! Smells like a sewer!" His face settled on a wretch, his skin turning green.

"Kzizn atmosphere, Commander," Lydia said. "In such a hurry to board, you can't wait for us to change the air? Hitting us with that tractor beam without warning injured my shipmate. If he requires medical care, you'll be getting the bill."

His face turned from green to red. "Inspect the ship!" he barked over his shoulder. "And you stay right here."

"Watch for Xsirh on the corridor floor," she told the marines as they surged past. She turned to Sarantos. "The next time you visit Kzizn, I'd like to offer you a complimentary kick to the testicles. Like the one you gave him."

A vein pulsed at his temple, his hand on his sidearm.

"Got the Kzizn, Commander!"

A blood-curdling squelch came from the back, Xsirh blatting in pain.

She whirled. "What are you doing to him?!"

Commander Sarantos slammed her to the bulkhead, his arm to her neck. "I said, `Stay'! Take the Kzizn aboard," he said over his shoulder.

"You can't do that! He's done nothing wrong!" she choked out, trying to push his arm off her.

"R'ev wlmv mlgsrmt dilmt!" Xsirh said.

The Commander made another face. "What the hell was that noise? It sounded like really bad gas. Is that speech? What'd he say?"

"He said he's done nothing wrong!"

They'd wrapped Xsirh in a net and were hauling him onto the other ship.

Commander Sarantos let her go. "I'd advise you lay low for the next few days, Ms. Procopio. Whatever business you have can wait."

"My first order of business will be to file a complaint with the embassy, and my second, to do whatever I can to get you bounced out on your incompetent backside!"

"It's just a Kzizn, Ms. Procopio."

"That's my father, Commander!"

* * *

Lydia frowned at the line ahead of her. A queue of a couple hundred people snaked away from the Imperial Infection Control kiosk at the Helios spaceport, all of them awaiting clearance.

"What's the holdup?" she asked the person in front of her.

A rough-faced old man, his back bent from years of labor, gave her a look up and down. "Where you been livin', some backwater bayou? Outbreaks on Pyrgos Five and Cygnus Twenty, both planets under quarantine." He shook his head at her. "Ought to surf the holonet more often."

She blinked blankly at him and snorted. "Brain rot," she said. Anxious already to get Xsirh out of custody, she was tempted to raise a stink just to get past the line. She was certainly going to file multiple complaints about the rough, unwarranted treatment they'd received. "Where are you coming from?"

"Neither of those places, thank the stars."

She estimated how long she'd be standing in line, saw immediately she'd have to postpone her appointment with the CEO of Titanide Aquafoods. And who knew how long it'd take to get Xsirh released. Or if. She didn't have a lot of faith in human bureaucracy.

"Lydia." She extended her hand to the half-bent old fart in front of her.

"Nick," he said, shaking. "Short for Nikephoros. Pleased."

"Mutual," she replied. "What do you do here?"

"What else on a soupy planet like this? I fish—run a trawler for Titanide. Not much else to do either."

Lydia saw a bureaucrat making his way through the line, asking quick questions of each person he passed. "Titanide? I'm here to see Orrin."

"Runs a tight ship, he does. What's he gonna do with a pretty one like you?"

Lydia blushed and snorted. "Strictly business."

The bureaucrat pulled a man aside and led him over to an arch, where a glowing biodetector sat, its bulk twice the man's height. The man walked under the arch, alarms sounded, the arch flashed red, and a squad of armed soldiers appeared from nowhere.

"But I've been inoculated!" the man said, his voice quailing with fear as they hauled him away.

"What'll they do with him?" Lydia asked.

"Sterilize him," Nick told her with a shrug.

"Will he be able to reproduce after that?"

"Depends on whether or not it kills him."

Lydia stared after the squad, the man in their midst struggling. "How long has it been like this?"

"Happens whenever there's an outbreak. And those quarantines may not be enough." Nick shook his head.

Lydia had read up a little on immunology and disease prevention. Her father Dorian had been a Professor of Xenobiology before he died in the shipwreck, and among his effects had been some preliminary research. The fact that Imperial Infection Control was screening people after they made planetfall seemed to her to border on incompetence.

The bureaucrat was back at it, asking people questions, passing most of them by.

"What do you suppose he's asking?"

"Whether they've been to Pyrgos Five or Cygnus Twenty in the past year."

Lydia frowned, having been to both planets multiple times on business. Pyrgos Five manufactured shipping containers, and Cygnus Twenty supplied packaging. "What's it like to fish on Theogony?"

"Terrible! Didinium are all over the place. They get in your boots, they get in the nets, they clog up the exhaust pipes, they swim up inside the sewers, and worst of all, they get mixed in with the catch. You ever see a didinium? Those slugs can grow to the size of your head."

Lydia grinned and nodded. "On Kziznvxrz, they're ferocious little beasts." In their early evolution on Xsirh's home planet, the Kziznvxrfn and Didinium had fought for preeminence across a million years, each devouring the other relentlessly, and only in the last five hundred thousand had the Kziznvxrfn waded onto dry land from the planet's primordial soup as the dominant species. And the Kziznvxrfn had never lost their liking for didinium, despite its being nearly extinct. "They're considered a delicacy. If you can catch them."

"A delicacy? They taste awful! Who in their right minds would think they're a delicacy?"

Lydia shrugged at him. "I have relatives with some pretty strange tastes."

The bureaucrat approached the old man. "Any travel to Pyrgos Five or Cygnus Twenty in the past year?"

Nick shook his head. "No, Sir, never been either place."

The head moved slightly in Lydia's direction, the bureaucrat's eyes remaining fixed to his palmcom. "Any travel to Pyrgos Five or Cygnus Twenty in the past year?"

"Several times to both," she said.

Nick instantly stepped back, as did several people around them.

"I've been inoculated," she told them all, "if that's any help." Lydia already knew nothing she could say would sway a bureaucrat, always gumming things up like didinium in the fishing nets.

"Inoculation didn't help five hundred million people on Cygnus Twenty," the bureaucrat said. "Is that a rash?" he asked her.

"Huh?"

"Those spots on your arm, is that a rash?"

"Oh, that? I don't know," Lydia said. "It's been itching off and on since I left Kziznvxrz."

"I'll have to ask you to come with me, miss. What's your name?" The bureaucrat gestured toward the glowing biodetector.

"Lydia Procopio." She followed him to the arch. Blue lights twinkled around its insides, the hum of its motors faintly audible. It soared over her, dwarfing her slight form.

"On my signal, just walk slowly through, Ms. Procopio. Don't make any sudden moves." The lights began to blink. The hum went up two octaves. "Go ahead, please."

She stepped slowly through the machine. When she reached the far side without setting off the alarms, Lydia turned to the bureaucrat. "I told you I've been inoculated."

Chapter 2

"Unlike Imperial Infection Control to revoke its clearances without warning," Orrin Stamos told the fetching young woman across from him. "And I'm so sorry they treated your ... father so badly. After her coronation, the Empress will be touring the outlying colonies. Based on the level of activity here, I'm guessing Theogony will be her first stop. I'm afraid an Imperial visit is going to complicate things."

The CEO of Titanide Aquafoods hoped she hadn't heard his hesitation. His company was the largest exporter of fish on Theogony. Orrin frowned, distressed at the way she'd been treated, but having difficulty believing the alien was so important to her.

Now their deal was about to fall apart.

Her company was the biggest importer of didinium on Kzizn. Trawlers on Theogony dredged up didinium by the trillions, the creatures ubiquitous. A carnivorous unicellular ciliate protist, its gelatinous texture nauseated the human palate. The didinium preyed upon Titanide's main catch, so throwing them back wasn't an option, and disposing their carcasses into the sea had earned the company the castigation of local environmentalists. Selling the didinium to the Kzizn seemed like the perfect solution.

Orrin didn't want to lose the contract because of a diplomatic snafu.

When he'd met her at the spaceport, Orrin had seen how distressed she was, and she'd insisted on being taken immediately to the consulate. En route, she'd been furious and disconsolate by turns.

"How's Xsirh's detainment being received at home?" he asked hesitantly.

"I don't know yet," Lydia replied, her gaze on the floor. "They probably won't release him any time soon, will they?"

"Difficult to say. Why do you ask?"

"My father's throwing a birthday party for me on Kziznvxrz three days from now."

"Well, I hope you don't have to spend your birthday here."

He could feel the contract slipping through his hands, as though coated in slime. He knew the creature who'd accompanied her to Theogony couldn't possibly be her biological father, but clearly, she regarded him highly. Her biographical information indicated she'd been reared by the Kzizn after being shipwrecked on the planet as a child. All right, Orrin asked himself, if I were visiting Kzizn with my father, and they detained him, how would I want to be treated?

"Look, why don't we go see him, make sure he's being treated all right?" Orrin knew he wouldn't be endearing himself to Immigration, but he was in exports, not tourism.

"Oh, could we?" she said, brightening immediately. "That'd be wonderful! They probably don't even know what to feed him. And he'll dehydrate within hours if he's not immersed. Oh, thank you, Orrin!"

She looks about to leap across the desk! he thought. Himself, he wouldn't mind, the young woman quite attractive, but his girlfriend certainly would. I'd better com her, he thought, I'll probably be late for our date.

Orrin had Lydia wait in the foyer while he made arrangements, having to reschedule two afternoon meetings with suppliers.

He wondered what he was getting himself into.

* * *

Carissa Minas, Warden at the Helios Immigration Detention Center, frowned at the uproar.

We're Immigration! she thought in disgust. We should be trained for this!

Instead of a calm and orderly detention, chaos had erupted from the moment the detainee had arrived, the Kzizn's odor causing revulsion and nausea. Carissa had nearly fainted when she'd entered the holding area.

Now, watching on holo, she struggled to keep her face impassive, her bowels grinding and heaving, just like everyone else's in the facility. The creature's stupefying smell pervaded the place, and the sights and sounds hovering above her desk made it worse.

The elliptical glob of shimmering muck squirmed and writhed on the cell floor, bright mucous green along most its length. The purple splotching on its midriff almost looked like bruises. And it emitted a constant stream of blurts, blats, phorts, and phlats, the sounds a human might make when undergoing extreme gastrointestinal ejection.

"Sounds like C-Diff in there," said the man across from her, Lieutenant Simon Hatzis, her second in command. "Smells like it, too."

"What? What's that?" Carissa asked, looking at him through the holo.

"Clostridium difficile," he said immediately. "A bacteria in the human intestine which releases toxins that attack the intestinal lining. Causes projectile diarrhea, highly infectious."

"It's infectious?!" she asked, pointing at the writhing creature. The recent infectious outbreaks on two nearby planets were causing considerable consternation.

"Well, not according to the ship's manifest," Simon replied, looking at a hand-held holo, text swirling above it. " `All passengers inoculated and assured to be free of infectious pathogens per interstellar protocols.' It's even signed off by Imperial Infection Control." He extended the holo toward her.

"I don't need to see it, thank you." She hated his manner, redolent of a teacher lecturing young boys on imitating bathroom sounds.

The holographic figure blatted sonorously.

"Oh, my! What I wouldn't give to have been able to emit such sounds in grade school!"

Her stomach cramped as if in sympathy, and she realized she had to pass gas.

No! she thought, not in front of Lieutenant Hatzis! She couldn't stop the flatulence, but thankfully, it was silent, and the cloud of miasma that seeped up around her head wasn't terribly different from the stench already pervading the facility.

It wasn't enough that Imperial Infection Control had issued a detain-all-aliens order for Theogony. Then that insufferable Field Commander, Sarantos, had foisted upon her a detainee that the facility was unprepared to care for, one who appeared to be in distress, perhaps injured. And then this idiot Lieutenant waltzes into my office and spews his discursive diffi-whatever dissertation! Carissa fumed, wondering what she'd done to deserve such a fate.

"Visitor to see the Kzizn, Warden," her intercom blatted.

Maybe someone from the embassy to tell us how to care for the creature, she thought. Carissa had commed them immediately after the alien's arrival, needing a translator. She'd quickly realized she needed more than translation. "Thank you, Stan, and can you ask environmental services to do something about the smell?"

"Yes, Warden." Stan's voice over the intercom was almost as unpleasant as the sounds from the cell, the equipment ancient.

"Shall we, Lieutenant?" She gestured him to go first. I'd do anything to get his officious ass out of my office! Carissa thought, carefully keeping her sentiments off her face.

He preceded her into the corridor and turned toward the foyer.

There, in the septic-smelling, antiseptic waiting room, they found not another Kzizn from the embassy but two humans, both of them looking distraught.

"I'm Orrin Stamos, CEO of Titanide Aquafoods," the man said.

"Lydia Procopio," the woman said. "I'm told my father is being detained here."

Carissa shook both their hands, introducing herself. Even in her distress, the woman was stunning. "I'm afraid you must be mistaken, Ms. Procopio. Our only current detainee is an alien."

"A Kziznvxrfn," the woman said. "I know he's here."

For a moment, Carissa was baffled. She'd never heard the full, non-diminutive name for the aliens spoken by someone fluent in the Kziznvxrfn language. Nonplussed by the bizarre sounds issuing from the beautiful woman's mouth, Carissa was befuddled by what she was trying to tell her. "Forgive me, a what?"

"A Kzizn."

"Your father's a ..." She coughed, taken aback. "Forgive me, but ..."

"He adopted me when I was four. He's the only father I've ever known."

Spoken with such simplicity, the words moved her. Further, the woman looked as if she'd been crying.

"I know he's here, Warden."

A bit difficult to disguise that fact, Carissa thought sardonically. "Yes, the Kzizn is here. Uh, er, what's his name?"

"Xsirh."

" `Sure'?" Carissa repeated.

"Well, almost. It's short for Xsirhglksvi, spelled X-S-I-R-H."

"Xsirh?" Carissa marveled that anyone could master such difficult sounds. She could see Lieutenant Hatzis suppressing his laughter. I'll pummel him later, she thought.

"Please, I have to see him. He was injured when Infection Control put a tractor beam on our ship. And he has to be immersed every few hours or he'll die from dehydration."

"Of course, Ms. Procopio." Even better than a translator from the embassy, Carissa thought. They didn't have a machine that could translate a language as difficult as Kziznvxrz. Even among human settlements across the galaxy, the proliferation of languages challenged even the most sophisticated translation equipment, despite the near ubiquity of Galactim, the lingua franca. "A few questions, first, if I may?" Carissa asked. "What was the purpose of your visit?"

"They were meeting with me to negotiate a didinium export contract," the man said.

Orrin is his name, she reminded herself. "Thank you, Mr. Stamos." She looked at the woman. "You mentioned injury, Ms. Procopio. How was he injured, and how severely?"

"He got up from his chair to get into an envirosuit after Infection Control said they were boarding our vessel. The tractor beam caused our ship to lurch, throwing him against the wall and bruising his micronuclei, the human equivalent of testicles."

Carissa saw the two men squirm. "Sorry to hear he was injured, Ms. Procopio. You mentioned immersion?"

"Yes, Warden, preferably in salt water to maintain his electrolytes. Fresh water will work for a day or two, but will eventually cause delirium, seizures, coma, and respiratory arrest."

"Lieutenant Hatzis, secure what he needs."

"Huh?"

She whirled on him. "Get on it, man! He's in our care. His health is our responsibility."

Hatzis hesitated again.

She stepped up to him, shoved her face into his, and ground her heel into his foot. "Now, please," she said sweetly. Carissa turned to the woman as the Lieutenant limped away. "Ms. Procopio, we'll do everything we can to insure he's well. Typically, visitors aren't allowed, but given the circumstances, we'll make an exception. If you'll give us a few minutes, I'll escort you back myself."

* * *

Wait for it! Erastus thought, wait for it!

He was Erastus Doukas, Agent Provocateur from the Imperial Bureau of Suspicion, and he watched the Immigration Detention Center like a hawk for anyone exiting.

He'd seen his target entering with an unknown man ten minutes ago.

Wait for it! he told himself yet again.

For the next two minutes, no one else entered or exited the building.

The detention center was isolated, sitting on the point, perched atop an escarpment overlooking the sea. Purposively so. No one got in or out without being observed. And there was only one bridge.

He surveilled the facility from across an estuary where rough seas surged. Erastus was somewhat dismayed at how close the facility was to the water. Not that anyone would dare try to escape into the roiling seas, waves battering rocks just a few feet below the facility's foundation. What do they do in a storm? he wondered.

But no matter. She'd gone in the facility, and hadn't come out.

And if everything went well, she never would. Not of her own volition.

He grinned, his mission nearly finished. "T-minus three minutes," he said into his com.

Rarely did he complete such missions so fast, but this one had been unusual from the start. A month ago, he'd been contacted by agent control in a brightly-lit alley on Lucina IX.

A woman wearing a fedora and a long trench coat was slumped against the alley wall between two malodorous bins of refuse, glaring radon lamps high overhead throwing every object into sharp relief. "Agent Doukas," she said, her eyes barely visible under the wide brim, her nose as perfect as an axe blade.

"If you're gonna do the cloak-and-dagger routine, you might consider a darker alley," he told her.

"What concern of yours is that?" she snapped. "Besides, dark alleys are spooky."

He could see the fine, classic lines of her face, the perfect nose, the luscious lips. "They don't find dead dames in bright alleys."

"Precisely my point, Doukas," she snarled, mispronouncing his name like a homophobic slur. "I've a special assignment for you. One which has the bouquet of a fine Metaxa."

He immediately went on high alert. As exalted as it was rare, Metaxa was a distilled blend of brandy, spices, and wine from Pelopone VI. Nearly no one except the Imperial Family could afford it. Nearly no one but the Imperials drank it. He knew what she meant but he didn't say it: Orders from the Palace.

"You are to travel immediately to Erato IV in the Mnemosyne Constellation. The planet is locally known as Theogony. You're familiar?"

"Adjacent to the system of that alien species with the unpronounceable name, right? The Kzizn?"

"That's the one. In fact, that's your task. Secure the planet under the Bureau's auspices, capture all aliens and their human companions, and ship them back to Gaea for interrogation."

"All of them?"

"Did I specify any exemptions?" Her tone was as sharp as her nose.

"What about indigenous species?"

"There's no intelligent life on Theogony!"

Taken aback, he realized the orders applied only to ... "Ah, sentient aliens," he said. Sentience was a characteristic ascribed to just a few elite forms of life in the galaxy, a category rumored to exclude Homo sapiens.

"Of course I mean `sentient,' idiot!"

Proving once again that an assumption on his part would have made an anatomical posterior of them both. She doesn't need my help in that regard, he thought. He suspected he didn't need hers, either. "How long do I have?"

"A month."

At first, he thought to object, Theogony just a parsec from Kzizn-vxrz. But how do I know any Kzizn are even there? he wondered.

"Relations between the two species aren't spectacular," the woman said, "so you might not have any difficulty at all."

"Which means very few human companions, too," he said, nodding. "What about the embassy?"

"Don't worry about it. Cleared by Immigration, and technically, not even Imperial Territory."

And he and a crew of ten subordinates had come to Theogony and had scoured the planet for any sentient aliens, not just Kzizn. Within a week, they'd secured their removal to Gaea for interrogation.

Done, he commed agent control to say he'd finished early. "What do you mean, I gotta stay?" he objected to the shadowy, fedora-obscured woman.

The blade-nosed face in the holocom nearly leaped from the machine into his hotel room. "I told you a month, do you hear?!"

And the very next day, Emperor Zenon died, throwing the Empire into an uproar. Fortunately, Princess Hecuba stepped into the breach and declared herself Empress, a startling move for a young woman at the tender age of twenty-four.

Watching events on Gaea from the border planet Theogony, Erastus couldn't help but notice that in the background of every vid or still of the Empress-designate lurked the Dowager Empress, Narcissa Thanos, the Emperor's surviving second wife. The first wife had died in childbirth some thirty years ago.

Doukas wasn't a genius, but he wasn't ingenuous either. Rot in the rarified air of a palace smelled the same as that in brightly-lit alleys. And something smelled rotten in Denmark, wherever that was.

And then, that morning, a Kzizn ship had commed Helios Control for permission to land on Theogony. Aboard were a Kzizn and a human. Intuitively, he knew his bird had alighted.

Watching the building to assure for himself that not a soul emerged from the Immigration Detention Center, he lifted his com to his mouth. "All right, katáskopos, time to capture our bird. Go, go, go!"

Hovers and ground cars descended upon the facility like a swarm of bees. Instantly, the place was surrounded, and the ordnance aimed at it was enough to blast it off the precipice and into the sea.

Doukas and two subordinates brandishing sidearms blew into the waiting room, badges out. "IBS," he intoned in his deepest voice, displaying his badge in one hand. With the other, he held his weapon at his shoulder, its point glowing and ready.

The stench was hideous, and he nearly gagged.

Behind partitioned glass, the receptionist quailed and slowly sank to the floor, his hands in the air.

Three agents surged in behind him, one going left, one going right, and one staying at the door. Three more entered behind them, all of them looking bilious.

Two agents on his heels, Doukas headed straight in, toward the holding tanks, already familiar with the layout. He opened his trake to the paging system, trying to contain his gag reflex.

"This is Agent Erastus Doukas of the Imperial Bureau of Suspicion." His voice boomed back at him from overhead. "This facility is being commandeered by Imperial authority. All planetary Immigration officers are hereby deputized as IBS agents under my command. You will lower yourself to the floor immediately. You will be shot after the count of five if you are not on the floor. Five, four, three, two, one."

Six agents reported all clear.

Doukas marched past wormwire-reinforced glasma panes toward a set of double doors.

A uniformed female burst through the doors. "What's the meaning of this!?"

"Hold your fire!" he told his agents, two guns trained on her. "Warden Minas, I hope. If you're not, you're dead."

"Indeed. What the stars is going on?"

"Your detention center is now under my command by order of her Imperial Majesty. All your staff are now my staff, and all your prisoners are now my prisoners."

"Fine by me. How are you going to care for the Kzizn?"

Doukas was taken aback, not quite the response he expected. "I'm not. It's to be transported to Gaea immediately for interrogation. And its companion, the woman it arrived with. Who's the man?" He strode through the next set of doors, the Warden on his heels.

"A business associate, a Theogony native."

In the corridor beyond, the stench intensified. "The Kzizn's through this door?" Doukas stopped abruptly before going through.

"In the holding tank, yes," Warden Minas said.

He signaled to the two agents with him, both of them female.

All three burst through the door.

Partitioned cells lined the walls, their shiny, carbo-nick alloy bars stretching from plascrete floor to plascrete ceiling. Bare loomglobes hung near the ceiling, bathing the scene in stark, surreal light.

A woman lay on the floor in front of the rear-most cage, her wide-eyed stare on the agents. Nearby lay a man, the Theogony native. Just beyond the bars lay a lump of green protoplasm, a large purple splotch in its middle.

The stench was overpowering, and Doukas nearly retched.

His two agents turned the same putrid green as the creature beyond the bars from the stench. They pounced upon the couple. His other two Kzizn detainees had worn envirosuits, the Theogony atmosphere eventually fatal to the Kzizn. None of them had had human companions.

"What's the meaning of this?" the woman asked, a plaster barrel to the base of her skull.

He saw she was exceptionally pretty, even face down on the floor. Doukas knelt where they could both see him. He flipped out his badge and repocketed it, so practiced at the maneuver that no one had time to peruse it. "Agent Erastus Doukas, Imperial Bureau of Suspicion. You're under arrest."

"On what charges?!" the man demanded. "I want to speak with my lawyer!"

"He wants his lawyer," Doukas mocked, his voice a high-pitch whine. "Sequester them," he ordered. "No further contact between the prisoners until after interrogation. Put the female in isolation and take the male immediately to interrogation room two. I'll question him first."

Other agents converged to assist, and as they hauled the female to isolation, Doukas was taken aback by her breath-taking beauty.

"My father needs help," she protested as she was dragged away. "He'll die if he' not immersed within an hour!"

Father? Doukas wondered, bewildered for a moment. Then he realized she was talking about the Kzizn.

"R'oo yv zoo irtsg uli z grnv," the alien inside the cage blatted.

Doukas cringed at the sound, as if to dodge projectile diarrhea. He stepped to the bars to look at the amorphous figure, its cilia writhing helplessly in the air. "Get a Kzizn envirosuit," he told the agent beside him, Lieutenant Special Agent Jace Eliades.

"Why do you suppose she called it 'Father'?" Eliades asked.

Doukas shrugged. "And then get me her dossier, Lieutenant."

"Yes, Sir."

Warden Minas stepped up beside him. "How soon can you get them going to Gaea?"

"An hour maybe. Lieutenant Eliades, secure transport. We'll be ready by the time they get here."

"Yes, Sir." Eliades had his hand to his ear, his lips moving soundlessly as he issued a series of orders.

"I can't believe the smell," Doukas said. "And she calls this thing her father?" he asked the Warden.

Minas shrugged. "Reared by the Kzizn since she was four, apparently."

He glanced over his shoulder toward the isolation cell where his agents had taken her, wondering what the palace wanted from her.

Erastus Doukas, Agent Provocateur from the Imperial Bureau of Suspicion, was convinced she was the reason he'd been sent to this backwater planet.

But why her? he wondered.

Chapter 3

"Colonel," the com squawked on her desk, "I've just received a request for a dossier on the subject."

Colonel Melanctha Remes looked up from her desk at the back of the theater at IBS Command on Lucina IX. Atop the fine classical lines of her face was a nose as sharp as an axe blade, perfect for cutting through the red tape of Imperial bureaucracy. She peered through the glasma pane separating her from operations.

Beyond the glasma was a darkened room lit solely by the myriad of holo displays hovering above the staff. Five rings of desks encircled a central pit, where her immediate subordinate stood, directing the surveillance technicians around him like an orchestra conductor.

"I'll be there in a moment, Lieutenant-Colonel." All squawk-box coms recorded, she wanted this information off-record, the mission to Theogony having that fine Metaxa bouquet.

Why the hell is the palace so interested in the Kzizn? she wondered, standing and making her way to the command theater center.

The entire Delta Quadrant under her surveillance, Colonel Remes was mystified by the sudden attention to an isolated planet on the outer Scutum-Centaurus Arm, where virtually nothing happened. Further, the focus on the Kzizn was downright enigmatic.

The Empire had somewhat recovered from the uproar over Emperor Athanasios Zenon's untimely demise three weeks ago, the initial shock throwing everything into chaos. Yesterday, Colonel Remes had floated an inquiry to IBS Command whether to abort the mission to Theogony.

The impersonal, imperious reply had been, "All current missions will be pursued in extreme vigor with all due diligence and dispatch." An emphatic no, and cloaked within the message, the threat of dismissal should the mission fail, worded vaguely enough to slather the communiqué with a viscous layer of plausible deniability.

And then this morning, Doukas had commed about a new arrival.

The original mission had emphasized the detainment of all sentient alien life and any human companions. The proximity of Kziznvxrz to Theogony had suggested the emphasis on the Kzizn, but they were such a reclusive race, devoid of hegemonic ambitions, languishing on their septic, swampy world like limp, amorphous blobs of protoplasm, that Colonel Remes wondered what threat they could possibly pose. They were a race of peaceful if repulsive aliens, no threat to anyone.

Had they had any such ambition, they'd be formidable, their aspects repulsive. Further, their advanced technological development gave them a tactical advantage over their Homo sapiens neighbors, their interstellar ships diaphanous and difficult to track, their weaponry virtually unknown.

Diplomatic relations with the Kzizn had always been tenuous, their appearance, language, and aroma all so repulsive to humans that missions to Kziznvxrz had been brief and unproductive. Theogony was the only planet where the Kzizn maintained an embassy, their diplomats exchanged yearly, their human hosts as attractive to the Kzizn as they were to the humans. Further, the Theogony atmosphere was deleterious to Kzizn health.

Colonel Remes threaded her way up the aisle, nodding to subordinates, most the technicians at their desks so focused on their work they didn't even notice her. On one holo was a feed from Gaea, the capital, the pomp and pageantry of the upcoming Imperial Coronation glutting the media.

Lieutenant-Colonel Urian Nikitas saluted her as she stepped into the conductor's pit, a holographic image of the Delta Sector swirling above them, multiple points of attention highlighted to indicate threat level, the Theogony region outlined in red.

"All coms off?" she asked.

Lieutenant-Colonel Nikitas nodded.

"Who's requesting the dossier?"

"Agent Doukas, on Theogony," Nikitas replied. "Damn it, Colonel, why him? Forgive me for asking, but he's as slimy as those Kzizn."

"I know it. I had to scrub my backside raw just to rid myself of his stench. Deny his request for the dossier. Don't tell him why, not even that it's ultra-confidential. Tell him there is none, all right? That'd be best. There is none." She questioned the wisdom of telling her trusted second-in-command what its status was, much less that it existed at all.

"Yes, Colonel," he said, giving her a brief salute.

She stepped back to the pit edge, watching as he commed Agent Doukas in the field.

"One moment, Agent Doukas," Nikitas said, turning to her. "Colonel, Agent Doukas says no transport's available for the two prisoners. He's asking for further instruction."

"No transport, in this day and age? There must be hundreds of ships he can charter, and thousands he can commandeer!"

"I told him the same. He swears up and down there's not a single interstellar vessel in the Mnemosyne Constellation except the vessel the two prisoners arrived on. Something about security measures being taken in the sector, he says."

"Security measures? But we're security," she protested. "If there're security measures to be taken, we're the ones to taking them. Unless..." Colonel Remes blanched, only one possibility coming to mind.

The Secret Service.

That small, ultra-clandestine law enforcement agency whose sole task was to protect the Imperial family. And the Empress-to-be.

If the IBS mission to Theogony had befuddled her before this, now it flummoxed her completely.

Colonel Melanctha Remes wondered what was going on.

* * *

Vasilios Xenakis, Imperial Secret Service Special Agent Ad-hoc, issued the order to halt.

A squadron of vessels stopped as a unit in the Oort cloud of the Erato subsystem. Highlighted on his holo were six planets orbiting a dull yellow primary. Their squadron was the main expeditionary force sent to secure the region prior to the Empress-to-be's arrival some three days hence.

Already, his pre-containment unit had interdicted any inbound ships, except for that slimy Kzizn vessel whose diaphanous hull had baffled all sensors, and whose sub-ether drive had obscured its emissions.

And just why, Vasilios wondered, would her Royal Assness choose this stinking backwater?

Xenakis wasn't bitter.

No, why would he be bitter?

In fact, he had every reason to be grateful. He was an upstanding officer in the most clandestine law-enforcement organization known to the Milky Way, and four weeks ago, he'd been awarded Employee of the Month.

Either I did something stupid or I'm about to be fired, he'd thought as he received the plaque at the awards ceremony back on Gaea. Or I'm about to get an assignment so reprehensible that I'll wish I could crawl back into my Petrie dish.

Mother, forgive me my thoughts, Vasilios said silently to the cockpit ceiling.

And the day before Emperor Athanasios Zenon died, the dreaded orders had appeared on his desk, commanding him to embark on his current mission.

Vasilios thought back through his last thirty years of service to the Imperial family, wondering where he might have slipped up. Where there might have occurred that single perceived slight to precisely the wrong person, whose ire he'd provoked and who'd harbored this most-minute of grudges for decades, the insult festering like a puss-filled boil on the buttocks of hindsight, seething with noxious poisons, its insidious discontent slowly oozing infectious dissatisfaction, until the diseased tumor had burst three weeks ago, and had unleashed its vitriol onto his otherwise-pristine career.

Twenty-nine years ago, he'd met the now-Dowager Empress, Narcissa Thanos, Emperor Zenon's second wife, then only a servant applying to his Majesty's service, whom Vasilios was considering as a new hire to attend upon the Empress Consort, Ambrosia Lillis.

The scion of a shipping magnate, Ambrosia Lillis was beautiful, as intoxicating to look at as her name. She'd have risen to fame without her father's wealth just on her looks alone. Cultured and suave, demure as a fog-shrouded sunrise, Ambrosia was introduced to Gaean high society at an Imperial ball thrown to announce the official appointment of the Imperial Heir, Athanasios Zenon, as the Regent Emperor.

At thirty-five years old, Athanasios was ready to assume the Emperor's duties and become the nominal Emperor, his father hale and hearty but seeking to assure a smooth transition and avoid a nasty interregnum. Single, and the most desirable bachelor in the Empire, Athanasios had taken few lovers and seemed annoyed with the usual crop of high-society debutantes being thrown under his feet by their scheming aristocratic parents.

Despite the ball having been thrown in Athanasios's honor, Ambrosia stole the evening. And the Prince's heart. The romance had set fire to wagging tongues and had torched the Imperial ambitions of many an aristocratic parent.

And it had immediately invoked Imperial Secret Service protection for Ambrosia, whose personal safety had become the charge of Special Agent Ad-hoc Vasilios Xenakis. Further, it had merited a retinue of personal servants, personally selected by said Special Agent.

One servant girl during the interviews had struck Vasilios Xenakis as incredibly competent and perceptive. Narcissa Thanos, her dossier had told him, was a peasant girl from a minor city on the far side of Gaea whose mother had died in childbirth and whose father's tsipouro vats produced only enough of the alcoholic beverage for him. Despite these desultory origins, Narcissa had worked her way quickly through several aristocratic Gaean families. Just after the Imperial ball, she'd applied to enter the Empress Consort's personal service as a Lady's Maid.

Ambrosia's personal safety his charge, Vasilios had screened Narcissa thoroughly. Her meteoric and blemish-less career in servitude had struck him as overly ambitious, but in multiple interviews, she'd assuaged his concerns, as had his interviews of all her previous employers.

At the bedside of the near-term Empress Consort, that competence had become starkly evident.

"I fear her Ladyship will have a difficult time," Narcissa had told him the day before Ambrosia went into labor. It'd been an odd pronouncement, quite in opposition to the opinion of a cadre of physicians in attendance upon the Empress Consort.

At the birth, medical personnel swarming around the Consort, and her favorite servant Narcissa right beside her, Vasilios had kept a personal eye on the Empress Consort for as long as he could, as if he might guard her from the clutches of Thanatos himself.

But no one had been able to protect her, and Ambrosia had died in childbirth.

Twenty-eight years later, looking down at the Erato subsystem, Vasilios Xenakis sighed.

Six planets orbited a dull yellow primary, the fourth one a pure blue marble, over ninety percent ocean.

How the hell did I end up here? he wondered, his task to secure a beautiful if backwater planet in a backwater system in a backwater constellation at the lightly-populated end of a galactic arm for the arrival of the Empress, the second daughter of Emperor Athanasios Zenon by his second wife, Narcissa Thanos.

Far from the center of power.

Far from the grave of the Empress Consort Ambrosia Lillis, the only person he'd ever loved.

* * *

Outside the door of the mausoleum where the ashes of the Empress Consort Ambrosia Lillis lay interred, a woman laid a single rose on the lowest step, said a brief prayer, and then moved on.

Drucilla Kanelos hadn't wanted to get any closer nor stay any longer.

Someone immediately took her place from a long line of waiting supplicants snaking through the graveyard into the distance, each with flowers, cards, and other mementos of sorrow in hand.

In two days, the usurper gets crowned, Drucilla thought, shedding a silent tear for Ambrosia and her unnamed daughter, wherever she was at, if she were alive at all.

A Laundry Maid who'd washed the personal undergarments of the Empress-to-be from the time she'd been an infant, and before that, who'd laundered the bed sheets of the Empress Consort Ambrosia Lillis, Drucilla hadn't let her lifetime of laundering dirty linens for the

Imperial family either corrupt her or depress her. She was proud to have laundered the matrimonial sheets of the Empress Consort.

But ashamed of those she'd laundered later.

For within that laundering duty had come the august responsibility of verifying the breach of hymenal tissues by the Imperial pestle.

It was a singular honor to have done it the first time for the Empress Consort, her Ladyship Ambrosia Lillis. And a person might think that a second such instance of this sacred duty might have lifted Drucilla to the heights of Laundry-Maid heaven.

Pulling her hood far forward, Drucilla Kanelos hurried away from the mausoleum for fear of being seen, casting furtive glances all directions.

She'd wanted to honor the deceased Consort on the anniversary of her death two days hence, but the usurper's mother had conveniently scheduled the coronation for that very same day.

Deliberately, at least in Drucilla's mind.

Hired from the same pool of Lady's Maids, Housekeepers, Head Nurses, Chamber Maids, Parlor Maids, House Maids, Between Maids, Nurses, Under Cooks, Kitchen Maids, Scullery Maids, and Laundry Maids, Drucilla knew Narcissa from previous posts among the Gaean aristocratic households.

If she finds out I came here, she thought, I'll wake up dead tomorrow.

Drucilla had had the singular disgrace of verifying the Imperial-pestle breach of the hymenal tissues belonging to the upstart maid-become-Empress, Narcissa Thanos, an act which might have earned Drucilla the Dowager Empress's undying enmity.

But somehow had not.

Hurrying back toward the palace, Drucilla made her way along a busy avenue, an occasional hover whining past, pneumatubes criss-crossing the air above her like spaghetti noodles, a rainbow of people inside the tubes being whisked to their myriad destinations like so many corpuscles. Only Drucilla used the sidewalk, other travelers safe in their vehicles or tucked in their tubes, secure in anonymity.

Footsteps behind her!

Bewildered, she glanced back.

An ungainly figure with an egg-shaped body and stick-like legs hurried along, going the same direction she was.

She increased her pace, the tap of feet behind her sounding not like shoes but more like metal spikes striking pavement.

The tapping increased in tempo. "Dzrg, kovzhv."

What the stars kind of language is that? she wondered. What Drucilla had just heard had sounded more like a bad case of flatulence. Galactim was used for the routine business of government, but the people of Gaea could be frequently heard speaking their native Greek, from which Galactim was derived.

"Wait, please." Similar sounds, but this time with a simultaneous overlay of Galactim. A translator! And somehow in the mechanized translation, hints of desperation were audible. The tinny steps were right behind her.

Drucilla saw an alley ahead. Much as any woman disliked being in a confined space alone with a stranger, she feared Imperial surveillance worse. She turned abruptly into the alley. Impersonal plascrete soared overhead on both sides. The whine of hover and whoosh of pneumatube were muted here.

She looked at the figure.

Below each dress-slack pant leg poked a metal spike. The slacks were hung from the rim of what appeared to be a gigantic egg cup, like the ones they used at the palace during breakfast, when they inevitably argued over which end to break first, the big-endians and little-endians often coming to blows over the issue. Attached to the egg-holder edges was a frame whose only purpose, it appeared, was to give the blazer some shoulders to hang from and someplace for the bizarre head to perch. It could only be called a head because of the position it occupied on the anatomy, the clownish features looking as if they'd been copied from some children's morning holo show.

But what really drew her attention was the green amoebic creature inside the egg holder, its cilia flailing at the controls of the contraption. Indentations atop the amoeba looked vaguely like eyes, and a pocket just below them opened and closed in time with the gurgles, burbles, and squelches.

"Thank you," it said.

She suppressed the urge to duck, the sounds reminding her of projectile emesis. "What the hell are you?" She saw a thin veil of some material between them.

"I'm a Kziznvxrfn," the creature said.

"A who-what?" She realized it wasn't a material at all, but some sort of field, one of those science-fictiony force fields.

The creature emitted a series of blats and burps, its translation machine beeping back in protest. "Ah, bewilderment expressed. I'm a Kzizn," it said, finally. "From beyond the Erato subsystem, in the Mnemosyne Constellation."

"One of them. Always wondered what you looked like."

"Diplomatic relations between our people are somewhat fraught with difficulty."

"I'll bet. You sound violently ill."

"Yes, a side effect of our aspiration and expiration."

"You're gonna die on me?"

Again a series of blats, burps, and gurgles, the machine blatting back in shrill tones. "Oh, uh, 'breathing' is the proper word, I'm being told."

"Oh, heavens, I was wondering. What's that shimmering around you, anyway?"

"A vovxgilnztmvgrx field to separate the air I breathe from the air you breathe."

"A what field?"

"Vovxgilnztmvgrx," it said. Its translator burbled back at it. "Oh, uh, I'm being told there isn't a translation for that particular concept. Hasn't been developed by humans, apparently. Anyway, it keeps your air from harming me and my air from offending you."

"Now, why would I be offended?"

"You don't want to know. Oh, this is all so difficult. Listen, I know your government doesn't want you talking to me—"

"Now, why would they be offended?" Drucilla knew the creature was right, but how did it know? She'd lived in the palace for the last thirty years. She'd seen the consequences of the slightest offense, many of them imagined. Among the offenses that wasn't a product of the imagination was simply knowing too much. Many a domestic servant hadn't survived until morning because, under the cover of night, or under the night covers, he or she had found out something damaging about his or her charge.

"Never mind," she told the creature. "What's your name, by the way?"

"I'm Svkszvhgfh Ezhrozprh. Just call me Ezra. You're Drucilla

Kanelos, Laundry Maid on staff with the Dowager Empress. You're going to Theogony with the Empress-to-be the day after her coronation."

"I am?" It was the first she'd heard about it. And usually the servants knew before members of the Imperial family. "How do you know?"

"I have a message for the Kzizn Embassy there, a message I can't get to them any other way."

She noticed Ezra hadn't answered her question. "And you want me to help? And get my ass thrown into prison?"

The translation machine beeped, clicked, clattered, and slurped, stuck on some word.

"Forgive me, but what is `ass'?"

She smacked her backside. "This thing."

"This is a colloquialism?"

"A who-what?"

"Bewilderment again. Immaterial. I understand `prison.' I assure you, you'll be protected, and there isn't any way you'll be caught."

"How do you know?"

The breathing orifice became a crescent moon, ends upturned; a mock smile. "The message is verbal, and they'll find you when you arrive. They're expecting you."

"What's the message?"

" `Gsv likszm rh uzi nliv gszm hsv hvvnh.' "

"Huh?"

"Bewilderment expressed. Pardon, but I'm wondering why you're puzzled. It's very simple. `Gsv likszm rh uzi nliv gszm hsv hvvnh.' "

"How am I supposed to remember that? What am I, a human voice recorder?"

"Oh, that's right, my apologies. I forget that humans have imperfect recall. A curious trait, that. Very well, I suppose I'll have to have you remember its Galactim translation. Ready?"

"All right," Drucilla said, "go ahead."

" `The orphan is far more than she seems.' "

Chapter 4

She should have died in the crash! Deion thought, sweating.

In the palace security center, buried five hundred feet below the palace proper, Chief of Palace Security for the Imperial Secret Service Deion Goulas reviewed the measures thus far implemented for the Imperial Entourage. Touring the Empire was de rigueur for all incoming sovereigns. Making sure the tour was safe was his responsibility.

And to his knowledge, Deion was the only person who knew the ultimate fate of everyone aboard the diplomatic mission to the Kzizn-vxrz home world a quarter-century ago.

Upon arrival, as the ship was entering the atmosphere, hull integrity had failed, and the burning hulk had plunged into the ocean. Those aboard had been killed instantly, the Ambassador, her husband, and their four-year-old daughter.

Or so everyone thought. Only Deion suspected otherwise.

Three years ago, rumors had begun circulating of a Human-Kzizn pair of entrepreneurs in the Mnemosyne Constellation at the end of the Scutum-Centaurus galactic arm. Since the region was beyond the reach of the major space lanes and nearly devoid of interstellar traffic, the pair had made a killing in shipping and commerce, quickly assembling a fleet of Kzizn-manufacture freighters whose diaphanous hulls and sub-ether drives confounded conventional sensory equipment.

Slowly, Deion had come to the personal conclusion that the human could only be the four-year-old Ambassador's daughter, now grown.

It hadn't been a conclusion he'd arrived at suddenly, but one he'd reached after years of random sightings, several dozen stills, a few security cam vids, and interviews of two people who'd done business with her.

Information which had previously been superfluous to his primary duty—Palace Security.

Until now.

Now, the Dowager Empress wanted to go there, the first stop on the Imperial tour.

Why there? he wondered, the information niggling at him in ways he couldn't quite fathom.

Further, he'd been unable to say just what it was about the crash twenty-four years ago that so intrigued him. The crash of an Ambassador's ship on a distant, swampy world of no particular diplomatic, cultural, economic, or military significance was a blip on the radar. Diplomatic missions went awry all the time, more often than the public realized, these events typically kept out of the galactic headlines.

The crash itself had not struck anyone at the time as particularly momentous. A minor Ambassador, Viscountess Basilissa Procopio had taken her Professor husband and four-year-old daughter on what was considered among the aristocracy a futile and repulsive mission. Not only was Kziznvxrz far from the centers of haute culture, couture, and cuisine, the planet was also revolting, triggering the basal ganglia of human beings in ways that nothing else could. The lizard brain of Homo sapiens had developed an aversion to vomit and excrement as one of its earliest neurological responses. Finding someone brave enough to resist these deeply embedded autonomic responses and live on a swamp at the threshold of oblivion had been a challenge. Not a single member of the aristocracy would touch it.

The Emperor, young Athanasios Zenon, had offered the Ambassadorship to any among the aristocracy who would take it, and for several years, that offer lay open, the position unfilled, without takers. Further, ruling with a benign autocracy, he'd been unwilling to foist it upon anyone, even those who'd incurred his displeasure.

Having just started as a junior officer in the Secret Service, Deion Goulas remembered the minor stir in the Imperial household, just four short years after the death in childbirth of the Empress Consort, Ambrosia Lillis, the event plunging the Empire into deep despair. But the stir, a tempest in a teapot, really, and such a minor breach of protocol that nearly no one outside the administration had noticed, had alarmed everyone in the Imperial household.

About a year after Ambrosia's death, Emperor Zenon took up with the servant girl, Narcissa Thanos, his deceased Consort's Lady's Maid. The affair would have scandalized the Empire, but everyone assumed it would fizzle out after a time. Except that it hadn't.

In three years, she'd taken over his bedchamber and had spread her influence like an insidious cancer throughout the Imperial household. The fait accompli of her coup d'état was to order Viscountess Basilissa Procopio to Kziznvxrz to take up the unwanted, perennially-vacant ambassadorship. The Lady's Maid wasn't so brazen as to order it outright, using instead a combination of poison and honey to engineer the appointment, but that was the effect.

A minor incident, to be sure, but of profound importance, for it had signaled a shift in power from the Emperor to his new unofficial consort. The move cemented her influence over Imperial affairs.

Deion remembered the incident vaguely, and the Ambassador's tragic end was even more obscure. All of these events, however, were being brought into sharp relief by a decision whose origin had left upon it the taint he'd come to know as the power behind the throne.

Why does the Dowager Empress Narcissa Thanos want her daughter Hecuba, the Empress-to-be, to start her Imperial tour in the Mnemosyne Constellation the day after her coronation?

* * *

Licensed Behavioral Technician Baptiste Tomaras knew he had it easy, his job as cushy as it got.

He was a member of the hand-selected team caring for the daughter of the just-deceased Gaean Emperor, Athanasios Zenon. When he told people what he did, sometimes they misunderstood him, and one response he often got was, "Oh, I didn't know she was so impaired!"

And then he had to explain that no, it wasn't the Empress-to-be, Hecuba Zenon, whom he cared for, but the Emperor's other daughter, the first one, Cybill Zenon, whose mother, Ambrosia Lillis, had so tragically died in childbirth.

"Cybill, this way, please," Baptiste said, trying to draw her away from the window.

She was pressing her face against the glasma again, an afternoon ritual for her. There wasn't any danger, the glasma impervious from either side to all but a boson-beam bomb.

He was simply implementing her behavior plan. He didn't know why the doctor didn't want her to mash her face against the glasma and slather so much drool that the window sill had started to soften. "Cybill wants to color, doesn't she? Coloring is her favorite."

"Cybill not like Bap," she said.

"Cybill doesn't like Baptiste, maybe, but she loves to color." He dangled a marker near the window where she could see it, even with her face plastered to the glasma.

Slowly, he lured her away, and soon she was at the easel, laughing and swiping randomly at the holocanvas. As much as they tried to stimulate her language skills, she was as about as expressive as she would ever get, the functional equivalent of a two-year-old.

And yes, as true of any two-year-old, she threw fits. A minor drawback of the job.

Most of the time, she was so zonked on limbic-system suppressants, she couldn't summon the adrenalin to throw them. It was rare she had to be restrained.

She threw a glance over his shoulder and said, "Bad room."

"Good coloring," Baptiste said instantly, attempting to redirect, already knowing he was too late. She was referring to the "quiet room" behind him, a door they typically kept closed. Inside the room was a bed with six-point mechanical restraints, there in case she ever got so out of control as to make chemical and manual restraints ineffective to insure her safety.

For some reason known only within the primal impulses regularly issuing forth from the underdeveloped brain of the twenty-eight year old woman, she'd begun to focus on the quiet room. Last restrained there six months ago, she would look longingly toward the room and then soil herself. Six months in her impaired retention might as well have been the Paleocene Epoch.

Another minor drawback of the job, Baptiste thought.

407

A few times, he'd redirected her without problem, distracting her successfully before these stimulatory signals traveled from her brain to her bladder. But once she got the words out, urination soon followed.

On cue, she wet herself, a bright yellow stain spreading down the legs of her pants.

Per the behavioral plan, Baptiste paid it no attention. "Time for Bap to go."

Two female co-workers, both behavioral techs like him, emerged from the office. One, Talitha, gave Baptiste a raised eyebrow as she passed. They escorted Cybill to the shower, Talitha talking happily, and per the behavioral plan, neither mentioning the incontinence.

Baptiste retreated to the office, where Doctor Jack Eliopolis waited, frowning at the surveillance holos, only the sounds from the shower piped into the office. "Drooling at the window, saying she doesn't like you, redirected, happily coloring, glimpses the QR, says, 'bad room,' and then wets herself." Doctor Jack looked at Baptiste. "Which one do you suppose was the antecedent?"

"We should have the QR door closed, frankly. I think it's seeing the restraints." Baptiste sat at a holoterm to do his notes, seeing his shift was over a half-hour hence.

"Good point," Doctor Jack said, nodding. "Let's do it, see whether the behavior changes."

Cybill their only patient, the team was able to refine their behavioral intervention plans with nuances not available to most facilities. The Emperor's daughter received the most advanced behavioral modification interventions and pharmacologic regimens.

"Good work today, Bap," Doctor Jack said as Baptiste was going out the door.

Navigating his way through palace security, Baptiste walked to the pneumatube station right outside palace grounds. Ten glasma tubes stood in a vertical row, the sun glinting off their shiny surfaces, lines of people at each tube, the pop-and-whoosh of capsules audible under inane music.

Rush hour, he thought glumly. Within a minute, it was his turn, and a capsule popped to a stop in front of him. He climbed in, and the pneumatube scanned his face and asked him, "Home?"

"Home, James," he replied.

The capsule took off with a whoosh, the pressure changes causing his ears to pop.

Bewildered, he watched the scenery around him change, the tube taking him toward the Acropolis at the center of New Athens. The pneumatube wasn't taking him home. Baptiste hit the emergency communicator inside the capsule.

A red light lit up, and the serotonic voice of automation asked him, "What is your emergency, please?"

"I'm being taken somewhere other than home!" he complained.

"Your vital signs are within normal parameters. Are you injured?"

"No," he said.

"Are you bleeding?"

"No," he conceded.

"Are you unconscious?"

"I damn well hope not!"

"Then it's not an emergency. Please restrict your use of the emergency communicator to emergencies. Thank you." The communicator went silent and the light went off.

Baptiste wondered what would have happened if he'd answered affirmatively to any of the annoying questions. The capsule took a side tube and dropped toward the ground. It eased into place at a station, and Baptiste stumbled to the platform.

The Acropolis was right in front of him. A symbol of civilization for four thousand years, the Acropolis on Gaea had been duplicated from the original on Earth, its soaring columns dominating the New Athens skyline.

"Inspiring, isn't it?"

The Galactim was mixed in with gurgling sounds which Baptiste could only associate with extreme digestive upset. Cybill had once eaten half a pillow before they could stop her and then had gagged for an hour, making similar sounds. He looked at the figure who'd emitted the sounds.

Inside a metal cup was a green mass of writhing goop, a thousand tendrils sliding over a control panel. Sockets near the top looked somewhat like eyes, and below that was an orifice which flapped in mistimed sequence with the sounds, "Rmhkrirmt, rhm'g rg?" The cup was held aloft at waist-height by a pair of metal extensors protruding from a motor housing mounted on the underside of the cup. A frame sprouted from the cup edges and met over the creature's head. A veil of distortion hung around the alien, like a sheet of plastic.

Baptiste quickly forgot his own distress. "What the hell are you?"

"A Kziznvxrfn. My name is Svkszvhgfh Ezhrozprh, but you can just call me Ezra."

"Uh, all right, Ezra." Baptiste glanced over his shoulder at the malfunctioning tube that had dumped him here. "I've never met a real Kzizn."

"We're really an affable bunch, once you get past the smell."

"And the sound."

"Yes, well, that too," Ezra said. The tendrils waved in unison in what looked to be a shrug.

Baptiste decided to venture a hunch. "So why'd you bring me here? How'd you bring me here?"

"You're a sharp one. Hmm, yes, the why and the how. You're one of the caretakers for Princess Cybill Zenon. She calls you Bap."

"It's the only part of my name she can remember."

"A terribly impaired young woman. Tragic, what happened at her birth."

"Tragic," Baptiste repeated.

Her mother dying in childbirth, and a life severely restricted by a stunted development. If the Empress Consort's death during childbirth hadn't been painful enough, the daughter's failure to thrive must have doubled the Emperor's grief. Not one, but two tragedies. It wasn't a wonder why Emperor Athanasios had succumbed in subsequent years to the wiles of the upstart Lady's Maid, Narcissa Thanos.

He looked at the creature. "Ok, so you know a lot about me." He opened his palms beside his shoulders.

"Er, uh, forgive me, I'm not completely conversant with Homo sapiens body language. What does that mean?"

"It means, so what? You know who I am, you got me here somehow. Now what?"

"This isn't going quite the way I expected. You humans are terribly impetuous. I didn't say that out loud, did I? Oh, my, I'll never figure out this translator." The cilia danced wildly in obvious distress, the longer tendrils slithering in circles.

"How did you get me here, anyway?" Baptiste was intrigued that the creature had managed to infiltrate the pneumatube control system.

"Electrons behave the same whether they're traveling along a wire or propagated as waves. It was easy to beam in an alternate set of instructions in response to your face."

"But the whole system's encrypted."

"You call that encryption? Hmligrmt! A newly germinated Kzizn-vxrfn could develop a cipher more complex than that."

The sounds the creature made were remarkably similar to those Cybill generated in her imbecile oblivion. "Ok, and now the why, please."

"Why? I don't know why your systems are so quaint. Perhaps it's the rudimentary human evolution."

Baptiste was getting annoyed. "Why did you bring me here, Ezra?"

"Oh, that, well, yes. Xovzirmtgsvgsilzg." The creature paused, all the tendrils going suddenly still. "The Kzizn think a great deception has been perpetrated upon the Gaean Empire."

* * *

Retired Governess Eugenia Ioannou considered herself a member of a specialized class of Gaean Citizen.

"Gigia, look at me!" squealed a child on the jungle gym.

"Look at you!" Eugenia replied, enjoying an afternoon in the park with her niece's daughter.

Governesses occupied a curious kind of social ambiguity. They cared for the female children of the aristocracy from the moment of birth until the age of majority, male children under the charge of governors. Governesses were typically unmarried, were considered unmarriageable, and often came from aristocratic families who'd fallen on hard times, either through misfortune, misadventure, or debauchery. Without the resources to live comfortably on their meager inheritances, they had to go into service to support themselves. Highly educated and cultured, they thought it unseemly for them to stoop to one of the myriad positions within the ranks of maids. As governesses, they were expected to bring their education and culture to bear in helping rear the scions of their more fortunate peers, and perhaps retain a modicum of dignity.

"Look what I can do!" the child screeched, hanging upside down, her dress falling over her face.

"Look what pretty panties you have!" Eugenia called back.

The girl screamed in mock dismay and righted herself.

Holding themselves aloof from the service staff, governesses were nevertheless looked down upon by their employers, in large measure because they represented what might happen to the family should similar misfortune befall them. Further, governesses represented contradiction, on the one hand retaining their gentility and on the other, having to work for a living. They typically were treated badly by their host families and the service staff. They had few rights, might be dismissed at whim, were expected to work all hours of the night, often found themselves victimized by male family members, and were inevitably blamed for the victimization that had been perpetrated upon them. Worse yet, they were expected to be disciplinarians and were prohibited from imposing consequences for misbehavior. They had to be models of comportment in the face of sometimes savage treatment.

"Come jump rope with me, Gigia!"

"I'm too old to jump rope, Darling," she called from the park bench.

Governesses however were glorified in vids that showed them granted privileges beyond those accorded house servants, such as walking through the front door. Partly because of that fictional depiction, retired Governess Eugenia Ioannou considered herself special, her status made loftier because of the family she had previously served.

The Imperial Family.

She was revered among governesses for a singular accomplishment within that service: She'd survived it.

She'd survived *Her*.

Yes, *Her*.

There was only one *Her*. And if an interlocutor didn't know whom Eugenia referred to when she mentioned *Her*, Eugenia dismissed that person as unworthy of her time and attention.

Her was of course the Dowager Empress, Narcissa Thanos.

Eugenia heaped contempt on anyone she had to explain that to.

Further, Eugenia had not only survived her service as governess to the Imperial Family and *Her*, she'd guaranteed that she and her family would be spared the Imperial Wrath in perpetuity. Although childless, she did have nephews and nieces whom she doted upon, and their future was secure.

Because she, Eugenia, had outsmarted *Her*.

The curious episode had begun with the tragic deathbed of the Empress Consort, Ambrosia Lillis, giving birth to the Princess Cybill Zenon. In preparation, they'd hired Governess Eugenia Ioannou, who was expected and prepared to care for the child from the instant she and her mother left the birthing chamber.

But instead of both leaving it, only one of them had.

The death of the Empress Consort Ambrosia Lillis had thrown her entire coterie of servants into unemployment, all of whom sought service positions elsewhere. All except the Lady's Maid, Narcissa Thanos.

Eugenia remembered that first terrible week, the palace in chaos, the Empire prostrate with grief over the tragic end to the fairytale romance. Having been enthralled with the courtship between the Emperor and his Consort, Eugenia was stricken too, having plunged herself nightly into immersivids of the royal couple, hurling herself into Ambrosia's part like every other female throughout the Empire, even sneaking home a few of the hormone-infused, black-market seduction scenarios, orgasm guaranteed or your money back. Against this backdrop of a fairytale romance and a fairytale pregnancy, the Consort's death in childbirth had left the Empire devastated.

Heartbroken, Eugenia hadn't been able to refuse the entreaties of the Lady's Maid, Narcissa Thanos, to see the baby, Princess Cybill Zenon.

Unlike everyone else, who seemed entranced by the vulnerable, day-old child, Narcissa recoiled, her hand to her mouth. "Don't you think she looks ... slow?"

"Not as if she'll have mastered several languages by now," Eugenia retorted.

"Well, no, of course not, but ... I must be mistaken."

And each time, twice per day, that Narcissa laid eyes on the child, she'd initially have that ill-concealed look of concern, as though something were abnormal about the child's development. The two of them took to having afternoon tea, Narcissa seeming disconsolate over the late Consort, berating herself for inattention in letting her charge slip away. During that first week, while the Lady's Maid secured the late Empress Consort's effects and quietly resolved the estate, these visits were not considered inappropriate, as long as they remained brief and untoward.

"I've applied to become your nurse assistant," Narcissa told Eugenia abruptly on day seven.

Taken aback, Eugenia did her best to conceal her response. It was presumptuous of a lowly Lady's Maid to think she might give succor to one so delicate as the Infant Princess, a task ill-suited to anyone not belonging to the aristocracy. Only a member of the lesser nobility might be entrusted with her care.

She was livid when she found the next day that Narcissa had been added to her staff. No coattail-riding upstart member of the service staff was going to wriggle her way into the Imperial Family's good graces under her watch. Not if Eugenia could help it!

But as Lady's Maid to the Empress Consort, Narcissa apparently had been consulted on a frequent basis as to the Consort's druthers, inquiries made on behalf of the Emperor himself, and to Eugenia's utter horror, by the Emperor himself, who it appeared had taken a liking to the Lady's Maid.

So Narcissa stayed.

Perhaps she reminds him of his lost betrothed, Eugenia told herself at the time. But as a precaution, being a suspicious one, Eugenia began archiving the nursery vid feeds. Just in case, she told herself.

"If it's all right with you, Lady Governess," Narcissa told Eugenia just a day or two into her new position, "I'd like to spend part of my day with the Procopio family. Their daughter's but a few hours older than Princess Cybill, and mayhap I might learn a thing or two from Governess Filmena."

She certainly needs to learn manners, Eugenia thought, welcoming any excuse to get the upstart commoner out of her hair for a few hours each day. Not that the social graces a princess was required to acquire could be imparted by someone so debased as a servant.

The Procopio family was of the lesser nobility like Eugenia herself, but unlike her, they'd enjoyed continued prosperity and Imperial favor, living just outside the palace grounds on an estate of enviable size. Eugenia did not begrudge them their good fortune.

She knew Governess Filmena personally, the two women consulting each other sometimes on matters of care. Eugenia pitied Filmena for the task ahead of her, for it was rumored that the Procopio child's genetic profile indicated a difficult development. While such genetic syndromes as fragile-x, Turner's, and de-novo dysmorphia had been eradicated from the gene-pool, new infirmities in gene structure cropped up as fast as old ones were eliminated. Many genetic disorders could not be traced to a single gene but were instead spread among several genes. In Lydia Procopio's gene structure, no specific abnormality had been identified, but an aggregate of lesser oddities prognosticated trouble for her development.

Princess Cybill Zenon's genetic structure was clear of any oddities.

"We should make a day of it, you know, an outing of sorts, on the palace grounds, of course," Narcissa said one day, the babies nearing two weeks old.

Eugenia thought hard, disliking the idea but knowing the grounds secure in every way, hard-pressed to demur without causing the overly-persuasive Narcissa to run to the Emperor in complaint.

Sugar pines encircled a glade whose succulent grasses glowed with emerald brilliance, dew scintillating in the morning sun, each baby in a carriage, gurgling happily.

"Eugenia, might I talk with you a moment?" Governess Filmena asked.

Eugenia looked at her, her counterpart from the Procopio household. The two of them knew a common tragedy. A swindler out of Bellona XI had suckered both their forebears into investing nearly all their assets into a pyramid scheme of massive proportion and had absconded with the lot of it, leaving a substantial number of the lesser nobility impoverished.

Narcissa was doting over the girls in their respective carriages, paying the two governesses no attention whatsoever.

Filmena looked to one side and inclined her head that direction, indicating her desire to speak privately. The two Governesses turned their backs on Narcissa with the two infants.

"What the hell is he thinking, hiring that strumpet?" Filmena immediately asked her the moment they were out of earshot, her voice low, her speech fast, her face furious. "Not that I'm questioning the Emperor's wisdom, but it's just not right!"

Eugenia was relieved that someone else shared her opinion. She'd not been able to garner an iota of support in her opposition to the strumpet's appointment.

"Anyway, seems she feels a bit miffed at your haughty treatment and tried to inveigle me into getting you let up a little on her. If anything, you're not hard enough with her, Eugenia. Seems to have assumed airs in her uppity little mind that she knows better than you how to rear a princess. The utter gall!"

The two of them twittered.

"I 'm given to understand Lydia's genetic profile doesn't look good," Eugenia said.

Filmena frowned and nodded, giving her counterpart that look.

The look Eugenia had seen on Narcissa's face.

Alarmed, Eugenia turned.

Fifty feet behind them, Narcissa was still bent over the two carriages, her lilting voice carrying across the meadow.

That look.

Her intuition screaming that Narcissa had just done something to Princess Cybill Zenon, Governess Eugenia scurried back to the carriages. "Got me a fright, I did," she said to Narcissa as she poked her head into the Imperial carriage.

The bonnet was a bit askew, but the baby stared at her, a bewildered look in her face.

Odd, Eugenia thought, she's usually happy to see me. Concerned, she lifted the infant out of the carrier. Immediately, the child began to cry.

"Oh, dear me, I've gone and upset you, haven't I?" And she hurried to take the squalling infant back to the nursery, carrying her the whole way, the afternoon outing a disaster.

Not terribly long after that, at the daily Imperial showing, a ritual in which Emperor Athanasios deigned to gaze upon his child, Eugenia saw something between the Emperor and the upstart Maid-turned-nurse. Just a glance, but enough to raise Eugenia's suspicion.

And she discovered shortly afterward that Narcissa was retiring most evenings not to the servant's quarters toward the rear of the palace grounds, but to the Emperor's chambers.

The information was nearly as devastating as the death of the Empress Consort, Ambrosia Lillis.

In her daily routine of bringing the infant to a viewing room to await the Emperor's arrival, Eugenia was sometimes alone with the Imperial infant, Narcissa with her at other times. Eugenia took advantage of the times she was alone to place miniature holocams in a few of the viewing rooms.

Within a month, she had on holocam the information she needed to secure Narcissa's immediate dismissal, the encounter reminding Eugenia of the seduction-scenario immersivids she'd furtively watched during the Emperor's courtship of his Consort.

First, before confronting the strumpet with the incriminating vid, Eugenia placed a physical copy in two secure locations and then rigged a dead-man switch. A term borrowed from days of yore when electrical devices ran on slim filaments of metal known as wires, a dead-man switch was a device that automatically signaled at regular intervals unless stopped by the person who held the switch. If the person ever died, the switch then flipped when no one stopped it. Eugenia's dead-man switch was her sending a message to ghost holomail account. If Eugenia didn't send the message once per week, the ghost account would then auto-send the incriminating vid to multiple news outlets and a frivolous litigation firm she'd employed named Dewey, Treatem, Likashose, and Howe.

"Gigia, look at that man!" the child on the jungle gym squealed.

Eugenia leapt to her feet, startled out of her reverie.

A bizarre-looking figure in a trench coat tottered toward her through the park.

She almost grabbed her great-niece and fled.

The features looked to be those of a clown, a bulbous red nose protruding from a garish, white-cream face, where two green-rimmed eyes were mounted, looking different directions, an oversize smile in ruby-red lips permanently plastered between the cheeks. The face might have come directly out of some children's morning holo show. A long, limp trench coat hung from narrow, angular shoulders, giving glimpses of a livid-green torso. Dress slacks hung from a bowlish, protrusive stomach, and from each pant leg protruded a metal spike, which rang with a metallic twang each time they struck the plascrete.

"Please, don't be frightened."

The words reached her over the nearly-simultaneous sounds of extreme digestive distress, "Kovzhv, wlm'g yv uirtsgvmvw."

The creature was now close enough that Eugenia could see that the livid-green torso was a mass of jiggling jelly covered with writhing cilia, a few longer tentacles slithering over a device mounted just inside the trench coat.

"Ewww!" her great-niece said, holding her nose.

417

"Did I leak a little? I apologize for my terrible-smelling breath."

"That's your breath?" the girl said. "And what are those sounds? Can you teach me how to make 'em?"

The creature issued a series of snarts and forkles, which sent the girl into a tizzy, and soon, Eugenia too was laughing uncontrollably, delighted to hear the girl's hilarity.

The retired Governess later wiped the tears from her eyes, unable to remember the last time she'd laughed so hard.

And by then the mass of alien green protoplasm was burbling contentedly, turning from one to the other, as if looking at each in turn with its optical organelles.

"Well, thank you, whoever you are," Eugenia said. "I haven't laughed that much in a long time."

"I am Svkszvhgfh Ezhrozprh, but you may call me 'Ezra,' if that is easier for you to pronounce. I'd like to talk with you about what happened in the days following the death of the Empress Consort, Ambrosia Lillis."

Chapter 5

"You're who?!" Lydia stared through the bars at the badge.

"Imperial Bureau of Suspicion," it said in bright red letters, the man's name, "Doukas," prominent below that. And then the man holding it whisked it away.

"What'd you say your name was?" she asked again with a sneer.

Furious that they'd imprisoned her father for no good reason, she was now doubly furious that she'd been detained. The foul atmosphere of Theogony didn't help, its air without the methanogens that thickened and sweetened Kziznvxrz. The atmosphere of her home world contained nearly five percent ammonia, hydrogen, carbon dioxide, and methane, giving it the sweet smells of anaerobic decomposition.

"Listen, Dickass, I'm a citizen of Kziznvxrz. You can't hold me against my will. You've got no jurisdiction."

The ugly face beyond the bars grew uglier. "You're in Imperial territory, where I can do what I damn well please."

"My father and I have been trading in Gaean territory with Gaean approval for over five years. We've never had a glop of trouble from any Imperial representative, and we've never had a ship impounded for contraband. Look it up, Detective Doukas. None of our ships have so much as a moving violation. Further, our company is under contract with the Gaean Empire to deliver critical lithofuels to Cygnus Twenty. If we give the word, Cygnus Twenty goes without."

"That's Agent, by the way," Doukas said.

"All right, Agent. What are we being held for?"

"Where'd you come from in that fancy vehicle?"

Not answering my questions, Lydia thought. Two can play that game, but is it a game I really want to play? All she really wanted was to wrap up the contract with Titanide Aquafoods and get off this foul-smelling Terran planet back to Kziznvxrz. Longing for the open, mud-brown expanses of semi-liquefied tidal flats, whose constant, quiet percolation burbled with such delectable aromas, Lydia sighed. "Look, we just want to go home, all right?"

"The faster you answer my questions, the faster you get home."

"I heard you talking to Warden Minas. You're planning to send us both to Gaea, halfway across the galaxy. You don't have any intention of letting us go home." She stared at him. "Deny it, Agent Dickass."

He stared at her silently, denying her even the comfort of being right.

"Look, whatever my father and I are being arrested for, Orrin hasn't done anything. How about we make a deal? You let Orrin go, and I'll stop calling you Dickass."

"I've been called worse."

Not budging. She should have expected as much and wondered whether he was amenable to bribery. Not that she'd consider it, but she'd been given to understand that the closer to Gaea one got, the more grease these Grecians expected.

"I've already turned him loose, by the way."

She saw the cold calculation in his dull, compassion-less eyes. I'll bet he thinks he can gain my trust by telling me that. Not that he's actually let Orrin go, either, she thought, knowing these humans capable of deceit.

When her father had first introduced the concept to her, he'd been telling her about the tragic accident that had orphaned her on Kziznvxrz.

"It may not have been an accident. Someone may have sabotaged the ship in such a way as to hide the fact they tampered with it," Xsirh told her.

"Why would someone hide anything, Papa?" the girl said, now eight years old, her memories of Gaea distant. The sight, sound, odor, and texture of the Kziznvxrfn were as familiar to her as her human parents had once been. Xsirhglksvi was particularly familiar to her, he who had reared her over the objections of his peers and despite the vehement opposition from a dissident Kziznvxrfn splinter group, the Wrwrmrfn.

Of course, technically, Xsirhglksvi Xlmhgzmgrmrwvh wasn't even male, the Kzizn able to perform in either role, changing their reproductive organelles as needed for the circumstance. Kzizn reproduced in four ways, most often preferring to reproduce asexually through fission, in which they would split in two by pinching through their long axis. They could also reproduce through an interaction with other Kziznvxrz known as heterogeneous conjugation, the human equivalent of copulation, either partner taking either role, or through endogenous autogamy, otherwise known as self-fertilization. Thus, they really couldn't be insulted by telling them to go procreate with themselves.

Something Lydia was tempted to tell this pinch-faced troglodyte in front of her. "Liar."

"Where'd you come from?"

It was clear to Lydia that the Agent was at least as stubborn as she was. And so she let loose on him, telling him to procreate with himself in his own back passage, something her variation on his name had already suggested.

The pinched face went purple, and he stormed out in a tizzy, leaving Lydia alone in the isolation cell.

Well, that was really effective in securing my release, she thought, looking around.

A set of carbo-nick alloy bars stretched from plascrete floor to plascrete ceiling. Around the cage door were solid plascrete walls, easily a foot thick. A single bare loomglobe hung near the ceiling, at a height at least double Lydia's. The walls on either side were more plascrete, and the back wall of her cell was the native bedrock. There were no windows, and she saw that the only vents were in the ceiling twelve feet above her, obscured by the loomglobe.

She stepped to the back of the cell and put her hands against the wall.

Somewhere close, she felt the pounding of surf, the wild seas of Theogony beating persistently against the few archipelagos that dared raise themselves like upstarts above the turbulent waters. The sounds of ocean transmitted to her hands through rock reminded Lydia of Kziznvxrz, and her longing for home returned.

She turned, put her back to the wall, and bunched her fists.

I will not cry! she ordered herself.

She slid down the wall, hugged her legs to her chest, put her forehead to her knees.

And wept.

* * *

"What do you mean, you can't get me a ship?! I have to endure this stench another day?!"

Colonel Melanctha Remes, commander of the IBS Command Outpost on Lucina IX, recoiled at the vituperation in the voice of Agent Erastus Doukas on Theogony. His holoimage hung above her desk like a miniature incubus. At any moment, she expected the diaphanous figurine to whip out a trident and sprout a forked tail. Immediately upon hearing that Agent Doukas hadn't been able to procure transport to Gaea, Colonel Remes had requisitioned a patrol from nearby Momus XVIII, but it had been forced to halt at exactly midnight GMT or Gaean Mean Time.

"Nothing is moving today, Doukas," she said, "not a single vessel anywhere in the Empire."

Today was the coronation of Princess Hecuba Zenon, daughter of the just-deceased Emperor Athanasios Zenon and the upstart Lady's Maid, and now Dowager Empress, Narcissa Thanos.

"Can't we get an exemption?" the IBS Agent asked, his holoimage distorted by multiple layers of encryption. "Didn't the palace itself order their detainment?"

"Don't say that!" Remes remonstrated, cringing. Now, she'd have to purge the transmission from any and all systematic recording and archiving devices here on Lucina IX, there on Theogony, and at every intervening re-transmission station between the two planets. She put in an immediate trace to record those holonet hops. But it wasn't the hours of work ahead she regretted. "Fool! You'll be lucky if you aren't detained for interrogation on Gaea yourself! Out!"

She cut the connection, and the incubus dematerialized from above her desk. Colonel Remes knew she was reamed, her career over.

Doukas really stuck his dick up his ass this time, she thought, and mine too. There was no concealing such a major blunder from the Imperial Secret Service, whose clandestine tentacles reached into every skeleton-filled closet throughout the Empire, no matter what level of encryption nor how many layers of security obscured it from scrutiny.

With bulldog persistence, Melanctha methodically retrieved the incriminating utterance from the Command Outpost archives and destroyed it, and then did the same for every holonet relay between Lucina IX and Theogony, her bowels grinding, her palms sweating, her hands trembling. Each relay would record her actions, of course. There was no obscuring the fact that she was destroying the transmission, but she hoped against hope that when she was tried for conspiracy in Imperial courts that her having done so would mitigate her role and perhaps result in a lighter sentence than she might have otherwise received.

She held no hope she wouldn't be arrested and tried. Those were inevitable from the moment Doukass had said "palace."

It didn't matter that it was true. All that mattered was he'd said it.

Once she was finished, Colonel Melanctha Remes summoned a live holofeed of the festivities on Gaea, finding comfort in Hecuba Zenon's coronation and its attendant Pangaea.

In ancient times, the festival of Pangaea consisted of numerous sacrifices to the Earth Goddess Gaea and her mate, the Star God Heaven, whose joining gave birth to all the lesser Titanide gods and goddesses, Oceanus, Coeus, Crius, Hyperion, Iapetus, Theia, Rhea, Themis, Mnemosyne, Phoebe, Tethys, and lastly the immutable Cronus. In modern times, Pangaea simply referred to the bacchanalia and saturnalia common to licentious celebrations.

Pangaean debauchery was already evident on Gaea, the spigots of the Imperial vaults opened wide, fueling a grand celebration.

The festivities helped to assuage Colonel Remes' feelings of impending doom.

* * *

Vasilios Xenakis, Special Agent Ad-hoc of the Imperial Secret Service, picked up on the transmission immediately, and before Colonel Remes had deleted it, he'd obtained a copy and was already forwarding it to his superiors.

Maybe it'll redeem my career and earn me a post somewhere closer to Gaea, Vasilios thought, closer to the grave of the only person I've ever loved.

He hadn't meant to fall in love with the Empress Consort, Ambrosia Lillis.

She'd be fifty years old today, he realized.

He'd been assigned to head security at another coronation at the innocent age of twenty-five. For a Kalamata native, an extraordinary first assignment, but not unexpected for a graduate of the Corfu Institute of Military Studies, the finest academy on Gaea. The coronation of Athanasios Zenon as Acting Emperor was as lavish as that being held today for his second daughter Hecuba. But that first one might as well have been Ambrosia's debutante ball.

Vasilios watched the festivities on one holo, and on another, he watched the planet Theogony in the Erato subsystem of the Mnemosyne Constellation. It did not strike him as ironic that the coronation of Hecuba Zenon was being held on the anniversary of Ambrosia's death.

It was deliberate, arranged by the Dowager Empress, Narcissa Thanos.

Agent Xenakis sent a com to the other nineteen ships under his command, their placement in the Oort cloud forming a perfect dodecahedron, ensuring complete visual and sensory coverage of the entire Erato subsystem. Each ship in the squadron acknowledged.

Like his counterpart in the domestic security branch, the Imperial Bureau of Suspicion, Xenakis knew precisely where his orders had originated, but he was not so foolish as to disclose it. Erastus Doukas had earned himself an early retirement to a dungeon on Gaea, or at least to a cell on Tyrintha, the prison planet.

From his position in the dodecahedron, Vasilios saw only one star beyond Erato, between him and the vast void of empty space, Andromeda the next nearest galaxy at 2.5 million light years away. That one star was a dull, blue-white primary with barely enough lumens to cut through the dense atmosphere of its only planet.

The Kziznvxrz subsystem was the outermost in the constellation, so far beyond the nearest space lane that the region had no strategic worth whatsoever. The Kzizn home world, a murky, muddy ball, hovered relatively close to the cold blue sun. The half-a-dozen diplomatic missions to the worthless planet had all ended abruptly, the two races mutually repulsive to each other. The last attempt to establish an embassy on Kzizn some twenty-four years ago had ended in tragedy, the ship coming apart on atmospheric entry.

Doukas's bungled efforts to clear Theogony of any sentient aliens would certainly aggravate diplomatic relations, especially his transporting the five Kzizn citizens to Gaea for interrogation, three of whom were already en route.

Vasilios had seen the notation that one of the two Kzizn citizens awaiting transport to Gaea was a human female. It had struck him as odd, the Kziznvxrz ecology offensive to human sensibilities and deleterious to human health. He couldn't imagine anyone living there, much less obtaining citizenship.

The image on the holo in front of Vasilios shimmered.

What was that? he wondered, examining the Kzizn primary closely.

"Agent Xenakis," his com squawked, "I've got some odd signals from Kzizn, unusual disruptions in the sub-ether. Spectral analyses appear normal. Please advise."

The shimmering, Vasilios thought. "Get me an analysis of the Kzizn propulsion technology."

"Yes, Sir."

Everyone knew their technology was superior. A reclusive race, the Kzizn had declined several entreaties for technological exchange. Further, all attempts to purloin one of their vessels had failed. The only reason the Gaean Empire hadn't invaded was the Kzizn's utter lack of ambition. And the fact that any such invasion was likely to be repulsed. As long as they didn't attack Gaea outposts or try to annex Gaean territory, the Empire seemed willing to let them alone.

No one had seen a Kzizn weapon either, although they were rumored to exist.

"Agent Xenakis, there, uh, apparently isn't an analysis to be had. The Kzizn propulsion technology hasn't been studied to any appreciable depth."

"There must be some information on it somewhere." Maybe their sub-ether drives are beyond our understanding, he thought.

"Just a few observations of their ships flying at low speeds. And

425

even then they're difficult to look at. They're often described as `diaphanous' and `illusory.' We've never been able to replicate the technology."

"In other words, we don't know how they travel, do we?"

"No, Agent, we don't."

"They could be invading Theogony right now, and we wouldn't know it."

"I guess that's theoretically possible, Sir."

Vasilios amplified Theogony on his holo.

As he watched, the planet began to shimmer.

Agent Xenakis hit the red alert.

Chapter 6

It's a party for them, but not for us, Drucilla thought, pausing to look at a holo.

Imperial Laundry Maid Drucilla Kanelos frowned at the bustle around her, all ten thousand of the Empress's personal staff in an uproar. In the middle of the night, the order to pack had descended upon the service staff like a cloud of locusts.

A tour of the Empire was an obligatory part of any Emperor's investiture. The service staff could have guessed they'd have to pack for an extended excursion. The Imperial space liner, the Prince George, named after the first Monarch of Greece back on Earth, was kept in orbit, stocked, provisioned, and ready to depart at a moment's notice for exactly such occasions. The exigencies of ruling such vast domains as the Gaean Empire were likely to whisk its ruling family anywhere throughout the galaxy, and the space liner's always being ready kept the chaos barely within manageable limits.

Drucilla and the other nine-thousand, nine-hundred-ninety-nine service staff members usually got wind of such excursions long before the departure date, but the untimely demise of Emperor Athanasios and the swift investiture of his second daughter Hecuba as Empress had launched the Empire into a state of high confusion.

Further, Drucilla was expected to make a compulsory appearance at the coronation and Imperial ball in a show of fealty. Disregarding this requisite duty would certainly invite the castigation of the Dowager Empress and an immediate dismissal, if not criminal charges of disloyalty.

And the Dowager Empress never forgot a slight. Not even the ones she'd imagined.

Drucilla was nearing retirement, at least ten years senior to Narcissa. She had trained Narcissa in the skills required of a Laundry Maid when Narcissa was but fifteen, newly entering maid service in the Procopio household, and as fresh from the provinces as a rutabaga from the ground. Like any attractive girl from a rural background nearing the age of legal consent, Narcissa had found herself in a swarm of male service staff. Only Drucilla's swift intervention had kept her from getting pregnant and therefore fired. But the incident had awakened Narcissa from her provincial slumber.

In Drucilla's mind, at least, it was probably the only reason she had kept her job and her life. She had to attribute her longanimous service to the Imperial family to something.

The Dowager Empress, it appeared, never forgot a favor, either.

She wasn't the only one with a long memory. Throughout her decades of service, Laundry Maid Drucilla Kanelos hadn't forgotten a single incident.

Especially not *the* incident.

Checking the Imperial bed sheets for hymenal blood on the morning after the Imperial consummation was the highest duty accorded to a Laundry Maid. A duty so sacred that Laundry Maids were sworn to secrecy before being initiated into the art. And not all Laundry Maids were initiated, only the select few who'd be handling the matrimonial linen. When a succession was in doubt, or when a blushing bride's extra virgin olive oil was thought to have been spoiled, the Laundry Maid handling the matrimonial linens was sure to be called upon to verify having seen the hymenal stains. The lives of many a Laundry Maid had been placed in danger to prevent verification.

This practice had spread throughout the nobility, and even upperclass commoners were said to have taken on the airs of this rare bird of passage, its spread accompanied by old maid's tales of how to mimic the telltale break, dyed-red robin's egg among them.

If you're that distrustful, Drucilla was inclined to tell them, just don't marry the meretrix!

And why commoners would adopt the practice baffled her completely, as if their ranks weren't already tainted with commoner blood.

The second time Drucilla was called to check the matrimonial linens had challenged her principles of propriety. The first time, she'd been deeply honored, the bride-to-be having been the Imperial Consort, Ambrosia Lillis, daughter of Countess Giorgi Lillis, hers a hymen worth breaking.

But the second had been that of Narcissa Thanos, she who'd entered the service profession as a Laundry Maid in the House of Procopio at age fifteen, a rutabaga who'd just fallen off the proverbial vegetable truck, whom Drucilla had trained in the arts of matrimonial linen handling.

And the ways a hymenal stain might be mimicked.

Try as she might, Drucilla hadn't been able to prove the hymenal stains fraudulent. Narcissa, she knew, was too cunning not to devise a foolproof guise. The Imperial succession depended upon it.

Drucilla remembered being called to audience with Emperor Regent Athanasios, his first Consort dead five years, his only child from that joining a functional idiot who required specialized, twenty-four hour care, his new wife ruling the Imperial household with an iron fist.

The dull gaze tracked her approach but seemed to be empty of the spirit that most forty-year-olds would have. His father ailing and having withdrawn years ago from any active role in governing, the Emperor Regent exerted full control over his empire, but he seemed to Drucilla to lack any control over his own life.

Pitiable, she'd have said, had she been asked to describe him.

"You're Drucilla, yes?" he said simply. The courtiers on either side of him had verified her identity five times in the last hour. And the Imperial Secret Service had done the same.

"Yes, your Imperial Highness, Laundry Maid to Her Imperial Highness, Empress Narcissa," she said, dropping instantly to both knees, the carpet so thick she thought she'd dropped onto a cloud. Drucilla kept her gaze on the floor in front of her. It was considered defiance to look upon his August Person. The guards lining the walls were ready to leap upon her at the first sign of the least hostility.

"Yes, and she tells me, the person who trained her in the very arts you've now employed on her behalf."

"Yes, your Highness." Respond only to the question asked, and do not elaborate, she'd been told by the courtiers who briefed everyone prior to entering the Imperial presence.

"Ironic, isn't it?"

"Some might say, your Highness."

"I ask you, Drucilla, Maid of the matrimonial laundry, to look at me."

She shuddered, the request unexpected.

"Please, it's important."

The request was elegant for its simplicity, and Drucilla raised her gaze. She was no spring chicken, of a similar age as Emperor Athanasios, and she knew he'd suffered. She found she was looking not at the ruler of the human-occupied universe, but at a person who found himself trapped by events seeking one bit of solace, the slightest consolation, that might make all his suffering worth something.

And the realization slammed into her mind: He wants me to deny she was a virgin.

Reeling, she struggled to keep her gaze on him, the walls warping, the room skewing. It was one thing to be asked such a question, but it was quite surreal to know that the person asking—one's own Sovereign Emperor—wanted a particular answer, a particularly damning answer.

"Tell me what you found this morning on the conjugal sheets, Drucilla."

Her throat closed on her, and sweat sprang up on her brow. Her heart thundered in her breast, and her palms were chill and clammy. Her bowels cramped and heaved, and her gorge rose in her gullet. "Your ... Highness," she said, her voice catching, "I found ... a stain that appeared to have come ... from a broken hymen."

"Appeared?" His gaze didn't change, as though he asked by rote.

"It passed all the required tests, your Highness."

He sighed.

An Imperial sigh was far too ambiguous for Drucilla's concrete mind to interpret. In retrospect, she'd wished she'd asked, but it would have been presumptuous of her to do so, in violation of all convention. And it would have certainly come to Empress Narcissa's attention.

She'd been ready to retreat, thinking the audience over, thinking she'd been dismissed from the Imperial Presence.

"You applied all the required tests to the best of your ability?"

This time, before answering, she glanced furtively to each side of the throne.

"Leave us," the Emperor said.

The courtiers glanced amongst themselves, hesitating.

"Now, please. Guards too."

"But—"

"Now, please." His voice hadn't changed, but something had.

And now Drucilla was frightened.

Being granted a solitary audience with such an August Person was analogous to receiving the Employee of the Month award. Either she'd done something stupid or she was about to be fired.

The moment they were alone, the Emperor sighed again. "And turn off the recording equipment," he said aloud to no one. "I order it!" He cast a baleful glare around the room as if to sear shut with just his gaze any lens that might still be open.

"You may speak freely, Drucilla. You know Narcissa as well as anyone."

Taken aback, Drucilla felt an inkling of hope, seeing now for the first time a spark of spirit. "She talks like a snake that bites its own ass," she blurted.

He looked at her, and then chuckled inanely. "But snakes don't have asses."

"You see how she twists things? Just what I'm talking about, your Highness."

"Not quite the question I was asking." He gave a giddy giggle. "Hymenal tissues be damned! Archaic practice that someone should have banned long ago. Tell me truthfully, Drucilla. Is Narcissa faithful?"

It was so direct a question that Drucilla couldn't have answered with anything other than a direct answer. "Panta pisti," she said in Greek. "Always faithful, your Highness." And then she looked at him directly. "To herself."

"And no one else, eh?" Emperor Athanasios threw his head back and laughed, then stopped abruptly. "Yes, that's my observation of the conniving bitch, too." He leaned forward and peered at her. "You tried very hard to prove that the stains weren't from her hymen, didn't you?"

And now Drucilla was no longer afraid. "Yes, your Highness. I tried to prove they weren't with every test at my disposal. And I'm disappointed to report that I was unsuccessful."

The Emperor grunted, frowning. "Thank you for trying, Drucilla. It appears we're now completely ensnared in her web, doesn't it?"

Twenty-odd years later, as she finished packing her bag for the requisite sovereign tour of the Empire, Drucilla glanced over at the holo.

An image of the Empress-to-be, Hecuba Zenon, waved at unseen crowds, a glittering, diamond-encrusted dress draping her to her feet, being paraded to the Parthenon in central New Athens to be crowned Empress.

Are you really the daughter of Emperor Athanasios Zenon and the Laundry Maid Narcissa Thanos?

* * *

Erastus Doukas, Agent Provocateur with the Imperial Bureau of Suspicion, stared dumbly at the woman in front of him.

She whipped out her badge and thrust it back where it came from with pickpocket agility. "Agent Nellie Roussos, Secret Service, Internal Investigations Unit. We're here to take your detainees back to Gaea."

He'd barely had time to read her badge. He looked over her shoulder.

A group of muscular suits in dark glasses and gum-soled shoes stood in two silent ranks behind her. And beyond them was a Gaean patrol cruiser, Imperial emblems emblazoned on its sides, the dull rumble of its idling engines audible. They'd managed to land the ship astride the estuary between the detention center and the main island, the seas roiling beneath the ship as though angry that it hovered just out of reach.

"I'm glad you're here," Erastus said. "I thought I'd have to languish in paradise another day. How'd you get permission to travel on coronation day?" He entered the building and headed toward the cages at the rear.

"Special dispensation," the woman said, following briskly, her nose wrinkling. "What's that smell?" Her speech was as devoid of expression as her face. The twin ranks of muscular suits followed her with uncanny precision.

"The alien. And most of the smell is now contained by his envirosuit. You should have smelled it before." Erastus pushed through the first set of double doors.

"The Kziznvxrfn, right? What's his name, Agent Doukas?"

He glanced askance at her. "You said that almost as well as the female prisoner. She calls him `Xsirh,' but his full name is much longer. You should hear her say it. Tongue-twister doesn't do it justice."

" `Xsirh?' "

"Yeah, just like that, better than I can pronounce it. You a linguinologist, or something?" The word didn't sound quite right to him. Erastus hoped he wasn't displaying his ignorance again. They went through another set of double doors. "I thought I was gonna have to suffer that stench for days. Oh, by the way, she calls him her father." He glanced at her.

"That is a curiosity, Agent Doukas," the woman said, looking at him dully.

"Yeah, funny thing, that. Raised her since she was four, she says." Doukas was put off by Agent Roussos, her nonchalant manner, her clipped speech, her abrupt manner, her impassive face.

"Four. On Kziznvxrz. How odd."

Perfect pronunciation again, Doukas noted. They approached the final set of doors, a guard of his on either side of it. "I put her in isolation so she couldn't talk to the alien. But if you need a translator, she's your man."

"She's a man?"

Erastus stopped and looked at Agent Roussos. "No, I said, `She's your man.' Never heard the expression before? Where you been livin'? Some backwater swamp somewhere?"

"Oh, pardon. A misunderstanding, Agent Doukas. Through these doors?"

"Her cell is beyond the door to the right, his is straight ahead to the rear. I'd suggest keeping them apart on that little boat of yours. They're pretty slippery, these two. Might start a mutiny if you let 'em near each other."

"I will note your suggestion, Agent Doukas."

They went through the doors, four of the muscular suits moving toward the alien in the last cell, four heading down a short corridor toward the woman's isolation cell.

Agent Doukas and Agent Roussos watched them carry the limp alien in its envirosuit, the reinforced material easily holding the creature's weight. Kzizn were terribly slow on dry land, far better adapted to mudflats and bogs.

Moments later, the other quartet of guards emerged with the woman, her wrists cuffed in bright glasma circlets.

Erastus was struck again by her breathtaking beauty.

"Lydia Procopio?" Agent Roussos asked, her voice as dull as ever.

"That's me," the woman said. "Who're you?"

"Agent Nellie Roussos, Secret Service, Internal Investigations Unit. You're not under arrest. We'd just like to ask you and the alien a few questions."

"We haven't done anything. We've both been inoculated. Where are you taking us?"

"Immaterial. Your ship will be safe in the meantime, won't it, Agent Doukas?"

Roussos hadn't looked at Erastus. "Uh, yeah, it'll be safe." He wasn't sure why, but he got the feeling there was more to Agent Roussos than met the eye. She was just too damned tidy.

"Well, all right," Lydia said, throwing a glance his way.

"Pleased to meet you, Ms. Procopio."

"Mutual, Agent Dickass," she said pleasantly.

He recoiled, blinking at her as they hauled her out the door and down the corridor. "While you're at it, Agent, beat some humility into her."

"Not authorized, Agent Doukas." The woman turned to look at him. "What did she call you? Was that a colloquial pejorative?"

"Uh, yeah, that's what it was." He smiled to cover his bewilderment and walked with her to the entrance of the building.

"Oh, uh, Agent Doukas?" Agent Roussos stopped just beyond the threshold and turned to look at him. "We weren't here."

"Yes, of course. You may rely on my complete dereliction." He hoped he'd said that right.

She hesitated momentarily. "Thank you." She shook his hand with a limb as limp as a fish and stepped toward her ship, its boarding ramp just a few feet from the base of the steps.

He watched the boarding ramp retract. The engines began to rev, the dull rumble escalating to a high-pitched whine.

Erastus Doukas, Agent Provocateur with the Imperial Bureau of Suspicion, couldn't quite pinpoint why the whole episode had been so disconcerting, from the clandestine meeting in a brightly-lit alley to this bewildering transfer of detainees on coronation day. It was all too bizarre for the small-minded Doukas.

Then the patrol vessel with Imperial emblems lifted slightly from its perch and dematerialized in front of him.

* * *

"What was that?!" Vasilios called to his navigator on the com. The image of Theogony on the holoscreen had shimmered again.

"More sub-ether disruptions, Sir," his com squawked over the roar of engines.

The second set of such disruptions from the surface of Theogony.

His vessel plummeted toward the planet, all engines blazing, the nineteen other ships in the flotilla also scorching their way toward Theogony.

Special Agent Ad-hoc Xenakis of the Imperial Secret Service began to sweat. Even if they managed to spot a Kzizn ship, the tractor beams aboard his ship would be unlikely to latch onto the slippery alien vessel. Not a physicist, Vasilios had a limited understanding of sub-ether principles. But he knew that a ship in sub-ether couldn't be latched onto or fired upon. Sub-ether was like a window into another universe, he'd been told. His Musca-class vessel was perfect for surveillance but a poor vehicle for interception.

The autopilot turned on the retros, the deceleration slamming Vasilios against the restraints.

You'd think I'd get used to this by now, he thought idly, his eyes glued to the holo, his face stretching. "Tractor beams ready?"

"Yes, Sir, but uh …"

"I know they won't work on a ship in sub-ether, but we have to try."

"Yes, Sir."

He didn't blame the young navigator. Theirs was a thankless task. They were as likely to be executed if something went wrong as not. Simply because the Dowager Empress had turned her face from him. She never forgot a slight, Vasilios knew.

Not that she needs one to order my removal.

"Contact Gaean Command and alert them to a possible alien infiltration of Theogony."

"Yes, Sir," the com squawked back at him.

You'd think they'd make better equipment in this day and age, he thought, his ship starting to shake as it entered the atmosphere.

White clouds streaked the surface of the blue marble below him, the capital Helios outlined on the holo. The detention center stood at one end of an archipelago, alone, only a bridge connecting the building with the rest of the city.

"Enlarge," he said. The holo detected what he was looking at and amplified.

The edifice ballooned to life on the holo. Two figures stood at the top of the steps in front of its doors, gesturing wildly at each other. Suddenly, they both looked up.

Toward him.

Twenty ships converged on the compound, his touching down on the bridge.

Vasilios leaped from the hatch, blasma gun poised at his shoulder, its tip white hot. "Special Agent Ad-hoc Vasilios Xenakis of the Imperial Secret Service," he said to the pair, one of them a low-browed gumshoe, the other a woman in an Immigration uniform.

"Where's your badge?" Low Brow said.

"I don't need a stinking badge."

"Yeah? Never heard that before. Your badge now, or I blow your head off." A kalashmakov pistol appeared in Low Brow's hand.

He'd be stupid enough to use it, too, Vasilios thought, sighing. He pulled out his badge. "The aliens got your detainees."

"How'd you know?" the woman asked.

"They were disguised as you guys," Low Brow said. "She said her name was Nellie Roussos, Imperial Secret Service, Internal Investigations Unit."

"I'm Carissa Minas, Warden, Helios Immigration Detention Center," the woman said.

They shook. "Pleased," Vasilios said, glad someone here had some competence. "Saw the sub-ether disruptions once on Kzizn, and then twice on Theogony," he told her. "On arrival, and then again on departure." He looked at Low Brow. "I'll have my assistant check on the identity."

"Erastus Doukas, Agent Provocateur, Imperial Bureau of Suspicion," the man said.

They shook. "Pleased," Vasilios said. All he's likely to provoke is gales of laughter, Agent Xenakis thought, keeping it off his face.

"How come you get to travel on coronation day?" Low Brow asked him.

"Lead containment contingent for the visit of her Imperial Highness." He jerked his thumb over his shoulder at the nineteen Musca-class ships hovering over the island. "Warden Minas, I'll need holos of the entire incident. Every minute from every cam since the alien detainee's arrival, please, not just today's events."

"That's a whole lot of holo," she said. "Let me get started on it. Back in a moment." She retreated into the building.

Vasilios commed the name he'd been given to his navigator. "Start from the beginning, Agent Doukas," he said. "Just the facts, Agent, just the facts."

Chapter 7

Lydia Procopio turned to her escort the moment they boarded the ship. "Thank you so much," she said in Kziznvxrz. She'd smelled them the instant they'd taken custody of her. If she hadn't lived among them for twenty-four years, she wouldn't have known they were Kzizn.

The four beefy humanoid-shaped Kzizn stared blankly at her. "Please proceed peacefully," one said, also in Kziznvxrz, pointing along the corridor.

"Aren't you going to take off these handcuffs?" Lydia held up her bound hands, the bright glasma circlets glinting in the dim interior light.

"Go, please."

"Where's my father?" she demanded, fear beginning to knot up her bowels. "He was hurt, and he may need medical attention."

"Xsirhglksvi will be taken care of. Your cell is that way. Cooperate, or we will escort you manually. Now, please."

Lydia obeyed immediately. Now, she was really afraid. "What are you, Wrwrmrfn?" she asked, not expecting an answer.

A Kziznvxrfn splinter group, the Wrwrmrfn had lurked for millennia in the remote bayous of Kziznvxrfn politics, their xenophobic philosophy and take-no-prisoners rhetoric at odds with moderate mainstream Kziznvxrfn views. She wondered how they'd managed to morph themselves into near-perfect humanoid shapes,

438

the female even mastering Galactim, a near impossible feat for a Kzizn.

But if she and Xsirh were now their hostages, it meant that the Wrwrmrfn had moved from rhetoric to terrorism.

They directed her through the ship to a cargo hold, where a cube stood, fifteen feet to a side, gleaming and polished as though newly manufactured. Its hatch stood open.

They took off the circlets. "In," the one Kzizn ordered.

"Pondscum," she snarled.

They shoved her into the cube and slammed the hatch closed, the sounds from outside indicating they were locking her in.

The cell was devoid of comforts. An excretory, a bed, a sink, a chair.

But at least they were all designed for a human. She sat immediately and secured the five-point, guessing they were taking off quickly.

The lurch of acceleration added its upset to the anxiety gnawing at her innards.

They've been planning this for a long time, Lydia thought. She wished she knew what "this" was. It didn't surprise her that they'd taken her hostage, the group having long advocated her extermination, the most vocal among those objecting to Xsirh's rearing her.

Xsirhglksvi had described the bureaucratic battles he'd had to wage just to keep her on Kziznvxrz. Everything from what school she attended, what immunizations she got, what food she ate, what to do with her excrement (which proved a powerful catalyst to Kzizn waste products), what clothes she wore, and even what air she breathed.

At four years old, all she had understood was that she wasn't looked upon favorably, and that Xsirh struggled every day just to meet her basic needs. Those first few years had been horrible for her, the atmosphere noxious, the swampy tidal flats difficult for her to navigate, and the wet, clammy weather giving her perpetual goose bumps.

But for Xsirh, the struggle had been worse, even though she hadn't known it at the time. The simple mechanics of providing for her basic needs had nearly overwhelmed him. The political opposition to his adopting her had nearly resulted in criminal charges. And of course he'd been ostracized from his pod for having taken on the care of this foul-smelling, funny-sounding, bizarre-looking offspring of that widely-derided alien race known as Homo sapiens.

Or as the Kzizn pronounced it, "Slnl hzkrvmh." The Galactim

approximation sounded like "Silinil" but lacked the glottal stops, affricates, and lateral clicks that thickened the Paramecium tongue.

Lydia examined the cabin thoroughly from her chair. Of standard Kzizn manufacture and materials, it'd been designed with human dimensions and physiognomy in mind. They must have copied some of my father's designs, she thought, the chair fitting her perfectly. Further, the air in the cabin had little of the sharp ammonium scents common to the Kzizn tidal flats. They'd invested considerable resources into manufacturing this cabin alone.

The more they'd invested, the greater her disquietude became.

Come on, she told herself, think!

She brought to mind what she knew about the Wrwrmrfn. A radical fringe group, they appeared to be an evolutionary throwback, preferring not the tidal flats where their moderate cousins lived but the gentle surf just beyond, a liminal existence inhabited by rotting seaweed, water-logged driftwood, and bloated graptolite, trilobite, and brachiopod carcasses. They eschewed the comforts of warm tidal pools, the lovely aromas of mud, the pleasant buzz of swarming cyclorrhapha. One of the pillars of their reversionary philosophy was their aversion to technology.

It doesn't stop them from using it to their advantage, Lydia noted, looking around.

Another of their philosophical pillars was the extinction of Homo sapiens and the takeover of the galaxy. They alone among the peaceful Kzizn had any ambition to extend the Paramecium dominion. Fortunately, theirs was quite a minority view, and war with the nearby Gaean Empire had never been considered a viable political option.

The Gaeans had never attacked Kziznvxrz either, despite each race finding the other repulsive. Their mutual indifference far exceeded their mutual revulsion, the Wrwrmrfn philosophy notwithstanding.

So what are they trying to accomplish by kidnapping me from Theogony? Lydia wondered, dreading the answer.

* * *

First among equals, Bishop of the Orthodoxy Dea Papadopoulos swept across the stage, the picture of regality, her smile affixed to her face with carbo-nacreous adhesive.

I don't know why I dressed up, the Bishop thought. The Dowager Empress has never graced our pews with a single thread from her satin-clad backside.

Bishop Papadopoulos, or "Bish Pap" to her intimates, was layered with the vestments of her office. A glittering kolpak or miter perched atop her head, its dome undercloth woven from the finest damask, its outer platinum cage encrusted with diamonds, and atop the miter, a cross of pure gold, the Savior depicted in fine relief. Beneath all her finery, she wore the humble alb, a pure-white garment reaching her ankles, a cincture girdling her waist. Over the alb, she wore the dalmatic, a long tunic with wide sleeves, today's color a shimmering gold lame. Over the top of that was the phelonion, or chasuble, usually the outermost vestment. On this august occasion, she wore on the top of everything the revered sakkos, its name derived from the ancient Greek word for sackcloth. This outer garment symbolized the tunic of disgrace worn by the Savior at his humiliation.

How apropos, the Bishop thought, I get to wear a sakkos at my humiliation. Even a fully-enclosed hazmat suit won't keep me from feeling sullied.

She was in her element, but out of her element. As the Deity's representative on Gaea, she was responsible for administering to the Lord's worldly affairs and for dispensing the ecstasy of eternity to the faithful. This was her calling. But today, the Bishop would minister to the High Thief herself and would consecrate the ascension of Princess Hecuba Zenon to the Empirate.

Bishop Papadopoulos halted at the Acropolis altar and knelt. Lit thuribles awaited, the burning incense inside sending its perfumed tendrils cascading down the steps. "Dear Lord," she murmured, sure no one was near enough to hear, "forgive me my blasphemy and save my ass today."

Then she rose, spread her arms elaborately, and turned to face the crowd, her robes flying around her in a whirlwind of cloth.

The seething mass of humanity below her roared. The cacophony was nearly a physical blow against her chest, leaving her gasping for breath. From her perch atop the steps of the Parthenon, she could see nearly all of New Athens, the city occupying a bowl ringed by mountains. Orbit-scraping structures spiked the valley floor. Pneumatubes noodled in between, a veritable bowl of vermicelli. Faces sprouted from every bit of open space between buildings and every window of every building, all peering in her direction.

This many people hadn't gathered for the coronation of Hecuba's father, Athanasios.

Bish Pap wondered why. Do they sense the presumption of commoner blood to the royal throne? The decline of Empire before their very eyes? The mad theater of mockery?

But it wasn't Hecuba's coronation they feared.

The Dowager Empress Narcissa Thanos watched like a hawk from the Imperial seats, a bunting-plastered box to one side of the Parthenon steps.

Atop the steps to one side of Bish Pap was a bejeweled pedestal, on it the Imperial Scepter, symbol of might. To the other side of her was the Imperial Shield, symbol of protection. To the immediate right of the altar was the Imperial Cloak, symbol of unity. And to the immediate left of the altar was the Imperial Crown, symbol of infallibility.

Princess Hecuba knelt at the base of the Parthenon steps, her head bare of her dainty tiara for the first time in her life.

Bish Pap couldn't remember seeing Hecuba without the tiara atop her revolting little head, the symbol of her position.

Eidolon of beauty, Hecuba wasn't. The pinched lips were poised in a perpetual pout. The nose was squished into the face between cheeks too close together. A wart the size of a snail perched on one cheekbone. The close-set eyes peered from beneath a beetled unibrow, the single line of black hair across her forehead looking like a giant umlaut. The hair was dull blond, the color of water used to wash a thousand dishes. The coif had been sculpted with the implements of modern hair-dressing for naught, the thin hair defying all efforts to tame it. She wore cloaks of silk and damask, so diaphanous and fine of manufacture they did little to hide the dumpy body beneath. Her appearance was a cracked foundation, through and through, and no amount of inspired cosmetology could straighten the building atop it. It would have taken a faceplant to improve her looks. She was ugly.

Bish Pap raised her gaze above the Princess and wielded her perfect smile across the crowd like a sword, slashing first one direction and then the other, palms in and hands up. Then she lowered them slowly.

And the roar died.

"Gaeans here and throughout the Empire, welcome today to this sacred event," she said, her voice booming across the assembled masses, her image appearing on a hundred trillion holos across the watching Empire. "We gather to honor the passing of our beloved Athanasios and to welcome the arrival of our adored Hecuba."

Bish Pap had almost said "adorable," but she wouldn't have been able to stomach such a blatant lie. "His Highness is dead, long live her Highness!" She thrust her arms into the air.

The crowd roared, their arms raised as well.

She brought hers down, and the crowd went silent. They're learning, she thought. "We gather for the coronation of her Highness, the Empress Hecuba, may she rule wisely and well. Long live her Highness!" Again, she thrust her arms into the air.

Again, the crowd roared, their arms raised.

She brought hers down, and the crowd went silent. Soon, I'll have them drooling at bells, she thought. "We gather in the might of our Creator and ask that He bless this Scepter, symbol of her power. Long live her Highness!"

The crowd roared and raised their arms in time with hers.

"We gather in the light of our Creator and ask that He bless this Shield, symbol of her protection. Long live her Highness!"

Again, the crowd roared and raised their arms with hers.

"We gather in the sight with our Creator and ask that He bless this Cloak, symbol of her unity. Long live her Highness!"

In synch with her, the crowd roared and raised their arms.

"We gather in the right of our Creator and ask that He bless this Crown, symbol of her infallibility. Long live her Highness!"

A last time they roared and raised their arms.

"Now," Bish Pap announced, "to place in the Imperial Hand the symbol of Her power, Chief Admiral of the Gaean Naval Forces, the handsome and honorable Hector Kritikos!"

A figure stood from the bunting-plastered Imperial box, his immaculate uniform bedecked in medals.

Bish Pap greeted him effusively. Then with great ceremony, she retrieved the Scepter from its mount, returned it to the altar, and knelt to say a prayer. She picked up a thurible and swung the smoking metal ball around her head once, its path leaving a trail of vapor. Standing, she handed the now-blessed Scepter to the Chief Admiral.

While she waited beside the altar, Admiral Kritikos carried the

Scepter reverently down the steps toward the waiting Hecuba. The young woman had not moved, her head bowed. While Admiral Kritikos hectored her in haughty tones, extracting from the Princess a solemn oath to exert her military power judiciously, Bish Pap wished he'd get on with it, already bored with the pomp and finery.

In the crowd beyond a solid line of kneeling guards, a figure perhaps twenty deep looked to be maneuvering through the crowd.

The Chief Admiral finally quit blathering and handed the Scepter to Princess Hecuba.

One down, three to go, Bish Pap thought. "Now," she intoned, "to place upon the Imperial Arm the symbol of Her protection, House Speaker of the Gaean Assembly, the high and mighty Elke Drivas!"

A figure stood from the bunting-plastered Imperial box. Her smart, slick suit shimmered in burnished blues. She looked like an immaculate angel devoid of taint.

Bish Pap greeted Speaker Drivas expansively. Then with great ceremony, she retrieved the Shield from its mount, and returned to the altar for the ritual purification by thurible. A trail of vapor ringing her, she handed the now-blessed Shield to the House Speaker.

She carried the Shield reverently down the steps toward the waiting Princess. While Representative Drivas driveled to Hecuba in a booming voice from her soapbox on the purity of politicking, extracting from the Princess a solemn oath to negotiate with bipartisan compromise, Bish Pap groaned at the utter folly, not a soul believing any compromise possible, the House already plotting its recalcitrant postures.

In the crowd, the figure looked to be wriggling his or her way nearer to the front.

Two down, Bish Pap thought, two to go. "Now," she pronounced, "to place upon the Imperial Shoulders the symbol of Her unity, Premier of the Gaean Administration, the hale and hearty Flavian Galanis!"

From behind the bunting-plastered Imperial box emerged a man. His sultry, smooth suit shone in black, like a dark devil of death. If Thanos weren't already in the Imperial box, the Bishop might have believed him death.

Bish Pap greeted Premier Galanis effusively. Then with great ceremony, she retrieved the Cloak and purified it, the thurible leaving its ring of smoke. She handed the now-blessed Cloak to the Premier.

Galanis carried the Cloak reverently down the steps. While he propounded in an amplified voice to Hecuba upon the efficiency of bureaucracy, Bish Pap sniggered at the blatant contradiction, even the Savior recoiling in spirit at the oxymoron, the administration ready to bury the next Imperial edict under mountains of red tape.

In the crowd, the figure now stood at the front line of the audience, just beyond a kneeling soldier's shoulder.

Three down and one remains, she thought, thank the Deity! "Now," Bish Pap announced, "to place upon the Imperial Head the symbol of Her righteousness, Chief Justice of the Gaean Empire, the right and holy Daphne Carras!"

The long black robes of the Chief Justice moved her stoically across the steps, like a wraith devoid of legs.

Bish Pap greeted Justice Carras reverently. She retrieved the Crown for purification, swinging the smoking thurible around her head not once, not twice, but thrice. Standing, she stepped through the triple rings and handed the now-blessed Crown to the Chief Justice.

While she waited beside the altar, Justice Carras carried the Crown down the steps toward the waiting Hecuba. While Justice Carras spoke in sonorous tones, extracting from the Princess a solemn oath to exert her righteous wisdom judiciously, Bish Pap wished she'd get it over with and crown the ugly bitch, trying not to wet her britches. She'd have fallen asleep if she hadn't had to pee so badly.

The Chief Justice finally blithered herself into silence. She raised the Crown and began to lower it into place upon Princess Hecuba's head.

"Stop!" the figure at the front of the crowd declared, the voice boomeranging over the crowd.

Chapter 8

It wasn't far from Theogony to Kziznvxrz, and Lydia didn't have much time.

She shrugged out of the restraints and immediately inspected the door to the container. The Kzizn were remarkably adept at harnessing fluids to their purposes, but equally inept with solids.

They'd put the hinges on the insides of the doors.

She smirked, shaking her head, and got to work.

Without prisons—or the need for them—the Kzizn were virtually without experience in containing each other. The first time Lydia had come across a jail cell on a human-colonized planet, she'd stared at it for hours, trying to warp her mind around what it meant. Depriving another creature of its liberty was as untenable to Kziznvxrz as a tidal mudflat to humans.

Patiently, she unscrewed the hinges using a hairpin, the process tedious.

She wished she were back on the tidal mudflats. The constant vertigo of standing upright on land for three days had been disconcerting. Her human trading partners seemed oblivious to the strain, walking around all day on their lower limbs as if born to it. On rare occasion, she'd heard them complain of sore feet. The one time she'd tried to describe mudflats to these land-based bipeds, the reaction had nearly sundered the contract negotiations. Lydia hadn't raised the subject again.

The last screw coming out, she wondered where they were keeping Xsirh, if at all.

Stepping back, she eyed the door.

On one human world, she'd taken a round of self-defense classes at the advice of another female of her species. "A pretty woman like you might have to fend off a lusty male," the woman had told her. In the classes, Lydia had learned just how remarkably effective her limbs were as weapons.

Okay, here goes, she thought. She raised her foot and kicked.

The door careened from its frame.

She poked her head out into the cargo hold. It looked unoccupied except for the container.

The Wrwrmrfn, the rogue Kzizn who'd captured her and her father, were probably having a round of distilled dihydroxyl with him, the beverage intoxicating to them. The purified beverage was ultimately poisonous, diluting Kzizn electrolytes quickly. In small amounts, it lowered their inhibitions and tended to put them in a convivial mood. Lydia had found ethyl alcohol to have similar effects on her.

She sidled up to the cargo bay door. She couldn't hear anything through it. Good, she thought, guessing they hadn't heard her kick her way from the container. They hadn't thought to lock the cargo bay door. Probably hadn't imagined she might escape. She slipped into the corridor beyond, the tubular shape easier to navigate than those rectangular human corridors.

She heard sounds of revelry from the galley. Similar in layout to her own Kzizn-manufacture ship, she guessed where the cockpit was, wondering how to commandeer the vessel. Do I disable the environmental systems first, create a diversion, or what? Lydia wondered.

Homo sapiens were frightening for their violence. The Kzizn had never been to war with themselves and had only developed weapons as a defense against the barbaric humans. Kzizncide was unheard of, and the most extreme conflict on Kziznvxrz was the horrific schism between the Wrwrmrfn and mainstream Kziznvxrfn, which had forced the latter to banish the former to the ocean surf. Ostracism was equivalent to death, for without the pod, how could a Kzizn survive?

Thinking through her options, Lydia decided direct action was probably the best.

She slithered up the corridor past the galley and into the cockpit.

Only the copilot was in her chair, the pilot probably in the galley having a little distilled dihydroxyl with the other Wrwrmrfn.

"What are you doing?" the woman said.

"Taking us home. I'm Lydia Procopio." In the Kzizn language, her name was pronounced, "Obwrz Kilxlkrl."

"I'm Mvoorv Ilfhhlh. Pleased to meet you." Mvoorv extended a tentacle in greeting.

Lydia grasped and shook it, recognizing her as the one who'd led the incursion into the detention center. The woman looked a lot different in her Kzizn guise, the human disguise having given her an unhealthy pallor. "How did you do that, Mvoorv?" She hiked her thumb over her shoulder to indicate Theogony behind them, a gesture she'd picked up on Eos XI.

"You mean imitate those Slnl hzkrvmh?"

Lydia giggled at the pejorative, the Kzizn name for Homo sapiens making a mockery of their supposed intelligence. What really amused her was how the Kzizn used the name openly to their faces, insulting humans without their knowing it.

"Our Slnl clandestine pods developed a short-acting catalyst to solidify our exoderms," Mvoorv said. "What I'd really like to get my tentacles on is that long-acting catalyst they're supposed to be developing."

"Long-acting? And look like me for the rest of your days?"

Mvoorv laughed aloud, her green mass jiggling like jelly, the sound not dissimilar to a series of human farts. "Xsirh said you'd be delightful."

Lydia grinned and squeezed herself into the pilot's chair. A perfect bowl, it wasn't very comfortable for her. Having bones, she didn't have the same fluidity as the Kzizn, who could fit into just about any space they chose to occupy. Similarly, her hands weren't as adaptable as Kzizn tentacles, and she really had to stretch her fingers to get them on the controls.

"What are you doing, Obwrz?" Mvoorv asked again. A Kzizn asking the same question twice was equivalent to astonishment.

Lydia had already answered and didn't repeat herself. No self-respecting Kzizn did. Say something once, why say it again? She took the controls and adjusted their course to take them to the Kzizn capital,

Dzhsrmtglm, near Xsvhzkvzpv Bay. The entire mudded-out west side of this gargantuan bay was the perfect environment for the miasma-loving Kzizn. The thought of home was comforting.

"How might I persuade you not to take us to Dzhsrmtglm?"

"You can't," Lydia replied. "I appreciate your rescuing us from that detention center, Mvoorv, but Xsirh and I don't agree with your philosophy. We're not going to cooperate. Whatever you hoped to achieve, you'll have to accomplish it without us."

Mvoorv issued a high-pitched blat, the Kzizn equivalent of a sigh. "We will accomplish our goal, you know. In fact, we almost have." Her tentacles slithered over the controls in front of her, and a sub-ether image appeared.

The image was a projection of events in the human capital of New Athens, on Gaea, adapted from a human holonet broadcast. The constant broadcast of images on the sub-ether created disturbances for Kzizn transport, all of which was powered by sub-ether drives. Modulating these ripples had required the Kzizn to retool their propulsion technology with built-in dampening units. The human invasion of the sub-ethernet had been cause for great concern among the Kzizn, since their sub-ether technology was all that kept Homo sapiens off Kziznvxrz. Humans were the worst invasive species known to the galaxy.

The image showed the front steps of the edifice known as the Parthenon. At the top of the steps was a thickly-clad human wearing a flamboyant hat, the high priestess of their bizarre religion. Spiritual practices among Homo sapiens were risible at best, in the opinion of Kzizn scholars.

Bishop Dea Papadopoulos, the subtitle said. She was swinging above her head a metal ball on the end of a chain, the ball leaving a stream of smoke, a cleansing ritual, Lydia knew. She was mystified how introducing toxins into the air was supposed to cleanse anything.

"Why are you showing me this, Mvoorv?" she asked.

"The new Empress will herald a change in our favor, Obwrz."

She looked over at the female Kzizn.

Gender roles among the Kzizn were temporary states, assumed for reproductive purposes. The multiple means of replication available to the Kzizn bewildered their human neighbors. Whenever Lydia tried to tell a Kzizn she would always be female, it usually provoked gales of

449

laughter, the concept of remaining one gender nonsensical to the multi-morphic Kzizn.

Lydia didn't like the look of evasion in Mvoorv's visual organelles, evasion a trait that the Kzizn had learned from their Homo sapiens neighbors. She wasn't telling Lydia everything.

"You don't need to cooperate with us any further," Mvoorv said. "You've already done your part."

Lydia raised her eyebrow at the woman. On the holo, the Bishop handed the Crown to the Chief Justice, who descended the steps toward the ugly Princess.

For some reason, as she listened to the Chief Justice spout a lot of nonsense, Lydia was convinced that that should have been her.

The Chief Justice lowered the Crown toward the head.

"Stop!" a figure at the front of the crowd declared, the voice boomeranging over the crowd.

Lydia recognized the Kzizn immediately. "Ezra, no!"

* * *

As the words reverberated across the crowd, Bishop Dea Papadopoulos wondered how the creature had infiltrated the public address system.

"I beg you, do not do this! It's a mistake!" the alien blatted, the sickening sounds of its own language underneath the monotone translation.

The first blasma blast blew a score of human spectators and a few guards into their next lives, the beam of destabilizing ions causing their flesh to disintegrate into sticky red plasma.

Bish Pap looked over just in time to see the Dowager Empress fire a second time, a shot that didn't miss its mark.

Alien slime splashed the crowd, and screams erupted as its acids etched their way into human flesh.

"Crown her, or you're next," Narcissa Thanos said, taking aim at Chief Justice Daphne Carras.

The woman in long black robes lowered the crown onto Hecuba's lopsided head.

* * *

450

Special Agent Ad-hoc Vasilios Xenakis watched the coronation ceremony over the holonet just as his vessel achieved escape velocity from Theogony for his return to the Oort cloud. Satisfied at least that the system had been adequately secured, Vasilios gaped at the holo, watching incredulously as Narcissa Thanos blasted the alien apart, then aimed the blasma gun at Chief Justice Carras. "Crown her, or you're next."

Justice Carras lowered the crown.

A curious burbling sound in the cockpit behind Vasilios caused him to turn.

A bright-green slug easily six inches around hurled itself at his face and wrapped its tentacles around his head. His hands came up too late, the creature already slipping tentacles into his mouth and nostrils.

The two tentacles in his mouth slithered down his throat, punched a hole in his esophagus and wrapped his heart in a vice-like grip. The other two in his nostrils punctured the ceiling of his nasal cavity and sent their spike-like tips into his basal ganglia.

Vasilios Xenakis died, at last joining his beloved Consort Empress in the afterlife.

* * *

Imperial Laundry Maid Drucilla Kanelos stood on the crowded ante-promenade deck of the Imperial cruise liner George the First with barely enough room to breathe. She watched a giant holo of the Dowager Empress aim the blasma gun at Chief Justice Carras. "Crown her, or you're next."

The top judge of the Gaean Empire lowered the Crown.

And the crowd aboard the cruise liner went wild.

The cold started just under the hem of Drucilla's evening gown and slithered up the insides of her thighs to her anus. She'd have liked the sensation in other circumstances, but in these, her titillation turned to terror as pain ripped through her innards, the mass inside her wriggling relentlessly toward her heart, shredding any flesh in its way. Drucilla's dying scream was drowned out by cheers in the crush of humanity around her.

And there the body of Drucilla Kanelos remained for several more minutes, suspended upright in the tightly-packed crowd.

451

Chief of Palace Security Deion Goulas watched a holo of the coronation from Security Command twenty stories beneath the palace, the ventilation system working overtime to cool the crowded underground compound. Deion leaped to his feet the instant the alien said, "Stop!" the voice booming over the loudspeakers, the figure at the front of the crowd a bright, lime green.

"Who let that alien get so close?!" Deion demanded.

Security Command erupted in chaos just outside his office.

"I beg you, do not do this! It's a mistake!" the alien said, the nauseous sounds of its language underneath the monotone translation.

A blasma beam blew a huge hole in the line of spectators, missing the alien. A fountain of liquefied flesh splashed the crowd. A second blast splashed green alien goop at least twenty spectators back, many of them writhing from the acids.

Narcissa Thanos took aim at Chief Justice Daphne Carras. "Crown her, or you're next."

Justice Carras lowered the crown.

Deion looked up at the vent. A ball of bright green goop slithered through the grill, a six-inch round globule of oozing protoplasm.

The same bright lime green as the creature at the coronation.

The slug launched itself at Deion's face, and his hands came up too late. The creature's tentacles in his mouth slithered down his throat and bit through his carotid artery. The other two in his nostrils wrapped themselves around his basal ganglia and squeezed.

Chief of Palace Security Deion Goulas was dead before he hit the floor.

* * *

Former Governess to Lydia Procopio, Filmena Sotiropoulos, who had resigned rather than accompany Ambassador Procopio to the planet Kziznvxrz, watched in dismay as the Crown descended toward the head of Princess Hecuba Zenon. It struck her as ironic, really, that Hecuba Zenon, the second child of Athanasios, born to him by his second wife, the Lady's Maid, Narcissa Thanos, would be the one to receive the Crown upon her repulsive little head.

An object splatted against the glasma of her sixteenth-floor apartment window, and Filmena stared at it dully. It looked like a large slug, its footprint against the glasma nearly six inches across. The creature convulsed and surged through the outer glasma pane, spreading itself across the inner layer. Filmena didn't know whether to be disgusted or alarmed. Then the slug convulsed again and oozed through the glasma into her apartment.

She stood, her terror rising, and stepped toward the door.

It flung itself toward her face as she turned and splatted against the back of her head. Screaming, she ran toward the door, but before she reached it, the creature wrapped her neck with tentacles and strangled her scream. Two more tentacles positioned themselves at her upper back and shoved their points between her third and fourth cervical vertebrae to sever her spine.

The body of Filmena Sotiropoulos fell against the inside of her apartment door, where it was found days later, partially decomposed.

* * *

Eugenia Ioannou, Retired Governess of Princess Cybill Zenon, attempted to watch a holo of the coronation from her barstool at the nearly-empty pub. She could barely keep her head up.

The first blasma blast stirred her slightly from her drunken stupor, the fountain of liquefied human remains splashing across the crowd. She just caught sight of the second blast, and she wondered why the fountain of flesh had turned a putrid green.

"Crown her, or you're next."

The voice of Narcissa Thanos penetrated through the alcohol-saturated cerebral cortex to Eugenia's amygdala, and fear sent a sobering shock of adrenalin shooting from Eugenia's hypothalamus.

We're in for it now, she thought, picking up her beer from the bar.

She didn't notice that the beer wasn't amber anymore but had somehow turned bright green. Thinking she was hallucinating, she upended the glass anyway. The thick sludge slithered into her trachea, pierced the lung and severed the aorta.

Retired Governess Eugenia Ioannou fell backward off the barstool, the glass shattering as it hit the floor at the same time she did, and she died.

Chapter 9

"Revered Leader, I bring you my fellow Paramecia, a group of Wrwrmrfn who have acted to the detriment of the pod, for whom I beg your forbearance." Lydia Procopio lowered herself to her knee. The six-inch layer of muck on the floor gave a satisfying squelch.

She had just arrived in the presence of the oldest Kziznvxrfn, Mrxlwvnfh Gzelfozirh.

Beside Lydia was Xsirh, looking wan but recovering from the injury to his reproductive organelles. The noxious human air and dry environment had done more to exacerbate the injury and damage his system than the actual impact with the corridor wall.

Behind Lydia and Xsirh was the group of Wrwrmrfn, looking abashed. Their leader, Mvoorv Ilfhhlh, stood at their front, her exoderm a sickly pale green, her tentacles drooping at her sides, her cilia flat and limp. She looked the picture of capitulation.

All thirteen of them were crowded into a room large enough to hold twenty people standing. The walls were a slimy brown color, shiny as though wet. Along each side wall a few inches off the floor were cups for sitting. On the floor was six inches of the finest putrescent mud to be found, none but the best for the Revered Leader.

Mrxlwvnfh Gzelfozirh, the Ivevivw Ovzwvi of the Kziznvxrz, occupied a similar cup, its position at one end of the room the only indication it held any importance. The closest approximate translation of his title, Ivevivw Ovzwvi, meant "Revered Leader," but it also carried with it hints of his age and lineage. Mrxlwvnfh Gzelfozirh was several thousand years old, had reproduced at least a hundred times in each of the four ways available to the Kziznvxrz, and had even outlived some of those he'd spawned.

Mrxlwvnfh looked past her to the group of Wrwrmrfn, and then returned his optical organelles to her. "The Homo sapiens have crowned a new Empress," Mrxlwvnfh said. "What do you know of these events, child Lydia?"

"Little, Revered Leader," she said.

He turned his optical organelles onto Xsirh. "What do you know, Grandchild?" Mrxlwvnfh was Xsirh's grandparent, having spawned Xsirh's spawner.

The term Mrxlwvnfh had used for Xsirh translated clumsily but literally as "offspring conceived through conjugation." The word was pronounced "luuhkirmt-xlmxvrevw-gsilfts-xlmqftzgrlm," and Lydia found it a tongue-twister, in spite of being reared by Xsirh since age four. There were subtle distinctions to parentage among the Kziznvxrz. How one was spawned made a huge difference in one's social status. The individuals accorded the most status were produced through the conjugation of two Kzizn. Since each Kzizn could choose to be the male, inseminating the female bearing the young, these were considered distinct and separate means of reproduction. Evolutionarily, these Kzizn tended to be more vigorous and hardy, and were subject to fewer infirmities. Kzizn spawned through fission, the pinching of a Kzizn through the center to form two new Kzizn, carried all the genetic irregularities that they'd been born with and any that might have developed during the lifetime of the Kzizn who had spawned them. Self-fertilization, the third method of reproduction, was also the most reviled. Offspring produced this way were derided as "jerk-offs."

Xsirh looked at his grand-sire, his organelles swiveling to focus. "Revered Leader, alas, I also know little. Svkszvhgfh Ezhrozprh left for Gaea some months ago. Lydia tells me Ezra tried to stop the Homo sapiens ceremony. I am aggrieved that the plasma of my pod-mate and my co-parent of five offspring has rejoined the food chain."

Lydia held out her hand to comfort him. Xsirh's tentacles wrapped themselves around it.

"I am sorry to hear of Ezra's loss," Mrxlwvnfh said. "He was a free-thinker."

Lydia blanched, someone's thinking for themselves and not in cohesive accord with the pod often taken as derogatory.

"He went to Gaea at my bidding," Mrxlwvnfh continued, "and if anyone is responsible for his rejoining the food chain, Xsirh, it is I. Forgive me."

"But surely, Revered Leader," Xsirh objected, "you didn't ask Ezra to stop the ceremony."

"No, you speak factually, I did not, but I did ask that he go to Gaea, which placed him there, where any Kzizn would object to such a wrongness." The Revered Leader's optical organelles swiveled toward Lydia. "Human child, I desire to confer with you in private. Let me dispense with these Wrwrmrfn, and then we will talk."

Lydia and Xsirh stepped aside, her father taking one of the side cups. Lydia knelt in the mud beside him, the cups too uncomfortable for her to sit in for long.

The dissident Wrwrmrfn moved toward the Revered Leader as a group, Mvoorv Ilfhhlh at their head. All of them melted to the floor in obeisance.

"You invaded a Homo sapiens planet by disguising yourselves as them," Mrxlwvnfh said. "Worse, you did it not to rescue your fellow Kzizn and his human daughter, but to incite our Homo sapiens neighbors. An act of provocation." He uttered the word with the full expulsive emission of his digestive tract—disgust.

Further, provocation was an act repulsive to the capacity of a Kzizn, a peace-loving species whose only predatory enemy on Kziznvxrz, the didinium, was nearly extinct. Lydia tried to understand what might have motivated the splinter group to take such an opprobrious action.

Mrxlwvnfh's upper cell sprouted livid purple spots, a sign he was furious. "Further, with this act of provocation, you have incited the ire of these Homo sapiens, and even now, they amass in the Oort cloud of our system in preparation for an attack.

"One that you provoked," he added. "What do you have to say for yourselves?"

Mvoorv Ilfhhlh raised her tentacles in supplication. "May I address the Revered Leader?"

"You may."

"Revered Leader," Mvoorv said, her organelles popping up from the top of her head, "there are subtleties within subtleties at work here. We are too timid a race to live beside these voracious Homo sapiens. We lack the spine—to borrow one of their phrases—to compete with them. Therefore, we must destroy them, as we once did the didinium. Our technology is superior to theirs, and all we lack is the will to extirpate all trace of them from the galaxy." She turned toward the imagers. "Rise up, pod-siblings, and—"

"Silence!" blatted Mrxlwvnfh.

Mvoorv went silent.

"You have revoked your right to remain members of the pod. You have demonstrated beyond all doubt that you are neither worthy of living in Paramecium society, nor of receiving the mutual support of its members. You are banished, all of you, to the middle of the sea."

Lydia gasped, and all the Kzizn in the room emitted exhalations of horror, similar only in feeling to her expression, theirs the rapid opening and closing of orifices around small pockets of air.

Already ostracized and living on the fringes of mainstream Kziznvxrfn society, these Wrwrmrfn were denied access to the mudflats, the rich primordial soup found on those vast stretches of semi-liquefied tidal basin whose yield of anaerobic organisms fed billions of Kziznvxrz. Forced to live in the surf already, they eked out a modicum of food from the cold, rough waves. Now these ten Wrwrmrfn were banished even from the surf. They would not survive long in the open sea, where microorganisms were too sparse to support a Kzizn and where the few remaining didinium prowled, voracious.

"Go now, unfaithful Wrwrmrfn," Mrxlwvnfh said, his voice deep and sad, "and suffer the consequences that you have brought upon yourselves."

Lydia watched as the goop of Wrwrmrfn slithered from the room, their cilia wilted, their tentacles hanging limp.

Xsirh murmured to her, "I need to attend to Ezra's affairs. Besides, I think Mrxlwvnfh wishes to speak with you alone."

She'd gotten that impression, too. "Give my love to his family," she said. Ezra had been one of her father's many reproductive partners, but they hadn't been on intimate terms since Lydia's first few years with the pod. She remembered him fondly. He'd been among the few pod members to have fully supported Xsirh by helping to nurture Lydia.

Why had Ezra tried to stop the ceremony? she wondered, waiting patiently in the mud while the Revered Leader's attendants replaced the six-inch layer of muck with fresh tidal-basin ooze.

The audience room restored to its original freshness, Lydia took a deep satisfying breath of the wonderful miasma, the air redolent of childhood mud-bath frolics with her father.

"Xsirh took great risks when he decided to rear you," Mrxlwvnfh said.

"I know, Revered Leader. He nurtured me beyond all expectation."

"Please, call me Marx," Mrxlwvnfh said, gesturing with his tentacles for her to approach.

She rose and eased herself into the fresh puddle of mud beside him. Instinctively, she leaned into his embrace. His tentacles wrapped around her, and his cilia began to massage her skin. Among Homo sapiens, such physical proximity and intimacy with one's leader was unthinkable. Lydia's excursions to multiple human-occupied worlds had taught her a few difficult lessons about their bizarre views of intimacy. The men just wanted to put their reproductive organelles into hers, and their female life-partners, whom they called wives, objected to that—vehemently, as Lydia had found out on one occasion. She'd been fortunate, Xsirh had later told her, not to have engaged in the act of conjugation with the paired Homo sapiens male.

"Your aroma has changed since you first joined us, child Lydia."

Twenty-eight years old, and they still call me child, she thought, bemused. At nearly six thousand years old, Mrxlwvnfh probably couldn't think of her as anything else. "You remember me when I was young?" she asked. Lydia did smell better now, her diet consisting of the thick zoylmwrtzh soup made from thickened algae. The main Kzizn diet of microorganisms was unsuited to her gullet, and no matter how many times she tried it, she usually ended up ill. As long as she stuck to a vegetarian diet, properly prepared, she experienced no adverse side effects.

"Of course I remember. We tried many times to return you to your people, but our entreaties fell on non-functioning auditory organelles. It was a trying time for us all. We were certain if we didn't return you that the Homo sapiens would surely invade Kziznvxrz to rescue you."

She turned her head to look at him. "Marx, why didn't they?"

The upper, sloped sides of his oblong shape slid upward—a shrug. "For a long time, we didn't know, but Ezra discovered a few things in his last days on Gaea."

"Why did he go there, Marx? Why did you send him there? Did he have to be punished because he won the Kzizn-of-the-month award?"

Mrxlwvnfh turned his upper nodule from side to side. "No, child Lydia, he went at my bidding to find out about you."

* * *

Lydia waded through the swamp toward home, pensive. What Mrxlwvnfh had told her was deeply disturbing. The coronation yesterday of Hecuba Zenon as the new Empress of the Gaean Empire was the culmination of a series of events that had begun before she was born.

Ezra's death had interrupted his quest for the truth, however, and the information he'd retrieved was incomplete. Amidst the information was a salient fact: Twenty-four years ago, a lowly Lady's Maid who was bedding the Emperor, Narcissa Thanos, had somehow engineered the appointment of Viscountess Basilissa Procopio, Lydia's mother, to the ambassadorship of Kziznvxrz. How and why Narcissa Thanos had done it remained a mystery.

Home for Lydia and Xsirh was inland somewhat, near the edge of the habitable tidal flat, where the thick slurry of mud began to dry, heights where seawater rose only during storms (Kziznvxrz lacked a moon), where amphibious creatures ventured to tread. There, at the edge of Kziznvxrz society, she and her father lived, their house one of the few structures with a dry floor, its above-water elevation making it difficult to access for the Kzizn, except with great effort. Fortunately, Xsirh was a young Kzizn, only a thousand years old, still vigorous with youth.

The wrong side of town, as the Homo sapiens said. Xsirh's choice of abode had been a cross product of social pressures and practicability. Members of his pod had disapproved of his decision to take on the care of the Homo sapiens waif. She smelled bad, made noxious noises reminiscent of their elimination process, and behaved like a child. Given that she was four years old at the time, there was a logical explanation for the latter. Further complicating the situation was her urine, which contained a catalyst whose interaction with Kzizn waste products precipitated the release of poisonous gasses. And on the practical side of things, the four-year-old simply couldn't have survived in the mud. She'd have drowned within a few days. So Xsirh had found an abode just above the tide line, among the least desirable locations. Lydia had been teased mercilessly by her Kzizn peers for living on the wrong side of town.

She waded from the muck and stepped through the doorway, glad to be back home, the familiar surroundings a comfort to her. She and her father weren't here much anymore, she realized, their business in trade frequently taking them off planet. Behind the house was an elevated platform, empty now of their amoeba-class vessel, which was still on Theogony.

How are we ever going to get it back? Lydia wondered.

She rinsed herself off in the cleansall just inside the doorway, a feature most Kziznvxrfn homes didn't have. Xsirh had outfitted the home in deference to Lydia's comfort, eschewing the six-inch layer of muck that covered the floor of every other home on the planet.

She stepped from the cleansall and opened the cupboard beside it to reach for a clean set of formalls.

A didinium leaped from the cupboard, glanced off her hand, and wrapped itself around her face.

Lydia dropped and rolled and managed to slip her hand between the creature and her cheek.

It tried to wrap its tentacles around her neck to strangle her.

Her arm in its way, she banged her forehead on the floor and stunned it somewhat. She brought her other hand up and pried the slug partway away from her mouth, and then spat into the didinium's intake orifice.

Her spittle hit its mark, and her pre-digestive enzymes catalyzed the lining of its intake exoderm. She ripped it off her head and flung it against the wall as the flesh began to sizzle. The slug slid to the floor, leaving an excrement-brown streak down the wall. The mass of protoplasm slowly fizzled into a puddle of protoplasm, smoke billowing up toward the ceiling.

Gasping, she stumbled to the door, the smell revolting.

She'd gotten lucky. She'd been reaching into the cupboard when it leaped out. Her hand had deflected it away from her lower face and neck. Had it landed where it intended, it would have choked her in less than three minutes.

She sat beside the door, breathing roughly, wondering how the didinium had gotten into the house. A deep-sea predator, didinium were rarely found near the coastal areas and almost never this far inland. The didinium and Paramecium had been mutual predators for nearly a million years, and only in the last five hundred thousand years had the Paramecium emerged as the dominant species, nearly wiping out the didinium in the coastal areas. Now, didinium was a delicacy among the Kziznvxrz, but one that Lydia couldn't stomach.

Relieved to have survived the attack, she set about cleaning up the mess.

Finished, she stepped into the cleansall a second time.

Not quite the homecoming greeting she'd expected.

Xsirh hadn't returned from visiting Ezra's pod, where he'd gone after their audience with the Revered Leader. Guessing he'd be home soon, Lydia set about preparing a meal, knowing he'd be hungry when he did return, fixing his favorite anaerobic soup, and preparing a lichen salad for herself.

From the direction of the tidal flat came the sounds of someone sloshing through the muck. Xsirh, she thought, recognizing his slither.

He came in on his exoderm, his cilia folded into his middle, a bundle of tentacles sprouting like a fern from the center of his abdomen. He set an object near the door and wiggled across the floor toward the kitchen. "I smell anaerobic soup! My favorite! You spoil me terribly, Lydia."

"A little spoiling makes us all smell better," she replied, the saying an adage as old as the Kzizn language.

"I have something to show you after we eat." He climbed into his seat at the low table, a cup that looked like a gigantic egg-holder.

Lydia sat in her own chair, one built for her physiology. As she ate, she reached across the table, and he wrapped his tentacles around it. Together they dined, home again, father and daughter, the picture of perfection. She told him about the didinium ambushing her from the cupboard.

"A didinium, this far inland?" Xsirh said. "I thought I smelled something when I got home. That's quite odd. How do you suppose it got in?"

Lydia shook her head, not knowing.

"Here, let me show you what I brought," he said. Xsirh slithered back to the door and returned with the object he'd set there.

Clearly of alien manufacture, the object was angular; bolts on the intact end held together a casing, the other end exploded outward, sharp shards of a dull gray metal protruding wickedly.

"What is it?"

"The casing of an A-warp core."

She laughed and shook her head. "Must be Homo sapiens in manufacture. They're the only ones using such a primitive technology."

"It is of human manufacture," Xsirh said. "You're familiar with how A-warp works?"

"It's third-grade physics, father, of course. The torsion to the foliated hyperleaves compresses space in front of the ship and expands space behind it, moving the ship across space faster than the speed of light. Simple stuff." She couldn't help but giggle. "Primitive, too."

His intake orifice curved upward at the edges. "What do you suppose caused it to explode?"

She looked at the exploded end, thinking through what she knew. Although not an engineer or physicist, she had mastered the rudimentary principles that governed A-warp technology alongside all the other Kzizn children. "Well, I couldn't say for sure, but there aren't any fissile materials in an A-warp core. Something foreign must have been introduced."

Again, Xsirh smiled. "Chemical traces of a thermonuclear microfusion event were found embedded in the casing."

"A microfusion generator? In an A-warp core? No wonder it exploded. Would have had to have happened at or near peak load, though."

"Exactly." Xsirh sat up, obvious pride in his optical organelles. "And peak load for any spaceship engine occurs when?"

"Leaving or entering a significant gravity well, most likely a planet." Lydia looked at him. "Who would put a microfusion generator inside an A-warp core? That's either outright stupidity or sabotage. Why are you showing this to me, father?"

Xsirh held up the A-warp core. "Ezra had this among his possessions. His notes indicate it's from the Homo sapiens ship that attempted to land on Kziznvxrz twenty-four years ago, the ship carrying Viscountess Ambassador Basilissa Procopio and her family."

Carrying me, Lydia thought, staring at Xsirh.

Chapter 10

She strode up the hill behind the house, perhaps the highest point of land for miles around, a place Xsirh had difficulty getting to, his exoderm not well adapted for dry, rocky terrain. She scratched an itch on her arm.

All Kziznvxrz lived on the planet's tidal flats. None of the other species on Kziznvxrz had risen from the muck and adapted to the environments on either side, the deep blue sea and hills like the one Lydia now climbed, nor had they developed the intelligence, language, and technology that the Kzizn had.

She was grateful that Ezra had recovered something from the crash site. The damage to the A-warp core casing indicated sabotage. Among other items her father had recovered from the crash site were tissue samples from both her father and mother, kept in zero-kelvin cryo. When Lydia had learned of the Homo sapiens death customs, she'd laughed herself silly. The Kziznvxrfn had nothing similar, probably since death was so rare among them, their life-spans often exceeding five thousand years. So her parents had never had a proper burial, or any sort of obsequy. Lydia wondered whether the Procopio family on Gaea had held any ceremonies for the deceased Viscountess Ambassador, her husband, and their daughter.

She reached the hilltop and stared at the stars. Nightfall on Kziznvxrz tended to be sudden and sharp. Without a moon, its nights were dark. Given the system's position near the edge of the Milky Way, only a slim strip of stars was visible in the night sky. She'd seen the night skies on worlds relatively close to the galactic bar, where brilliant bands of stars bathed planets with near-daylight intensity. Lydia didn't sleep well in the presence of light—any light—and she couldn't imagine living on a planet with a moon.

The Kzizn didn't have the Homo sapiens equivalent of a religion. Having an average lifespan of five thousand years, they'd never developed the concept of an afterlife. The thought of one was ludicrous. Why would anyone have any desire for an afterlife after having lived five thousand years? They were ecstatic when it was time for them to contribute their protoplasm to the food chain. After that amount of time, Kzizn were practically begging to be released from the doldrums of existence.

Lydia wondered which star was Gaea's. She knew for a fact she couldn't see it, but she might have found a smidgen of comfort in looking its direction. It was where she'd been born. While the Kzizn had nurtured her and given her succor, they weren't her people. They'd allowed her to live with them, had educated her, and had made allowances for her human foibles, such as her lack of an eidetic memory, which all Kzizn had, but they wouldn't ever be able to bring her fully into their society. She simply would never live long enough, her life expectancy a fraction of theirs.

The thin strip of Milky Way stars directly above her stretched across a twenty-degree arc of sky. So far away, Lydia thought, wondering why someone had felt it necessary to sabotage the Ambassador's ship twenty-four years ago. As if the post itself weren't remote enough.

What possible threat could my mother have been to the ambitious and cunning Lady's Maid, Narcissa Thanos? Lydia silently asked the stars. She didn't know, and Xsirh didn't either.

"Known only to the stars," the Homo sapiens adage went.

Lydia looked at them overhead, wishing they would tell her.

The thin strip of stars shimmered.

What's that? she wondered. And as she watched, the patch of shimmering stars grew slowly wider. They shouldn't be doing that!

The oddity was like an artifact you could see only in your peripheral vision, the objects beyond it distorted. The artifact grew larger as she watched, its size difficult to gauge against the nearly black sky.

It settled just below the hilltop, on the other side of her house, a faint hum audible.

Then it appeared. From behind a diaphanous curtain manifested her amoeba-class vessel, the one she'd left on Theogony.

But who's flying it? Lydia wondered.

* * *

Erastus Doukas, Agent Provocateur with the Imperial Bureau of Suspicion, leveled the blasma pistol at the young woman. "Hands up, Lydia Procopio. You're under arrest."

She put her hands in the air instantly.

He hustled down the boarding ramp. Pistol aimed with one hand, he clamped a circlet onto her arm and twisted it down behind her back.

"Oww!" she complained.

"Now the other," he said, reaching up for it and wrenching it behind her back. There, he clamped them together. "All right, aboard." He grasped her upper arm with his free hand and dragged her toward the boarding ramp.

She didn't resist. "Where are you taking me?"

"A little out of the way place I know called the Andromeda Galaxy. Where do you *think* I'm taking you?" He couldn't believe how stupid she was, asking him something so simple. Doukas herded her onto the ship, and the ramp retracted behind them.

"You're taking me to Gaea, then. Guess I deserved the sarcasm. You'll let them know you've captured me?"

"No, I'm going to waltz right into an audience with the Empress and her fatuous mother the Dowager Empress saying I've a pleasant surprise for them personally." He guided her over to the cup-shaped Kzizn chair and strapped her into it, and then took the pilot's chair. Erastus felt her eyes upon him, watching his every move. He struggled to keep his attention on what he was doing.

She was so beautiful, all he wanted to do was look at her. He'd felt the same when he'd first taken custody of her on Theogony. If she hadn't called him that taunting pejorative he'd heard all his life, he might have remained spellbound, transfixed by the elfin face and bottomless-blue eyes.

Focus! he told himself, looking over the bewildering, unfamiliar controls. The Kzizn ship was difficult to fly, his hands ill-adapted to the controls, better suited to tentacles than hands. It'd been a challenge to fly it here from Theogony.

"The blue button, over there," she told him.

Oh, yeah, he thought. A low hum became audible, a far more pleasant sound than the dull roar of Gaean-designed ships. He'd actually found it quite pleasant to fly, other than the difficult controls. "Ridiculous for these ships not to have any type of security systems," he said, activating the engines.

"Well, when you don't have theft, you don't worry about thieves," she replied.

Sensing sarcasm, he grabbed the nav, spreading his hands across a two-foot square of fine-motor controls. The ship began to rise, wobbling awkwardly.

"It's got voice command," she said.

"But I don't speak that awful-sounding language."

"I adapted it to Galactim, too."

"Why didn't it say so?" He looked at her suspiciously. "You're not going to take over the ship, are you?"

"No, of course not."

"Ship, take us into orbit, and then set a course for Lucina Nine."

"Orbit, and then set a course for Lucina Nine, acknowledged," the ship said in Galactim, and then it repeated itself in Kzizn, "Liyrg, zmw gsvm hvg z xlfihv uli Ofxrmz Mrmv, zxpmldovwtvw."

"Eww!" Erastus cringed at the sounds. "Any way to turn that off?"

"Ship, Galactim only, please."

"Galactim only," the ship said. "Tzozxgrn lmob," it repeated.

"You sure it'll obey?" he asked the young woman. "That language is awful enough to make someone vomit!"

"It'll obey."

The ship engines engaged, pressing him into his seat. He glanced over at her.

She was pressed into the cup awkwardly, looking uncomfortable in the upended hemisphere, as if in pain.

She seems to be taking this all without much complaint, Erastus thought, wondering why.

The planet below retreated in the holoscreen, its left side lit by the setting sun. The mudded-out bay they'd just lifted off from was cloaked in darkness, no lights to indicate inhabited areas, as on most human-occupied worlds. Thinking the lack of lights odd, Doukas asked her about it.

"Their optical organelles perceive a wider range of frequencies than our eyes. And they're much more sensitive to ambient light, no matter how little of it there is."

"You mean they can see better." He didn't know what organelles were, but he didn't want to seem stupid by asking. He struggled enough with that as it was.

"Orbit achieved," the ship said in its dreary monotone. "Course plotted for Lucina Nine. Engage at what speed, please?"

Shoulders hunched up near his ears, he cringed, waiting for the ship to start blatting in that foul-sounding language.

The ship didn't say anything further.

Erastus threw her a glance. "How fast can this thing go?"

"Sub-ether transport requires no time at all. We can arrive at Lucina Nine in moments."

"Captured the Kzizn transport technology and the most wanted criminal alive, all in one trip." Erastus could feel the glory already. "Ship, open a sub-ether channel to Colonel Melanctha Remes, IBS Command Outpost, Lucina Nine."

"Warning, sub-ether transmission will disrupt our drives," the ship said without emotion. "Engines will have to be shut down while transmitting. Open sub-ether channel?"

"So we sit here vulnerable while I transmit, eh?"

The young woman shrugged at him. "No one's chasing us, in case you hadn't noticed."

He had noticed, and he thought it odd. "Why aren't your people chasing us? What's the matter with them? And why are you just letting me kidnap you?"

"It's not complacency, I can tell you that. I am uncomfortable, and I'd appreciate it if you'd take off these bracelets."

Startled, he nearly got whiplash looking at her. "You'll go with me willingly?"

"Of course."

He stared at her, aghast. "But why? You should be doing everything you can to get away from me!"

"If taking me to Lucina Nine stops the Empire from attacking Kziznvxrz, then take me."

Not exactly a genius, Erastus had to think through what he was doing. Not that he cared one whit whether Kziznvxrz was annihilated with a planetary core detonator, turning the ball of mud into a ball of fire. All he wanted was to clear his name of the fiasco on Theogony, where somehow the Kzizn had impersonated Imperial Secret Service agents and had whisked the human captive and her father from under his very nose. He didn't care what happened beyond that.

An Agent Provocateur, he cared nothing about interstellar relations and even less about the bizarre interest that the Palace seemed to have in the young woman now in his custody. All he cared about was avoiding looking bad, his physical appearance notwithstanding. Like the newly-crowned Empress, his ugliness was irremediable.

He turned to the control consol, happy he wasn't being pursued. "Ship, open a sub-ether channel to Lucina Nine."

"Shutting down engines, opening sub-ether channel to Lucina Nine."

"One of these days," the woman said, "you humans will devise a better means of communication."

He snorted at her, and realized the sound was uncomfortably like a word from the Kzizn language, which he didn't speak. "You've got room to talk."

"I'd have more room if I didn't have these bracelets on."

Trusting that she wouldn't try anything, he got up to remove them. He took one off, watching her carefully.

"Thank you," she said, giving him a brief smile.

Her charm sent warmth coursing down into his toes. He smiled back and then took the other one off.

"Channel open."

"Agent Erastus, is that you?" A holo of Colonel Melanctha Remes materialized above the controls.

"I have a present for her Highness, the Empress Hecuba." He gestured at the young woman.

Remes' jaw dropped, and her face blanched. "Fool!" Remes snarled, and the holo collapsed.

Erastus stared at the empty space above the control panel,

wondering what had happened. Not the reaction I expected, he thought, wondering why she hadn't been overjoyed.

"I don't think she wanted to hear that," Lydia said.

He whirled on her. "Shut up! What do you know?!" Flummoxed, he didn't need his captive telling him what he already knew. "Engage course!" he snarled.

"Passengers in unsafe locations," the ship said. "Please secure all passengers."

"I said `engage'!" he screamed at the holoscreen, tendons popping out at his neck, a vein wriggling at his temple.

"Engaged."

The acceleration slammed him into a bulkhead, knocking him unconscious.

* * *

"Colonel Remes, incoming!" Lieutenant-Colonel Urian Nikitas squawked on her com. "Vessel of unknown make and model just appeared in orbit above Lucina Nine!"

Colonel Melanctha Remes of IBS Command nearly soiled herself. "Sub-space disruptions?"

"Yes, Colonel."

"Kzizn! Squadrons three, five and eight, scramble! Intruder alert! Squadrons three, five and eight, scramble! Intruder alert!" What the Hades is Dickass thinking? she wondered.

"Squadrons three, five and eight scrambling, Colonel!"

Klaxons began to sound, lights dimmed, and red strobes took over.

Now I can't see a blasted thing! she thought, tearing out of her office into the command theater. The five rings of monitoring stations had come alive with activity, Lieutenant-Colonel Nikitas at the center, spouting orders.

She reminded herself that she wasn't certain it was Doukas, but his transmission hadn't contained the sub-space signatures built into all Gaean ships, military or otherwise, indicating he'd pirated a vessel of Kzizn manufacture. Melanctha had ordered a scan of the Kziznvxrz system immediately after closing the com channel, and sensors had detected sub-space disruptions just moments after the holocom. It was a fair assumption that the Kzizn-manufacture ship was piloted by Doukas, but it was still an assumption.

The fiasco just yesterday on Theogony had set them all on edge. The Kzizns' disguised as Imperial Secret Service personnel purloining the captives from the Detention Center was an interstellar incident of major proportions. Melanctha had placed IBS Command for the Delta Sector on high alert, prepared for the order to assist the Gaean Armada in its assault on Kziznvxrz. Ships were now amassed in the Oort cloud of the lonely system at the edge of the Mnemosyne Constellation, more collecting every moment. But thus far, no attack had been ordered.

Colonel Remes joined Lieutenant-Colonel Nikitas in the center ring. "Status?"

"They're surrounding the unknown vessel now, Colonel," Urian said.

On high alert already, they'd been able to scramble quickly. "That's the second time in two days that Gaean territory has suffered Kzizn encroachment."

Nikitas shot her a glance. "You don't think this is Doukas?"

"I do, but he's caused me more work in the past week than a bureaucrat from Gaea." She rolled her eyes. "I'd rather blast his ass into the next galaxy and apologize later. Get me a secured channel to all three squadrons, and then a separate unsecure channel to the Kzizn vessel, muted."

"Channels open," Nikitas told her moments later.

"All fighters, arm neutredoes at full power. This is the second Kzizn incursion in two days. Prepare to blast."

She waited until they acknowledged. "Unmute," she ordered, awaited his nod and then said, "Attention Kzizn vessel, you have violated Gaean territory. Shut down your engines immediately or be blasted out of the sky."

The static of a regular radio signal screeched from the speaker. No holo appeared. "Agent Doukas is hurt and needs immediate medical attention," an assertive female voice said. "I'm taking him to the hospital. Out."

"Non-sub-space transmission, Colonel," Nikitas told her.

"Belay there, Kzizn vessel," she said.

"It's gone!" squawked their com. "The Kzizn ship has vanished!"

Several monitoring stations confirmed. "Slipped away without a trace, Colonel," one tech said.

"Colonel, sub-space disruptions detected at Tyrnavos Hospital."

"On screen!"

The sprawling hospital complex appeared, and atop the tallest structure perched a gleaming blue-metal vessel, its sleek design nothing like any ship of Gaean manufacture that Melanctha had seen. The boarding ramp was already out, and a figure awkwardly carrying a bundle stumbled down the ramp. A hospital crew hustled out to meet them.

A close-up showed medical personnel taking a limp and bloody Agent Doukas from the arms of a young woman, blood covering the front of her formalls. Her hair brown, her face triangular and soft, and her eyes a vivid blue, the young woman was striking for both her bloody clothes and her elfin beauty.

Melanctha Remes drew a sharp breath, the face unforgettable.

Chapter 11

Lydia walked along an endless corridor inside a tight cordon of captors, keeping her composure in spite of her fear.

For Kziznvxrz, she kept telling herself, anything to avert an attack on Kziznvxrz.

The squad of uniformed soldiers had converged on the hospital helopad within minutes of her landing. A hundred blasma rifles aimed at her, they'd ordered her away from the ship and then had swarmed around her, bundled her into a waiting hover, and whisked her away to a military compound surrounded by barbed wire, gun emplacements, and watchtowers.

On arrival at the compound, they'd whisked her over to a gigantic biodetector, the arch twice as tall as her, its sides glowing blue.

"But I've been inoculated!" she'd insisted. They'd shoved her through it anyway, and the machine had turned green, indicating she was clear of pathogens.

The phalanx of soldiers marched her down the corridor. At a checkpoint, where carbo-nick alloy bars reinforced clear glasma panes, female soldiers replaced all the males in the phalanx, and they took her down another corridor, this one equally sterile. They passed through three more checkpoints, ID-ing the prisoner and every member of her escort each time.

A woman at the last checkpoint stepped up and stuck her face into Lydia's. "I'm Sergeant Glavan. Your Kzizn pals try any of their tricks here, and they'll have *me* to deal with." She poked a thumb at her own chest.

"Yes, Ma'am."

"Now, if you agree to cooperate, we'll get you out of those bloody rags and into a shower. One wrong move, and we blast your ass."

"Yes, Ma'am." Lydia would have saluted if she could have done so without irony. Doukas had bled all over her, and all she wanted was to get out of the sticky, clingy garment.

They led her into the containment area. Two of the female soldiers indicated a cleansall stall, and a third retrieved a fresh pair of formalls. "Slowly now," one of them told her. "No sudden moves."

Methodically, she stripped, trying not to feel naked.

"Just leave it. Into the stall."

"Stunning, isn't she?" one said to another.

"Plug it!" the detail commander said.

She got into the stall, its door clear glasma. She closed her eyes, and the cleansall cycled through a wash, a rinse, and a dry. A hairhelm descended from the ceiling and gave her a quick, utilitarian coif.

She stepped out and dressed in the pair of proffered formalls.

They led her along another sterile corridor to a cell. "In," a soldier said, "Chow in five. You hungry?"

She entered the cell, wondering what they'd be feeding her. "Famished," she said, "and I'm a vegetarian."

"This ain't the Hilton, sister."

She bit her tongue on a sarcastic reply. She'd never been able to stomach the protein-rich protozoa steaks on Kzizn, and standard human fare hadn't proved any more digestible.

They closed the door and locked it, the carbo-nick reinforced glasma giving her no privacy.

Another cell, the third in three days, Lydia thought. The cell wasn't terribly different from the one on Theogony, the materials more durable here. Detainment cells didn't differ much, she surmised. On Kziznvxrz, there weren't any, so she didn't have much to compare them with.

What the hell did I do? she wondered. Easing herself to the bunk, she squelched her despair. For Kziznvxrz, she told herself again.

She looked up to find a woman staring at her.

Her ramrod posture declared her status as loudly as the epaulets on her shoulders. She had a sharp, blade-like nose. "Colonel Melanctha Remes, IBS Commander here at the Lucina Nine. Lydia Procopio?"

Lydia nodded.

"You could've escaped—easily. Instead, you took Doukas to the hospital. And then you stayed there on the helopad until we got there, again giving up an opportunity to escape. Why did you want to be captured?"

"Maybe stop an attack on the Kziznvxrfn," she said, shrugging. She felt the woman's scrutiny, as though Colonel Remes recognized her.

"At the Immigration Detention Center on Theogony, you called the Kzizn your father."

"He reared me since I was four. My mother, Viscountess Ambassador Basilissa Procopio, and my father, Professor Dorian Procopio, were killed when our ship broke up entering the Kziznvxrz atmosphere."

"And you've lived there ever since?"

Lydia shrugged. "Nearly twenty-five years now. My father and I have a small shipping company. We have every Imperial clearance we need, Colonel. I've been to three dozen Gaean planets. We've never had a problem before. And it was a dissident group called the Wrwrmrfn that kidnapped us from Theogony. They're trying to stir up conflict between Gaea and Kziznvxrz."

"Kziznvxrfn Dissidents?"

"You pronounce that pretty well, for a human."

"Thank you."

"Why all this trouble, Colonel?" Lydia asked. "We didn't do anything wrong. We've both been inoculated."

The other woman's face was impassive.

Either she won't tell me or doesn't know, Lydia thought, and she doesn't want to betray which it is. "Look, you don't have to tell me anything, but you could do something for me."

"What would that be?"

"Make sure they don't attack my home."

* * *

475

"I can't make any guarantees, Lydia," Colonel Melanctha Remes said, looking over the waif.

Her small frame and elfin face gave the impression of adolescence. The refulgent beauty of her face was compelling, as though an angel had stepped from heaven into the cell. Lydia Procopio had the heroic face of ancient tales, like the ones Melanctha had heard as a child. A face so perfect and fine that it caused the breath to catch and the heart to skip. Further, the face reminded Melanctha of someone. The face of someone she'd never forget.

"I've ordered double vegetables and half the meat. No guarantees it'll be anything like your usual diet on Kziznvxrfn." Then Melanctha met Lydia's gaze. "I'll do what I can about the naval buildup."

She turned and was headed out the door when a faint "Thank you" followed her from the cell far behind her.

Your first duty is the Empire's security, Melanctha remonstrated herself, the face of her captive threatening to break through the hard shell that she'd built over the memories of her youth, layer by layer.

"Get me a secure channel to Kastela. Admiral Vlahos on holo," she said to the air, striding down the corridor, knowing Lieutenant-Colonel Nikitas was monitoring her.

"Yes, Colonel," he said. "Obtaining channel."

Melanctha gritted her teeth, her jaw muscles rippling, her stride nearly the march of an automaton. No, she ordered herself, you will not think about him! She took the stairs rather than the lift, blindly charging through the checkpoints, her face carefully composed, her mind in turmoil.

"Colonel, I have an encrypted channel to Rear Admiral Vlahos, Kastela Headquarters," Nikitas said. "Go ahead."

She passed the last checkpoint. "I need privacy for this one, Urian." Melanctha hoped using his first name would soften the request. She turned a corner toward her personal suite.

"Certainly, Colonel. Monitoring off."

She entered the underground apartment she'd occupied for six years, a palatial suite of five rooms.

Rear Admiral Cleon Vlahos was waiting for her, leaning against the mantel in the living room. His holo image, rather.

"Clever bastard," she told him. "How are you, my friend?"

"None the worse for the wear and tear of acquiring a new Emperor, Mela," the holojection said, coming away from the faux hearth. "Good to see you, my friend. I've missed you, but I'm glad you were spared the hullabaloo here on Gaea."

"I don't know what shocked me more," she told her boss, "seeing the narcissistic bitch aim her blasma pistol at doddering Daphne or watching the High Justice soil herself again in public."

The Rear Admiral's image threw his head back and laughed. "Classic Narcissa, wasn't it?"

"In fine form, the both of them," she replied, laughing too.

He sobered suddenly. "But you didn't com me for that, did you?"

"I've got the girl, Cleon."

The sharp intake of breath told Melanctha all she needed to know.

"Not another word," she told him. "For your safety and mine, eh?"

"That's wise, Mela. Thank you for the caution. It's too easy to think the encryption impenetrable."

She smiled. He hadn't said, and wouldn't ever say, that the IBS had incorporated backdoor decoding methods into every type of encryption used throughout the Empire. "Two things I need, Cleon. And what I don't want is a word of assent or even acknowledgment."

"Not and maintain plausible deniability, of course," the Rear Admiral replied. "Not a very clear transmission to start with, Colonel. Your image is fuzzy, difficult to hear you through the static." His image was perfect, his voice crystal clear.

She smiled. "First, see if you can delay the attack on Kziznvxrz. A splinter group called the Wrwrmrfn carried out the extraction raid on Theogony. Second, get me the file on Count Terzi's only child, the one who died at age ten."

"What? What was that, Colonel Remes? The signal is really bad. I didn't hear a thing you were saying. I can't even see your face anymore, Colonel. Colonel Remes? Colonel? Oh, blast it. Signal's gone. Holo out!" The expression on his face as the holovid collapsed was a broad grin.

Melanctha felt the smile slide off her face like a mud mask at a beauty parlor, and she lowered herself to the divan, the memories too vivid to contain anymore. Memories of the freak hover accident and horrific explosion that had taken the life of her childhood friend right

477

in front of her. The life of Count Terzi's son, Icarus, the next in line for the crown after the new infant child, Hecuba Zenon.

Colonel Melanctha Remes wept.

Chapter 12

Lydia looked up from the half-eaten meal.

A lab-coated man stood in front of the glasma door, a biometer in hand. "Nurse Galen Liakos," he said. "Please step out of the cell so I can examine you. Colonel's orders."

She frowned, bewildered. The female guards on either side of the nurse looked as puzzled as she felt. "I'm a prisoner. Why would Colonel Remes give a grape leaf?"

The nurse shrugged. "Patient refusing to cooperate," he said to the air, as if reciting to a machine.

"I didn't say I wouldn't cooperate." She rose and stepped to the door, which slid aside.

The two guards held their blasma pistols at ready, their tips glowing.

"Step this way and stop here," the nurse said. "Now turn around. Pull the formall off your shoulders and lower it to your waist."

Lydia did as she was bidden, the chill air on her exposed back and front making her skin prickle.

"These leads will be cold."

Icy points of sticky tape pegged her, one to each shoulder just below the clavicle, one to each side on the lowest rib. Her skin sucked in the adhesive, accustomed to environments much more moist than this one.

"Breath deep and release," Nurse Liakos said.

She did so dutifully, feeling a bit warmer on the exhale.

The sterile setting helped her feel somewhat comfortable being half-exposed in front of the man. On Kziznvxrz, she rarely wore clothes. The humid environment and constant presence of mud made it difficult to keep anything clean. A quick rinse just before entering the house was far easier without clothes to contend with. Studying a human-occupied world before she'd arrived, she'd been bewildered by the outer coverings they always wore. And she'd learned what a disturbance the sight of an unclothed woman caused without having to experience it firsthand.

He ran the biometer up and down her back while she breathed, the hand-held machine humming. "Is that a rash?"

"Huh?"

"Those spots on your right arm, is that a rash?"

"Oh, that? I don't know," Lydia said. "It's been itching off and on since I left Kziznvxrz. I've been inoculated."

"All right, taking off the leads now. These are usually pretty sticky." They came off easily, with only a slight tug. "That was odd. Formalls back on, please."

Lydia pulled the cloth back over her shoulders, wriggling into the form-fitting suit. While she secured it in front, Nurse Liakos started asking her questions.

Endless questions. As many questions as Imperial Immigration had asked when she'd first applied for a trade visa. Personal questions about her procreation history (none), psycho-chemo alteration history (none), abuse history (what's abuse? none), family history (unknown, orphaned at four), violence history (none), ad nauseam.

At the end, Nurse Liakos thanked her politely and apologized for the invasive questions.

"Galen," she asked, "did your parents want you to be a doctor?"

He grinned at her. "Couldn't tell from my name, could you?" With a nod, he punched a few buttons on the biometer, and the hum died. "Pleasure to make your acquaintance."

"Likewise," she replied as the guards herded her back into the cell.

He nodded and nearly ran into Colonel Remes as he exited.

Lydia watched them retreat into the corridor, unable to hear their conversation from inside her cell. She saw Colonel Remes slip something into her pocket as she entered the detainment area.

"Come with me, Ms. Procopio."

"Where are you taking me?"

"Gaea, Ms. Procopio. You're going to Gaea."

* * *

Lydia boarded the mini-cargo vessel waiting on the tarmac, her phalanx of guards walking her up the ramp.

The cell aboard the ship was a container in the cargo hold beside her amoeba-class Kzizn vessel, looking as sleek as a wasp.

They'll dismantle it and try to re-engineer its drive, Lydia thought, knowing the sub-ether transport technology superior to the Homo sapiens' A-warp drive.

The phalanx of guards marched her into the cell, a sterile box with seat, toilet, shower, and bunk. It looked remarkably like the cell aboard the Wrwrmrfn vessel that had taken her back to Kziznvxrz. They secured the door behind her, the carbo-nick reinforced glasma giving her a view of the cargo hold entrance. The guards left the ship, and mechanical whining indicated the boarding ramp was retracting.

She strapped herself into the seat, guessing lift off was imminent.

Another twenty minutes passed however before warning lights began to flash.

Gaea finally, Lydia thought.

It'd always been a curiosity, that distant planet she was supposedly from. Not that she had much interest in going there, just that it was an unknown feature of her life, a place she'd heard about and imagined things about, where her relatives were thought to live. She'd always had a faint yearning to visit Gaea, and once she'd even inquired into the process. The bureaucratic hurdles had seemed daunting at the time, far greater than her vague desire to overcome them.

And whatever family she might have on Gaea, they'd either lacked the will or the political influence to persuade the government to have the accident investigated. Kziznvxrfn requests to have the Homo sapiens take back the Ambassador's surviving daughter had been met with silence.

Lydia didn't understand why they hadn't, nor did she begrudge it.

She'd been so overwhelmed with the sudden loss of her parents, the horror of the crash itself, and the difficulties of her new environment, that she'd given little thought to Gaea. And she'd been four years old, barely old enough to know what death was, bewildered that Mommy and Daddy weren't ever coming back.

As to the things that Mrxlwvnfh Gzelfozirh, the oldest Paramecium, had told her, information gathered by Ezra on Gaea before the coronation, Lydia didn't quite know how to put it in context. It seemed such a pastiche of random facts, splotches of paint spread out on a canvas, no two splotches touching, no way to connect the information together.

The ship rumbling under her, the acceleration pressing her into the seat, Lydia hoped she was making the right decision.

Going to Gaea seemed the only way to stop an attack on Kziznvxrz.

Why, she couldn't have said. What possible interest could I be to these Homo sapiens now?

The acceleration eased, and the warning lights blinked off.

She unbuckled herself and looked at the bunk. She was tempted, the utter boredom inside these cells difficult to endure. Ironic, she thought, that I've become such an expert on prison cells.

Somewhere, a hatch opened.

Lydia looked toward the cage door.

Colonel Melanctha Remes appeared beyond the glasma. Without a word, she opened the cell. "Join me in the mess? There's a proper synth we can program to your liking."

She stared at the other woman, really looking at her. Not much experienced at estimating age, Lydia guessed the woman was in her late forties, early fifties. She held herself stiffly erect, but beyond the sharp-bladed nose, her gaze was gentle, her face having a hint of regality, plain but not unpleasant. Soft confidence exuded from her, the confidence of command.

"I didn't expect to see *you* aboard, Colonel Remes."

"I've taken the initiative to bring you to Gaea personally. Given circumstances, it seemed the prudent thing to do."

"What circumstances are those?" Lydia still hadn't moved, bewildered.

"The back and forth, and the interest in you displayed by our capital. Come along, then. Provided you won't try to escape, there's no need for you to remain in that cell."

Lydia shrugged. "I won't, which you already knew."

"I did."

She stepped toward the door, and the Colonel led the way. The rectangular corridors were disconcerting to Lydia, Kzizn ships having tubular passageways. As they moved through the ship, Lydia got the distinct impression they were alone, no one else aboard. In the galley, the table and chairs were uncomfortably high, Kzizn cup-seats just inches above the floor and their tables usually not more than a foot.

Colonel Remes gestured her to sit and stepped to a machine.

Lydia watched as the device beeped and blipped back at the Colonel.

"Stubborn thing doesn't have a setting for vegetarians. Call me Mela, by the way."

"Pleased," Lydia said. "Thank you, Mela."

"What do the Kzizn call you?"

"Obwrz," she said. "They have as difficult a time pronouncing Galactim as we do Kziznvxrz."

Melanctha sat across from her and pushed a steaming bowl toward her.

The green bubbling liquid looked appetizing and smelled delicious. "What is it?"

"Protoplasm soup. I had your stool sampled, by the way, and this concoction is as close to your usual diet as I could get. Hopefully, it's adequate."

Lydia tasted it. The warm protoplasm soup was good. Somewhat odd in taste, but not objectionable. She found the Homo sapiens animal protein diet nauseating, and this soup was a welcome change. "Thank you, very kind of you." She looked at Melanctha. "Why the personal interest, Mela? What am I to you?"

Lydia saw the woman change. It wasn't overt or dramatic, but enough to indicate something profound had once happened to her.

"I had a friend in childhood, and I saw him die. You look uncannily like him, Lydia. His name was Icarus Terzi, and before Empress Hecuba Zenon was born, Icarus was the heir apparent, the next nearest relative to Emperor Athanasios Zenon."

* * *

Rear Admiral Cleon Vlahos, Chief of the Imperial Bureau of Suspicion, brought his gaze up from the dossier of Icarus Terzi and looked out the window of his office at Kastela Headquarters on the outskirts of New Athens.

Initially, he'd delegated obtaining the file to his administrative assistant.

"Sir, my apologies, access to Icarus Terzi's dossier is restricted."

"But you've got top-secret clearance."

"Access requires top-top-secret clearance, Sir."

"So I have to retrieve the damn thing myself, eh?"

"Yes, Sir, I'm afraid so."

"Why do you suppose that is?"

Outside the triple-paned glasma window, in the distance, the palace gleamed like a jewel.

Icarus Terzi had been the son of Count Ilias Terzi, cousin to Emperor Athanasios Zenon, and the heir-presumptive if the Emperor failed to spawn a viable candidate for the throne. At the time of the boy's death, the Emperor's first daughter, Cybill, was beginning to show signs of developmental difficulties. Her failure to meet several expected milestones was generally perceived as a sign she would be passed over for the succession. More than one member of the aristocracy had cast an envious eye in the direction of Icarus, the next obvious heir apparent.

Tragic, Cleon thought, how the boy died. A hover had veered out of traffic, had upended, and had plummeted to the ground, erupting in a fireball, right on top of Icarus Terzi. A freak accident, few hovers malfunctioning in such a spectacular way.

The boy had been playing on the private grounds of the Terzi estate with his friend, Melanctha Remes, the two ten-year-olds being watched from a distance by his governor, an old gentleman named Giles Sotiropoulos. Blameless in the boy's death, Giles had been fired nonetheless, and the file indicated that he'd committed suicide not long afterward, destitute and without the means to support himself.

Vlahos got up from his desk, disturbed by the similarity in feature between the boy, Icarus Terzi, and the captive, Lydia Procopio.

The aristocracy, being a somewhat insular group of scions, most of them so fabulously wealthy that fortunes might be made in their footsteps, were not immune to trysts, liaisons, and infidelities. In fact, it might be said that they had far more opportunity to indulge themselves in such foibles.

Rear Admiral Vlahos remembered the Kzizn ambassador, Viscountess Basilissa Procopio, a suave woman of immaculate breeding whose husband, Dorian, was a Professor of Xenobiology and a scion from among the lesser nobility. Vlahos had admired Viscountess Procopio's staunch resolve in accepting the ambassadorship to such a distant backwater.

He'd been a newly-appointed sub-secretary of Military Intelligence to the Imperial Bureau of Suspicion and had been at the palace to brief the Emperor on an uprising along the outer Perseus Arm. So it was just by chance he'd been present when Emperor Zenon had formally asked Viscountess Procopio to take the appointment.

Palace personnel had become aware of a subtle shift in the bureaucracy. No official documentation of this shift could ever be found, but the upper echelons felt its impact on daily-decision making. The guerilla bureaucracy adjusted to such changes with alacrity. Power was like water, having an undeniable need to flow, finding its way around or over obstructions, eating away at vulnerabilities until it had etched a channel where it might flow unrestricted, often seeping silently through thicker obstructions, eroding insidiously at the bedrock of people's moral character, saturating their inhibitions and slaking their thirst for power. Everyone had become aware that Emperor Athanasios had lost his grip on power. Four years of grieving for his beloved Consort, Ambrosia, had wrung him dry as a sponge.

Power had begun to flow through a new, unofficial consort, one whose station prevented her from ever being recognized in any official capacity, the Lady's Maid, Narcissa Thanos.

Newly-appointed to a position didn't mean Vlahos was new to bureaucracies. Thirty-three years old, Lieutenant Vlahos had previously served as Chief of Counter-Intelligence in the Gaean Navy. His graduation at twenty-three from the Hellenic post-graduate naval academy with triple degrees in encryption, linguistics, and interstellar relations had nearly guaranteed him a fast-track to Admiral. Alas it was not to be, the IBS having somehow pulled some strings to get Vlahos transferred to a civilian intelligence role. Strings, he'd discovered, that had been closer in size to hawsers. They'd hauled his career ship by its hawsers over to civilian intelligence.

Now, as he compared the two stills, one of the boy, Icarus Terzi, and one of the captive, Lydia Procopio, the Chief of the Imperial Bureau of Suspicion knew his ship had come in.

He considered his options: withhold the dossier from Colonel Melanctha Remes, his erstwhile lover with whom he'd shared many a romantic evening; take his information directly to Empress Hecuba and the Dowager Empress Narcissa; consult with his colleague the Chief of the Imperial Secret Service; or simply take the initiative and annihilate Remes and her captive en route from Lucina IX.

Vlahos knew the latter the most prudent course.

It was what the Empress would order him to do, anyway. And if he didn't do it now, he was likely to incur the Dowager's wrath in having hesitated.

If he'd had some way of killing the captive without hurting Melanctha, he wouldn't have blinked.

And since they're both going to die, Vlahos thought, why don't I send the information anyway? In his estimation, it wouldn't hurt. In fact, if he didn't send it, Melanctha might become suspicious.

In the dossier on Icarus Terzi, he saw a genetic profile. He was certain Melanctha had obtained a tissue sample from her captive. A comparison of their genomes would prove irrefutably what Melanctha certainly suspected: That the captive, Lydia Procopio, daughter of the Ambassador to Kziznvxrz, Basilissa Procopio, was a close relative of the just-deceased Emperor Athanasios Zenon.

How and why was immaterial.

Emperors don't think the same way as normal people, Vlahos told himself. They hold in mind the long view and aren't averse to a little intrigue.

Not averse to a little intrigue.

He smiled at his minimizing Imperial misdeeds.

Perhaps Athanasios had impregnated Basilissa as a hedge against his legitimate children through Ambrosia not surviving childhood. Likely targets of assassination from multiple directions, the aristocracy included, such children rarely lived lives with a modicum of normalcy, under constant guard, their food and water always taste-tested, every interlocutor screened heavily and vetted thoroughly.

Vlahos was convinced Lydia was of Imperial blood. His only question was the degree of consanguinity. No matter what the degree, however, the Dowager Empress wanted her dead.

Looking out his office window, Vlahos queued up a holomail message for Melanctha and attached the dossier on Icarus Terzi. In the distance, the palace sparkled.

"Encryption, please," he said, as though to the air.

"What level encryption, Sir?"

Cryptology one of three degrees he'd earned at post-graduate, Vlahos smiled. "Quadruple, please." With such deep encryption, even someone with his considerable skills would have difficulty decrypting it.

"Ultra-top-secret priority, Sir?"

"No. In fact, no priority at all," he told his desk computer. Better not to bring attention to it, he thought. "Send immediately."

"Sir, there is no subject or message, only an attachment. Send anyway?"

"Send immediately," he repeated.

"Message sent, Sir."

Rear Admiral Cleon Vlahos admired the wonderful view from atop Kastela Headquarters on the outskirts of New Athens, the city spread before him in the bowl-like valley, the ring of mountains on one side soaring into the clouds, the seas on the other like blue blankets of water.

The splat against the glasma didn't alarm him, the window triple-paned and impervious. The smear on the other side looked odd, like some gigantic gastropod without a shell. It burrowed a hole through the first pane, and then began to work on the second.

Disbelief and revulsion held Vlahos entranced. His mind tried to apprehend what chemical synthesis might be required to tunnel through the impervious glasma.

The slug burrowed through the second pane and spread itself onto the third.

Should I be alarmed? Vlahos wondered.

The innermost pane of glasma melted quickly. A tentacle leapt to his throat and yanked his head into the glasma, splattering his brains across the lovely view.

Chapter 13

"Huh? You took a tissue sample?!" Lydia didn't know whether to be honored or alarmed. "Forgive me, but what possible importance does my genetic profile have? What's going on here, Mela?"

The other woman looked at her from across the table. In her gaze was a terrifying concern. She had just told Lydia she'd received the dossier on Icarus Terzi.

Lydia continued when the only response she got was silence. "First, you tell me I look like the Emperor's nephew, once removed, and now, you want to compare my genes with his? What in Hades is going on?"

"Don't get upset, Lydia. I realize how difficult this must be for you. Detained by Imperial Infection Control, kidnapped by a faction among your own people, arrested by the Imperial Bureau of Suspicion. And now all this."

Lydia snorted. "Upset? Why should I be upset? Not a single Homo sapiens has exhibited a whit of interest in me for the last twenty-four years. The moment Empress Hecuba gets crowned, they're all coming after me with fishing nets. The next thing you know, the Imperial Secret Service will try to kill me. Why should I be upset?" She heard her own voice echoing back at her from the galley walls, and she realized how loud she'd gotten. "I'm sorry, Mela." She took a deep breath and sighed, looking down at the empty bowl in front of her.

"All true," Melanctha replied.

"When I got back to Paramecia, my father showed me the A-warp casing from the shipwreck twenty-four years ago. Traces of a thermonuclear microfusion event were found in its lining." Lydia watched the Colonel's face as the information worked its way to its logical conclusion.

The color drained from Colonel Remes' face. "Your mother's ship was sabotaged." She stared at the wall behind Lydia.

"And did you see those obituaries the day after Empress Hecuba's coronation?"

"Obituaries?"

"Of Drucilla Kanelos, Eugenia Ioannou, and Filmena Sotiropoulos?" Lydia had happened to see a name from among the list of people on Gaea whom Svkszvhgfh Ezhrozprh had interviewed. The time of death had coincided with Hecuba's coronation. Alarmed, Lydia had searched the holonet for the other names. "All of them died when Hecuba was crowned. Ezra spoke with them in the days leading up to the coronation."

"Must be a coincidence, Lydia."

"Do you even know who they were?" Lydia recited their positions. "The Laundry Maid to the Dowager Empress, the Governess to the first-born child of Emperor Zenon, and my Governess when I was an infant. You tell me, Mela, how do all three die on the same day at the same time that the second-born child is crowned Empress?"

Colonel Melanctha Remes was shaking her head.

"I don't know, either, Colonel," Lydia said quietly. "But it certainly isn't a coincidence."

"Let me contact my superior, Cleon. He's the Bureau Director. He'll have some ideas."

Lydia watched Colonel Remes' jaw work, the mouth moving as the woman subvocalized on her trake. She'd considered getting similar hardware when she'd found out at twenty years old that ninety-eight percent of Homo sapiens had such electronics installed between the ages of eight and ten. Somehow, she'd never gotten around to it. Only the aristocracy eschewed such implants.

"What do you mean, he isn't available? He just sent me an h-mail!"

Lydia didn't like the sound of that. She put her hands on either side of her chair as if to steady herself. Fixed in place to the floor, it offered insubstantial comfort.

Remes stood as if to head to the cockpit. "Well, damn it, then, check on him!"

She probably doesn't realize she's verbalizing, Lydia thought.

The ship lurched and howled, Remes careening into a wall, the empty bowl with her. Lydia clung to her chair, the momentum threatening to hurl her too.

Tractor beam! Lydia thought. Klaxons blaring, the ship slewed the other way, steel complaining, her bowl bouncing back the other way, the unconscious Remes slamming into that wall. Then the motion ceased.

All the loudspeakers blared, "Micro-cargo vessel, this is the Department of Infection Control, prepare to be boarded."

This isn't a coincidence either, she thought, her heart pounding heavily, panic threatening to overwhelm her. Lydia didn't hesitate. Remes was insensate and bleeding from a head wound. Lydia grabbed Melanctha by the waist and hauled her into the corridor, the gravity at a half-G helping. She carried the unconscious woman into the cargo hold to the entrance of her amoeba-class vessel.

A heavy thunk struck the micro-cargo vessel amidships.

Boarding party, Lydia thought. The amoeba's boarding ramp seemed to take hours to extend itself.

"Power up," she called to the ship as she hauled Melanctha aboard. The boarding ramp retracted behind her, the amoeba coming alive under her. Lydia secured Melanctha in a sleeping net.

"Direct sub-ether jump!" Lydia dived for her chair, the holo display coming to life. She buckled her restraints.

Fists pounded on the amoeba hull. The display showed three figures in full envirosuits outside.

"Destination, please?"

"Anywhere!"

One of the three drew a weapon and aimed it.

"Jumping," the ship replied. And the vessel shifted, leaving Lydia with that slight twinge of nausea she always got.

The display changed, stars wheeling around the ship in scintillating profusion.

"Where are we?" Lydia didn't recognize the configuration of stars, their brilliance causing her to squint. Why are there so many?

"Two parsecs from the Galactic core," the amoeba said, "three parsecs from Gaea."

Too close to the capital. "Jump to Istra Six," she said immediately, the first place she could think of.

"Jumping," the amoeba said. Again, that nausea, and the stars around the ship changed.

A planet three-fourths covered in jungle appeared below the amoeba. Istra VI sat half-way out the Scutum-Centaurus arm on a side spur, a politically unimportant system whose primary attractions were its lush jungles and fabulous beaches. She and Xsirhglksvi had gone there once, and she'd had a wonderful time, Xsirh not so much, the climate wet enough but far too hot for him.

"Orbit, please." She struggled out of her restraints.

Colonel Remes was barely conscious as Lydia checked her wounds. The bleeding had stopped on its own. Globules floated around the cabin and coagulated on multiple surfaces.

"Where are we?" she said groggily.

Lydia told her. "They hit us with a tractor beam and boarded."

"I know you're not an engineer, but any idea how they did that while we were in A-warp?"

She shook her head. "We need to get you examined. You hit the wall pretty hard both times."

"Both times? I barely remember the first." The other woman smiled at her weakly. "You're pretty resourceful. You saved our lives, you know."

Lydia shrugged. "I did what I could."

"Thank you." Melanctha tried to struggle free from the sleeping net. "Here, help me out of this thing. Look, uh, we can't go planet side. We'll be ID'd instantly."

She's right, Lydia told herself, helping Melanctha into the cockpit. Lydia sat the other woman in her chair and wiggled her behind awkwardly into Xsirh's cup-chair. "We need to get you medical attention. What do you suggest?"

"I know a few shady characters on Amphitrite Three who might be able to help. At the Bureau of Suspicion, we get to know a lot of the local pondscum."

"Jump to Amphitrite Three," Lydia ordered. Pondscum was one of her favorite dishes, repulsive to the eye but delectable to the palate.

"Jumping," the amoeba replied, and she felt that twinge of nausea.

A blue-white ball materialized on the holoscreen. A cold, forbidding planet, nearly all the infrastructure underground, Amphitrite III seemed to Lydia the perfect place to go underground for a few days. "How do we avoid being ID'd here?"

"I'll take care of that," Melanctha said.

"Sub-ether holomail received," the amoeba said.

Lydia and Melanctha exchanged a glance. "Who do you suppose—?"

"Identify source," Lydia said. Who would be contacting us? she wondered.

"Holonet trace indicates the origin as Lucina Nine, and sender identified as Lieutenant-Colonel Urian Nikitas."

Again, Lydia exchanged a glance with Melanctha. She wondered how he'd acquired her holomail address.

"Let's see what Urian has to say."

The Lieutenant-Colonel's face protruded from the holo. "Colonel Remes, are you all right? A-warp disruptions were detected along your flight path. It appears that the Department of Infection Control has seized your ship. To search for infectious pathogens, I suppose. I've lodged a complaint against them. Ridiculous for them to be suspicious of the Bureau of Suspicion. I'm h-mailing you just to make sure you're all right. Why are you personally taking the prisoner to Gaea in the first place? Let me know what your disposition is, Colonel." The face collapsed.

"They weren't searching for infectious pathogens, were they?" Lydia asked.

"I'm afraid they weren't," Melanctha said. "Can you get a visual on the micro-cargo vessel?"

"Not from this distance," she told the Colonel. "We'd have to be within a parsec. Are you going to reply?"

"You don't have any special equipment aboard to prevent its being traced, do you?"

Lydia shook her head. "They tell me that Kzizn vessels are difficult to trace because of their hulls and sub-ether drives, but the holomail that this ship uses is Gaean technology, not Kzizn."

"Then perhaps I'd better not reply. It's odd. I've worked beside Urian for six years now, but I can't really say I know him."

492

"I'd say we've got bigger problems than that. Why do you suppose Director Vlahos wasn't available?"

"I don't know. Suspicious, how he sent that dossier, and minutes later couldn't be raised."

"Do you have access to other dossiers?"

Melanctha looked at her.

"The two governesses and the Laundry Maid."

"Not easy to obtain without someone at headquarters to get them for me," Melanctha replied.

"Gl szwvh drgs rg zoo!" Lydia cursed in Kziznvxrz, and then switched back to Galactim. "We need more information, Mela."

Melanctha turned to look at her. "Such as what's really going on on Gaea."

* * *

Licensed Behavioral Technician Baptiste Tomaras knew he was hip-deep in human waste.

Ever since that Kzizn had commandeered his pneumatube capsule, Baptiste had felt he'd been thrust into some really bad spy movie, spooks following his every move, the feel of eyes on his back like an ice pick between the vertebrae, blasma rifle sights queuing up his head for the next shot.

And what does the Kzizn do after I get him a tissue sample from Princess Cybill Zenon? Baptiste asked himself rhetorically. Goes and gets splattered by the Dowager Empress herself!

If Baptiste hadn't felt paranoid before that, the sight of liquefied alien flesh spewing in a green cloud of spray on holovid was certainly enough to cause him to void all over himself.

Hip-deep in his own waste.

Baptiste hustled from the pneumatube station toward the palace. Going to work each day was a task now so onerous he could barely face it.

He joined the long line of palace employees getting their daily biodetector scan. The pathogen check had detected the empty vial, but he'd justified his having it on some pretext. Now, three days after the Empress's coronation and that idiot Kzizn's sacrificing himself, Baptiste

493

shuffled forward, sweating profusely, his heart pounding in his ears like a bass drum.

"Hey, you all right, Bap?"

Oh, no, his coworker, Talitha. He'd been trying to avoid her. She was far too perceptive. It didn't help that he'd fallen instantly in love with her their first day on the job two years ago.

"You're not all right, are you?"

Consumed with guilt, afraid he'd be shot dead any moment, terrified his name and face would be plastered across the galactic tabloids, certain he'd be cited in the Encyclopedia Galactica as a traitor. "I'm fine," he said. His quavering voice betrayed that he wasn't. "Of course, I'm fine." A little better, a little more convincing.

"Then why are you sweating? A touch of fever, Bap?"

He nodded mutely. He wished Talitha wouldn't call him that. It's what Princess Cybill called him. It's all she could remember.

The line ahead was getting shorter, the biodetector an arc that glowed green as people passed through it. The guards on either side looked terribly bored. They seemed to focus as he and Talitha approached.

They asked the usual questions, got the usual responses.

"He ok? Looks ill," one guard said to Talitha.

"Touch of fever, I think."

The biodetector arch glowed green, and he was through, Talitha right behind him.

She walked the long path to the palace beside him in silence, the immaculately manicured grounds on either side like some fairyland paradise, preserved in perfect symmetry.

Baptiste saw none of it, the cold nipping at his cheeks.

The employee entrance looked as if it might have once served lesser dignitaries. A huge portico crowned a colonnaded entrance, the flaking gold leaf paint on the handrails the only indication it wasn't public anymore.

"Come with me," she said the moment they entered the building. Instead of heading toward Princess Cybill's wing, she hauled him toward the break room.

She wrestled him into a chair and got him a cup of coffee. "You've been acting like a ghost for a week, Bap. Something to do with the coronation?"

He realized he'd been on edge since Ezra had asked him to obtain the tissue sample. At the time, it'd seemed like the right thing to do, given the circumstances. What the alien had told him was deeply disturbing. And getting a sample of Cybill's tissue for analysis had seemed not only prudent, but deeply patriotic.

The morning of the coronation, he'd delivered the sample to Ezra.

The alien, whose name was impossible to pronounce and even more difficult to spell, had thanked Baptiste. "You will know a deep satisfaction when the lie is exposed."

"What are you going to do with it now?" he'd asked the green, pulsating blob of alien flesh.

"Genetic analysis," Ezra had said, his real voice burbling under the translator's soft contralto. "Try to prove that she's unrelated to Emperor Zenon."

And within hours, live on galactic holo, Ezra had been reduced to a bubbling pool of protoplasm. Baptiste had no idea whether Ezra had had the opportunity to do the analysis.

"Bap, you've got to tell me what's going on."

He looked up at Talitha, so beautiful, so vulnerable, so naïve. "You're being very kind, and I'm grateful, but it's better if you don't get involved. The fewer who know, the better."

She just stared at him, a soft smile on her face, the silent question in her eyes.

Baptiste knew he couldn't resist her entreaties. When she looked at him that way, he couldn't have denied her if she'd asked him to scrub a toilet with his own toothbrush. "Why don't I tell you after work, over dinner?"

"My place," she said instantly. "I'll fix."

He met her gaze and nearly wept in relief. The burden of knowing what he knew, of doing what he'd done, had somehow become lighter. "I'd like that."

On their way to Princess Cybill's wing, he looked over at her. "Thank you."

"You're welcome." She met his gaze and giggled.

And for the first day since he'd obtained the tissue sample from Princess Cybill, Baptiste felt as though he were really present with his charge, doing his job with all the mindfulness that a Licensed Behavioral Technician should have.

Chapter 14

"Incoming holomail," the amoeba said.

Her head pounding, Colonel Melanctha Remes threw a grin at Lydia. "That'll be my contact." She'd sent a holomail to the top bottom-feeder she knew on Amphitrite III and had secured the amoeba a landing berth at an off-grid spaceport near the South Pole. Geologic analysis indicated Amphitrite III was deep in a quaternary glaciation, its fossil record revealing rich and varied fauna and flora extant during previous interglacial periods.

Nearly all underground, the planetary infrastructure seemed ripe for the kind of illicit traffic the Bureau was empowered to interdict: Exotic substances with psychogenic properties, illegal weapons of poor manufacture, enslaved hordes of humans, and businesses catering to licentious libidinality, catering to every whim, no matter how depraved. Every conceivable form of power, pain, and pleasure might be had on Amphitrite III, all of it obscured under thick ice sheets, if not bed sheets.

Melanctha glanced at Lydia for permission to activate the message. The amoeba was a strange ship, all smooth surfaces inside, not an angle to be found. She supposed if she were a soft-skinned inverte-brate, she'd have designed her vessels similarly.

"On-screen," she said. Despite her pounding head and possible concussion, Melanctha was relatively confident they'd be able to get the care she needed. Even criminals need medical care, she told herself, especially cosmetic surgery.

A face materialized, obscured by a fedora. Melanctha realized how ridiculous she must have looked to Agent Doukas back on Lucina IX.

"The boss doesn't like you Imperialists hanging around, so you can't stay long, all right?" The fedora and the face underneath it collapsed.

Imperialist was the name given Bureau agents by the underworld— anyone remotely connected to Imperial authority.

Embedded in the message were the coordinates of the spaceport entrance, which likely consisted of a gigantic hole in the side of a glacier. Such entrances could be quickly constructed and quickly destroyed, making them ideal for smugglers.

"Plot course for coordinates," Lydia said to the ship. "You sure about these people, Mela?"

"Of course not," Melanctha admitted. "They're a slimy bunch of slugs. But at least we'll have the chance to recoup and recover."

She thought about Icarus and what he'd meant to her. They'd fallen in love, the two pre-teens, to the degree two pre-teens could fall in love, a latency-age infatuation. Many of their games on the grounds of the Terzi Estate had consisted of how to outwit the boy's Governor.

"Listen, Lydia," she said, "about Count Icarus Terzi."

The young woman looked over when she didn't continue.

On the holo, licks of bright red at the edges accompanied a slight rumbling. The deceleration pressed Melanctha into her seat. Her headache grew sharply worse.

"Entry," Lydia said, her face looking drawn.

The atmosphere of Amphitrite III was low in carbon dioxide, the surface below them so bright it was difficult to look at.

"The reason he and I were playmates as kids, that I spent long hours at his family's estate on the outskirts of New Athens," she said, turning to look at Lydia, "was that my father and his mother were having an affair. I was ten years old and infatuated with him, and in my child-like mind, my father took me there under the guise of cementing my marriage to the future Count. Years later, I realized otherwise. Anyway, Countess Terzi ended up pregnant, and her son, the current Count Ioan Terzi, is my half-brother."

"Ioan," Lydia repeated, as if fixing it in her memory.

The amoeba's shuddering ceased as their speed dropped, and the young woman took the controls, a flashing cross-hairs on the holo indicating their destination.

"You're telling me this because you think Count Terzi will help me?"

Melanctha nodded. "Ioan never knew his older brother, and the scandal around his mother's affair with my father was widespread enough that everyone knew he wasn't Count Ilias' son, and therefore—"

"Not a threat to the succession."

She looked over at Lydia. "You're sharp. Yes, an illicit child. But Count Ilias refused to disown him, perhaps out of grief for his own son, who died so tragically."

"He'll be younger than me, won't he?"

"He's twenty-three now," Melanctha replied, watching the craggy, ice-locked landscape below. "A year younger than Empress Hecuba."

Amphitrite III was the kind of world few people dreamed of colonizing, especially at the poles. The equatorial regions weren't much warmer, the small oceans unfreezing for just a single month during the equator's two summers, only a narrow band of earth directly below the sun experiencing a thaw. Nearly all the planet's surface water was locked up in ice, the oceans briny and inhospitable except to the hardiest of aquatic species. Nearly all agriculture on the planet was hydroponic. The little arable land was difficult to till and couldn't be farmed with Terran crops due to the foreshortened growing season. A few indigenous specimens with rapid gestation cycles were farmed, but produced too little food to sustain the populace.

The spaceport entrance, she saw, was a hole at the base of a glacier. As the ship dropped in elevation and the landscape revealed its features, Melanctha watched in awe.

Miles-tall mountains of ice sawed at the sky with jagged teeth. Many of them glowed a deep blue with trapped air, a sign of rapid freezing. Sheer escarpments jutted from mountainsides, their edges wicked, as though slashing at the passing ship.

"Not a place I'd come for vacation," Lydia said.

Melanctha felt cold just looking at the landscape.

In a cleft between two mountains, where a snow-filled crevasse hid activity from all but the most prying of eyes, was the spaceport entrance. At first it looked to be an overhang, the massive slab of ice above it looking ready to smash to smithereens anything under it, but the area underneath kept reaching farther and farther back under the mountain.

The amoeba was soon enveloped in darkness, the overhang having long since become a cave.

Lydia was poised above the controls and looked ready to punch in an evasion course.

"Can you get us out of here if this cave collapses?"

"I can try," she replied.

Melanctha prayed she could. She'd been to the planet once before, and its ever changing glacial landscape at the equator—floods, storms, avalanches—had frightened her.

The cave became a tunnel, rock replacing ice all around them, its scale large enough to contain whole cities. Structures began to appear in the cave sides, and the floor below them began to sprout buildings, vehicles darting between them like ants.

"You could fly an armada out of this place."

Melanctha nodded, seeing a clearing ahead, the crosshairs on the holoscreen indicating the area as their destination. On the tarmac was a variety of vessels. All of them looked like private vehicles, and she didn't see one among them that looked to be from a law-enforcement agency.

Did I expect them to meet us here? she wondered.

As she thought about it, the possibility seemed very real indeed.

* * *

Lydia stepped through the biodetector at the hospital entrance. The arch above her glowed green, indicating she was clean of pathogens.

"I'm Chelsais Bouras, but you can call me Steve," the man said.

Lydia shook his hand, his grip firm and confident. "I'm Lydia, Steve. Pleased." She wasn't pleased at all. He struck her as a thew-bound thug with beefy shoulders.

The man turned to Melanctha, who'd also just stepped through the biodetector. "Boss wants to see you once you're done here." He glanced at her wound.

"Of course, Steve," the Colonel said.

"How'd that happen?"

"Ship got hit with a tractor beam while I was in the galley."

His eyes searched hers.

Lydia could see the conclusions he reached with just that little amount of information. She'd heard his name before when she and Xsirh had visited the region two years ago. They'd been warned to steer clear of him and his organization.

They stood at the emergency room nursing station just a few miles from the spaceport, where she and Melanctha had been immediately escorted. Steve had walked in moments later and then had sidled up to the counter to the front of the line.

Steve turned to the nurse behind the counter. "Nurse Wretched, get my friend here some medical attention, would you?"

"The name's Riga," the nurse said, "and she'll have to wait her turn, like everyone else."

His fist slammed the counter and he pointed to himself. "The name's Bouras. Get her some attention, or your name will be wretched."

Nurse Riga's eyes widened, and she hesitated.

"Please," Steve added, spreading his hands in apology.

They were soon in an examination room, a doctor asking rapid-fire questions, Steve listening placidly from the door, his gaze on the corridor.

Lydia imagined he was constantly vigilant.

"Let's get that imaged," the doctor said. "She was unconscious how long?"

Lydia shrugged. "A few minutes, maybe, not more than ten."

"And the wound occurred the first time she struck the wall, or the second?"

"First time, if I recall correctly."

"Is that a rash?" the doctor asked.

"Huh?"

"Those spots on your arm, is that a rash?"

"Oh, that? I don't know," Lydia said. "It's been itching off and on since I left home."

The doctor brought a machine down from the ceiling. "If I could ask you to step over there near the door, Ms—?"

"Procopio," Lydia said, complying and moving toward the door.

Steve glanced at her and returned his gaze to the corridor. "Where were you going?"

She didn't know how much to tell him, but given his activities, she suspected that the less he knew, the better. "A little excursion to the Maldives," she said. En route to Gaea, the Maldives had been in the direction they'd been headed.

"Sleek little rig you got. I ain't seen its like before. Who's the manufacturer?"

Difficult to hide where it's from if someone really wants to know, she thought. "Outer Scutum-Centaurus arm, near Theogony." She watched the doctor tend to Melanctha, not looking at Steve. For a human male, he hadn't given her much attention. She was accustomed to drawing numerous prolonged stares, particularly from the males.

The sexual dimorphism among Homo sapiens was a curiosity to her. Reared among the Kziznvxrz, Lydia had found the preening of her female peers and male paramours annoying. They seemed to be constantly posturing toward each other, as if continuously fertile. The monomorphic Kzizn transformed themselves as needed and found the posturing superfluous, even risible.

She felt Steve's glances, which were fewer and shorter than the stares she usually got.

"You're good," Steve said. "I don't blame you for being cautious. The bloodsuckers around here will drain you dry the moment you drop your guard."

"You included?"

"Me included."

She was startled by the honesty of his response.

"You come back and see me, next time you're in the area. I like you."

Not much chance of that, Lydia thought.

* * *

The hover ride took them up the side of the gargantuan tunnel. From inside the amoeba, it hadn't looked daunting, but walking in open air below the jagged crystalline roof of stone and ice gave Lydia the constant feeling of impending doom, as though it were about to collapse.

Riding up the slope in a hover helped somewhat, but not much.

"What holds up the ceiling?" she'd asked Steve immediately after they'd left the hospital.

"Antigrav units," he'd said, paying more attention to her now, while driving, than he had before.

"Hey, watch out!" Melanctha said from the back seat.

Steve swerved to avoid another hover, bleating the horn and shaking a meaty fist out the window. The air coming in was frightfully cold, but he didn't seem to feel it.

What have we gotten ourselves into? Lydia wondered.

"We just need a place to lay low for a few days," Melanctha was telling him.

"You're in the right place," Steve reassured her, grinning madly at Lydia, paying no attention to Melanctha, as if she hadn't spoken.

She didn't feel reassured and kept herself from glancing back at Melanctha. There was something in Steve's manner that left Lydia feeling … sticky. As if she'd just waded through a hip-deep pool of mud. Kziznvxrz didn't have criminals, and although Lydia had heard about them among human populations, she'd never knowingly inter-acted with one. Until now.

The experience wasn't exactly pleasant.

His intimidating the nurse at the hospital hadn't endeared him to her. And his brusque and truculent manner with nearly everyone else was at odds with how he treated them.

Lydia could make a pretty good guess which one was the true Steve.

The hover climbed steadily, the road narrowing and the drop-off getting increasingly steep.

"Where you goin' after this?"

The extent of his speech seemed to be two-syllable words and five-word questions. Lydia wondered if multiplying them gave his approximate IQ. Feeling naïve, she let Melanctha answer the ill-disguised probes for information. A brilliant conversationalist, Steve was not.

"Here we are." The hover pulled up under an escarpment that jutted out from the tunnel wall nearly a hundred feet. "The boss would like to see you before you get settled."

Another vehicle pulled in behind them as they got out. Lydia hadn't realized they'd been followed. She saw the overhang was encircled by guards spaced every thirty feet. Lydia suddenly felt trapped. Melanctha didn't look capable of an escape attempt, not with a new bandage on her head.

"The boss just wants to talk," Steve said, grinning and gesturing to a door.

Columns framed a corridor leading up to the door, and Lydia glimpsed one last slice of the far cavern wall as she and Melanctha were herded inside.

She was startled by the flooring. The soft, cushioned layer of deep burgundy fabric on the floor silenced their progress. She thought she was walking on a cloud. Steve led the way through corridors decorated with statuary and portraiture. Holo-flame sconces lit their way, their joyous flames even giving off wisps of holo-smoke.

They turned a corner and approached a set of double doors. On either side of them stood a large man in a bulky suit. At Steve's nod, they opened the doors outward.

In a sun-drenched courtyard, a man in a white three-piece suit enjoyed a mai-tai at pool-side, fanning himself.

The near-tropical warmth hit Lydia as she stepped into the room, the smells reminiscent of her vacation to the jungle-shrouded world of Istra VI, the scents of palm and coconut battling a thick, salt-brine breeze.

But how … and then she realized that it was all artificial, that the environment had been manufactured. Tropical climates simply didn't exist on Amphitrite III.

Steve led them toward the pool. "Father," he said, "this is Melanctha Remes and Lydia Procopio."

The man in the white suit turned his head slowly to look at them. First at Melanctha for thirty continuous seconds, and then at Lydia for a full minute.

She began to feel uncomfortable under his scrutiny, and offered a tentative smile.

"You may call me Dmitri," he said finally, his voice a half-whisper.

"Pleased to meet you, Dmitri," Melanctha said. "Thank you for your assistance today."

"Don't be a γουρούνι, Son, and get them chairs." He looked at Lydia. "Forgive him, he hasn't learned manners yet."

Steve got them chairs, and Lydia thanked him as she took hers. She hadn't caught the word his father had used but it'd sounded derogatory. Steve didn't look the slightest bit nonplussed by the interaction.

"May I get you something to drink?" he asked.

"Thank you, yes. Some water, please."

"We have a variety of beverages from all points of the galaxy, Ms. Procopio," Dmitri said. "Are you sure you won't try something a bit more exotic?"

"No, thank you, Dmitri. Water is sufficient." She'd found their alcohol-infused concoctions quite overwhelming.

"A martian on the rocks, stirred, not shaken," Melanctha told Steve.

"Aristocratic names you both have," Dmitri said the moment Steve was gone. He looked around his pool and leaned his head back for a moment.

The walls were painted to look like a beach somewhere near New Athens, where the winds might be hot siroccos off the Meditian Sea. As a child, Lydia had found a still of one such beach on Gaea and had projected it on all four walls of her room.

"Not often that members of the nobility seek sanctuary among their less-fortunate cousins." He turned his head slowly their direction, his gaze alighting on Lydia. "You're the Viscountess Ambassador's daughter."

She nodded. "Reared by the Kzizn when my mother's people wouldn't accept me back."

His gaze shifted to Melanctha. "Your father was acquainted with Count and Countess Terzi."

"He was," Melanctha replied.

Steve returned with their beverages and then retreated.

Dmitri sipped slowly off his drink, a dark brown liquid so turbid it looked as if it absorbed light. He set down the glass and adjusted his cuff. Then he returned his gaze to Melanctha, his eyes on the bandage. "The doctor seems to think you'll live."

"I think I will," she replied, a smile touching her face.

Dmitri's gaze grew unfocused. "It is fate that brought you here. Princess Hecuba tours her domains, our new sovereign deigning to show the people the trappings of her majestic person." His gaze bore into Lydia. "Trappings it is said that belong to another."

"We know the true power behind the throne," Melanctha ventured. "She who threatened the Chief Justice."

"True power, Colonel, or false power? The power of the pretender. Yes, mighty power, but illegitimate. It is sad that the first child of Emperor Athanasios is so … incapacitated, no? The power of a pretender cannot hold fast against the truth. But for fate, you yourself might have been an Empress, married to the Emperor Terzi. Is this not a fact, Colonel?"

Melanctha's gaze dropped to the tile. "Yes, Dmitri, I might have."

"And yet you're here with an orphan on a planet known for its ties to the guerilla economy, to put it delicately. How strange fate is."

Lydia looked between the two, sensing more than what was being said. Clearly, Dmitri knew far more about the inner workings of the Empire than his tenuous position on its periphery should allow.

"I have a friend on Gaea you should see," he said, looking at Lydia, "if you ever find yourself there. My enturm, Chiron Likashose, a counselor who sees after my affairs on the capital, is to be trusted in any circumstance."

"Thank you, that's very kind," Lydia said, bewildered that this man, this criminal, would extend such generosity.

"You're welcome, Ms. Procopio. I would be delighted if the both of you could join me for dinner this evening. Between now and then, I imagine you'd like to freshen up." Dmitri looked over toward his son. "You may show them the guest wing, my son."

505

Chapter 15

"Mela, Why do I get the impression that all he wanted was to tell us about this counselor on Gaea?"

"He has a cunning to him, that's for certain," Melanctha replied, admiring herself in a mirror.

"He's pretty resourceful too," Lydia said, looking at herself beside the other woman.

Their suite of three rooms was palatial. One common room contained a kitchen-dining area and a lounging area, floor-to-ceiling glasma on one end overlooking the gargantuan tunnel. On either side of the common room were bed-bath units, the accommodations commodious enough for a princess.

After changing Melanctha's bandages, Lydia had retreated to her unit and availed herself to the cleansall. Her meager wardrobe consisted of a clean pair of formalls. Frowning, she looked in the closet and found an evening dress scandalous for its scantiness, and in her exact size. In the jewelry case on the vanity was a necklace, earrings, and bracelet, the diamonds shining with the blue-white brilliance of glaciers, all matching. Melanctha had found similar couture in her room.

They both looked stunning.

"We're going to leave them gasping," the Colonel said, turning from her reflection.

Lydia smiled, feeling beautiful and wondering how Dmitri had managed to make such arrangements in so little time.

There was a knock on the door, and Melanctha went to answer. "Time already?" she asked. "We'll be along in a moment."

The plush corridors obscured the sound of their passage even from them. The high heels were somewhat awkward for Lydia, and she was afraid the stiletto points would puncture the floor. "I hope I don't have to run from anything," she said.

Melanctha threw a grin over her shoulder. Her stern, sharp face seemed softened somehow by the diaphanous dress hanging tentatively from her shoulders. "Maybe from Steve. But your heels are lethal, if you know how to use them."

My lessons in self-defense might be helpful, she thought.

They entered the dining area, where a long table of the finest Zortaxian pine split the room, whorls of blond and tan spinning through the tortured wood.

Steve greeted Melanctha first, and then looked at Lydia. His eyes bulged from their sockets, and his complection flushed. "M-M-Ms. Procopio," he managed from around a tongue twisted from titillation. He seemed rooted to the floor, his eyes fixed to her bosom.

Melanctha sniggered.

"Mr. Bouras," Lydia replied, giving him a slight curtsy, wishing now she'd just worn formalls.

"Ah, you're here!" Dmitri said, entering with a flourish. "Lovely, the both of you. I do hope I wasn't presumptuous in my choice of dress for you. Ms. Remes, you look positively statuesque. And Ms. Procopio, oh my!" He put the back of his hand to his forehead and feigned a swoon.

Once they were seated at the far end of the table, Melanctha across from Dmitri and Lydia across from Steve, the glasma window looking out onto the glittering tunnel just feet away, Lydia began to relax. Anything that put distance between her and the clearly-enamored younger man across from her was a comfort.

He looked besotted, flush creeping up his neck to his jaw. His father was focused almost exclusively on Melanctha, his admiration plain, but at least he kept his eyes on her face. Steve couldn't seem to get his eyes off Lydia's bust. Melanctha, oddly, seemed to be drinking in

Dmitri's attentions like a parched traveler alone and forsaken in the desert.

Ubiquitous but unobtrusive servants served them dinner.

Lydia could see how the other woman's evening was going to end, but she wasn't interested in her evening ending in a similar fashion with the brute across from her. She wondered as she dined how she was going to engineer a graceful exit.

A blob of protoplasm smacked the glasma. It looked like a giant slug, its footprint against the glasma nearly six inches across.

"What is that disgusting thing?" Dmitri asked. "Apologies, my darling Melanctha, while I dispense with this nuisance."

Lydia knew exactly what it was: A didinium, a deep-sea predator, scourge of the Kziznvxrfn, their roasted flesh considered a delicacy. Their digestive acids ate through nearly everything. This one looked to be of similar size and ferocity as the one she'd killed upon returning home. Was that just three days ago? Lydia wondered, amazed so little time had passed.

Dmitri returned to the room. "An attendant is taking care of the pest."

"They're pretty voracious," Lydia said. "How many panes of glasma are there?"

The didinium convulsed and surged through the outer pane, spreading itself across the next layer.

"Uh, three," Steve said, his eyes now bulging for a different reason. "You know what it is?"

The attendant stepped out onto the balcony from another door, a scraper in hand.

She didn't know they lived on planets as cold as this one. She'd always thought they thrived only on semi-tropical worlds. It occurred to her that the staff might not know how to handle a didinium. "Mr. Bouras, does your attendant know what to do?"

The slug slung a tendril at the approaching attendant, wrapped his neck, and hurled him off the balcony. A distant scream faded from earshot.

"Apparently not," Dmitri said, his eyes bulging too.

Again the slug convulsed, and squeezed itself onto the innermost pane.

"Oh my god, it's coming after us!"

Lydia rose and approached the glasma. She positioned her face right in front of the creature and readied herself.

"What are you doing?"

"Our spit is poisonous to them, but only if they ingest it. Their exoderm neutralizes it. So I have to spit into its intake orifice."

The slug convulsed itself through the glasma and slung a tendril at her. She caught it, pulled it aside and spat into the didinium's intake orifice. Her spittle hit its flesh, and the slug disintegrated with a sizzle, its protoplasm streaking down the glasma in brown, excrement-colored smears, smoke wafting upward both inside and outside the triple panes. The smell was noxious.

"What the Hades *was* that?"

"A didinium," she replied. "One of the most ferocious predators on Kziznvxrz. The Didinium and Paramecium fought for dominance for nearly a megaannus."

"A what?" Steve asked.

"Me-ga-an-nus," Lydia repeated, separating its syllables. "A million years."

"Oh, I thought you were calling me names."

She'd considered it. "But what's it doing here? This planet's climate can't possibly support a creature like that."

Dmitri threw a glance at the cavern beyond the glasma. "We've been infiltrated. Steve, double the guard and alert the perimeter to an intruder. The question is, who was it after?"

"One tried to get me on Kziznvxrz just three days ago," Lydia said.

"How dare they try to assassinate you in my home?!" Dmitri seemed more offended that it had occurred under his roof.

"That also means they know where you're at," Melanctha said. "Mr. Bouras, I'm afraid I can't put your household at further risk. My apologies for the inconvenience we've already caused and for the attendant's death. We'll leave immediately."

"But where will you go?" Steve asked, managing somehow to compose a five-word question.

"There's only one place we *can* go," Lydia said, hating the word as it came out of her mouth. "Gaea."

* * *

"This is syndicate spaceport control," the computerized contralto voice intoned. "There's a delay in your clearance for takeoff. Please wait."

Lydia and Melanctha exchanged a glance. They both wore their evening dresses. Necks had broken as Lydia strode swiftly through the spaceport, heads spinning in her direction, the haute couture better suited for a fashion runway than a spaceport runway. The high heels hadn't slowed them at all.

And now they wanted Lydia and Melanctha to delay their departure. The spaceport tower on the holoscreen brooded at them, the small, squat building staring back at them with darkened glasma panes, like some secret agent.

"Doesn't smell so good, does it?"

"Sure doesn't. And besides," Melanctha added, "what self-respecting thief pays attention to rules?"

Lydia's fingers danced across the controls, her fingers splayed over the Kziznvxrfn controls.

On screen, several vehicles spat from the terminal and headed their direction.

"Engage course!" she told the amoeba.

"Engaging course," it replied. "Vmtztrmt xlfihv," it repeated in Kzizn.

The ship shuddered and rose above the tarmac, and then swung up toward the tunnel ceiling. The ship lurched sharply, the screen flashing. "Hit taken to starboard!" the amoeba said, repeating it in Kzizn.

"Maintain course with evasion," Lydia told it. She glanced at Melanctha, strapped in her usual chair, Lydia buckled into Xsirh's egg-cup. "Hold on."

"Those fools'll bring the ceiling down!" she said, throwing a glance at Lydia, a sudden swerve throwing her to one side.

"Close up of tarmac!" Lydia said. A second swerve threw them the other direction.

The holoscreen zoomed in. Ten people in plain business suits stood in two even rows, their weapons aimed up at the ship. To one side stood their commander, her sidearm in hand at her waist.

"They look like IBS," Melanctha said.

Lydia was afraid of that. It meant they'd been traced, somehow. "Amplify sound," she told the ship.

"Hold your fire!" the commander was saying. "We found 'em once. We'll find 'em again."

"That's Lieutenant Christakos from Infection Control. Get us out of here, Lydia."

She programmed in a jump for the Thalassa Constellation. "If we jump from here, Mela, our sudden displacement will cause a sonic shock."

"Enough to bring the ceiling down?"

Lydia shook her head. "I don't know, but I don't think we should risk it. Not here, with all those people below us."

The amoeba's acceleration had taken them much farther along the immense tunnel, icy rock glittering above them. The way so far was clear as the syndicate settlement receded farther behind them.

"How do you think they found us?"

"Not sure," Melanctha said. "Not only found us, but infiltrated the base within hours."

Lydia turned to stare at the Colonel. "The didinium that came after me …"

The other woman returned her gaze. "What are you thinking?"

"The second in three days—first on Kzizn, and now here. There's a faction on Kziznvxrz whose tenets include the extermination of humankind and the takeover of the galaxy."

"The ones who kidnapped you from Theogony?"

Lydia nodded. "They live in the surf, at the edge of Kzizn society, much closer to the deep sea, where the didinium still survive. The didinium are endangered due to overfishing, but I wonder if it's possible …" She looked at Melanctha. "Does your species ever domesticate other species?"

"Well, yes. Many, as a matter of fact. Cats, dogs, horses—quite a few."

"I wonder whether the Wrwrmrfn have domesticated the didinium."

"Or perhaps breed them in captivity?"

"More likely, given how feral they are."

Ahead, the tunnel bent sharply to the right.

Beyond was a phalanx of starships, an entire squadron of undercover, patrol-class vessels armed to the teeth, blasma cannons mounted between their incisors.

"Amoeba, jump!"

A tractor beam hit them, and the ship slewed as it entered sub-ether. And the tunnel disappeared from around them.

Chapter 16

"Where are we?" Colonel Melanctha Remes looked over at her companion.

Lydia shook her head. "Coordinates, please."

"Navigation module damaged, galactic positioning unavailable." And then it repeated, "Mzertzgrlm nlwfov wznztvw, tzozxgrx klhrgrlmrmt fmzezrozyov."

Melanctha cringed, the awful-sounding language more nauseating than the maneuver they'd just executed. She had no idea how a tractor beam might affect sub-ether navigation, but she knew what one did to A-warp.

"Kzizn translation off," Lydia said.

"Paramecia translation off," the amoeba said. "Kziznvxrz gizmhozgrlm luu."

"Attempt to determine position visually," the young woman said, sighing. "We could be anywhere."

"Attempting," the ship said.

Melanctha glanced at her. "What now?"

Lydia met her gaze. "Now, we wait. If the ship can't figure out where we are, we try a jump to a known location. Risky, but it's one way to do it."

"Don't we have to know where we're at first before we can jump someplace?"

Lydia shook her head. "Not necessarily, since all locations in the galaxy are pre-determined. Sub-ether engines are calibrated to the galactic core, and all jumps are simply translations in space to a fixed distance and direction from that core, irrespective of origin."

"Instantaneous translations, too. A-warp is pretty primitive in comparison, isn't it?"

Lydia nodded. "Compressing space does seem somewhat elementary compared with translating across it."

Melanctha could see Lydia was trying not to smile. We must seem so backward to her, she thought. She tried to wrap her mind around the Paramecium lifestyle, living in near-complete harmony with their environment, experiencing none of the ills that plagued human society. No robbery, no wars, no prisons, no poverty, no slavery.

The worst abuse they ever inflicted on each other was ostracism, and from what Lydia had told her, it wasn't often imposed. Very rarely was someone banished to the open sea, as the Were-wormer contingent had been.

"Location visually determined," the amoeba said. A map appeared on the holoscreen, their position highlighted, nearby systems aglow. "Our coordinates are thirty-three-point-two-three-two degrees by eighty-seven-point-two-three parsecs, two-point-two parsecs above the galactic plane."

"Isn't that the Thalassa Constellation?" she asked.

"Not too far away from our destination," Lydia replied. "We must have escaped the brunt of the tractor beam."

"I wonder what our jump did to the cavern." She exchanged a glance with Lydia. "Why here?" Melanctha asked.

"I've an old friend on Eris Eleven, Economics Professor Zenais Demo. She helped me organize my business plan when my father and I started the shipping company. The Kzizn know virtually nothing about business. She can help me get in touch with Father."

Melanctha heard the strain in the younger woman's voice. "You miss him, don't you?"

Lydia blinked rapidly, nodding. "And I'm worried about him."

"You think the Were-wormer faction might try to hurt him?" She'd pronounced it the best she could.

"Either them, or the faction on Gaea that seems to be after me."

* * *

Professor Zenais Demo stepped off the shuttle and into the crowded transit station in the town of Irakleio, a backwater of no significance on Eris XI. She saw Lydia instantly, standing beside a taller, older woman whose ramrod posture and sharp, sere face bespoke a military discipline, a fact not obscured at all by the plain civilian formalls.

"Lydia, how are you?" she said effusively, giving the young woman a peck on each cheek. "You look wonderful. How's business?" She exchanged pleasantries with the other woman as Lydia introduced them.

Then Zenais leaned in close and spoke rapidly in Lydia's ear. "Now, I know you're not here for a social call. The proprietor of the Caged Bull Tavern six blocks away can insure we'll have privacy. Follow me but only at a distance." She stepped back and smiled broadly. "So nice to see you here. Call me soon, and we'll have lunch. So long!" She waved and walked off.

Zenais had instantly been alerted to Lydia's distress by the odd location she'd specified, a backwater town halfway around Eris XI from the university. Irakleio lacked any attraction whatsoever and didn't even have a spaceport, the nearest one in Kifissia, six hundred miles away.

A consultant on the side, Professor Demo had helped Lydia and her father, the only Kzizn she'd ever met, assemble a viable business plan for the trading firm they'd wanted to start. After the consultation, Zenais had looked into Lydia Procopio's past, placing a few delicate inquiries with colleagues at the University of New Athens.

The Procopio Family had been among the most prominent of the noble families until falling into disfavor for reasons no one could seem to fathom. Viscountess Basilissa Procopio was suddenly appointed Ambassador to Kziznvxrz, a post vacant for nearly ten years, its location utterly remote and its conditions onerous. Living on tidal mud flats under a cloudy gray sky on a lonely planet at the end of the Scutum-Centaurus galactic arm wasn't anyone's idea of paradise.

The Ambassador's ship had crashed on arrival, all passengers presumed deceased, the vessel lost under the vast seas of a nine-tenths water planet. Or thought to be deceased. How Lydia Procopio had turned up on Kziznvxrz twenty years later, alive, well, and thriving, was remarkable.

Professor Zenais Demo's delicate inquiries had stirred up a minor tempest on Gaea, and one of her colleagues had warned her that the information she was seeking was so sensitive that it was redolent of a fine Metaxa.

Zenais didn't need to have it spelled out any further.

At the pub, she greeted the proprietor and asked for the most private booth he had. "Meeting with friends from out-of-system," she said simply.

He showed her to a back room, where the heavy smoke of illicit substances clung to the walls like ghosts. Customers liked to mix their pleasures, legal and otherwise. The dimly-lit room heralded a long-past age on Earth, when men on massive beasts thrust lances at each other to win over maidens whose chastity exceeded their beauty.

Zenais didn't have to wait long, the other two women arriving within minutes. "Mythos all around," she told the proprietor.

"Oh, I'd love a Mythos," the taller, older woman said.

"Melanctha, right?" Zenais asked, wondering whether she'd remembered correctly.

"Indeed, but call me Mela."

"This Mythos, does it have any ethanol?" Lydia asked, sitting across from Zenais.

"You mean alcohol? Of course, it does."

The young woman demurred. "I'm afraid I can't, Professor. At the first sip, I melt to the floor in a puddle of protoplasm."

"I'll have hers," Melanctha said.

Zenais shrugged. "Something to do with where you grew up?"

"I think so. My tissues seem to absorb fluids more readily."

She talked pleasantries with them while they were being served. A large tankard of brew in front of her, Zenais turned her attention to Lydia. "After you and Xsirh consulted me on your start-up trading firm eight years ago, I looked into your past. Not something I usually do, but I was curious. My inquiries were met with silence, mostly, but a few of my colleagues at the University of New Athens knew your father, your human one. Xenobiology Professor Selene Toccim, in particular, was very helpful. I suggest you see her when you get to

516

Gaea." Then Zenais took a deep draught from her tankard. "Is that a rash?"

"Huh?"

"Those spots on your arm, is that a rash?"

"Oh, that? I don't know," Lydia said. "It's been itching off and on since I left Kziznvxrz. I've been inoculated."

"Anything come up during the screening?" Zenais knew they'd been screening for xenopathogens since the outbreaks on Pyrgos Five and Cygnus Twenty.

Lydia shook her head, frowning.

Zenais frowned back. "You're in trouble."

The young woman nearly burst into tears and began a tale that left Zenais amazed and gasping. At first, she just let the young woman talk, sensing her need to vent. As her speech grew a little less pressured and her story a little more coherent, Zenais inserted a question or two to help clarify the tale. "And these didinium are deep-sea creatures, you say. They can't live on worlds as cold as Amphitrite Three."

"Exactly. But we don't know who's planting them or why. It's easy to think they're after me, since it's happened twice now. Finding one in my home might have just been chance. Someone's trying to assassinate a syndicate boss wouldn't be unexpected, either."

"The method is rather insidious," Zenais said. "Gives me the shudders. Anyway, it's clear there's an effort to capture or kill you. How can I help you?"

"I don't have a way of contacting my father without giving away my location."

"I was wondering why you contacted me using a public holocom."

"And they found us on Amphitrite Three, so I think they tagged my ship with a galactic-locator."

"They fired on us as we were taking off from Amphitrite," Melanctha added. "Damaged the nav unit."

"So you need him to bring you a new vessel."

Lydia nodded. "I know I'm asking you to take a risk. Just meeting with us is risky, but I just don't know where else to go."

"Except to Gaea," Zenais said.

The young woman met her gaze. "But on my terms, and not as a captive."

* * *

"There've been some new developments," Xsirh told her. The machine beside him babbled in Galactim so Melanctha could understand him.

Lydia turned around in the pilot's chair. "New developments?"

He'd dropped in an archeota from orbit around Eris XI into an abandoned warehouse on the outskirts of Irakleio, where Lydia and Melanctha had been waiting, and had immediately launched. The ship had been outfitted with two human-style seats. Like her amoeba-class vessel, this archaeota was equipped with a sub-ether drive, capable of instantaneous transport. Further, it was smaller, sleeker, and far more nimble. They'd already executed several jumps to deter any followers.

They hovered in orbit over Kziznvxrz, Lydia now at the controls, ready to drop her father off at home before venturing to Gaea to confront the fate that awaited her.

"What new developments?"

Xsirh's optical organelles swiveled toward her, and his intake orifice turned downward at the edges. "Remember those tissue samples I kept in zero-kelvin cryo?" Xsirh asked.

Lydia felt the blood drain from her face, knowing where this conversation was going. "You did a genetic analysis."

The upper portion of Xsirh's physiognomy bobbed up and down. "Yes, Lydia, I did."

"And you compared my parents' genes with mine."

Again, Xsirh nodded.

"I'm not their daughter, am I?"

"No, child, I'm afraid you aren't."

Lydia had experienced difficulties in the past. The death of her parents, the wreck of their ship, the struggle to adapt to the alien environment and learn the alien language. The limitations of her physiology had caused her terrible trials in more than the environment and the language. She'd never really fit in with the other Kziznvxrfn, as much as she might have liked to. They were a gentle and loving people who rarely quarreled even amongst themselves, and those around her had extended themselves in a thousand ways to help her feel more comfortable.

But she'd never been one of them and never would be. And one tiny dream had helped Lydia to keep going when she felt she couldn't go on any longer, when her school subjects seemed overwhelming or her peers treated her condescendingly because her neurology prevented her from remembering the way they did and from learning at the pace they learned, when she had to wade awkwardly through miles of mud while her peers swam effortlessly and gracefully to their destinations within minutes, when she hadn't thoroughly cleansed residues of her eliminations from her hands and accidentally injured the Kzizn around her, her excretory enzymes catalyzing even the tough Kzizn exoderm. Whenever these events seemed nearly overwhelming, she'd always held to the thought of one day returning to Gaea to meet the members of the Procopio family, imagining their joy in finding out that she, Lydia Procopio, daughter of Viscountess Basilissa Procopio, had survived the shipwreck and was returning home triumphant.

The one tenuous thread connecting her with Gaea, the fragile link to her past and her heritage through her parents, her mother a Viscountess and Ambassador and her father a University Professor, was abruptly severed.

And in spite of having overcome extreme difficulty in losing her parents and in adapting to a terribly foreign environment, Lydia had never let any of it defeat her.

But this?

How was she supposed to cope with this?

The one saving grace, the one place where she knew she belonged, the family left behind on Gaea, who cared for her the way her mother had cared for her, in whose arms she might find the comfort and security that she'd once found in her mother's arms.

Gone.

* * *

Colonel Melanctha Remes looked over at Lydia.

After the young woman's tearful departure with her father, a scene that had evoked a few tears even from the thick-skinned Colonel, Lydia had collapsed into the co-pilot's chair and had turned the helm over to Melanctha.

"Just get us to Gaea," she'd said.

It'd been rather eerie to watch Xsirh embrace Lydia, his bright green protoplasm wrapping its folds nearly all the way around her, as if to swallow her whole.

After muddling through a few test jumps to insure she had a rudimentary understanding of the controls, Melanctha had taken them far afield, generating random jumps to baffle any pursuit.

And then she'd brought them to Pontus XIII, a financial services sanctuary, where anyone with a fortune could go to hide it, just a few systems over from Gaea.

Melanctha set the ship adrift in the Oort cloud and swiveled the pilot's chaise toward Lydia's. Then she reached over and turned the co-pilot's chaise toward her.

"What?" Lydia looked at her listlessly and then dropped her gaze back to her hands.

Melanctha stared at her, wondering what approach would work best. "Not good news, was it?"

A tear slid down Lydia's cheek.

"If you go to Gaea now, they'll dip you in hummus and have you for an appetizer."

Another tear, and then another.

Melanctha leaned forward and took Lydia's hands.

The young woman began to shake with soft sobs, her face a wreck.

The Colonel waited, wishing she could do something to ease the other's pain. There wasn't, and it infuriated her that they'd subjected this child to such a terrible fate, sending her to her death aboard a ship set to disintegrate as it entered its destination's atmosphere. All of which begged the question: Why?

And the other question nagging Melanctha, now that they knew Lydia wasn't the Ambassador's child at all.

Was that why no one on Gaea had come forward to claim the lone survivor of the Ambassador's shipwreck? Or had the entreaties simply been ignored?

Remes didn't know, the past mystery as bewildering as the current one.

"Sorry, Mela," Lydia said, wiping her face. "I guess I'm not handling this well."

"Nothing to be sorry about, Lydia. You've been served a plate of rotten scraps. Of course you're upset." She evaluated whether the young woman was ready and suspected she was. "The question is, if you're not Basilissa and Dorian Procopio's daughter, then whose child are you?"

Chapter 17

Lydia hove into orbit around Sol IV, a cold red planet named after some long-forgotten culture's god of war, Mars.

Gaea was the next planet inward, but getting there from outside Sol's Oort cloud required a full bioscan of all ships and an auto-decontamination, or A-decon, of all travelers. Fortunately, while drifting at the edge of Pontus, Lydia and Melanctha had contacted the lawyer of Dmitri Bouras on Gaea, Chiron Likashose. To all appearances, he was a partner in a legitimate law firm whose primary focus appeared to be government lobbying, Likashose looking after the Bouras Syndicate interests in the Hellenic Parliament. From him, they'd secured false identities complete with dossiers, a contingency frequently required of the Syndicate, apparently.

"I'd think having A-decons at every stop would catch any xenopathogen, wouldn't you?"

Melanctha just shrugged at her.

"Probably wouldn't help to tell them I've been inoculated, would it?" Lydia sighed and pulled the archaeota into line behind the other passenger vessels seeking permission to land on Gaea. It extended halfway around the planet. She groaned, wondering whether they'd be stuck in orbit above Sol IV for days, no way to get around the bureaucratic red tape. She threw a glance at Melanctha. "Mela, you didn't have to do this as an IBS agent, did you?"

The other woman shook her head and glanced down at her plain formalls.

It occurred to Lydia how much Colonel Melanctha Remes was risking in coming with her to Gaea this way, as a fugitive. "This won't look good on your resume, will it?"

"No, probably not," Melanctha said. "Mind if I turn on the news?"

Lydia shrugged. "Not at all." She found it bewildering, the penchant these humans had for constantly filling their heads with extraneous information. But there really wasn't much else to do while they waited.

Melanctha reached for the holovid controls.

"And in other news," a busty anchor said, "efforts to curtail the outbreak on Cygnus Twenty failed spectacularly as the Panthovirus continues to spread, having achieved a saturation rate of ninety-five percent. Further, local contingents of the Imperial Infection Control Authority appear to be in disarray, calling upon the Gaean Central Command to take over the pathogen interdiction efforts. Evidence indicates that the quarantine is in tatters. A similar subsequent outbreak in the Maldives Constellation points to the possibility of a Typhoid Mary—some individual or agency spreading the pathogen deliberately, bringing the total number of infected worlds to twenty-five. For more on this phenomenon—"

"Imperial Infection Control, prelim inspection vessel requesting permission to come alongside," the override com said, a bespectacled bureaucrat replacing the busty anchor. A prelim inspection vessel pulled alongside theirs, the other vehicle small, a single-passenger minnow-class ship. "Any declarations?"

"I do declare this is an onerous process," Lydia snarked.

"Look, lady, make my job easier and just say no. I'm asking about offworld plants, animals, or other biologic living material, all right?" The poor, bored bureaucrat looked as if he could use a vacation.

"No declarations," Lydia replied.

"Inbound from where?"

"Eris Eleven," she replied. "It's all in the manifest."

"Yeah, saw that, gotta ask anyway. Sleek little ship you got, by the way. Expensive?"

Lydia decided to lob a wobbler. "I'm not sure. Daddy bought it for me. Must be, though. He said I should take better care of it than the last one."

The Inspector snorted, his gaze going to his screen for the first time. His eyes grew big around. "Who's your daddy, Ms. Castellanos?"

"Zorba Castellanos, Duke of Pyrgos." The lie came easily to Lydia, the name part of the dossier, but the position a complete fabrication.

"I'm afraid I have to ask you to follow me, Duchess." The image collapsed.

She exchanged a glance with Melanctha.

"Now, you've done it."

"But what have I done?" Lydia engaged the engines and followed the minnow. They passed frigates and cargo ships, huge passenger star liners, personal yachts, quite a few commuters, and several tankers.

The minnow led them to a side-dock at the inspection station, where their holo lit up again. "We'll have you both step off your ship and through the A-decon," the inspector said, "and then we'll give it a bioscan and get you on your way."

"Why, thank you," Lydia said, delighted.

"My pleasure. Please follow the signs."

They stepped off the archaeota through a compression hatch into a long corridor. In one cubicle, they had to disrobe and step into the next cubicle for the dousing. Getting doused with a demicrobiating agent was like taking a shower in a thick, clear mud. Lydia didn't mind it, having grown up in mud, but it was clear Melanctha detested the process. They stepped to the next cubicle for a rinse, and then at last one, dressed themselves in a fresh set of formalls. Then back through the compression hatch into the archaeota.

"Cleared for Gaea," the ship's transponder beacon now declared.

"I wonder if they do that for all the nobility," Lydia said.

En route to the blue-gray planet, she reviewed Ezra's information again, knowing she would have to retrace his route.

First, Selene Toccim, Professor of Xenobiology at the University of New Athens.

Then, Chiron Likashose, the lawyer on retainer for Dmitri Bouras on Gaea.

Finally, picking up where Ezra had left off.

"I'm always amazed at how beautiful Gaea is each time I see it," Melanctha said, its image large on the holoscreen.

Lydia glanced at it with a fair degree of ambivalence. The place she'd been born that had once been her home, Gaea held both joy and dread for her. Joy at the possibility of being reunited with the family she'd always thought was her own, dread at discovering what really lay in welcome for her. Would they embrace her as the Viscountess's daughter, or reject her as some interloper from an alien planet at the rim of the galaxy? And what about her real family, the one she was truly descended from?

As she looked at the city of New Athens, perched on a craggy peninsula on a huge inland sea, Lydia became aware of an itch on her right forearm.

Absently, she scratched it.

* * *

"Professor Dorian Procopio? Yes, of course I remember him." Selene Toccim, Professor of Xenobiology at the University of New Athens, looked over the lectern at the pair across from her. She'd just concluded a lecture on microbial variants, and students had begun filing from the room when the two strangers had sidled their way into the lecture hall. "What about him?"

"What do you remember about his wife's appointment as Ambassador?"

Selene looked the younger woman up and down, struck by how attractive she was. Even the plain formalls couldn't obscure the fact that the young woman had the face and figure of a goddess. I wish I were that attractive, she thought. She'd always been short, blond, and skinny, with an acne-scarred face. Pumps, pads, and face-caking had never done much to obscure the fact that she just wasn't attractive.

The other, older woman was plain if statuesque, perhaps of an age with Selene, and disciplined in her mien, as though accustomed to command, her face sharp.

"I think they did it to silence Dorian," the Professor said bluntly.

The other two exchanged a glance, looking taken aback.

"Come with me," Professor Toccim said, and she strode from the room, heading toward her office on the fifth floor. The ground floor theater had disgorged its occupants into the confluence of students flowing through the corridors. She headed through the crowd for the stairs, not waiting to see if the other two would follow, knowing she'd rather be using her time to prepare for her next lecture.

It was the third time someone had inquired, and she'd have liked to dismiss them outright.

Except that she'd known Dorian well and had been hired by him twenty-five years ago to help with his research.

Except that just before the coronation, she'd had a similar inquiry from a creature whose sight, sound, and smell had been so bizarre as to be offensive.

Except that days later, the Dowager Empress had splashed that same bizarre creature with a disintegrator gun when it had stepped forward to protest.

On the fifth floor, she stopped at her door and glanced at the next door down.

His office door, once.

It hadn't helped that she'd been enamored of him, Selene a young researcher just hired as an adjunct professor by Professor Procopio to assist him with his research, highly impressionable and slightly giddy at having an office right next to one of the most prominent experts in the field of alien microbiology. It hadn't helped that Professor Procopio's wife was a Viscountess and very nearly royalty, twentieth in the line of succession.

Professor Toccim palmed the lock and pushed her way into her office, her guests not far behind. "Please, have a seat." She set her holopad on her desk and slipped off the Proctor's robe to hang it on the rack behind the door.

Shelves of Vilasian twistwood climbed to the ceiling on two sides, most of them occupied with placards of honorarium, among them a few still shots of the Professor with prominent politicians and other mementos of a lifetime in Academia. The desktop was a single slab of Istralis crystal, the milk-white rock glittering with a subdued, subtle glow. The deeply-padded chairs were upholstered with cured Gurlagian cowskin, the tanning esters making the office redolent of a bank.

The other two sat across from her.

On her holopad, Selene summoned a diagram from the research results that Professor Procopio had been finalizing for publication at the time of his wife's appointment. A blue, green, and red hologram hovered above the desk.

"I had a visitor two weeks ago, a creature from the very same planet where they banished Dorian and his family. When I showed him these preliminary results of Dorian's experiment, it got very excited."

"Ezra was here?"

Professor Toccim looked sharply at the young woman, startled. "You knew the creature?"

The woman nodded. "He and my father were close friends."

"Your father?"

"Oh, uh, sorry, my adoptive father, Xsirh. My ... human father died when I was four years old."

She sat down abruptly, the realizations cascading into her brain. "I remember ... You were so pretty then, even at four years old. You survived the crash! How ... they told us there weren't any survivors. I can't believe it! Oh, I'm so grateful." She stood and stepped around the desk and folded the young woman into her arms, remembering the delightful girl, the daughter of her colleague. You once wished you'd have a child like her, Selene remembered. And when she'd heard that the Ambassador's ship had crashed on arrival, Professor Toccim had wept in private, as though the family had been her own.

The young woman pulled away, as if uncomfortable with the embrace.

"What is it?"

"I'm ... It's ..." She didn't seem to be able to speak.

The taller woman spoke up. "Xsirh did a genetic analysis. Lydia just learned hours ago that the Procopios aren't her parents."

Selene felt the blood drain from her face. She looked at the hologram, having imagined for years that it'd been the Professor's research that had offended someone in power.

"Professor Toccim, what was so exciting about the research?" the taller woman asked.

Selene glanced between the young woman and the holo above her desk. There were layers to this situation far beyond her comprehension. "His research proved that infectious diseases were—and are—infiltrating human habitations on xenogenic planets throughout the galaxy at a rate far greater than we have the technology to track."

"I don't understand, Professor. Why's that so important?"

"The model he was devising predicted that within thirty years, a pathogen with a ninety-five percent transmission rate will infect

527

colonies throughout the Milky Way." Professor Selene Toccim looked at both women. "A pathogen so virulent it will kill ninety percent of the population and wipe out humanity as we know it."

Chapter 18

Lydia read through her father's work, startled at its clarity and gravity.

Infiltration of human pathogens by alien microorganisms was inevitable. Humans had spread throughout the galaxy far too fast for the research on alien pathogens to keep pace. Once an infectious vector had been compromised by an alien genome or had mutated in its exposure to extreme environments, it had the potential to spread among humans with a savagery unseen for centuries.

In one pandemic on pre-diaspora Earth, a pathogen had infected a quarter of the population and had killed a quarter of its victims. The Spanish Flu of 1919 had killed fifty to two hundred million people after infecting over twenty five percent of the human population. This haemagglutinin-1, neuraminidase-1 virus, or Influenza H1-N1, an admixture of swine and avian viruses, had made the leap into its human variant and had spread throughout the world within months.

Key to any pandemic was its lethality. The rhinovirus, or common cold, despite being highly infectious and likely to reach fifty to sixty percent of the populace during any given cold season, was rarely lethal, its victims nearly always succumbing to some secondary opportunistic infection rather than the rhinovirus itself. Contrary to myth, no part of the rhinovirus was an aphrodisiac. Despite its high penetration rates and near-ubiquity in virility enhancements, it killed very few people.

A highly lethal virus, such as the haemagglutinin-120, neuraminidase-240 strain, Influenza H120-N240, otherwise known as the tyranovirus, was infamous for shredding the meat off a human skeleton in one bite. Difficult to transmit, the tyranovirus was rare, its rampages confined to prehistoric theme parks. However, if it ever developed the transmissibility of its rhinovirus cousin, a lethal pandemic would instantly ensue.

Professor Dorian Procopio had extended standard epidemiological models to the spread of humans throughout the Milky Way. Encounters with new alien microorganisms occurred daily. Professor Procopio postulated that no matter how robust the human immune response, such exposure rates would inevitably overwhelm its ability to adapt. Incorporating travel patterns, settlement rates, trade volumes, and xenomicrobial profiles, the Procopio model predicted with a ninety-five percent certainty that an alien pathogen would infiltrate one or more of the human viruses within thirty years, and cause a pandemic so widespread that interstellar travel was likely to collapse. Further, the model incorporated xenobiologic lethality potentials, a relatively young field of study, which had identified only a handful of alien microbes inimical to humans.

And it was this small proportion of inimical versus benign alien microbes that detractors had used to silence Professor Procopio's work. Peer reviewers had consistently derided the research over this weakness in his arguments.

Reading through the work, Lydia now understood the human paranoia regarding infectious diseases. She also understood that the lynchpin of the research was the lethality potential. It only took one lethal alien pathogen to infiltrate a high-penetration viral vector to create a pandemic.

One section of the work was devoted to an analysis of environments most likely to produce such a pathogen, among them watercovered planets whose temperatures ranged just below those at which the human metabolism operated.

Kziznvxrz, for example, Lydia thought. And then she read the next line.

"Kziznvxrz, just beyond Theogony in the Mnemosyne Constellation at the end of the Scutum-Centaurus arm, is a prime example of a world likely to produce a pathogen with a high degree of lethality. Its nine-tenths water surface and ambient temperature of 36 degrees Celsius make it the perfect Petri dish for culturing an organism inimical to the human physiology."

How ironic, she thought.

Lydia looked out over New Athens University from Professor Toccim's office and sighed. Still deeply sad at finding out that the Procopios were unrelated to her, she still felt a curiously-detached pride in the work her father had done prior to leaving Gaea. The vague memories she had of her parents contained that high degree of security fundamental to any developing human. There wasn't any question in Lydia's mind that Basilissa and Dorian Procopio had been there for Lydia as parental figures. The fixed place they held in her psyche could not be contravened by something so superfluous as not sharing their genetic heritage. She was as much their child as any biological offspring might have been.

Lydia had chosen to come to the University of New Athens first, both because her mother's positions as Ambassador and Viscountess tended to overshadow her father and because the Noble Procopio family was far more intimidating and, at least in Lydia's mind, best approached last.

Before Xsirh's revelation that she was not a genetic descendant of the Viscountess, Lydia had hoped to prove she was Basilissa's daughter through a simple genetic test. She'd imagined approaching the family through an intermediary, perhaps the enturm, Chiron Likashose, the lawyer of Dmitri Bouras on Gaea.

But now, her heritage in question, Lydia didn't know how she was going to prove she was the daughter of Basilissa Procopio and there-fore the rightful Viscountess.

Declaring herself the long-lost daughter of a member of a noble family was itself fraught with difficulties, a process likely to upset the status quo and invite the enmity of the current Viscountess, if not that person's homicidal intentions.

I might as well declare myself the Empress, Lydia thought.

Her other task before approaching the Procopio family was to retrace Ezra's steps on Gaea. Her father's breeding partner when Ambassador Procopio's ship had crashed on Kziznvxrz, Ezra had helped to care for the orphaned girl and later had advocated with the Kzizn government to allow Xsirh to adopt the child.

Despite transmitting regular progress reports to Kziznvxrz, Ezra hadn't been able to finish his investigation and had assembled only a disjointed, incomplete picture of the events leading up to the Viscountess's being appointed Ambassador.

Colonel Remes and Professor Toccim returned from the cafeteria with a tray full of food.

Lydia blanched. The smell was nauseating, the human propensity for animal flesh one of their most disgusting characteristics. The vegetarian sandwich they'd managed to procure from the cafeteria was a dry slab of carbonaceous fibers cooked in a vat of animal lipids and slapped onto a stale pastry made of a milled grain kneaded with more animal lipids into a puffy lump whose moisture had been baked out of it. Further, the "psomi" had been slathered with a thick yellow sauce made from the ground seeds of a known carcinogenic plant and another white sauce made from more animal lipids and the whites of a domesticated bird's reproductive embryos. The "mustard" and "mayonnaise" condiments did more to condemn the sandwich to inedibility than rescue it.

But Lydia was hungry. And they'd brought her a beverage to help lubricate her epithelial digestive tissues. The combination wasn't as bad as she'd thought, except that she had to chew more than she was accustomed to, the Kzizn diet consisting primarily of liquefied microbial proteins.

"Find anything interesting in there?" Melanctha asked around a mouthful of food, throwing a glance at the holo still hovering above Professor Toccim's desk.

Lydia nodded. "Very similar to what I studied on Kziznvxrz in college." Or what passed for college on the planet, a vastly different structure than that she'd seen on human-occupied worlds.

"Not too technical?" the Professor asked, gravy dripping off her roast beast.

She tried not to stare at the nauseating spectacle. "No, not at all. I found the commentary from the peer reviewers specious at best. They seemed bent on refuting the model based on speculative ratios of benign versus inimical xenomicrobes, as if they were in any better position to evaluate the threat."

"For having been reared by the Kzizn," Toccim asked, "you have a surprising command of Galactim."

"Xsirh was adamant that I study it. I guess he always knew I'd return to Gaea."

* * *

"Duke of Pyrgos?" Chiron Likashose III, JD, Esq., threw his head back and laughed. A doctorate in jurisprudence hadn't deterred him from taking the most lucrative position to be had: Personal counselor and governmental affairs advisor to Syndicate Boss Dmitri Bouras, a choice of position most lawyers would call imprudent.

Like any law office, bound volumes of the current code of regulations filled every shelf, de rigueur for impressing clients with the gravity of the work that lawyers did. The expense of having so much printed matter on the walls was impressive by itself, particularly since the only purpose of such an expense was to impress. He never consulted the voluminous material, his law clerks doing the legal grunt work and searching the holonet anyway.

He looked across his desk at the beautiful young woman in plain formalls. "I'd be happy to add that to the dossier, Ms. Castellanos." He glanced at the older, hatchet-faced woman behind her. The woman's bearing gave her the air of nobility and command. Accustomed to privilege, Chiron thought. "And how about you, Ms. Giorgiadis? Is everything in your file satisfactory?"

"It certainly is, Mr. Likashose. Thank you for your assistance."

"By the way, it's pronounced Like-as-hose." He could ruin her career with a flick of his pinky. A Colonel in the Imperial Bureau of Suspicion escorting a fugitive to Gaea under an assumed name was enough to send her to prison for life. The younger woman was intriguing, daughter of a Viscountess who'd died on an ambassadorial mission gone awry to a planet at the galactic rim.

"Beyond that little modification to the dossier, Mr. Likashose," the younger woman said, her gaze piercing, "you do understand the delicacy of the issue at hand, don't you?"

"I certainly do, Ms. Castellanos. The long-lost daughter of a deceased Viscountess appearing after a quarter-century absence will upset quite a few applecarts. Let's just say that the worms will writhe when they find out they've bit into a rotten apple." He saw her brow crease. "Sorry, an old adage. It's best at this point to speak in vague generalities to preserve your plausible deniability. Don't you agree?"

"Of course she does," the older woman volunteered.

He saw from her look that she would explain in more explicit terms later. Chiron stood, stepped around the desk, and extended his hand to the young woman. "I want you to know, Miss, that restoring what's rightfully yours will be handled with the utmost discretion. Whatever you do from this point forward must compromise neither your current identity nor your purpose in having come to Gaea—particularly not using that name we both know. Please, on your way out, see my assistant for contact instructions—the how and when we will meet in the future. On this point I must be firm: You must never come back to this office. Katalavino?"

The young woman blinked at him, looking bewildered.

"Understand?" he repeated in Galactim, belatedly realizing she didn't know Greek.

"Oh, uh, yes, I understand. Thank you, Mr. Likashose."

He saw them to the outer office, nodded to his administrative assistant, and then returned to his desk.

The problem, Chiron thought, is that the current Viscountess Procopio won't be the person most upset by the return of the long-lost Ambassador's daughter.

It'll be the Dowager Empress Narcissa Thanos and her puppet, the Empress Hecuba Zenon.

But pissing off Empresses was what his boss wanted him to do.

Chapter 19

Lydia looked over New Athens and nearly cringed.

She stood in the kitchenette of their suite, as far from the balcony as she could get.

The sight of the city packing the bowl-like valley nine stories below caused her heart to thunder and her breath to rasp. Her skin crawled and grew clammy, the fine, cilia-like hair on her arms prickling.

Melanctha's standing on that very same balcony, leaning against it, and looking as if she were going to pitch over the side to the street below, didn't help.

Lydia forced herself to sit in a chair, and when that didn't assuage her panic very much, she turned her chair to face the other direction.

Her back to the window, she was finally able to relax somewhat, her heart slowing and her breathing becoming easier.

"Not a comforting sight, eh?"

She started to look Melanctha's direction, but quickly became overwhelmed.

"Here, why don't I tint the glasma?"

The room darkened appreciably and the interior lights brightened to compensate.

Lydia tried to look that direction and found the darkened wall to be a little less daunting than the precipitous drop several stories down. As though a fuscous landscape made it somehow less tangible. "Thanks, that's much better."

"Never seen anything like it, eh?"

"Actually, I have, but my response has always been the same. Father says it's a trauma response."

"To what? Your parents' ship falling out of the sky?"

Lydia nodded, knowing it a neurological flight response, something the Kzizn didn't understand, their endocrine systems under direct prefrontal control, and not subject to the vicissitudes of their basal ganglia.

Looking at Melanctha, Lydia wondered again what to do about her. I can't ask her to put herself at any further risk on my account, she thought, knowing that Colonel Remes was now vulnerable to exploitation. The law offices of Dewey, Treatem, Likashose, and Howe had surely recorded every moment of Remes' visit.

"Melanctha, I want you to know how much I appreciate all you've done. It's more than anyone could expect of another person. Thank you."

The other woman smiled. "Before you go on, I want you to know something. Whatever else happens, Lydia, remember that you have allies. In a lot more places than you might imagine." Then Colonel looked levelly at Lydia. "You were saying—?"

"But I can't ask you to risk your livelihood or your life any further."

"If I felt that way, I'd have told you."

Lydia considered her perspective. Given the degree that the aristocratic Colonel had extended herself, Lydia felt she could no longer leave unsaid how much danger there was in continuing the enterprise. "I know you're here because you feel a sense of purpose and obligation. I really admire the depth of your loyalty in doing so, but I can't in good conscience ask you to accompany me further."

"You don't have to ask."

She looked at Melanctha, standing so tall, easily six inches taller than Lydia, her sharp features perfect for chopping through bureaucracy, her posture as straight and proud as an axe handle. Lydia smiled sadly. "I'll miss you, Mela."

"No, you won't."

Taken aback, Lydia shook her head. "It would be foolish for you to continue, Mela."

"I know the risks, and I'll walk face first into them, willingly."

"Mela, I can't let you do that."

"Lydia, you can't stop me."

She stared at the other woman, not sure what to say, bewildered by the other's persistence.

Melanctha stepped to the table and pulled out a chair to sit facing her. "You're courageous and very considerate to take on this challenge alone. Whatever your reasons for not wanting me to continue, whether it's because my career is in jeopardy or that I'm likely to be extorted by the syndicate, they don't hold up in the face of my reasons for continuing. I can't be dissuaded."

Lydia opened her mouth to argue.

The other woman held up a single finger. "My childhood friend died a strange and tragic death." She raised another finger. "The aristocracy is being undermined in subtle and insidious ways by some erosive poison eating away at its foundation." She raised another finger. "What happened to your parents could happen to any of the noble families. Yes, I'm risking everything, but that's because everything I know is at risk." Melanctha sighed and glanced toward the balcony.

Lydia looked at the older woman and saw in her face the lines of her age. But in the creases too was the wisdom of an ancient lineage that extended deep into the past, her heritage in her wrinkles. And rather than weigh her down with the centuries, this heritage strengthened her and gave her courage in the face of longanimous suffering.

A scion's death at age ten had scarred a young Melanctha, but that scar had hardened into a callous. And the older, wiser Melanctha saw an opportunity to get at the heart of an imbalance wobbling nearly twenty-five years out of equilibrium.

Lydia saw all that and more, and saw it because it was the same fiber from which she herself was woven, the Procopios having passed along to their daughter the determination that comes with quiet resolve. They were nobility, and theirs was to endure whatever vicissitude their sovereign commanded of them.

"What if Empress Hecuba tells you to arrest me and bring me to the palace?"

"What if Metaxa were brewed from the bitter grapes of ambition?" Melanctha retorted.

Lydia smiled and took the older woman's hand. "Thank you."

* * *

"Who're you?" Baptiste Tomaras, Licensed Behavioral Technician, had just walked into his apartment to find two women waiting for him, both in dark sunglasses and utilitarian formalls.

One was tall and statuesque, with a face like a blade, and the other was the perfect height, with perfect proportions, perfect hair, and a perfect face.

The face of a goddess.

He stopped short, as taken aback by her beauty as he was by finding them both in his apartment. He was certain he'd locked his door. Further, it was a palm lock, impervious to decryption.

"Agent Giorgiadis," said the tall one from behind dark tints.

"Agent Castellanos," said the pretty one, hers equally dark.

They weren't pointing guns at him, but they might have been.

"Where are your badges?"

Their heads moved incrementally toward each other, as if to exchange glances. Then the pretty one said, "We don't need badges."

Baptiste's gaze narrowed. *What did I do, just walk onto the set of a bad immersie?*

But the fact that they were in his apartment bespoke an abridgement of his privacy by some powerful surveillance agency inoculated from the constraints of law. "Agents of what?"

"The Imperial Bureau of Suspicion," the taller one said.

Baptiste felt his scrotum crinkle. His feet grew cold and he couldn't feel his hands. He stood gaping at them, mute, not daring to speak, his teeth sure to chatter in fright and his lips sure to blurt his confession.

Here it was, the dreaded moment when Imperial law enforcement finally moved in to arrest the alien collaborator. Accomplice to the Kzizn agent who'd conspired to disrupt the crowning of Empress Hecuba Zenon. They must have retraced Ezra's steps, Baptiste thought, certain his wide, staring eyes and trembling knees gave away his guilt.

"We need your help," the shorter one said. "We're not here to arrest you. Our apologies for breaking in, but we had to make sure we weren't seen."

Baptiste heard something in her voice, the catch of a silent plea, the desperation of someone unmoored from all that anchored a person to the past. "You want to know about the Kzizn, Ezra."

She seemed relieved, her shoulders easing back a little. "Yes, Mr. Tomaras."

He caught the faint odor of an organic compound, the smell redolent of Ezra himself. "You knew him, didn't you? You aren't ... related, are you?"

"He was my stepfather, and he came here to help me."

Bewildered, he looked her over. She didn't look alien. She looked to be as delectable a human specimen as he'd ever seen, her soft, soulful eyes a window into her unusual past, her elfin, heart-shaped face begging to be cradled in loving hands. There wasn't a trace of alienness about her, except that she was so trusting and vulnerable. Her mien of complete trust invited him to extend the same trust to her, which he found himself doing despite multiple reasons not to.

"Stay for tea?" he asked, setting down his bag and moving into the kitchen. Comprised of three modest rooms, his apartment was comfortable, a bedroom and bath to one side of a living room, on the other a small dining-kitchenette. "Have a seat, and I'll put some water on."

He didn't even have three chairs, his guests taking the two that he did have. The water was instantly hot, and he poured them each a cup, having to wash the one that he'd used at breakfast. As cushy and well-paying as his job was, he still couldn't afford a luxurious life. Not in New Athens, the most expensive place in the galaxy to live.

"I'll stand," the taller woman said.

"You sure, Agent ...?"

"Giorgiadis," the sharp-faced woman said. "Yes, I'm sure." She leaned against the window embrasure, her cup in hand.

Baptiste settled across from the pretty one, Agent Castellanos. "What do you want to know?"

"Do you know why Ezra was here?"

"He said that his people thought the Gaean Empire had been deceived."

Chapter 20

How does a person deceive an entire Empire? Lydia wondered, reviewing her mental notes.

Neurologically, the Kzizn were able to remember everything, unlike humans. All sensory input was encoded into a hextuple neuropeptide brain that doubled as a genome. Whenever a Kzizn reproduced asexually through transverse binary fission, all memory and knowledge was transmitted to both offspring. Hence, Lydia's neurological limitations had bewildered them, the alien species not understanding for years why she had such difficulty with learning. Eventually, they'd helped her to develop skills to improve her memory to the point of nearly eidetic recall.

Incorporated into her mental notes were the dossiers of the two Governesses and the Laundry Maid, dossiers that Colonel Remes had pilfered from the archives of the Imperial Bureau of Suspicion. All three of them had died on coronation day.

Baptiste Tomaras had told them he'd given Ezra a tissue sample from Princess Cybill Zenon, also on coronation day.

"What do you suppose Ezra did with it?" Melanctha asked, looking over the holo coming slowly to life under Lydia's hands.

She'd begun putting her ideas together in a gigantic holographic mindmap on her palmcom, consisting of two clusters, the small one a tight ball of clear ideas around a nine-tenths water planet known as

Kziznvxrz, and the large one a tangled web of mysterious clouds around the third planet orbiting a small yellow sun.

"Took it somewhere to be analyzed, I guess," Lydia replied. She drew the orb representing Icarus Terzi, son of Count Terzi, toward her. "What did you say was the name of his governor?"

"Giles…" Melanctha began, squinting and turning her head to the side, as though she might roll the information out of her ear. "Sotir something."

Lydia looked over at the dossier on her governess, Filmena, whom she barely remembered, whom her parents had left behind on Gaea when Lydia was four years old. "Sotiropoulos?"

Melanctha's gaze narrowed. "I think so. How'd you know that?"

She expanded the dossier on Filmena, the globe enlarging enough to reveal the information contained therein. Among her vital statistics was the notation of a marriage to a man named "Giles."

Lydia and Melanctha exchanged a glance. The years of the marriage overlapped with the years Filmena had been her governess. "Can you get his file?"

"I can try, but I don't want to do it from here. If a trace is run, it'll lead directly to us. How about the Pantainos Library?"

A famous public library in New Athens, it'd been named after Titus Flavius Pantainos, a benefactor of ancient Athens who'd dedicated his private library to public use in the name of the city's patron goddess, Athena.

"Let's go," Lydia said, snapping the palmcom shut.

* * *

Three galleries surrounded an arboretum whose soaring glasma ceilings enclosed a virtual microcosm of the Gaean biosphere, nearly every type of flora represented among its sixty different microclimates.

Lydia drank in the scents as she and Melanctha wound their way toward the holonet terminals, every volume in the vast library accessible on the holonet. The heavy encryption shielding the IBS archives from public view recorded every request for access and its source. Accessing the archives from a place so public as the library might enable them to avoid being traced.

At the entrance, they'd seen the inscription above the door dictating proper library etiquette: "No work is ever to be removed from this collection, either by fiat or edict, nor to be made inaccessible out of political expediency. Down that road lies tyranny."

The library was situated to the west side of the Agora, near the Gate of Athena Archegetis, considered the most revered site after the Tower of the Winds and the Parthenon itself, the gate made of four Doric columns on a base of pentelic marble. Manufactured of synthetic pentel, the library soared thrice as high as the Archegetis Gate, dwarfing the ancient structure. Its glasma panes and geodesic roof gave the library the air of an open festival or bazaar, sans the calls of vendors endlessly hawking their wares.

Instead, under the hush of a place devoted to deep study and contemplation murmured the babbling of multiple streams, bringing their life-sustaining waters to a diversity of plants.

"Magnificent," Lydia whispered, walking the lichen-splotched flagstone path beside Melanctha.

"I couldn't get enough of this place as a child," the other woman said, stopping outside the portal leading to the holonet terminals. "You should stay here, Lydia. They're sure to have holocams."

Lydia nodded, spotting a fern-infested glade surrounded by trellis. Micromisters saturated the air with humidity so thick she could see the mist. "I'll be over here." She retreated to the chosen glade as Melanctha entered the holoterminal area.

Sitting on a damp bench under ferns, Lydia relaxed for a few moments, the microclime reminiscent of Kziznvxrz's humidity and fecundity.

"May I rest for a moment?"

Lydia looked toward the voice.

An old woman stood there, her gray, curly hair escaping a checked scarf tied tightly under her chin. She wore a long wool coat that reached her ankles, and carried a woven-straw handbag looking too insubstantial for the weight it seemed to be carrying. She sat without waiting for permission. "Not as young as I used to be, you know. Hope I'm not a bother. I'm Giorgi Lillis, by the way." She stuck out her hand.

Lydia shook the wrinkled claw, the name vaguely familiar for reasons she couldn't name. "Do you have far to go?"

"It isn't the distance ahead that tires me; it's the distance I've traveled." The old woman looked Lydia up and down with an upper body

542

stiffened by age and infirmity. "You're a pretty one, child. You remind me of someone I once knew, someone who embodied a dream, and whose death was a tragedy long forgotten."

"Good and bad memories, all in one," Lydia said, seeing the old woman's joy and sadness.

"Our greatest triumph sometimes becomes our most humiliating defeat."

Not minding the old woman's prattle, she smiled. "The opposite is true too, sometimes."

"Yes, child, sometimes."

"You! Old woman! How many times have I told you not to bother the patrons?!"

Lydia looked up.

A uniformed security officer was bearing down on them. "Get up, and get off with your old carcass! Go on!" He reached for the old woman's arm.

Lydia stood and shoved her face into his. "Excuse me, she's not a bother. She's my grandmother!"

He recoiled, backing away a step, blinking rapidly.

"Next time, ask! Who's your supervisor? Eh? Out with it, man! Harassing old women unnecessarily. Ought to be ashamed of yourself. Come on, Grandmama. Here, let me help you to your feet."

Later, as they approached a pneumatube station, the old woman said, "You needn't have done that, child. Here, let me give you my address. Come and see me, if you've a mind. You know, the more I hear you speak, the more you remind me of her."

"Who, Dame Lillis? Who do I remind you of?"

"My daughter, Ambrosia," the old woman said, a tear trickling its way down her cheek, "dead now nearly thirty years."

* * *

"You did what?" Melanctha recoiled as if stung.

The two of them had just stepped out of a pneumatube and now strode through the Chaidari neighborhood toward Agias Paraskevis, on the western outskirts of New Athens, a set of sharp, short peaks between them and the Gulf of Elefsina. After Melanctha had retrieved the dossier on Giles Sotiropoulos, which contained his last known address, they'd come here to this part of the old city to check the dwelling. Walking up the steep hill, Lydia wondered that the houses here still stood, packed side-by-side on narrow tree-lined streets. She marveled that they'd not slid into the valley through erosion or succumbed to the area's frequent seismic activity.

"It wasn't right, what he was doing," Lydia said.

"We're supposed to be undercover, Lydia, not drawing attention to ourselves."

"Sorry, but I couldn't let that pompous idiot treat her that way." Lydia knew she'd jeopardized their mission by defending the old woman in the arboretum.

"I'd have probably done the same." Melanctha glanced at her hand-held and then looked at the apartment buildings on both sides. "This one," she said. "Let's hope Mr. Sotiropoulos still lives here, eh? According to public records, he committed suicide shortly after being dismissed from Count Terzi's service. But the IBS dossier says otherwise."

None of the houses looked in terribly good shape, paint peeling from walls, cracks in the foundations from subsidence. Melanctha had indicated a three-story structure set back from the street by only a few feet, behind a thin strip of ill-kempt grass. On either side of the walk stood a tree struggling to eke out enough nutrients. The entry held a com system for the six apartments in the building, two on each floor.

A door swung open before they'd even read the labels. "It's me you're looking for, isn't it?"

Lydia was startled by how direct he was. She saw that his face was the same as the image in the dossier.

"May we come in?" Melanctha said.

He let them inside and gestured to a darkened living room. "Please, have a seat. I'd get you something, but I don't get around so well anymore."

Lydia's eyes adjusted, and she realized that the only source of light was the shaded balcony looking out over the street, through which he'd seen them approach. The air was thick and closed, as if the occupant never opened the windows or left the apartment.

"Thank you, Mr. Sotiropoulos. We appreciate your time."

"What else am I going to spend it on? I'm retired, nothing else to do but wait for Thanatos to come claim my soul." He hobbled to the chair opposite a low table, his step infirm and his breathing heavy.

"You probably don't remember me, Sir."

"Of course I do, clear as a bell. You're—"

"Agent Giorgiadis, Imperial Bureau of Suspicion. We're here on a highly classified mission requiring the utmost discretion."

The gaze shifted to Lydia and then back to Melanctha. "They've been here three times already, asking me about her. We divorced twenty years ago, rarely saw each other since then."

It was a silent complaint. "And you already told them everything you know," Lydia said. "Agent Castellanos, by the way. The circumstances of her death were odd, to say the least."

"An alien life form attacked and killed her in her apartment on the day Princess Hecuba was crowned. A bit more than odd, wouldn't you say?"

"A bit, Mr. Sotiropoulos," Melanctha said. "We're here to ask you about another time in her life, when you were married."

"You know, my dear, you and that young man would have married."

Melanctha looked at her feet.

She and Icarus Terzi, son of Count Ilias Terzi, Lydia knew. She could tell Melanctha was struggling to maintain her composure. "Mrs. Sotiropoulos was governess to Viscountess Procopio's daughter, Lydia," Lydia said.

Giles nodded, his eyes not leaving Melanctha. "She was. Unusual for a married woman to be a governess. We were planning to divorce before the girl got much older. But Viscountess Procopio was appointed Ambassador and left for that godforsaken place on the galactic rim." He swung his gaze over to Lydia. "I can't ever remember its name."

"Did Mrs. Sotiropoulos mention anything unusual during her four years as Lydia's governess?"

"Chatted endlessly about the household scuttlebutt to any who cared to listen. Volumes, you might say."

"Anything unusual?"

Giles looked out the single unshaded window and shrugged. "There was an incident, early on, which I happen to recall for very personal reasons. Filmena told me that they expected the child to have some difficulties."

Lydia frowned. "Difficulties?"

"Yeah, you know, developmental difficulties."

Melanctha asked, "As in mental retardation?"

Giles nodded and spread his hands. "Some cluster of infirmities in her gene structure. No specific deformity, Filmena said, just a number of weaknesses. How did she say it? `An aggregate of lesser infirmities,' I think. Odd that Princess Cybill became the functional idiot. The two were born the same day, you know."

Lydia exchanged a glance with Melanctha.

"Anything else, Mr. Sotiropoulos?"

He looked at Melanctha and shook his head. "It was nearly thirty years ago. Difficult to remember much else, after all this time."

"Did she know Eugenia Ioannou, the Governess to Princess Cybill?" Lydia asked, knowing the two governesses had both died on coronation day.

"They were friends, as I recall. And Filmena did mention taking Lydia onto palace grounds once for a little picnic with Eugenia and her charge. I thought it odd, since the two infants weren't more than two weeks old. Filmena said a third person was there, someone I wouldn't have expected."

Lydia exchanged a glance with Melanctha. "Who was that?"

"The Lady's Maid of the Empress Consort, Ambrosia Lillis, who died in childbirth."

"Lady's Maid?" Melanctha said. "Very odd that she was there. Do you remember her name?"

"Her name? Why do you want to know some Lady's Maid's name? I don't remember it. She wasn't anyone important."

Chapter 21

Near sunset, they were back at the library, Melanctha at a holoterminal, Lydia waiting for her in the arboretum.

Lydia was hoping to see the old woman again. She hadn't realized at the time that Giorgi Lillis was the mother of the deceased Empress Consort, Ambrosia Lillis, who'd died giving birth to Princess Cybill on the day that Lydia herself had been born.

A prim old man sat at the other end of the bench under the ferns, the trellis reaching high overhead. There was no sign of Countess Giorgi Lillis. Beyond him, she could see the entrance to the wing of holoterminals, where Melanctha had gone.

"Have you got a tube fare you could spare?" he asked, his voice a croak.

The request struck Lydia as odd. Earlier, she'd offered Giorgi enough money to take the pneumatube home, but Giorgi had declined, saying the tube was free to the elderly. So either she'd declined out of decorum, or this prim old man was panhandling. "How much is it?" Lydia asked.

"Ten drachma," the old man said.

She fished that much out of her pocket. "Here you go," she said. "I thought the pneumatube was free for the elderly."

"I thought everyone knew the tube fare was ten drachma," he retorted. "You some rutabaga from the provinces?"

Why she had the feeling she was being insulted, she didn't know. She did notice he'd evaded her question. "Ten drachma won't get you a pint of mead, if that's what you're after."

Melanctha emerged from the holoterms and strode toward the fern-filled enclosure, saw the old man, and abruptly turned toward the library entrance.

On alert, Lydia resisted the impulse to follow her.

"The devil mead, why would I want any of that?"

Same reason most people would, Lydia thought idly. "Better get going, old man. They don't like vagrants around here."

"Who says I'm a vagrant? Do you know who I am?"

Lydia shook her head. "Who are you?"

"Death himself, Thanatos incarnate! Impudent wench!" The old man staggered to his feet and wandered off.

What the stars was that all about? Lydia wondered, getting to her feet and going the other direction.

She found Melanctha outside the main entrance, at the bottom of the long, wide staircase, near a marble lion with one paw in the air.

"You didn't recognize him?" she asked as Lydia descended the last few steps. "That was IBS Agent Provocateur Erastus Doukas, whom I recruited on Lucina Nine, in disguise. I wouldn't have recognized him if I hadn't monitored his work for years."

Lydia went cold, frightened that IBS had managed to track them to Gaea somehow.

* * *

"Before taking over command of Lucina Nine, I was in counterinsurgency," Melanctha was saying.

Lydia was exhausted, the two of them having taken multiple tube trips across the city, changing clothes in boutique dressing rooms, split-ting up and taking different routes to the next rendezvous, waiting at each stop to see if someone followed them.

It seemed hours later when they finally decided there wasn't a chance someone could have followed. Night had fallen by then, and Lydia was hungry and tired.

"We'll have to rent new lodgings each night and leave each place as if we're going to return. I'm glad Likashose gave us that encrypted holomail address. He hasn't responded yet, but in his business, he's sure to know someone who's good with disguises."

They ate awful food at a lipid utensil and rented a room in a low-down high-rise. The noise kept Lydia awake half the night, and the vermin kept her awake the other half, the comings and goings of other patrons audible through the film-thin walls. She debated which would be worse: the elevators at one end of the hallway or the restrooms at the other, the noises from each equally lurid.

In the morning, she took a look at the shared cleansall and decided she didn't need a bath. The scum-covered walls might have supplied her a meal, but she didn't have a kitchen to prepare it in.

"This way," Melanctha said, going out the back door.

The alley contained the city's normal assortment of trash: addicts, criminals, and prostitutes. Two women in formalls appearing in their midst caused a minor stir. They looked at Lydia like a delicacy, but a baleful glance from Melanctha warned them off.

The address that Likashose had commed to them wasn't far away, off another alley with equally unsavory characters loitering in its shadows.

"Somebody's got to loiter in alleys, might as well employ the trash to do something," the woman told them. "Call me Polly. You don't need to know more than that."

In a short few minutes, Polly had concocted disguises for them both. "Let me look at you." She stood back, gave them a once-over, and shook her head. "You," Polly said, pointing at Melanctha, "you're fine, but you, girl, you've got just too much of whatever you high-born types are born with. It's gonna show through any disguise I give you. The big one's got it too, but at least she hides it. You just don't know how to hide, do you?"

Lydia frowned, her brows drawn together in bewilderment.

"Here, I'll demonstrate." Polly turned to face away, wriggled her shoulders, and then turned back around. She looked completely different. Her comportment was that of a Duchess at an Imperial ball, her head held high, her back as straight as a pole, her shoulders back, her bosom stuck out proudly, her gaze traveling over everyone's head.

"That's how I look?" Lydia asked.

"It's worse than that, Rutabaga Pie," Polly said, "That's who you *are*. If I didn't know better, I'd say you were Empress Hecuba, except prettier. Ugly as pondscum, that woman."

Lydia giggled, having thought the same. "So what do I do?"

And Polly proceeded to show her, contorting Lydia's limbs in uncomfortable ways.

"Well, can't say it's a complete failure." Polly sighed. "It'll have to do. Oh, uh, and Chiron said to give you that." She pointed to a package near the door, a three-by-three-by-six inch oblong rectangle. "It was making some odd noises, so I just left it where he put it."

Lydia recognized the outer materials as Kzizn in origin. She picked it up and knew instantly what it contained. How had Xsirh obtained them? And how had he sent them here without setting off every alien biologic matter detector between Kziznvxrz and Gaea?

Outside, Melanctha told her, "Polly's right, you know."

"Huh? About what?" Walking toward the tube station beside her, Lydia tried to carry herself the way Polly had told her. It was so depressing!

"There's no hiding who you are. What's in the package?"

"Trained didinium, two of them, like the one that tried to kill me on Amphitrite Three. Our revered leader told me just before I left Kziznvxrz that Wrwrmrfn dissidents had tamed wild didinium."

Xsirh's note just under the wrapper indicated that these two didinium had been neuro-sensitized to Ezra's scent, but that they were still voracious predators, to be handled with extreme caution. They were trained to obey Lydia exclusively and attack any Kziznvxrfn instantly. Also in the note, he'd warned that the dissident leader, Mzixrhhz Gszmlh, who hadn't been seen on Kziznvxrz in many years, was now thought to have gone into exile for safety. Xsirh had written the note in the Kzizn script, which no Homo sapiens had ever deciphered, Lydia the only known human who could understand it.

"What now?" Lydia asked, a three-inch cube in each pocket. Her hair now blond, and a thick brow ridge giving her the visage of a throwback, Lydia resisted the urge to scratch. Polly had given them enough in supplies to last a few days, warning them to remove the disguises every night and re-apply them every morning, or they'd start to slough off.

"Now we try to track down the others Ezra saw. By the way, Lydia, what was he thinking?"

"What was who thinking?"

"Ezra, going up there and spouting off like that in front of the Gods and everybody? Didn't he know he'd be splashed?"

Now, in retrospect, it did seem to be ill-advised. Lydia would have felt compelled to do the same in those circumstances. "On Kziznvxrz, it would be expected."

"Dorothy, you're not on Kzansas anymore." She glanced at Lydia. "I don't want you doing something similar, all right?"

"Yes, Mela," Lydia said, trying not to grin.

* * *

Agent Provocateur Erastus Doukas of the Imperial Bureau of Suspicion hurled himself into the bushes as the pair of women strode past him. He felt ridiculous in his flower-delivery disguise, complete with winged helmet and winged shoes, a gold, glittery, one-piece body suit emphasizing his muscular figure and giving him the physique of a god. The outsize genital cup was the whipped cream atop the hot-fudge sundae of his humiliation, the prominent bulge emphasizing his cherries.

They must be laughing off their posteriors back at the office, he thought, peering from the bushes toward the two women who'd passed him. The dark-haired taller woman with the stooped shuffle didn't concern him. The smaller one with the troglodyte brow ridge, however, carried herself with the ease of an Empress, not at all like somebody who was irremediably ugly.

Agent Doukas had lost his quarry yesterday after seeing the pair enter the Pantainos Library twice in one day. The first time, he'd seen the young woman, the Procopio scion, on a bench speaking with a decrepit old hag. He'd shadowed the pair as they'd taken a pneumatube to a neighborhood on the outskirts of New Athens and then had followed them back to the library. There, he'd ventured to sit on the same bench with the uppity brat. How dare she imply all he wanted to do was drink his life away!

And then they'd slipped away, somehow, and he hadn't been able to find them.

With a still of the decrepit old woman, Erastus had obtained her dossier and had come to her address, on the off-chance the Procopio woman would appear.

Problem was, Countess Giorgi Lillis lived the high life, her mansion surrounded by a thick hedge of rhododendron twenty feet high. Erastus couldn't get onto the grounds, and the estate was so large, he couldn't monitor the four entrances all by himself. It didn't help that he'd been given a disguise so blatant and flashy that it was downright gauche. No self-respecting spy would be seen in such a get-up.

The two women were far enough past that he was able to extract himself from the hedge.

He emerged just in time to see them turn toward the gate. His jaw dropped as they entered the grounds.

That's them! Erastus thought, kicking himself in the cherry cup for having let them past.

And then he wondered, why are they visiting Countess Giorgi Lillis?

* * *

"Why have you come to see me?" the old woman across from them asked. "Forgive me, I'm having difficulty understanding why you're here."

Melanctha had tried in vague terms to explain the reason for their visit.

"It's delicate," Lydia said. "We don't want to endanger you, but we need your help. I need your help."

"Help with what?"

Lydia looked around the parlor, its carpet a thick Naltrexian wool, the furniture of Wirtassian origin, the elaborate moldings done in Mildanian beetle-wood. This was the kind of parlor her parents had had, where trillion-galacti deals were cemented with a smile and a toast, where truces between antagonists were discussed over sips of fine Metaxa.

Emperor Athanasios had been entertained in this parlor, an event Lydia was convinced would never be held for the wart-faced Empress Hecuba.

Lydia turned her attention back to Countess Lillis. "My parents were sent to Kziznvxrz to their deaths, their A-warp engine sabotaged to explode on arrival."

The elderly woman looked at her with a level gaze. "It was a strange time. Go on."

"I've been pursued across the delta sector by Gaean security agents and a dissident Kzizn faction for no apparent reason. After discovering the sabotage, one of my Kzizn caregivers, Ezra, came to Gaea to research my past. Twice now, that dissident Kzizn faction has tried to assassinate me. And just before coming to Gaea, I found out that Viscountess and Professor Procopio aren't even my parents."

"What?"

Lydia struggled to keep from bursting into tears. "My Kzizn father kept tissue samples from my parents' bodies in zero-kelvin cryo and compared their genomes to mine. I'm not a genetic relation to either one." A tear slipped down her cheek. "And yesterday, we were spotted by an IBS agent at the library arboretum. Somehow, they traced us all the way from Lucina Nine."

"Not the child of Basilissa and Dorian Procopio?" The old woman stood and began to pace before the hearth, its mantle carved from a single piece of cured Filgastic bone, the huge beasts five times larger than any creature ever to have roamed Gaea. The Countess Lillis looked deep in thought, her brow wrinkled and her gaze on her feet.

"We haven't told you everything, mostly because there's so much to tell."

"And you shouldn't, child. I probably know too much already." She stopped and looked at Melanctha. "Your family probably isn't in a position to help?"

"No, Lady, and I fear I've placed them in jeopardy already, simply by being here."

"Certainly true. But what's been done to the Procopios might be done to any among the nobility."

Lydia exchanged a glance with Melanctha. "Or already has," she said.

Countess Giorgi Lillis stopped in her tracks, her gaze fixed on Lydia. "How can I help?"

Chapter 22

"Somewhere in the Gaean government, a faction is conspiring with the dissident Kzizn to destabilize the Empire."

Melanctha whirled toward Lydia. "Feels that way to you, too, eh?"

They were headed toward the nearest pneumatube station after leaving the Lillis estate. Lydia felt conspicuous, the long empty stretches of wide avenue emphasizing their presence. There simply wasn't a way to access the area on foot without looking obvious. The occasional passing vehicle was inevitably a luxury-class hover. The hedge-lined streets rarely saw a vehicle worth less than the gross domestic product, and pedestrians were an endangered species.

As if to contradict her very thoughts, a flower-delivery vehicle hove around the corner, engines whining, its gold-glitter exterior outlandished by a pair of blinding-white wings.

"What insensate marketing executive would subject a company's employees to parading around in such gaudy vehicles?"

The hover careened toward them and slewed to the side, skidding to a halt. A figure leapt from the cab, his musculature emphasized by the skin-tight, one-piece, gold-lame body suit, a large genital cup giving his physique a protrusive pubis. The man leveled a blasma pistol at them. "You're under arrest!"

Lydia burst into laughter, and she'd have fallen to the ground in stitches if the pistol weren't aimed at her. She recognized him as the pompous idiot who'd commandeered the Imperial Detention Center on Theogony.

Melanctha was sniggering behind her hand. "Stars above, Erastus, is that the best Clandestine could do for you?"

"Awful, isn't it?" he said. "You're still under arrest."

"All right, all right," she said, her arms up, her body half-bent over with laughter.

Erastus stepped up behind her and wrestled her wrists into cuffs. Melanctha would have looked forlorn in the glasma bracelets if she weren't laughing so hard.

"Just be careful with the didinium," Lydia said as the agent provocateur approached to cuff her.

"What's a didinium?" Erastus asked, hesitating.

"The creature in my pocket. Take a look." Lydia kept her arms above her head.

He fished the three-inch cube from the side pocket of Lydia's formalls and stepped back, keeping his blasma barrel on her. Underneath the clear material writhed a swirl of organic goop. "Ewww!"

"They're really very affectionate," Lydia said.

He looked at her, doubt clear on his face. "Do they smell as bad as those Kzizn?"

"No, sweet as ambrosia, in fact. Take a whiff."

He popped the container open, and the didinium leapt upon his face and wrapped itself around his head. Lydia grabbed the barrel and shoved the pistol at him to keep him from firing it. The two of them tumbled, his hands going to his face to claw the creature off him. Lydia fell onto him, the bulk of her weight landing right on his outsize crotch cup. She tore the weapon from his hand and got to her feet.

The pistol aimed at him, she pulled the didinium off his face. At her bidding, the creature withdrew its tentacles from around the man's head and settled onto her arm.

Erastus was too busy holding his bruised reproductive organelles to give her much attention. She nicked the key off his belt and helped Melanctha out of the glasma bracelets.

Melanctha took the weapon from her, and Lydia put the didinium back into its protective enclosure. Despite being trained to obey her commands, a creature so feral might still turn on her.

"Get into your vehicle," Melanctha ordered.

"I'm hurt, bitch! Can't you see—"

Melanctha kicked him in the gonads, and he curled into a ball. "Help me out, Lydia."

They each grabbed a handful of his gaudy suit at the shoulder and hurled his fetal form headfirst into the equally gaudy hover. Melanctha leaned into the cab and fiddled with the controls, then slammed the door shut.

The glittery hover took off down the avenue on autopilot.

"Where's it taking him?" Lydia asked.

"The palace, where he'll get a welcome reception," Melanctha replied, grinning and shoving his pistol into her belt.

"If they don't cut apart the hover as it approaches," Lydia added, turning to look at Melanctha.

The other woman met her gaze. "I guess I'm all in now, aren't I?"

Lydia nodded, knowing now there was no turning back for either of them.

* * *

Just before they stepped from the pneumatube, Lydia rigged a leash of sorts for the didinium. The glasma restraint circlet fit around the didinium perfectly. To the glasma circlet, she attached an elastoband. Any time she wanted to rein in the didinium, she reduced the band's elasticity, and the didinium snapped back toward her. Lydia had been looking for some way to leash them, not wanting to let them completely loose while tracing Ezra's scent throughout the city.

"Nice little contraption," Melanctha said, looking at the elastoband in Lydia's hand. "Is that a rash?"

"Huh?"

"Those spots on your arm, is that a rash?"

"Oh, that? I don't know," Lydia said. "It's been itching off and on since I left Kziznvxrz. It can't be anything contagious; I've been inoculated."

They stepped out of a capsule into the transit plaza closest to the palace. The maze of tubes overhead made this one of the busiest, most-chaotic tube stations on Gaea, being just east of the Acropolis, surrounded by major attractions such as the Temple of Zeus, the Parliament, and the National Gardens.

The crush of crowd swept Lydia and Melanctha toward the exit, neither able to resist the surge. This side was all exits, people popping out of tubes like gophers on an arcade game. Beyond the tube station, Melanctha stopped at a crossing, where hovers on the street whined dangerously close to pedestrians, all the machines moving at a crawl.

Ahead was the main entrance to the palace, the public entrance, multiple guards both inside and outside the gate.

Weaving her way through the crowd, Lydia walked toward the Parthenon, dominating the Acropolis above them. "Ezra was standing at the front of the crowd when he was splashed." She made her way across the plaza toward the base of the Acropolis. Relatively empty now, just a few pedestrians around, the square looked vastly different. She couldn't tell where Ezra might have been standing. "You saw the coronation too, right, Mela?"

The other woman nodded. "Let's try over here."

Lydia followed her. Oddly, her own nose alerted her to the faint ammonia esters that still lingered.

"Look at the green splotches."

Spots of bright green were splattered across a twenty-foot area, each spot showing evidence of attempted clean-up. The acidic heptoneuropeptide biochemistry of the Kzizn was a challenge for any detergent.

Lydia pulled the didinium from its enclosure and slipped the circlet around it. The slug-like blob of protoplasm bulged from both sides of the glasma ring. She set it on the ground and increased the elastoband's elasticity.

Like a dog, the creature darted this way and that, pausing momentarily and extending a tendril, as if sniffing. It was remarkably adroit at avoiding pedestrians, seeming to sense when it was about to be stepped on. It helped that most pedestrians found the creature repugnant.

A slug on a leash, Lydia thought.

The didinium then darted across the square, back toward the palace gate.

At the crosswalk stood a fire hydrant, where the didinium suddenly froze. One tendril shot straight up, and a stream of dark green liquid doused the hydrant.

Then the didinium moved to the curb, right beside the traffic lane, and prowled parallel to the sidewalk, one short tendril feeling the curb edge. Lydia and Melanctha followed. Again, it stopped, this time extending two tendrils at ninety degrees from each other, one vertical, the other horizontal. Slowly, it turned in place, and then began a frantic dance, its horizontal tendril pointed toward a building.

"Target acquired," Lydia said.

Melanctha looked that direction. "Dedalou Medical Plaza," she said, reading the sign. Her brow furrowed, and she looked at Lydia. "Why would Ezra go there?"

"I wonder ..." She calculated quickly. "Baptiste said he gave Ezra a tissue sample from Princess Cybill on coronation day. This was probably the laboratory closest to the ceremony." She grinned at Melanctha. "Come on."

The didinium strained at the elastoband, pulling them at a rapid clip toward the building.

An explosion behind them echoed across the square, and Lydia whirled. Near the palace entrance, a hydrant head crashed to the pavement, a spout of water beside it reaching fifty feet in the air, people scattering in panic.

"Pretty caustic, looks like," Melanctha said. "Better not let it urinate on anything else."

Lydia nodded, exchanging a glance with her. They entered the building, strode to the elevator, and took it to the second floor to a laboratory, the didinium leading the way.

The clerk leaned over from behind steri-glasma to peer at the creature on the floor. "No pets allowed in the building."

"It's a service animal. Can't a girl get some comfort?"

Looking nonplussed, the clerk gaped at her, like a fish gasping for water.

He might look pretty cute in gills, Lydia thought. "A friend of mine dropped off a tissue sample for analysis," she said. "His name was Svkszvhgfh Ezhrozprh, but he might have just given his short name, `Ezra.'"

Again, the clerk peered at the didinium. "Was his skin the same vomit green as that?"

"About, yes." Ezra would have been mightily insulted at being compared to a didinium, the gentle Kzizn manner antithetical to the feral creatures.

"Ah, it's been waiting for him," the clerk said. "I was wondering when he was coming back. Ezra's the name, you said?"

Lydia nodded. "He's not coming back. He's deceased."

"Oh, uh, sorry to hear that. One moment, please." The clerk retreated behind a panel, shelves visible behind the service counter. A moment later he returned, a memnode in hand. "That'll be a hundred drachmas."

"Usurious!" Melanctha said.

Lydia paid without complaint, sliding a chit into the sterile exchange tube, the irradiation cleansing it of any microbes.

The clerk slid the memnode into his side of the exchange tube.

She plugged the memnode into her handheld, and the machine beeped at the upload. "Oh, uh, I'll need another analysis." She produced the vial of blood she'd obtained from Countess Giorgi Lillis.

"There's a kiosk to your left. Put the new sample into a steri-sample envelope, please, located at the kiosk. We'll have your results in twenty-four hours."

She stepped to the deposit kiosk, filled out the form, deposited the Countess's blood sample into an envelope, and slipped it into the receptacle. The machine whirred and hummed.

"Deposit accepted," it said, and spat a receipt at her.

Lydia reeled in the didinium and returned it to its enclosure.

"Good idea," Melanctha said as they made their way toward the elevator. "Where to, now?"

"I'm famished. How about you?"

"I know a place nearby called Petit's."

"Does that refer to the price or the portion?"

The two of them made their way to the restaurant, dodging hovers and wading through the crowds. The restaurant's circular, green-and-red emblem was emblazoned upon bright orange shades. Inside, they were seated near the back, Melanctha facing the front. "We should be safe in our disguises, as long as we can see who comes and goes," she muttered, eyes on the door. Lydia ordered a Kalamata olive salad, hold the lipid-based dressing, and Melanctha ordered similar. "Guess I'm adapting a little to your diet," she said.

Lydia smiled. Someone's gorging themselves on the cooked, fleshy remains of a meaty bovine was a disgusting sight. She realized that her favorite, algae soup, was just as disgusting to them.

While they waited for their order, Lydia pulled out her handheld. On it were four sets of genetic analysis. Hers, one for each of her Procopio parents, one for Princess Cybill. She programmed in a comparative analysis of all four genomes, similar to the analysis Xsirh had already run, the one establishing that she couldn't be the Procopio's natural child.

"One more gene sample," Lydia said, wondering what they'd do for twenty-four hours while the laboratory analyzed the genome for Countess Giorgi Lillis.

She sighed and ate her salad in silence, anxious to get the results.

Chapter 23

That night, they rented a room at a posh, run-down, flea-bag hotel called the Miramare, located almost due south from the Acropolis. It should have been called the Nightmare. Its one redeeming feature was the sound of surf, which found its way in through the alley that their window faced. When the cats weren't caterwauling, and the street toughs weren't scuffling, and the drunks weren't belting out some forlorn, besotted memory. It was better than the one they'd stayed in last night, but not by much.

And the room had its own cleansall. Without moss-caked walls.

Lydia luxuriated, her parched skin sopping up the water like a sponge.

"You gonna use all the hot water?" Melanctha called after awhile.

After a few more minutes, Lydia got out. "Hand me a pair of formalls, would you?" she said around the door.

Melanctha did so, getting a glimpse of Lydia. "You've got a body to die for, girl."

She blushed, stepping into the formalls. "Thanks."

"And a face to launch a million ships."

It was wonderful to feel admired, especially given her recent travails. Dressed, she stepped out to the main room, where Melanctha was watching a news report on the holo.

"They just sterilized a whole fucking planet."

"Huh? Sterilized?" Lydia hadn't heard Melanctha cuss before.

"Watch. Maybe they'll replay it." Melanctha turned up the volume.

"...pathogen appears to have been neutralized," said the anchor, her bulbous breasts defying gravity, "but all recent travelers to Ananke Ten have been placed in mandatory quarantine for sixty days. Nearby quarantine centers are overwhelmed with the number of detainees, many of whom had relatives on Ananke Ten. At one such center on Pales Three, our very own News Center reporter, Pompous Pompadour, spoke with one grieving family member."

The view switched to a man's face and impossible coif. They protruded from the holo into the room. Behind him was the crowded quarantine center, the low hum of multiple voices in the background. "Thanks, Bustine. We're here at the Imperial quarantine center on Pales Three with Serge Thalamis, who just disembarked after visiting his father on Ananke Ten. What was it like there, Mr. Thalamis?" Pompous shoved a microphone into a man's face.

Tears streaked his cheeks. "My father was healthy! He had no symptoms whatsoever! Why did they have to do that?" Thalamis plunged his face into his hands and wept.

The camera switched back to the bulbous-breasted anchor. "Again, breaking news, Ananke Ten sterilized just hours ago after the outbreak there couldn't be contained."

The vid switched to a blue, cloud-shrouded planet, green continental swatches across its surface. Thousands of flares began to lance the land masses from space, pinprick points of light flashing at each point of contact, until every land surface on Ananke Ten was engulfed in flame.

"I remember visiting there about five years ago," Lydia said, her gaze blurring. She sat on the bed, biting her lip.

The reporter's face replaced the burning planet, his hair easily five inches tall, curving up and out over his forehead like a tsunami. "The last outbreak of this magnitude was three years ago on Quirinus Eight," Pompadour said. "A similar loss of life ensued when Imperial Infection Control was required to inoculate its atmosphere with a caustic enzyme. Back to you, Bustine."

"Thank you, Pompous," the busty Bustine said. "Epidemiologists tracking the outbreak aren't sure about its source but do say that anyone who's traveled to Ananke Ten in the last five years should be immediately screened for symptoms. These symptoms include itching, wheezing, coughing, fluid buildup in the lungs, and increasing respiratory distress. With us in the studio to talk about the outbreak is Professor Selene Toccim, Chair of the Procopio Institute of Xenobiology at the University of New Athens. Welcome, Professor."

The holo switched to a woman in a lab-coat.

"That's not Professor Toccim." Melanctha frowned at Lydia.

She gaped at the image. Professor Toccim had been short, blond, and skinny, with an acne-scarred face. The woman on screen was medium-tall, brunette, and almost as buxom as the anchor.

"Thank you for having me on your show, Bustine."

"Tell me about this particular pathogen."

"Well, Bustine, it appears to be a hemagglutinin-sixty variant, cross-bred with a xenobio organism of unknown origin and incubated in a human host for a substantial period. What's remarkable is both the virulence and transmissibility of the H-sixty variant. Further confounding the situation is our vulnerability to the pathogen. Once it began spreading on Ananke Ten, there wasn't any way to stop it."

"Explain what you mean by virulence, Professor."

"Virulence is the speed with which a pathogen causes symptoms of disease and distress in its victims. It also refers to the severity of these symptoms. The H-sixty variant causes a rapid buildup of fluids in the lungs, or pulmonary edema. The virus colonizes almost exclusively in the lungs. The onset of symptoms is so rapid, in fact, that people literally drown within hours. Further, the incubation period appears to be minutes, the onset so brief that people barely have time to seek help."

"How about transmissibility?"

"This term refers to the ease with which a pathogen spreads from one person to another. Some diseases are spread through vectors, often parasitic organisms. These pathogens are usually neutral to these parasites, on occasion weakening them but rarely debilitating them. Some vectors are inert, such as water droplets, a frequent culprit in respiratory infections such as the H-sixty variant. We cite these as `airborne,' but in fact, standard droplet precautions are sufficient to reduce the rate of infection. But on Ananke Ten, even droplet precautions proved inadequate, as if the pathogen had evolved or had been cultured to produce its own airborne vector."

"Professor, pardon me, but the way you're speaking makes it sound intentional."

"We haven't ruled that in or out, Bustine," Professor Toccim who wasn't Professor Toccim said. "The incubation period is just one of many assumptions we've made in trying to establish how this pathogen developed."

"Professor Toccim," the anchor-breasted anchor said, "didn't the founder of the Procopio Institute of Xenobiology try to warn us of precisely these kinds of outbreaks? Didn't Professor Dorian Procopio's research predict to a ninety-five percent certainty that we would have a virulent outbreak of a xenopathogen within twenty years?"

"Well, Bustine, his research certainly did indicate that an outbreak was a remote possibility, and it remains the basis for much of xenoepidemiology today, but no, his work made no predictions with that degree of certainty or that extreme a result. No one could have foreseen the magnitude of events on Ananke Ten."

Lydia gaped at the holo, having read the research. "How dare she lie about my father's work?!"

"Hush," Melanctha said.

"But Professor Toccim, there's a small community of scientists who advocate otherwise and a slim compendium of literature to support their view. They all claim that Ananke Ten and Quirinus Eight are the natural consequence of mankind's spread across the galaxy. And that Professor Dorian Procopio predicted these events."

The fake professor put up a façade of indifference. "Not a single word from Professor Procopio's published work says any such thing."

"Earlier, we were discussing intent. Is there evidence that points to someone's having concocted this pathogen?"

"Bustine, it would be preliminary even to discuss this aspect of the outbreak. However, a review of alien visits to the planet did turn up an interesting event. In this holo segment from the main spaceport on Ananke Ten taken five years ago, you'll see an alien step off a ship."

The holo switched to an amoeba-class vessel of Kzizn manufacture. A blob of bright-green protoplasm in a two-legged egg cup tottered down the boarding ramp.

"That's Xsirh!" Lydia shrieked.

"How do you know?" Melanctha asked.

From the ship behind the Paramecium walked a pretty young woman in formalls. Lydia, five years younger.

"We've issued an all-sectors-bulletin for this pair," the fake Professor said. "Anyone who's seen them should report the sighting to their nearest Imperial Infection Control authority. Further, it's not the alien we suspect of having been the carrier, but the young woman in the background. Alien-to-human transmissibility is a relatively rare occurrence, and human-to-human transmission is nearly always implicated in a pathogen this virulent. Our Typhoid Mary in the Ananke Ten outbreak is almost certainly the unidentified companion of this giant Paramecium."

"Liar!" Lydia leapt to her feet and shook her fist at the holo. "You slimy, bottom-feeding, pondscum liar!"

Melanctha wrapped her arms around Lydia. "Hush, child," she said quietly.

Lydia struggled for a moment, straining to get at the smug face of the fake Professor.

The older, larger woman held her securely, calmly reached around her, grabbed the remote, and killed the holo.

Lydia turned inside Melanctha's arms, put her head to the woman's shoulder and wept.

Chapter 24

"Typhoid Mary," Lydia later learned, was a figure from Old Earth, Homo sapiens' planet of origin, now a gigantic archeological ruin devoid of life, rendered uninhabitable by its original occupants. The dissident Wrwrmrfn held as one of their basic tenets the belief that Homo sapiens was doing to the galaxy what they'd done to their planet of origin, fouling their own nest. Somehow Homo sapiens had managed to escape the planet before annihilating themselves.

Among the tales attributed to Old Earth was this Typhoid Mary, a Kitchen Maid in the households of primarily wealthier families. Her lack of simple hygiene had caused the spread of the salmonella typhi bacteria, the woman preparing food without washing her hands after contact with her own feces and urine.

Now I'm Typhoid Lydia, she thought, lying awake that night, the sound of surf seeping in through the alley window.

Melanctha snored sonorously beside her, oblivious.

Unable to sleep, Lydia pulled a chair to the window. An occasional puff of breeze carried the comforting scent of brine. How she wished she were home on Kziznvxrz, where the brine was rich in microorganisms and electrolytes.

Over and over in her mind, she replayed the interview. Lydia wasn't sure what bothered her more, the anchor's gargantuan breasts poking like armed missiles from her chest, the imposter's trying to represent herself as Professor Toccim, or being accused of spreading a raging contagion.

At least mine are proportional and real, Lydia thought. Hers are sure to be prosthetic and filled with helium for buoyancy. If I had breasts that big, I'd have to stand on my head!

And what did they do to the real Professor Toccim?

Why are they assassinating my character in this propagandistic hatchet job?

Unable to sleep, Lydia slipped out of her nightclothes, slipped into pair of formals, and slipped out the door. The hotel was pin-drop silent. The last hotel had stayed raucous with saturnalia nearly till dawn. This one appeared to retire early. On the ground floor, she sidled past a snoozing night concierge, a spike-haired younger woman tattooed in brilliant colors.

A half-block away was the ocean, the coastline rocky but the seas gentle. The breeze here was stronger, bringing with it the smell of strong brine. Lydia breathed deeply and walked parallel to the ocean, an occasional hover whining past. A few streetlights along the road stole her nighttime anonymity. The stars glistened overhead, scintillating with brilliance. This close to the galactic core, nighttime skies were daunting for their fusillade of stars, so different from Kziznvxrz on the galactic rim, where only a handful of stars and the vague dust of the Milky Way hung in the night sky like a ghost.

What am I going to do? she wondered.

It was clear the government had concocted the Typhoid Mary charade to justify publicizing a still of her in its efforts to detain her. Why they sought her so avidly was a mystery. She hadn't done anything to them. Why were they persecuting her?

A hover roared past, and she nearly wet herself in fright.

She hadn't heard it coming, wrapped deeply in her thoughts. She realized how vulnerable she was. If the IBS agent had traced her before, others could certainly do the same. And out here, on a lonely strip of ocean-front road, she was easy pickings.

Lydia turned back toward the hotel.

The night concierge was awake. "Sneak out the back door?" the woman asked, her muscled arms rippling under tattoos as brilliant as the night sky. "You look better without the disguise, by the way."

Lydia grinned, stifled a yawn, and stepped to the elevator.

"Hey, uh, Ms. Castellanos, I almost forgot. There's a message here for you. Don't you have holomail?"

"Not where I come from," she said, returning to the desk. She and Melanctha hadn't dared connect to the holonet, except anonymously through a desk term at the library. She took the proffered envelope, its texture the fine flim used on Kziznvxrfn. Made from a dried and flattened colonial protist, the flim was edible, one of her favorite snacks. "Thanks," she told the concierge. How did Xsirh get this to me? she wondered, turning.

"Hey, watch out for that old curmudgeon on the top floor, ok?"

Lydia stopped to look at the woman.

"I'm Buster, by the way."

"Pleased to meet you. Who on the top floor?"

"Old guy, one of those lesser nobility, fallen on hard times, too uppity to work, too poor to continue the debauchery he's accustomed to steeping himself in. About five years ago, he bought the penthouse suite and disappeared into it. We maybe see him once a year. Nobody goes in, nobody comes out. Every once in a while, I get a complaint when he harasses somebody in the elevator. Don't take him seriously. Just an old, disaffected grouch."

A bit more information that I needed, Lydia thought, suspecting the concierge was lonely. "Thanks, appreciate the warning. Good night, Buster."

"Good night, Lydia."

She stepped into the elevator and opened the envelope.

* * *

Lydia my darling,

I hope you're well. May you find the scum of the galaxy nourishing. I've taken great risks to get this letter to you. The outbreak on Ananke Ten made it imperative that I get you our latest intelligence information on the dissident Wrwrmrfn.

We've discovered that they're far more subversive than we ever gave them credit for. Revered leader Gzelfozirh ordered a raid on dissident headquarters. We arrested nearly a thousand Wrwrmrfn and discovered a plan to destroy the Gaean Empire and annihilate humanity. They plan to infect human-occupied worlds with a virulent pathogen that they've been incubating for over twenty years. We're working to isolate the pathogen now.

The outbreak on Ananke Ten was a test run, and by Wrwrmrfn standards, a successful one. Their plan is to infect all major settlements throughout the Gaean Empire in similar fashion, including the capital, Gaea. And while it appears the Imperial Bureau of Suspicion has accused you as the carrier in its efforts to find and capture you, we fear that the actual carrier is far more pervasive and ubiquitous.

Further, we're still not able to locate the Wrwrmrfn dissident leader, Mzixrhhz Gszmlh. She seems to have disappeared, and even her closest adherents either won't or can't disclose where she's hiding. Worse, the documentation we recovered in the raid indicates that Wrwrmrfn researchers perfected a long-acting catalyst to solidify the Kziznvxrfn exoderm years ago. If dissident leader Gszmlh is using this catalyst, it means she may be in hiding among the Homo sapiens, masquerading as one of them. She could be on Gaea itself, and no one would know it.

Oh, and on a personal note, the instability in the Empire has caused a spike in essential-goods prices, and the company profits are higher than ever. For now, I'm placing all profits in those clandestine accounts that you had me set up on Pontus XIII years ago. I'd wager you didn't think you'd ever need them, did you?

Profits should remain high into the near future, just as long as our customers don't know I'm running the company. Xenophobia is running rampant throughout the Gaean Empire. After Ezra got splashed at the coronation ceremony and a holo of you and me was shown yesterday on the interstellar news, our people have had to flee Homo-sapiens occupied planets. Some didn't make it off planet and were killed by rampaging mobs of these unsapient sapiens.

It would be easy in these circumstances to adopt the dissident philosophy and condemn the entire race as primordial bottom-feeders or some deep-ocean-trench algae, but when I think of you, and how kind and gentle you are, and how beautiful, I'm reminded that all life is worthy of respect, even these pondscum human specimens rioting and killing Kziznvxrfn.

I send you the warmth and love of all our people, and I pray to the Almighty Single-Cell Organism that you return to us safely.

Yours,

Xsirh Xlmhgzmgrmrwvh.

* * *

Lydia clutched the letter to her chest and sighed.

She stood in the corridor outside the room she shared with Melanc-tha, early morning light beginning to seep through the glasma door at the end, which read "fire escape."

She stepped down the hall, not quite ready for sleep, wanting to think through what Xsirh had said, but mostly wanting to bask in his warmth and affection. She stepped out onto the fire escape. Hungry, and knowing Melanctha wouldn't be awake yet for breakfast, Lydia gobbled the letter, the dried and flattened protist fizzing with effervescence on her tongue.

From her vantage on the fire escape, she saw where the avenue intersected the coastline, the white foam of the soft, gentle surf just visible in the approaching light of dawn.

"Peaceful, isn't it?" said a voice from above.

Lydia turned and looked up.

An old man leaned on the balustrade above her.

"I had no idea there were rooms up there."

"Just the penthouse suite. Care to enjoy the view and watch the sunrise with me?"

The fire escape did extend to the roof, she saw. "All right." For a gruff, old curmudgeon, he seemed awful nice. She climbed up to the roof and saw that the "penthouse" was a rundown tar-paper shack beside a conglomeration of roof-top air-conditioning equipment. Must get noisy up here in summer, Lydia thought.

"Looks better inside," he said, "but it does get noisy in the summer months, all those air conditioners going. You'd think by now we'd have come up with a more efficient heat exchange system, wouldn't you?" He was easily six feet tall and perhaps seventy years in age. His hair was jet-black with some gray at the temple, and his features were those of a patrician god, classic Athenian lines similar to the ancients depicted in statuary throughout the capital. He carried himself with the equanimity of the self-assured, as though born to privilege, and although his face bore clear indications of his age, his posture reflected none of it, still proud and straight, in spite of his plunge into penury.

"I'm Horace Drivas."

"Lydia Castellanos."

They shook, and his eyes searched the area behind her. "Curious, not a name from among the nobility—not even those in disgrace, as I am." He returned his gaze to her. "And yet you carry that nobility in the way you move. Your beauty is startling, too."

Lydia blushed. "Thank you." She remembered the make-up artist, Polly, saying something similar. She wondered about his name, thinking she'd heard it before.

"Where dost thou come from, Princess Anonymous?" he asked in an affected accent, bowing gallantly.

She giggled, not quite believing she was succumbing to his charm. "Well, you might say I went to a really special finishing school."

"Oh, pray tell, where was that? I'd like to recommend it to our new sovereign, her Highness Empress Hecuba. Oh, but her visage is incurably ugly, isn't it? No amount of charm will ever lend her a smidgen of comeliness."

"I'm afraid not," Lydia replied, "but her looks don't matter, do they? Have you noticed who's in the background of all the stills and vids of Empress Hecuba? What matters is the power behind the throne."

"Indeed, Ms. Castellanos, indeed."

Lydia looked out over the ocean, the sky slightly lighter.

"Not only do you have the carriage of nobility, your face is somewhat familiar."

Anxiety blossomed in her gut like a bloom of algae.

"The Typhoid Mary of Ananke Ten."

Now I have to kill him, Lydia thought.

"Why would they level such an accusation, except to assuage their guilt at carrying out that massive slaughter?" His gaze went to the eastern horizon. "Its transmissibility and virulence would have slowed the pathogen substantially. Kill your host too fast, and you kill your means of spreading." Then he looked at her. "Such gloomy talk does little to brighten the coming day."

"You don't think I'm the carrier?"

He shook his head. "Of course not. How could the pathogen incubate in Ananke Ten's populace for five years, spreading asymptomatically, and then suddenly activate all at once? No, child, unless there's a catalyst."

"What if it's built into the pathogen?"

"As with some RNA clock? No, because such a clock would have been reset at the time of infection, and we'd have seen a gradual spread of symptoms across Ananke Ten, not an abrupt, widespread onset."

Lydia cheered up a little. He reminded her somewhat of her father, Dorian Procopio. What little she remembered of him consisted of a warm voice and warm arms, and a gentle affection and adoration.

"Then there's the little coincidence of your looks."

She remembered with a nudge of panic that she wasn't wearing her disguise. "You, too, eh?"

"Others have said something similar?"

Lydia nodded. "Countess Giorgi Lillis."

Horace's gaze narrowed, his brow creasing between the eyes. "Mother of the now-deceased Empress Consort, Ambrosia Lillis, to whom you bear a startling likeness."

"Who died giving birth to Princess Cybill Zenon."

"The poor child, condemned to a life sentence in a mind barely capable of reason."

"A child who looks nothing like her mother." Lydia exchanged a glance with Horace. His face grew suddenly brighter, and Lydia looked.

The sun peeked over the eastern horizon and grew visibly larger as she watched. Soon it was too bright to look at, its warmth chasing away the chill of night. Lydia let the light pour into her soul, understanding why the ancients had worshipped Helios as a god.

"No, Lydia, whatever else you are, you're not the carrier. Don't believe their lies."

Chapter 25

Disguised, Lydia picked up the results at the lab the next day, Melanctha waiting outside.

"I'd swear we're being followed," the older woman had said the instant they'd left the hotel.

Lacking experience in clandestine activities, Lydia couldn't have named so succinctly that creepy feeling in her spinal column, the cilia standing on end, the skin crinkling as it twitched at the touch of a hostile gaze. She'd thought she was being paranoid until Melanctha had said something.

They'd split up, rendezvousing at random pneumatube stations throughout New Athens, surveilling each other in their attempts to find whoever was surveilling them.

Unable to ferret them out, they went to the lab shortly before noon, where Melanctha waited downstairs.

"Where's your slug-dog?" the lab tech asked.

In her backpack, but she wasn't about to tell him. "At home with my friend."

The tech looked disappointed. "If you don't mind my asking, a romantic friend? I was thinking of asking you out."

She smiled and shook her head. "No, not a romantic friend. But I am involved, sorry." She took the memnode the clerk gave her and plugged it into her handheld.

In the elevator, she incorporated the sample into the ongoing analysis, which still wasn't complete. With the additional gene sample to analyze, the projected time of completion increased to forty-eight hours. Her palmcom had a really slow processor.

Lydia sighed, wondering what she and Melanctha were going to do in the meantime.

As the elevator door opened, a young man tried to step on and then backed away at seeing her. He held the door, his skin fair and his hair dark.

"Thank you," she said, passing him. She caught a whiff of miasma, like pondscum or algae.

The didinium in the backpack lurched, tugging her to one side and nearly throwing her off-balance.

He lunged as if to catch her. "Almost tripped there, eh?"

"Almost, thanks," she said, righting herself, wondering what the didinium were doing. On a whim, she tore the backpack off her back and opened it.

Both didinium leaped onto the young man's face.

He clawed at the green slugs, his scream muffled, and fell backward across the elevator threshold. Then his hands turned into jelly, his body went flaccid inside his clothes, and his flesh morphed into a blob of bright green protoplasm. The two didinium began feeding lustily on the still-quivering Kziznvxrfn flesh, his cilia writhing in his death throes. The elevator doors thunked against the body and retracted.

Lydia backed against the wall, gasping.

Melanctha appeared beside her and whispered harshly, "Quick, get your pets and let's go."

She squelched her terror, stepped to the Kziznvxrfn, and gingerly plucked the two didinium from atop the carcass. The elevator doors thunked against the body and retracted. Tucking the didinium close to her body and walking half-hunched over to hide them, she followed Melanctha from the building, throwing furtive glances over her shoulder.

"I don't think anyone saw us," Melanctha said. "Come on, let's get the tube out of here. Keep walking hunched over like that."

At the pneumatube station, the taller woman shoved through the lines of people waiting for tubes. "My friend's hurt, sorry," she said multiple times, elbowing people out of the way, Lydia hunched over.

They stepped into a double capsule and Melanctha punched up a destination. "Why'd you have your critters loose in the backpack anyway?"

Lydia shook her head. "I was thinking they'd be easier to pull out if I didn't have to take them out of their enclosures." The image of the gnawed carcass caught in the elevator doors wouldn't leave her mind.

"Better put 'em back in now."

Lydia did so, juggling them while the capsule curved and swerved toward its destination, the two-person capsule a tight squeeze. The noon-time traffic was moderate, and they arrived just as Lydia finished containing the second didinium.

"We can bet that he wasn't alone. Take a tube to the Gerakas station, find a public restroom, change your disguise, and ten minutes later, get in a tube to the library station."

She stepped from the capsule and navigated her way to the pneumatube to Gerakas. A capsule popped to a stop in front of her. She stepped aboard, and it shot her upward. Her terror began to subside, and in its place blossomed the ugly fruit of guilt. She was grateful she'd had the didinium to help detect the Kziznvxrfn in disguise, but she felt terrible she'd killed him. As the city whisked past below, the capsule sledded through a series of tubes, upended, and plummeted toward a station in the northeast suburbs.

She found the public washroom and changed her disguise in a stall. The various getups that Polly had given them were easy to don, and with a few helpful pointers, such as changing stance and posture, the difference was startling. She changed in three minutes and went back to the tube station.

Waiting the full ten minutes before stepping into another capsule took forever. People came and went, none of them announcing themselves as spies. What does a spy look like, anyway? Lydia wondered, her doubt and ambivalence growing. Did I really need to kill the spy? she wondered. Had it really been necessary to turn the savage didinium loose on the Kziznvxrfn?

Lydia didn't know.

She saw ten minutes had passed and boarded a capsule for central New Athens, feeling terrible that she'd killed a Kzizn, never mind he'd been one of the dissident Wrwrmrfn who'd attempted twice now to kill her.

* * *

"What are we doing here?" Lydia asked.

"More research," Melanctha said, looking around suspiciously. The Colonel looked Lydia up and down. She's looking a bit shook up, Melanctha thought. Probably the first time she ever killed someone.

The canopy of verdure under the geodesic glasma roof was snarled with all the danger of an urban jungle. Melanctha hadn't wanted to come here, knowing any pattern of movement likely to betray them to their surveillers. If the IBS had traced them once already to the library, they were sure to be monitoring the location. Now, though, with the IBS, Infection Control Enforcement (ICE), and the dissident Worm-Worm all pursuing them, Melanctha had to call upon her contacts in New Athens, no longer able to keep Lydia safe by herself. She looked over at the younger woman.

The disguise couldn't hide her beauty. Lydia had the legendary comeliness that caused the balladeers to croon love songs and poets to gush iambic pentameter. Even Lydia's obvious terror at being pursued couldn't dim the beauty radiating off of her, as though she were a blue-white star in her own right, shining with her own light.

Melanctha saw the toll the Kzizn's death was taking. There was a hollow look to Lydia's face that hadn't been there before. How many times have they tried now to kill her? the Colonel wondered. She'll have to get accustomed to eliminating her enemies pretty fast. Sympathy for one's nemesis was a self-culling trait.

"Sit down," Melanctha said inside a copse of thick olive. Adapted from the olive groves of Earth, this particular copse was engineered to grow densely, its fruit to mature simultaneously. She could barely see through the thick olive canopy to the tessellated glasma overhead.

"You're mad at me, aren't you?"

She realized she was. She sat and faced the young woman. "These Worm-Worms aren't your friends. They've tried to kill you thrice now."

"The Wrwrmrfn? But—"

"No 'buts,' Lydia. No quarter is to be given an enemy, do you hear? You have to kill swiftly and remorselessly, because that's what they're trying to do to you."

"I think you're wrong."

Melanctha blinked at Lydia, befuddled.

576

"I had my back turned to him, and I was off balance. If he'd wanted me dead, he'd have killed me right then."

She couldn't believe her entreaty was falling on deaf ears. "What about the other two times?"

The young woman shrugged. "I don't know, Mela. Some other faction? Some infiltrator? I just don't feel that I'm in that much danger. Yes, we're being watched, and it feels hostile, but I don't sense they want my death."

There was a kernel of truth deep inside what she was saying, Melanctha realized, a feeling that had been niggling at the Colonel ever since they'd arrived on Gaea. Even before that, when Infection Control had slapped their ship with a tractor beam while it was in A-warp. As big and powerful as the Gaean Empire was, it had chosen thus far not to eliminate them both. She knew what the intelligence apparatus was capable of, and if it really wanted to find and eliminate a minor annoyance like this pair of women, it could have done so long ago.

"You're right." Melanctha sighed, because the implications were astounding. "Well, the reason I'm here, actually, is that I need allies. I can't continue to protect you on my own. I just don't have the resources. And if the Empire doesn't want you dead, it begs the question, `What does it want?' "

* * *

"I came as soon as I heard," said the middle-aged man across from them.

Lydia looked him over. He had that same patrician posture that Polly had told her couldn't be disguised. His hair was styled fashionably, and he wore a suit impeccable in cut and fashion, the seams just so, the spats and cufflinks twinkling in matching gold, the cravat perched under his chin like a toy poodle, the slacks creased to the floor like naval prows.

She and Melanctha were huddled under an umbrella in front of the Estiatorio Milos, a side-street café hidden from the main avenue by a screen of trees. They each could see over the other's shoulder and had spotted the man's approach from a long way away. At his approach, Melanctha had asked Lydia to remove her disguise.

"Mela, you look dreadful," he said, and then he turned toward

Lydia. "And you, young lady, are an absolute eyeful of radiant grace and beauty. Surely, a duke or baron has already asserted his claim on your hand in marriage?"

Lydia blushed. "You're being ridiculous, Sir, but pray tell, don't stop at my protest."

"I assure you, I wouldn't, if I weren't happily married. I'm Hadrian Kritikos, son of Hector Kritikos, Chief Admiral of the Gaean Navy."

She shot a glance at Melanctha. "You know I'm being sought, don't you?"

"Indeed, Miss. I'd be concerned if Ananke Ten hadn't been a thorn in the Empire's foot."

"So it was politically convenient to kill two trillion people?"

Hadrian nodded in acknowledgement, his eyes boring into her. "Another reason that reduces my concern. My government is—oh, how might I say it?—imbalanced."

"And your father doesn't have similar concerns?"

Hadrian's gaze darted to Melanctha, and he raised an eyebrow at Lydia. "You never knew Emperor Athanasios—a good man led astray. He'd have never sanctioned the sanitizing of an entire planet. My father would denounce me publicly if he knew I were here. And privately praise me. Such are the exigencies of political office. What he thinks is secondary to what I know. And what I know, simply by looking at you, is that a terrible betrayal has taken place."

"Why do you say that?"

"You're twenty-eight, aren't you?"

"How did you know?"

"And the daughter of Basilissa and Dorian Procopio."

Lydia stared at him silently.

The eyes probed hers. "Missing now for nearly a quarter century, and presumed dead in the crash on Kzizn."

She held herself absolutely still.

"But you're not the daughter, are you?"

She neither acknowledged nor refuted his assertion. She didn't know any longer what to think. She desperately wanted to believe she was the devoted daughter of Viscountess and Professor Procopio, but genes didn't lie. Her palmcom held the secret, churning away relentlessly on its comparative analysis of five different gene profiles.

"You were born the same day as Princess Cybill Zenon. Her genes were as pristine as a dewdrop on a summer morning, daughter of Emperor Athanasios Zenon and Empress Consort Ambrosia Lillis, the both of them breathtaking eidolons of human beauty. And yet, somehow, Princess Cybill is not fit to rule." He looked into the distance, and then brought his gaze back to her. "But you—"

Lydia felt the swelling in her throat, not ready to hear what he was saying. "Please, stop." She felt Hadrian's eyes probe her soul, his face blurring. "I'm sorry. Please, you mustn't."

Melanctha took her hand in both of hers.

All the evidence pointed toward the conclusion Hadrian was about to state, and the comparative gene analysis running on her palmcom would prove it. But it was a conclusion so far beyond anything she could have imagined, with repercussions that would shake the foundation of the Gaean Empire and poison its relations with its tiny neighbor, Kziznvxrz, that Lydia wasn't able to face it.

A conclusion likely to plunge the Empire into confusion and perhaps civil war. A conclusion certain to place in danger her home planet and the alien race who'd nurtured her since she was four years old. With only a tiny armed navy, Kziznvxrz would be immediately vulnerable, and Lydia's enemies wouldn't hesitate to exploit this weakness.

She simply wasn't ready. "We don't know anything yet, Lord Kritikos. And ultimately, it's better left unsaid."

"For now, young lady, yes. The day will come, however, when the truth cannot be denied. How will you stay safe until then?"

She met his gaze.

Hadrian Kritikos stared back at her. "And more importantly, lovely Lydia, how do you prepare for that day? How do you prepare for that truth?"

Chapter 26

"What are you here for?" a hotel-lobby denizen asked her.

She and Melanctha were in the lobby of the Value Palace. Melanctha stood at the barred-glasma window negotiating a room from the proprietor of this New Athens underworld hotel, by far the worst place they'd stayed in their traipse along their downward spiral.

Warped and stained paper with faded patterns peeled from the walls. The portrait of someone who might have been famous leered salaciously at them from a canted angle. The carpet admonished them to walk only within the blackened strips, where the nap had worn through to the warp and weft. The furniture declared itself unfit to sit upon, stains in multiple, overlapping penumbras attesting to urine-soaked occupants, the upholstery pattern long since lost in the tides of incontinence.

"What'd you say?" the man asked.

Lydia looked him up and down. The man hadn't changed his formals in several days, and his aroma was redolent of a bovine dish left out in the alley. The dried, scaly toads of his feet poked through the frayed formall toes. His hair hung lank over a face gaunt with dissipation. His beard looked like the back side of a bear that had rubbed it too hard against a tree, the half-inch, red-brown stubble glinting in the poor light. His lips were sunk into an edentulous mouth, puckered from years without teeth. His eyes held an amused despair, a cynical ennui, as if to say, "This is what I've got to give."

"What do you mean, 'What am I here for?' " Lydia asked.

"Everyone's here for something, kid," he said, "You name it, I got it."

"I'm not interested."

"Everyone's interested in something. I've got heroin, cyclidine, opiates, cocaine, amphetamines, hallucinogens, inhalants, psychotics, cognates, cognacs, weed, worm, snake, slither, slime, slug, barbiturates, neurolytics, neuroloptics, neurolactics, and neurolumptics. I can get anything you want, 'cause when you got nothin', it's all the same."

As he named off the drugs, sensations flared in each region of her body that she imagined was involved. She'd heard about people like him, the tales so tall she hadn't believed anyone could stoop so low. "I'm not interested."

"Just a babe in the woods, aren't you?" His eyes grew round, and he rolled forward on the balls of his feet, as though to pounce. He didn't lick his lips, but he might have. The man shot a glance toward Melanctha at the window. "You renting by the hour with your friend? Too bad you go that way. A girl like you could troll the Ritz-Carlton."

Lydia blinked at him, not quite following. What's taking Melanctha so long? she wondered. "I'm not interested," she repeated.

"The questing is how you want it. Do you want to shush, push, gush, flush, blush, brush, busche, crush, cush, dush, frush, grush, hush, kusch, lush, mush, plush, rush, slush, thrush, woosh, douche, bouche, or do you want a complete and total scaramouche?"

The patter of his chatter was bamboo beneath her fingernails. "I got slugs. You want slugs?" She whipped out an enclosure. Beneath the clear exterior, the knot of green slime swirled.

"Ooohhhh, and phlegm green too, the best kind. Trade a slug for a slug?"

"Let the guy alone, Lydia," Melanctha said, stepping up behind him.

The man whirled, bewilderment in his gaze. "What did you say?"

"Sorry, was she bothering you, sir? I see she's got her soulcatcher in hand. You know you're not supposed to use that here, Lydia. Put it away."

"Soulcatcher?"

"She's from Lunoid Twelve, doesn't know any better. Left to her own devices, she'd take the soul of everyone in the building and leave behind a bunch of zombies. Come on, Lydia." Melanctha guided her toward an uneven stairwell, the steps groaning in their inclination to collapse.

Lydia threw a glance over her shoulder. The dirty, dissipated man was looking after them, befuddled as a zombie.

They went up six flights, Lydia following by a few steps, not wanting to risk both of them on a single step at the same time, a recipe for a disaster.

"People like him are the reason it's called the Value Palace, you know."

Lydia met her gaze and giggled.

Their room was in better shape than the lobby, but not by much. She stepped to the window. The hotel sat inland on a saddleback between two valleys. Far to the north stretched a pastiche of rooftops, hovels glinting under the harsh, unforgiving sun. Chaotic lines of foot traffic threaded their ways in between hovels, the slum-dwellers without hovers, and the area absent the usual skyful of pneumatubes. Hotels of similar quality as the Value Palace lined what looked to be a main thoroughfare. She suspected this hotel was no better or worse than most.

Lydia backed away from the window, sat on the bed, and nearly wept.

"Somewhat of a reduced circumstance, I'd say," Melanctha said, sitting next to her.

She leaned into the other woman, biting off her despair. "I feel so helpless."

Melanctha nodded. "It's difficult, having to wait on other people."

"I just wish we could walk into the palace openly, without a disguise, and tell the Empire that a great wrong has been perpetuated upon them."

"You don't like all this intrigue and subterfuge."

"It feels so ... dishonest."

Which, as she thought about it, was precisely the point. Reared amidst a race of beings biologically disinclined to deception, Lydia felt the wrongness of her current circumstance like a crushing weight on her chest. It pressed the air from her lungs and left her gasping for breath. As though the oxygen of truth and forthrightness couldn't be found in the atmosphere of Gaea. As if New Athens lived off the noxious odors of fraud and artifice, chicanery and stratagem.

It wasn't how Lydia wanted to live.

"Mela, if this all resolves the way we think it will," Lydia asked, phrasing it with the delicacy of avoidance, "will I be like them?"

Melanctha pulled away and adjusted her position to face Lydia directly. "Taking over the apex doesn't require you to adopt the rot. Absolutely not. You're your own person, Lydia. You always have been. Xsirh, Basilissa, Ezra, Dorian, and all your other mentors saw to it that you developed the inner resources to be your own guide and resist the blandishments of convenience and exigency. No, Lydia, you won't be like them, not at all."

It was comforting to hear her say that. Lydia's doubts stemmed not from her lack of experience with such circumstances—and she had none, a royal rutabaga indeed—but from her insecurity about what would happen next.

Seeking some distraction, she turned on the holo above the bed. The holo was mounted on an articulated joint and could be positioned to be viewed from any place in the room. Lydia saw her own face staring back at her.

"Looks as if the previous occupants enjoyed watching themselves."

Lydia blushed, guessing that antics on the bed were often pictured on the holo. She switched the channel to the local news.

"And in interstellar matters," the busty Bustine said, her twin zeppelins threatening to lift her out of the studio completely, "the Empress Hecuba Zenon arrives tomorrow, back from her tour of the Imperial Domains, having circumnavigated the galaxy. Other than some minor route deviations to avoid the outbreaks, the new Empress was received by her subjects with all the pomp and circumstance at their disposal. Today, her Royal Highness issued this statement through her shameless self-promotion department."

The holo switched to a still 3-d image of the beetle-browed Empress, the wart on her cheek at least as big as one of the didinium slugs in Lydia's possession and almost the same puke green.

"'My blessed subjects, citizens of the Empire, Gaeans all, on the evening of my return tomorrow night from touring the Imperial Domains, I do declare a holiday in celebration of the effusive welcome

I received from all my loyal subjects. Further, since I so love a masquerade, all the attendees will come dressed up as members of the royal family and a contest will be held to determine who has most closely masqueraded themselves as one of us. Everyone is invited and no one shall be turned away."

The still image appeared to be looking directly at Lydia, as if daring her to come.

* * *

She and Melanctha were at breakfast the next morning when they heard the news.

The restaurant was a Spanish bistro. On its walls pranced beefy male bovines with outsized horns, waltzing to the strains of a soft violin on a warm summers' day. Lydia was having a breakfast berry crisp topped with creamy salmon spread and a side of radish hash browns with a cucumber-avocado shake, a fair compromise to the meat-laden dishes that these Homo sapiens seemed to consume at every meal.

In the corner, above all the patrons and drowning out the threnody-wailing violin, was a holonews broadcast, full of market-opening ticker numbers and sniggering about the upcoming Imperial Masquerade, none so brazen to comment on the one currently in progress.

"Coming up: An outbreak of a virulent respiratory infection this morning on Amphitrite III, and what Imperial Infection Control is doing about it. But first, this word from our sponsor."

Lydia frowned, raising an eyebrow at Melanctha. "Do you think the Syndicate will let the Imperium proceed with its usual blasma-cannon approach?"

"I'll bet Likashose is busy this morning," Melanctha replied. "Speaking of whom, we need to get more supplies for our disguises. I didn't realize we were out. You shouldn't be seen in public without one."

Lydia didn't mind, having grown tired of slapping the rubbery props onto her face, of the itching and sweating and worrying whether the make-up was sloughing off. She'd known they were running low and had forgotten to say anything. She and Melanctha had left their things in the hotel room, intending to fetch a quick breakfast and return afterward for their effects, Lydia bringing only her palmcom.

With both Countess Lillis and the Admiral's son Hadrian gathering support among the noble families, and the genetic comparison nearly finished, Lydia couldn't wait to get on with things. The last thing she wanted was to attend an Imperial Ball.

"You should waltz into the palace and claim the throne," Melanctha quipped.

Her palmcom on the table beside her plate beeped. "Comparison finished," it flashed.

Lydia just stared at the machine.

"Are you going to look at it? Most people would be anxious."

A life hangs in the balance on the thread of its result, she thought, knowing what it would say, knowing she wasn't prepared for its conclusion. There simply wasn't a way to prepare. Hadrian had said as much. What does a person do to gird herself for the moment she finds out that she isn't who she thought she was, but someone far more important, someone fated to change the course of the Empire, someone fated to restore a balance thrown into a chaotic wobble by someone so wicked that all innocence and purity was disillusioned and sullied.

I am who I am, even if I never knew it, Lydia thought. The existential swirl of sophistry and supposition, of who was who and who was perceived as whom, threatened to consume her in its solipsistic slobber.

I am, she thought, and my only task is to be the very best person I can.

She punched up the results.

Princess Cybill Zenon, purported daughter of Emperor Athanasios Zenon and Empress Consort Ambrosia Lillis, was no relation to her supposed grandmother, Countess Giorgi Lillis, to a ninety-five percent certainty. Princess Cybill Zenon was a direct descendant of Professor Dorian and Viscountess Ambassador Basilissa Procopio, their daughter to a ninety-nine percent certainty. Lydia Procopio, purported daughter of Professor Dorian and Viscountess Ambassador Basilissa Procopio, was no relation to them whatsoever to a ninety-nine percent certainty. Lydia Procopio was a direct descendant of Countess Giorgi Lillis and was, to a ninety-five percent certainty, her granddaughter.

A tear trickled from her eye.

Lydia wiped it away and handed the palmcom to Melanctha.

The Colonel read the results, her face growing sharper with disdain. "I'm sending this to Countess Lillis, if you don't mind."

Lydia nodded her to go ahead, her mind aswirl with the implications.

Somehow, the two girls, Lydia Procopio and Cybill Zenon, born the same day, had been switched shortly after birth.

And the daughter of Emperor Athanasios Zenon and Empress Consort Ambrosia Lillis was supposed to have died in the wreck of the vessel carrying Ambassador Procopio and her family to Kziznvxrz. A vessel sabotaged with the intent of killing the Emperor's daughter.

But she'd survived the crash.

Lydia, the Emperor's daughter, looked across the table at Colonel Melanctha Remes, Commander of the IBS Outpost on Lucina IX.

The Emperor's daughter, Lydia told herself.

"Your Highness," Colonel Remes said, bowing her head. "It's my privilege and honor to offer you my everlasting fealty and service and those of my descendants in perpetuity, may you rule wisely and well."

The doors crashed open. A beam zapped Melanctha in the back and hauled her toward the door, her arms flailing, the palmcom flying. Blasma barrels shattered through windows on all sides, every rifle aimed at Lydia. Patrons hurled themselves to the floor.

A uniformed man stopped just inside the door as Melanctha was towed past, the tractor beam hauling her out of the restaurant.

"Nikitas!" she snarled at him, her arms now pinned to her side by her captors.

The uniformed man approached Lydia. "I'm Lieutenant-Colonel Urian Nikitas, and you, Lydia Procopio, are under arrest."

Lydia considered attempting to flee but knew she wouldn't get far. "I'm a sovereign citizen of Kziznvxrz," she said. "You can't arrest me."

"I don't care if you're the Empress, bitch. You're under arrest." And he clapped a glasma bracelet on one wrist, spun her around and cuffed the other, and then hiked them both up between her shoulder blades. "Come quietly, and you won't get hurt."

The Emperor's daughter, and rightful heir to the throne.

Not much good it'll do me now, Lydia thought.

Chapter 27

The cell wasn't any worse than the others she'd been in. I've become a connoisseur of confinement, Lydia thought.

What differed was the level of security surrounding it. The Bogiati Military Prison on the island of Aegina was encircled with the elite corps of brigadiers. The island itself was surrounded by a fleet of ocean-going vessels whose combined deck space exceeded the island's square footage. Overhead circled a fleet of aircraft whose sides bristled with so many guns they looked like porcupines. In subspace orbit was an armada of spacecraft equipped with so many blasma cannon that they could have seared the surface of Gaea with one fusillade.

You'd think they were greeting an arriving Imperial, Lydia thought sardonically. Oh, that's right, the Empress Hecuba returns from her Imperial tour tomorrow.

The booking process seemed more akin to a military induction, with strip, shower, body scan, medical screening, cavity searches, cuticle cutting, toe-jam inspection, and a variety of unmentionable indignities.

"What's that rash on your forearm?" the doctor asked.

Lydia looked at her blankly. "What rash?"

"Right there, those red spots."

She looked closely at the area indicated. On the interior of her fore-arm, three inches in from her wrist, tiny red dots sprinkled an oval patch of skin one inch wide and two inches long, each dot so small as to look like a pinprick. "That's a rash?"

"How long has it been that way?"

Lydia shrugged. "I don't know, a while, I think." She tried to remember if she had it the last time she'd left Kziznvxrz.

"Does it itch?"

She shook her head. "Well, on occasion," she amended, remembering having scratched it before.

"Bioscan is clear, no infectious pathogens aboard," the doctor said, looking at her handheld. "Must be a histamine response to some allergen."

Then they gave her an orange pair of formalls and hustled her to a cell deep underground.

A grill in the ceiling high above issued a stream of chilly air. The solid granite block walls yielded no clue to what lay beyond. The door was set in a wall of carbo-nick alloy reinforced glasma, the door itself a single sheet of clear glasma. Beyond the door stood four guards, two more than she usually had. The bunk was a thick slab of travertine sitting directly on the floor. The toilet was a ring of porcelain on a pedestal in the corner, the sink an indentation in the wall sticking its lower lip into the room. Two bare loomglobes hung near the ceiling, in excess of the requisite lone-source lighting.

Fancy, Lydia thought, feeling spoiled to have so much light.

She put her face in her hands and wept in despair.

* * *

The woman appeared without warning outside the cell door.

Lydia had been in the cell for about four hours, without a way to mark the passing of time. She'd looked away from the door for a moment, and when she looked back, the guards were gone and the woman was there, unannounced.

She needed no announcement.

Her face had lurked in the background of every appearance by Emperor Athanasios or Princess Hecuba for the last twenty years. A hawk face, watching relentlessly. A predatory face, ready to pounce at the least sign of intransigence, resistance, or disobedience. She was the Dowager Empress Narcissa Thanos.

She wore a slick jacquard uniform, similar in style to the ones worn by all the Imperial Guards, but hers of a far finer material, with embroidered accents at hem, knee, waist, breast, and neckline. Her shoes were form-flow flats, meant for mobility and comfort, whose only concession to style was a sequined clasp. On one hand she wore a brass ring that was green with corrosion. Her hair was tied tight at the nape and fell straight to her mid-back, leaving the hawk face sharp and ready to peck.

She stood there, silent, staring at Lydia through the clear glasma door, like a patron at a zoo watching a confined animal. She did not move nor evince any change in expression for five full minutes, her eyes boring through Lydia like lasers through granite.

Lydia didn't have in her the ramrod steel hardened in the forge of politics, but she knew the purpose in such stares.

And she refused to cower, not to this one, not to the usurper. Not to the mastermind of the scheme that had put the Princess and Heir to the Throne on a ship bound for the galactic rim, its engines sabotaged to explode on arrival. Not to the scoundrel who'd subsequently eliminated any other proximate claimant to the throne through cunning, stealth, and intrigue, one of those victims having been Icarus Terzi, son of Count Terzi, Melanctha's betrothed.

No, Lydia would not cower to the usurper.

The silence stretched between step-daughter and step-mother, neither ceding ground by speaking first, two she-wolves pissing on opposite sides of the same tree.

"I served your mother, once." The voice was sultry, an octave lower than expected.

Lady's Maid Narcissa Thanos to her Imperial Highness, the Empress Consort, Ambrosia Lillis, whom the Emperor Athanasios Zenon had married posthumously. The Lady's Maid hadn't had a solid enough grip on the Emperor's affections to stop the post-mortem nuptials, the marital obsequies.

"You killed her, didn't you?"

Thanos laughed softly, not a hint of smile reaching her face. "Of course, dear Lydia—or perhaps I should call you Cybill, since that's your birth name. How else could I claim my place? But my deeds of yore are such a bore."

Lydia saw no one behind the woman and sensed no one else in the corridor outside the cell. Was she completely alone, no one to bear witness to her acknowledging Regicide? Had she turned off the holocams?

"No, dear Lydia, there's no one listening and no devices recording. We're alone, child, just you and me."

Completely alone meant completely vulnerable. So why doesn't she kill me? Lydia wondered.

"Why don't I kill you? You're of use to me, a distraction for the masses. Oh, they'll never know I switched you and the retarded Procopio whelp when you were infants only two weeks from the womb, but they *will* know of your conspiracy with the Wrwrmrfn when you attempt to assassinate the Empress Hecuba. Homo sapiens will finally declare war and stir those indolent Kziznvxrfn from their centuries-long slumber."

Lydia was taken aback at the woman's perfect pronunciation of the two foreign words. I thought I was the only person who spoke perfect Kziznvxrz. She smelled the faint miasma of an algae-rich tidal flat. Her Kzizn father Xsirh had asserted in his last letter that the dissident Wrwrmrfn leader might be in hiding among Homo sapiens, masquerading as one of them, using the long-acting catalyst to solidify the Kziznvxrfn exoderm. Lydia stared at the Dowager Empress.

"I see you're beginning to understand, Lydia. You humans are notoriously stupid and impulsive. Not that the Kziznvxrfn are absent all flaw, certainly. Yvuliv blf zxxfhv nv, gzpv z ollp zg blfihvou."

Lydia automatically translated the aphorism. "Before you accuse me, take a look at yourself."

"Our tolerance of your pesky race has gone on far too long. We should have ground your endoskeletons down to calcium centuries ago, before you managed to escape the cesspit you'd made of your own nest."

"You're her, aren't you?" Lydia asked, gasping. "Mzixrhhz Gszmlh, the Wrwrmrfn dissident leader!"

This time, a smile did reach the face of Narcissa Thanos, but there was no humor in it, only the simple necessity of inflicting death. "Now, Lydia, I have to kill you. But not before I use you to wipe out three-quarters of humanity and stir those lazy pacifist Paramecium brethren of mine into wiping out the other quarter."

And then she was gone.

Lydia had been looking right at her and had not seen her leave. The Wrwrmrfn Leader in human disguise had simply vanished. And she'd vanished so quickly that Lydia was surprised she hadn't heard the pop of a vacuum suddenly filling with air.

Staring at the spot where the woman had been, Lydia wondered how to stop her. I'll escape and denounce her at the Imperial Ball! she thought, realizing instantly how idiotic it was to think she might escape the most secure prison on Gaea.

Somewhere, a door slammed open, an order was given, and a contingent of guards marched in, halting in front of her cell door at another order.

The woman at their fore turned toward the cell door. She alone among them wore a single, floor-length robe of fine, shimmering, night-black silk. "Lydia Procopio, daughter of Viscountess Ambassador Basilissa Procopio and Professor Dorian Procopio," the woman announced in grave tones, "you are hereby found guilty of conspiracy to spread virulent pathogens to numerous worlds, including but not limited to Amphitrite Three, Pyrgos Five, Quirinus Eight, Lucina Nine, Ananke Ten, Eris Eleven, and Cygnus Twenty, requiring their sterilization. You are sentenced to death."

"But I plead not guilty!" she protested. "Besides, you missed four, six, and seven." She wondered why Erato IV wasn't mentioned, a planet she'd visited several times, the planet where she and Xsirh had been detained, known locally as Theogony.

"Great stars above, Ms. Procopio, what do you think this is, some backward style of government, like a democracy? Now that you've nothing further to say for yourself, you're to be taken to the steps of the Parthenon for public execution by a firing squad of your peers."

"But I was reared on Kziznvxrz," she protested. "Where are you going to get twelve of my peers to shoot me?"

"Uh, well, uh, I hadn't thought of that. We'll have to consider that, but of course it won't delay your execution by a moment. Come with me."

"Who are you? You haven't introduced yourself."

"Me? Oh, sorry, I'm Daphne Carras, Chief Justice of the Gaean Empire. I thought everyone knew my name."

A legend in her own mind, apparently, Lydia thought. The cell door swung aside with a whoosh. She stepped forward to the indicated place in the midst of the soldiers, the Chief Justice beside her. They placed a pair of glasma circlets on her wrists.

For the second time that day, Lydia smelled the faint miasma of an algae-rich tidal flat.

On the Chief Justice's order, the contingent did an about-face and escorted her from the facility.

* * *

Aboard the military ferry between the island of Aegina and the mainland, Lydia stood encircled by guards near the prow, the ship shrouded in thick fog, the thrum of engines under her feet. Gulls circled the vessel overhead, calling out antemortem laments. To starboard, port, astern, and ahead, barely visible, were auxiliary ships in the flotilla escorting the prisoner to the mainland.

They can't even wait until Empress Hecuba returns, Lydia thought bitterly, despair threatening to overwhelm her.

The Chief Justice in her floor-length robe stepped into the circle of guards and nodded amiably.

It's not your execution, Lydia wanted to say.

"It's not your time, child," Chief Justice Carras said with a wink. "Hold your breath."

Astounded, Lydia took a deep breath and held it.

The flock of gulls dispersed, the sky above them shimmered, and the guards surrounding Lydia fainted, each of them slumping to the deck unconscious. Lydia caught the faint odor of a soporific.

A boarding ramp dropped from nowhere, and Daphne nudged her forward. The diaphanous hull made the Kziznvxrz ship nearly invisible in the thick fog.

Her heart thundering with excitement and disbelief, Lydia ascended the ramp and boarded the vessel, Daphne right behind her. The sub-ether drives engaged, Lydia bracing herself against a bulkhead.

Daphne's human physique melted into a blob of green protoplasm, which squirmed from beneath the robe and sat up on its exoderm. Xsirh swung his optical organelles at Lydia and opened his tentacles toward her.

Weeping, Lydia stepped into her father's embrace.

* * *

"Father, no, I can't let you do that. Don't you understand? I'm the one who has to expose her. Remember what I told you about Homo sapiens? They're as likely to crucify me as to crown me. Some politician could blame me at any time for infecting all those planets. As much as I'd like your help, this is something I have to do on my own."

Lydia and Xsirh were sitting across from each other in a corner table in the ship galley, the gigantic Kzizn Armada Flagship half in subether, half in the physical universe, hovering in the shadow of the moon. The Kzizn Naval Commander, Chief Admiral Svxgli Pirgrplh, sat to one side of the table. The way he watched them reminded her of a Licensed Family Counselor doing therapy for a kid from a broken home.

Lydia wanted to tell him she wasn't broke. She had just told them about Mzixrhhz Gszmlh, the Wrwrmrfn dissident leader, and her grand plan to destroy humanity by inciting a war between the races.

"Well, yes, I guess I understand," Xsirh said, taking her hand in his tentacles. "Who am I lying to? Of course I don't understand. You humans are beyond understanding. But I don't need to understand. I just need to let you handle this the way you feel is best. They're your people and it's your planet. One of my people may have messed up your life terribly, but you're in the best position to fix it—or even know how."

Well, at least he understands part of it, she thought, sighing. Would he ever understand the rest? The human group-think, the prideful face-saving, the urinary competition? Probably not.

"Here, take this, Lydia." Xsirh pushed an ampule toward her.

The vial was soft-surfaced and compressible, with a spout formed on one end. "What is it?" she asked, picking it up. It had an organic feel, clearly made from the outer membranes of a large, single-cell protozoon.

"It's an antidote to the exoderm-solidifying catalyst. Squeeze the ampule to spray her with it, and she'll melt into her natural shape."

Lydia tucked it into a pocket. "I hope I can get close enough to use it. She's pretty slippery."

Admiral Pirgrplh got Lydia's attention. "So you won't need me to attack the palace?"

"No, Admiral, I'm afraid not."

"Oh, thank the One-Cell-Over-All for that! I thought for certain I'd have to fire a weapon. Ghastly things. We only have them aboard in case of a hostile confrontation." He swung his optical organelles toward Xsirh. "You know, Xsirhglksvi, I'm not even sure they work."

A warfaring race, the Kzizn were not.

"So, your Imperial Highness," Admiral Pirgrplh said, "tell me where I can let you off, and signal me if some need arises."

"Thank you, Svxgli, that's very kind," she said, knowing it'd take her years to become accustomed to the title. "And please, just call me Lydia."

"But I could never do that, your Highness, not now, not with—"

"It's not official until it's official," Lydia interrupted. "When they crown me their Empress, then it's official." She sighed. They were such sticklers for protocol. "You can set me down in Countess Lillis's garden."

"Yes, your Highness." He bowed to her, rolled onto his exoderm and squirmed toward the door.

Xsirh looked at her from across the table, his tentacles intertwined with her fingers. "Promise me you'll be careful."

"I'll be careful, Father, I promise." And she leaned across the table to kiss him somewhere in the vicinity of his cheek.

Chapter 28

The bedroom on the fourth floor of the Lillis Estate in central New Athens was bedecked in silks, satins, sequins, and squawkadoodles.

"I don't know why Ambrosia liked squawkadoodles," Countess Giorgi told Lydia. "She was half-crazy for them and insisted on wearing them everywhere she went. I persuaded her to forego them for the Imperial Ball the night she met Prince Athanasios, and I'm sure she'd have worn them at her wedding if she hadn't been ..." The older woman turned away, her voice catching.

Lydia had stepped off the Kzizn Armada Flagship into the garden behind the Lillis mansion. By the time she'd turned to wave, the ship had already vanished, and the old Countess had swept up Lydia into her arms, weeping profusely and squealing in delight. The comparative analysis results had reached Countess Giorgi Lillis that morning, just before Lydia's arrest at the Spanish Bistro. Then, arm-in-arm, grandmother and granddaughter had entered the house, Grandmama taking Lydia directly to Ambrosia's suite on the fourth floor, where the Consort-to-be had prepared herself for the fateful Imperial ball. "Where you're going to prepare for quite another Imperial ball," Countess Giorgi said.

The two of them stopped in front of the dressing dummy that still displayed the gossamer, robin's-egg gown Ambrosia had worn, its silicoid-alloy threads impervious to the depredations of time and inattention. A sash of similar material trailed to the floor on one side, and a bodice of gathers barely covered the dummy mammaries.

Lydia eyed the dress doubtfully, knowing her bust already the object of too much testosterone titillation. The ballroom floor will be awash in hormones if I wear that! she thought.

"Not nearly inadequate enough to show off your fine figure," Grandmama leered, "but it's what your mother wore. In the palace, there's a portrait of her wearing that dress, you know. Makes me weep to think about that night, when it seemed that every girl's dream was to be in her shoes, and every boy's dream to be in his." Countess Lillis put her palm to her chest. "Oh, and when they kissed, the stars burst with joy and brilliance!"

For a moment, Lydia thought the old biddy was going to swoon.

"But you won't have your prince tomorrow night. It'll be just you and all the other guests against that bitch upstart Lady's Maid."

Lydia smiled and patted the ampule in her pocket, wondering whether she should tell Grandmama Giorgi about the alien in disguise who'd ruled the Gaean Empire from behind the throne for the past quarter century. Better let it be a surprise, Lydia thought, guessing the Countess wouldn't be able to keep it to herself.

"I've invited a few friends over for dinner this evening, my darling. I hope you don't mind."

"Oh, no, not at all, Grandmama," Lydia said. "Uh, who would that be?"

"Her Excellency, Bishop Dea Papadopoulos of the Divine Orthodoxy, Admiral Hector Kritikos, Chief of the Gaean Naval Forces, the honorable Elke Drivas, Speaker of the Gaean House Assembly, his honor Flavian Galanis, Premier of the Gaean Administration, and her right honorarium herself, Daphne Carras, Chief Justice of the Gaean Empire."

Lydia blanched, particularly at the latter, the Chief Justice certain to be under suspicion for having let such a high-value detainee escape from her custody.

"What's the matter, dear? It's important we have their support before the coup, don't you think?"

"Uh, well—"

"Did you think the five most powerful people in the Empire besides the Dowager herself were going to throw their weight behind you the instant you expose that rotten, bottom-feeding, scum-sucking rutabaga for the deceitful, power-hungry, concupiscent slut she is?"

"Uh, well—"

"They're a bunch of—"

"Grandmama, that's enough."

She stared at her granddaughter, her eyes wide.

As if I've roused her from a trance, Lydia thought. "You're right, of course. It's important that I have their support. I just hope they don't get distracted by the lure of power, too. It's certainly corrupted the Dowager Empress, hasn't it?"

The eyebrows rose and furrowed together. "I hadn't thought of that. I guess we'd better tread carefully. They'll be here in an hour."

* * *

Lydia greeted each in the atrium of the Lillis mansion with a perfect smile and a perfect manner, wearing a lime-green evening gown whose neckline curved modestly down toward her cleavage to give just a hint of its promise without flaunting the proud, full bodice. She wore a didinium like a corsage, slung over one shoulder, the creature's protoplasm hanging elongated to her hip and attached to the slim belt of emeralds encircling her waist. The greens complemented her skin, giving her the vibrant glow of a blushing bride, offsetting the hue given her by her chlorophyll-rich diet.

First among equals, her Excellency Bishop Dea Papadopoulos of the Divine Orthodoxy was the first guest to arrive, ordering her passel of priests to wait outside. She was bedecked in layers of vestments, an elaborate chasuble over an intricate dalmatic, and beneath it all the humble alb, a pure-white robe reaching her ankles. The miter she wore atop her head was a modest cap of intertwined gold bands, a far cry from the church steeple she'd sported at the coronation.

"Lady Giorgi, who is this dear, beautiful child?" Bishop Papadopoulos asked, her eyes wide as she took in the sight before her.

"Your Excellency, may I introduce my granddaughter, Lydia," the Countess said.

The Bishop's head whirled so fast that her miter almost took flight. "But you don't have ..." She swung her gaze back to Lydia. "My darling, it's such a pleasure. Surely, Grandma Countess will explain herself in due course."

"The pleasure is all mine, your Excellency," Lydia replied, curtseying and kissing the ring of the Bishopric. "And with luck, all the mysteries will be revealed tomorrow evening."

Admiral Hector Kritikos, Chief of the Gaean Naval Forces, was next to arrive, a contingent of commanders marching in lockstep up to the entryway behind him. He doffed a gold-rimmed tricorn, tassels dangling merrily from the two rear horns, and bowed to her elaborately. His uniform was so bedecked with medals that it tinkled like a windchime as he straightened. His spats shone like mirrors and brass tacks trimmed his slacks.

"Did you say `granddaughter,' Dear Countess? Wherever on Gaea ...? Pardon my discomfiture, my child, it is a shock, to say the least, to behold the apparition of one so dear to us all. A pleasure to meet you, Lady Lydia."

"Mutual, Lord Kritikos," she said, curtseying and not minding the way his gaze traveled the length of her body. "I so enjoyed lunch with Lord Hadrian a few days ago. Please give him my regards."

The honorable Elke Drivas, Speaker of the Gaean House Assembly, arrived next, a bunch of bureaucrats bickering bitterly amongst themselves behind her. She looked relieved to be shut of their banter as she stepped through the portico into the atrium. The jacquard jacket and herringbone skirt seemed somewhat at odds with the business pumps on her feet, but then pumping the flesh was a politician's occupational hazard. The precise cut of her pageboy and no-stick, perfect face signaled how impervious she was to ridicule and blackmail, like an immaculate angel devoid of taint.

"Lydia, dear, so honored to make your acquaintance. Where has the Countess Lillis been hiding you all my life?"

"A pleasure, Honorable Speaker," Lydia replied, curtseying.

Her right honorarium herself, Daphne Carras, Chief Justice of the Gaean Empire, swept in moments later on robes made of wings, like a wraith on strings, floating into the atrium from within a coterie of legal aides, their faces planted in giant tomes of legal codes.

"Your Honorarium," Lydia said forthrightly, before Countess Lillis introduced her. She knelt at the feet of the Chief Justice and bowed her head. "Please forgive me for the debacle earlier today aboard the ferry."

"Oh, that?" A light laugh tittered off her tongue. The woman helped Lydia to her feet and clasped her by her shoulders. "Never you mind, dear girl. It'll take more than that to tie my robes into knots. Her Highness Empress Hecuba owes me some latitude. After all, I crowned the bitch. Very nice to meet you, Lady Lydia. Did you say, Lady Countess, that she's your granddaughter? You didn't have to, since it's so clear. Lydia, my child, you look just like your mother, who was beholden by Gaeans everywhere."

Lydia smiled and sighed, basking in the Chief Justice's regard.

"Oh, but where's our colleague, his honor, Premier Flavian Galanis?" Justice Carras asked.

Countess Lillis dropped her hand from her ear. "I've just received a com from him, your Honorarium. He sends his apologies that he's been delayed, and he's asked that we not wait dinner for his arrival."

Grandmother Giorgi extended her arm to Lydia, and together they led the way into the dining room.

Tablecloths of damask and napkins of silk cushioned silver flatware so shiny it might have burned through the table. The seven-place setting of fine Hardassian cerasteel service scintillated under a chandelier of Crgrtrzm crystal, its thousand bulbs so diffuse and subdued that illumination appeared from thin air. The centerpiece of Litressan lilies sprouted from slim, graceful stalks, a single flower spreading its pure, pale petals in front of each plate, the flower the family namesake.

"A toast and a prayer," Bishop Papadopoulos said, standing and raising her Crgrtrzm crystal chalice. "To the return of Countess Lydia Lillis to the warm embrace of her family, may all her rightful privileges and positions be restored forthwith! Eis igian!"

"Eis igian!" everyone repeated.

Lydia raised her chalice with the others, in hers water tinged with a dye to make it the same gold-brownish color as the Metaxa in their chalices. She metabolized ethyl alcohol so quickly it was disorienting for her to drink. And she knew she'd need a clear head tonight.

And so it went, each guest toasting Lydia with praise and good wishes so effusive it was intoxicating. And finally it came round to her.

Lydia stood and smiled demurely. "I'm honored and humbled by your welcome. In some ways I know you honor the memory of my mother, Ambrosia, and if I have any regret, it's that I'll never know her as you did, to bask in the warmth of her smile and the grace of her presence. I am my mother's daughter, and I'm also the child of Viscountess and Professor Procopio, who reared me until I was four, and the child of the Kziznvxrfn, who reared me after that. Equally Gaean and Kzizn, I'm a child of the galaxy, and I pray I'll be able to serve the people of the Gaean Empire to the best of my ability. Thank you for honoring me tonight. Long live the Empire!"

"Long live the Empire!" everyone repeated.

"And let's eat before the Metaxa goes to my head," Speaker Drivas drawled.

On a signal from Countess Lillis, servants began to bring out appetizers.

"What is that thing you're wearing on your shoulder, Lady Lillis?" Admiral Kritikos asked. "It almost looks alive."

Her laugh was light, and the night felt like magic. "It *is* alive, Admiral. It's a didinium, a single-cell protist ciliate from Kziznvxrz." She took it off her shoulder and rolled it into a ball to hand to him. "It's an excellent hygienator, since it feeds on all microorganisms it comes into contact with. On Kziznvxrz, it's a fierce predator."

The Admiral peered at the ball of protoplasm skeptically. "If I may, I'd rather pass, but thank you."

Sounds of a disturbance came from the atrium.

The bombastic voice of the Premier Flavian Galanis floated into the room. Suddenly, he was at the doorway. "Pardon, Lady Countess, for my tardy arrival. Fashionably late and all that, eh?" Over the top of his suit, he wore a silk tabard embroidered with the Imperial Crest, as clear a declaration where his loyalties lay as the scorn upon his face, his eyes immediately finding Lydia.

The ball of protoplasm in Lydia's hand sprouted spikes as it bristled, shot out two tendrils, one at the chandelier and the other at the far edge of the table, and it slung itself like a rocket right at Galanis.

The Premier clawed at the alien stuck to his face as he stumbled backward and fell with a whump to the floor, pulling at the goop. His hands turned to goop themselves, going green, and his body melted into a mass of slime, the didinium snacking lustily on the Premier's Kzizn face.

600

"What in Hades?!" Members of the dinner party crowded around the quivering mass in a tuxedo, gawking.

"Stand back," Lydia said, reaching over to pull the didinium off its victim. The ball of protoplasm strained against her hold, trying to leap from her hands to return to its feast.

The Kzizn corpse quivered in its death throes, and then was still.

"What's that horrible smell?! Is that a sewer leak?"

"Where did this alien come from?"

"That creature at the coronation, the one that the Dowager Empress splashed, wasn't it similar?"

"What has it done with Flavian, the poor boy?"

"Lydia, dear, do tell us what's going on, please?"

She looked among them and sighed. "This is a dissident Kziznvxrfn who disguised itself as a human, one of several Kziznvxrfn who are conspiring to topple the Gaean Empire. It's such a long story that I don't know where to start."

"Well," Bishop Papadopoulos said, "start from the beginning. How about, `In the beginning …'?"

"Maybe not that far back," Countess Lillis said.

"Probably not a good idea," the Bishop said. "I always get bogged down in the begats. But go on, my girl, take all the time you need."

Lydia looked among them, sighed again, and told them what was happening.

* * *

Waking the next morning in the suites that had once belonged to her mother, Ambrosia, Lydia felt both elated and encumbered: Elated at the warm reception and near-unconditional support she'd received from four of the most prominent Gaean citizens, and encumbered with guilt for the havoc created by the Wrwrmrfn faction from Kziznvxrz.

As much as she tried, she couldn't shake the feeling that she was somehow responsible for their having suborned at least two high-placed Gaean officials. It was guilt by association, and with that guilt was the worry that regular, peaceful Kziznvxrfn would be blamed for the betrayals perpetrated by a few dissidents.

And the question left in everyone's mind last night after Lydia had finished her story was, how many more dissident Kziznvxrfn had infiltrated the nobility?

Further, the Imperial Masquerade Ball was tonight, and Lydia was overwhelmed with the preparation and the coming confrontation with the Dowager Empress, Emperor Zenon's second wife, Narcissa Thanos, otherwise known as the Wrwrmrfn dissident leader, Mzixrhhz Gszmlh. The confabulated cabal of conspirators last night had all agreed: Bish Pap and Admiral Kritikos would investigate Premier Galanis's disappearance, and Lydia herself must publicly expose the fraud.

No one knew how long the alien had occupied the Premier's position. A factor most humans overlooked was longevity. The Kzizn lived such long lives that subsuming oneself into the life of a comparatively short-lived human was not nearly the sacrifice that it would be for a Homo sapiens.

The combined guilt by association and the anxiety about tonight's confrontation weighed heavily on Lydia.

"I have to get out of the house, Grandmama," she told Countess Giorgi at breakfast. The weight of luxury around her added to the burdens she already carried, the mansion palatial.

"Certainly, take a stroll down at the docks. The fish market is not to be missed, and perhaps it'll remind you somewhat of home. But do take the scullery maid Melpomene with you. She's a sharp eye for miscreants and a sharper knife she keeps hidden in her bodice."

"Thank you, wonderful suggestion, Grandmama."

Melpomene was a substantial woman easily two inches taller than Lydia and nearly twice her weight. And it was weight well proportioned, the woman thick through both limb and torso. "It's my big bones, they say," she said, clasping her own meaty forearm in demonstration.

Lydia mocked herself up in the smock of a Scullery Maid and pulled a bonnet tight to obscure her looks.

The pneumatube ride was uncomfortable, the double capsule still not quite large enough for them both, Melpomene complaining she was too large for a single capsule and had to pay double to get anywhere. The tube popped them out just one street over from Pireas Bay in Attica, where smaller sea-going vessels clotted the small inlet's waters, pontoon wharves branching out in between. Many among these were private fishing trawlers, their captains and crew weathered by a life at sea. Stalls lined the streets facing the inlet, fishmongers calling out their catch for sale, screeching to be heard over the gulls. Brine and sea floated off the bay in the light breeze.

Toward one end were larger fishing trawlers, the industrial size, their cargo holds wheeled directly onto transport hovers for shipment to the canneries.

"Why we goin' here? They won't be sellin' none of their catch to the likes of us."

Reminiscent perhaps of a not-so-distant time in her life, Lydia mused, trawler hulls towering over them on either side of the wide quay.

A vaguely familiar man was stepping down a gangplank. He stared at Lydia and Melpomene as they strolled past. "Pardon, aren't you ...?"

She knew the voice. "Orrin, right? Orrin Stamos of Titanide Aquafoods, yes? We met on Theogony. I'm Lydia."

"Of course, yes, now I remember, much as I might like to forget," he said, looking abashed. "Terrible, the way they treated you and your father. How is he, by the way?"

"None the worse for the experience, thanks for asking. What brings you all the way to Gaea?" She was pleased to see someone she knew who didn't suspect her of Imperial ambitions and wasn't wanting to arrest her.

"Those didinium you were going to buy from me, as a matter of fact," he said, grinning. "I'm researching a possible niche market for them as a hygiene product."

"Surprised you got here, as paranoid as everyone is about these outbreaks." He seems genuinely pleased to see me, she thought. "How'd you get past Imperial Infection Control?"

"They're the ones who may be buying them. Despite the outbreaks on several planets in the Delta Quadrant, I noticed Theogony is virtually unaffected. Given its industry, nine-tenths water and all, I suspect the didinium might have a role, they're so ubiquitous. We're researching their anti-contaminant properties now."

"The ones on Kziznvxrz are so ferocious they'd be lethal. They're tamer on Theogony?"

"Certainly are. Say, Lydia, do you want to have lunch? My next appointment's not until three ...?"

"I can't, Orrin, sorry. I have an engagement tonight I'm preparing

603

for." She sighed and shrugged, seeing Melpomene was anxious to go. "But thank you, Orrin, very kind of you."

"Maybe tomorrow? How long are you on Gaea?"

She didn't know whether she'd be alive tomorrow, much less what her availability was. "I'm committed to a project for the next several days, but send me a holo, and I'll see what I can do. Very nice to see you again, Orrin."

"Nice to see you too, Lydia." He nodded and headed up the quay.

She watched him go, lamenting that she couldn't take him up on his offer. She'd sensed more than a desire to talk business, and she couldn't exactly say she'd had much of a social life recently.

"We're going to stand around here all day for what?" Melpomene said.

Lydia signaled she was ready to go. On their way back to the Lillis estate, she pondered the encounter, knowing her simple wish to go to lunch with a friend a distraction from the terrifying fate that awaited her at the palace tonight.

Not knowing its outcome.

Chapter 29

She wore the same dress her mother had on the night she met Emperor Athanasios.

The blue chiffon glowed with the color of the sea at high noon, the back open to the waist and gathers at the shoulders. In the front, the neckline dropped to the base of her sternum, the mountains on either side forming a rift valley hinting at the delights to be found there. A slim belt in sky-blue sequins trimmed the waist, and the material dropped to the floor, slit up the sides to mid-thigh, edged with a strip of azure lace. Matching heels in sequined straps winked from beneath the hem.

Around her neck she wore a single string of aquamarine and lapis lazuli, and from each ear dangled a two-inch trail of the same, a matching bracelet at one wrist. The jewelry was the same as her mother had worn, except for a few touches Lydia had added. Dangling from the bracelet was the green ampule given to her by Xsirh, and around one ankle was a lime-green ring of didinium, contained in an elastoband torus.

Grandmother Giorgi wore a dress similar to Lydia's but more modest in mien, exposing considerably less in both skin and form. Lydia and Countess Lillis were among thousands of guests heading toward the palace, the streets jammed with hovers. Traffic was stopped intermittently and hovers were moved aside as escorted hovercades were given room to pass, the glitterati getting favorable treatment.

"I could have insisted we get an escort, I guess," Countess Giorgi said.

"No, it's all right, Grandmama," Lydia said. "The less attention we get, the better, eh?"

But the longer it took, the more her anxiety mounted, her bowels tied up in knots by the time their vehicle floated up the long drive toward the palace entrance.

The Zenon Palace sat just north of New Athens, filling the saddleback between the Acharnes and Kamatero neighborhoods, the ridges on either side funneling winds off the Bay of Elefsina. The sprawling complex climbed both sides of the saddleback, all servicing the main palace structure. The palace itself brooded like a toad, framed on four sides by towering, black-stone turrets out of some medieval nightmare. The architecture was some deranged architect's blend of random historical themes. Multiple minarets poked their domes above the main roofline like obstinate children, none so bold as to challenge the corner turrets. Framing the main portico was a colonnaded walk between marble columns marching out from the entry like sentinels. And for the Imperial ball, miniature lights sprinkled every surface, the palace aglow like some tawdry house of depravity and dissolution.

And inside skulked Lydia's nemesis, the Dowager Empress Narcissa Thanos.

"Whatever happens, child, remember to smile," Countess Giorgi said.

Their hover pulled up to the entrance, and servants swarmed to assist them from the vehicle.

"If you could step this way for a bioscan, your Excellencies?"

Lydia followed the Countess under an arch. The glowing biodetector flashed green as she passed through it, the didinium at her ankle escaping detection.

One step behind the Countess, Lydia followed along the colonnaded walk toward the main portico, the columns on either side growing ever larger. By the time she reached the soaring doors, she felt extremely small.

Smile as Grandmama told you, she admonished herself.

The concierge took the Countess's calling card, swiped at a holodisplay to find their names, and passed the card to a footman. The footman's tails flapped happily as the servant led them deeper into the palace, the soaring ceilings and thick plush carpet absorbing the noise of their passage. The corridors were so sound-absorbent that had Lydia spoken, Countess Giorgi wouldn't have heard her. Walls of alabaster and marble leaned heavily inward, many showing signs of pictures recently removed.

The footman led them into the main ballroom, a vast hall already crowded with thousands of people. Twenty-one chandeliers hovered above, the central chandelier so ponderous she was convinced it had to be supported by antigrav units. At various points on the walls and on pillars throughout the hall perched portraits, hundreds of portraits, each one of a past member of the royal family, all mounted above head-height. Moved from the corridors into the ballroom for this occasion, Lydia guessed.

People nearby fell silent and stared at her.

The footman handed the card to the maitre d'. He glanced once at the card, glanced down his nose at them, and glanced at the card again, his brow furrowing. He gestured the footman close, pointed to a place toward the front of the hall, and whispered something.

The footman's eyebrows shot up. "Yes, Sir," he said. The footman handed Lydia a small flag on two-foot stick and said in a low voice, "Here is your number, Lady. At the time of the voting, hold your number just above your head, and good luck in the competition. This way, your Excellencies."

As he led them through the crowd, people turned to look, falling silent as Lydia walked past.

Countess Lillis nodded to many of them, her smile never faltering.

Lydia nodded to those who would meet her gaze, letting the hint of a smile reach her face. She caught up with the Countess and murmured, "This is all too easy, Grandmama."

"It is, isn't it?" The Countess shot her a look, her smile slipping not a notch.

The footman led them to the front of the hall, near a semi-circular dais raised three steps above the ballroom floor. Just yards from the dais stood two pillars. On one was a portrait of the Emperor, Athanasios Zenon, resplendent in full uniform, his spiked helmet tucked under one arm. At the pillar base stood a coterie of at least thirty imposters, each dressed as elaborately as he who was pictured. Mounted on the second pillar was a portrait of the Empress Consort Ambrosia Lillis stunning in a chiffon dress the blue of the sea at high noon. No one stood at the base of this pillar.

Countess Lillis looked up at the portrait above Lydia, and then brought her gaze down. Her hand leaped to her mouth, and her eyes filled with tears.

That was when Lydia realized that the ballroom had gone silent.

"Ravishing!" rang a voice. "Absolutely ravishing!" From the crowd stepped Orrin Stamos, CEO of Titanide Aquafoods, bedecked in uniform, a spiked helmet tucked under his arm. He stopped a few paces away and bowed elaborately. "Lady, I had no idea I'd find you here. A pleasure to see you again."

"Mutual, Mr. Stamos, and I see you're dressed the part." She gestured at portrait of Emperor Athanasios. "Good luck this evening, especially since it appears you have quite the competition."

"There's no competing with you, Lady. Tis clear you've already won." He stepped close to her and murmured, "What do I call you?"

"Lady Lillis is fine, or your Excellency. Mr. Stamos, this is my grandmother, Countess Giorgi Lillis." She introduced them, noticing that conversation in the room was returning to its previous low-level rumble.

"A business associate?" the Countess asked Lydia, looking flustered.

She can't help it, Lydia knew. The thought of working for a living was antithetical to the very ethos of nobility. "It wasn't long ago, Grandmama, that I discovered who I was."

"Thank the stars, you did. Wouldn't want your backside calloused from a chair, heaven spare you that terrible fate."

Lydia didn't roll her eyes at Orrin, and she saw he was trying not to grin. Suddenly, his grin faltered, and he went to his knees. Everyone else in the room bowed too, silence falling again.

Only Lydia still stood, feeling the stab of eyes in her back like a knife. She didn't need to be told who was there. Deliberately, impertinently, she remained standing in the presence of her royal Highness the Dowager Empress, not caring what offense it implied.

Had Narcissa Thanos wanted her dead, it would have been done, and Lydia would not now be standing beneath a portrait of her mother, wearing the same gown. The former Lady's Maid would have quietly rid herself of Lydia long ago, had she wanted it.

So Lydia remained with her back to the Dowager Empress, the only person in the room on her feet.

"Yes, he's right," hissed the soft, sultry voice, the lower octave menacing. "You do look stunning, dear Lydia."

The didinium around her ankle strained against its elastoband containment. Lydia fingered the ampule on her bracelet. Lydia pitched her voice so everyone in the room would hear. "And who, Lady Dowager Empress, are *you* impersonating?" Then she turned.

Beside Narcissa Thanos was Empress Hecuba.

Immediately, Lydia went to her knees. "I humbly beg your pardon, your Highness, for my unforgivable breach of protocol. I thought it was just the usurper behind me."

The Empress Hecuba Zenon threw a glance at her mother, her eyes going wide. In her hand was the royal scepter, a gold staff three feet long with a fist-sized diamond capping its head. She was sitting upon the semi-circular dais three steps above the ballroom floor, the Dowager Empress standing beside her. Second child of Emperor Athanasios Zenon, Hecuba wore a dress identical in design and materials to that in the portrait above Lydia, complete with lapis lazuli and aquamarine jewelry. The bright green wart the size of a banana slug on her cheek dispelled any hint of resemblance. Her dishwater hair was done up in spiraling vertical coils like some cultured, miniature plant. The single brow was almost a precipitous cliff above the close-set eyes. Her perpetually pouty lips puckered, as if in displeasure at the confrontation suddenly brewing in front of her.

"Why do you call her the usurper, Lady Lillis?"

"Because, your Highness, she murdered my mother, the Empress Consort Ambrosia Lillis," Lydia said.

The narrow gaze went to the Dowager Empress, Narcissa Thanos.

The former Lady's Maid to the Empress Consort gazed placidly back at the Empress.

"You don't deny this, Mother?"

"No, your Highness, why should I? Oh, perhaps not my proudest moment, but after all, I did it for you, dear. If I hadn't, her child would now be sitting where you are."

Lydia couldn't believe what she was hearing. The brazen admission of murder was so unexpected, laid out in so forthright a manner, without the slightest hesitation and with only the slightest compunction, that Lydia gawked at her nemesis.

"Do spare me the theatrics, Lady Lillis. Surely, your mother taught you better than that?" Then Narcissa issued an impertinent little laugh and put the back of her hand to her forehead. "Oh, sorry, I forgot about your upbringing. An orphan reared by giant slugs at the galactic rim. How desultory, how utterly despicable, how incredibly rutabaga!"

"Your Highness," Lydia said, keeping her voice under control, "the usurper switched the Emperor's first child with that of Viscountess and Professor Procopio, and four years later, sent Ambassador Procopio and her family to their deaths in a vessel sabotaged to crash upon arrival on Kziznvxrz."

Empress Hecuba looked quizzically at Lydia and then turned her gaze toward her mother. "You did all that, Mother?"

"I'm assiduous in my efforts not to be so industrious, I really am. Do I look like the kind of person who would do such dastardly deeds? Of course I did them. But not everyone died in the wreck, did they, Lady Lillis?"

"You mean ..." Hecuba glanced between her mother and Lydia, looking befuddled.

"Yes, your Highness," Lydia said. "I'm your half-sister, Cybill Zenon, daughter of the Empress Consort Ambrosia Lillis and firstborn child of Emperor Athanasios Zenon."

"Well then, who's that?" Hecuba pointed toward the forward corner of the ballroom to her left, where a woman in a blue evening gown scribbled furiously on a wall with a crayon, attendants attempting to sop up endless ribbons of drool.

"That is the child of Viscountess Ambassador Basilissa and Professor Dorian Procopio," Lydia replied. "I have the genetic analysis to prove it."

Empress Hecuba turned her stare upon the former Lady's Maid. "Mother, you could have warned me at least."

"What, and spoil the fun? But you're absolutely right. My apologies for not telling you sooner, your Highness." Narcissa peered slyly at Lydia.

"Your Highness," Lydia said, bowing, "what's done is done, and you're the Empress now. None can gainsay that, nor undo it. I'm not here to claim something that's not mine, but I am here to beseech your Highness to bring to account the perpetrator of these foul deeds and to administer justice both swift and merciless upon the person responsible." Lydia straightened. "Thank you for considering my request."

The Empress scowled at the Dowager Empress. "What do you say, Mother Highness? Are any of these foul accusations true?"

Again, Narcissa Thanos laughed, the low, sultry voice carrying over the crowd. "I've already admitted to these deeds, Daughter. You act as if you don't believe me. What would I gain by denying I did them?"

"Utterly wretched and despicable acts, Mother. Of course I believe you did them. I just can't believe you'd admit to them so readily. What am I supposed to do with that, Mother?"

"Who am I to tell you, Daughter? *You're* the Empress. I've always said you'd be on your own one day. It's happening a bit sooner than you expected." Narcissa glanced toward Lydia. "Aren't you going to greet your half-sister, your Highness?"

Lydia and Hecuba both stared at the woman as if she'd lost her mind.

"Your Highness!" Daphne Carras, Chief Justice of the Gaean Empire, stepped forward. "Forgive me my intrusion into this little family reunion. In light of the admissions made freely by the Dowager Empress Narcissa Thanos, I must insist that she be detained immediately."

Empress Hecuba's eyes darted to Narcissa, then to Lydia, and then finally rested on the Chief Justice. "Your honorarium, please administer to this supplicant before me the sacred oath of fealty."

"Yes, your Highness, it would be an honor." Daphne Carras stepped to the base of the dais. "Your Excellency Lady Lillis, kneel before me."

Lydia stood and knelt before the Chief Justice. She was five feet from the Empress and a similar distance from the Dowager Empress.

Almost close enough.

Chief Justice Carras raised her right arm. "Raise your right arm, your Excellency."

Lydia dutifully raised her arm. From the bracelet on her arm dangled the ampule, practically begging her to use it on the Wrwrmrfn dissident leader Mzixrhhz Gszmlh, standing but feet away in the guise of the Dowager Empress Narcissa Thanos.

"Do you, Countess Lydia Lillis, daughter of Empress Consort Ambrosia Lillis and first-born child of Emperor Athanasios Zenon, swear upon all that you hold sacred to serve the crown and uphold the laws of the Empire to the best of your ability as a citizen of Gaea, with all the rights, responsibilities, and obligations thereto implied?"

"I do, your Honor."

"Swear it to her Highness, the Empress Hecuba."

Lydia bowed to her half-sister Hecuba. "I swear, your Highness."

"She must foreswear any claim to the crown," the Dowager Empress said.

The Chief Justice glanced at Empress Hecuba, who nodded. Carras turned to Lydia. "And do you, Countess Lydia Lillis, swear to forego all claims, past and future, upon the throne of the Gaean Empire, for as long as you shall live?"

"I do, your Highness."

This time, it was the Empress herself who spoke. "And now to the truth."

Chief Justice Carras nodded. "And do you, Countess Lydia Lillis, swear to the veracity of what you have attested today?"

"I do, your Highness."

"One more, your Honor," Empress Hecuba said, throwing a glance at her mother.

The judge nodded gravely and turned. "Your Highness, Dowager Empress Narcissa Thanos, you stand accused of the murder of Empress Consort Ambrosia Lillis, to which you have admitted. Do you swear to that admission?"

"I do, your Honor," Narcissa Thanos said nonchalantly. "For the record, I killed Empress Consort Ambrosia Lillis with the full intent of murdering her. I admit this deed volitionally with the expectation that the most severe of punishment is to be levied upon me in penalty. Would you like to know how I killed her?"

"Spare us the despicable gloating of this foul wretch!" Countess Giorgi Lillis wailed, dissolving into tears, collapsing into the arms of Orrin Stamos.

Lydia wanted to run to her grandmother and hold her.

"Your Highness," the High Justice continued, "you also stand accused of kidnapping Princess Cybill Zenon, conspiracy to commit regicide upon her, attempted regicide of her, and of the murder of

Viscountess Ambassador Basilissa Procopio and Professor Dorian Procopio, to which you have also admitted. Do you swear to these admissions?"

"I do, your Honor." Narcissa smoothed a wrinkle in her evening gown, as though bored with the proceedings.

"Guards, contain her," Empress Hecuba ordered.

A contingent of guards converged on her and began to haul her away.

"No, we're not done with her," Lydia said.

Empress Hecuba held up her hand to stop the guards and looked at Lydia. "Lady Lillis ... Sister Lydia, kneel before me."

Lydia stood and stepped forward, approaching the dais and stopping the requisite five paces away. She began to kneel.

"Closer, please." Hecuba tapped a spot in front of her with the butt of the royal scepter. "Here."

She kept her astonishment off her face and stepped to the indicated spot. She knelt, her knee against the royal scepter. Then she bowed her head. "How may I serve thee, my Sovereign?" She could feel the gaze of the Dowager Empress burning upon the right side of her face. The ampule dangled from the bracelet on her right wrist.

"You said, Sister Lydia, that you're not here to claim something that isn't yours."

"Yes, your Highness."

"You don't want the throne, despite being deprived of it through intrigue and machination?"

"I do not, your Highness."

"You said you want justice, Sister."

"Yes, your Highness, that's all I desire, if it's possible for justice to be administered."

Empress Hecuba stared at her and then nodded slowly. "But there's more, you say."

"Yes, your Highness, quite a bit more, I'm afraid."

"More foul than what we've already witnessed? How can this be, Lady Lillis?"

"Much more foul, your Highness, sorry to say."

"Expose the rot, please, so that we may cut it from our midst, Sister."

"Yes, your Highness. If I may divagate for a moment to describe

613

what I'm about to show you?" At Empress Hecuba's nod, Lydia continued. "Among the Paramecium who reared me is a faction of dissidents known as the Wrwrmrfn—"

"Were-wormer-what?"

"—who hold as a basic tenet that Homo sapiens is an invasive species deserving only extermination. The leader of this faction has been in hiding for many years, using a long-acting catalyst to solidify her exoderm and disguise herself as a human."

Empress Hecuba threw a glance toward her mother. "Her? Unbelievable! Completely without basis in fact!"

Lydia indicated the ampule on her bracelet. "I have the antidote, your Highness."

"Please, Lady Lillis, show us this dissident leader."

Lydia bowed and rose. She stepped toward the woman being restrained by guards. Bending, she pulled the didinium off her ankle. "You know what this is, don't you?" The creature squirmed and writhed, trying to get at the Dowager Empress.

Some emotion besides utter boredom manifested on Narcissa's face. "How dare you bring such a foul creature into the palace?!"

"How dare you bring your foul backside into the palace?!" Lydia replied. "This is a didinium, your Highness," she said over her shoulder to the Empress, "a carnivorous unicellular ciliate protist native to the Kzizn homeword, one that feeds voraciously on Paramecia."

The didinium struggling in her right hand, Lydia reached for the ampule with her left. The rash on her right forearm flared, and she scratched the itch. Then she grasped the ampule between two fingers, aimed it at Narcissa Thanos, and squeezed.

A cloud of fine, green mist enveloped the Dowager Empress. Her face began to melt and change color, livid chartreuse spreading across the flesh. The melting spread up over the head and down the neck. The head sank into the upper torso and the arms retracted into the body as the upper half became what looked to be a giant yellow-green...

"Slug! Ewww!"

The transformation spread to the torso, and the evening dress fell away, the legs fusing and the torso sinking to the floor onto them, until all that was left was a potato-shaped lump of ugly green protoplasm.

The didinium strained against Lydia's grip, frantic in its efforts to feed.

"This, your Highness, is your culprit. Her name is Mzixrhhz Gszmlh, and she remained disguised as a human with the ultimate intent of provoking Homo sapiens into attacking Kziznvxrz."

"But why?!" Empress Hecuba asked.

"So we could wipe our asses with your faces," Mzixrhhz Gszmlh blurted, her words oddly clear through her burbling intake orifice, despite her physiology's lacking the parts necessary to produce human speech.

"You have asses?"

"Asses far cleaner than yours, you wart-faced runt."

"Why, you little ball of slime, I—"

"Your Highness, forgive me," Lydia interrupted. "But this creature only wants to provoke you. If we succumb to the temptation and go to war against her people, she and the other dissidents win. The Kzizn technology is far superior to ours, your Highness, and they'll quickly defeat us in any war we launch against them."

"Is that what she's been after all these years? To provoke us into attacking their world? To incite these peaceful if repulsive slugs to destroy us?"

"Yes, your Highness."

"Well, then we just won't attack them, will we?"

Lydia sighed and shook her head. "I wish that were all, your Highness."

Empress Hecuba groaned audibly. "Can't I just stage an Imperial ball? Stars above, Sister, what else could there be?"

"I suspect that Mzixrhhz has ulterior motives for admitting so readily to my mothers' murder and my kidnapping. I'm not completely sure, your Highness, but I think she's trying to hide the fact that she's behind these recent outbreaks of disease."

Hecuba stared at her, looking pale. "How so? She's never been to any of those worlds."

"No," Mzixrhhz Gszmlh said, "but my agent has, and we'll wipe you Homo sapiens off the ass of the galaxy one way or another!"

"Agent? What agent?"

"Your low-brow Highness, allow me to introduce the Typhoid Mary of my disease." Mzixrhhz Gszmlh pointed a tentacle at Lydia. "Her!"

Lydia stepped back as if struck by a physical blow. The room began to warp and skew, a nightmare threatening to envelop her.

"You short-sighted humans have it all wrong." Mzixrhhz Gszmlh laughed, the sound similar to a severe bout of flatulence. "I didn't try to kill you, Lydia. Far from it! No, just those uppity Procopios, so you'd have to live among my people throughout your life. Excellent way to incubate a pathogen. You're a walking Petrie dish, darling. Fifteen years in the primordial soup of the Kziznvxrz mudflats was more than adequate to gestate a viral strain strong enough to kill off eighty percent of Homo sapiens. Too bad you don't have the insight to exterminate the other twenty percent yourselves. Wherever you've gone, Lydia, disease and death has followed!"

Of course! she thought, a dark cloud beginning to engulf her. Why didn't I see it? They virtually told me I was the carrier. The media had levied the accusation after the Ananke Ten outbreak. I've been to every one of the infected worlds. The itch on my right forearm! Lydia thought, the blood draining from her face. She stared at the rash, the tiny red bumps so faint they could hardly be seen.

Professor Dorian Procopio had predicted such an outbreak. Her father's research had proved clairvoyant, prognosticating the development of a highly-infectious and highly-lethal pathogen. Except for one small detail: It hadn't developed spontaneously. The dissident Wrwrmrfn Mzixrhhz Gszmlh had developed it, her intent to exterminate humanity.

Lydia felt someone at her side. She was so disoriented she didn't know who it was. The person eased her to a seat, the ballroom swirling around her like a typhoon. The colors in her eyes tasted bad, the sounds in her ears felt like sandpaper, and the taste in her mouth looked black and ugly.

Melanctha was at her side, whispering assurances.

"Mela?" Lydia wondered where she'd come from. Lydia's anchor in the recent weeks of chaos, Mela had been the one person she'd been able to count on when all else had come crashing down around her.

"I'm here," Melanctha said. "Come on, Lydia. Don't let her win. You've survived so much. You're so strong and courageous. You can't be defeated. You've been through so much that you can get through anything. And you know it. All you have to do is to reach deep inside for that extra dose of strength and courage. Let's see what you've got."

The ballroom settled around her, the maelstrom subsiding.

She was sitting on the dais, the didinium struggling to free itself from her right hand, the rash on her right forearm itching terribly.

Over one shoulder was Empress Hecuba. "Are you all right, Sister?"

"I think so. Sorry, just a bit of shock." She looked around.

Melanctha was nowhere to be seen among the spectators.

"Where's Colonel Melanctha Remes, your Highness?"

"I'll have to look into that." Empress Hecuba shot a look at a staffer, who took off running. "I'll find out."

"Thank you, your Highness." She looked at Hecuba. "Forgive me, Sister. I didn't know I was the carrier. I thought I was inoculated."

"It wasn't you, Lydia. You didn't cause this to happen."

"I know, your Highness, but somehow... somehow ..." Lydia frowned at the blob of protoplasm lazily waving its cilia just a few feet away, unable to dispel the feeling that somehow she should have known. She looked at Empress Hecuba. "I've now infected Gaea too, your Highness. There must be something we can do to stop the outbreak."

"There's nothing you can do," Mzixrhhz Gszmlh said. "If we had enough time, we Kzizn could simply sit back and watch you exterminate yourselves, but you'll turn the galaxy into a trash heap if we wait. Kill me now, if only to deprive me of my delight in watching your pathetic race die."

Lydia got to her feet and looked down at the oval mass of slime.

"Narcissa Thanos," Empress Hecuba said, drawing herself erect, "in the interests of swift and merciless justice, I sentence you to death by diddily, or whatever that thing is in Lydia's hand." She lifted the gold, diamond-topped staff and brought the butt crashing to the floor. "Go ahead, Sister," Empress Hecuba said. "Kill it! Kill the filthy creature now!"

* * *

It was surreal.

And in that moment, as she gazed upon the dissident Wrwrmrfn who'd condemned her to a fate worse than death, who'd marooned her on an alien planet, who'd incubated a pathogen inside her, who'd chased her across the galaxy to turn her into an interstellar Typhoid Mary, Lydia realized that she wanted nothing more than to destroy the agent of her transmogrification.

And yet … Exhorted by the Empress herself to carry out a death sentence, Lydia hesitated.

It was all too surreal. Too pat. Too tidy.

Too convenient.

She glanced between mother and daughter, between Dowager Empress Narcissa Thanos and Empress Hecuba Zenon. The didinium in her hand strained first the mother's direction, and then the daughter's.

Lydia pivoted and hurled the didinium into Empress Hecuba's face.

The slug parachuted and wrapped itself around her head. Her hands came up to claw it away from her face, the staff falling aside. A muffled scream emitted from the beneath the green-slime facial, and the Empress's hands lightened, morphed, and turned into tendrils. The didinium sank into the alien as its head sank into its body, green exoderm replacing human flesh. The tentacles flailed one last time and then were still. The dead Kziznvxrfn's limp mass sloughed off the throne onto the dias. The slurp of a happily-feeding didinium filled the ballroom.

"She was one of them," someone said in a breathless voice.

Lydia looked over at Mzixrhhz Gszmlh.

The dissident leader's cilia looked wilted, as though with disappointment.

"She was your daughter cell, wasn't she? And you planned this all along, didn't you?"

"Yes, we did." The frank admission was uttered with the monotone of fact. The Kzizn were incapable of lying, per se, but they could certainly be deceitful. Mzixrhhz Gszmlh didn't seem bereaved at her daughter's death, only disappointed in the mission's failure.

"Gaeans all," Dea Papadopoulos, Bishop of the Orthodoxy, called out to the silent ballroom, "I hereby propose that Lydia Procopio, also known as Lydia Lillis, also known as Cybill Zenon, be granted immediate authority to act as Empress until such time as we can hold a proper coronation."

"I second that motion," said Chief Justice Daphne Carras.

618

"I too back her candidacy," said Hector Kritikos, Chief Admiral of the Gaean Naval Forces.

"The hell with it! Let's crown her now!" said Elke Drivas, House Speaker of the Gaean Assembly. "The Empress is dead. Long live the Empress!"

A roar filled the ballroom, hats and scarves flying into the air.

Lydia blinked the tears from her eyes, shaking her head.

Countess Giorgi Lillis stepped to her side and took her to the pillar where the portrait of Empress Consort Ambrosia Lillis was mounted. "Do it for her, Lydia. Your mother would have wanted to see this day."

Lydia looked among their faces, seeing a people cast adrift by the deep-seated betrayal perpetrated upon them and the sudden demise of their sovereign.

If I don't become the Empress, they'll launch a war on Kziznvxrz and the dissident Wrwrmrfn will have won.

"Your Honorarium," Lydia called to the Chief Justice, "Swear me in as Empress, please."

Chapter 30

In fairy tales, they live happily ever after, Lydia thought, frowning at the blob of green protoplasm through the cell door, carbo-nick alloy bars reinforcing the glasma between them.

"Hasn't said a word since we put ... it in there, your Highness," the guard said. Beyond her, the detainment center Commander nodded in confirmation.

The optical organelles stared at the floor, not even pivoting to follow the conversation, laying flat against the upper torso above an intake orifice as limp as the rest of the creature. Mzixrhhz Gszmlh looked defeated.

"I don't think she's going to help us," Orrin said. After the ball, he'd spent the night at the palace in one of the bazillion guest rooms and, at Lydia's request, had joined her to see if they might extract information from the dissident leader imprisoned in the dungeon. Beside him stood Colonel Melanctha Remes, whom they'd found last night in a cell nearby, forlorn and forgotten.

Lydia surmised that Mzixrhhz Gszmlh had gotten pregnant by self-insemination. The records indicated that the Imperial Laundry Maid, Drucilla Kanelos, had indeed verified Narcissa Thanos's loss of hymenal tissue on the night of the her wedding to Emperor Athana-sios, but an alien as crafty as Mzixrhhz could easily fake the bloody sheets. The greater difficulty must've been fabricating the development of a human child with a Kziznvxrfn body, not an impossible feat given the advanced biotech available to the species.

Lydia hadn't slept well, going over and over in her mind the terrible suffering being inflicted by a pathogen beginning its rampage across the Empire. "She has to know something," she said. "We've got outbreaks on thirty worlds, and we have to find some way to stop the infection."

Automatic quarantines had been ordered for any planet where signs of respiratory distress were reported. Another thirty worlds, Empress Lydia thought, and I'll have to order an Empire-wide quarantine. Two million occupied planets in the Gaean Empire depended on a swift containment of the disease.

"Mzixrhhz," Empress Lydia said, "look at me."

The optical organelles shifted slightly, now aimed in her direction.

"You've lost, and you'll never achieve your goal. Your daughter cell is dead and your resistance movement has been dismantled. Humanity is going to survive this plague, and you know it. How do we stop the pathogen?"

"Go dump yourself in the deep blue sea," the creature burbled listlessly at her in Galactim.

"Where the feral didinium reign supreme." Lydia sighed, knowing they'd get no help from the creature.

"What about your father's research?" Melanctha asked.

She looked at the Colonel. "Certainly worth looking through. Maybe he had some ideas. Let's go."

The Empress visiting the University of New Athens was no simple task. The campus was locked down immediately, as if a mass murderer had gone on a rampage. "Surround the building," she ordered as her hover approached the University. "No one's to go in or out."

"Yes, your Highness."

Within seconds, the building was sequestered. The Royal Hover dropped into the quad.

Empress Lydia with her inevitable entourage swarmed the building that housed the offices of Selene Toccim, Professor of Xenobiology. She who still had a closet-full of Professor Dorian Procopio's effects. She who had appeared on a galactic broadcast, looking very different from the Professor whom Lydia had spoken with when she first arrived on Gaea.

An advance guard penetrated the office, blastols ready.

The short, blond, skinny Professor with an acne-scarred face stared wide-eyed from behind her desk at Empress Lydia, clearly petrified by the multiple barrels aimed at her. "Your Highness, it's an honor, I think."

She took the chair across from the other woman. The guards all stepped back at her wave.

Orrin took the chair beside hers, and Melanctha stood behind her.

Lydia introduced Orrin. "And you remember Colonel Remes, Professor Toccim. Everything my father predicted has come true, except that the pathogen is worse than he thought and it's been manufactured rather than incubating naturally on its own. I know what the media is calling me. Typhoid Bloody Lydia." A conflation of Typhoid Mary, the typhoid carrier from Earth's nineteenth century, and Bloody Mary, a murderous queen from Earth's fifteenth century. "But I'm also in the best position to stop the contagion. By the way, who was that on the interstellar news?"

Professor Toccim shrugged her slight, bony shoulders. "Some fatuous idiot the administration selected, didn't know her ass from an infectious disease."

"I'm glad you're all right, given the spate of abductions. Do you know of anything in my father's research about the likely means of transmission, the structure of the viral sheath, the RNA sequence—anything that could give us some edge in containing this contagion?"

The woman gave Lydia a mirthless smile. "Dorian didn't speculate too much on the internal viral structure, but he did speculate on the means of transmission, or vector, which every plague has—some way of getting from one victim to the next. The Bubonic Plague used fleas, and Lyme disease was carried by ticks. Most influenza viruses are transmitted by droplets, but they can also live on an open surface in the right conditions for about forty-eight hours.

"Dorian speculated that the next virulent contagion would adapt to live on an open surface for far longer, perhaps by entering a dormant phase, much as ticks do. He also speculated that such adaptation to extant conditions might include its viral sheath becoming impenetrable to the most commonly-used antiseptics, even bleach."

"Rendering contact precautions ineffective," Orrin said.

"Exactly," the Professor said, glancing at him. "If either one is true, your Highness, then the infection is going to be far more difficult to stop than any plague we've ever seen. And given this pathogen's eighty-percent death rate, if it has developed both dormancy and an impenetrable sheath, humanity is doomed."

"And every world I've ever visited is now infected." Lydia dropped her face into her hands. Empress to a dying Empire. How ironic. She forced herself to look at the Professor. "What about the other twenty percent?"

"Who develop immunity or aren't infected?"

"The ones who develop immunity," she said. "Can't we engineer an inoculation or immunization?"

"By the time you develop an antigen, your Highness," Professor Toccim said, "seventy-five percent of the victims will be dead. The incubation period appears to be minutes, and after the onset of symptoms, death follows within hours. I was looking at the statistics just before you arrived." She gestured at the air, and a holograph appeared above her desk. A tally of infected worlds and the number of dead from influenza. The graph was steep already. "These are only the reported numbers. The actual numbers, your Highness, are sure to be worse. And mounting."

"Please look again at my father's research, Professor. There has to be something."

"Yes, your Highness, I'll keep looking." Suddenly, she turned her head into the crook of her arm and sneezed. "I'll look right now, in fact. Your Highness?"

"Yes?"

"Is it true you aren't even Dorian's daughter?" Her voice was mangled by a stuffy nose.

Lydia nodded sadly, her memories of Professor Dorian Procopio obscured in a thick haze. She blinked away her tears, the loss of her parents at four years old still hurting. "He was as much a father to me as anyone. Thank you, Professor Toccim."

"You're welcome, your Highness." Professor Toccim sneezed into her arm again.

* * *

Outside, Empress Lydia headed toward the Royal Hover. Nearly every person in the Royal Entourage was sneezing.

Except her and Orrin. Even Melanctha two seats over was seized with a fit of sneezing, sweat beginning to bead on her forehead.

Buckling herself in, she looked at Orrin. "Not quite the lunch date you were expecting, is it?"

He chuckled gently despite the despair evident in his eyes. "Your Highness, would you marry me if I were the last man on Gaea?"

She threw her head back and laughed. "Even if you weren't," she replied, warmed by his affection. Then she gave him a bewildered look. "Doesn't the CEO of Titanide Aquafoods have business he needs to be conducting?"

"Oh, I suppose," he said. "Given the circumstances, not too many people are interested in buying my hold full of didinium."

Lydia seized his arm. "Didinium! That's it!" Her heart thundering in her chest, she threw her arms around him and hugged him tightly. "That's what we need!"

"What—?"

"Where's your ship?"

"Huh? My ship?"

"That hold full of didinium you're trying to find a buyer for. Where is it?"

"Uh, at the spaceport. Why? What's going on?"

"Pilot, New Athens Interstellar, immediately!"

The Royal Hover banked sharply toward the north.

"Your Highness, are you all right?" Melanctha asked. She sneezed again. "Have you lost your mind?"

"Not yet, Mela. Orrin, didn't you tell me that the populace of Theogony is virtually unaffected? Nearly everyone on Theogony handles the didinium. They're in every trawler hold, they cling to the nets, they get in your fishing boots. If you're a fisherman on Theogony, you can't avoid the didinium. They're everywhere. Didn't you say you're researching their anti-contaminant properties?"

His eyes went wide, his hand to his mouth. "I'll send the crew a com." His cargo vessel sat on the tarmac near a distant corner of the spaceport, guy lines and grav units holding it in place, its engines running at a dull hum to keep its cargo hold refrigerated.

Her guards insisted on sending a contingent aboard first, their noses running, sneezes seizing them. Lydia followed Orrin and Melanctha aboard.

On the cargo-hold deck, the symptom-free crew stood around a vat full of a thick, swampy liquid, its smell redolent of Kziznvxrz. Inside the vat swam several hundred globules of bright-green protoplasm, each didinium about as large as two hands held tightly together in a double-fist.

"I need a volunteer. Colonel Remes?"

"Certainly, Lydia, uh, your Highness." Melanctha turned and sneezed into the crook of her arm. "My apologies. If this bug is going to kill me within hours, I'll do anything to get better. What do you need me to do?"

"Here," Lydia said, putting her hand into the thick muck. One of the six-inch balls of green slime swam over to investigate her hand. She grabbed it and put it against the Colonel's neck. More tame than the didinium on Kziznvxrz, the one from Theogony settled complacently into the curve between the chin and collarbone. "Let it spread out, Mela."

Her eyes wide with fright, her hands trembling, she nodded. "Yes, your Highness."

It slithered down her chest under her uniform, worked its way all the way down to her toes, then up her backside, and up to her shoulders again. She squirmed at its progress, her face contorting with disgust.

"Now into your lungs."

"Eh?" And she sneezed, sneezed, sneezed again. Sweat beaded on her forehead, and her complexion grew red.

She's already getting a fever, Lydia thought in despair. "Let it crawl into your lungs, Mela." To a crew member, she said, "Get her a chair."

One appeared instantly, and she sat.

"Just relax, Colonel."

Terror in her eyes, Melanctha nodded and leaned her head back.

The didinium crawled onto her chest and slid a pair of tentacles up her neck and into her mouth. She began to squirm, a strangled gargle emitting from her throat.

"Just relax," Lydia said again, glancing at Orrin.

The CEO's face was white. He signaled to two of his crew.

Colonel Remes put her hands to her face as if to tear the didinium away.

The two crew converged on Melanctha and pulled her arms back.

The two tendrils grew turgid. The gargle intensified. It sounded as if she were strangling. Then the Colonel passed out. Lumps of gray-green phlegm surged through the tentacles, the didinium's mass swelling.

The didinium gave a final slurp and withdrew its tentacles from Melanctha's throat.

"She's not breathing!" one crew member said, his cheek near the Colonel's mouth.

"I'll start compressions!" Orrin said.

They laid her out on the deck, and Lydia took the didinium off the Melanctha's chest. Oh, Mela, she thought, terrified at the thought of losing her friend.

Orrin ripped open the shirt and positioned himself over the Colonel. Ribs crackled at each compression. "Where's that defibrillator?!" Orrin shouted.

The machine wheeled itself into place and attached its pads to the Colonel's chest while Orrin continued to give compressions.

"Get help. Stay calm," the defibrillator said. "Analyzing heart rhythm, do not touch the patient."

Orrin brought his hands up and leaned back. "Everyone clear, analyzing rhythm!"

"Shock advised, stay clear of patient. Administering shock, stay clear of patient."

The body leaped six inches off the deck.

"Resume compressions," the machine said.

Orrin leaned forward and put his palm to the sternum, about to restart compressions.

Melanctha twitched, and her eyelids fluttered open. "What happened?" she asked, her voice a whisper.

"Analyze rhythm," Orrin shouted at the defibrillator, withdrawing his hands.

"Analyzing heart rhythm, do not touch the patient," the machine said.

"Why does my chest hurt?" Melanctha looked down at the pads, her eyes wide.

"Normal sinus rhythm detected. No compressions needed. Get patient to hospital immediately."

Other than her sweat-soaked brow, Melanctha looked all right, her color returning to normal.

"How do you feel?" Lydia asked.

She took a deep breath and coughed experimentally. Her cough was dry, her lungs sounding clear. Melanctha looked at her in wonder. "I'm in pain, but it worked."

The Empress stepped back and looked among the other members of her entourage. "Who wants to go next? How many defibrillators do you have aboard, Orrin?"

He grinned at her and turned to a nearby crew member. "You, get the other defibrillators, every single one of them." He turned to a cluster of other crew. "You, you, you, and you, go get the defibrillators off every vessel nearby." Then he looked at Lydia. "You did it, your Highness."

She knelt beside Melanctha and embraced her. "Thank you, Mela. On behalf of the Empire, thank you."

The Colonel sat up, wiped the sweat from her forehead and pulled her blouse closed. "What are you thanking me for? Getting sick?"

"For volunteering."

"You're welcome, your Highness, but you were the one who thought of it. You're the one we owe our gratitude." And Colonel Melanctha Remes bowed from the waist to her.

"I'm glad I could help." Empress Lydia bowed back, relieved.

Epilogue

The fleet of five hundred Kzizn vessels filling the air above the New Athens spaceport fired off a brief blast of their retrorockets simultaneously.

A tiara upon her head, Empress Lydia Lillis saluted the fleet, and then waved as the diaphanous vessels slowly rose and faded into the sky. "Goodbye, Father," she whispered as the fleet disappeared, feeling as if she'd never see Xsirhglksvi Xlmhgzmgrmrwvh again.

The Kziznvxrfn of the impossible name who'd reared Lydia since she was four years old was going home and taking the Kzizn fleet with him.

Wiping away a tear, Lydia chided herself for thinking such disastrous thoughts, knowing he'd be at her side instantly whenever she asked, knowing she would see him again.

Maybe it's because I've spent so much time with him in the past six months, the Empress thought, Xsirh at her side nearly every moment throughout her battle with the virulent contagion.

Receiving a salute from her escort, Empress Lydia descended from the bunting-clad platform, her entourage preparing for departure. The Kziznvxrfn had endured hours of speeches as the assembled humans had honored the Kziznvxrfn for their assistance in the battle.

We couldn't have done it without them, Lydia thought, reaching the tarmac.

"Well, your Highness," Orrin said, bowing from beside the steps, "stopping a plague in the first six months of your reign was quite the feat, wouldn't you say?"

She flashed him a grin. "A plague today, poverty tomorrow, and the next day, who knows?" she replied. "Maybe I can cure ambition, too." They shared a laugh.

Lydia felt exhausted as she walked along the red carpet toward the Royal Hover.

On the seven hundred worlds that the plague had eventually spread to, nearly five hundred million people had died, but another two hundred billion on those same worlds had survived. Only with extreme quarantine methods had they kept the pathogen from spreading to more worlds. The Kziznvxrfn with their sub-ether drive vessels had been central to the quarantine and the didinium distribution, risking their lives to get trillions of the creatures to the infected worlds.

Very few patients had needed a defibrillator, they'd discovered early on, most people easily cured within minutes. Further, the didinium thrived off the virus, phlegm, and other pathogens that they removed from patients and underwent binary fission after treating three to four patients, making more didinium. Study of the didinium exoderm had helped the Kzizn and Homo sapiens researchers to develop a biochemical agent able to penetrate the pathogen's tough viral sheath, improving antisepsis dramatically.

She stopped at the door to the Royal Hover and looked over her shoulder.

Orrin was deep in conversation with Melanctha near the bunting-clad platform.

"One moment," she told her staff. And Lydia walked back over to the pair, both of whom immediately bowed to her. "Did I remember to say thank you to you both?"

The two of them exchanged a glance. "You're welcome, your Highness," Melanctha said, grinning.

"You're welcome, your Highness," Orrin said with a nod.

"And by the way, Lord Stamos," Lydia told him, "I've been considering your offer, and I'd like very much to have lunch with you. Are you free tomorrow, by chance?"

About the Author

Scott Michael Decker, MSW, is the author of nearly thirty novels in the Science Fiction and Fantasy genres, mucking about among the sub-genres of space opera, cyberpunk, paranormal, spy-fi, and sword and sorcery. His biggest fantasy is to sell a book or two, maybe more.

* * *

To learn more about Scott Michael Decker and discover more Next Chapter authors, visit our website at www.nextchapter.pub.

Beyond The Horizon
ISBN: 978-4-82417-748-3
Paperback Edition

Published by
Next Chapter
2-5-6 SANNO
SANNO BRIDGE
143-0023 Ota-Ku, Tokyo
+818035793528

12th April 2023

www.ingramcontent.com/pod-product-compliance
Lightning Source LLC
Chambersburg PA
CBHW021111020225
21278CB00020B/121